LIFE, LOVE AND LAUGHTER IN THE REIGN OF LOUIS XIV

LIFE, LOVE AND LAUGHTER IN THE REIGN OF LOUIS XIV

A.W. Preston

A new translation
of Robert Challe's novel

LES ILLUSTRES FRANÇAISES

Book Guild Publishing
Sussex, England

First published in Great Britain in 2008 by
The Book Guild Ltd
Pavilion View
19 New Road
Brighton, BN1 1UF

Typesetting in Baskerville by YHT Ltd, London

Printed in Great Britain by CPI Antony Rowe

A catalogue record for this book is available from The British Library.

ISBN 978 1 84624 249 6

This book is dedicated to my mentor and supervisor in the Department of Romance Languages, University of Texas, Professor Leland J Thielemann, who introduced me to
Les Illustres Françaises;
and to Frédéric Deloffre, Professeur Emérite à la Sorbonne, Officier de la Légion d'Honneur, with gratitude for his generous help and friendship.

Contents

Preface

Robert Challe's novel *Les Illustres Françaises* appeared early
in the eighteenth century, though the events it depicts are
set in a period some years earlier, in the latter part of the
seventeenth century. The work was first published in 1713
in The Hague and was popular throughout the eighteenth
century, with many editions appearing between 1713 and
1780. But eventually its popularity waned. Over the course
of sixty or seventy years, history moves on, fashion shifts, the
new eclipses the old, and what was once in vogue loses its
prestige.

In the case of *Les Illustres Françaises*, the irony was that, as
if to balance the long-standing esteem it had enjoyed in the
eighteenth century, the work dropped out of sight, and was
well-nigh forgotten in the nineteenth century. It remained
almost unknown until more than halfway through the
twentieth century, when it was rescued from this obscurity
by Frédéric Deloffre, who published the first modern edition of the work in 1959.[1] Today, it is recognised as a
remarkable book, both for its modernity and originality at
the time it was written, and for the enduring interest of the
picture it draws, not only of France in the latter part of the
seventeenth century, but of human nature as it was then,
and as we still know it today.

Challe was born in 1659. He travelled widely between the
years 1681 and 1692, in North America, and as far afield as

India and Siam, at times as a trader, and sometimes with the position of ship's writer. He is the author of the *Journal d'un voyage fait aux Indes orientales*, published in 1721, and of a philosophical work, the *Difficultés sur la religion proposées au père Malebranche*, which foreshadows some of the pre-occupations of the philosophical movement of the eighteenth century. But *Les Illustres Françaises*, if not his only work of fiction, is at least the best-known.[2]

In discussing *Les Illustres Françaises*, one is in something of a dilemma as to whether the work should be called a novel or a collection of stories. It takes the form of a series of stories told by a group of friends, either about themselves or about acquaintances. Two time frames are therefore in operation. The events recounted in the stories, of course, took place in the past, mostly during the previous ten years or so. But secondly, there is a period of a few days 'in the present' during which the friends meet several times to hear the stories as they are being told. These meetings provide a framework outside and largely independent of the stories themselves. This framework can be called 'the novel', distinguishing it from 'the stories' – though the same major characters are found in both. Though it is by far the smaller element of the two, this 'novel' contributes an atmosphere and a content of its own, which contrast in some ways with those of the stories.

The novel opens with the arrival in Paris of a traveller. He is on horseback, muddy and dishevelled, and is being jostled on all sides as he tries to make his way through a seventeenth-century traffic jam – a seemingly impenetrable confusion of horsemen and carriages. The traveller's name, we learn, is Des Frans, and he is returning to Paris after an absence of several years. By good fortune, he is recognised by an old friend, a Monsieur Des Ronais, who takes him into his carriage until the throng disperses. Des Ronais also offers the new arrival a lodging in his home until more permanent accommodation can be arranged.

Another friend, Dupuis, is also eager to welcome Des Frans when he hears of his return, and joins the pair two days later at Des Ronais's house. They exchange news about themselves, about mutual friends, and about all that has happened during Des Frans's absence. Several questions emerge during the course of their conversation. Why had Des Ronais's intended marriage (to Dupuis's cousin Manon) not taken place? What is the mysterious link connecting another friend, by the name of Gallouin, with Des Frans and a young woman called Silvie? How can the reported death while in exile of a certain Monsieur de Jussy be reconciled with his recent appearance, alive and well, in Paris? And what lies at the heart of Des Frans's misogyny? These questions cannot immediately be answered, either for lack of time, or because information is missing. It will be over the course of the next few days that the answers come to light, as the friends meet at each other's houses, and those in possession of the necessary information recount the stories, revealing what they know.

Since there is no good equivalent in English for the French title, *Les Illustres Françaises*, I have given this translation a new one. To begin with, the work gives us some insight into life in France in the latter part of the seventeenth century, during the reign of Louis XIV. The characters belong mostly to the ranks of the lesser nobility, who may mingle with wealthy and successful members of the bourgeoisie. We also catch glimpses of those who belong to the underclasses – those who do the bidding of the upper ranks and undertake more of the work of the world: lackeys, servants, waiting-women, maidservants, a steward, priests, monks and nuns, cobblers (with their mobile-huts), a peddler, a brothel-keeper, a midwife, a scrivener and his wife – among others.

Love, not surprisingly, is the theme of the stories. Each of the first five stories hinges on the efforts of a pair of young people to overcome some obstacle which stands in the way of their freedom to marry. The raw material of these stories therefore is not particularly original. Challe's originality lies in the range of situations he puts his characters into, the varied responses with which the young people face their problem, and not least, in the memorable and independent-minded characters he sometimes draws.

The laughter occurs particularly in the light-hearted atmosphere among the little society of friends as they assemble, disperse and reconvene to hear the stories, commenting on them, expressing opinions, agreeing, disagreeing and teasing each other. An atmosphere of such familiarity and good humour as we encounter here is rare in fiction of the period.

One element in the French title, however, is lost in the English one. Challe's title makes it clear that his emphasis is on the heroines of the stories. His purpose is not merely to draw a picture of life – 'to hold a mirror up to nature' (in the phrase current in the eighteenth century) – but to highlight the women who are central to his stories. It is their outstanding qualities which deserve the reader's admiration. Women are not depicted as the weaker sex: they are at least equal in courage and steadfastness to their male counterparts. His heroines are 'illustrious' not because of their high birth or fame, but because of their beauty and strength of character.

There are seven stories in all, varying considerably in length. The first five are relatively short, and together occupy roughly half the total number of pages, while the last two fill the second half of the book. A pattern is established in the earlier stories, in which (as already mentioned) two young people meet, fall in love, and must then decide how to act in the face of (potential or explicit) opposition – a decision which will lead to happiness or tragedy. Having gained confidence with the use of this formula, Challe, in the second half of his book, seems more ambitious and is ready to extend his scope. By the time Dupuis prepares to tell the last story, it is clear he is embarking on the account not merely of a single – if central – event in his life, but on his life story.

The most perturbing aspect of the structure of Challe's novel for the modern reader is perhaps that the latter is asked to believe that all these stories are being told aloud, with a small audience present. How, one begins to wonder, could this be so? Even the shortest story, that of Monsieur de Jussy and Mademoiselle Fenouil, would take two or three hours to tell, and that of Dupuis is more than four times as long. The reader's credulity is strained as he tries to believe that the narrator's stamina and the listeners' patience could last so long (though, while actually reading, one is carried along by the thread of the story and not consciously disturbed by the improbability of the situation). It is true that there are occasional interruptions, but these are rare and do not lessen the problem.

We must remember, of course, that in the seventeenth century people belonging to the class Challe is describing had an abundance of leisure time at their disposal. Looking back enviously from a perspective of three centuries later, we may well wonder how they filled it. The answer is that they probably occupied much of it in visiting, frequenting salons, conversing, and in other similar sociable pursuits. Though there were books and theatres, their world was not saturated with ready-made entertainment, so the return of an old friend who had not been seen for several years would doubtless provide a welcome opportunity for celebrations and reunions, where detailed accounts of happenings and experiences could be exchanged between the traveller and those who had remained at home.

But this explanation will not satisfy the reader's misgivings where the last two stories are concerned, and in order to understand why Challe puts his stories into the mouths of narrators, we need also to see the work in the context of literary history. At the time *Les Illustres Françaises* was written, the novel as a genre was considered inferior to those of poetry, drama and history, which had been inherited from the Classical era. In order to enhance its status, critics and arbiters of literary fashion argued that it should dissociate itself from imaginary tales of fantasy and adventure and seek a more serious, didactic role. Instead of the rulers and princes who had been the protagonists in the nobler genres, the novel would use ordinary people and show them in situations which arise in everyday life, and by giving an accurate and believable representation of the world, it could have a positive moral value, illustrating the relationship between actions and their consequences.

But, in order for such illustrations to be valid, the argument ran, they must record actual events. Otherwise, how could their lessons be trusted? An invented story with a happy ending proves nothing about real life. It is no more than a fairy tale. 'Truth' in this reasoning tended to become equated with historical fact – something which had actually happened – and 'fiction' with invention, which was unreliable and could be misleading.

The concept of plausibility – that is, of something being 'true-to-life', even though it had not actually happened – received little attention, while the argument which insisted that a true story was intrinsically superior to an invented one was, for a time, widely accepted, at least with lip-service, by those writers who wished their work to be seen as serious literature. They therefore went to great lengths to prove – or at least to claim – that their stories were true, and by no means mere products of the imagination. A writer might say that a friend had left a journal in his keeping and he was now able to offer its contents to the public, or that he had discovered a bundle of letters in an old trunk, revealing a long-hidden love story, or that he was recording stories which had come to his knowledge from some unimpeachable source and knew to be true.

In using the device of a storyteller who is recounting the events of his own life, or repeating a story told to him by the person to whom it had happened, Challe is therefore following the convention of his day. In his Préface to *Les Illustres Françaises*, he tells us that the stories are ones that he has been told on various occasions, which he has collected together and written down in his spare time. They are true accounts of events which actually happened, he says, and he has added nothing of his own invention. Neither has he omitted anything, he seems to claim, since he says he had to include even the most unlikely incident in the book – that of Dupuis's attempt to kill himself for love of Madame de Londé – since it really happened. These protestations of accuracy need not be taken too literally. Frédéric Deloffre and Jacques Cormier have indeed uncovered a number of earlier mentions of people and ideas or incidents which appear in *Les Illustres Françaises*,[3] but these are merely fragments which Challe has incorporated into his work. They do not provide its basis, and do not detract from its value, nor from the credit due to the author.

There is only one part of the work, Challe acknowledges somewhat apologetically, which is of his own invention. This is the first few pages, describing Des Frans's arrival in Paris and the renewal of his acquaintance with his friends, and it must be assumed that this 'invented part' includes all the linking passages between the stories, the parts which we have called 'the novel', and even the occasional interruptions from the listeners during the telling of the stories. In writing this part, Challe says he used 'the first idea that came into my head which would serve to link the stories together'.

We cannot avoid noticing something of a paradox here,

for it is those scenes which the author admits to having fabricated which are perhaps the most lively and realistic, and which give depth and vigour to the whole, while the ploy used in the effort to prove the authenticity of the stories is liable to arouse scepticism. One is tempted to feel that Challe inadvertently disproved the theory that the novel could best achieve authority and validity as a literary genre by confining itself to the representation of true stories and real events.

Literature shows us people whom we recognise as more or less like ourselves. However different their existence and the environment they live in may be from our own, we can understand and share, at least to some extent, their wishes and motivations and emotions. We admire and enjoy Challe's work, *Les Illustres Françaises*, not only because it transports us to a different era and gives us a glimpse into history, but even more because he shows us characters whose feelings we may at times share, whom we delight in, and whom we recognise as true to life, whether or not they actually lived.

Notes

[1] Robert Chasles, *Les Illustres Françaises*, Edition Critique publiée avec des documents inédits par Frédéric Deloffre, Bibliothèque de la Faculté des Lettres de Lyon (Société d'édition 'Les Belles Lettres', 95 boulevard Raspail, Paris, 1959), 2 vols.

There are two further modern editions: Robert Challe, *Les Illustres Françaises*, Edition nouvelle par Frédéric Deloffre et Jacques Cormier. Textes Littéraires Français (Librairie Droz, S.A., 11 rue Massot, Geneva, 1991); and Robert Challe, *Les Illustres Françaises*, Présentation et Notes par Jacques Cormier et Frédéric Deloffre. Bibliothèque Classique (Le Livre de Poche. Librairie Générale Française, 1996).

[2] Challe was also the author of a continuation of *Don Quixote*, published in 1713, though written several years earlier. A new edition of this work

appeared in 1994: Robert Challe, *Continuation de l'Histoire de l'Admirable Don Quichotte de la Manche,* Edition Critique par Jacques Cormier et Michèle Weil, Droz, 1994. In 1705 Challe had also sought permission to publish three other works of fiction, but permission was not granted, and no trace of these works survives.

[3] See Introduction to the 1991 edition of *Les Illustres Françaises.*

Life, Love and Laughter in the Reign of Louis XIV

When our story opens, Paris did not yet enjoy the benefit of the fine thoroughfare which runs from the bridge of Notre-Dame to la Grève – a benefit it owes to the generosity of Monsieur Pelletier, who later became a well-known government minister. He himself modestly gave this carriage-way the name of Quai du Nord, or North Quay, but the general public still continues to call it the Quai Pelletier, thus keeping alive the memory of this illustrious dean of the Merchants' Guild. It happened, then, on a certain occasion that a horseman – fashionably dressed, but whose muddied coat, boots and steed showed that he had travelled some distance – found himself caught up in one of those traffic congestions which at the time occurred daily at the end of the rue de Gesvres. And, unfortunately for him, because of the carriages which were streaming in from all sides, he found himself unable to turn in any direction. A valet riding behind him was having the same trouble, and both were in danger of being crushed between the wheels of the carriages if they attempted the slightest forward movement. The distinguished appearance of the rider attracted the attention of those in the carriages around him. Seeing the danger he was in, they hastened to offer him a seat in one of their coaches, and he, ready to accept, was deciding which one to choose, when someone from one of the carriages – a gentleman wearing the robe of a Counsellor in the Judiciary – called out to him more loudly than all the rest. Scrutinising the man on horseback, he had apparently recognised him, and, almost throwing himself out of his carriage window, he was shouting: Here, Monsieur Des Frans! Ah, Monsieur, the horseman answered, dismounting. What luck to have found you here! He climbed into the carriage, greeting its occupant with an embrace, and had his footman climb up behind, preferring to risk his horses rather than leave the young fellow in danger of being hurt. This action did not go unnoticed, and persuaded the onlookers that the newcomer was indeed a man of quality, and they enjoined their coachmen the more to avoid causing any injury to his horses. These instructions were effective, and, when the crush dispersed, the horses were unharmed. The valet regained his mount and, leading his master's horse by the bridle, followed the carriage.

How pleased I am to see and embrace you, my dear Monsieur Des Ronais, the new arrival exclaimed as he climbed into the carriage. And for me, too, answered the Counsellor, this is the happiest moment I have had for a long time. You are returning then to your friends, who have so long been made downhearted by your absence? Yes, answered Des Frans, I am returning to my friends, to my family, and to myself, by returning to my home country, from which I have been so long banished by my misfortunes, and it bodes well for me to have met the dearest and truest of my old friends at the very moment I arrived! There is no need to enquire after your health – I can see it is good – but you will allow me to ask if you can give me news of my family?

Your honoured mother is dead, said the Counsellor. That I have known for some time, answered Des Frans with a sigh. But have you any news of my uncles? No, answered the Counsellor. All I know is that neither of them is in Paris. That is a pity, said Des Frans, since in that case I don't know where I shall find a lodging. Have you forgotten that we are old friends? the Counsellor answered, laughing. My house is big enough for both you and me, and now that I know you have made no other plans for your stay, I shall feel slighted if you go anywhere else! I believe I can make you reasonably comfortable. Not long ago, I was on the point of being married and therefore furnished a vast house – which I am now living in alone. I will not refuse your offer then, answered Des Frans, since it seems I shall not be inconveniencing you. I am only too happy to renew our old ties of friendship. You will be doing me a favour, said Des Ronais, and I would be seriously upset if you were to think of staying anywhere else!

By this time the carriage had reached the house. Des Ronais showed his guest to a room and gave orders that dinner should be served promptly. Will you find it acceptable if we do not stand on ceremony with each other? Des Frans asked his host. That would be my wish, answered Des Ronais. That being so, Des Frans continued, do not be offended if I do not join you today for dinner, nor perhaps for supper either. I have engagements elsewhere which require my immediate presence. It was on this condition alone that I was able to be here – and in fact I can only stay with you at present just long enough to put on some fresh clothes and to be measured for a new suit. Could I ask you to send for your tailor? What! said the Counsellor, you won't dine with me? No, replied Des Frans, I beg you to excuse me, but you must believe that it is only because matters of weight and honour call me elsewhere that I flout the norms of politeness in this way. You are your own master, said Des Ronais amiably, but at least while we wait for the tailor, you will join me in drinking a glass to my health? Even three or four, if you like! answered Des Frans, laughing. Just give me time to change. I feel a fright until I change out of these filthy clothes!

Des Ronais left him with his servant, who had brought in his bag. Des Frans put on some fresh clothes and then rejoined his friend. He enquired after many of his old acquaintances, particularly Dupuis and Gallouin, and learnt that the former was still alive and well, but that Gallouin was dead. Dead! exclaimed Des Frans. Yes, answered the Counsellor, he is dead. His death was that of a saint – a death that will surprise you when you hear how it came about. Four years ago, he entered a monastery. Can this be true? interrupted Des Frans. Gallouin was a monk when he died? He would have continued, but at that moment the tailor arrived. Des Frans was measured and gave the man money to make him a fashionable and expensive suit of clothes by the next day, as well as an outfit for his valet. Then he left, telling Des Ronais he was extremely sorry to disappear so precipitately, because, he said, not only do I enjoy your company, but also because I am more eager than you can imagine to hear whatever you can tell me about Gallouin and how he died. There are circumstances you do not know about, and which I will impart to you in due course. If you see Monsieur Dupuis before I do, give him my greetings and assure him that I have returned as much his friend as ever. Des Ronais enquired when his guest might be expected to return. The answer was that it would be at the earliest possible moment – and with that, Des Frans took his leave.

Des Ronais, who was Dupuis's closest friend (in spite of the rupture in his plans to marry Dupuis's cousin Manon), had lost no time in sending to inform him of Des Frans's arrival. On receipt of this news, Dupuis came to Des Ronais's house, but found Des Frans had already left. Nor did he find him there on three subsequent visits; in fact, Des Frans did not reappear until the third day. Wherever have you been all this time? said Des Ronais, as soon as he saw him. I have been to see a woman of exemplary faithfulness,

4

and to be present at her wedding, which took place on the very evening that I arrived in Paris. Don't tell me! said Des Ronais, laughing. You have already found escapades to get embroiled in, and you've only been back two days! Yes, replied Des Frans, laughing, and very surprising ones. At first, I was just a spectator, observing events with curiosity, but in the end, I decided to play a part and perform a service for a very worthy gentleman, if he should need me to do so. I will tell you all about it some time. But for the present, let's talk about other things. Begin by telling me what you have been doing while I've been abroad, and tell me all you know about Gallouin.

I know nothing but what everyone knows, said Des Ronais, but Dupuis, who will be here shortly, can give you a more accurate account, for those two knew each other's secrets right up till Gallouin's death, which took place not long ago. Dupuis has been here four times hoping to see you. I have just sent someone to tell him you are back, and I have no doubt he will soon be here. It should have been I who went to see him, said Des Frans. But never mind. Since you have asked him to come here, I will wait for him, and he can tell me what I wish to know. But tell me what has been happening to you. You said you were about to be married, but the wedding has not taken place? I should like to hear why. Was it a love match, or something more concerned with financial considerations?

I will tell you about it whenever you like, answered the Counsellor. Then start right now, said Des Frans. There isn't time just now, said Des Ronais, because Dupuis will be here at any moment, and I would not wish to talk in front of him about my quarrel with his cousin. Why, was it the beautiful Mademoiselle Dupuis, who served with me one time as a godparent, whom you were to marry? asked Des Frans. Yes, no other than she – the most faithless woman in the world – Dupuis has no other cousin. I am surprised that you accuse her of infidelity, said Des Frans. People always praised her so for her sincerity and honesty. She is utterly changed, answered Des Ronais, sighing. She put on an appearance of uprightness for so long that I myself was almost taken in by it, but in the end, just as the marriage arrangements were about to be concluded, I was disabused. I will tell you all about it, as soon as there is an opportunity. The arrival of the tailor, who had been sent for, put an end to their conversation for the time being. The tailor produced the clothes he had made; Des Frans was satisfied and was once again able to cut a fine figure.

A few moments later, Dupuis arrived. He and Des Frans greeted each other as two very good friends who had not seen each other for a long time might be expected to do – not in the studied and artificial manner that has become habitual nowadays, but with genuine feeling. Des Ronais, as master of the house, did the honours. They sat down to eat, conversed about their old friends, and gave a general picture of what they had been doing since they had last seen each other, postponing detailed accounts until more time was available. There, concluded Dupuis. That is how things are at present. And we are all still sorely distressed by Gallouin's sad death!

I too am touched by it, said Des Frans. I was not his enemy to the point of wishing misfortune on him. You would have been wrong to do so, continued Dupuis. He held you in real esteem and felt sincere friendship towards you. It was, in fact, as a result of the wrong he did you that he went into the monastery. He had done me no wrong! said Des Frans, in some embarrassment. Whatever you say, he discovered in the end what the true situation was, Dupuis went on. I know more about your story than you think, but don't worry; I am the only one who knows your secret, and no one else will know it without your permission.

I will tell you the whole story if you wish to hear it, said

Des Frans. There is no longer any reason to hide anything, and I have already promised to tell it to Des Ronais: you may speak as openly as you wish.

In that case, said Dupuis, I can be more frank in front of him than I would otherwise have been. I beg his pardon for having kept anything from him, but when he learns the truth, he will understand that it was not something I could reveal without your consent. But since you no longer wish, you say, to keep the matter secret, I can now assure you that Gallouin was at first unaware that he was wronging you, since he did not know that you were united, you and Silvie, by the Holy Sacrament. I can also assure you that she did not deceive you voluntarily, since she was forced into what she did by a power stronger than nature. I am not surprised that you have not asked for news about her, since you must be better informed in that respect than we are. However, we could not help guessing the truth because of a letter Silvie wrote to Gallouin, about six months after his departure and your own.

Silvie wrote to Gallouin! said Des Frans in great surprise. And you say the injury she did me was involuntary? Yes, answered Dupuis. She wrote to him, but don't let that cause you any pain: Gallouin had by then entered a monastery and become a Capuchin monk – and now he is dead ... He can no longer injure you. And it was in fact this very letter which persuaded him to enter the monastery. Silvie wrote it from the convent she had entered, telling him she had decided to withdraw from the world, but without telling him where she was. What! Des Frans interrupted, clasping his hands together. You are telling me that Silvie was dishonest enough to write to Gallouin and say she was a nun! And he was fool enough to believe her and follow her example! That is what happened, said Dupuis.

But, Des Ronais interrupted, speaking to Des Frans, what is all this to you? Why are you so distressed? It has everything

to do with me, Des Frans answered. It is something you do
not know about, my friend, added Dupuis, addressing Des
Ronais. But you, interrupted Des Frans, turning to Dupuis,
how did you discover all this – which I thought no one else
on earth knew about? I will tell you, answered Dupuis, when
I tell you all that has been happening to me. Meantime, do
not allow the thought of the letter to cause you distress. It
was wholly Christian, written by someone imbued with
religion, who was concerned only with salvation – her own,
and that of those she knew. I will show you a copy, which
Gallouin allowed me to make. But tell me what has happened to her, and where she is. She is dead, answered Des
Frans. Then they are both dead, said Dupuis sadly, and
perhaps they both died violently? No, answered Des Frans.
Silvie's death was natural. It is possible that the austerities
she embraced may have told on her, but at least no outside
agency hastened her end. You are right, said Des Ronais,
showing great surprise, to say that the things I am hearing
are entirely unknown to me. It would never have occurred
to me that you had ever had anything to do with Gallouin
and Silvie; nor that the duel you fought with him was over
her. It is those two, however, who have been responsible for
all that has befallen me, and it is they who turned my native
country into a hell for me, said Des Frans. I will tell you the
whole story when I have rested and regained the composure
I will need. Monsieur de Jussy, whose name you already
know well, will vouch for all I have to tell you.

Is he in Paris? asked Des Ronais and Dupuis together. Yes,
answered Des Frans, we arrived together the day before
yesterday. We have spent the last two years together. It was
his wedding I attended the day I arrived. He has married his
mistress at last, the lovely Babet Fenouil. He told me the
first part of his story, and the rest – I saw with my own eyes.
It must be an interesting tale! said Dupuis. It is indeed,
asserted Des Frans. Always in the thick of things! said Des

Ronais, laughing. The very day you arrive, you are present at the wedding of a man who was exiled for more than ten years for the sake of his mistress, a man whom all of us in Paris believed had died four years ago – and yet who returns and finds his mistress has been true to him all that time! She had to be, for the sake of her good name, said Dupuis. I too was impressed to see such loyalty, said Des Frans.

It is rare to find such constancy in a woman these days, said Des Ronais. You don't have so much cause for complaint as you make out, said Dupuis. I've tried a hundred times to open your eyes, but you are so attached to your own misconceptions that you refuse to listen either to me or to anyone else. Perhaps you will pay more attention to Monsieur Des Frans, and as soon as I have a chance to talk to him alone, or as soon as he has been to call on my cousin – an invitation she asked me to convey to him – we will get him to try and make you see reason.

In what way can I be of service to my charming friend and fellow godparent? asked Des Frans. The fact is, answered Dupuis, that Monsieur Des Ronais here is determined to be at odds with her over a certain letter. My cousin has done everything in her power – and even more than could reasonably be expected – to explain the matter to him, and several of their friends have intervened on her behalf, but all to no avail! He is determined to be angry, whatever people say, and refuses to believe anything but his own misguided opinion. I have mentioned your arrival to my cousin, and she begs you to call on her. She doesn't believe you will allow Monsieur Des Ronais's ill-temper to persuade you to refuse her request. No, I certainly will not, answered Des Frans. I know where my duty lies and have no need of instruction on that. I will call on her tomorrow.

She will explain the whole matter to you, said Dupuis. I would tell you the whole story myself, here, in Des Ronais's presence, but I must leave now to go and meet Madame de

Londé. Who is this Madame de Londé? asked Des Frans. She is Gallouin's sister, and Monsieur Dupuis's fiancée – whom he should by now already have married, answered Des Ronais. She is the one they used to call Mademoiselle Nanette, and is now the widow of Monsieur de Londé, one of the best and finest gentlemen you could find, answered Des Ronais. I remember her, said Des Frans. Be on your way, he continued, speaking to Dupuis. A mistress's company is always more agreeable than that of one's friends! Indeed I cannot excuse myself from going there today, said Dupuis, but I promise to be here tomorrow morning, and to stay with you as long as you wish. But now, forgive me, I must take my leave. He went, and Des Frans and Des Ronais being left alone, the former asked his friend to take this opportunity to recount what had happened between his fiancée and himself, and how the misunderstanding between them had come about. He did so in the following terms.

The Story of Monsieur Des Ronais and Mademoiselle Dupuis

There is no need for me to describe my family background – you know it well enough, since we have been neighbours from birth. Nor, since we grew up together, do I need to tell you about my early life. All I need to relate is what has happened since you left the country – an event which took all who knew you by surprise. Some thought you had rejoined the army; others surmised that your uncles, fearing you might become embroiled in another quarrel with Gallouin – which might prove even more serious than the first – had had you removed to some safe place; others again – apparently nearer the mark – said you had gone off with Silvie, who disappeared at the same time as you did, or very soon afterwards. So it was that everyone expressed an opinion, asserting as proven what in fact was merely conjecture. Only your family kept aloof from the discussion. Your mother was even more reserved than the rest, giving rise to the belief that she must have had something to do with your disappearance. Gallouin and Dupuis did everything they could to discover your whereabouts, but failed in this; and as Dupuis has told you, six months later, Gallouin entered a monastery, with no apparent reason but a distaste for the world, though in fact there were reasons unknown to me, about which Dupuis can enlighten us in due course.

Your disappearance, or departure, while it remained for

some time a subject of conversation and a cause of sadness among your friends – particularly in the case of Mademoiselle Grandet, who had felt she had a certain claim on your heart – affected people differently. Some consoled themselves quite quickly, others took longer, and certainly Mademoiselle Grandet did not recover easily. She eventually married, but the marriage was unhappy, and had it not been for her mother, who forced her into it, she would still be single, and that because of you. She is now a widow, more beautiful than ever. Being her own mistress, she has refused several advantageous offers of marriage, rather than stifle once again the tender feelings she has always had for you. I know this from Mademoiselle Dupuis, whose information I trust entirely, because she and Madame Mongey – the former Mademoiselle Grandet – are inseparable and have no secrets from each other. This is probably what Mademoiselle Dupuis wishes to speak to you about ... I am extremely flattered, Des Frans interrupted. I do not deserve the devotion of such a perfect creature. Others will corroborate what I tell you, answered Des Ronais. I myself will say no more. However, your departure left her inconsolable, though she kept her pain secret. She became much more reclusive and ceased to be seen in society. Those who wanted to see her were forced to go to her mother's house. As I was a near neighbour, I went there often, and the pleasure of her conversation appealed to me so much that, though I was by no means a suitor, I nonetheless attended her with assiduity and became one of her close friends.

While I was there one day, Mademoiselle Dupuis came in with her mother. She was only fifteen or sixteen years old: you knew her at that time – you and she had been godparents together not long before. She had left the convent, where she had lived since the age of six, to spend some time with her father, but after about three months she returned to the convent because her mother didn't like it to be seen that she had a daughter of that age. Her mother prided herself on her youth and good looks – with some justification – but this vanity sometimes made her appear in a light which compromised her reputation. She was an honest woman nonetheless, and though her concern to appear youthful made her a less than perfect model of good behaviour, no one but her husband ever doubted her virtue. If she did misbehave, Dupuis was certainly the only one to have discovered it. Let me show you what sort of man he was: you will be able to judge for yourself when I tell you what he did the day his wife died, about four and a half years ago.

Dupuis, as you know, was a military man, who had seen a great deal of the world. He had journeyed to distant parts – and had returned none the richer. He was a lively, intelligent man, gruff and honest, who was never underhand with anyone but his daughter and me – and where we were concerned, he made out all the while it was a trifling matter, of no importance. He had never been successful with money; none of his endeavours had borne fruit. And this is why his daughter, although she is an only child, is not anything like as rich as her cousins, Dupuis and his brother, although their fathers inherited equally, and although the brothers' inheritance is divided between two and has not been increased by additions from any other source. Dupuis, as I was saying, had had some terrible losses. But it was at least fortunate that he recognised before it was too late that he was not born to make a fortune, and that he had therefore better make up his mind never again either to rely on providence – nor to tempt it.

He had in his early days led an extremely dissolute life. At the siege of Charenton he was seriously wounded and on the point of death. He made a general confession and the last rites were administered, but the priest refused to give him absolution unless he promised to reform and to marry the woman with whom he was living. The ceremony took place at his bedside. When he recovered, they spread it around that he had been secretly married for a year, but had not wished to announce the fact for fear of angering Monsieur le Prince de Lonne, who had earlier offered to arrange a match for him which he had refused. And since there are always those who are ready to pry into other people's affairs, the gossip-mongers noted that Mademoiselle Dupuis (for he never allowed his wife the title 'Madame') had a child about six months after her husband had been wounded, and claimed that the consummation had therefore preceded the benediction by more than three months. However that may be, she gave birth to her only child, the beautiful Manon Dupuis – the person about whom I am telling you – and with whom you once served as a godparent.

After the birth of Manon, Dupuis's wife led a perfectly respectable life, but since she was young and extremely attractive both in face and figure, Dupuis, who was more than fifty-eight years old, and worn out from his years of travel and fighting, fell prey to the malady of old men and became prone to jealousy. Contrary to the norm, he claimed to know more about his wife's misbehaviour than anyone else did, and their union was not one of the closest. He was mistaken about his wife, however: even her strongest detractors never went beyond asserting that she enjoyed being seen and admired, and never cast doubt on her virtue.

She died, as I told you, about four and a half years ago, at Carnival time. On the very day of her death, her husband disguised himself with a mask and went to the Marquis de Verry's. The evening had started with a supper, after which there was to be a masked ball in honour of a very high-born young lady whom the Marquis was to marry in four days' time. He had been told of Mademoiselle Dupuis's death

14

and was clearly saddened by the news. He had indeed been one of her friends, but not her lover, and never spoke of her but with respect and with the highest regard. Dupuis, incognito behind his mask, went into the room, where he found himself in a distinguished company, and proceeded to gamble, bidding fifty gold louis. The Marquis accepted the bid, and lost, not only at the first call, but at a second when the bids had been doubled, at which point he retired from the game. His place was taken by one of the guests, who also lost, as did several more who played against Dupuis that evening. The latter won six hundred louis. This was, he said, the only day in his life when fortune had smiled on him, as if his wife's death and his gambling success both belonged to one and the same fortunate turn of events.

As he had played high stakes, he was taken to be a man of substance, and his manner tallied with this assumption. He was urged to take off his mask, and though at first he appeared unwilling, in the end he removed it and revealed himself. When the Marquis saw who it was, he gave a cry. What! he said, A man whose wife has just died masks himself and goes to the dicing-table! For shame! he continued. Is this the way you shed tears for a wife who was one of the world's most beautiful and virtuous women? Gently, Monsieur le Marquis, answered Dupuis. Calm yourself! My wife's death is a greater loss to you than to me. The difference between us, as I see it, is that I was the owner and you the beneficiary. The one is as good as the other. As for masking myself and twirling the dice, if I had lost my money, I would perhaps have wept, or at least have felt sad – and thus I would have ingratiated myself with the ladies, who would have thought I was mourning my wife. But, as it is, I have every reason to be happy: I have lost a wife who caused me grief, and I have won six hundred louis. I have matter for rejoicing, while you do not, having on one and the same day lost both a Cloris who cost you nothing, and your money.

15

And so I give you Good Evening. And with that he took his departure, without waiting for a reply.

You can imagine the effect of this sally on his audience – they burst into laughter. The Marquis called him a madman and a brute, begged his friends to keep the incident quiet, and warned his servants not to talk of it, declaring before God that he wished for no more virtue in his own wife than he had found in Mademoiselle Dupuis. Meanwhile, Dupuis, who was no fool, and whose uneasy relations with his wife were common knowledge, feared he might come under suspicion concerning her demise, the more so when whispers about poison began to circulate. So he sent for doctors and surgeons, had an autopsy performed, and, before interring her remains, obtained certificates attesting that her death had been due to natural causes.

You can see from this story that Dupuis thought himself better informed than anyone else about his wife's conduct, but it was his own mistrust that fed public suspicion: there can be no doubt of the truth of the maxim that says a man who suspects his wife invites others to believe ill of her.

As for his daughter, he could not deny he was the father: she was the image of him. But what surprises me most is that as she grew older, she grew both more beautiful and more like him – yet he is one of the ugliest men you can imagine; his only good features are his forehead, his eyes, and his bearing. She remained in the convent for a time even after her mother's death: Dupuis did not want the trouble of looking after a girl of sixteen or seventeen and did not bring her home until the management of his affairs began to be too much for him. She started to be seen in society about three years ago, when she took over the care of the property which would one day be hers. She was about twenty years old. I had seen her, as I told you, some four years earlier, at Mademoiselle Grandet's, and although her appearance had already been extremely pleasing, it was

16

nothing compared to the striking effect her beauty had on me at this second meeting, which also took place at Mademoiselle Grandet's, though the latter had by now married a certain Monsieur Mongey. I won't attempt to draw her portrait – it is beyond my powers to describe her. Imagine, if you will, a fine figure, with the bearing of a princess, a youthful charm, and a complexion of dazzling pallor and delicacy, such as is fostered by convent life – where a young person is less frequently exposed to the harshness of the elements than one who lives in the outside world. Her black eyes are set wide apart, not sunken, sultry in repose but bright when she is animated; her forehead is broad and smooth, she has a well-shaped nose, a small rose-red mouth, and teeth like ivory, and her whole face is sweet and pure. For the rest, her bust is perfectly proportioned, her arms are plump and dimpled, she has beautiful hands and a well-turned ankle; her step is firm and sure. Though her conversation and movements can be lively, she has a certain natural modesty which completely stole my heart. In a word, she is a vision of perfection. I was overwhelmed, and abandoned my heart to her. Until then, it had been untouched – but this was so no longer. I loved her – or rather, I adored her – from the moment I saw her. One is not master of one's heart. For a moment, I recalled the gossip there had been at the time of her mother's death, and recollected also that she had little wealth, and on the strength of such thoughts as these, I decided that, although she was the most beautiful person I had ever seen, I would think no more of her. But the next day, I saw her at Mass, and a tender glance she directed towards me undid all my resolution and made me think again: her mother had been innocent, her father was nothing but a ruffian and a brute. No one, I reasoned, but a wholly virtuous woman could have given birth to such a perfect being. I gave way to my passion, and my attentions were well received. I spoke, and she listened, but without vouchsafing any clear response. I remained in a state of uncertainty for some time and was only extricated from it by a small incident which showed me that she cared enough for me to think seriously of me as a possible husband.

One day, there was an ecclesiastic at her house. We were talking about a variety of things and, insensibly, the conversation turned towards marriage, and what impediments could prevent it or make it invalid. The ecclesiastic said that formerly the Church had been stricter than it was at present: nowadays, Christians were growing negligent and corrupt in their ways and the Church had consequently been forced to relax its position. As an example, he said that, in earlier times, those who had served together as godfather and godmother to a child were not allowed to marry, but that this was no longer seen as an impediment to matrimony, and that these days two young people connected in this way did not even bother to obtain a dispensation before marrying. Nonetheless, he said, such a spiritual alliance ought to preclude a marital alliance: daily experience showed that children born of such marriages, just like those born of parents related by blood, were always a prey to misfortune and, moreover, often showed signs of depravity in their behaviour. God made it clear, the churchman said, by withholding His blessings, that such marriages were abhorrent to Him, even if the Church had given its dispensation, which it did most often out of charity and in order to avoid controversy.

Now I must tell you that living nearby there was a very respectable fellow, whose wife was about to give birth. They had told Manon more than once that they would like her and myself to be the godparents. The baby was born the day after this conversation with the ecclesiastic; the husband came to see me and, in answer to his request, I promised to be at his house in the afternoon. I thought Manon would be the godmother, as did the infant's parents – but we were wrong. She had taken the clergyman's words to heart, and when the father made his request that she serve as godmother, and told her that I had given my assurance that she would do so, since she had previously appeared willing, Oh! she said. I spoke without thinking when I agreed! I did not intend it as a commitment, and I beg you not to insist! Indeed, it would put your child's life at risk were I to be godmother, for whenever I have stood godmother in the past the child has died – out of more than twenty, not one is still alive. This was not true, for the only time she has served as godmother was on that occasion with you, and the child is in fine fettle. The fact is, she did not want to be a godparent with me, and however hard we tried to persuade her, she refused to be my partner. I was shocked at her behaviour, which I thought uncivil, and I spoke to her about it the same day. She only laughed at my reproaches, and as I reiterated them, she indirectly reminded me of what the man of God had said. His words were not wasted on me, she said, blushing, as she left me. This comment, coming unprompted as it did, was a little daring for a girl to make, and though its import could not have been more clear, it was accompanied by such an air of modesty that, while taken by surprise, I was nonetheless charmed by it. Everything the ecclesiastic had said suddenly came back to me, though up till then I hadn't given it a second thought. The child was baptised with myself and Madame Mongey – whom Manon herself had proposed – as godparents, and Manon joined us for the collation which followed.

I thanked her for letting me know her feelings in this way. We talked to each other and came to an understanding. It was resolved that I would ask her father for her hand in marriage. I was of an age to be my own master, was accountable to no one, and my circumstances were such that Dupuis should not have been unhappy that I sought his daughter in marriage. My family was of a rank equal to his and my wealth greater than his, and I could have been expected to seek a more advantageous alliance. For these reasons, we thought the proposal would no sooner be made than accepted, but we were wrong. In reply to those who spoke to him on my behalf, Dupuis said he was very grateful for the honour I wished to do him, but that he was unable to accept it, for the reason that he could not provide a dowry for his daughter without relinquishing a good part of the capital which enabled him to maintain an acceptable style of life, and which, if he shared it with a son-in-law, would become very mediocre; he had saved it from the shipwreck of his inheritance only with difficulty and felt he had a right to enjoy it in peace for the rest of his days. He said he had brought his daughter home to look after him and be a solace to him in the latter part of his life, not for her to be taken into the arms of some man who, when she became a wife, might prevent her from giving him the consideration and attention she had shown for him as a daughter. He added that, if she were unwilling to conform to his wishes, he knew very well that what he had belonged to him, and that she could ask only for what came from her mother – who, as she well knew, had not had two pennies to rub together before her marriage. If Manon wanted to inherit anything after his death, he said, she would have to earn it during his life by caring for him; if she was not willing to do so, he knew where his rights lay. Finally, he declared, this was his last word on the matter, and nothing would change it. He begged them, therefore, never to talk to him again about his daughter's marriage if they wished to remain his friends.

Such an unequivocal reply was a serious blow to our hopes. Manon wept, I was in despair, but there was nothing to be done. Dupuis was immovable; he had made up his mind long before, and it was impossible for us to make him change it, although we used every ploy we could think of, including one which, far from improving matters as we had intended, came nearer to destroying our hopes beyond repair.

Our idea was to have his confessor talk to him, to the effect that his daughter might not find a second suitor of such good standing, that she was getting to an age where she would be less marriageable, and that the time had come when it would be wise for her to secure an establishment. The priest told him that I would marry her without a dowry, the only condition being that, in the marriage contract, she would be named as his inheritor; he would therefore be able to enjoy the income from his property for the rest of his life without diminution. It was pointed out to him that, having a son-in-law, there would be two people to care for him, instead of only a daughter; and moreover, it behoved him to consider her moral well-being, and to forestall a thousand possible temptations to which a young woman in love might be subject; that daily examples of such calamities should make him concerned lest his own daughter follow suit; that it was therefore in his own interest, and for the sake of his own honour, that a prompt marriage should protect her from such a disaster. The confessor presented these ideas with all the inventiveness that his earnest Christian rhetoric could supply – all to no avail. He was dealing with a man who had been embittered by mis-fortune, who knew the ways of the world, and who coun-tered each argument with his own imperturbable logic.

He acknowledged that the match appeared, on the sur-face, to be very advantageous, but said that, in fact, he had divulged his own worth to no one, therefore no one knew if there were indeed more on one side than the other, and that, perhaps, on his death, his daughter would appear as advantageous a match for me as I now appeared for her. As far as her age was concerned, it was not yet so advanced as to make it necessary to rush into an alliance – three or four years would not make an old woman of her; indeed, by marrying a few years later, he said, she would have fewer children, and they would be stronger and healthier; by that time also, she would be more mature and would conduct her household more competently, having outgrown the frivolities of youth. With regard to his property, which I was offering to allow him to retain during his lifetime, it seemed to him I had a certain gall, to make a virtue of allowing him to keep the profits on something of which at present he was the absolute owner. In fact, both capital and income now belonged to him, and he intended to keep both until his death – it not being his practice to undress until he was ready to go to bed.

If he were to give up the right to do as he pleased with his own fortune, his daughter and son-in-law would look on anything he spent during the rest of his life as being stolen from their inheritance. He was not unselfish enough to die just to please them, nor did he want to lead them into the sin of wishing for his death. The world, he observed, offered only too many examples of old men who had made themselves miserable through foolish generosity towards their children. The latter, flouting all the precepts of piety and religion, often enough showed them no consideration but rather despised them, having got what they wanted. He did not wish to find himself in this position. He thought it better for his daughter to be dependent on him rather than that he should risk being dependent on her and a son-in-law. He was well aware, he said, that children were only too ready to make the finest promises in order to get what they wanted, and then, once the documents were signed, the promises were forgotten. For his part, he swore to God that his daughter would never break her word and use him in this way, since he would never give her the chance.

With respect to his son-in-law's support: this he did not

need. His affairs needed neither protector nor advocate; they were straightforward and in good order, and there was no danger of seizures or lawsuits, since he owed no one a penny. As for himself, he needed only a valet, his cook, and a nurse if he were ill – and a walking stick, and for that, the stick they used to beat the dust from his mattress would do well enough. Regarding his conscience, he was not much of a casuist, but since conscience was not supposed to be at odds with common sense, he did not see how his own salvation could depend on the marriage of his daughter. It looked to him as if they were trying to make him fear some fall from virtue on her part for which he would be responsible through not having allowed her to marry. He had only one thing to say in reply: he agreed that parents were responsible for any dereliction in their children's behaviour if they forced them against their will either into a marriage or into a convent, but in that respect he was blameless, since he did not plan to give Manon in marriage to anyone during his lifetime, and when he was dead, she could choose for herself. Neither did he intend to put her into a convent – on the contrary, he had brought her home from one, and she was useful to him where she was; though he wouldn't prevent her from returning if that was what she wanted, which didn't seem likely, since she was so eager to be married. He acknowledged that parents might also be blamed if, because of their niggardliness, their children had to look elsewhere for their needs to be met, but again this was not so with his daughter who not only had enough money for all her needs, but also for all the little extras she might want – whether for her attire or for her diversion. He had never refused her anything, but rather had always anticipated her wants, giving her money before she asked for it (which I have to admit, said Des Ronais, is true, for he was very good to her in this respect). In a word, Dupuis continued, she spends what she wants, without having to account for it. Therefore, if she were to stray from virtue, it would not be for any reason other than her own pleasure. And against such a calamity he knew of an infallible remedy, which was never to let her out of his sight or, at least, out of that of her waiting-woman; the latter should accompany her whenever she went to Mass, and beyond that, he would never let her out of the house except in the company of people whom he could trust: he would allow none of this scurrying hither and thither in devotions and pilgrimages.

As for letters and billets-doux, he would not forbid them, he said, as he knew very well it was not by their means that the race multiplied. He didn't even mind if Manon and I were to see each other, so long as we were not alone toge-ther. And if, in spite of all, we found the means to pull the wool over his eyes, she would be the loser, not he, before God and before men: before God, since God would not damn him for someone else's sin, and before men, because he would disown her absolutely and take no further interest in her than in the most indifferent member of the human race. However, he believed she was too sensible and too well brought up to do anything foolish; and, if she did, she would be the one to suffer. She would get nothing from him; and moreover, he would treat her as Mademoiselle de l'Epine had treated her daughter – an example still fresh in people's minds.

Who is this Mademoiselle de l'Epine? Des Frans inter-rupted. She is, answered Des Ronais, a woman whose daughter entered into a marriage without her mother's knowledge, a marriage in which the ceremony had not been entirely in order. The daughter became pregnant and went to her mother's house when the baby was due. The mother, in order not to offend Monsieur Des Prez, the girl's father-in-law, turned her away, so the young lady was taken to the paupers' hospital, and died the same day. I remember now, said Des Frans, I heard the story from a traveller who had arrived from Paris while I was in Lisbon. He probably knew only the common gossip, said Des Ronais. Dupuis knows the whole story. We should get him to tell it to us sometime. It is an unusual tale, worth hearing. In due course, said Des Frans, but forgive me for having interrupted. Let me hear the end of Monsieur Dupuis's long reply. It seems to me somewhat harsh, but full of good sense nonetheless. That was the end of his reply, said Des Ronais, but not of the conversation with his confessor. He heard a slight noise, and guessing that his daughter and I were eavesdropping (as indeed we were – and feeling highly mortified by the manner in which he had turned the tables on us), he continued his harangue in terms which so distressed Manon that she was overcome with tears. This forced us to withdraw, having heard the sermon which he had preached, pretending all the while he did not know we were there.

For, said he to his confessor, am I not to be pitied? I have worked and struggled all my life, more than you can imagine, but nothing I set my hand to prospered; through my misfortunes, I lost nearly everything I owned. Yet it was no fault of mine, but the will of God, and I do not complain. Now I am at the end of my life, plagued by gout and hardly able to move, and they want to deprive me of the remnant of my fortune. And who is it that would do this to me? A daughter who is indebted to me for all she has, and who will inherit everything on my death. They want me to give up the modicum on which I live and hand it to a man who may never feel any gratitude to me for it. For, after all, my daughter is not so exceptional as to have found a man who is different from all the rest. I judge him from myself: I would have sworn when I became enamoured of her mother that I would love the woman for ever, and she, being fool enough to believe me, let me have my way. Yet the truth is, that the only real happiness I had with her was our first three or four nights, which we spent together

25

secretly; after that it was no longer love which drew me but only desire. Certainly, I would never have married her, in spite of all the vows I had made and the promise I had given her, had it not been for the fact that she was pregnant, and that I was so ill I believed I had no hope of recovery; for it is true that a woman whose virtue is too easily overcome soon disgusts a man.

I married her only because of the child she was carrying, and because the Jesuit who heard my confession forced me into it (though I did my best to resist his arguments) – making it the condition of my redemption. I am always amazed when I think of how I was talked into marrying her. But they told me again and again that I was on the point of death, and hearing it so often, I began to believe it was true. The fear of death warped my judgement. When you are in that state, things do not look the same as when you are in good health. They said my mistress was an honest woman, so I believed it; and that my only hope of salvation lay in marrying her, so I did, not out of love, but to legitimise the child, and to assure my entry into Paradise – which, however, did not happen, since I am still on earth. But at least I didn't go to Hell. Instead, I've spent eighteen years in Purgatory with her, as penance for escaping death!

She finally decided to die, which to tell the truth caused me no distress. The fact that barely an hour after the marriage ceremony I had had a will drawn up which would allow her just enough to live on but which denied her any rights over my estate (which I left to the child) – this fact will show you that all my affection for her had vanished by the time the marriage took place. But since she died before me, the will never came into effect.

I lived with her in relative tranquillity, since I had no choice; but had it not been for my daughter, whom I have always loved, and still love, my wife would have fared less well. I turned a blind eye on all her misconduct, not because I was unaware of it, but because I have no relish for scandal. I did not wish to publicise my own dishonour and bring disgrace on my daughter. Besides, my wife took care to maintain an appearance of virtue, and that is, after all, the essential with regard to a woman's behaviour; what she actually does is of less matter, in my opinion.

I tell you all this, my dear sir, in confidence, as being my confessor, so that you will see how I have always been a prey to misfortune: from the days of my youth, when all my endeavours came to naught; during my marriage, when my wife managed to do exactly as she pleased, while forcing me to keep silent; and now, in my old age, sick as I am, when my daughter, for whom I have done everything, wants to leave me and reduce me to poverty – and will probably look on me as her persecutor into the bargain!

But, since she cares so little for me, I will teach myself not to care for her. From now on, if anyone comes and talks to me about allowing her to marry, and if I know she is behind it, or if I ever hear she is misbehaving, I shall wash my hands of her and give all my worldly goods to some institution where I can take refuge and be allowed to depart this life in peace. That was all I heard. Manon, thoroughly upset by what – through her own curiosity – she had overheard, and even more by the fact that I too had heard it, left her hiding place, obliging me to do the same.

We suspected that he had been trying to undermine our trust in each other's affection by what he had said – hers, by his own example, and mine by that of her mother. Our embarrassment was such that we dared not look each other in the eye. At length, the priest came to report what her father had said, without, however, mentioning her mother, or anything that might disturb our feelings for each other. He merely told us that we must give up all thought of marrying at present, that it was just so much time and effort wasted. He advised us not to broach the matter again, saying that Manon's father was adamant, and that we would only make matters worse for ourselves if we made any further efforts to influence him. For his part, he said, he would never say another word to him on the subject, were Dupuis to live to be a hundred. Heaven forbid! I exclaimed – and must have said it with such feeling that both Manon and the priest burst into laughter.

After the priest had left, her father sent for Manon, and she went up to his room, telling me to call on her later that day, and saying we could spend the evening on the porch, even if we could not go out together. I agreed, and she went up to her father.

It's not the end of the world, he said as soon as he saw her, as she recounted to me that evening. Did you think, he went on, a priest could help you win your case, as with your mother? No, no, don't try that on; one is not at the mercy of such weakness every day. Don't try to tell me what I should do, I'm too old for that. Do I give you lessons on how you should behave? I let you act as you think fit. All the same, make sure you don't give me cause to complain. My first idea was to forbid you to see this devoted suitor of yours, but I thought better of it. It would only give the chatterboxes matter for gossip, like your mother did, and I want to save you from that. If you want my good opinion, don't start any of that. Make sure you and your sweetheart conduct yourselves in such a way that neither I nor public opinion can find fault with you. You know me, and you know it is not my way to stand over you and tell you what to do. I have never lectured you, and I believe your conduct has always been of good report, and I hope it always will be. I will not speak to you again on the subject, I promise, but don't give me reason to act. It would take only a moment of weakness on your part to destroy your happiness and give you cause to weep for the rest of your days.

After that, he fell silent. He kept his word. From then on

he never opened his mouth on the subject again. And left me with the choice of either giving her up, or playing the role of the perfect hero of romance until his death – which in the event took place about eighteen months later.

I had every reason to believe she loved me. I was granted all legitimate favours. I saw her every day. We walked together quite often. I was made welcome at her home, and Dupuis showed me every friendship, though he must have known that, had it been up to me, I would have dispatched him promptly into the next world.

I was obliged to go to Angoulême on family business. I expected to be away for six weeks at most, but my absence turned out to be far longer. Before I left I asked Manon to give me a portrait of herself. After some small show of hesitation, she agreed, and asked for mine in return. I agreed and was the first to make the gift, as she had wished. My portrait was encased in a simple silver-gilt box with a mirror to the right of the picture. She didn't give me hers until the day of my departure. It was far richer and more elegant than mine. It was in enamel, beautifully made, and a fine likeness, with a ring of pearls around the picture and another round the mirror. The outside of the case was also done in enamel, with a picture on the back of the portrait representing the flight of Aeneas: Dido on a funeral pyre, a dagger in her hand, and behind her a multitude of ships sailing into the distance. Around the picture were the words, 'So would I do'. On the other side, behind the mirror, the picture was of a knight on horseback whose galloping steed was led by a winged figure representing love, leaving behind him a town and several maidens. The words around this were: 'Nothing delays the lover who hears love's call.' It was a gift of great value. When I showed it to the craftsmen who had made mine, they declared it to be of the finest quality, worth at least two hundred louis. The images were apt – the horseman urging me to avoid delay and spurn temptation, while Dido assured me that my beloved would be faithful unto death. Dido, however, proved false – though we have not yet reached that point in my story.

You can imagine my expressions of gratitude and the promises of constancy I gave, all of which were reciprocated. I left and, in spite of the considerable length of my absence, I returned more in love with her than on my departure. She, too, seemed more ardent and more demonstrative in her affection than when I had left. I had written to her regularly and, similarly, received letters from her. I had even sent her small gifts on occasion.

I had always admired her wit in our conversations and have never known a young woman able to express herself with more ease. She doesn't dwell beforehand on what she is going to say, yet she speaks with more precision than many of those who spend time preparing their thoughts. But her letters are even more striking, and I was charmed by them. Her style is concise and polished, sincere and sensitive, and she expresses herself with a certain warmth of personality which makes her writing speak straight to the heart, more powerfully than the spoken word – even with its accompaniment of gestures – can do. I was so proud of the perfections of my beloved that I showed her portrait to some of the great ladies of the province to excuse my apparent indifference to the local belles. They admired its splendour and exclaimed at her beauty, but claimed that the design and inscriptions might not be of her own devising, saying that she would indeed be perfect if she was as intelligent as she was beautiful. I assured them it was all her own invention and, in order to prove her abilities, I showed them a letter which I had received from her less than an hour before. I still have all the letters she wrote and can show them to you should you wish – it is all I have left of her; I wrote and told her when our engagement was broken that I had burnt them, to dispense me from the obligation of returning them. Let me read this one to you, since it fits in at this point in my narrative. With these words, Des Ronais took out a small box containing several letters, opened one, and read aloud:

If I heeded my better judgement, I would not be writing to you. I am very angry with you. Could anything be less compli-mentary to me than the good spirits you display in your letters and the perfect good health you take care to tell me you enjoy? You told me a thousand times that you loved me, and I believed you; you promised to return in a month and therefore I let you go. And yet, four months have passed, and you are happy and well? How fortunate you are to have a heart which is proof against absence and jealousy! Unlike you, I am fur-iously jealous, to the point where I could wish that everyone hated you, so that, spurned by all, you would have to return to me. Yet this thought is too hard on you to remain with me long: the next instant I wish the opposite, and tell myself that the more you are loved, and the more doting admirers you have, the more justified is my attachment to you; then I wish that all would see you through my eyes, yet that you had eyes only for me. I want all those who love you to have true merit, so that my own is enhanced by your rejection of them. But no, do not believe a word of this. It is pride which makes me speak in this way. I do not wish for any sacrifice, only your love. I beg only that you do not betray me. If you have done so already, do not tell me, and I will blind myself. But how can I ignore the testimony of your letters, your unconcern, the length of your absence, and your perfect health? With so much evidence against you, how can I overlook it and persuade myself that you still love me? I feel a kind of certainty that you are unfaithful. The provincial beauties have supplanted me; the attractions of those who are near outweigh that of one who is absent. All you have of me is a portrait, which is nothing but

31

an outline painted on paper. Would that I had never given it to you! You will compare it to the charms of those nearby, who delight you, and will find it no longer pleases you. Such temptation is enough for an inconstant heart! How many reasons there are for you to desert me! When will you return? Shall I never see you again? Have you forgotten me? If you loved me as much as you try to tell me, would that love not come before all else? Can you give me no other mark of your passion than a few written words which I cannot trust? Farewell. I am in such anguish, my despair makes itself visible even on the page. I had meant to be angry when I began my letter but thinking of you has made my anger vanish quite away. Mademoiselle Maillet has taken her vows today and is now a nun. How happy she must be if her heart is free! But how unhappy, if she still remembers Beaulieu with any of the feelings I have when I think of you!

This letter clinched my portrait of Mademoiselle Dupuis. The ladies were enchanted by it and without further prompting from me became my confidantes. I made as much haste as I could to conclude my business but was still delayed nearly two months more in Angoulême, during which time Manon's letters to me formed the subject of our conversations. I was congratulated on my choice and encouraged to be faithful to someone who seemed of such great merit.

Yet I had a rival in Paris, the son of an officer of the King's household, who, towards the end of my absence, had taken it into his head to try his luck at winning the heart of Mademoiselle Dupuis; but as he was merely a stripling barely out of law school, as witless as any Parisian who has never been further afield than his own parish, she merely made fun of him, and wrote to me in a vein so amusing that it would have dissolved even the gravity of a Cato. She ridiculed him with verve. I showed what she had written to my circle of friends, and they shared my appreciation of her satire. Her manner of writing, and the love which she displayed in her letters, won over all those who saw them – and there were many who did.

I returned to Paris, as I have told you, more in love than when I left and with the resolve to do all I could to hasten the day of our marriage. Dupuis had seen some of the letters I had written to Manon on this subject and had taken his precautions, as you will shortly hear. You can hardly imagine how tenderly we embraced on my return, an event which we had both awaited so eagerly. We shed tears of joy. I lay almost senseless at her feet, and she was scarcely less overcome. After a little time, we recovered our composure, and I determined to make a final attempt to obtain her hand, on whatever conditions her father wanted. So I went to see Dupuis, the very next morning, while Manon was at Mass, a time which I had chosen deliberately.

I threw myself at his feet and asked him for his daughter's hand, just as she was, without any financial settlement: I offered to marry her, that is, without any dowry, without any commitment on his part, and even without expectation of anything from him. I asked him just to let me marry her, and I would let him draw up the documents; and without her bringing me a farthing, and without expecting ever to receive anything, I would settle on her whatever he asked and would declare that I had received a dowry of whatever sum he wished to name.

Could I have done more? He appeared embarrassed by my ardour, but since he had to some extent anticipated it, as I told you, having read some of my letters, he answered that my long absence had made him conclude that I was no longer interested in his daughter and that the situation had changed since my departure. I have come to an agreement with one of my close friends whose son is as devoted to my daughter as you are, and whom, I think, she likes well enough, he said. I have promised her to him, and all the devils in Hell could not make me go back on my word. However, I have no desire to pressure her against her will; if she does not agree to the engagement I have made for her, we will think no more of it. Then let us settle the matter, I said, throwing myself at his feet again (a position from which he had previously raised me), and since you will at last agree to let her marry, give her to me, if that is her wish.

In my eagerness, I added several more reasons which I no longer remember but which finally moved him to the point where he promised to give her to me if she chose me – and if she chose the other suitor, I would have to look elsewhere for a wife. I readily agreed. It will not be difficult, I believe, to find what her decision is, and I have no doubt as to where her choice will lie, I said. So much the better for you, said Dupuis. If that is the case, she is yours, but don't be too sure. You don't know what young women can be like. They are more devious than any man would imagine. I don't think, said I, that your daughter has anything hidden from me that would cause me distress. So much the better for you, he repeated, and I could get no more out of him. But in leaving the choice to his daughter, my victory seemed assured. He had wanted to make me jealous and had succeeded to some degree, but my jealousy soon faded.

I waited downstairs for his daughter, and she returned soon after and was surprised to see me there at such an early hour, since I usually went only in the afternoon. She was even more surprised when I told her what had brought me. We are lost, she exclaimed. Acting like this without consulting me will be disastrous. You should not have taken such a step without my consent!

This response angered me. I told her I had no reason to fear the outcome, and if there was anything to fear, it was for her to worry about. It appeared, I said, that perhaps her father was right to doubt whether her choice would fall on me, and that it seemed perhaps she did prefer the new suitor. I was so dismayed and took her reproof with such ill-grace that I might have added further harsh words, but she stopped me. My father told you I had a new lover? she said in great surprise, wringing her hands. Yes, that is what he told me, I replied. Furthermore, he told me that you returned his affection. Listen, she said calmly, this makes me suspect he has some trick up his sleeve. I have never given you cause to doubt my sincerity. What we say here will be overheard, and we need to be cautious. Meet me at three o' clock this afternoon in the Jardin de l'Arsenal and we can discuss this without interruption, and I will explain the whole situation to you and give you all the reassurances you need. This was said with an appearance of absolute honesty and I agreed to the rendez-vous.

We met and talked together at length. I told her word for word what I had said to her father and what he had replied. I don't know what to make of it, she said. I am more at a loss than you. The respect I owe my father prevents me from saying anything against him; however, my best judgement is that he is playing a trick on us, for he knows very well that I would never consent to marry anyone but you, and as for that, he will not allow it during his lifetime. As for the suitor he says I have, I don't know whom he can be thinking of. I haven't seen anyone but young Dupont since you went away. His father is a friend of my father, but as regards being in love with him, the way I wrote to you about him should convince you that this is not the case. Even my father looks on him as a mere child. What I don't know is whether his father can have spoken to mine on the matter. Anyway, there is an easy way to find out. He told you we could marry if I gave my agreement, and that I can do without delay. I am ready to declare my feelings whenever you like – although he knows them already. But I will do it once again, in front of you and the whole world if necessary, this very day if you wish. I don't think I can make myself clearer. Tell me what you want me to do and I will do it now. Believe me, we should make haste and bring him to the point. Since he gave you his word, let us put him in the position of having to keep it: let me speak my mind to him once and for all. I took her at her word and begged her to do so immediately.

We both got back into the conveyance which had brought her, which was a cab – since we had not wanted to use a carriage belonging to either her father or mine – and arrived back with the intention of speaking to him and having our yea or nay from him there and then. But we were dealing with a man whose moves could not be predicted. The ardent love which had manifested itself in my words that morning had elicited a moment of sympathy in him such as even the most hard-hearted feel at times. He had agreed to my request for his daughter's hand, but had immediately regretted doing so, because he was really determined not to let her marry. He had therefore sought a means of escape from the promise he had given me. But he didn't want me to be able to blame Manon for the rupture since he did not really want me to break off completely with her. He thought of me as her future husband – after his death. He wished only to delay our marriage, not to prevent it. Therefore he had in the interim spoken to Dupont's father even though he did not in fact want to give his daughter to someone of so little merit and such limited fortune as the young Dupont. And since he realised I would endeavour to force him to make good his word, he had taken steps to forestall us. This is what he had done.

He knew that Manon and I had arranged to meet. Scarcely had she left the house than he sent for his friend Dupont on what he called 'urgent business'. Monsieur Dupont came at once while, as chance would have it, his son had come to call on Manon at the same moment, so that they arrived together. When Dupuis saw them, it occurred to him he could catch out both them and us at one stroke. After they had exchanged greetings, he told Dupont senior that he had been thinking about the marriage of their children, of which they had previously spoken; and that, being old and frail, he had made up his mind to settle the matter as soon as possible. Young Dupont, delighted, broke in first, not giving his father time to reply, and showed more love than wit in his answer. He threw his arms round the neck of his presumed father-in-law-to-be, saying this was a happiness he had not dared to hope for, but which he received with the greatest pleasure. The father, in a more restrained manner, thanked Dupuis with as much sincerity as if the offer had been made in all seriousness, and accepted immediately, the proposition being very much to his advantage.

They discussed the terms of the contract. Dupont would transfer his position at court, which it was in his power to dispose of, to his son, and he agreed to all Dupuis's requests. Altogether it was as if the matter were already settled, and Dupuis would not have been able to extricate himself if his daughter had agreed to it, which however he knew very well she would not do. And, of course, it was purely to outmanoeuvre her and force her to appear to oppose him that he had devised the ploy. Thus, without running any risk, he was putting on a comedy, in which the actors were playing themselves.

We arrived while they were still discussing the terms of this supposed marriage. I fell silent at the sight of Dupont and his son as I did not know who they were, but I was enlightened before long when the son began to speak. Mademoiselle, he began, addressing himself to Manon, allow me to express my joy at your father's promise to give me your hand in marriage – for I cannot suppose you would oppose his wishes. He would have continued in this vein had I not interrupted: Monsieur Dupuis has agreed to a marriage between his daughter – and you? Yes, Monsieur, he answered. Well, said I, Monsieur Dupuis promised me this very morning that he would allow Mademoiselle herself to make the decision. I claim her too – and my claim is at least as well-founded as yours! However, I leave it to her to make the choice. And you, dear Monsieur, who think her too obedient to defy her father's wishes, I believe you are too well-bred and too honourable not to submit to her choice in the matter. Let us hear your decision, Mademoiselle. There could be no more opportune occasion. She blushed, but did not hesitate for a second. She fell on her knees before her father, without a glance at Monsieur Dupont and his son, and I heard her express herself in my favour as honestly, intelligently and passionately as it is possible for a young woman to do. She finished by assuring her father that she would never do anything contrary to virtue or which might displease him, but she begged him not to make arrangements for her future that went against her wishes.

I also spoke up on my own behalf, and although I had no doubt it was all a charade arranged by Dupuis, I presented our case with such effect that young Dupont's father, who is in truth a good-hearted, honest man, took our side and told Dupuis that he would never have contemplated the agreement they had just drawn up if he had known about Manon and myself, and that Dupuis's best course of action, in his opinion, would be to unite two persons who had so much mutual affection, and this was the course he, as a reasonable man, would recommend and, as a friend, would beg him to pursue.

Dupuis, who had not expected this turn of events, was momentarily nonplussed, but since his resolution was not to be shaken, he maintained that it was shameless of his daughter to speak up so boldly in front of all the company, that she was forgetting her duty towards him and the modesty she owed herself, and that, as punishment, he would leave her as she was. He would not force her into a marriage she did not want, since he had always promised not to do this, but since she refused to conform to his wishes, neither would he consent to her choice. But, I interrupted, you promised to give her to me if she consented, and I call on you to keep your word! Piffle! he replied. I was not serious. You caught me off-guard and took advantage, and I had forgotten I had an understanding with Monsieur Dupont. I release you from our agreement, intervened Dupont. That need not prevent you from reaching an arrangement with Monsieur Des Ronais. I will do nothing of the sort, fumed Dupuis, turning over in his bed to face the wall; and we could get no more out of him.

Monsieur Dupont senior hardly knew what to make of this. His son was in despair at seeing his hopes evaporate. Manon left the room in tears. But I, fully aware of how I had been cheated, could not remain silent. I have been courting your daughter for many months and, as you know, she returns my affection. Yet you bring this gentleman here, out of the blue, and put his claim ahead of mine. I do not have the honour of his acquaintance, but I flatter myself that any difference in position between us is in my favour, and I think he would not dispute this, however little he knows me. Certainly, I would have no wish to change places with him in any respect. I am sorry to have to speak so plainly, but I am forced into it by the injustice you have done me. However this may be – and whatever your motives – it behoves me to follow your daughter's example and say nothing further, for fear my anger may lead me to utter words I would regret having used to the father of the person I love and adore. With that, I left the room and went to join Manon. I found her bathed in tears, and though I was in need of consolation myself, her sorrow touched me more deeply than my own. We poured out to each other all that we felt in our hearts, but were unable to come to any other conclusion than to love each other for ever despite all the hurdles her father could put in our way. She could not help betraying a fear, which touched me to the quick, that I might be so discouraged as to relinquish my suit, which I countered with vows of eternal devotion.

Monsieur Dupont and his son left about half an hour later. I expected to have a quarrel on my hands, but this turned out not to be the case. The father is a gentleman and told me he had not taken offence at the way I had spoken, nor at the scorn I had cast on his son, but that he attributed it all to the state of my feelings, and that it would be unreasonable to expect anyone so thwarted in love to be reasonable. This generous attitude prompted my apologies, and Manon went even further, for, after excusing herself for having had to speak so plainly, she turned to the son and said, You must realise, sir, that one does not dispose of one's heart as one wishes. If I had met you before Monsieur Des Ronais, I would have recognised your worth, but I saw you after I had already given my heart to him, and I can therefore offer you only my esteem. You are too much of a gentleman not to understand this and the request I therefore make of your father that this matter should go no further. You are right, Mademoiselle, said Monsieur Dupont – for all this was beyond the wit of the son. I give you my word that my son will give up any pretension to your hand, and I tell him here and now to bid you a final farewell. And, speaking to his son, he continued: A gentleman never intrudes where he is not wanted. You have played an unfortunate role in this affair. Let this be the end of it. Promise Mademoiselle that you will never call on her again, and since you were not able to win her heart, let your merit lie in your submission to her will. The young man reconciled himself to this and we separated with a thousand expressions of regard on either side.

In this way I was relieved of my rival without being any the better off for it. Manon and I were well aware of how we had been used by her father, but it was clear there was nothing further we could do. Our only hope lay with the passage of time – but during this time I was consumed with frustration at seeing him still alive! He never mentioned the subject of Dupont and myself to his daughter, any more than if the incident had never happened. He treated her neither better nor worse than before – nor me, either, and my frequent visits to the house continued as before. He maintained a silence on everything to do with our situation which we hardly knew what to make of. But we had nothing to fear. He harboured no ill-will. He had foiled us and we had no further weapon at our disposal. This was all he had wanted, and he was satisfied..

As I told you, his aim had been to prevent our marriage, and to do this without giving me any grievance against his daughter, since I was the man he wanted her to marry eventually. What I haven't told you is that, in fact, he liked me. But this was true, and about a month later he proved it to me with a very generous action in my favour.

I must explain that I had already received approval for my appointment to the judicial position I now hold, which had become vacant with the death of the previous incumbent. It was thus merely a question of paying the purchase price. I had about two-thirds of the necessary amount, but I had agreed to pay the whole sum at once. Unfortunately, a banker who was holding twenty thousand crowns of my money died just at this time, and as is often the case with that sort of person, he had been cutting a fine figure at his creditors' expense. His affairs were in no state to allow for my immediate repayment, and I considered the money to be either lost, or at least in serious jeopardy. I tried every avenue to obtain a loan but my credit was not sufficiently well established at the time for me to find such a considerable sum, particularly as there had just been a spate of bankruptcies and cash was hard to come by. I was therefore in a desperate position. I don't know how Dupuis heard of it, as I had said nothing to Manon and she was unaware of it until he sent her to me. He had borrowed money here and there – even pawned some of his silver – and just when I least expected it, she arrived at my door. She told me that her father, having heard I was in need of ready money, was sending me twelve thousand crowns, and that if this was not enough, I was to let him know and he would stand guarantor for whatever further sum I needed. With what I already had, this was more than sufficient. She told me that when she had seen her father in such haste to borrow money and sell his effects (she thought the silver had been sold) she feared he was planning another farce, but that when she found out his real purpose she was overjoyed.

I was greatly touched by his generosity, for I received the money around midday and the payment was due that same afternoon. I went immediately to express my gratitude and told him that indeed he had saved me from a serious embarrassment. He interrupted me and, without changing his usual manner towards me, told me to be on my way and get the affair settled, saying only that one finds out who one's real friends are when one is in need, and that he was one of mine, more than I suspected, even though he was well aware I must wish him to the devil. Think no more of it, he said. Come and have supper with us tonight. Seeing he did not wish me to stand on ceremony, I did as he wished: I went off and, with the benefit of his help, was able to bring the matter to a successful conclusion.

I took supper with him that evening and tried to renew my expressions of gratitude, but he interrupted me, exclaiming: For Heaven's sake! If you will not leave the matter alone, you will have to hear what I have to say too. Is it not true that if I had agreed to your marriage with my daughter and had given her her inheritance I would not have done you this service, either because I would not have been able to, or because you did not need it? Is it not also true that if you had married my daughter without any inheritance, as you wanted, you would have thought it was merely your own property I was giving you, and not mine? Is it not true that since you have no claim on me you feel more obligation to me for what I have done than would be the case if you were my son-in-law? Is it not true that you feel more gratitude and are more affected? I admitted that all this was true. And that is the point, dear friend, he went on, tapping me on the shoulder. Keep hold of what is yours, and let your children, when you have them, be beholden to you rather than the other way round. It is better to be master in one's own home. You will have children one day. Do with them as I have done with you and Manon (for I regard you both as my children) and you will have their devotion and respect.

Although his principles were the cause of much fury and frustration to me, I could not help but admit there was a lot of good sense in them and that, if everyone followed them, the younger generation would have more respect and consideration for their parents. For, as he said, it comes naturally to parents to help their offspring, but young people are not always ready to help their parents. And indeed it is shameful to be dependent on those one brought into the world, whereas it is part of the natural order and of divine law that we should depend on those to whom we owe our birth.

I couldn't help admiring this man who felt his fortune was safe in my hands but who would not countenance my marriage to his daughter because of an absolute determination not to be deprived of his independent means. But, after all, he liked me, and trusted me so completely that he never even asked me for a receipt or note, and when I returned some of the money, which was more than I needed, and gave him a written acknowledgement for the rest, he took them, but asked me if I were planning to die before he did, and said that between gentlemen there was no need of such precautions, which smacked of mistrust.

If this incident made me realise that he would go out of his way to protect my interests, another, which took place shortly thereafter, showed me that he would do as much to protect my person.

There was a rather pretty young girl who also lodged with Madame de Ricoux, where I was living at the time. It is only since Dupuis's death and since assuming my position as Counsellor that I have had my own establishment. Before then I resided at the house of this lady, who is a relative of mine. My only servants were a coachman, a valet and a manservant, and I gave them money to find their own board and accommodation, while I took my meals with my kinswoman. The girl was said to be of good family, and her manner and appearance seemed to confirm this. She came quite often to my apartment and into my room, to clean it, or to collect my laundry and see to any mending. She came four or five times in succession when I was alone, without any very good reason. I was tempted. I made love to my betrothed only as one does with the angels – whatever my feelings may have been, no physical expression of them was permitted. This girl was willing and good-natured, and I was led into a dalliance with her; and since the devil intervenes in all we do, before long the two of us had made a third. This had all been going on quietly for some time and no one suspected anything, but in the end it came to light.

Dupuis had friends everywhere: he heard that the girl was about to give birth, that she was suing me, and that she had that morning obtained a warrant for my arrest. At this time I did not yet hold my official position. He told me of the danger I was in, which threw me into the worst panic of my life. He had tried to speak to me when Manon was not present, but she was listening anyway, so I was not much better off. It's not such a serious matter, he continued. But if you were arrested, it could cause you trouble. It would not do your reputation any good, particularly just as you are about to take up your appointment, which calls for a man of sober character, above the pleasures of the world. Stay in my house, he continued. They won't look for you here, and it should be possible to reach some accommodation. But it would be as well to know whether, on the first occasion when you yielded to the girl's charms, you made any promise to marry her, or if you gave her some present? I made no promises, I told him, but I gave her thirty gold louis. A high price to pay for a mortal sin, he said, laughing. And since that time, have you not given her anything? No, I answered, she has refused to take anything, though I have offered her presents several times. She had her reasons, he said, but it is of no consequence: she succumbed for money the first time, and thereafter it was pleasure which brought about her downfall. Leave it to me, he continued, and all will be well. Stay here, and wait for me. He sent for a sedan chair – it having been a long time since he had used his carriage, which was now entirely at his daughter's service – and in spite of all that she and I could say, off he went, though it was six months since he had been over the threshold – for he even had permission to have Mass said in his own home.

He went here and there as needed; I don't know how he did it but in less than four hours he returned with a piece of parchment in his pocket. Here you are, he said, showing me it, 'emplastrum contra contusionem': your temptress can no longer have you arrested; the tables are turned and you can now have her arrested. I don't suppose you would be so heartless as to have the poor thing thrown into prison, but we must put the fear into her that such a thing could happen. The bailiffs know you have a warrant for her and she will soon know it too. Let her realise what is happening, and she will learn to be compliant. And he sent for a sergeant who he knew was friendly with the girl, and handed him the warrant, though he stopped short of giving him money, in case he should feel obliged to proceed with the arrest to earn it; he only promised to pay him later. The man did as Dupuis hoped – he warned the girl, who now saw that she might find herself in a serious predicament if she continued to pursue me for breach of promise, since she was up against people with infinitely more resources and power than herself. At the same time, an offer was made to come to terms with her, and Dupuis managed it all so effectively that the matter was settled in two days, at little expense. It is true, there was some money involved, and I promised to pay for the child's care; but it only lived two weeks, so its death spared me the expense of its upbringing. Dupuis and his daughter did even more to smoothe over the affair: they arranged for the girl to marry a country gentleman. Dupuis gave her a sum of money on her marriage and made me contribute to her dowry.

Manon was somewhat ruffled by this affair, claiming I had been unfaithful to her. She was distant with me for a time and would have no peace until the girl and the man she had married were safely departed. Her father only laughed about it all. The subject gave rise to some of the most entertaining conversations you can imagine among the three of us. Dupuis was not in the least disposed to make any special allowances for the fair sex, and made no effort to tone down his opinions or mince his words because his daughter was present. The desires of the flesh are a terrible thing, he would say, especially for a young woman. Every day she is confronted with examples of what can happen, but it doesn't make her any the wiser: on the contrary, the more loose women there are around today, the more there will be tomorrow. I can imagine, he continued, the sort of chatter they bandy among themselves: 'Some women get pregnant and never manage to retrieve their good name, but this is only because they don't have the wit to hide their condition. Not like (they name someone) – whom no one even talks about. Madame so-and-so had a baby only six months ago – she suffered horribly having the child, her life was despaired of and she herself thought she was dying. She swore to God and on her soul that if she survived she would never let her husband near her again. She swore never to have relations with a man again. Yet in spite of what she went through and all her vows, here she is, pregnant again. And it's not only her husband – they say she has a favoured lover too. It proves that there must be enormous pleasure in being with a man.' Thinking about it rouses their senses, and curiosity leads them on, until some galant catches them in a moment of weakness. They resist for a while for the sake of their pride. Finally, in a moment of temptation, they give way, and in the end it becomes a habit. Nothing but the initial resistance costs her anything. At the start of an adventure, a young girl feels some shame; a remnant of modesty makes her disguise any pleasure she may feel; she merely accepts her lover's attentions. But time gradually emboldens her and in the end it is she who takes control. Then, fol-de-rol, they have changed places: the lover tires, the lady begins to enjoy the game, and finds someone new, and in the end both horse and rider go to the devil.

One couldn't help but laugh when he got on to this subject. As he was by nature caustic and irreverent, he spiced his observations with a mockery and tone of voice which were irresistible. His daughter would make as if to leave the room when she saw him start on this theme, but he somehow made her stay in spite of herself, sitting her at a table in the corner. She had gradually got used to hearing him; she even answered him back at times, defending her sex, but without changing his opinions. But, she said to him one day, if you are so persuaded of the fallibility of young women, why do you let me, your own daughter, live as I do, unchaperoned? Why are you not afraid that I shall be as foolish as all the rest? Do you think that by some special dispensation I shall behave properly, you who maintain that no young woman can be trusted? For, after all, if I had wanted to misbehave, what was there to stop me, since you give me total freedom? If I had wanted a beau, I could easily have found one, without looking far afield. Our friend, Monsieur Des Ronais, who is here present, has offered more than once to oblige me and is still ready to do so, if I am not mistaken. You are not mistaken, I broke in. And I am ready to say now, in your father's presence, that you are a fool not to justify his opinion of young women by your own example. Ah, but I have no worries on that score, exclaimed Dupuis. People, wherever they are in the world, live according to the customs of their own country. I am not Spanish, or Portuguese, or Italian or Turkish: I do not count on locks and bolts to preserve a woman's chastity. A woman's good behaviour is worth nothing unless it depends on her own virtue, not on external constraints. It is true of everyone – and especially of women – that whatever is forbidden has a particular attraction. This is why there are more women of easy virtue in Italy and Spain than there are in France, where it is rare at least for a woman to make the first advance. True virtue in a woman consists in being tempted, and resisting the temptation. This is why our women in France who remain virtuous deserve a thousand times more praise than the women of the other nations which I have just mentioned, because, being in the world, they are always open to temptation, yet they resist; whereas those others owe their virtue solely to the walls which surround them; the result of this is that the first time a man finds himself alone with one of them, he goes straight to the point, like a brute, without preamble. And although they call Spain the country of love, those who are connoisseurs of the art of gallantry in fact prefer a woman who is sparing of her favours, or who refuses to give them altogether. This reserve – more typical of Frenchwomen than of those of any other nation – is what delights their lovers and holds their admiration. But wherever there is constraint, far from taking pride in her virtue, a girl finds it oppressive and is ready to accede to her lover's wishes, regardless of the consequences.

For example, he went on, talking to his daughter, if, when I refused permission for you and Monsieur Des Ronais to marry, I had forbidden you to see him, can you, with your hand on your heart, say that you would not have disobeyed me? Now, when a young girl has a clandestine rendez-vous with her lover, the time is stolen and she will not waste a moment of it. A lover will make more headway in a quarter of an hour with her than he would in six months with a woman he sees openly every day. In those circumstances, I might have feared you would go astray; whereas, since I allowed you to be with Monsieur Des Ronais as much as you liked, he has spent his time complaining and wishing me dead and with the devil. He has left you alone, as would not have been the case had you been having secret meetings. Anyway, I had little to fear from Monsieur Des Ronais, since I knew, when I looked back on my own past, what his behaviour would be.

I was young once, he continued. I was in love with a girl whom I wanted to marry. She loved me. And although I was bold enough with other young women, for her I felt only respect; that is to say, the love I had for her, though passionate, never allowed me to make the sort of advances I always tried with other women. So I know by my own experience that one's behaviour towards the person one hopes to marry is different from that towards someone else, even if she is of the same rank. Am I not right? he continued, turning to me. Is it not true that if you and Manon had spent your time elsewhere it would not have been as innocently employed as it was here in my house? I cannot say how it would have been employed, I replied, but I believe I would have been no less respectful towards her, and she would have been no less modest and demure in her behaviour. And I do not think so, he said. I am sure, in any case, that you would not have preached the value of virtue to her, and I fear she might have listened to you, for when a girl puts her trust in someone, she is guided by him, and God knows where your persuasion might have led. But what pleasure do you have in putting Manon and myself in danger of succumbing to temptation then? I protested. Why do you not consent to our marriage, since you do not disapprove of it? Our conversations usually ended this way, and in reply he would either change the subject or say there was time enough.

In this manner, the time passed. I was constantly at his house, I ate there every day, and the only thing needed to make me the son-in-law in fact was to share the daughter's bed. I did my best to make her consent to this, but it was useless for me to remind her of the favour with which her father treated me or of his affection for her – which would guarantee his accepting our marriage if it should somehow come to light that we had thus taken matters into our own hands: all my efforts at persuasion failed to move her. She let me talk to my heart's content, but was not convinced. She always answered with a laugh that she loved me too much to risk losing me, and that my little escapade, and the things her father had said on the subject, were enough to safeguard her. What is the hurry? she would say, laughing. You are quite capable of finding what you want elsewhere. Not true, I replied. I may be able to find elsewhere a little sensual pleasure, but only with you can I find true happiness. Well, I declare! said she. The distinction is mostly in your own head, I do believe.

I could never get beyond this point with her. In the end, as time passed, I settled into a way of life which I myself can hardly credit. Every day, I saw a man whose very existence caused me the utmost despair, yet whom I could not dislike, for apart from all he had done for me, he treated me like a son and made me laugh. Every day, I saw a woman with whom I was madly in love, and who loved me – as I believed – and yet I did not suffer the torments one usually feels when one is in love. The only explanation I have is that, recognising the futility of our endeavours after so many thwarted attempts, my heart and my senses had learnt to submit to my thought and my reason.

In the end, after living together in this way for some considerable length of time, Dupuis suddenly fell into a great weakness. His strength gave way in an instant. He had lived long enough to have thought about death. He prepared himself, like a good Christian, and since, this time, he realised there would be no reprieve, he wanted to make his peace with me and unburden his heart. After receiving the sacrament, he sent for Manon and myself. Everyone else left the room. He made Manon sit on his bed, and I sat on a chair beside his pillow. He traced the story of his life briefly and without self-flattery. I saw in it a long succession of losses and misfortunes, but beneath all these disasters – and some dissolute behaviour – there was visible an underlying foundation of probity and honour. He was certainly one of the most upright of men and had a firm, clear conscience; and if he had been less honourable – apart from the fact that some of his misfortunes would never have happened – he would have amassed a sizeable fortune. This, however, he preferred to forego rather than compromise his sense of fair play and decency. He said that the belief he had long held, that he had not been born for good fortune, had always persuaded him to anticipate the worst. He had never doubted that his daughter and I would treat him well if he had allowed us to marry, but he admitted that he had never been able to overcome a fear of the future. It is not I who give you my daughter, he said, she belongs to you, for all sorts of reasons. I beg forgiveness of you both for having so long opposed your union, but I hope to be excused rather than condemned for having been unable to suppress the fear I felt in my heart, and which the approach of death alone has removed. I know you love her truly, and that I could not leave her in better hands than yours. I commend her to your care, both for her own sake, and also, out of consideration for me. Now that my end is approaching, I can own that I have always liked and esteemed you. Take each other's hands. I hope she will remain as dear to you after your marriage as she has always been, since I hope she will be true and will never make you repent of the honour you do her.

I pray that God's blessings may attend you both, and I give you mine, he continued, speaking to his daughter, on condition that you earn it by your virtue, and by your sincere and loyal devotion to Monsieur Des Ronais. Be grateful that God has given you a man like him. Give him your affection and gratitude for the honour he does you – for his birth would have entitled him to seek a person of higher rank for his wife; show him, with simplicity and sincerity, all the constancy, submission and respect that an honest woman owes her husband. So you will have my blessing. Come, he said, turning to me, tell the priest what I have just told you and ask him to perform the marriage ceremony here and now, in this room. I have nothing else to hope for in this world and I would die happy if I could see you married and my daughter's future secure. Any number of unforeseen events could intervene when I am gone. Hurry, if I am to have this satisfaction. I feel my strength dwindling. I have only two or three hours of life left.

It almost seemed as if he foresaw what was to happen after his death. And since he was so favourably disposed, I wanted to take advantage of his goodwill. I didn't think he was as near to death as he said, for I saw that his thoughts and expression were still clear, his voice strong and his eyes alert. Yet the poor fellow knew himself better than I did. I was indeed saddened to see his decline, and I was moved by his daughter's tears and distress. I admired the quiet gentleness with which he consoled her; he died with the utmost calm and stoicism, showing no sign of impatience and no desire to cling to life.

I spoke to the priest as Dupuis had requested. The priest told us that he could not perform the marriage ceremony without permission from the Archbishop of Paris, but that he felt confident it would be given in the present circumstances. We begged him to go and request it, which he did, taking with him a note of our names and rank, and leaving another priest with Dupuis. Manon and I also stayed with him. And so, I must say, I witnessed a spirit of complete and sincere acceptance in a dying man, and a true detachment from earthly things; in a word, the spirit that I would hope to have myself when I reach that moment. He recited the following lines to us, which he himself had composed:

Dupuis – On Dying

Soon entombed in deepest sleep,
*   And new enrolled among the dead,*
Soon – escaping all earth's grief,
*   I shall no longer see the sun.*
My spirit freed from earth's dark hold,
Life's endless strife forever done.

The death I welcome seals my eyes,
*   Sky's burning orb will shine in vain,*

Its lustre will not trouble me.
    Misfortune wracked my every day,
No longer need I fear its sway,
Death frees me from its endless pain.

Death is no curse;
    It brings surcease.
All Nature's laws we must obey:
    They ruled my birth; they close my day,
Life's baleful path is now complete
And gratefully my end I meet.

You mortals who are born today
    I envy not the world you claim –
Man's troubles here outweigh the gain.
    Had they been known before I came,
Had I been master of my Fate,
Fain would I have forsworn the game.

New misfortunes daily plague us,
    New torments daily strike our limbs;
Prey to pain and every sickness
    Till decay unmakes our bones:
This, poor mortals, paints the picture,
Crave no peace while life still holds.

Death brings freedom from this anguish,
    My chastened spirit hails its peace,
In life's end there is no sadness,
    Death proves Our Maker's boundless grace.
Life's travail ended
Gives us each our sweet release.

Since I didn't recall ever having seen these lines before, I asked Dupuis if he were the author. He said yes, and that he had composed them several months before. I asked him to dictate them to me, which he did, and these were almost the last words he uttered, for, taking my hand, and asking us to pray, he expired in my arms. I wept at his death and fully shared his daughter's grief, which was intense.

Permission for our marriage arrived only after Dupuis had breathed his last, and did us no good, because of the obstinacy of the priest. He argued that the Archbishop had given his permission only to satisfy the wish of a dying man, to prevent his spirit being further troubled by the matter and to bring him peace. He said that he would have been perfectly willing to perform the ceremony had Monsieur Dupuis been able to witness it, but that the latter's demise had changed everything; and since we two were now the only persons involved, there was no longer any justification for dispensing with the usual formalities required by the Church.

There was nothing we could do; we had to accept his decision. Though my behaviour towards this priest since then may have appeared pleasant enough, the truth is that I bear him the strongest ill-will, for it is he who is responsible for all the unhappiness that has befallen me since that time. Strictly speaking, there may have been some justification for his stance, but, after all, a sacrament is a sacrament and, for my part, I would have considered myself just as surely married as if the Pope himself had performed the ceremony – with all of Europe in attendance! Our priest was more punctilious, and all my efforts at persuasion were in vain, as were those of Dupuis's sister-in-law, and of her son, our friend Dupuis. Both of them, like me, did their utmost to convince the priest to change his mind. The sly Manon, however, who had laid her own plans and had apparently been restrained only by the thought of her father's dis-approbation, was, I imagine, relieved. Yet I was blind enough to believe she was in earnest, when, stifling her tears for an instant, she begged the priest to perform the marriage, even offering him a large sum of money to do so. She must have realised that the man was too obstinate to be swayed.

Since, apart from his refusal to let us marry, no one could have been a better father than Dupuis, Manon's grief at his death was acute. I shared her sorrow and did my best to console her. I brought her here, to my house. (After the affair with the girl – for which Madame de Ricoux blamed me, saying it was I who had seduced her – I stopped taking my meals there, so there was no longer any reason for me to continue lodging with her, and I moved into this house.) I therefore brought Manon here, as well as her friends, Mademoiselle Grandet – at the time a widow – and Madame de Contamine to keep her company. I myself returned to Dupuis's house, where I had left his nephew and sister-in-law, and several other relatives, who all now looked on me as head of the household and allowed me to make all the arrangements as I thought best. Manon had given me the keys for her father's rooms and her own. I had everything sealed by the bailiffs, though the seals were lifted two days later. I made arrangements for the funeral, and for the prayers to be said, and took care of everything – in a word, I acted as if I were indeed head of the household. When the inventory was taken, I looked after everything as carefully as if it had been my own property. Manon, however, was letting me do the work on another's behalf, but I was unaware of this. I told her what to sign and she signed it, what not to sign and she didn't. In a word, she relied on me for everything, and has not had cause to regret it. As her father had not left a ha'penny of debt, and as she was the only daughter and sole heiress, there was no question of the will being contested. She merely had to go through the legal formalities to establish her position as an independent minor, with her cousin Dupuis as her guardian, this having been agreed to by all the family. She came into possession of everything her father had left, and when all was settled, I took her back to her house, in such a state of despondency that I did not dare to bring up the question of our marriage.

Her aunt, Madame Dupuis (our friend's mother), whom she had apparently prompted, made the observation in my presence that it would cause comment if she married too quickly after her father's death, that people would misconstrue the facts, and that she ought therefore to let some time elapse. The argument was, in truth, not very strong, as everyone had known the situation, but I accepted it nonetheless. Manon was the first to suggest postponing our marriage, since she was really just looking for time to find a pretext to break off our engagement, and she asked me to accept the delay. It distressed me, but I did as she wanted. I was not in the habit of opposing her wishes, and I was more ready to agree than would otherwise have been the case as a problem had again arisen in Angoulême which made it desirable for me to go there. I expected to be there for about a month and this, plus the time taken for the journeys there and back, was about the length of time Manon wished to delay our marriage. Her aunt also pointed out that it would not be proper for an unmarried woman on her own to be head of such a large household, so I advised her to spend this time with her aunt, hoping the company she would find there – especially that of her good-natured cousin – would gradually help her spirits revive. She took my advice, went to live with her aunt – and that is where she still is.

Two weeks or so later, on the eve of my departure, I went to see her and found her writing some letters for the post. This did not worry me, as I was aware that she was now mistress of her property, some of which was in the provinces, and that she might need to communicate with her overseers by letter. I noticed, however, that there was one letter whose address she was anxious to hide from me. To try to hide something from one's lover is an invitation to his curiosity. We were on terms which would have allowed me to ask to whom she was writing. I didn't do so, however. Instead, I dropped one of my gloves, and, as I picked it up, I raised my head in such a way that I saw the name 'Gauthier' on the envelope. I was unable to see the town where he lived, as this was written on the underside. The address was written in her hand and sealed with her seal, but never having heard of anyone by that name I gave the matter no further thought.

I left for Angoulême with the expectation that we would be married on my return. Our farewells were even more tender than on my previous departure. This time I was a man impatient to claim his prize. I saw only those people with whom I had business. I gave up some of my rights, in order to conclude the more promptly, and I was back in Paris two weeks earlier than expected.

I went straight to where Manon was staying, even before going to my own house, but she was not at home. While I was there, a postman arrived with two letters for her. Her maid, who knew how matters were between us, let me take them. I told her not to say that I had been, so that I could announce my return by putting a letter from me in one of those I had taken. This would be a way of taking her by surprise, and would provide a source of amusement for us. The girl promised not to say anything, and I went home to take off the boots I had been travelling in – for, as I told you, I had gone straight to see her. I had assumed the letters were concerned purely with her inheritance, and that she would not mind if I opened one, which I therefore did without a second thought. But what a letter it was! No one but myself can imagine my rage and despair on reading it. There could be no mistake about it. The postman from whose hand I had taken it was the same who delivered the letters to my own door. The letter was signed by someone called 'Gauthier'. This brought back to my mind the trouble she had taken to hide from me the address of someone of this name. I did not know what to say or think. You are probably impatient to know what was in the letter, and you have a right to know. Here is the exact text:

It was with the greatest joy, Mademoiselle, that I received your letter of the 14th instant, and learnt that you are no longer a slave to your father's tyrannical authority. I have been filled with admiration at your complaisance towards him all this time, and the patience with which you endured his uncertain temper. I would not have believed that filial piety could lead a daughter to tend a father as you did yours during his illness. Now that you are free, I give God thanks daily, both for your sake and for my own. I shall be away only a short time longer, and in two weeks at most, I hope to be with you and able to taste the pleasure of a mutual love which has overcome so many barriers, and the threat of a rival favoured by the person on whom you were dependent. Whoever that rival may be, I swear to dispatch him as soon as I arrive, or my death will preserve me from the misery of seeing you in his arms. Since you wish to belong to me, nothing will prevent me from succeeding and from proving to you that no one is more faithful or more loving than Gauthier.

From Grenoble . . .

Tell me, dearest friend, what would you have done in my place? What would you have thought? People do not die of despair, or I would have died that instant. I sat there more than an hour, as if deprived of my senses, so stunned was I by such an unforeseen blow. Anger followed grief – I heeded nothing but my rage and resolved to anticipate this man, who had sworn to kill me even before seeing me. I took up my pen; I do not remember what I wrote in the tumult of feeling that engulfed me. I sent the letters I had taken from her apartment back to Manon, without looking any further, and with them I sent what I had just written. I leapt on my horse and went post-haste to Grenoble with the intention of seeing whether this Monsieur Gauthier was as much of a blackguard at close quarters as he was at a distance. Anger gave me wings. I was there in thirty hours, and taking no rest, I both sought this man myself and sent others to search him out, wherever information might lead us, but I could discover nothing. Foiled in my efforts, and ever more enraged against my faithless betrothed, I passed through Lionnais and Le Forest, and returned to Angoulême, determined to remain there till I had blotted her from my memory. Four months were not enough. I should have stayed longer, but my official position demanded my presence and forced me to return to Paris about three months ago – more incensed with her than ever.

She came to see me the day after I returned. My servants informed her I was not at home, and I instructed them not to admit her should she ever return. This order they have followed. She has written to me; I have returned her letters unopened, along with her portrait and other trinkets which I had received from her. Since then, her cousin and others have tried to make peace between us, but since her treachery was too heinous and too self-evident I have refused to talk or hear of her. For her part, she has returned nothing to me, and I ask nothing of her, except that she leave me in peace. She remains unmarried, and I do not know what can have prevented her from marrying, for apart from her Gauthier – whom I have never been able to discover – two other suitors, of higher station than herself, and whom she should not have refused, have sought her hand. I have not tried very hard to find this Gauthier because I thought my best revenge was to ignore them both.

I don't know what she wants to say to you now, but I know

I have told you nothing but the truth, and I believe that you would not do other than I have done, which is to pretend complete indifference, though this is not in fact what I feel. For to tell you the truth, I still have moments of tenderness, which draw me towards her. But it seems to me her betrayal was too crass for me not to give rein to my spite and defend my wounded honour.

If Mademoiselle Dupuis, answered Des Frans, has in fact deserted you for someone else, I can only applaud your behaviour. In that case, she would not deserve an honest man's attentions. But since I am able to be more open-minded about this than you, I would swear that there has been some mistake. Indeed, how could she let you down after having done so much to forward your suit? Why would she be trying so hard to see you? What can have become of this Gauthier? Why does she write to you? And finally, if she has forsaken you, why does she seek a reconciliation? There is some mystery here, which you should not have allowed to persist for so long. I am sure there is some mis-understanding; you have jumped too rapidly to a conclu-sion, and she has left something open to misinterpretation on her side. If not, she is the most deceitful, worthless woman in the world – I say this, since Silvie is dead.

I don't know what the truth of it is, answered Des Ronais. I admit, I am at a loss myself, and the facts do not seem to accord with each other. When you see her, if you happen to talk about me – as I expect you may – try to discover the truth. A long look, which she cast in my direction the day before yesterday half melted my anger; that is why I don't want to speak to her myself. I am more than willing to do as you ask, answered Des Frans, and I can even let you know the outcome today. I promised Dupuis that I would visit him tomorrow, but it is only five o'clock, the weather is fine, I am suitably dressed and have no other engagements. If you agree, I will go now and will be able to tell you what I learn

61

over supper when I return. I will stay only long enough to find out what we want to know, for to tell you the truth I need some rest, since I have had none these last two nights at Monsieur de Jussy's wedding, and I was already tired before that from my journey.

Des Ronais thanked him for his offer but accepted it only for the following day, as he was going out after dinner. The next day Des Frans went to visit his uncles, who were back in town, and who welcomed his visit since he was not asking for anything from them. He told them that he wished to settle in Paris, and asked them for advice about purchasing a government position such as he wanted, and then went to spend the rest of the afternoon with Dupuis and the young lady Des Ronais had been engaged to marry.

They greeted each other with the greatest cordiality. The charming Mademoiselle Dupuis asked Des Frans a thousand questions, all of which he answered, concluding with the remark that, on arriving home almost a stranger in his own country, he had had the good fortune to encounter Monsieur Des Ronais, who, with his generous welcome and offer of hospitality, had made it clear that the friendship which they had formed in their earliest years was as strong as ever. He is, continued Des Frans, a really fine person, and I would be only too happy if I could be of service to him in any way. You certainly can, interposed Manon. You could do him a service by bringing him back to his senses, which he took leave of eight months ago. He seemed perfectly sane and in his right mind to me, responded Des Frans. Yet the fact is, he is mad, she replied, and you yourself will say so when I tell you the ridiculous way he has been treating me. He told me what has occurred between yourself and him, said Des Frans. And has he told you, she interrupted, the nonsensical fantasies he has filled his head with? At first I felt sorry for him, she continued, and I did everything I could to undeceive him. Not only did I go to his house several times – even though he had the discourtesy from my very first visit to have his servants refuse me admittance. His behaviour shocked everyone who heard of it, but in spite of it I persevered in my efforts. I have written to him time after time, but he returns my letters unread. What is even worse, whenever he sees me, far from showing even the minimum civility expected from a man to a woman, he turns away and ignores me. And all this because of a letter, the reason for which I have tried to explain to him a thousand times, while he refuses to listen to me. Don't you honestly think, she went on, it is surprising that a man who is crazy enough to go as far as the Dauphiné in order to provoke a fight with a supposed rival should refuse to take one step to give the woman he loves a chance to explain a misunderstanding to him? For though he puts on the pretence of hating me, he is deceiving himself. I know him too well to be taken in. For my own part, I cannot deny that, though I ought to be discouraged – after all I have done – by his unwillingness to trust me, I too still love him. I tried to make him jealous, so that he might decide to listen to me, but it was a waste of time. Had I wanted, I could have made a very good marriage by now, but he is the only man I care for, and if I don't marry him, I shall die an old maid. I still consider him my intended husband, not only because of my father's wish and behest, but because I love no one but him. I wept for a long time over his desertion, or rather, his obstinacy, and I am still as disconsolate as ever, but this cannot go on. You are his friend. Pity the pass we are in – he and I. I am tired of tormenting myself with futile efforts! Find out when he will give me a chance to explain what happened. It will take but a few moments. I need only tell him what I have already written several times in my letters. And if we can put an end to our quarrel, the credit will be yours. And if you do not make it up, said Des Frans, laughing, what credit will I get? As far as I am concerned, she answered, you will have the credit for having convinced me to enter a convent – and that before the week is out. But I believe we shall make our peace, as I am sure he still loves me as much as ever; and you will see how much I love him if I am still ready to talk to him after having received a shocking letter such as this from him – which you may read. She put a letter into his hands, and on opening it he read the following:

Chance has revealed your perfidy, and I herewith return to you your lover's letter; to whom, for my part, I shall convey my own reply. It seems you have told him he need not fear me, since he swears to defeat me before ever having seen me. I look forward to meeting this would-be Mars. Either he will take my life, or I shall finish his. I do not fight for your hand – you do not deserve such esteem. It would be beneath me to take up my sword for someone so untrue. I wish only to prove to your new lover that you misled him in saying I lacked courage. As for you, it is sufficient revenge to despise you as beneath my contempt. I consider you a lost soul more to be pitied than hated. Adieu. My vengeance lies in the destiny that awaits you. I have no doubt in due course you will attract some empty-headed fop whose merit will match your own. I return anything I have received from you which is in my possession. I have burnt your letters. Your mind is too fertile in invention to need them for a model. I esteem your favours no more than those of a courtesan.

You see, she continued when he had finished reading, how completely your friend is in thrall to his fantasies. No doubt I ought to leave him to shift for himself – but no, I love him too much not to take pity on his wilful self-delusion. I have shown this letter only to two friends of my own sex. If my cousin had seen it, he and Monsieur Des Ronais would not be on such good terms as they still are. I give it into your keeping for you to return it to Monsieur Des

Ronais. I have always thought of him as my husband, and for that reason I forgive his bad humour and will treat him as I should if I were in fact his wife – as I shall be as soon as he wishes. So, I overlook the lack of respect which he would owe me as an unmarried girl. But if he refuses my offer this time, you may tell him, it will certainly be his last chance.

Let us get this clear, said Des Frans. The letter he opened was addressed to you. It accorded with your circumstances; it came from a requited lover – and therefore I cannot see that Monsieur Des Ronais was altogether unjustified to have taken offence. It is true, she said, that the letter was addressed to me, but it is not true that it was for me. This is what I will prove to him as soon as he will let me. The man who wrote it and the young lady for whom it was intended are married to each other and are both here in Paris. It would be good if the explanation took place in their presence, so that Monsieur Des Ronais could speak to Monsieur de Terny – who is the 'Gauthier' of the letter. Monsieur de Terny will show him his handwriting, and will tell him why he was using a borrowed name, and why the letter was in a cover addressed to me. I will send for both husband and wife tomorrow to come and have dinner here. I am sure they will come, and I invite you to come too, and to bring Monsieur Des Ronais. I shall be extremely surprised if we are not all good friends by the time we separate. And what if Des Ronais refuses to come, what shall I tell him? said Des Frans, laughing. That you will have him locked up in the madhouse, she answered, laughing too. And to prove that you are acting on my instructions, here is my portrait, along with his fine letter, which I am sending back to him. Give it to him, and tell him from me he is a fool to have returned it to me, and that I still have his, and will keep it all my life. I am sure, said Des Frans, laughing, that your reconciliation will soon be accomplished, for, if you love him, I am certain that he also loves you, and his behaviour stems from vexation and misunderstanding. The fact is, she interrupted, he is hotheaded and obstinate – and is now furious with himself for not having let me clear the matter up before now.

While this conversation was taking place a lady dressed in the height of fashion arrived to call on Mademoiselle Dupuis. Des Frans prepared to take his leave, but Manon prevented him from going. Do you not recognise who this is? she said. You are not paying attention. He therefore looked more attentively at the lady. I beg your ladyship's pardon, Madame, he said, if I do not immediately recognise you. I think I have met you before, but do not remember exactly where. So much has happened since that time, the lady said, that I am not surprised if you cannot exactly place me. Not many people spared me a glance, only six years ago, and I was of so little significance in the world that, whatever ideas you may have, you will not be able to guess who I am at present. I do not know what your present position is, he answered, but your features remind me of a girl who lived in a house I often visited. I dare not mention who she was because of the great disproportion in station there is between the person I see now and that girl. However, you are not mistaken, the lady answered. Is it possible, he said, that it was you whom I saw in those days – so different to what you are now? Yes, Manon broke in happily, Madame is indeed the person whom you used to know as Angélique, and who owes her present position to her beauty and her merit. She is now the wife of Monsieur de Contamine. Ah, Madame, can what Mademoiselle Dupuis tells me really be true? Yes, Monsieur, answered the lady, it is true. Everyone knows my former lowly station, and I myself will always remain aware of it, and acknowledge my gratitude to Monsieur de Contamine, and also to Mademoiselle Dupuis, who went to much trouble on my behalf. You are aware of how I was indebted to her in my early life, but you

66

do not know the help she gave me subsequently, to which I owe the position I now hold – and which I am ready to tell you about more fully whenever you wish. I have done nothing for you, Madame, to deserve these expressions of gratitude, said Manon good-humouredly. You owe your position to your own conduct. You provide me with an example which enables me to say that there are times when virtue is indeed rewarded by good fortune. I do not know in what ways Mademoiselle Dupuis may have been of service to you, said Des Frans, but having seen you as you were formerly and seeing you now the wife of Monsieur de Contamine, I have to acknowledge that the change is almost more than I can credit, and well-nigh unbelievable. If that is the case, said Manon, go back to Monsieur Des Ronais. He knows Madame de Contamine's story – she told him it herself. Ask him to recount it to you – you will not be disappointed – and I am sure Madame de Contamine will not be displeased for you to hear it. Apart from the fact that there is nothing in it which is to her disadvantage, I have often heard her speak highly of you, so I think she will not be unhappy for Des Ronais to tell you how her good fortune came about.

I shall not be in the least displeased if Monsieur Des Ronais tells Monsieur Des Frans what he knows about me, said Madame de Contamine, and if I were in the least troubled about anyone hearing my story, it would be only because he had learned my history without allowing me into his confidence and telling me about the events of his own life. Mademoiselle Dupuis told me yesterday, she continued, that you were coming to see her today, and that is why I myself am here. You are a friend of Des Ronais. Give him this message from me. Tell him I am scandalised by his lack of courtesy. Tell him he should listen to me when I try to talk to him about Mademoiselle Dupuis; that is the least he can do – out of respect for me as a woman, if not for his own sake. Tell him that it is because of him that she is growing thin, and that I am very angry with him. Tell him, however, that I am not spiteful, and that, rather than repaying him, as I could, by encouraging Mademoiselle Dupuis to take offence at his unmannerliness, I have always maintained that the rift between them was nothing more to begin with than a lovers' misunderstanding, which arose from a generous action on her part, but which was prolonged out of all proportion by his wilful pride.

Manon told her of the conversation she had just been having with Des Frans. Des Ronais is extremely lucky, Des Frans asserted, to have such an understanding friend and such a loving mistress. And I swear that if he does not take heed of what I tell him it will be the end of my friendship with him. All we want is that you should bring him here, said Madame de Contamine with a smile. My husband and Madame de Cologny will be at Saint Germain all day tomorrow, and I will dine with you all here – I hereby invite myself! And I do not doubt that we shall make him more humble and docile than a postulant before his Superior! Des Frans gave his promise and left.

Des Ronais was awaiting him impatiently. Well, he called out as soon as he saw him, have you good news to tell me? No, laughed Des Frans in reply, but I am to berate you on behalf of your betrothed, who is entirely innocent concerning the letter of which you assumed she was the heroine; also on behalf of Madame de Contamine, who came to call on Manon while I was there. You are very lucky in having such a good friend, and in your sweetheart. The latter still loves you and is sure you still love her. She says you are crazy as well as discourteous – and she is not far off the mark! She is ready to marry you, and in token of this, here is her portrait, which she is returning to you, along with the fine letter you wrote to her. All the circumstances will be revealed to you tomorrow at dinner, to which you are invited. The so-called 'Gauthier' – a name plucked out of the air – will be present. He is Monsieur de Terny, who assumed the name and address of his serving-man, for reasons you will hear. He will demonstrate his handwriting before your own eyes, to prove it was he who wrote the letter, and his wife (to whom he was betrothed at the time) will give you her word that she received it. They will tell you why these letters were addressed to Mademoiselle Dupuis, and why she also forwarded the replies. In a word – all will be explained. Your ill-temper and discourtesies will all be forgiven, and your Manon is ready to marry you, if that is your wish. If not, to prove that she cares only for you, she will retire from the world and spend the rest of her life in a convent.

This is what I have been instructed to convey to you. I was further enjoined to warn you that you should take this opportunity – for it will be the last. If you refuse it this time, there will be no other. I have promised either to bring you to our gathering when we meet tomorrow or to cease thereafter to call you my friend. I will keep my word in either case. It is for you to decide which way it is to be. And now, I am not interested in your 'perhaps' and 'maybes' – all I want is for you to tell me Madame de Contamine's story. She told you it herself, and both she and Mademoiselle Dupuis request that you recount it to me.

You are assailing me with so many ideas and requests all at once, said Des Ronais, that I don't know which one to start with! How can it be that a letter addressed to a young lady, which so closely fits her own circumstances, which she receives through the post, is yet not for her? That is all true, answered Des Frans, and is acknowledged, but it is the consequences you draw from these facts which are denied. All will be explained tomorrow. I shall be there too. And I can assure you that the changes you have noticed in Mademoiselle Dupuis's appearance are the result solely of her distress over the way you have treated her. She loves no one but you; her happiness depends on you – that I can promise you. She has tried to explain everything to you, either face to face, or in writing. She has done everything she could to enlighten you, and it is through no fault but your own that the misunderstanding has persisted for so long. That is all I can tell you, since it is all I know. Tomorrow everything will be explained, and at present I am extremely anxious to hear all about Madame de Contamine, and to find out how a girl whom I first saw as a servant in the household of the mother of your sweetheart has been able to rise to the position of prestige and fortune she now holds. It is something I find incomprehensible.

If you did not feel that way, you would be the only person not to be amazed at such a transformation. Everyone who hears of it is equally surprised. But the most astonishing part of it is that she married Monsieur de Contamine with the consent of his mother, who is the most ambitious woman in France, and who always intended her son to marry into one of the wealthiest families in the country. And it is also true that Angélique, now her daughter-in-law, did not use any discreditable means to ensnare her son. On the contrary, it was her virtue which won him to her, and which persuaded him to marry her. Moreover, though it is true that her refusal to yield to him drove him to despair, he was also, in his deepest heart, grateful to her for acting in this way. And, in the end, it was the unfailing uprightness of her behaviour, and his own concern not to displease his mother, which persuaded the latter to give her approval to the marriage.

We will leave the question of Manon until later, continued Des Ronais. I hardly know what to think at present. But if you are ready to listen, I will tell you the story of Madame de Contamine, which you wish to hear. But before I begin, I must tell you that Monsieur de Jussy came to see you. I did my best to persuade him to wait for you, but he was too busy to do so. I accompanied him to his carriage, where his wife was waiting, whom I thought extremely beautiful, and whose appearance made me eager to learn their story.

I will tell you it some time, said Des Frans. I should be very happy for Monsieur Dupuis, Madame de Contamine and Mademoiselle Dupuis to hear it too. And it might also serve to bring about a reconciliation between Monsieur de Jussy and Madame de Mongey. It is true, said Des Ronais, that she does not count him as one of her friends. She considers him a deceitful scoundrel. I can tell you why she has that opinion, said Des Frans. We will call on Jussy and his wife tomorrow, if you like. But now, let me tell you about Monsieur and Madame de Contamine.

The Story of Monsieur de Contamine and Angélique

In order for you to understand the enormous disparity in station between Monsieur de Contamine and Angélique, I had better remind you of what their positions were before they were made equal by the sacrament of marriage. I will begin with Monsieur de Contamine. He is the son of a barrister who was extremely rich, and who, over and above his initial wealth, had made immense sums of money through certain important positions he had held in the service of the state – not by any underhand dealings, but by wholly legitimate means. He was of noble rank, being of a house which has always distinguished itself by personal devotion to our kings – more in the administration of justice than on the battlefield, however – though some members of the family have nonetheless served with distinction in the army. As well as the wealth he possessed in his own right, he increased his fortune through his marriage to the daughter and sole heiress of an enormously wealthy tax collector; all her brothers and sisters died before their parents, though after her marriage to our hero's father. This is the person who is now Angélique's mother-in-law.

Although her marriage to Contamine's father was long and happy, they had only one child. She was still young enough to have remarried when she became a widow, being no more than twenty-nine or thirty years old at most –

72

having spent fifteen of those years with her husband. But she preferred widowhood, and the pleasure of raising the six-year-old son left by a husband she had loved dearly, to all the offers of marriage she received – though there were some among her suitors who included, perfectly legitimately, a crown in their coat-of-arms. Her son and daughter-in-law, Angélique, live with her, and the latter has so won her affection that, a short while ago, when Madame de Contamine went to visit an estate not far from here, Contamine had to keep his wife hidden away, because her mother-in-law cannot do without her and, wanting her always on hand, would have tried to take Angélique with her. In fact, she has several times said in jest that if Angélique were in danger, she would throw herself after her, either to save her or to share the danger, but if it were her son, she would be satisfied with calling for help and shouting 'every man for himself'.

Contamine is slightly above average height, of good build, but a little awkward. His eyes are black, as are his beard, hair and eyebrows; his complexion is pale, his face open, his features pleasing; he has a broad forehead, a mouth which is delicate for a man, his teeth are white and regular, he has a strong, pleasant voice, his hands are chubby and dimpled – in all, he can be called a fine figure of a man. He doesn't lack wit, though he is not assertive. He is reliable, generous, a good friend, very gentle – but he can display considerable determination. He is capable of shedding tears: this has been a great asset to him where his mother is concerned, since women are very susceptible to tears. He is a man of integrity, whose word can be relied on; the story of his marriage is enough to ensure this reputation, and there are other actions of his which confirm its accuracy. He was, as you can see, a man who, by his wealth, his person and his temperament, might make a woman very happy, both in terms of his ample means and of his personal qualities, and he could have aspired to choose a wife from among the highest families in the land. His mother proposed several such parties for him, who have subsequently made excellent wives for those who married them, but he refused them all and cast his eyes on a girl whose station appeared vastly inferior to his own.

It was on Angélique that his gaze fell. You saw her earlier today, and you knew her when she lived in the home of the wife of Monsieur Dupuis senior. Angélique's father was a gentleman from Anjou, the youngest son in his family, whose fortune consisted of nothing but cloak and sword, and who, to make matters worse, married a young lady from his own part of the country who was no better off than himself. To his misfortune, he served under Monsieur le Maréchal d'Hocquincourt and was killed fighting for a faction opposed to the King. His death left his wife burdened with a daughter and entirely without resource. Furthermore, the Maréchal d'Hocquincourt was himself killed shortly afterwards, leaving Angélique's mother quite unable to provide for her daughter, and forcing her to seek some situation which might afford her a livelihood. Monsieur Dupuis let his wife bring Angélique into her home, out of charity rather than anything else, since at the age of seven or eight, which she was then, she could not perform much in the way of service. His wife, Mademoiselle Dupuis, who was very good-hearted, looked after her well. She had her taught to read and write, so that Angélique could help her look after the household accounts. Her husband was not usually interested in the details of her petty expenses, but sometimes, to annoy her, he insisted that she give him an account of all that she had spent – though he never demanded anything like that of his daughter. Angélique stayed there six or seven years, and when his wife died, Monsieur Dupuis wanted to send her to join his daughter at the convent where she was being brought up. But it happened that just then, the daughter of one of his wife's good friends was about to become maid of honour to Madame la Princesse de Cologny, and asked Monsieur Dupuis to let Angélique serve as companion to the young girl. Dupuis, knowing this woman to be perfectly reputable, willingly agreed. He spoke to Angélique, treating her as if he were her father. In fact, he did take a fatherly interest in her, for Angélique's father had been standard-bearer for the first company of Dupuis's regiment, and he had known him to be a thoroughly good man.

This, then, was how Angélique's good fortune began: instead of joining Monsieur Dupuis's daughter in a convent, she entered the service of Mademoiselle de Vougy, a young lady of about her own age who, within the next two or three days, became a lady-in-waiting to the Princesse de Cologny. By then, Angélique was fifteen or sixteen years old. I hardly need to draw her portrait, as you have just seen her. She is small, but her figure is ideally proportioned; her features are perfect and regular. In a word, she is a most beautiful and accomplished example of Nature's handiwork. The proof of this is that she succeeded in captivating a man whose gentle, reticent character would not have seemed likely to predispose him to such a fierce attachment. She has wit and wisdom, and can bend him as she wants: indeed, she needed all her wit to get to where she is. She is well read and has an excellent memory; she sings delightfully, dances extremely well, can paint a very pretty miniature – in fact, she has every quality. Her conduct is beyond reproach: at least, there is every appearance of this being so; if it had not been, she would not have achieved her present position. Contamine tried every inducement to obtain his goal without the sacrament; she rejected everything and preferred to lose all, rather than obtain a part by a means which would sully her honour. She succeeded, but she had luck on her side: without it, all her beauty and all her virtue would not have carried the day. She is self-assured, without false modesty, and thus people generally agree that she deserves her good fortune. She is devout, kind-hearted, generous, she is a good friend, and very discreet – she never gossips, or maligns people. It may be that her virtue is merely put on – but if this is so, and she is merely acting a part, she does it very well, since everything she does looks artless and perfectly natural.

So she became Mademoiselle de Vougy's companion. Her mistress studied singing and dancing and all the other accomplishments suitable to a young lady of quality. Angélique, who always accompanied her, benefited more from these lessons than her mistress. She learnt perfectly everything Mademoiselle de Vougy was taught, especially Italian and music, although the teachers rarely spoke to her directly.

Mademoiselle de Vougy was obliged to attend on Madame de Contamine on behalf of a relative of hers who had a dispute with this great lady. She took Angélique with her; Contamine saw Angélique and instantly fell in love with her. He did not speak to her at first: he only looked and admired. The matter in which Mademoiselle de Vougy had undertaken to mediate for her relative had to do with a road which had been moved back by one of Madame de Contamine's farmers, and now ran on the property of Mademoiselle de Vougy's cousin. The pretext was that this made the route shorter and more direct, but in truth it was a ploy on the part of the farmer who wanted to cause trouble for his neighbour and increase the area on his own side. This did considerable injustice to Mademoiselle de Vougy's relative, diminishing the size of his holding, but he was only a poor country gentleman of little account in comparison with Madame de Contamine. And to avoid a lawsuit against her, he had asked Mademoiselle de Vougy to endeavour to settle the matter amicably. However, there appeared to be some justification on the farmer's side of the argument, and the matter could not be settled in an instant; and fate had decreed that Angélique would play a part in reaching the settlement.

Her mistress was forced to go quite often to see Madame de Contamine and always took Angélique with her; and Contamine, who always saw her, became more and more enamoured. On one occasion, Mademoiselle de Vougy went into Madame de Contamine's room alone and left Angélique in the antechamber. Contamine came into this small room. It has given me the greatest pleasure to see you here so often, my dear young lady, he said. So it would seem, Monsieur, answered Angélique, judging by the necessity your mother and you impose on Mademoiselle de Vougy of coming here daily. Does this displease you? he asked. It certainly does not make me very happy, she replied, not only because I fear that Mademoiselle de Vougy is wasting her time, but because she is put in a demeaning position. Perhaps you should add, said he, that you are annoyed at having to sit alone in a house where you know no one, and where you are wasting the time you would much rather spend with your lover.

I have no answer to that remark, Monsieur, she said. Being alone in a respectable house like yours cannot cause me any misgiving, particularly as I am so near to your honourable mother; and supposing I were, in fact, regretting the company of a lover, your position is too elevated for you to be interested in hearing my confidences. But whatever the reason, were I the mistress, I would not care to press my case any further with people who, not having had the goodwill to accede at the first request, are not likely to accord it whatever solicitations one makes. How do you know there is not some other motive for the refusal, since it will always ensure a repetition of your visit? If that were true, she replied, I would say that such a hidden motive were improper, and that those who wish to see Mademoiselle de Vougy here so often have little consideration for her, since they give her all the trouble, some of which they could spare her by taking their turn and coming to see her.

But if it were you, and not she, that they wished to see, what would you say then? I do not know how to reply to such a suggestion, she said. Those people here who may wish to see me have certainly not enough influence to be concerned with the matter which brings us, neither would they feel it beneath them to come to Mademoiselle de Vougy's themselves. And if it were I? said Contamine, blushing, would you consent that I should come and see you? Most certainly not, she replied. And why not? he asked her. Because, she replied, the visits of a man like you to a person like me would be bound to give rise to a suspicion of wrongdoing, and I do not wish to provide any grounds for scandal. But go no further, Monsieur, in this vein. A man like you thinks he is doing a favour to a young woman like me when he speaks to her, but I assure you that I do not aspire to this favour, and that in fact it would cause me considerable chagrin. Then you must not be surprised, he replied, if I prevent Madame de Contamine from granting Mademoiselle de Vougy's suit, since I have no other way of seeing you than by ensuring that you and she continue to come here.

Go no further with this jesting, Monsieur, she said, in some confusion. Because of my lack of fortune, I am at your mercy, but be mindful that it is not becoming for a gentleman to insult a person whom fortune has placed beneath him, above all, a person of the weaker sex. I am not insulting you, I think, he replied, if I say I could not endure to forego the opportunity to see you, and that you are the loveliest person I have ever seen. I do not know, Monsieur, she said, whether you see any difference between insulting me and teasing me, but it seems to me that you are doing both. That is not so, he answered. On the contrary, I have the highest admiration and respect for you, and I would be in despair were you to take my words, which are utterly sincere, as jest. Yes, he added, let me say again, you seem to me the most adorable person in the world, and I love you more than anyone in the world. Find a way of letting me see you, do not deprive me of the chance of seeing you, and from this very day, I promise that we will no longer require your attendance here, since these visits vex you.

I would have to be mad, she said, to give any credence to what you say. But, no matter: I will pretend to believe you, if you promise that we will no longer be compelled to make these visits. Bring the paper that Mademoiselle de Vougy requires, give it to her at her home. She will be grateful for the courtesy and will not refuse if you ask permission to visit her. That is true, he said, but in that case it will be she whom I see and not you, whereas you are the one I wish to see. I am always with her, Angélique replied, and when you see her, you will see me. That may be so, he answered, but even if I saw you, I would not be able to speak to you. If this is a second condition, she said, which you are trying to add to the first, you will achieve less by insisting we come here than if you came to Mademoiselle de Vougy's; for I vow that I will never again open my mouth here, whereas at her house I will not stop you from taking any opportunity to speak with me that chance may bring about. I shall even take into account all the footsteps you have saved us!

You are playing with me, he said. You are making these fine proposals only so that I deprive myself of the means I have at present of seeing you, and then you will laugh at me. Not so, she answered. But since, by your own admission, you have it in your power to give us satisfaction, and yet you refuse to do so in order to make us continue our visits, I swear that I will not come here again: that from today I shall beg Mademoiselle de Vougy to release me from my duties as her companion when she comes to see Madame de Contamine. That would be a harsh blow and would make me very unhappy, he replied. I do not seek to make you happy, she answered, since you are not in the least desirous of obliging us.

But if you did have an obligation to me, what would you do to show it? he asked. Anything you like, she responded. That sounds like promising all in order to do nothing, he said. But promise less, and perform what you promise. And what do you ask me to promise? she asked, laughing. I ask you, he said earnestly, to believe that I love you. I will believe it, she said. What proof will you give me? said Contamine. Whatever you like, she said, providing it is within my power, and I am able to give it. At that point, Mademoiselle de Vougy came out of Madame de Contamine's room and carried Angélique off home with her.

Angélique did not mention the conversation she had had with Madame de Contamine's son: it meant far too much to her; but from that moment, it is certain she began to lay great store by what he had said. She felt quite sure that Contamine had spoken from the heart, but to test it, she resolved not to accompany Mademoiselle de Vougy on her visits to Madame de Contamine in future and found a pretext for staying at home on Mademoiselle de Vougy's next visit four days later. The latter made no more headway on this occasion than previously and came home infuriated by Madame de Contamine's continued refusal to come to terms. Angélique, who heard her complaints, flattered herself that before long the desired agreement would be forthcoming, but she took good care to give no hint of this. Her expectation was proved right. Contamine came in fact the next day, but since it was not Mademoiselle de Vougy he wanted to see, he called at a time when she was out with the Princesse de Cologny. He had known very well she would not be at home, but told the footman he would await her

return. He was shown up to her room, where he found
Angélique alone, as he had hoped.

Are you satisfied, dear Angélique, with what you have
done? he asked her. You kept your word by not coming to
the house with Mademoiselle de Vougy; will you also keep it
by showing the gratitude you promised me? Here is the
document, he continued, showing her a piece of paper. We
are granting more than was asked for: what thanks will you
give me?

I owe you none, she replied, laughing. Your generosity is
not altogether disinterested, and I therefore consider the
conditions of the bargain are not entirely binding. Do not
make a joke of it! he said. I am in earnest. Will you not be so
too? How can I be serious, she said, about something which
is quite nonsensical? Do you think I am simple enough to
believe that it is just for my sake that you are now granting
Mademoiselle de Vougy what you formerly refused her? I
would have to be a simpleton to believe that, and it would
be pure folly on my part to take you seriously. Nonetheless,
it is absolutely true, he said, it is wholly because of you that
we are making this settlement, and were it not for you,
neither she nor her cousin would have obtained anything
from my mother and myself. And as I am a Christian, I swear
I love you more than anyone has ever been loved before.
Now, after that declaration, do you think it would be so
foolish to take me seriously? There can be no further doubts
about the sincerity of my love, so believe me and answer me
in all seriousness. I came knowing Mademoiselle de Vougy
was out so that I could see you alone; and a moment or two
before she returns, you will see a lackey bring a message
requiring my departure, so that I shall have to make
another visit and will have another chance to see and speak
to you. So do not prevaricate: answer me truly and honestly.

Indeed, she answered, what you have just said has
impressed me so strongly that my frivolity has quite

vanished, and I am as serious as I have ever been in my life, and will answer you as you would have me do. I believe you love me, since you tell me so; but what is your intention? To love you for ever, he answered, and to be loved by you. Suppose that you are not loved, what will you do? said Angélique. I shall be forever unhappy, he said, but I will not cease to love you. And suppose on the other hand that I, in turn, do love you, then what? I will do whatever you wish in order to make you happy. What I wish may not be what you would want, she said. The love that a man of your rank has for a person of mine dishonours her if it is known, or dishonours him if he gives way to it and lets it rule him so that he marries beneath him. Give heed to what I say, she added. I prefer to remain poor for the rest of my life, rather than become rich by any dishonourable means. The only possession I have of value is my virtue and I will not sell it. Therefore expect nothing of me which will do me dishonour; neither do I expect anything on your part which would bring scorn on you, or for which people would blame you. Though I am born a gentlewoman, my lack of fortune debars me from marriage with you; yet I have too much virtue and self-respect ever to be your mistress. You asked me to give you a serious response. I think you will agree I have done so.

Yes, said he, you have done so. I anticipated a part of your reply, I admit, but I hardly expected it to be so forthright. As to marrying, the whole world would blame me if I were to marry someone who ... I am well aware, she interrupted sharply, that I am a mere dependent in someone else's household. You need not remind me of that, but I also know that if, in order to change my station, I am required to do something disreputable, I shall remain a dependent all my life. You are not the first person to offer me your help – others have done so. But both my religion and my upbringing have taught me that poverty is not a vice, and that before both God and men a penniless woman who is virtuous is more honoured and more estimable than a rich courtesan. These are my beliefs; let yours conform. I do not ask you to marry me. I can expect no such thing, but I beg you to make no other demands of me, but to leave me in peace. Wait for Mademoiselle de Vougy or do not wait; that is of no matter to me, nor is your piece of paper. And now, rather than give ear any further to your talk, which it is not fitting I should hear, I take my leave. She tried to leave the room, but he restrained her. Stop, he said, my dearest Angélique, you have heard only part of what I have to say. Perhaps, said she, but I know your thoughts, and I take them as said, and she left in spite of him.

He chose to leave too, without seeing Mademoiselle de Vougy. He was in despair as to what course of action to take: as to marrying her, he could see no possibility of that; he did not even consider it at that point; but as to renouncing her, this he could not contemplate either. For her part, she had seen in his eyes how much he loved her, and she resolved to follow her fortune as far as it would take her. She knew he was too ensnared to be able to free himself, and felt sure that, with time, she could bring him to the point of asking her to marry him, so she resolved to proceed, with all the virtue and pride she could muster, yet without ever antagonising him by the slightest arrogance or discourtesy; and in truth, no one ever steered such a delicate course more skilfully.

She told Mademoiselle de Vougy that Contamine had been to see her, without giving any further explanation, for fear of misrepresenting him or saying something he might not have wished. He returned the next day, once again when Mademoiselle de Vougy was out. As he entered the room, Angélique gave a low curtsey, but didn't say a word; before even returning his greeting, she went and brought another young woman into the room. Angélique then spoke to Contamine and told him that Mademoiselle de Vougy had been informed of his visit the previous day. She does not know, Monsieur, the reason for your visit – whether it was to grant her request, or on some other errand – but only that you were here, and if she had not gone out again with the Princesse today, she would have spared you the trouble of returning; but I have no doubt that she will call on you this evening, though it will be late, since she is at the Palais du Luxembourg. And I do not advise you to wait for her. If what I had to say to her were important enough to warrant that I await her return, would you not agree to keep me company? he asked. I have nothing to say to you, Monsieur, and I do not think there can be any conversation between us capable of holding your interest. You must certainly be needed elsewhere; it is better for her to come to you this evening, as she plans; for after you have waited a considerable time, it may well be that a lackey will come for you, and you would still have to leave without seeing her. You are malicious, he said, with your lackey. But there is no need for Mademoiselle de Vougy to trouble herself to call on me. She will do so gladly, provided it is for the last time, she said. He stayed the whole afternoon, but was given no opportunity to see Angélique alone: her attendant never left her side. In the end he left, with a civil salutation, which she returned, and let him go.

Mademoiselle de Vougy called on him that same evening, but he was not at home. She spoke to Madame de Contamine and learnt from her that a document had been duly drawn up, and that he wanted to bring it to her himself. And in fact he came the next day and gave it to her, with the utmost civility, apologising for the fact that it had taken so long for an agreement to be reached, and pointing out that her cousin was receiving more than he had originally asked for. The young lady thanked him sincerely, in Angélique's presence, adding that she felt particularly indebted to him.

Your mother, she said, seemed so little disposed to come to any understanding the last time I spoke to her that I thought the case was hopeless, but she told me yesterday she had not been able to withstand your insistence on an even more favourable disposition than we had requested – that you had even persuaded her to give up a piece of ground of greater value to my cousin than the one he had asked for. So it is to you, Monsieur, that I must express my gratitude for this result. I thank you, Monsieur, and so will my cousin – who is a very respectable person whom you will not be sorry to have helped. He replied in a thoroughly proper manner and concluded by asking if he might be allowed to call on her from time to time, to which she agreed.

As he left, he tried to give a letter to Angélique; she did not take it and appeared not even to have seen it, although, in fact, she was extremely grateful for his perseverance and for what he had done for Mademoiselle de Vougy. He came back the next day and continued his visits for more than a month, making it appear that he was in love with Mademoiselle de Vougy. Everyone teased her about this; the Princesse de Cologny herself said it would be a great conquest for her. Mademoiselle de Vougy did not deny it; she admitted that she would be very pleased with such a match; that, not to mention his property and his fortune, she found Contamine himself very attractive; but she told the Princesse – who offered to broach the matter on her behalf – that he had not declared himself, and she begged her to wait and allow him to speak first. This young lady is quite good-looking, and pleasant; clearly the intervention of the Princesse would have been embarrassing for Contamine and would have caused Angélique to despair. She was distinctly alarmed, and it was for this reason that the next time he tried to give her a letter, Contamine was not rebuffed. She took it, trembling, as if she were doing something wicked, and as soon as she was alone she read it. This is what it said:

This is the sixth letter I have written to you, beautiful Angélique, and I do not know if it will have more success than its predecessors. I will not say I love you: I flatter myself you do not doubt this. I don't ask you to trust my words, but to believe my actions. I do not say that I am ready to marry you – you yourself do not expect this. Neither do I renounce the desire for a legitimate union. It would be useless for me to try. My heart is in torment. Leave your present lowly position; withdraw to some place where you will be your own mistress. Move from a neighbourhood where you are too well known; accept the means which I offer you, merely to oblige me, without in any way engaging yourself. If we were in some place where you were not known, I would not hesitate an instant: you would be mine, if you so consented. But in Paris! However irresistible your charms, and however strong my love for you, would I be forgiven if I married you as you are now? I do not say this to destroy your hopes; but I ask you to save me from becoming a public spectacle. Allow me a moment's conversation alone with you; you will disentangle the feelings of my heart, which are so confused that I cannot unravel them myself. I await your reply – as a sentence of life or death – with the utmost impatience. Farewell.

The tone of this letter led Angélique to believe that all was possible, so long as she kept her head, and made no false move; and in fact, she never lost her composure. Contamine returned the next day: he was sure that she would speak to him, or agree to meet him somewhere. He was mistaken. She had no intention of making things easy for him. He was obliged to wait for an opportunity to see her when Mademoiselle de Vougy was out, which did not occur for another week, and during all this time she appeared indifferent to his distress and his impatience – but inwardly, she rejoiced in her power over him. Finally, he found her alone, and by this time she, too, was grateful for the occasion because some words of the Princesse's had reawakened her jealousy.

What have you decided, then, dear Angélique? he asked her. Are you going to lead me to despair? Am I not sufficiently submissive? Are you trying to heighten my love even further? I assure you, that is not possible. Tell me what my fate is to be – what is to become of us? I want you to leave me in peace, she answered. I understand your reasons for not wishing to marry me; therefore, understand mine for wishing never to see you again. Do not pursue the matter further; you would merely be wasting your time and making me unhappy, were I credulous enough to listen to you.

But tell me, he repeated, what you would have me do. I will do anything. I want you to consider marrying Mademoiselle de Vougy, she said. She thinks of you, she would be a suitable match for you, and I am not. I have no desire to think of her, he said, and would to God you were really jealous of her – the sacrifice I would make of her would convince you where my real feelings lie. Then, she said, make this sacrifice for me, and stop coming here. Then I would not see you, he said. But you would convince me the more, she interrupted. So be it, he replied, this will be my last visit. Your orders will be obeyed, and the sacrifice of my visits to Mademoiselle de Vougy costs my heart nothing. But dear Angélique, he added, throwing himself at her knees, his tears streaming on to her hands, I cannot live without seeing and speaking to you. You know how to write, she said, and I will not refuse your letters.

But, he said, you will still be in a position which makes it impossible for me to pay court to you. Change it, I beg you. I have sufficient means to provide for you to live elsewhere, more suitably, and in more distinguished fashion. I cannot

bear to see you any longer forced to spend your time performing a service which is unworthy of you and of me – time
which I would like you to spend thinking of my love for you.
Take up lodging elsewhere, be your own mistress. Bring
your mother to live with you. My visits then will not be
improper. What would people say if they knew that, well
received by the mistress, I prefer her waiting-woman? I will
not come here in future, since you forbid it; I will write to
you, since you permit it – but who will bring your answers to
me? Who is there whom we can entrust with a secret of such
great moment to us? If you lived in a neighbourhood far
removed from here, where neither you nor your mother
were known, and changed your style of living, what you are
at present would be forgotten. And if you will agree to save
appearances, I will do the rest. Consult your mother. I will
ask no favours of you which might endanger your reputation. In return for any presents I give you, I ask only the
pleasure of giving them, and of seeing you in a position
which does not force me to disguise the tenderness of my
regard. You yourself would not approve if I were to declare
publicly that I was in love with a chamber-maid. But I shall
soon be forced to this, if you will not put out your hand and
save me from the precipice. But, by changing your manner
of living and disguising your lack of fortune, I shall not be
dishonoured if I let my feelings for you be known.

The feelings you have expressed, she replied, are perfectly honourable. You are quite right, I could not approve
of your declaring yourself the suitor of a mere servant; I
should esteem you less were you to do this. But can you
approve of my accepting the means you offer me of escaping from my present situation? Would my reputation not be
in jeopardy? Should I not in effect be selling myself if I take
the help you offer me? What will people say if I suddenly
appear in a different guise? I shall be recognised – what will
not people believe to my disadvantage? How could your

visits appear innocent? You will agree with me that it is not enough for a woman to be chaste and virtuous – albeit that is the essential – she must also appear so. Would I appear so, if I did as you wished? Would people believe you were doing so much for me out of simple charity, and that I was not buying your gifts with criminal favours? What would become of me if, having taken up a train of life beyond my means, I were abandoned by you – for whatever cause. I do not speak of a change in your feelings – I trust in your constancy, or at least in your generosity – but you are mortal. How could I maintain the manner of living I had adopted? The butt of everyone's scorn, should I then be reduced to support by real debauchery the lifestyle which had formerly merely had that appearance? I accepted the justice of your reasons, but are mine not also just, and do you not admit this?

Yes, dear Angélique, he answered. Till now, I adored you for your beauty, but at present I admire you for your good sense and virtue; and since you are at last willing to discuss the matter with me, allow me to tell you what I am determined to do. I have arranged ... As he was about to continue, Mademoiselle de Vougy came in. He remained only a moment with her, then went home, intending to write to Angélique telling her what he had been going to say. He did so, but had no chance to give her the letter either that day or the next. In the end, he heard that her mother had been taken ill, and that Angélique had gone to look after her, since they did not have the means to pay anyone else to perform this service. He had a great deal of difficulty discovering where she and her mother were living, but by dint of endless enquiry he found out and went there.

Angélique was completely amazed when he came to this house, where she had had so little expectation of seeing him, but he was even more shocked to see the poverty in which she and her mother were living. He realised they were in very straitened circumstances and in need of his help. His visit was short. Angélique's first thought was that she would never see him again, and this idea caused her great pain; but after a little reflection she came to a different conclusion. Indeed, he returned in half an hour.

You are in no position for me to be able to speak to you here, dear Angélique, he said. I do not even dare to stay for any time, but I will come every day for news of you and your mother. Take good care of her, but don't neglect your own health, which is extremely precious to me. I am grieved to learn of her illness and to see you in a place so unworthy of someone I adore. I must not stay now. Don't let anyone go to your cupboard; I shall find out tomorrow how much regard you have for me. He left immediately and she went to look in the cupboard. In it she saw a very fine purse, which she took and opened. It was full of gold coins, and it also contained a letter. Angélique took the letter out and read the following words:

You are in no position, dear Angélique, to refuse the help which I offer for your mother. Her state of health demands that I provide for her needs. It is not for you that my gifts are intended; they are solely to supply what your mother requires, and you would be responsible before God for the course her illness might take if, out of pride, you refused the means to relieve her. You are in no way indebted to me for what I do; it is done out of pure charity, and the only obligation you have is the proper use of what I am giving you. See if you can improve the furnishing of your quarters. This can be done quietly and without fanfare; and I shall know if you have any esteem for me by that which you show for your mother, both with regard to improving the comfort of your rooms, and to obtaining what is needed to preserve her life and enable her to regain her health.

Angélique had never before been in such a quandary about what course of action to take as she was when she read this letter. She was in need of many things and her mother was seriously ill and required assistance. It was being offered to her, but by her lover. If she accepted, she was afraid of being indebted to him. She later told Mademoiselle Dupuis and myself that she had been at a loss as to what she should do, and that she would not have been able to make up her mind so readily had it not been for a Capuchin monk, who had come to hear her mother's confession and whose advice she sought. She told him under the seal of the confessional exactly what her position with regard to Contamine was, and he told her that she could accept the latter's help with a clear conscience, and do as she was bidden in the letter, without being under any commitment to him.

So she took advantage of Contamine's offer and was very relieved that the opinion of a man of God coincided with that of her heart. For in her heart she was not sorry to be indebted to a man whom she loved, and who was acting in such an honourable and generous way. She bought a tapestry for the wall, and some chairs, and generally made the room, if not luxurious, at least respectable enough to receive visitors in. Contamine came to see her the next day. He approved of what she had done, and thanked her for doing as he had asked. She in turn thanked him for his generosity and explained frankly that she had decided to accept it only after consulting her mother's confessor. He laughingly reproved her for such unnecessary cautiousness and repeated that she was under no obligation to him. However, dear Angélique, he continued, I have one more request to make, which will put me under an obligation to you if you agree to it, and which is also for your mother's sake. You are not strong or sturdy enough to endure the strain of nursing a sick woman day and night. You are too young to stay awake all night attending your mother. You must engage a woman to look after her at night-time. Buy a small bed for yourself, so that you can sleep out here in this room, not in the enclosed atmosphere of a sickroom, which you are unused to. Your mother will be better cared for, and I shall not be so afraid for your well-being. Angélique was grateful to him for such thoughtfulness, and though she appeared to agree only reluctantly to what he asked, she was actually quite pleased to comply.

He sent her a ewer, two serving dishes, two plates, two spoons, two forks, two large candlesticks and a small candleholder – all of silver – and also all the things that might be required by a sick woman. He refrained from sending more than this for fear that Angélique would absolutely refuse to take it. All this kind generosity began to soften Angélique's reserve.

Contamine asked permission to visit her every day: she consented unwillingly, and to avoid gossip and ensure that his visits did not become known, only on condition that he come in the evening, so late that nobody would be about, and above all, on condition that he leave his carriage and servants some distance away. I do not want people to have any suspicion of who you are, she said. You want me to hire a nurse for my mother, and I will do so, to please you; but so that this woman will have no reason to wonder about your visits, it would be as well for us to tell her you are my cousin – my mother's nephew. No such person exists, but she is not to know this. We will even say that your days are not your own, and that you are only free to come in the evening. Your visits will appear to be those of a dutiful relative. And I trust your behaviour will be as proper with me as it would be if I did indeed have the honour to be your cousin.

He did as she wished, and no day passed without his going to see her, and without his either taking or sending some present, which she had no choice but to accept. Though appearing reluctant, in her heart, she was highly gratified by his generosity. In the presence of the nurse, he behaved as if he were indeed Angélique's cousin, and since he always went late in the day he was never seen or recognised.

Gradually her mother's health improved. Contamine was as pleased as if she had been his own mother, and Angélique felt grateful to him for this. He asked the convalescent if she could now eat something. The nurse, answering on her behalf, said she would be able to, and that she would give her some grilled chicken for her supper the next day. Then I will join you, Aunt, he rejoined promptly. I will have supper with you. Don't worry about the food. I will take care of it. I will be one of the family tomorrow, my dear cousin, he continued, speaking to Angélique. She was so taken aback by his sudden decision that she didn't say a word. Early the next morning he sent a locked box to her, and a quarter of an hour later he sent the key, with a note, in which he told her to open the box at some time when the nurse would not be present to see the contents. She therefore opened it while she was alone, and inside she found the rest of the beautiful silver dinner service, from which nothing was missing. It was carefully packed, with cotton wadding tightly filling the spaces between all the pieces. Seeing a note just inside the box, Angélique took it out and read it. It said:

It would be a pity, my charming cousin, if your table lacked suitable tableware and were not properly laid. Take the service out of this box, and put it in your own box, or in the cupboard, so that the nurse does not realise that it has been brought especially for this evening's supper. It will be soon enough for it to appear this evening – which I am looking forward to impatiently. Had I waited for an invitation, I fear I would never have had supper with you, so I invited myself – and believe I was right to do so.

Nothing could have been more galant than this present, and the way in which it was given made it even more precious. Contamine arrived at suppertime, carrying the food he had bought. He came early, enveloped in an enormous cloak, to avoid being recognised. While the nurse saw to the cooking of the chicken, he and Angélique sat together by her mother's bed. Angélique tried to thank him for his present, but he continually interrupted her, telling her how delighted he was to be sharing a meal with her for the first time. Angélique, on the advice of her confessor and with Contamine's consent, had told her mother who he was. The ailing woman was amazed to see such love for her daughter in a man of his rank, and to see with what delight he had himself arranged an opportunity to share their meal – an honour beyond anything she could have expected. She knew about his gifts, and his kindness towards herself, which had contributed in no small measure to the recovery of her health, which was daily improving. As for the supper, no one had ever looked happier or more contented than Contamine, and Angélique has told us that it was on this occasion that she was finally persuaded of the sincerity of his intentions towards her.

As soon as Angélique's mother was well enough to leave her bed and get up, Contamine found an opportunity to speak to her and ask for her support in persuading Angélique to agree to what he wanted to do for her. He sent the nurse into town on some pretext and, with Angélique present, spoke to her mother. I do not need to tell you, Madame, he said, that I am in love with your daughter. I am sure she has told you this, and my actions must have made it clear to you. My intentions towards her are completely honourable. I intend to marry her. However, this cannot be for some time, for, in spite of my love for her, I can never forget the respect I owe my mother. She has always been too good to me for me ever to wish to cause her the least pain, and you yourself will recognise that there is no possibility that I can ask her permission to marry your daughter, and even less that she would consent. I know that she is determined that I should marry, but I shall reject all those she suggests as possible brides, and I shall never belong to anyone but my dearest Angélique. She can be assured of that. Nonetheless, you can see that it would be extremely awkward for me to marry someone who had been known to be a serving-maid. What is done is done, but for the future I beg you both to adopt a different style of life. I have asked Angélique to move to a different neighbourhood, and now I ask you to agree to this. The woman who has been looking after you does not know who you are and need never know. Let her stay with you for the time being, until you have your own servant, and until Angélique has a chamber-maid and a boy to run errands for her. I will provide for all you need in the way of household furnishings and clothes. And since it is true that I am mortal, and if God were to take my life, you would be unable to pay all the bills you will incur, here, he continued, drawing three parchments from his pocket, are two bonds which I have bought in her name and which I give her – one issued by the city of Paris, the other by another community. These will provide her with an income. And thirdly, here is the deed of a house near the Porte de Bussy, which I also give her. If, because of my death, I do not marry her, she will be able to maintain a decent style of life for the rest of her days.

But, dearest Angélique, he went on, turning to her, since you might think these gifts will give me some hold over you, and that I might wish to obtain from you favours contrary to your virtue and to the respect I have for you, I am going to ask your mother always to be present while we are together, and I promise that from now on I will never come to see you except with your permission and, indeed, so rarely that my visits will give no cause for gossip. I promise that I will have as much respect for you as if you were as far above me as you would be if your fortune were in keeping with your merit. Can you now have any doubt as to the purity of my intentions? I will do more. One is not master of one's feelings: if it should be my misfortune that you cannot willingly give yourself to me, you are free. What I am giving you will enable you to find a good husband. If I can know that you are happy and contented, I feel that I shall be so too. On the other hand, I should die of misery and despair if, in marrying you, I did not make your whole happiness, as I hope you will make mine.

Angélique, who had had no expectation of such a gift or of such generous and honourable behaviour, was so moved that she could not find words to reply. She threw herself at Contamine's feet, with a bursting heart and tears in her eyes. Don't mock me, dear Angélique, he said, kissing her hands, which he was holding; and she, out of gratitude, or love, or some other feeling which she could not control, threw her arms round his neck and embraced him with all her strength. He returned her kisses and kept her in his arms as long as he could. In the end, she drew away, confused and ashamed of what she had done. Dearest Angélique, he said, do not regret having shown me that you are not as completely indifferent towards me as I had feared. This is the first token of affection you have given me, and I am a thousand times more delighted with it than by any words you could have spoken. I do not know, she said, whether I did right or wrong, but although I was too forward, and even shameless, I do not regret it. How happy you make me, he answered, clasping her hands. So tell me, do you agree to my proposals? I will do whatever you wish, she said. Your actions have been too kind and you have been too open with me for me to have any further misgivings. I accept your gifts, so that I shall be less unworthy of you. And I believe you will find my mother, too, quite ready to give her approval. You promise then to be my wife? he asked, embracing her. And I swear I will be your husband as soon as I am my own master and it can be done without risking our future. Will you accept, he continued, smiling and putting a string of pearls round her neck, the chain which binds you to me, and this ring which assures you of my faithfulness? She let him give her both without more ado. Remember, he said, that it is not in reality such things as these which bind us to each other, but the feelings of our hearts. He then enjoined the two women to buy themselves some good furniture and some more fashionable clothes. The next day he brought Angélique three times as much money as she and her mother would need, and told her that as soon as she was ready he would take her to see her house, in which he had reserved the first apartment for herself. Before leaving, he begged them to make the preparations to move from their present lodging and into their new home as soon as they could.

This they did. Before long, Angélique began to look very different, dressing with great elegance. Contamine took delight in providing her with fine petticoats, headdresses, lace and all the niceties a man can buy for a lady; and since everything was of the finest quality, Angélique took on an added radiance. He took her to see the house; she was completely satisfied with her apartment and thought the house itself beautiful. He introduced her as the owner to the lawyer who occupied the rest of the house, and then waited two weeks before paying his next visit, giving Angélique and her mother time to procure furniture and settle in without any appearance of involvement on his part. When he next returned, he was highly satisfied with what he saw: nothing was missing, everything was perfect both in style and comfort.

Angélique had a serving-maid and a young boy to do her errands, and her mother had a woman who also did the cooking. Angélique had one splendid room for herself and a second smaller room, also very fine; her mother had a large, well-furnished room with an antechamber. There was another room for the chamber-maid and the cook to sleep in, and a very large, well-appointed kitchen with all the utensils one could need, where the lackey slept. Thus there were six rooms on the same level, which led into each other, starting from the antechamber, without using the front staircase; Angélique had even had the doors which led from her rooms to the staircase walled up, so that one had to enter from the courtyard by the back staircase. The court-yard had an iron gate which was always kept closed. This courtyard was also separated by an iron railing from the garden, which Contamine had decreed was for Angélique's use alone. This garden was reached from her apartment by some steps, without going through the courtyard. In the garden, Contamine, or rather Angélique herself, had installed two painted garden houses, with tables and chairs in them, and on the other two sides were leafy, arched walkways.

The apartment that Angélique and her mother lived in, then, was on a single floor from front to back, and the rest of the house was taken by a man of law who himself rented out part of it to a merchant and to some other tenants, so that Angélique, comfortably lodged herself, received two thousand francs in rent for the rest of her house. From this description, you can see that it is a roomy, attractive place, of considerable value, especially when you consider its location. It still belongs to Angélique, just like everything that Contamine has given her since their marriage, for they were married with separation of property – and he can die whenever he pleases; she will still be able to maintain her present style of life, with five sturdy lackeys behind her carriage, and all the rest to match.

Contamine was pleased with everything he saw in the

house, and not least with Angélique, who, far from showing any lingering traces of her days of poverty, displayed all the graces of a high-born woman of quality. He asked her to take up her lessons in singing and dancing and music again, and in all the other womanly accomplishments. This she did with great success, and in her leisure time she read a great deal. She decided to learn to paint miniatures, and at this, too, she was successful, and in less than a year Contamine agreed to sit for her, and she was skilled enough to paint his portrait. She also did a self-portrait by looking at herself in a mirror, which she gave to Contamine, as well as a number of other miniatures which she had painted. To him, these were presents of the highest value. She was the admiration of all those in the neighbourhood who knew her. She went out very little, however – partly so that she would not be seen and partly also so that Contamine would always find her at home when he called. He didn't visit her often, and there was never any suspicion of scandal. When he found her in the company of the others who lived in the house, he stayed, and had no private conversation with her, and so no one had occasion to speak ill of them. I don't think anything improper happened between them; it certainly doesn't seem plausible to me that Contamine would have married her if she had given herself to him without the sacrament. It was not for want of asking, though, or for want of propositions which others would not have refused – but they were all rejected; indeed, the more grateful she felt towards him, the more circumspect she became.

She now displayed, as I said, the air of a noblewoman and behaved like a lady of high breeding; and it is true that she had lived and been brought up in houses that could be called schools of good manners. But the same could not be said of her mother, who did not undergo a similar transformation. Angélique feared with some justification that her mother might let fly some angry word which could have been very damaging; she therefore indulged her every whim and took care not to upset her in any way. Angélique herself, however, was often put to some trouble, particularly with regard to going in or out of her room, since this necessitated going through her mother's room. Angélique frequently spent part of the evening in her garden with the young girls who lived in the same house, and others from the neighbourhood, and her mother went to bed earlier than she did. Her mother's irritability arose from her frequent indispositions, her advancing years and the misfortunes she had suffered, which had embittered her; besides, her manners had never been polished, since she had always lived either among country folk in the provinces, or with lower-class people in Paris. Nevertheless, she and Angélique lived together in this way for more than two years, at the end of which time she had a relapse and died. And the only thing left to say about her is that on her deathbed she had the good sense to thank Contamine for all he had done for her, to recommend Angélique to his care, and to remind Angélique herself always to cherish her virtue, and to comport herself in such a way that he would always retain the same feelings of love and respect as he had for her now. Angélique hardly needed this advice: she already knew how incumbent it was on her to conduct herself wisely, and that her whole future depended on it.

Angélique arranged a very proper funeral for her mother and realised that, being now on her own, there might well be times when her lover would visit her and when she would forget her strict resolutions of prudence and virtue. She was aware that on several occasions, it had been her mother's presence which had obliged Contamine to observe the rules of decorum, when this might not have been the case had she been alone. She wanted him to maintain his respectful behaviour, and being alone was not the way to ensure this. Her chamber-maid could not be counted on to resist the presents of a man of as liberal a disposition as Contamine and might be persuaded to leave her alone with him. She recognised the danger she was in – either of allowing him some favour which would be her ruin (which would have been only too easy, so she admitted to us, because she loved him as much as he loved her), or of rebuffing his advances and appearing to reject him. She therefore determined to take precautions against herself, and to find some external means to guarantee the propriety of her behaviour.

To this end, she asked Contamine to allow her to move into a convent. She had no intention of doing this, and knew very well that he would not agree: in order to get the smaller concession she really wanted, she began by asking for a larger one. Contamine was indeed dismayed by the request, and refused to give his consent – while saying she was nonetheless mistress of her own conduct and he would not impose his will. Angélique did not insist. Instead, she asked him if he would agree to let her reduce the size of her establishment, which was now larger than she needed. She wanted to dismiss her cook and take her meals with the family of the lawyer who occupied the second and third floors of the house. Contamine smiled when he heard this proposition, whose motive was not too difficult for him to penetrate, and gave her permission to do whatever she thought best. Although he realised that this arrangement was not to his advantage, he esteemed her the more for suggesting it, and told her so with a smile, saying he was pleased to see he was not quite as harmless as he had thought, since the idea of being alone with him apparently alarmed her. So she began to take her meals with her neighbours in the house, and it was this which led to her ultimate good fortune, as you will see. For if she had not made this change, Mademoiselle Dupuis would not have heard her spoken of on a certain occasion, and would not have been able to help her as she did.

101

Angélique went even further. So that there would always be someone nearby who could vouch for her actions, she lent the room next to hers, which had been her mother's, to the two daughters of the man who occupied the rest of the house, and in whose household she now took her meals, allowing them to sleep there. This gentleman was, as I've already said, in the legal profession and had been living in the house a long time. He was a very decent, upright person, and his wife was a very good sort too. His only children were a boy, the oldest, who was by way of being a lawyer too and worked in his father's office, and the two daughters, who were about the same age as Angélique – well brought up, presentable, good-looking girls. It was with these two that Angélique was particularly friendly: in fact, the three of them were nearly always together.

The older of the two girls had been a boarder at the convent where Mademoiselle Dupuis had been brought up, and so there was a degree of acquaintanceship between them. One day they chanced to meet in the arcade of shops at the Palais de Justice, and since a light rain had begun to fall they started to chat to each other. Mademoiselle Dupuis, finding that her friend was going in the direction of the Faubourg Saint-Germain, offered to take her in her carriage. The girl accepted and on the way painted such a dazzling portrait of Angélique's beauty, wit and wealth – without naming the person she was describing – that Mademoiselle Dupuis became quite desirous of meeting her, and when they reached the door she stepped out of her carriage and came into the house. She saw Angélique and eyed her closely, trying to remember where she had seen her before. Angélique recognised her immediately, but gave no indication of this in front of the others, so that at first Mademoiselle Dupuis thought she must be wrong. But when she heard the name de la Bustelière (which was Angélique's father's name) she knew she had not been mistaken. She bethought her and realised it was the same young lady that she had seen at her mother's house.

Two days later she went to the house again; she ate lunch there and stayed part of the afternoon; and since I joined her there, I also saw Angélique, her house, and how well it was furnished. We went into her private apartment, where Mademoiselle Dupuis was thrown into the utmost astonishment by the magnificence of what she saw. Angélique was not unaware of this and said she wanted to show her something more. She opened a jewellery box which contained jewels of enormous value. It is certain that Contamine intended to marry her – he would never have given such a fortune to a mistress. This jewellery box and the gems it contained would in themselves have constituted one of the richest marriage settlements. May I have a word with you? said Mademoiselle Dupuis, amazed by such a display of wealth. Certainly, answered Angélique, smiling. I know what you are about to say. All I ask of you is that you keep my secret. What I have just shown you was to prepare you for what I have to tell you, which is what you want to know. Mademoiselle Dupuis gave her word not to betray any secret Angélique confided to her. They changed the subject and talked of other things while we were there, and then, when we had rejoined the others, they went off into the garden and walked there by themselves.

It would be pointless to try and dissemble before you, Angélique said to her. You recognise me and, on the understanding that you will keep my secret, I will explain my present circumstances to you, for I am sure you must have come to a conclusion which is contrary to the truth. No, answered Mademoiselle Dupuis, I have not made any rash judgement about your situation. What I think is that you have contracted a very advantageous marriage which has not been made known to the world. I promise I will not give you away, if you are ready to confide in me. I am still unmarried, said Angélique, and as much a virgin as on the day I was born; and yet it is to a man that I owe everything you have seen. Then she told the whole story to Mademoiselle Dupuis, who was very much surprised, as you will easily credit. Certainly, to begin with, she did not believe Angélique to be as chaste and blameless as she claimed. Nevertheless, she promised not to betray her secret, while at the same time she took pains to ascertain more about how Angélique conducted herself, and about who visited her. She found nothing which did not agree with what Angélique had told her. She learned that Angélique never went out except to church, or to go walking, and never alone, always accompanied by the two sisters, and usually with their mother; that nobody but Contamine ever came to see her, and that he rarely spoke to her in private, and never out of sight, and that in fact his visits were not frequent; that she led a simple, retired sort of life and went little into company; that her chamber-maid slept in her room with her, and the two sisters slept in the room one had to pass through to get to hers; and that no one could get into her apartment without being seen by the people who opened the iron gate leading into the courtyard – the only entrance there was – and which always remained shut, since it was weighted to close itself. Mademoiselle Dupuis told me all this, and I thought it was all a fine façade covering a less blameless reality. She begged me not to divulge any of what she had told me: I promised, and kept my promise. And my suspicions were in fact unfounded: there is no doubt that Angélique's behaviour was exemplary.

She lived in this way for nearly two years after her mother's death – and would probably still be doing so, except that good luck was on her side; and this is what remains for me to tell of her story.

One day the Princesse de Cologny went to the Foire Saint-Germain. Mademoiselle de Vougy, who was still in her service, accompanied her. The Princesse wanted to buy two crystal chandeliers from a glass merchant and had been bargaining with him over the price, which they had not been able to agree on. The only people she had with her were Mademoiselle de Vougy, her groom, a page and two footmen. She went into a china shop which was opposite that of the glass merchant. While she was in this other shop, Angélique went into the glass merchant's with the two sisters who lived with her. She wanted to buy a pocket-mirror to give to Contamine, and the merchant was showing her some. I must add that she was magnificently attired, with gold embroidery, a necklace, a diamond crucifix, buckles, rings, earrings, clasps – nothing was missing, and all of the finest quality – also the most exquisitely delicate lace that Contamine had been able to find, which he had given her as a New Year's gift – nothing had been spared. She dressed in this fashion because it was Contamine's wish and he was constantly urging her to do so. If she had fol-lowed her own inclination, she would have dressed far less ostentatiously. On this occasion, she had arrayed herself in her greatest finery at Contamine's particular request, as he was to be at the Fair himself with some relatives and wanted them to see her, as if by accident. Her footman and maid-servant followed close behind her. The glass merchant, taking his cue from her appearance, addressed her as Madame. The mirror, whose price they were discussing, was the most beautiful in the shop. Just then, the Princesse de Cologny returned, intending to improve on the price she had offered the merchant for the chandeliers.

She caught sight of the mirrors, walked towards them, considering them, and asked the price. Angélique, who had recognised her, moved towards the door, but was unable to leave without attracting the Princesse's attention: the latter, in spite of the immense difference between Angélique's present condition and what she had been before, and in spite of the four intervening years, recognised her at once. Angélique's obvious surprise at the meeting confirmed the Princesse in her recognition, and she could not refrain from speaking. You are extremely elegant, Madame, she said. Your fortune has improved considerably since you left my household! Who may your husband be? she continued allowing no time for Angélique to recover herself. If you had informed me of your good fortune – as it seems to me you should have done – we should not have sought to spoil it; on the contrary, Mademoiselle de Vougy, all my household, and myself would have taken the greatest joy in it. But who can your husband be, who enables you to appear in such finery? These words plunged Angélique into the most abject disarray. I am not married, she answered, in supreme embarrassment. You are not married! the Princesse repeated with a wealth of disdain. A fine thing, indeed! she added, turning her back on her, and regarding her with the height of scorn, for she took Angélique to be someone's mistress, who had acquired her finery at the price of her honour.

Angélique was transfixed. She was in despair at having been recognised, and at having been so misjudged. It was what she had always dreaded might happen. She pulled herself together, however, and left the shop – taking the mirror at the shopkeeper's price without further discussion. The two girls who were with her were horrified at the sarcastic comment made by this grand lady, who was unknown to them. They scarcely knew what to make of it, or of Angélique's confusion, since she had had no time to justify herself. Indeed, as she has told us since, she was so mortified by the Princesse's scornful remark that she wished she could die on the spot. She left the Fair on the instant, without attempting to find Contamine. She got into her carriage and tried to explain away to her companions what had happened. She told the two girls that the lady was the

Princesse de Cologny, whose lady-in-waiting she had formerly been; that she had left her service against the Princesse's wishes, saying she was to be married; that she had not dared to dress so fashionably in those days, as the Princesse was extremely high-minded; but that since she had left her establishment, she had changed her style of dress, being free to do as she pleased and wealthy enough to do as her vanity dictated; that her embarrassment derived from the fact that the Princesse thought she was married and, finding she was not, had realised that Angélique had wished to leave her service and had made up an excuse to do so. As this was all quite plausible and accorded well with what the Princesse had said, the girls readily accepted it and thought no more about it.

Contamine came to see Angélique that evening. She didn't give him time to ask why he had not seen her at the Fair. She gave him the mirror she had bought, and he thanked her; he cherished any gift she gave him. He asked her if she was unwell, as her eyes were very bright and her colour high. She said it was nothing much, but proceeded to describe her encounter with the Princesse de Cologny. She left nothing out – not the greeting, her reply, the rejoinder nor the parting shot. It gave Contamine the utmost pain, the more so, as he could tell Angélique was struggling not to break into tears in front of the others who were there and who were listening. It was obvious she and he needed to discuss the matter together, and so they went into the garden to do so, in spite of the weather being rather cold.

You see, Monsieur, she said, bursting into tears, that what I feared has happened. I am dishonoured. I can never be consoled for the bad opinion Madame de Cologny now has of me. I love you, Monsieur; you know it too well for me to deny it; my love stems from both gratitude and inclination. I owe you all I have. You are more to me than everything else in the world, but you are not so dear to me as my reputation, for which I will sacrifice everything. I cannot bear to be known as a woman of easy virtue. I must redeem myself in the Princesse's eyes. I will return everything you have given me; I renounce all the hopes you have had the generosity to raise in me, but let me reclaim my good name. I shall go to the Princesse early tomorrow morning. I would rather tell her all, and lose all, than be taken for a woman of ill-repute.

Contamine was aghast at Angélique's determination to reveal the truth to the Princesse. Is that what you are resolved to do, dearest Angélique? he said. You are prepared to give me up? Four years of mutual constancy count for nothing in the face of a moment's distress? This moment of distress will stay with me the rest of my life, she answered. Moreover, your own reputation requires that the honour of the woman who will share your bed should be above suspicion, since she has nothing else to bring you. Alas! she added, weeping even more and embracing him. It is you who have brought this misfortune on us. If you had not persuaded me to dress with such show, the Princesse would never have noticed me. I should not have been any the less yours, and my reputation would have remained as unblemished as my innocence! But it makes no difference, she went on, my mind is made up, and even if I were to be the most miserable of creatures for the rest of my life and return to my former lowly estate, I will not allow anyone to think so ill of me. I shudder to think that the Princesse has so low an opinion of me, and I would rather sacrifice my whole happiness than be so misjudged. Nothing you can say will change my mind. I should die of mortification if I were not to undeceive her. If I lose you, I shall die – but if I must die, allow me at least to die with my reputation untarnished.

Contamine spent more than two hours with Angélique trying to make her change her mind, or at least to delay any action, but he was unable to sway her. Her determination was unwavering, whatever might be the result. She refused even to delay. If I delay, she said, the Princesse de Cologny will certainly have recounted what she saw of me to Mademoiselle de Vougy and her groom and told them what she thinks of me; they will tell others, and the story will become public knowledge, which will reach and dishonour me even here, and make me totally unworthy of you. Whereas, if I forestall this, the rumour can be quashed before it spreads, and will not harm me. But, countered Contamine, do you think she will accept you at your word? I shall name you, she replied, I shall not hesitate to do so, and you are too honest to deny your part. But if they believe neither you nor me, then what will you do? he said. Ah! she exclaimed, her tears flowing the faster, that is my fear. If we are not believed, and you are willing to give me what little I will need, my mind is made up: I shall seek refuge in a convent for the rest of my days. For as to remaining in the world after the loss of my reputation, with people doubting the uprightness of my behaviour, that is what I could never tolerate.

You do not love me, he said. On the contrary, she answered, if I loved you less, I would not be so concerned for your honour, which is bound up with that of the person you wish to marry. And I should cease to love and esteem you if you were so indifferent on this point as to make your life's companion of someone who – though innocent – was not believed to be so.

He could make no further headway, and her obstinacy convinces me that their love had remained chaste, because if he had had any hold over her, she would never have taken such a step against his wishes. It would have been in her interest to indulge him, and if he had been satisfied, she would have had to make the best of it; but in doing what she wanted to do, she was renouncing him, in order to prove her virtue. This delicacy on the score of her reputation heightened his admiration and increased his love and esteem. Nonetheless, it plunged him into a state of despair, and twenty times he threw himself at her feet and implored her to think better of it. It was of no avail. But it was written that this same action of hers, which seemed certain to separate them for ever, was what in the end would lead to their union.

As soon as Contamine left, Angélique retired to bed and thought about what she must do. She was determined to make the facts known, but the best way of doing this was not immediately clear. She was afraid she would not be given access to the Princesse if she herself went to see her. She even feared some slight on the part of the servants, who would very likely have adopted the Princesse's own opinion. Suddenly, she thought of Mademoiselle Dupuis and resolved to ask her to do this service for her. She wanted to go straight to see her, but she felt so ill that she could not get out of bed. It was barely daylight when she sent her lackey out to find a carriage and deliver the following note, which she had written to Mademoiselle Dupuis:

An unexpected event occurred yesterday which forces me to impose on your good nature to forestall its consequences. You will understand from the state I am in how serious is the blow which has befallen me, and you will realise that I depend on you to save what is – after my salvation – my most precious possession. In God's name, come as soon as you are able.

It was no more than seven in the morning when she sent this note and the carriage, but she knew that Mademoiselle Dupuis lived in complete independence, and that her message would be delivered without delay, which was the case. The messenger told Mademoiselle Dupuis that his mistress had been in the greatest distress during the night, and that she awaited her with the utmost impatience. You know Mademoiselle Dupuis, and that she is never happier than when she can be of service. She took time only to put on a simple garment and climbed into the carriage which had been brought for her. Angélique was in a very weakened and feverish state, and was suffering from such violent stomach pains that she could scarcely speak.

When she saw Mademoiselle Dupuis, she sent everyone else out of the room, even the doctor and apothecary who had been sent for. With tears in her eyes, she recounted what had happened. If she had enough strength to get up, she continued, she would do so in order to throw herself at her friend's feet to beg her to go to the Princesse de Cologny's residence and find out what was being said about her. You know Mademoiselle de Vougy personally, she added. She is both a relative and a friend of yours. In God's name, find out what they think of me. I don't ask you to clear my name, if you cannot, but do what you can to persuade her and the Princesse to suspend their judgement for today. Persuade them to allow me to speak in my own defence and to listen to me. Persuade them to let me prostrate myself before them and give them a true picture of the way I have lived. The way the Princesse treated me yesterday has pierced me to the quick; the blow is mortal, unless you can bring me the remedy. Don't delay, I beg you; my anguish only increases as time passes. Go, she added, and save what is dearer to me than my very life! Her words were constantly broken by sobs, tears and sighs, and it was not in Mademoiselle Dupuis to refuse. Without wasting time trying to console her, she returned to the carriage and was driven to the Princesse's mansion.

She arrived just as Mademoiselle de Vougy was rising; the latter was surprised to see her there at such an early hour, and even more surprised to hear the reason for her visit. Will you save Angélique's life? said Mademoiselle Dupuis as she entered the room. It is within your power to do so. What can I do for someone who has thrown away her good name?

111

asked Mademoiselle de Vougy. Do not condemn her without a hearing, replied Mademoiselle Dupuis, and help to restore her to the good opinion of the Princesse de Cologny. I can vouch to you that her behaviour is above reproach. If this were not so, I would not be interesting myself on her behalf. She was so grievously wounded by the Princesse's scorn yesterday that she is unwell and unable to leave her bed this morning. Here is a note she wrote me. Her distress was such that I could not refuse to undertake this mission for her. She humbly begs permission to come and explain the true situation to the Princesse and to you. I know she is innocent ... But, Mademoiselle, interrupted the other, how do you account for the fact that a girl who had been penniless, like Angélique, should now go about arrayed in such finery? Riches do not come so promptly by honest means. This is what she herself will explain, if you will only agree to hear her, answered Mademoiselle Dupuis. But tell me, what has the Princesse said about her? The Princesse, replied Mademoiselle de Vougy, has said very little, but enough to make her opinion known, and every member of the household is apprised of it. I am sorry to hear this, said Mademoiselle Dupuis. Angélique can never regain her good name if such a slur is spread about. Would it not be possible to prevent it from going any further? She does not deserve to have her reputation destroyed. The fact that she wishes to meet with you and the Princesse should convince you that she has not forfeited her honour. If the Princesse condemns her, everyone will believe her to be guilty. The Princesse, who is good-hearted, would not wish to tarnish the reputation of someone who was once your maid-in-waiting, and of whom it might almost be said she completed her education in the Princesse's own household. The Princesse, answered Mademoiselle de Vougy, will be extremely surprised to hear that Angélique is so sensitive on the point of honour. This is nonetheless the case, said

Mademoiselle Dupuis, and more so than you would think. If you will accept my word, I do assure you that she has done no wrong. Your word is enough, said Mademoiselle de Vougy, and in the light of your assurances I am willing to reverse my opinion about Angélique. I will speak to the Princesse. She is not yet risen, but I believe, in this instance, she will pardon any indiscretion.

And she went to find her and related what Mademoiselle Dupuis had been saying. It seemed so improbable that the Princesse sent for Mademoiselle Dupuis to hear for herself what she had to say. The latter, as you have heard, had presented her case with some force. She emphasised it even more strongly to the Princesse, telling her all she had heard from Angélique, but as if she knew it at first hand. She added that the Princesse could learn the full story with all the detail she wanted from Angélique herself, and begged her not to condemn Angélique without hearing her. The Princesse gave permission for Angélique to come, adding that she was very gratified to find that she was so concerned about her honour, and that she was persuaded therefore that her conduct must have been upright. And, she said, to prove to her that, on the strength of what you have told me, I have no further doubt as to her honesty, take news to her of what you are about to witness.

Thereupon, she sent for all her servants and retinue, and when they were assembled she spoke to them as follows: There is something I wish you all to hear. Yesterday evening, I spoke disparagingly of Angélique, whom several among you knew when she lived here. I was misled and did not know then what I now know. I therefore take back what I said, and apologise to Angélique. I now know her conduct to be beyond reproach. Therefore, erase my harsh words from your minds. I would be distressed should an ill-founded suspicion on my part do her any injury.

I need hardly point out, said Des Ronais, interrupting his

narrative, the nobility of this gesture. Everyone knows Madame la Princesse de Cologny to be an example of all Christian virtue, and remembering what her station in life is, I cannot imagine a more generous action than this, towards a servant – for she had always considered Angélique as such, not knowing at that time that she was of a noble, though impoverished, family. She went even further, for she sent Mademoiselle de Vougy back with Mademoiselle Dupuis, to report to Angélique what she had done, and to assure her that she could come as soon as she wished and would be well received.

When these two young ladies reached Angélique's house, they found she was not alone. Contamine, who had left her the previous evening very impressed by her virtue and very dissatisfied by her refusal to be guided by him, had returned early the next morning, to find out what she had decided to do. He wanted to try again to dissuade her from proceeding with a course of action which seemed to have every likelihood of separating them for ever. He had even decided to affect a certain indifference, in order to unsettle her, but when he saw the state she was in, any such stratagem was forgotten. She had a fever, and he trembled for her, and felt half-dead with anxiety. Without a word, he dropped to his knees at her bedside. Both wept, unable to speak. He held one of her hands, bathing it in tears. For more than an hour they had been thus, when Mademoiselle de Vougy and Mademoiselle Dupuis arrived.

When she saw them, Angélique gave a cry, which roused her lover from the despair in which he had been engulfed. He stood up and greeted the two young ladies with all the civility he could muster. There was a moment of embarrassment between Mademoiselle de Vougy and himself, but Mademoiselle Dupuis quickly dispelled it. I have been successful, dearest Angélique, she cried. Here is Mademoiselle de Vougy, come on the instructions of Madame la Princesse de Cologny, to prove it. It is up to you now to explain everything about your present situation to the Princesse. She is waiting and ready to hear what you have to say. Mademoiselle de Vougy has come to tell you what the Princesse has already done to redeem your good name – a most striking and impressive gesture which she has made on your behalf. She then related all that had taken place, and what kindness the Princesse had shown. Mademoiselle de Vougy added that the Princesse had been surprised the previous day to see Angélique in such finery and had assumed she was married; but that if she were not married, her dazzling appearance had seemed inexcusable; that the Princesse had, nevertheless, attributed her apparent fall from virtue not to weakness – as she had known her to be serious and well behaved – but to necessity, which she assumed must have stifled the virtuous sentiments she had learned in the houses where she had spent her formative years.

Angélique thanked her for her kind words and asked her forgiveness for having disappeared and hidden herself away when she left her service. She told her the whole story, in the presence of Contamine, who confirmed it all. She concluded by saying that, with appearances so strongly against her, she was not surprised that Madame de Cologny had believed the worst, and that if she, Angélique, had not now taken steps to prove her innocence, she would have thought herself deserving of those suspicions. But, Mademoiselle, she exclaimed, could I have done less than I did for a man whom I love, and to whom I owe everything? And could I have refused to comply with his wish that I make myself appear more worthy of him? I am delighted by what I have been hearing, this young lady answered. Others in my place, she added, laughing, might have felt some resentment at having served as the pretext for Monsieur de Contamine's visits. But no, the strength, constancy and innocence of your relationship have won me to your cause, and I am ready to be of service to you in any way I can. I hope I shall have your friendship, and you can both count on mine. I will speak to the Princesse and am sure I can win her to your side. Have no fear on that score. But you must see her yourself. I do not need to tell you that your first visit, as soon as you are able to leave the house, must be to the Princesse. Till then, I will be your spokeswoman and will prepare the way. Angélique and Contamine thanked her warmly for all her kindness, with a thousand words of friendship. Contamine asked her forgiveness for having used her in order to see Angélique. She only laughed, and said good-naturedly that marriages are made in heaven before the parties meet on earth, and besides, the head does not rule the heart. On a signal from Contamine, Angélique gave Mademoiselle de Vougy a diamond and begged her to accept it as a gift. They both insisted with such determination that she could not refuse.

Angélique, having now recovered her spirits, invited the visitors to take lunch with her. Mademoiselle Dupuis accepted willingly, and Mademoiselle de Vougy likewise. The two girls of the house and their mother had joined the company and been welcomed earlier, and they also partook of the meal, which was short but not melancholy. It was set out beside Angélique's bed. Mademoiselle Dupuis and her companion departed together when it was over. Contamine and the two sisters remained. Angélique then requested that they leave her and go into the next room, and since the distress which had made her ill had now given place to the joy of having retrieved the situation, and perhaps even improved it, she slept peacefully and woke six hours later without fever, though still weak. She spent the rest of the day in bed, and the two sisters, who had served as witnesses of her conduct, and who by now knew her story, kept her company, along with Contamine.

116

Mademoiselle Dupuis and Mademoiselle de Vougy returned the following day. They were delighted to find Angélique so much recovered. Mademoiselle de Vougy told her that the Princesse was extremely anxious to see her, and Angélique said she would attend upon her the next day, which she did. Her dress was elegant but restrained. Contamine had lent her his carriage, and she charmed all who saw her. She threw herself at the Princesse's feet and kissed the hem of her gown. The Princesse raised her and remained cloistered with her for more than three hours. Angélique related her story down to the last detail. She made it clear that she could not have acted differently, except at the risk of remaining always poor, and of foregoing the chance of happiness which appeared to have sought her out. For, Madame, she concluded, could I have refused the presents he offered me, and which he really intended I should have, unless I wished to lose him and see him desert me? The promise given in my mother's presence, always to treat me with respect; his request to her that she never leave us alone; and, since her death, the company of the girls with whom I take my meals, who never leave me; the care I take never to be alone with him, either in my own room or in any other place out of sight: all of this, does it not announce publicly that I have always lived chastely and honourably? And the reasons I had for being prudent, and avoiding any weakness – which might have destroyed Contamine's respect for me, and cost me my good fortune – are these reasons not enough to ensure that I did not yield to temptation? If I had given him any hold over me, I would have been dependent on him: he could never have permitted me to deceive you with a false representation of the facts, for fear of the scandal it could cause. I could have done nothing without his consent, but, thank God, I am free to defend myself without his permission. I am sacrificing him to the fear of losing him – and yet, he is more

117

devoted and trusts me more, now that he knows I could not tolerate even a suspicion of dishonour.

The Princesse agreed that everything pointed to Angélique's innocence; she understood the reasons behind her behaviour; she rejoiced in her good fortune and was unhappy that she had been the cause of any pain; and, in an access of great kindness, she promised to do what she could to help her. Angélique accepted the Princesse's invitation to dine with her, and the carriage was sent back to Contamine, as the Princesse promised to provide one for her return journey. After dinner, they had another very long conversation, in which the Princesse learnt that Angélique was indeed of noble birth. She sent to request further information from Monsieur Dupuis. Mademoiselle Dupuis came as her father's emissary to say that he had known Angélique's father, who had been of a very old family from Anjou and had been one of the highest-ranking officers in his regiment.

The Princesse expressed her satisfaction at this news. She expressed the opinion that virtue is to be found in all classes of society but that, in the nobility, it had a lustre which was all its own. And, perhaps already contemplating what she would do two days later, she asked Angélique to promise to bring Contamine to see her the next day. Then she ordered her carriage and, taking Angélique and Mesdemoiselles Dupuis and de Vougy with her, was driven to Angélique's house. She was anxious to see her quarters, where she inspected everything. She then went alone to question the girls who lived in the house, and their mother. In the evening, on her return from the Palais du Luxembourg, she called for Mesdemoiselles Dupuis and de Vougy, and reminded Angélique that it was extremely important that she bring Contamine to see her, and that she would be waiting for them both the next afternoon.

Contamine came to see Angélique that evening to find out what had taken place during her visit with the Princesse.

Angélique gave him an account of all that had happened, and he was delighted by the Princesse's kindness. That is not all, said Angélique. She wants to see you and has made me promise to take you there tomorrow afternoon. You won't make me break my word? No, dear Angélique, he said. I take too great an interest in all that concerns you not to be elated by the thought of what such a highly-placed princess can do for you. I gladly agree to the meeting and will be able to add my thanks to yours. I will come for you tomorrow and we will go together. Write a note to Mademoiselle Dupuis and ask her to join us. But, dear Angélique, though to me you are quite charming in your everyday attire, tomorrow, take pains to outshine yourself and impress all those who will see you. As you wish, she said. I will try not to shame you and will dress in such a way as even you have not yet seen.

She wrote a note to Mademoiselle Dupuis, as Contamine had requested. He conveyed it to her himself. Mademoiselle Dupuis promised to be ready at the appointed time. It was she who told me how things stood at that point. I was impressed by what the Princesse had done so far, but it looked to me as if she was not absolutely convinced by Angélique's account and wanted to hear what Contamine had to say. Mademoiselle Dupuis shared my opinion; we considered, therefore, that this visit was going to be crucial in deciding Angélique's fortune. I eagerly awaited the outcome, which I would hear from Mademoiselle Dupuis when it had taken place.

Contamine came at the appointed time. I asked him to take me with him to Angélique's house on the rue Dauphine: I wanted to see how she looked now, and I was not disappointed with what I saw. She was radiant, not only in herself, but by dint of the diamonds with which she was adorned. I left, to allow them to keep their appointment with the Princesse.

119

Mademoiselle de Vougy led them into the Princesse's apartment, where they were received with the utmost graciousness. The Princesse conversed with them for a short time on generalities, then she took Contamine aside into her own room. She made him go over all that Angélique had told her. He corroborated all that she had already heard, and with such fervour that he succeeded in overcoming any lingering doubts she might have had and in winning her over completely. She asked him why he did not marry Angélique, since he was of age and did not need anyone's consent. The fact that you have not done so, she said, leaves me with some misgivings as to your real intentions. You admit that you have, on occasion, tried to advance your cause in ways that seem to me somewhat improper. You must be hoping that in the end she will succumb?

That is not in the least my object, Madame, he replied. And to convince you that my intentions are completely honourable, I would, if I dared, ask Your Highness to take Angélique under your own roof: in that way you could be sure of our actions, both Angélique's and my own. If I have not married her in secret, nor even suggested this to her, it is, as I have told you, solely because of the deep respect I have for my mother. A thousand accidents, which no amount of care could forestall, might reveal such a marriage to her. It is not the fear of being disinherited which holds me back, but my appreciation of the consideration with which my mother has always treated me. It is the tenderness which she has always shown towards me which has instilled in me a habit of respect which I cannot violate, and which would be too ill-rewarded if I were to cause her pain. I would rather forego my own happiness for ever than show myself ungrateful. For her sake, I sacrifice the fulfilment of my desires, but my heart belongs to Angélique. My mother has several times proposed advantageous matches for me, but I have refused them all on various pretexts. For this reason, she began to suspect that my heart was already engaged, and I admitted that this was so; but I confess to you that I have never dared to tell her who was the object of my love. I begged her not to try and discover my secret, and she promised that she would not. For my part, I promised not to enter into any marriage without her knowledge, and she agreed not to pressure me into an unwanted alliance. She has kept her part of the bargain, and I intend to keep mine. I have even limited the number of visits I pay to Angélique, for fear they might reveal where my attachment lay. I have sometimes gone whole months without visiting her. I love her with the greatest ardour, but I love without hope. I do not anticipate my mother will ever agree to my marriage with Angélique, and I will never ask her to; yet I have too much affection for her to form an engagement which is contrary to my duty and to the respect I owe her.

The Princesse approved of all this and told him that, in view of all the circumstances she now knew, she herself intended to bring the matter up with Madame de Contamine. Ah, Madame, exclaimed Contamine, throwing himself at her feet, I beg you not to do so. She would give her permission, without doubt; your intervention would demand her compliance; but her permission would be given under duress. I could not be completely happy unless my mother's consent were freely given. Your affection for your mother and your love for Angélique are both admirable, the Princesse told him, and what is more, you seem to me a thoroughly honourable young man. Leave it to me; I will not betray your wishes. If I succeed, you can thank me; if I do not succeed, or if I see that agreement is unwillingly granted, nothing is lost, and I will see that no blame attaches to you. It availed him nothing to oppose her; her mind was made up, and he left her presence uncertain of how he should feel: whether he should be pleased to have such a powerful ally, or whether he should be displeased that his mother was at last going to learn his secret.

On leaving the Princesse de Cologny, Contamine went back to Angélique and told her what the Princesse was resolved to do. Angélique was delighted at the news and was unable to refrain from showing her happiness with a thousand little caresses. His joy was equal to hers: they congratulated each other on having the support of the Princesse, whose wish Madame de Contamine would not be able to refuse. What felicity they envisaged! They saw themselves on the point of achieving their hearts' desire. They made known their good fortune to Mademoiselle Dupuis and Mademoiselle de Vougy, and these two young ladies responded warmly and shared their joy; embraces and tear-filled eyes abounded. Madame de Cologny sent for Angélique and told her she was ready to accede to Contamine's request and would take her into her own house. Angélique would eat and sleep at the Princesse's, and would have a room there. Angélique thanked her a thousand times for her kindness, and from that day on, while she lived with the Princesse, Contamine had no further private communication with her. He brought Mademoiselle Dupuis home, where her father and I were waiting for her before starting our supper.

The two lovers had parted filled with the hope that they would shortly see a happy conclusion to their story, but as soon as they had left each other's company they were no longer quite so sanguine. Their hope now seemed like a chimera which had been a delusion. Angélique could no longer persuade herself that Madame de Contamine – ambitious as she was for her son – would ever consent to their marriage. And should she refuse to give her consent, Angélique could see no future for herself but in a convent – serving thereafter as a cautionary tale for all those who came to hear of the exaggerated hopes she had entertained.

Contamine, for his part, was no more tranquil. In Angélique's presence, his love for her had given him confidence. Being married to this beautiful creature was all he could think of, but when solitude allowed room for other thoughts, he again became aware that it was unfair to extract his mother's consent by using an intermediary whose request he knew very well she could not refuse. He realised that to obtain her consent under such pressure would make him no less culpable, in the eyes of a generous mother to whom he owed so much, than dispensing with her approval altogether. He feared this blow would be taken deeply to heart by the one who had given him birth, and he was dismayed at the thought of so ill repaying her kindness. The good son in him silenced the lover, and though not renouncing his love for Angélique, he nonetheless determined to follow the path of duty.

He went home to his mother's house so troubled by these cruel reflections that she noticed something was amiss. She asked him if he were ill, and showed such solicitude and concern for his well-being that, overcome by remorse, he now resolved even to vanquish his passion for her sake. It is over, he said aloud. I will think of it no more. His mother thought he had succumbed to a sudden fever which had affected his reason, and that he must be extremely ill, and sought to try and relieve his distress. Have no concern for me, he said, my sickness is not of my body; it is only my spirit which is disturbed. I crave your pardon for having, even for a moment, consented to something which would cause you pain. Dismiss the servants, so that we are not disturbed for a while, and I will tell you all my misdeeds and give you proof of my repentance.

Madame de Contamine gave the order for them to be left alone. Her son threw himself at her feet and remained there, in spite of her efforts to make him rise. He hid nothing from her of his love, he allowed her to see its full force; he told her all that he had done for the one he adored, and by what chance the situation had come to be known to Madame de Cologny; his visit to the latter's home, and how she had promised to obtain from Madame de Contamine her consent for the marriage. He admitted that at first he had been unable to resist the happiness this gave him. He explained the remorse he had later felt, which had led to his present state. By the end of this recital, he was bathed in tears. He asked his mother's pardon for the Princesse's unwelcome intervention; he promised her he would think no more of the marriage, or, at least, that he would never speak of it to her again; and said that he would leave Paris if she wished, to allow time for absence to uproot from his heart a love which was so unworthy of her approval. He admitted it had been the reason for his rejection of all the matches she had suggested during the last four years. In all, he revealed at one and the same time, both a most tender-hearted and passionate love for his sweetheart and the deepest regard for his mother.

Madame de Contamine had every reason to be satisfied with her son. He had always been attentive to her wishes in every respect other than that of marriage. He had never abused her kindness, and had always repaid her affection with sincere filial respect. She let him complete his confession without interrupting; she was affected by his distress and consoled him as best she could; then she sent him to get some rest. She herself went to bed, uncertain as to what she should do: but before she fell asleep, her resolution had been taken.

She was woken by her maid, who said that a gentleman from the household of Madame la Princesse de Cologny wished to speak with her. He was allowed to enter: he told her that he had come to enquire at what time the Princesse might come to discuss with her a matter which could be communicated only to her. She asked him to wait for her, and went promptly and dressed, having already learnt from him that Madame de Cologny was at home and could receive her. She took a carriage and, accompanied by the gentleman, went to the Princesse's. It had long been her wish to see her son married, and since the person in question was well born and of a good family, she had made up her mind to overlook the question of property. She had been very impressed by the strength of her son's love for Angélique, and she was also well satisfied with his respect towards herself and his efforts not to displease her. While she was dressing, she had sent someone to find out how he was. She was told that he had had little rest, that he had tossed and turned all night, and had only just fallen asleep. She did not wish to interrupt his slumber, so left, with the injunction that he was not to be told where she had gone, for fear this should increase his disquiet.

When the Princesse heard that Madame de Contamine, instead of waiting for her visit, had herself come to the Princesse's, she was pleased at this gesture of civility. She went to meet her and reached the stairway as Madame de Contamine was climbing it. She embraced her, and they withdrew to the Princesse's room. After a good two hours, they reappeared, and Madame de Cologny sent for Angélique, who all this time, as you may imagine, had been on tenterhooks. On the Princesse's orders, her ladies had dressed her in the magnificent attire she had worn the previous day; she was in a daze and hardly aware of what was happening. She was expecting to be called, but was surprised when it happened. When she entered the room, a certain shyness in her expression won Madame de Contamine's heart. Come, Angélique, said Madame de Cologny, taking her hand. Here, Madame, is the young lady you wished to see, she went on, presenting her to Madame de Contamine. Tell me whether your son could have made a better choice! Like him, you will love and esteem her when

125

you discover that her outer beauty is but a reflection of the beauty and virtue of her soul.

Angélique's confusion was such that she scarcely knew what to do. She did not hear what was being said, and it is only from Mademoiselle de Vougy's account that we know the beginning of this scene. I have to admit, said Madame de Contamine, embracing Angélique, that if my son has been in any way at fault, at least he had a beautiful excuse. There can be no more comely young person in Paris. However, it is not your appearance, she added, speaking to Angélique, that has won my consent for your marriage. I give it firstly because of the recommendation of Madame la Princesse de Cologny, and because of your principles and virtue which she has spoken to me of. It is to her that you owe thanks. I give my consent secondly because of the respect and obedience my son has always shown me. I hope that I can expect the same from you, and that I shall never repent of having accepted you into my family. While the Princesse was present, Angélique replied only with tears and a deep curtsey.

Madame de Contamine recounted what her son had told her the previous evening, and what he had done. This example of a good son's devotion to his mother was much admired. The Princesse went into her room for a moment to find a reliquary which she wished to present to Madame de Contamine. Angélique, left alone in the room with Mademoiselle de Vougy and the mother of her future husband, lost no time in doing what she had not dared to do in the Princesse's presence. She fell to the ground before Madame de Contamine, kissed her hands, gave her a thousand thanks for her kindness, and promised her the same veneration and respect as she received from her son. Madame de Contamine endeavoured to lift Angélique to her feet. When the Princesse came back into the room, she caught sight of this little scene, and expressed her approbation. I am happy, she said, raising Angélique from the ground, to see that you display the true essence of good manners. Your action does you credit, and I am persuaded that you will prove worthy of Madame de Contamine's trust in you. She insisted that Madame de Contamine accept the gift of the reliquary – which was indeed the gift of a princess. She had learnt that Contamine had forced Mademoiselle de Vougy to accept a diamond and had taken this debt upon herself. She then expressed her great joy at having contributed to the satisfaction of one and the fortune of the other. She said she wished to be responsible for the wedding arrangements and wanted Angélique to stay with her until the marriage took place. She will not bring him a dowry, she added, speaking to Madame de Contamine, but he need not worry. I will take it on myself to look after his interests, through my own credit, or that of my friends. He can count on my protection, and he may see the effects sooner than he thinks.

They were all invited to stay for dinner, a meal at which Mademoiselle Dupuis was also present, and from that day until her marriage Angélique ate with the Princesse – an honour accorded only to those of unquestioned probity and of the highest merit.

In the afternoon, Madame de Contamine herself took Angélique, Mademoiselle Dupuis and Mademoiselle de Vougy to visit her son. He kept his bed, and was very unwell, and it was his illness that delayed the wedding, which did not take place until two months later. Angélique never left him, except at mealtimes, and whenever the Princesse was not dining at home she stayed the whole day. Angélique did all she could both for Contamine and for his mother, who became so fond of her that it was only with considerable impatience that she accepted the postponement of the ceremony. Finally, two years ago last Easter, the marriage took place. They still live with his mother, except when he is obliged to leave Paris for more than two days, in which case Angélique accompanies him. She has already had two children and is pregnant again, and it looks as if they will have a large family – she doesn't even wait a full year to have the next child! Both her husband and her mother-in-law adore her, and can't bear to let her out of their sight. She is constantly with Madame de Contamine, or with Madame de Cologny, who goes for her nearly every day, so that they can walk together, and who has her stay the night when Contamine is away from Paris. She visits Mademoiselle Dupuis very frequently, and the latter frequently returns the visits. All I can say is that she is the happiest of women, that she has the gift of being able to charm people, and that no one who knows her story envies her good fortune, because they believe she deserves it. I leave you to decide whether she does not bless the day she went to the fair in the Faubourg Saint-Germain, when disaster seemed to strike – since it was that occasion which led to her marriage and to her happiness, as well as to her husband's advancement at Court, for it is a fact that, if he were of the Princesse's own blood, she could not do more to promote his interests than she does at present.

So, said Des Ronais, that is the story of Madame de Contamine that you wanted me to tell you, and I leave you free to come to your own conclusion as to her conduct. But what I can't stop wondering about is how Mademoiselle Dupuis is going to explain away that letter! She will do so, and to your complete satisfaction, you can be sure of that, Des Frans assured him. As I told you, the time appointed is tomorrow morning – have you made up your mind to be present? I am not sure, said Des Ronais. You are not sure? laughed Des Frans. Well, that's an honest reply! But, let me remind you, if you don't promise to come – or if, in fact, you do not come – I shall break off all commerce with you. Why so much shilly-shallying? he went on, shaking his head. You are no longer really angry, but only putting on an act! In your heart, you wish you had already made your peace with her. The only thing holding you back is your own shame at having been so over-hasty. So, what is it to be? Will you come? Yes or no? How insistent you are! Des Ronais objected, laughing. Well, since I do not wish to lose your friendship, tomorrow you can do with me whatever you will.

At that moment, Dupuis arrived. He had come to invite them to have supper at his house. I did my best, he said, to persuade Manon to stay too, but Madame de Contamine, who had brought her, took her back home with her. However, Madame de Contamine invited me to join them for the midday meal tomorrow. She assured me that you would be there, he continued, speaking to Des Frans, and that you would be bringing with you one of your friends, whom I knew. Would that by any chance be Monsieur Des Ronais? You have guessed aright, answered Des Frans. Then, continued Dupuis, addressing Des Ronais, you have finally decided to become my cousin? I don't know what is going to happen, said Des Ronais, with a laugh, but that is what Mademoiselle Dupuis seems to want. It must be pleasant, Dupuis went on, in his bantering tone, to be so eagerly sought after by the ladies! And even better when one is able to boast about it! But are you really not eager to marry her? I leave you to guess! said Des Ronais, laughing. Then I believe you do want to marry her, said Dupuis. Am I wrong? Leave poor Monsieur Des Ronais alone, interrupted Des Frans. Can't you see the poor fellow doesn't know what he wants!

The three friends then went to Dupuis's house, where thay ate a splendid supper. They discussed their future plans. Des Frans told his friends what he and his uncles had been talking about, and said he had made up his mind to settle in Paris and seek a government appointment. Dupuis told him he knew of one which might be suitable. They decided to make enquiries about it and see if agreement could be reached on terms for its purchase. It was late in the evening by the time they separated.

The next morning, they went to enquire about the appointment and open negotiations for it; and since, on the one hand, someone wished to relinquish it, and on the other, someone wished to acquire it, agreement was soon reached. It was already one o'clock in the afternoon, however, when Des Ronais reminded his companions that Mademoiselle Dupuis was expecting to see them at the midday meal. At which, Des Frans and Dupuis both exclaimed, laughing, that they were pleased to see he had not forgotten.

A goodly company was already assembled when they arrived, and they were scolded for being late. Dupuis did not apologise, however, but said that at least it was not Monsieur Des Ronais's fault. For, he continued, leading Des Ronais towards Manon, we should not be here even now, if he had not reminded us of our engagement for dinner and told us he could not endure any longer for the misunderstanding between you to continue. And it was for this reason, Dupuis concluded, that we hastened our steps. Des Ronais blushed and smiled at these words, but Madame de Contamine did not give him time to make any rejoinder. She took him by the arm, laughing. Come over here, you numbskull, she said. Kneel before your sweetheart and ask her to forgive all your nonsensical behaviour!

But, Madame, Des Frans interposed, joining in her laughter, you are not keeping to the terms that were agreed on! I brought Monsieur Des Ronais here not to ask forgiveness but to be given an explanation! Everything will be taken care of, have no fear, she answered, still in her lighthearted vein. But he must do as I say. Make haste, she said to Des Ronais. Your true love is ready to pardon you, but you must ask her forgiveness, so do so with a good grace. Wherever have I brought you, my poor friend? said Des

Frans to Des Ronais, shrugging his shoulders and laughing. To a den of cut-throats, it seems, Des Ronais replied. Very well, Madame, he continued, speaking to Madame de Contamine. I beg pardon with all my heart. And it is by you, he added turning to Manon, that I hope to be forgiven. I can see from your eyes that you are innocent. My past folly and wilfulness fill me with shame ... All is forgiven, the lovely Manon replied, embracing him, with tears in her eyes. I have no quarrel left with you. All I ask, in agreeing to forget the distress you have caused me, is to beg you in future not to rely solely on appearances, for they are often deceptive. You should have known my heart. Come, she said, taking his arm, sit here and let us have dinner. After that, all will be explained to you.

And it will be for me to give you that explanation, Monsieur, said an extremely good-looking gentleman to him. I am the supposed Gauthier, who was responsible for leading you into such a transport of rage. It is only right that, after causing so much heartbreak between you and Mademoiselle Dupuis, I should be the one to reestablish harmony and understanding between you. Seeing you, I no longer find Mademoiselle Dupuis quite so blameworthy! Des Ronais replied. I might almost begin to understand her temptation! A man so full of qualities as yourself might well test a woman's constancy! Not so fast, Monsieur, a beautiful woman who had not previously spoken interjected laughingly. There is no need to heap such flattery on my husband! Were you a woman, I might almost begin to feel some jealousy – something I would not wish to happen! You yourself know only too well what suffering it can cause! All you need to know is that the letter which sent you on a mad cross-country goose-chase was written to me. I was at the time betrothed to the writer. He is now my husband. And, in order to remove any remaining doubt you may have, we will explain why it was that Mademoiselle Dupuis was in receipt of letters which were not for her. But in order to do this, we will need to tell you the whole of our story, and, if you are willing, we will delay the account until we have all dined.

So everyone sat down at table. Monsieur Des Ronais and Manon sat next to each other. Des Frans sat between Madame de Contamine and another lady to whom he had not yet been introduced, and who had so far not spoken. He noticed that she had attempted to leave, and would have done so had Madame de Contamine not intervened. He became aware that she turned her head away from him, and then, looking at her more closely, he recognised her as someone he had formerly known – someone, in fact, whom he had formerly given the appearance of having a disagreement with. Ah! Madame, he cried, suddenly embracing her, what happy chance has brought you here? The lady, somewhat surprised, answered that he owed their meeting to Mademoiselle Dupuis. And, she added, had I known you were to be here, Monsieur, I would not have come – but I was deceived. And are you displeased that I am here, Madame? he continued. No, Monsieur, she replied, since it is you who have brought Monsieur Des Ronais. But Madame de Contamine interrupted their conversation: This is no time for you to start a discussion and examine events of long ago, she said. There will be another chance for you to unravel what happened between you. But for the moment, let us have dinner, and then hear the adventures of Monsieur de Terny. Those of Monsieur Des Frans and of Madame de Mongey will have their turn.

This admonition was accepted, and an excellent dinner was enjoyed by all. During the meal, lovers' tiffs were the subject of conversation, and how it often happens that the actions of one party cause distress to the other. They agreed that the quarrels which sometimes ensued gave a new spice when the misunderstanding was repaired; though they

acknowledged that however great the pleasures of reconciliation they did not equal the pain suffered during the
discord. For example, said Monsieur de Terny, here are
Monsieur Des Ronais and Mademoiselle Dupuis, tasting all
the joy of reconciliation, after a lengthy estrangement (and
indeed, their happiness and affection were very evident).
But what pain and torment they suffered during the misunderstanding! How ready they were to hurt each other!
And what a state they were both in! Therefore, in order to
provide Monsieur Des Ronais with all the information he
needs to prove that Mademoiselle Dupuis is innocent, let us
keep our word and relate the whole story concerning the
letter which aroused his jealousy.

Yes, Monsieur, Madame de Contamine interrupted. You
do right to tell your story – but it is also right that we should
be able to hear and pay full attention to it! Therefore before
we begin, she continued, addressing Des Ronais, come and
sit next to me here, in Monsieur Des Frans's place; and you,
Monsieur Des Frans, she went on, come and take his place
next to Mademoiselle Dupuis. I may appear indiscreet,
nevertheless I must separate some of you: you, Monsieur
Des Ronais, because you must pay careful attention to what
Monsieur de Terny has to say; and as for you, Monsieur Des
Frans, in order to repay you for your incivility to me at
dinner, during which you never addressed two words to me,
but talked the whole time in a low voice to Madame de
Mongey.

Ah, Madame, exclaimed Des Frans, you are drawing
everyone's attention to things they would not otherwise
have noticed. It is true, she answered, with a laugh. It is only
I who keep my eyes open! But your private conversation
might distract us from Monsieur de Terny's story – and you
are sitting right next to him – except for his wife. Besides, I
might overhear something which you would want to keep
secret. Ah! Madame, we will not interrupt the proceedings, I

promise, answered Des Frans, showing some embarrassment. So be it, she said, smiling. You wish to keep the seat
you have: take care then to earn it with your silence, or you
may be certain we shall make you move! You can start your
story, Monsieur de Terny. We are all waiting and attentive.
Terny started with a private word to Des Ronais, but the
latter reiterated that he was fully convinced of Manon's
innocence and did not need to hear the whole story of how
she came to have his letter to prove it. That may be so,
exclaimed Manon. But I wish to hear the whole of your
story, and I beg you to begin. And so he began his story, in
the following words.

The Story of Monsieur de Terny and Mademoiselle de Bernay

I was not born in this city, but I was so young when I first arrived here that I consider myself a native. I am of good birth but my home is in a distant province. My name is well known in the region where I was born, but not elsewhere, except in certain places beyond the frontiers of France, where it was taken by relatives who had employment – and eventually established themselves – in foreign parts.

I was very young when my father sent me here to study military matters, the art of warfare, and all subjects suitable to a young man destined for a career in the army. France was at the time enjoying a period of peace and tranquillity, which her neighbours did not allow to continue for long. I had barely mastered the art of riding a horse, and little else, when a group of us, of whom I was the youngest, set out for Flanders. I won't dwell on my experiences there – you have not come to hear about that, but rather, to hear the story of my wife and myself. I was wounded and made arrangements to be transported to Calais, partly because I would receive better care there, and partly because I had relatives in England, from whom I was able to obtain help more promptly than from my family. In Calais, I met an officer, a Parisian, a little older than myself, who had also been wounded. Our acquaintance grew, and we developed a friendship which lasted all his life. His name was de Bernay.

He was the son of an extremely rich man: here is his sister, he continued, indicating his wife. He and I came back to Paris together. I returned to the military academy, and in the next campaign I served with the musketeers, after which, once again, I returned to Paris for the winter. Bernay was there, and our friendship grew stronger. I left the musketeers, took a company in the same regiment as his, and we fought together in two campaigns; in short, we became inseparable. His father, whom I had been fortunate enough to impress favourably, treated me with the greatest goodwill, which later turned to an equally strong malevolence.

Bernay fell in love with a very beautiful woman. This did not diminish our friendship; on the contrary, he liked me even better as a result, as I could be of service to him. I chided him at times, for I did not approve of his habit of being absent from his quarters all night, as he often was. He answered that the greatest pleasure in life was to have a mistress and to be loved by her. I scoffed at this attitude and would have continued to do so had I not met his sister. I was twenty-six or twenty-seven years old at the time. He told me one day that he and Madame d'Ornex, his sister, were going to visit their two younger sisters who were boarders in a convent several leagues outside Paris. The expedition was to take place the following day, and they would return the same day, and he said I would be very welcome if I wished to accompany them. I knew Madame d'Ornex, but had not previously heard his two other sisters mentioned. Being eager to meet all my friend's family, I readily agreed to join the party, the more so, as it was clear from the way he spoke of her that he was very fond of the elder of these two girls.

I had never been in love, I saw her, and was charmed. In fact, she was at the time at the height of her beauty. Have I changed so much, then? Madame de Terny interrupted. To other eyes, you may not have changed, said Terny, but to mine, you have, particularly in the last two months since we have been married. Though my wife may not appear very good-looking at present, he continued, with a twinkle in his eye, I thought then that she was beautiful. And since she has changed so much, I will have to draw you her portrait. We have the original before us, said Madame de Contamine. Pray proceed with your story! I am delighted by this charming impatience on your part, Madame, said Terny. It shows how anxious you are to hear my story, with all its twists and turns, and how the conclusion was reached! To me, the simple garb she wore made her look like an angel in black. She was in mourning for her mother, and my sympathy was awakened by her bereavement. During the journey, I had learnt that her father intended that she should take the veil, and her sister too. The look in her eyes, with their hint of rebelliousness, did not seem to me sufficiently subdued for life in a convent, nor did her alert, discerning air or the unconstrained manner she had, and it made me angry to see her forced into a path for which she had so little disposition. I could not remain silent. What is this! I expostulated to Bernay. You talked on the way here of your two sisters as of two girls who were ideally suited to the religious life. You didn't tell me that Mademoiselle was as beautiful as an angel! Only the ugly and disfigured should be hidden away in a cloister, but as for a beautiful, attractive young woman and one as vivacious as your sister seems, it is pure sacrilege! I do not necessarily share the opinion you expressed as to my beauty, Monsieur, Clémence interposed, but even if you were right, I do not see that it would be a sacrilege for me to embrace the religious life. On the contrary, it would be sacrilegious to offer to God only what the world rejects. Do not allow yourself, Mademoiselle, I said, to believe that you are being offered to God because you are beautiful: other considerations are involved, and piety has little to do with it. You are not being sacrificed in the service of God, I continued, but in the interests of Monsieur and Madame, your brother and sister, pointing to Bernay and Madame d'Ornex. If you had been the oldest daughter, or born a different sex, there would have been no question of the cloister. And if you were to follow your own inclination, there would be none either, or I am a poor judge of physiognomy. Admit it, you may take the veil, but it will be your family's vows you offer to God, not your own.

My sister has too much sense, interrupted Madame d'Ornex, who was extremely shocked by my words, to commit herself to a way of life to which she is not called. One must have a vocation to become a nun, and I do not know of anyone who wishes to force her to do so against her will. If Mademoiselle is free to choose, I answered, she will no more be a nun than you yourself are, at least if she heeds my advice. On that subject I shall follow the advice of my own reason, said Mademoiselle de Bernay. I admit, it has not been easy to resolve to spend my life here, but I have finally made my decision. The little I have seen of the world, which did not greatly please me, and my conversations about it with the nuns here, have persuaded me so well of the difference between the serenity of the life they lead and the hurly-burly of life in the world that I have become disenchanted with the latter. Have your nuns also shown you, I asked, the difference between the pleasure a woman can find in the arms of an honourable man and the harsh discipline of life in a convent? Your words are ill considered! exclaimed Madame d'Ornex, reddening with anger. Let me put it to you, Madame, I responded. Tell me, do you wish at present that you were a nun? Yes, I do, she answered with a sigh, and I noticed there were tears in her eyes. I did not persist, and a few days later Bernay told me the reason for her tears and melancholy.

I had been very outspoken in this conversation, and I feared it had not endeared me to Madame d'Ornex and, moreover, that it had unsettled Clémence in her resolution. As for Bernay, he had not appeared to take much notice of it. Indeed, he confided to me later that he did not approve of his father's decision to put some of his children in a nunnery in order to advance the fortunes of the others. I dawdled in the convent parlour as long as I could, and I noticed that Clémence's eyes were not reluctant to turn in my direction.

On the return journey to Paris, I pursued our conversation in the same vein, but I spoke with even more openness since I was now being heard only by a man and a married woman and did not have to moderate my words for the innocent ears of the young girls. Madame d'Ornex affirmed that I would not ingratiate myself to her father by putting such notions into her sisters' heads. I do not expect to return to the convent again, I declared, and though the words did not match my intention, I was not unhappy to mislead this woman, who was a little too perceptive for my liking. It is for their directors of conscience to instruct your sisters about their religious duty, I said, and for a man like me to voice regret that they are leaving the world. My age and appearance are not those of a catechist. It would be ridiculous for me to expatiate on visions and ecstasies and renunciation and such things, about which I am ignorant. I leave that to others, but as for telling her the pleasures of society, that is something I know about. I would have spoken in the same way to any girl in her position, and even more freely, for I would not have had to take into account how her willingness to renounce the world affected the fortune of yourself and your brother. I did all I could to undo the impression I had made on Madame d'Ornex by having spoken with so much candour, but I did not succeed. She made sure I was excluded from a second expedition to the convent which took place soon after.

With Bernay, however, I did not need to disguise my true

feelings. I was reassured by his response, in the course of which he told me all his family's secrets. I am not surprised by what you have told me, he said, embracing me. I have been expecting it since we left my sister's convent. If there is anything I can do to be of service, I will do it whole-heartedly. But you will have enormous difficulties to over-come, not the least of which is my father's determination that they should both take their vows, particularly Clém-ence, whom he never liked and whom my mother hated – since she was always far from compliant to her wishes. For myself, I have always been extremely fond of her, and I know she returns my affection. But what is to be done for her, since we all depend on a father whose whim is law and who cares nothing for his children's preferences? Madame d'Ornex was forced to marry against her will. Not that she didn't wish to marry, but she did not wish to marry d'Ornex. My father, without forewarning, made her choose between marrying d'Ornex and spending the rest of her life in the convent. She is miserable with d'Ornex, who is a ruffian, and who treats her very badly. Her health is suffering, yet she has no recourse. On the contrary, between her father and her husband, she is driven to despair; and then they use her to overcome the resistance of her younger sisters. They are both in the convent as willingly as wild birds in a cage, and though they have no religious vocation they have no choice. The family inheritance has been shared between Madame d'Ornex and myself. A very large sum of money was settled on Madame d'Ornex in her marriage contract and I myself had to fight tooth and nail to defend my rightful inheritance and not be sacrificed like my younger sisters. It is not, he continued, that I would not willingly give up a part of it in your favour, but I do not believe anything is to be hoped for while my father, who is the most stubborn and self-willed person in the world, is alive.

You misjudge me, I said, if you think that considerations

140

of fortune might prevent me from seeking your sister's hand. I am, thank God, rich enough to take care of both myself and her, and expect to be even wealthier in due course, so I give you my word that I shall never trouble you on that score and will leave you master of all your property, were it even twenty times greater than it is.

You will still have to convince my sister, he said, and she is the proudest and most determined young woman in the world. Once she has settled on a course of action, nothing will deter her. Not long ago, my father had no intention of making her a nun; she was in the convent only because he was unwilling to have a young girl living at home. Madame d'Ornex only left the convent in time for her wedding gown to be made, and so that she could more properly receive the visits of her future husband. My father wished to have both her and Clémence married at the same time. Madame d'Ornex acquiesced, but Clémence, being extremely wilful, far from following suit and obeying my father, called him a tyrant and told him she could see she would never be happy in this world, since the choice lay between marrying a man she disliked and staying in the convent against her will. Consequently, being unable to achieve salvation here, she would be damned in the next world, but at least she would have the satisfaction of not finding herself in the arms of a devil on this side of the grave. This was how she referred to the man my father had chosen for her, who was in truth a very repulsive person. But my sister was a fool. Apart from the fact that the marriage would have given her a means of escaping from the convent, the man might well have died first and left her a widow. My efforts to persuade her to change her mind were futile. She made things even worse by refusing to speak to my father when he left after visiting the convent; and, as for my mother, she said that if she found the would-be husband so attractive she could keep him for herself – no one would suspect any wrongdoing –

his very appearance was enough to safeguard any woman's reputation. In the end, her temper carried her to express herself in such terms that my parents all but disinherited her. Perhaps she regrets it, but it is too late now. My mother died only a month ago. She showed some remorse for having treated Clémence so harshly, and for having forced her elder daughter into an unhappy marriage – but what was done could not be undone. If she had to choose again, I think Madame d'Ornex would do as Clémence did and would prefer to be in the convent still. All this being so, I do not hold out much hope for your prospects. If you want to try your luck, however, I will give you all the help in my power.

I accepted his offers and went to see Clémence. She spoke to me as a girl who had entered a convent willingly might do, but her eyes spoke differently. I told her what I felt for her; I expressed my dismay at seeing her in a cloister and promised that, if such was her wish, I would find a way to obtain her freedom whatever bars, locks, walls or parents might stand in the way. She still replied as before, while making signs with her eyes which I did not understand. I was perplexed by them, as well as by her answers, but all became clear, for after giving a final sign, biting her lip and raising her eyes to Heaven, she abruptly left, asking me to be good enough to call in the afternoon and collect a letter which she was writing to her brother. I saw a nun slip out of a corner, where she had heard all I had said, and whose presence it was that had prevented Clémence from speaking frankly.

I left in a fierce temper, returned in the afternoon and gave her a note in which I swore my love for her and told her that I was prepared to do whatever might be required to remove her from where she was at present. I told her I would return in three days for her reply, and asked her to suggest what she thought would be the best means of releasing her from her prison. I mentioned briefly the conversation I had had with her brother. She gave me the letter she had written to him, which proved when he opened it to be a tissue of nonsense. She asked him not to allow me to go and see her again, because my improper proposals had upset the nun who had overheard them, and she had had the utmost difficulty in persuading this nun not to report what she had heard. She said that the eavesdropper had agreed only on condition that Clémence receive no more visits from me. For her own part, Clémence said, she had not been able to respond to what I had said, since she was settled in her vocation, but this was not true of the other nun. Clémence therefore asked him to go and see her, as he had promised he would. It was this that showed us the letter was intended for me, and that it had been written in the presence and under the eyes of her guardian. This was in fact the case. I begged Bernay not to say anything about all this, and he gave me his word and repeated his promises to help me in any way he could, so long as this did not damage his relations with his father, who would never forgive him should any involvement of his ever become known. I accepted these conditions, determined as I was to persevere in my undertaking, and to set fire to the convent rather than leave Clémence there against her will. I returned three days later, but Clémence's companion had not remained silent, for when I asked to see Clémence this girl came to the parlour and, having recognised me, said bluntly I could go back where I came from for I would certainly not see Clémence. I took not only the rebuff but Clémence's absence also to be her doing, and since my reply was none too courteous, she took exception to it. I was no more polite to the Mother Superior who arrived on the scene, called me a demon, and was ready to have holy water thrown on me to ward off the peril I presented.

I had achieved nothing by my visit. I asked my friend

either to go himself or to send one of his servants to the convent. He said he could not leave his father, but that he would send a lackey if I wanted. He asked me to be more careful than ever in my actions, as the nuns had written saying a man had been to the convent to see Clémence and had tried to turn her against the religious life. They said this man was of good appearance, and there was a danger she might give way to his persuasion; and that since his visits she had seemed less concerned with her devotions and more distracted than previously. Bernay wrote a letter to his sister, telling her she could entrust the man who brought it with anything she wished to send me. I added a postscript in my own hand to the same effect. This letter was to be secret, and he wrote another in which he said he was surprised by the complaints they had received from the convent about her, saying that she was allowing a man to visit her and cause a scandal. He said she was wrong to do this, that he did not know who this man could be, and didn't want to know as this would lead to serious trouble, but that the man must be someone of quality since he was prepared to offend both his father and himself and to arouse their resentment. He added that, in order to avoid the risk of laying a servant open to bribery should he always send the same man, he would use a different messenger each time he communicated with her. In short, the letter contained little but platitudes and instructions of this kind, since he had no doubt but that it would be intercepted by his father and was taking the opportunity to appear to good advantage. Moreover, the procedure he mentioned provided more freedom for my actions.

We sent a lackey with these two letters therefore, who was in fact one of my men dressed in Bernay's livery – one whom I knew to be quick-witted. I gave him my instructions, and he brought back a reply such as I had been hoping to receive. One can proceed much more rapidly with a girl who is in a convent than with one whom one meets in society. This is because for someone confined within closed walls, every man she sees is a source of temptation; furthermore, since notepaper does not blush, girls who are cloistered express themselves much more boldly than they would in speech and commit themselves further. They even develop the habit of using the tenderest of endearments; and after that, when a lover sees them alone, he has very little trouble persuading them to translate into action what they had promised in writing. This truth was confirmed by the letter which I received from Mademoiselle de Bernay, which I have here.

At this point, Madame de Terny tried to stop her husband from reading the letter aloud, but was unable to do so. In fact, this only made the company more eager to hear it. And as the letter was rather forthright and she was embarrassed to have said so much, she withdrew from the room. Never mind, said Terny. I was a little constrained by her presence. I shall be able to speak more freely and won't have to hide one or two circumstances which I would not have mentioned had she been present. I have brought all her letters with me: they are long, but nuns are short of neither time nor paper, and give full rein to their emotion, which, since they lack any other occupation, is all they have to think about. And since her letter didn't bore me, I hope you will not be bored either. Here, he said, giving the letter to Des Ronais, read it out. Des Ronais took the letter and read as follows:

I find it difficult to know in what terms I should answer you. I am afraid of saying more than a young girl ought, yet not enough to excite your compassion. I am afraid you might desert me, yet I am afraid if I refuse your help, that I might find no other way of escaping from here; and I would indeed be happy if it were to you that I owed my freedom. But if I accept your help I am afraid I may lose your respect. I do not know what course to take. I would like to leave the convent; I would like you to know that it is only because of you that I wish to leave, but I do not want you to think that my affection is so easily won, for, from what I have heard, men judge the value of their conquest by the degree of resistance they encounter. You read in my eyes, the first time you saw me, my aversion to life in the convent; did you not then also detect the trouble which your presence caused in my heart? I have had no experience of the world: what I am saying seems to me too frank and too bold for a young woman; at the same time it seems too feeble and timid to accurately express what I feel. I fear I could not support life's struggles, if what I have been told is true; but I cannot resolve on renouncing the world because then I would not see you. Yet I must refuse to see you: everyone in the convent is aghast at what you said to me. They say you are a demon from Hell who has come to tempt me. I am the only one who believes what you say. My heart hears only its own voice, which agrees with you and will not be silenced. You say and you write that you love me, and I believe you are as honest as I am when I say I love you.

I will not accept your offers; no one is forcing me to take my vows. As long as I am not being pressed to make a commit-ment, I will remain as I am. But if they try to force me, I shall remind you of your promise. Don't wish for them to force me. Though my wishes would then perhaps coincide with yours, it would be more than I could bear for us both to want the same thing at the same time ...

What destiny brought you to my convent? Why did you take my part with such generosity? Why did you make me dis-satisfied with the religious life? When I thought of all the sorrow my family had caused me, it made me believe the con-vent was the only safe harbour against the misfortunes of the world. The suitor I was given was so repugnant to me that all others appeared distasteful too. I had never seen anyone but priests and ecclesiastics, who were too old and repulsive to arouse any tender feelings in me. They spoke to me only about the troubles of life. The only man I had ever known was my father, who was unjust and violent. I had never met any but my brother who was pleasing. He was my brother and to love him was forbidden. Therefore I found my situation here tolerable. I saw you: this reasoning evaporated. My sister's unhappy marriage no longer inspires me with fear. My convent has become a terrible prison, and I am no longer afraid of the pitfalls of the world. Continue your friendship with my brother: we may need his help. Deliver your letters to me and receive mine to you through him. Our relationship is not in his interest, and perhaps I am foolish to assume he will help us. But he is honourable, and I believe in his goodwill ... Be cautious. I am not mistress of when we can meet. If you attempt to see me, I shall only be the more securely guarded; if you do not try to see me, I shall be in despair; do as you think best. Send only dependable servants here, and let your letters be full of pious sentiments as I am obliged to show them to the Mother Superior. But let others be passed to me secretly, and I will do likewise. I hope I do not write at too great length, but pardon me and attribute it to the lack of occupation afforded by the life I lead and to the fact that I am at present more disturbed than I ought to be by the state of my heart and with the hopes and fears which torment me.

I showed this letter to Bernay. You are not wasting any time! he said, laughing. And she is not backward for a girl of eighteen who has no knowledge of the world! I would say you have made a good deal of headway in a short space of time. It is indeed true, he went on, that parents put a great deal of strain on their children's virtue when they force them to adopt the veil without a genuine calling. But tell me honestly, what steps will you expect my sister to take? I can see that she will never become a nun. I know her. She will do whatever you ask, I am sure; but what do you expect her to do? I do not want anything of her which would damage her reputation, either in the sight of God or of men, I said, but I am determined that she shall not be forced into taking her vows. And I am as worried by the thought of your father's anger as I am about the winds that blew a thousand years ago. I wish to marry her and I ask you not to oppose us in achieving that end.

You can count on me, he said. But listen to what I have to say. I will promise by all the oaths you care to ask of me that I will serve you in any way possible and against all obstacles; that I will maintain the strictest secrecy; that I will help you to extricate her from the convent, if that is necessary to enable you to marry her. But I want you to swear to me in return that you will not make any arrangement with her to escape from the convent without my participation, for, foolhardy as she is, if you were knave enough to take advantage of her you would easily have your way, and this would result in either your death or mine. I gave him my word, and we bound ourselves to each other with such undertakings that from that time on we were like brothers.

He wanted to remain in Paris because of a dalliance he was involved in, and so did I, because of his sister. We should have liked to stay indefinitely, but the King did not consult us. We were given orders to leave at the end of January – not the best time to go to war, but the King, who spared himself no more than he did the rawest recruit, had, over time, accustomed the army not to wait for good weather. We therefore had to make up our minds to leave. I didn't want to go off to war without seeing Clémence. I went to the convent with her brother; he saw her and spoke to her, but I was not allowed to enter, whatever show of anger he displayed. Clémence's father, who had been told what had happened previously, had given specific orders for-bidding her to see anyone except members of her family.

Bernay told me how sorry he was about this, and I was in despair, but I was not so easily defeated. I considered a number of ploys and finally lighted on a suitable one.

I had a valet called Gauthier – the one whose name has caused Des Ronais so much jealousy. I've always trusted him, and he is still in my service. He has something of an artistic bent. I explained my problem to him, and we tried to think of a solution and decided that I would disguise myself so completely as to be quite unrecognisable. I asked Bernay if he would not be going to see his sister again; he said no, but that he had some books to send which she had asked for. I collected them from him, as well as a suit of the livery his servants wore. Gauthier transformed my face with something they call 'pastel' and changed both my features and my colouring so that I did not even recognise myself. Thus disguised, I went to see my friend, giving him a note from myself, to which I requested a reply. I was wearing livery borrowed from one of my own servants, and Bernay did not recognise me. But since he knew all my servants, he asked me how long I had been in Monsieur de Terny's service. I couldn't restrain my laughter, and this gave me away. He was very impressed and used the same means of disguise himself the same day to go and say farewell to his mistress, whose jealous husband had become aware of her intrigue and had been planning for some time to teach them a lesson.

You laugh, said Terny, interrupting his story. You think this disguise is pure invention and sounds like something out of a novel – but it is absolutely true ... I can vouch for it, since it was I myself who used it. My wife and servant are both alive ... We believe you, interrupted Madame de Contamine, laughing. The pastel was most timely and so convincing that neither your eyes nor your voice would betray you! I swear, said Terny, there is not a word of invention in what I am telling you! So, since I no longer had

149

any fear of being recognised, I set out for the convent and asked for Clémence on behalf of her brother. I carried with me a letter from him and one from me, in which I told her that I was the bearer. I gave them to her, disguising my voice as much as possible. I said I would return in the afternoon for the reply. I stayed only an instant to avoid arousing suspicion. I even put on the air of a simpleton. She seemed changed and downcast; and her sister, whom I also saw, looked as if she would be far more at home in a ballroom than in a convent. In fact, she did not stay there long – while I thought I was working solely to free Clémence from the convent, as time passed it turned out that as a result of my activity the youngest daughter also gained her liberty. Although she hates me with all her little heart, she none-theless owes it to me that she is no longer in a cloister. I returned in the afternoon: both sisters gave me letters, and while I still behaved like a half-wit, Clémence and I said much to each other which only we two understood. I left bearing a letter filled with pompous sentiments for my friend, and this is what Clémence wrote to me. Please read it aloud. Des Ronais took the letter and read as follows:

I may be required to do penance for your visit, though the joy it gave me was incomplete. I found no hint in your features of those which are so deeply etched on my heart. Your disguise was effective beyond belief: how could a casual observer have recognised you, when I was unable to? Come again if you are able. Since you leave tomorrow, I do not suppose it will be possible. What will become of me? Did I meet you only to lose you? You promised to secure my release, yet you are going away and leaving me here. Ought you not to put me in a position where it would be necessary for me to follow you? You could have disguised me so that I could be close to you, just as you disguised yourself to be near me. But what am I saying – my reason deserts me when confronted by my despair at your departure. I am no longer myself. What sort of life will I lead? And what guarantee have you given me that you will not forget me? Am I to believe your letters and your promises? Does your departure not give the lie to them? What guarantee have I for the future? Do I not rather feel certain that you will desert me? I am not like you. I shall keep my promises more faithfully than you have done. I shall never forget you, and amid all the bitterness which will engulf my life, you will be the one thing I shall cling to. Alas! It is now that the convent has become my sanctuary. What pleasure can the world give me? You have won my heart completely, and you despise your victory! I refused to marry the man who was offered to me, and the man I offered myself to abandons me. Unfortunate that I am! I too will abandon everything, in return. Farewell, Monsieur. Your departure teaches me never again to count on you, and nothing else in the world has any value for me. Henceforth leave me to the tranquil life I seek here.

But no! I shall never be able to quiet the confusion the mere thought of you arouses in my heart! Your letter, your disguise speak in your favour. My pride tells me you still love me, while your departure says the opposite. Which then am I to believe? I accept the arguments in your favour. I believe you love me – but does it prove it, to go off to war with a carefree heart and risk your life for something in which your love for me has no part? Though honour may order you to leave, does not love forbid that you do so? You discard me for the first distraction that calls you, whereas I see nothing, except as it is connected with you.

I will follow your instructions and take pains to avoid making enemies. I will try to regain my father's goodwill – you recommend this course and that is sufficient reason for me. But if it comes to the point where I am required to give you up completely, farewell all dissembling. I shall be myself again. I will keep you informed of all that happens to me, love will teach me to find a way of doing so; I shall leave it to you to

151

find a means to effect my escape. And if you do not rescue me, believe me, death will deliver me from the need to make any vow other than this: I will belong to you by any means that may offer. I overrun the bounds of modesty, I am aware, but my love overwhelms my reason. Farewell. Take care of my brother. Remain always good friends. Tell me all that you do, and return at the earliest opportunity that offers.

Bernay and I left the next day, Terny continued. We went as far as Fribourg together. I went with Monsieur de Turenne to Strasbourg and he left with a detachment under the command of Monsieur de Duras. I will not describe the campaign to you here, though it was one of the most glorious of those made under the leadership of this great man, whose death came not long after. We repulsed the Germans and gave them pursuit, and when I thought I would be seeing Bernay again, I discovered he had been killed in an engagement near Offenbourg three days earlier. I will not dwell on the sorrow I felt at his death – it was too acute for me to wish to reawaken it. From Paris I received other news: Clémence wrote to tell me her sister Madame d'Ornex had died, cursing her father and her husband, both of whom she had refused to see until an hour before her death; and that she herself had been sent for and was now at home with her father. You can imagine how I felt on hearing such news. I was saddened by Madame d'Ornex's death, as she had always appeared to me to be a wholly virtuous woman. I hoped that Monsieur de Bernay would be moved by this recent and fateful example, and would no longer exert pressure on either Clémence or her sister, who had now become rich heiresses. I hoped that he would let them decide their own future, or at least that he would not force them into any course against their wishes. I rejoiced at the thought that Clémence was no longer in the convent. I thought there was now good reason to hope that she could belong to me, and that we may even be able to obtain her father's consent for this, and I returned to Paris with this hope, which, however, was not fulfilled.

I found Clémence at home with her father. He had fallen ill, not because he was grieving over the deaths of two of his children – he was too hard-hearted to be afflicted by these events – but as a result of his exertions in plaguing d'Ornex for the recovery of the dowry he had settled on his eldest daughter. As these two men are cast from the same mould, when the union – which had been to their mutual benefit – was broken, they each embarked on a struggle to gain the advantage. The father-in-law haggled with the son-in-law who, on his side, was no less grasping: each one had found an adversary who stood his ground, and it was a pleasure to see them arguing their case in court. The trial, from being a civil suit, moved into the criminal court, each party accusing the other of having caused Madame d'Ornex's death. The father-in-law cited all the instances of bad treatment to which his daughter had been subjected, describing them in the most harrowing detail. His lawyer constructed a new character for him, to make his concern for his daughter the more convincing, investing him with all the tenderness of a good father and with heartfelt pity for her suffering. D'Ornex, for his part, set out to expose this deception, but by declaring that he had married his wife against her will, he covered himself in confusion. His aim was to show how indifferent her father had been to her feelings, as well as to those of her sisters, whose lack of religious vocation was brought into the argument. He held forth on the father's bad behaviour, particularly on how he had treated his daughter, whom he had been guilty of striking even since her marriage. In short, the pair made themselves a public laughing-stock. Eventually their mutual friends brought the scandal to an end, making them come to an agreement. But Monsieur de Bernay had been so consumed by the affair and had pursued it with so much tenacity that he had fallen ill, both mentally and physically. I hoped it would be the end of him. I prayed every day for his death. My prayers were not answered; he recovered from his illness, after keeping to his bed for about four months, during which time I saw Clémence every day, without his knowledge, for as soon as he had heard of my return he had forbidden her either to see or speak to me.

Someone had told him it was because of me that his daughter was no longer content to remain in the convent. This is the only reason I know of which could have caused him to dislike me, and I really believe that if his daughter and I had not loved each other he would have consented to our marriage. This is his nature: it displeases him to see people on good terms with each other, and for him to be happy there must be continual discord. Not knowing that she had been forbidden to see me, I went to his house. The welcome I received from him was muted, but I thought this was because of his illness. I saw his daughter, who, hoping to re-establish herself in his good graces, was undertaking the most menial tasks, which not even a servant would have been expected to perform – unless hired specifically for such work – far less a young lady of good birth. I have never beheld a more violent and demanding patient. He cared so little about my presence that he struck her while I was there and threw a glass of water which she had given him in her face. My visit was short. I was too uncomfortable to prolong it. I left the room and waited outside for his daughter, and when she came we went into a room downstairs, where we held and caressed each other and were able to talk alone with each other for the first time. I expressed my sorrow at seeing her situation, and she told me I had not seen the worst and that her life was misery. We arranged to see each other every day. Since all the servants were horrified by her father's harsh and unreasonable behaviour, and were angry to see their young mistress treated so cruelly, they all showed their affection and did what they could to help her. So I saw her every day, and every day I heard of a new extravagance she had endured from him. But whatever complaints she had, I must give her her due: she never departed from the respect a daughter owes a father, however imperfect he may be. She told me she wished she were still in the convent, and that her only reason for staying with him was that it enabled her to see me.

Since this was how she felt, it was not difficult for me to persuade her to elope with me. But in order to justify such a step, I asked for her hand in marriage, having received my parents' consent – which was none too willingly given, and which in fact I did not need. I may say, without undue arrogance, that on all sorts of counts Clémence could not have found a better match than myself. Everyone I spoke to assumed there was no question but that my suit would be accepted; neither she nor I thought so. Her father knew that I loved his daughter and that she was not indifferent to me: this was enough to make him refuse his permission. He answered that his daughter was not for me, and that I was not to his liking. It was true: I was considered a decent, fair-minded person, and this was enough not to be counted amongst his friends. He gave no reason for his senseless refusal – merely saying he would rather his daughter marry the devil than me. We had expected just such a response and were not surprised, and finally made up our minds to elope and leave France and marry outside the country. There were several compelling reasons why we could not marry clandestinely in Paris, not the least of which was my religion, for at that time I still belonged to what you call the dissident flock and what we called the reformed flock. This had not prevented Clémence from falling in love with me, or her brother from being my very close friend, and it was not one of the reasons for her father's refusal, for he believed me to be a Catholic like himself.

155

We therefore planned to go to England, where I would have found support and protection. The truth is, I was a good Catholic at heart, but had refrained from converting because of an elderly aunt in Grenoble from whom I expected an inheritance and who would have disinherited me – as had happened with one of my cousins – had I done so. She was extremely wealthy, so I disguised my true religious beliefs, and was counting on her support. She had promised me it more than a year earlier, when I had told her that I intended to rescue a girl from being forced to become a nun against her will. She said this was a most charitable deed and had expressed forceful views against convents. I wish I had her letter here to have the pleasure of showing you how she expressed herself. She was in a position to say whatever she wanted. She considered the vow of chastity to be deplorable. She had so little sympathy for this virtue that the death of her fourth husband when she was fifty-two had sent her out in search of a fifth. Since she was wealthy, she had found a candidate, but the authorities had refused to countenance such a scandalous union. I had no doubt but that she would give me her encouragement, and in this conviction I wrote to her. In order to enlist her full support, I said that the young lady concerned, who was the one I had previously spoken to her about, was ready to go to England with me and convert to the reformed religion. I put it to her that this was an opportunity to save a soul for God by rescuing her from the Papist persuasion. In fact, I made myself sound like a veritable Huguenot. She would certainly have acceded to my request and sold whatever she could to send me money, but, as God would have it, my letter did not arrive till two days after her death, an event of which I received word just as all the preparations were under way for our flight.

I told the news to Clémence and begged her to endure her father's ill-temper a little while longer. I explained that

156

it was of the utmost urgency that I go to Grenoble and ensure my inheritance. I promised to return soon with as much of the proceeds as I could readily encash. We changed our plans. Instead of going to England, we would go to the Papal domains in Avignon, where I would make acquaintance with those who could facilitate my acceptance into the Catholic faith. I had sworn to Clémence that I would become a Catholic, and I kept my word and went to the priests of the Oratorian order – one of whom had given me instruction in the Catholic faith more than four years earlier – to abjure the Protestant religion. In this way, I was obeying both my conscience and my mistress.

It was necessary for us to take precautions to protect the secrecy of our correspondence, since her father had powerful contacts with the Directors of the Postal Service, some of whom were his close friends. Clémence had known Mademoiselle Dupuis for many years. They had been boarders together and good friends over a long period of time. She confided in her and asked her to receive and then pass to her my letters, which I would write using the name 'Gauthier', and similarly, to forward to me her replies, which would be addressed to Gauthier. We used the family name of my valet de chambre since he came from the region I was going to, where this name is well known. It is not the name he uses here. I wish now, he said, turning to Des Ronais, that Manon had refused to be our intermediary, since this resulted in the rift between you, of which we were therefore the innocent cause. Here then is the solution to your mystery. But there is more to tell you. I left Paris the day after I had made the abjuration of my Protestant faith. I then took the post-coach (as you did subsequently) and arrived soon afterwards in Grenoble, at the house where my aunt had lived. My relatives were surprised that instead of a zealous Huguenot I had now become a good Catholic. My change of religion enabled me to complete my affairs more quickly, and in Grenoble I was able to bring them to a conclusion. I was there when I received a letter from Clémence. Please read it out, he said to Des Ronais. It is the one which elicited the reply which you saw, and which caused you so much anguish:

I had promised you that I would endure my father's ill-treatment until your return. For more than two months, when he knew that you were no longer in Paris, it was redoubled. I won't tell you how he treated me, you know what he is capable of. It is amazing that he seems to think of me rather as a servant than as a daughter. He could not tolerate having anyone but me serve him; I set my hand to every task; I did whatever he wanted, and my only recompense was to be ill-treated. I would have kept my word to you, however. For your sake, I had gradually become accustomed to his harshness and accepted it with patience, but I could not acquiesce to his attempt to separate us. When his health recovered, he initiated a new persecution. He wishes to force me into a marriage of his choice. Within a period of two days, he made arrangements for me to be married on the third day. He tried to force me to sign a contract of marriage with a military man, whose only interest in seeking the alliance was to augment his wealth, but when he had seen me, love entered into the calculation, and the persecution increased. He is a man of quality, but one with so little consideration for me that he still wished to marry me even after I had told him in all simplicity and honesty that my heart was not free and I could not love him. I love you too much to be unfaithful. I was locked up for two days in an effort to force my compliance, but my love is proof against such treatment, and I would rather die than belong to any other than you. My father's steward took pity on my plight and helped me to escape. I stayed with Mademoiselle Dupuis for two nights after which I took refuge in a convent, not the one I was in before, where my father has too many friends, but one which is unknown to

158

him. I entered under a false name and am not known here: all this so that I can leave as soon as you return – hasten then to come for me. Continue to direct your letters to me through the good offices of Mademoiselle Dupuis. But try to bring the answer to this one in person. Do not use any envelope – the name alone will make it clear whom your letters are for. Mademoiselle Dupuis will put them into an envelope, with the address in a woman's hand, and have them delivered to me. I wait only for you. On your arrival, I will throw myself into your arms. I am ready for whatever may happen. I believe God will hold my father's harsh treatment responsible for such actions as my despair may lead me into. His cruelty towards me dispenses me of the duty either to ask for or to await his consent. I see him only as a tormentor and a tyrant. My despair at present is such that, if your help fails me, I shall certainly end my misery by a prompt and self-inflicted death. I beg you once again – come quickly. Farewell, I am your faithful

Clémence de Bernay

I returned to Paris, Terny continued, with all possible speed. I made my way to my usual lodging house. Bernay, who did not know where his daughter was, and who guessed I would know, had set his people to watch out for me. They told him of my return, and he had me followed. I went first of all to see Mademoiselle Dupuis, whom I found in tears, because of the misapprehension my letter had caused, and which she told me about. I was in despair for her sake and wanted to apprise you of the truth, but you were not in Paris. I wrote a letter to Grenoble, but it was returned to me, and since then I had never been able to make contact with you because I have not been in Paris. My wife and I returned here only three days ago. Mademoiselle, he continued, pointing to the charming Manon, told me in which convent Clémence had taken residence, and I made my way there. I

159

found her determination even more resolute than I had expected, and we agreed that she would leave the convent the next day and we would be on our way. If I had taken her with me then, I could have been convicted of abduction – but God oversees all our actions for the best.

Enough, Monsieur! Des Ronais interrupted. You have said enough! I am fully persuaded that my dear Manon is innocent, and it was more in a state of repentance that I came here than with the need that your story would provide proof of her innocence. You will soon see a happy ending to our trials and tribulations, if she is willing. And, as for your own story, it seems clear the happy ending must have followed your return? It was nearly six months later before it took place, was Terny's rejoinder. We had not yet encountered the most difficult obstacles. May we hear about them? asked the charming Madame de Contamine. I should like to, I own, as it is clear your marriage did not take place with the blessing of Monsieur de Bernay, who is still alive and, from what you say, is hardly one of your friends.

It is true, Madame, answered Terny, that we became man and wife in spite of him, although the ceremony took place in his presence. We do not yet count him one of our friends; I am happy enough that he no longer makes trouble for us. My wife and I have not seen him since we were married. However, if he sincerely sought a reconciliation, we would welcome it and go halfway to meet him. But judging by appearances, we shall not receive what we are justly entitled to except by inheritance; he will not give us justice until he is about to face it himself in the next world; even then, we would be well enough pleased, as this could avert a long-drawn-out legal process. But we do not expect anything. He is a man who delights in disaccord, and he will leave the seeds of disharmony to flourish after his death. However, since you wish to hear the rest of our story, I am ready to satisfy you!

Bernay found out, by having me followed, which convent

his daughter was in. He went there the next day and berated her in no uncertain terms. He had used my name to gain admittance and speak to her. I leave you to imagine how she felt when she saw him; she turned away and left the room without saying a word; this gave him all the time he needed to talk to the Mother Superior and make sure Clémence would not be allowed to leave.

I arrived with a carriage. My high hopes sank when I saw how the lie of the land had changed. We were not on good enough terms, he and I, to put on a semblance of friend-ship. We looked daggers at each other. Though he was the father of the person I loved, we would have come to blows had our age and professions been more equal, but since he was a government official – not a soldier – I restricted myself to words, calling him a ruffian and a rascal. He replied in kind. I raised my cane and would certainly have done something of which I would still be repenting to this day if my valet – showing more wisdom than his master – had not held me back. I realised my mistake, and returned home without having seen Clémence. Bernay returned home too. I learnt later that he had wanted to bring a case against me for abduction of a minor, but no crime had been com-mitted and, as one cannot be punished for the wish, he was advised not to pursue the matter. Since his vengeance was thwarted in this respect, he tried to attack me through his intended son-in-law, but here too he failed.

Since I had now returned to Paris, I went to see Made-moiselle Dupuis. I understood her unhappiness and did my best to console her. I told her my own situation, and she commiserated with me. I was heartened the next day when she handed me a letter from Clémence. Here it is. Des Ronais took it and read:

Are we not beset by misfortunes, my beloved? You would still be happy if you had not met me and taken my part. My misfortune extends to all those around me. I am now more closely guarded than a prisoner; however, I am free to write to you: as long as I do not attempt to leave the convent, nothing else is forbidden. I shall continue to use Mademoiselle Dupuis as an intermediary for my letters; ask her to be good enough to continue her good offices. I am dismayed at the trouble her kind help has brought on her, but a few words of clarification are all that is required to bring her lover back to her. Our troubles are more grievous. Mademoiselle Dupuis's friend here has promised me faithfully not to betray us, and you may use the same means to convey your reply. The people here assure me that my father cannot force me to leave this convent, and I shall remain here in spite of him; but I am penniless: please take pity on me and pay what I owe for my lodging here, so that the convent will allow me to remain, and so that I have no obligation to Monsieur de Bernay, whom I no longer regard as my father. When I belong to you, you can claim my inheritance – he cannot refuse what is due to me from my mother. Until then, I have little to hope for, and that happy moment is still distant. These are the best years of my life which are being spent in suffering. It is of no account, dear one; we must wait. My love can withstand any trial. What I fear is that time and trouble will discourage you, and that they will tarnish the youth and beauty which you have admired in me. I am afraid that I shall no longer be attractive in your eyes. This is the care which occupies my thoughts. All else is of no account, and if you remain faithful you will see me scorn things which would make another woman tremble. If you cease to love me, I myself will bring an end to my misfortunes. I shall bear the punishment for the crimes of my father and the depredations of time which have destroyed what you loved. Until then, my days are occupied by thinking of you – write as often as you can.

I answered this letter and though I sent her a great deal more money than she needed, it was not sufficient for a circumstance which I will tell you about. I made up my mind to wait either until Bernay died or until Clémence came of age. I promised to be faithful and wait for her as long as necessary. I no longer entertained any thought of elopement: there was no possibility now of pursuing such a course. Meantime I was soliciting for a place in the King's household, like the one I expect shortly to assume. I was negotiating for it, but I didn't have time to conclude the matter. I believe I have already said that Bernay was never happy unless he was creating mischief and that his greatest pleasure was to foment a quarrel. He had not changed. The husband he had intended for Clémence was indeed a military man, who had achieved a certain reputation. Bernay's wealth would have proved very useful to him in rebuilding his ruined fortunes; moreover, he had naturally found Clémence attractive. He was therefore furious that the marriage had been thwarted. He knew that I was the culprit, and he knew my name. Bernay spoke of me as a young whipper-snapper in need of a hiding, and the rejected lover decided to pick a quarrel with me. He searched me out and, since I was not trying to hide from him he soon found me.

He came up to me in front of a large crowd of people and addressed me without specifically challenging me, but in a tone that might have unnerved a callow youth. He asked me if I would be willing to take a walk with him. I was quite happy to have him challenge me as there were plenty of people present, so I replied that I had business which required my presence here in France and didn't want to put myself in danger of having either to leave the kingdom or face the scaffold. He thought therefore that what Bernay had told him was true and that I was unwilling to take up a challenge and defend myself. He became so enraged that he lost all composure and started to shout at me and bully me: this was exactly what I had wanted in order to win the onlookers to my side. When I saw he had completely lost his temper, I said very quietly, I beg you, Monsieur, to desist and to discuss the matter reasonably, as I am beginning to lose patience myself, and if we are both angry at the same time, one or other of us will come to harm. The calm, unruffled way in which I said this made the people around who were listening laugh. My rival flushed with anger, seized his sword, and before I had drawn mine, he pierced my arm. The sight of my blood stung me in turn, and though the company tried their best to separate us, I thrust at him twice, and on the second stroke he fell to the ground.

Since he belonged to a powerful family, it did indeed become necessary for me to think of removing myself from the region. Depositions were made by the witnesses, all of which were favourable to me. I had good friends in Paris, who promised to work on my behalf. I delayed only long enough to write a short message to Clémence, saying I would write explaining what had happened when I was at a safer distance from Paris. On hearing this news she fell ill, but I did not know this at the time. I was not very upset at having to leave Paris. I believed Clémence was safe and thought that her father might treat her more humanely when I was not there. I was wrong. He could not live without stirring up trouble.

I was not followed. I boarded a ship in Calais and went to England, to a close relative who enjoys a certain standing there. I didn't stay long, but moved on to Holland, to travel round that beautiful country, which I had wanted to see. It was extremely cold, and all the waterways were frozen, making the ground underfoot quite dry. From Holland, I wrote to Clémence and to some of my relatives who were seeking to obtain my pardon. On receiving their reply, I was able to return to Paris, where everything had happened as I had wanted. My letters of pardon were confirmed, and I also received word from Clémence, who told me her father was

not causing her trouble, and that there had been a reconciliation between them. She said he often came to visit her
without proposing any new suitor; that she had spoken to
him about me, though to no purpose; and that, except for
that, all was well. I wrote to say I would return to England, to
while away some of the time that remained before she could
leave the convent. I returned to my relative in England and
remained there for more than three months, without
receiving any news from her. I grew worried and was about
to return to France to find out the reason for her long
silence, when a man, dressed in shabby travelling clothes,
and whom I recognised as having been a soldier in my
company, brought me my answer. He gave me the letter I
have here – but before reading it, I must enlighten you as to
what had happened.

Immediately after my second departure, Bernay had
withdrawn Clémence's younger sister, Séraphine, from the
convent in which she had been living all this time. And
since Séraphine was now, to all appearances an only child
(and it was his intention that this was what she would
indeed become), he had found an extremely good match
for her. Séraphine is neither beautiful nor ugly; she is not
unattractive and has a very good figure, but as for her
character she is the meanest-natured girl you have ever met.
She takes after her father – that is to say, she is cunning and
deceitful and more rapacious than a Jew. Bernay had been
visiting Clémence at her convent and had overwhelmed her
with kindness, and she had been duped by this masquerade.
He had promised the convent that he would give a large
endowment on her behalf if she took her vows and became
a nun. The sum he offered was so great that the good sisters,
for fear of losing such a valuable donation, had tormented
Clémence until, in the end, she had agreed to take the first
step and become a novice. Her sister, who was only waiting
for Clémence to take her vows so that her own marriage

could take place, and her father, who only wished it to be all settled and accomplished, were both putting on a show of the greatest affection towards her.

It had been discovered which of the sisters in the convent it was who had been acting as our go-between and she had been confined to a separate room. Clémence, and most of the others in the convent, had been led to believe that this girl had moved to a different convent; only the older nuns knew the truth. All this had been done so quickly and secretively that Clémence had not had chance to inform me about it. Mademoiselle Dupuis had gone to see her and had been told that Clémence's father had moved her to another convent. In a word, Clémence was totally isolated and unable to communicate her plight to anyone. She confided in another nun, who proved untrustworthy. Clémence was told that I had moved to England and was married. Though she didn't believe it, when she had no one to talk to, doubts began to creep into her mind; the more so, as her father, her sister, the other nuns, her confessor and director of conscience – all were urging her, with the greatest insistence, to agree to take her vows. They even tried to make her sign a request to the Archbishop, begging him to allow her to reduce the length of her novitiate and to take her vows after three months, instead of the usual twelve, in view, they said, of her strong vocation for the religious life, the fact that she had resided in the convent in her youth and absorbed its precepts from her earliest years, and a variety of other reasons, all equally untrue. This final assault roused her to undertake an action which was to be our salvation.

She agreed to sign the request, but said she owed a large amount of money which she had borrowed from people when she was outside the convent, and wanted to repay this before giving her life to God. She asked for three hundred gold louis. She was told not to worry about it – all her debts would be settled for her. She said she was not willing to name the creditors and that she wished to repay the money through her confessor or someone else whom she could trust. She said also that she wanted to be fully in control of this money and that, therefore, to make sure no one could find out to whom or by whom it was being disbursed, she would only sign for it three days after she had received it and disposed of it, for fear that otherwise it might be withdrawn. After that, she said, she would sign whatever they wanted, but if she did not receive the money within two days, she would sign nothing. They knew her to be resolute and immovable when she had determined on a course of action, and they gave her the money – the more willingly as it was only three weeks till the day she was to take her vows, and they didn't think that, in such a short time, and with all the precautions they had taken to prevent any communication between us, I would be able to receive any news and respond to it. And indeed, she was not far from being outplayed by time. Thank God she was not! Here is what she did with the money, with an ingenuity and determination worthy of our love for each other.

There was in the convent a lay sister who served as the gatekeeper and who did not appear to Clémence to have any more aptitude for the religious life than she herself did. It was to this girl that she uncovered her plans. She threw herself at her feet and promised to provide her with as much money as she would need to enable her to marry a good husband if she could get a letter to me; and, as a foretaste of her gratitude, she gave her a third of the money she had obtained. This girl was delighted with the glitter of a hundred louis and the prospect of a husband – two very important considerations for a girl whose only reason for being in a convent was financial necessity – and she agreed to do what Clémence asked, promising her every possible assistance. She had a brother who was an artisan in Paris; she went to see him and promised him heaven and earth if he would take a letter to England and bring back the reply. The inducement of two hundred louis which Clémence gave him was even more persuasive than words. He was told exactly what to say to me and where he could find me. He was told, if I were not in London, to go wherever he heard I might be found. He vowed to waste no time and departed the same day. It was a lucky chance that he had been a sergeant in my company and liked me, and so his heart was in his errand; but he was not an experienced traveller and his progress was not as swift as it might have been. He arrived, however, and finding me at my relative's house he told me what I have just told you and gave me the letter which you have in your hands, which you can now read to us:

I am writing this to you, Monsieur, without hope of receiving a reply. I will not spend time in pointless complaints against you: your indifference towards me for the last three months, during which you have not even written to me, has thrown me into a state of despair. I have written more than twenty letters to you, and am assured you have received and ignored them. I no longer flatter myself you care for me. Everything is over for me. What has become of your promises? Having resolved that I will put a dagger through my heart, I am allowing myself the sorrowful consolation of revealing the last moments of a life whose unhappy beginning you already know. I lived only for you. It is because of you that I valued my life, which had meant nothing to me until you took an interest in it. You are no longer interested, and I accept the sentence your indifference imposes. I repeat – everything is finished for me. Those around me tried to warn me that you would be unfaithful: your silence has convinced me they were right. They have shown me how little trust one can put in a man's promise. The only thing they have not been able to do is to make me hate you, but I have become disenchanted with the world.

My sister is at home with my father and has been to see me several times. She says she is not happy, but can one be unhappy when one is free? I wish I were at liberty; I would come and reproach you for your inconstancy. They have taken advantage of my weakness and have made me do as they wanted. They have persuaded me to take the veil, and the term of my novitiate has been reduced. I have yielded to all their wishes. Yet no! I am misled! They have deceived me. They have been too zealous. I cannot believe they are disinterested. The number and urgency of their requests make me suspicious. I do not doubt it! You are faithful to me – and yet you will lose me! I have consented to leave you. I deserve to be punished – though it is only my hand and my mouth that are guilty; my heart has never betrayed you. I was overwhelmed on all sides by the nuns, whose gain was my loss. I did not see through their praise and their flattery. They gave me no peace, and I gave in to their pleas and those of my family. I agreed to all they asked of me; their feigned affection caught me unawares. Yet now, this pressure from all sides to make me take vows which I find repugnant rouses me from my lethargy and forces me to discern a conspiracy. But I will play my own trick on them.

They asked me to sign a petition to the ecclesiastical authorities, requesting that I be permitted to make my profession of faith three months after taking the veil – because of my strong vocation, they said. What a travesty! My father hid his tiger's claws and put on sheep's clothing – but a tiger is even more fearsome when it is disguised. He appeared affectionate, my sister even more so, and the nuns followed suit. How could I resist, without you to turn to, in the face of such constant solicitation? I promised to sign their request on condition that I was given the money I asked for. It was not easy to secure it. But at last I have it, and will sign whatever they want. I am to take my vows the day after Trinity. This is less than a month from now. I have allowed myself to believe that my letters were not delivered to you, and I have used the money to send a

169

messenger who I am confident will deliver this into your own hands.

This is what I have done. The following is what I will do: until the day when I am to profess my vows, I shall rue the day I was born, learn to count my life as nothing, school myself to endure a mortal wound, and prepare to stab myself through the heart in the sight of all those present at the ceremony and at the very feet of my cruel father. I have a dagger, which I carry with me at all times, for fear it will be discovered if I hide it. I will sacrifice myself to my misfortune and refuse to make of myself a sacrilegious and unwilling offering to God. I said I would not blame you, and I do not blame you: to do that would be to make myself doubly unhappy. On the contrary, I wish only to take pride in myself so that you know that it is only because of you that I sacrifice myself. If I were sure that you were unfaithful, I would account you responsible for my death, but I want to be able to say, when I die, that I am dying only because I cannot belong to you. Alas, if the time were not so short, I believe I would see you and not die. The thought of you revives my desire for life, and belies my despair without completely dispelling it. But no! the fateful day is too near, already the preparations are being made. What misfortune is mine! What need for so much preparation and splendour merely to accompany a victim of hatred and ambition to her death? I shall leave this life willingly; it has been filled with too much misfortune for me to regret its end. Death will save me from a sea of evils more cruel than itself. What would I do in a convent? Am I worthy to be among the brides of immortal God, I who long for a mortal? Is not the very sanctity of such a place profaned by my presence? No, true sanctity does not reign here. I see within the convent only ambition, avarice and envy. My companions tell me that when, after taking my vows, I have no hope of returning to the world, I shall no longer feel any attachment to it. What a distortion! Would it not be proper, if one had a true vocation, to be detached from the world before renouncing it? And is it not nobler, having always been unfortunate, and having been born to be so, to put an end to so much unhappiness, rather than to suffer any longer, since I have no hope of happiness? Farewell, my dear love. Preserve the memory of me in your heart. Do not follow my path, live on; this is the only request I make of you.

This letter and the account the messenger had given me filled me with dread, continued Terny. There was only one week left. I set out without a moment's delay, bidding no one Goodbye. But to add to my desperation, a strong contrary wind in Dover and a heavy sea held up my crossing for three days. Finally, I sailed to Calais and reached Paris on Trinity Sunday itself, the day before that on which Clémence was to pronounce her vows – or rather, the day before the last act of the intended drama. This time, I took care not to go to my usual lodging house, fearing Bernay's spies might still be on the alert. I remained in the Faubourg Saint-Denis until nightfall. I sent the messenger, who had accompanied me, to tell his sister of my arrival. I gave him a note for Clémence, in which I asked her to devise some means for me to speak to her that evening; I instructed the man to give his sister the same message. Some half-hour after he had left, I set out on a fresh horse towards the convent and waited at a place we had agreed on for the reply. It came and was such as I had hoped for. I was admitted to the courtyard, and into the room of the girl who kept the gate. I gave her a generous gift and added the promise that I would look after her for the rest of her life. Clémence appeared almost immediately and clung to me, and was unable to utter a word for half an hour; finally she spoke, and I leave you to imagine what we said to each other. Bernay was blackguard enough to say that his daughter became my wife that night and that we profaned the sanctity of the convent. The gatekeeper, who is still

Clémence's chamber-maid, never left her side. Clémence was distraught, and it was not the pleasure of a moment that I sought. It was something we did not even think of – we had more serious concerns. We set our minds to our plan of action for the morrow.

I left the convent fully resolved to secure Clémence's release and to carry her away with me, come what may, and in defiance of her father, her sister, the intended husband, all her family and all the nuns in the convent. If I had heeded Clémence, I would have carried her off there and then, but the gatekeeper opposed this, and I convinced Clémence that, to forestall a thousand unforeseen eventualities and possible legal challenges, it would be better for her to proclaim publicly that she gave herself to me, rather than that we should leave secretly as she wanted. She resisted these arguments at first, but in the end she gave way to my reasoning. Here is what happened.

When I left the convent, I mounted my horse and rode with the utmost speed to the residence of Monsieur le Duc de Lutry. I am a relative of his and have the good fortune to enjoy his favour. Even though it was two in the morning when I arrived, I was taken to his bedchamber. I recounted the situation to him and what I planned to do, and begged him to provide a sanctuary for us. He agreed to do so, and went even further, for he promised to come to the convent with a posse of men who would be ready, if necessary, to provide armed support. And indeed, he came, under the pretext of stopping to hear Mass as he was passing and stayed for the ceremony. This being arranged, I retraced my steps to Paris. I hired a carriage and eight good horses, and installed a coachman and a postillion, whom I knew I could trust. I have some good men who will render me service in case of need. I went to see them, and they promised to do whatever was required in my service. I took them to where I had left the carriage, and there I revealed the enterprise we were embarked on and provided them with horses to go to the convent. It was their readiness to take up my cause which ensured the success of the undertaking.

We took a back road from Paris to the convent to avoid being seen, and halted a short distance away. It was no more than eight in the morning when we arrived, and as far as we could tell, no one had preceded us. As you see, I had wasted no time. I was so weary and tired, I could scarcely sit upright, but love and anger gave me strength. We ate a hearty breakfast while awaiting the moment of action, which would be just before noon. We remained in hiding all this time. I had sent Gauthier – the only one of my men who had come back from England with me – into the convent church, so that he could alert me when it was time for me to appear. He was so well disguised the devil himself would not have recognised him, and, moreover, his dress made him appear of a lowly station. And to secure our position, I had sent eight strong, well-armed men into the church with orders to make sure Clémence did not go back into the cloister once she had left it; I was confident that the rest of the troop would come to the rescue at the least sign of trouble. All my other friends hovered outside the convent, prepared to seize control of the entrance at a signal and ready to make short work of anyone, whoever they might be, who gave any hint of resistance.

Everything being disposed in this way, I awaited the moment when I should make my entrance. Gauthier signalled me at the appropriate moment, that is to say, shortly before the vows were to be pronounced. I had the carriage and my friends' horses brought closer, and those who were outside mounted their horses and took control of the door, to prevent anyone else from entering after me. People had noticed that Clémence appeared sad and pensive until my arrival, but her colour changed when she heard me enter. I was wearing my travelling clothes – the ones in which I had arrived from London – more caked with dirt than if I had been wallowing in a mud-bath, wearing boots, spurs, an unkempt wig, a week-old beard, and carrying a postillion's whip in my hand. The noise I made as I entered made everyone turn. Bernay recognised me and realised that the ceremony would not be completed quite as peacefully as it had begun, now that I, uninvited as I was, had made an appearance. He also realised that the ceremony was by now too far advanced to be halted, and that I had taken measures, and was in a position, to ensure that it could not be delayed and carried forward at some future date; moreover, his daughter was in a position to speak her true mind in front of all those assembled.

I made my way to the front. Monsieur le Duc de Lutry, who had kept his word, and who was occupying a privileged place, with nothing but an empty space between him and Clémence, did me the honour of embracing me, as if we had not met for a long time, and offered me a place beside him, close to Clémence herself. I knelt for only a moment, then stood up and, without a glance at the gathering, bowed low before the would-be nun, who stood firm, betraying no emotion, and did not even lift her eyes. The colour which rose in her cheeks, and a certain contentment which seemed to suffuse her person in a moment, was observed by Monsieur le Duc de Lutry, who whispered in my ear, with a laugh, that she had not always looked so satisfied, and that he guessed she had been ready more than once to accuse me of tardiness and irresolution. I laughed in agreement; Bernay, who noticed this, turned red in the face and, as far as I could make out, was apoplectic with rage. The ceremony continued. It was of so little interest to me that I cannot tell you anything about it. I watched only Clémence and thought only of her, who, when asked what she wanted, answered with decision, as we had agreed: I wish to have Monsieur le Comte de Terny for my husband, if he will have me for his wife, and at the same time she threw herself headlong into my arms. My friends and Monsieur de Lutry's men – who had, it appeared, been given this order – surrounded us and kept everyone else away.

The father, the daughter, the intended son-in-law, and all the honourable assembly were astounded by this answer – which they had not expected. The nuns were shocked, and the clergy were aghast. A great and not very respectful murmur arose, despite the presence of the Holy Sacrament which was laid out in preparation for the culmination of the ceremony. I had taken Clémence in my arms and had kissed and embraced her before the entire company, right there in the church. The priest who was conducting the ceremony was so overcome that he could not say a word. He stood without moving, his eyes wide open and his mouth agape. He seemed either to have been struck motionless or to be lost in ecstasy. At any other time, his appearance would have been cause for mirth, but I had other things to think of.

As the murmuring continued, I became impatient. In a voice sufficiently loud to be heard by everyone, I addressed Bernay. At my first word, everyone fell silent. Monsieur, I said to him, God wishes to call to His service only those who give themselves willingly. Should it be otherwise, His sanctuary would be profaned. He did not wish your crime to be accomplished, because, through it, innocent people would suffer. Only He can know what is in our hearts, and it is for you to see what is in your heart and repent of your evil design. Here is your daughter, whom I take as my wife, in God's presence, Who is extant in our most revered sacrament. I take her as such before all those assembled here. Do you accept me for your husband, Mademoiselle, I continued, speaking to Clémence. Yes, Monsieur, she replied. Raise your voice, I said, so that no one can remain in doubt. Yes, Monsieur, she said, I accept you as my husband. Then I thee wed, Mademoiselle, I said, placing a ring on her finger,

175

and embracing her a second time before the company. I then continued to address Bernay: It is clear, Monsieur, I said, your daughter's will is neither forced nor constrained, and it would be in vain for you to oppose it. You recognise that she is of age to decide her own future, since you agreed that she was old enough to take her vows and become a nun. I am of a family which is by no means inferior to your own, and she rejects the choice you made for her, and gives herself to me – which gives me the greatest pleasure, and your disappointment is not my concern. I make no request for a dowry, though I would be justified in asking for at least the same sum as you were willing to donate to the convent; but this is a matter of which we will talk at some later time. Neither she nor I renounce what she is entitled to from her mother's estate. For the rest, Monsieur, we hope that when the time comes for you to account to God for your actions, you will bequeath the part of your heritage to which she is entitled to your daughter, as you yourself will wish to receive God's redemption. Will you give our marriage your benediction? I said, turning to the priest who had been conducting the ceremony. If so we shall be well pleased. If not, she and I will have to dispense with it. Speak, Monsieur, I urged. Which is it to be? No, Monsieur, he said, I am not able to do so. Then we will make shift to do without, I replied. Come Mademoiselle, I said to Clémence. Take your leave of the company. She did so with a low curtsey. May I kiss her? said the Duc de Lutry, taking her hand. Of course you may, I said, smiling. He kissed her, and whispered to her that he admired what she had done, and told her to go on her way and not worry; he would make sure no one could cause us trouble.

She walked with a strong, firm step, and the excitement and warmth of what had taken place added a glow to her appearance which made everyone think she was the most beautiful person they had ever seen. She seemed so to me. I was entranced. Neither she nor I looked at anyone as we left. My friends made everyone give room for us to pass, and we climbed straight into the carriage. The church door was closed to prevent anyone from following us. We took the lay sister with us, our friends followed on horseback, and we sped towards Lutry. As soon as we arrived, we retired to the room prepared for us, and her nun's attire did not prevent me from making her my wife. Nor did I refrain from announcing this, so that there should be no doubt about it, as I still feared we might be subjected to further harassment. We spent the rest of the day happily enough not to envy whatever pleasures any others might be enjoying.

We were not followed. Monsieur de Lutry and other well-intentioned people who declared their approval for what we had done were able to subdue the most violent manifestations of Bernay's fury, since at that juncture he was beside himself with rage against us. They ate the feast which had been prepared to celebrate the profession of faith, and which turned into Madame de Terny's wedding-feast, though she herself was not there to share it. For her part, she conducted herself with the utmost good grace; while we were at table, and in the company of my friends and the lay sister, she handed me a dagger, which had in fact been hidden about her person – though I had not detected it, in spite of having been very close indeed to her, and of having unobtrusively searched wherever I surmised it might have been hidden.

We spent two weeks at Lutry, while my wife settled into her new style of life and changed her outward appearance from that of a person destined to live in a convent. Twice during this time, I sent to find out from her father, as I did again yesterday, whether he would allow us to pay our respects to him. Each time he has refused, and I consider the matter closed. My wife and I then went to an estate I own in the provinces, and we returned only the day before yesterday, so that I could take up the government position which my friends had negotiated for me.

This, then, Madame, Terny continued, directing his words to Madame de Contamine, is what you wished to know about Madame de Terny and myself. As for what has happened since, it is for her to tell you if she is dissatisfied. If she were here, I might not tell you my real feelings, but since she is not listening, I can tell you honestly that I do not believe there is any man in the world who is happier in his marriage than I am. Her affection has not diminished, and without dwelling on the private relations between a man and his wife, our footing with each other is like that of a lover and his mistress. I am delighted with her. If her father does eventually wish to be on friendly terms with us, I shall be extremely happy – so long as it brings us some material gain; if it is only a question of our good standing, we do not need his help. If he leaves her anything, so much the better. If he does not leave her anything, so be it. Since my wife did not deserve his harsh treatment, I will not love her any the less because of it. And why would you not say all this in front of me? said Madame de Terny, taking his head in her hands, and kissing him. Ah, he said, turning round, there you are! You know very well I do not believe a word of it, and I am only saying this to save appearances and make myself feel better off than I really am.

This story gave rise to a quite lengthy and very good conversation among those present, because they were a lively and intelligent group of people; but as it was beginning to get late, and Monsieur and Madame de Terny were to have supper at Versailles, they bade the company farewell and left.

It is clear, said Madame de Contamine, when they had gone, that loyalty to each other is very praiseworthy. It always triumphs over the obstacles in its way, when virtue and good sense are on its side. This is what your own experience has taught you, Madame, said Dupuis, who had only just returned, not having heard Terny's recital, since he already knew the story. You speak, Monsieur, she said, as one who holds an opposing view. This does not surprise me. Your infidelities are so well known that it is necessary for you to disagree with the proposition that loyalty is a quality worthy of high praise.

He is capable of loyalty, however, Des Frans interrupted. His forthcoming marriage to Madame de Londé is proof of that. I didn't know, Monsieur, she said, turning to Des Frans, that you were listening to our conversation! You seemed, you and Madame de Mongey, to have been paying so little attention up till now to what we were saying, and to have been so busy talking to each other, that I am surprised to hear you speak to us. It must be to take your mind off some more worrisome concern. Upon my life! Madame, answered Des Frans, in the same bantering tone, you are a dangerous woman to have around. You claim to know what Madame de Mongey and I have been talking about, and are ready to hold us up to ridicule in front of our friends, but ... No! said Madame de Contamine, interrupting him, I don't claim to know what you were talking about. On the contrary, what I was going to do was to suggest you and Madame de Mongey as examples of people who have shown admirable loyalty. We too were talking about constancy, said Des Frans, though not in relation either to herself or to me, but only because I wished to persuade her to be reconciled with Monsieur de Jussy.

Talking of whom, said Des Ronais, one of my servants has just been here to tell me that Monsieur de Jussy has been round to my house again asking for you. You had promised to tell his story to Monsieur Dupuis and myself. You had even wanted Madame de Mongey to hear it. She is here now, and we would be very pleased to hear the story, if you would tell it to us.

179

There could be no better time, agreed Dupuis. It will keep us entertained until supper, and Madame de Contamine will have the pleasure of hearing it too. I should be delighted to do so, said Madame de Contamine. Monsieur de Contamine will not be returning until very late, with Madame de Cologny; and my mother-in-law is at her country residence, so I have nothing to do at home until supper. If that is your only reason for needing to return home early, said Dupuis, I have already given orders to prepare an evening meal here. Manon gave you all a midday meal so that you could hear Monsieur de Terny's story, and now it is my turn, and I will give you supper, if you all agree. Madame de Mongey has no other engagement either. She can even spend the night with Manon. That she certainly can, said Manon good-naturedly.

Since no one has any other urgent commitments, said Des Frans, I am quite ready to do as you wish. But how about you, my friend? he went on, with a laugh, speaking to Dupuis. Will this not interfere with your private affairs, if you remain here to entertain us? What will Madame de Londé say if you spend a whole day without visiting her? There is no need to worry on that account, said Dupuis. You will see her this evening. She is in my mother's apartment, and they both sent me away. Ah, so we are merely a second-best source of entertainment for you, said Madame de Contamine, laughing. You are not very flattering to us. And she got up and made as if to leave. Let me show the way, she said. We are not going to let ourselves be used as a pretext to invite your mistress to supper. For heaven's sake, Madame! he answered, putting on a pretence of anger, while making her resume her seat. You are in a disputatious mood today! First it was Monsieur Des Ronais; then it was Monsieur Des Frans and Madame de Mongey who were not spared, and now it's my turn! Yes, he said, I have to make do with your company, and therefore I shall not tell you that in fact my interests are better served by my absence from my mother's room rather than by my presence there, for you would discover that I am to be married in five or six days' time, and my mother is agreeing to some very advantageous terms on my behalf. Well, then, Madame de Contamine replied, since you are in such frayed temper, we shall tell you that we are not interested; whereas, at any other time, we would have been overjoyed to hear of it. But before we tell you this, we shall have to wait for you to regain your good temper. So, Monsieur Des Frans, tell us what you know of Monsieur de Jussy's story.

The Story of Monsieur de Jussy and Mademoiselle Fenouil

I will begin, Madame, said Des Frans, but before recounting Monsieur de Jussy's story to you – as he himself told it to me – I should tell you that he and I became friends when we met two years ago in Portugal, and that since then we had been constantly in each other's company until the day before yesterday, which was the day of his marriage; and also, that, when we arrived in France, he obtained a certificate stating the day on which he had landed at La Rochelle; and that, all the way from that city to Paris, we covered whatever distance he wished each day, and at each place where we spent the night there were letters waiting for him. At first, this procedure, which I was at a loss to understand, worried me, but since it is not in my character to probe into my friends' affairs further than they wish, I did not enquire as to why he was doing this, and it was not until the day we reached Paris that he explained the reason for what I had inwardly been querying for some time. We arrived at Bourg-la-Reine at seven one morning. I wanted to press on to Paris, but to persuade me to restrain my impatience, he told me his story in the following words – or ones which are the equivalent.

Since we are now in Paris – or as good as – and before we part company, not only is it right that I should enlighten you as to my reasons for having left my country in the first place, but to do so will also give me an opportunity to express my gratitude for the way you have been my companion these last two years. You will then also understand my reasons for obtaining certificates each day since our arrival in France, and further, you will see that all my hope of happiness in life depends on the constancy of one girl – or rather, woman. Since in all our conversations about the fair sex, you have seemed to me to be less than favourably disposed towards them, and seem even to consider them incapable of remaining loyal to an engagement they have entered into, I want to prove to you, by telling you of my own experience, that, though there may be some who are fickle, there are others who will remain faithful and true in the face of all obstacles rather than renounce their choice, once it has been made.

I was born in Paris of a good family belonging to the upper bourgeoisie, but I had so many brothers and sisters that, after the death of my father and mother, we were unable to live in a style consistent with what a young person's normal ambitions might aspire to. My father was a lawyer, and my brothers and I followed in his footsteps, some from choice, others – of whom I was one – from necessity, rather than for any other reason. When I had completed my studies, I took up my position at the Bar, and foreseeing no possibility of ever being anything other than a lawyer, I gave myself up entirely to my work; and I flatter myself that I would have acquired some reputation, if love had not intervened and raised a thousand hurdles which forced me to give up everything I had achieved, just as I was beginning to make a name for myself. There is no need to tell you about my appearance or what sort of person I am: for the former, you can see me with your own eyes; and the time we have spent together has given you some insight into the latter. I need only tell you that I was fortunate to have the gift of an exceptionally good voice and a sensitive ear for music. It was these faculties which gave me access to the house of Monsieur d'Ivonne. This man had several children, among whom was one of the same age as myself – twenty-six years old – whom I knew well. He was extremely wealthy, and his family was of considerably higher standing then my own. Living with the family, there was a niece, who, after the death of her father and mother, had become a ward of Monsieur d'Ivonne. She was an only child and very rich. As her guardian, Monsieur d'Ivonne was responsible for her affairs, and he brought her up as one of his own children, the only difference being that her dress tended to be somewhat more fashionable than theirs and that she had one or two servants of her own. As it is she who is the cause of all my adventures, I had better tell you what she looked like when I saw her, more than eight years ago, though her appearance must by now be changed. She is now in fact twenty-five years old.

Mademoiselle Fenouil was tall and graceful and of a fine build; her skin was soft and her complexion pale; her eyes, set far apart, were large and bright and, like her eyebrows and hair, black; but when she was in the least upset, her eyes showed her distress and aroused sympathy from all those on whom they rested. Her brow was broad and smooth; her nose well shaped; her face was oval; she had a dimple in her chin and a small red mouth; her teeth were white and even; her nose was narrow and slightly aquiline; her neck and arms were perfectly formed; her bosom high and rounded; and her hands were the most beautiful a woman could have. You can see from this description that I can be excused for having loved her – even to the extent of risking all for her. Her physical beauty, however, is not what is most admirable about her: her inner self is beautiful too. She has a strong and honest personality, and is not swayed either by flattery or disapproval. She is warm-hearted and generous; bold and imaginative; what she promises, she performs. She is better educated than a girl has any need to be. She is well versed both in religious knowledge and in history; she reads and understands the poets, both ancient and modern. She even knows something of astrology – but this subject, which sometimes goes to people's heads and makes fools of them, is nothing but an amusement for her: whatever she reads in the stars, she adjusts to fit the case, whether serious or galant. She has a ready understanding; her speech is lively and natural, and she is fortunate in having a good memory; she writes correctly and well, and even writes verse occasionally. I have seen things she has written which have won the approval of connoisseurs. Her humour can be scathing, but if I believe the evidence of her letters, the reverses of fortune she has suffered have had on her an effect contrary to what is often the case and have softened rather than embittered her. She dances beautifully and sings with great charm.

She was as I have described her at about seventeen years of age when I met her. This meeting came about through my acquaintance with her cousin, who told her one day that he had a friend who was an extremely good singer. She asked him to take me to see her. He told me about her, and since those who are interested in one of the arts are naturally interested to meet someone else who is proficient in it, I accepted the invitation and went to see her that very evening. She was modest about her own singing, and I was embarrassed to sing myself when I had heard her. She had sung Lambert's famous variation on 'The Rocks', one of Lully's songs, and it was as if she had a thousand nightingales in her throat. Then I sang; she seemed satisfied and suggested we should meet regularly so that we could introduce each other to any new music that we discovered. I agreed and, on this basis, there was no day when I did not visit her. We had opera every day at her house! Mademoiselle Fenouil and I always had some new tune to show each other. We sang together sometimes; and in this way, for more than four months, I found it necessary to go there daily. And gradually I fell in love without realising it.

During all that time, there had inevitably been some moments of private conversation between us. I had found so many good qualities in her that I began to love her too much for my own peace of mind, and it seemed to me too that she was not entirely indifferent to me; her eyes, and quite frequently even her gestures, indicated that she felt for me what I was feeling for her; but there was so much distance between her fortune and my own that I had not dared take any of the opportunities that had presented themselves to declare my feelings. The songs I sang were all songs of love. In them I bemoaned my enforced silence, but this did not advance my cause – she sang them too, just as I did. Finally, I decided to speak so directly that there could be no mistake. I wrote the following verse and gave it to her, and since I am near the end of my long separation from her, I cannot refrain from singing it for you. And he sang these words:

My eyes are fixed on you
They speak my deepest feeling;
You know that this is true
In spite of my concealing.
You do not hear my call.
My love is hidden in song.
For you the notes are all –
The words do not belong.

As poetry, the lines are worthless, but the melody is agreeable and complements the words. The thought seemed to appeal, and I was asked who wrote the tune and the words. I said that I was the composer of both, and that I had written them for a girl I had been very much in love with. I looked at Mademoiselle Fenouil as I said this, and could tell she had understood me. Immediately, she sang the same piece and performed it better than I had done. I was grateful to her for this, but it was not enough – I wanted her to admit her feelings too. I was convinced that an outright declaration on my part would not have been ill received. I didn't press my case, however. I wanted to be practically certain of a favourable response before I did so; but a marriage proposal which came my way did more than I could have anticipated.

My family had found a very attractive match for me. This was a young girl of the same age as Mademoiselle Fenouil, who was not only beautiful and very attractive but also rich. Since my chances of succeeding with Mademoiselle Fenouil seemed very remote, I had allowed the marriage negotiations to proceed. Indeed, the proposed alliance was extremely advantageous to me in all sorts of respects and exceeded all I could have hoped for. These were, Madame, said Des Frans, turning to Madame de Mongey, the very words that Jussy used. But I will continue – you will hear what follows. Mademoiselle Fenouil, he went on, heard of this proposed marriage and even devised an opportunity for herself to see Mademoiselle Grandet – who was the person concerned. She was alarmed to see Mademoiselle Grandet's beauty, and she abandoned all restraint when she heard that the marriage contract was to be signed that day, or the one after. I had not been to see her for two days. On the morning of the third day – that which the marriage contract was to be signed – I received this note:

Do not be too hasty with regard to your marriage, or you may come to regret it. A better offer than the one you are considering has been found. Come to see me immediately. I am waiting for you.

I went, hoping to be back in time to attend the meeting with my relatives. I found her alone in her room, deep in thought. Her eyes were moist and red, and I saw she had been crying. I am here to receive your orders, Mademoiselle, I said, as I entered. I have come to find out what you want of me, and what this other offer may be? She reddened at this question. Before telling you that, Monsieur, she said, I must know whether you sincerely love the young lady you are to marry, and whether you are guided by your heart or your interest? No, Mademoiselle, I said, if I followed only my heart, it is certain I would not marry Mademoiselle Grandet. She is thoroughly amiable. But before meeting her, I had met another to whom I gave my heart. But my good sense opposes what my heart craves. Her rank is too far above my own for me to aspire to her hand, and my reason has persuaded me that, having no hope of achieving happiness in that direction, I must try to forget her by whatever means possible. My relatives offered me such a means, which I am accepting, in the hope that the duty I would owe to a wife, the responsibility of a household, and the need to stifle sentiments which would no longer be permissible, added to the demands of my profession – in the hope that all this would free me from my first love.

And who is she, this first love, whom you wish to cast from your heart? she said, with some effort. Now that I am here and have said so much, I answered, I can no longer hide the truth. My eyes, my behaviour, my confusion – all this must have made it plain that it is you yourself who have aroused these sentiments in me, which I had never experienced before, and which I am now expressing for the first time. Yes, Mademoiselle, I said, clinging to her knees, it is you whom I adore. I have always treated you with the respect which is due to you; I have remained silent, I would still be silent, if you had not brought me here. A true hero of romance! she exclaimed. You love me, and if I understand aright, if you did not love me, you would not be contemplating marriage? That is true, I said. If my heart were free, there would be no need for me to undertake the cruel burden of marriage. It is only my despair at being unable to belong to you which demands such an extreme remedy and forces me into the arms of another. And what is the basis for this despair? she said. The position of my family is so inferior to that of your own, I answered, that I could not hope to be considered worthy of you, and the disparity between your wealth and my own is so great that I could not allow myself to believe it would be possible to overcome such a great obstacle.

Do you love me as much as you would have me believe? she asked, looking me in the eyes. Yes, Mademoiselle, I replied, and you do me wrong if you doubt it. Well then, she said, who has told you that you could not hope for an alliance with me? The only obstacles between us are those of birth and wealth. As for the wealth, it is my own, and I shall have the power, when I am of age, to do exactly as I want with it, and I swear that I will place it in your hands. As for birth, I do not see that there is such a great difference between us. Mademoiselle Grandet is of higher birth than I am. She is of noble birth, whereas my position derives only from a place at court held by an ancestor of mine at his death; and one day you yourself could buy such a place, since I can give you the means. My uncle is my guardian, and he has control of my wealth, but he does not own it. I will be able, before long, to take control of it myself, receive the income, and do with it as I wish. Do you not think the offer I am making you is more advantageous than that of Mademoiselle Grandet, since, so you say, you love me, while for her you have merely respect, and not love?

How happy I should be, Mademoiselle, I answered, to hear you express yourself so favourably towards me, but how little would I be worthy of your generosity if I were ready to take advantage of it! No, Mademoiselle, I continued, you deserve a suitor very different from myself. A better fortune than I can offer will be yours. I cannot contemplate allowing you – not only to reduce your expectations, but also to diminish the rank to which you were born. Choose some-one worthy of you, and think of me with sympathy, not affection! I hardly expected such advice from you, she replied. Your refusal is a little too forced to be convincing. I see you do indeed love Mademoiselle Grandet, since my offer is so ill received. Be on your way, Monsieur, she con-tinued, scornfully. I will not delay your happiness. Go, and boast about the sacrifice you have made. Leave me to take care of my own future. I offered it to you, and you refused the offer. A convent's walls will save me from any such futile gesture in future.

No, Mademoiselle, I exclaimed, catching hold of her and clasping her knees, for she was attempting to leave. I love you with all the ardour a heart is capable of. I am over-whelmed by your generosity, but how can I accept? You are very young; your family will always oppose what you and I would want. Your feelings may change, and I would become the most unfortunate of men, after allowing myself such a flattering delusion.

Leave concerns about the future to me, she replied. There will be time and occasions to overcome the objections of my family. And as for me, it would be possible, she added, blushing, to take matters so far that you would be safe from any fear of betrayal on my part. Break your engagement with Mademoiselle Grandet, but do so in such a way that I am left in no doubt that the break is final. I shall hear what occurs, and I promise that I shall act accordingly and hold you to account. Go now and meet your family as arranged, or you will be late. Do not attempt to see me again until you have broken the engagement irrevocably – but do not reveal the reason! I want it to be me alone who knows what part I have played in the matter. I am jealous by nature, and it is in your interest to leave no shadow of doubt in my mind.

I will break off the affair so resoundingly, Mademoiselle, I said, that you will be left in no doubt. I foresee the dismay my family will feel and the distress this will cause a girl who is rejected for no legitimate reason; but I am prepared to do it gladly since it is a way of proving to you that nothing has any importance for me except your love or hate. You will receive news this evening, either in writing or by word of mouth. Go then, she said, and come to see me as soon as you are able, but do not come until the break is final and you are free. Thereupon I left, in considerable embarrassment as to what pretext I could find to extricate myself from the engagement, without it appearing to be my fault.

I went to Mademoiselle Grandet's home, where her relatives and mine were meeting. I thought she looked as beautiful as an angel. I regretted losing such a beautiful prize – one of which I could be certain – but my regrets did not deflect me from the action I had determined to take. I bowed to her as I entered, and placed myself next to her. I left the families to discuss the details of the settlement, and while I sought an excuse to break off the agreement, I told Mademoiselle Grandet harshly that I thought her dress unnecessarily showy and ostentatious; that I was not of a humour to tolerate such extravagance, and that a woman who is concerned to please only her husband has no need of such finery. She answered quite reasonably that what she was wearing was what her mother had always had her wear, and that there was nothing out of the ordinary in her apparel. She said that, until our marriage, she would continue to follow her mother's wishes in the matter, but that, thereafter, I could be the arbiter of what she wore and could require something simpler if I considered her dress too magnificent, and that she would conform in every way to whatever I wanted.

I was nonplussed by such a reasonable and submissive answer, but did not desist. I talked to her about the sort of company she could keep and about gambling – as if I were brutish and narrow-minded – and ranted on far more even than a jealous husband would be likely to do. I quibbled and harassed her about everything and led her to deduce that if she married me she might expect to be forever downtrodden and unhappy. I made her cry, yet I continued to criticise and chide her, until in the end she could not refrain from saying that she was dismayed that the arrangements were so far advanced, and that after what I had been saying, it would be only with the greatest repugnance that she would marry me.

It was a trick worthy of an out-and-out scoundrel that I had played on her. I had no doubt that Mademoiselle Grandet was a mild and sweet-natured person, as indeed her conduct showed her to be after she married a man at whose hands she endured all a woman can be subjected to from someone who was in fact as jealous and ill-tempered as I had pretended to be, and whose widow she now is. I knew that she had all the qualities needed to make a man happy. However, since my aim was to break off the engagement, I was quick to seize on the opening this reply offered me. You will marry me only with repugnance? I repeated, loudly enough for everyone to hear. Then, I have no desire to marry you against your will; indeed, I find I am not far from reciprocating your feelings. There is no need, I declared to my relatives, for you to go to any further trouble to arrange a contract between Mademoiselle Grandet and myself. We were not meant for each other. She wishes to withdraw from the arrangement, and I release her without regret. Of all the conversation we had had, only the last few words had been spoken loudly enough to be heard by the company. Every-one thought the poor girl had accidentally said something to offend me, and they tried to smoothe out the disagreement between us. They wanted to placate me and make me stay, but I ignored their efforts. I merely said that, since Mademoiselle Grandet had stated that she would marry me only with repugnance, I did not, as an honourable man, wish to use her parents' authority to make her marry me against her will. And then I left.

They questioned her as to what had happened. She told them exactly how she had replied to what I had said. Since I did not have the reputation for being so boorish as she had described me – and as in fact I had been – no one believed her, the more so as the marriage would have been very much to my advantage and it was not reasonable to suppose that I would have broken it off lightly and without good cause. Her mother in particular flew into a rage and railed at her. It was thus Mademoiselle Grandet who received all the blame for what had happened, and her parents were so angry with her that, in order to escape from their constant nagging and rebukes, she was forced, about a year later, to marry a certain Monsieur de Mongey, a very rich country squire and man of quality, who had seen her, fallen in love with her, and asked for her hand. He was assuredly one of the most disagreeable and disreputable people you could find. For more than four years, she endured all the hardship that an elderly, jealous and violent husband can inflict on a perfectly virtuous and irreproachable wife – and I was the cause of it all, for which I am extremely sorry. Mademoiselle Fenouil wrote to me in terms which showed that she too commiserated with this innocent victim, the more so since she also bore some responsibility for her suffering. Monsieur de Mongey finally died two years ago, and his wife became a very rich widow, being now not only in possession of her own fortune, but also of what she inherited from him. She had no children, for the marriage had never been consummated. Although I have been away for seven years, I have been kept informed of all this through the regular correspondence I maintained with Mademoiselle Fenouil during my absence, as you will soon hear. But as for Mademoiselle Grandet, that was how I broke off my engagement to her, and, as you see, she had every right to believe me a wretch and a scoundrel.

I did not interrupt Jussy at that point in his story, said Des Frans, interrupting his own narration and speaking to Madame de Mongey. I did not tell him then that I had the honour of your acquaintance – but let me continue De Jussy's narrative, and you will hear all in due course. After this unworthy exploit, I returned to Mademoiselle Fenouil and told her what I had done. She certainly disapproved of the stratagem I had used to disengage myself from my commitment to Mademoiselle Grandet, since it had exposed the latter, who had behaved with perfect modesty and decorum, to the anger and disapproval of her parents. I could not disagree and was full of remorse myself, but when I pointed out that I had been unable to think of any other means of breaking off the engagement – when it had already reached such an advanced stage – she blamed me less.

A week or so later, I reminded her that I had given up this excellent matrimonial prospect only because I had been given hopes of an alternative. She understood what I was saying, and realised that I wanted her to give me some proof that she would make good on her promise. I told her I was afraid that, sooner or later, when she was least expecting it, her uncle would present her with plans for her future; I said I knew that in this case she would not comply without a struggle, but that in the end she might give way – for reasons of prestige, or financial advancement, or through an unwillingness to displease, or a mixture of all of these. I reminded her further that she had said it would be within my power to take matters so far forward that she would not be able to retreat from her commitment. Her love for me added all the persuasion that was needed. We each made a promise of marriage to the other and, with nothing but a scrap of paper to serve as guarantee, we swore eternal loyalty to each other and lived henceforth as man and wife.

I do not think there is any greater pleasure in the world than such a relationship. We enjoyed it for six months without trouble, our only fear being that we might be discovered when we spent the night together, as we frequently did. And these were the only happy moments I have had in my life, as they were also the cause of the misfortunes which overtook us.

She became pregnant, which threw us into disarray, the more so since, just as her condition was about to become apparent, her uncle decided to arrange a marriage for her. A very good match was found, which everyone considered very advantageous for her. It was not her wealth which most attracted the suitor. Though she is very rich, he could certainly have sought a partner with even greater wealth. He was a man of very high rank, very personable, a man with a good intelligence and a good reputation; in a word, a perfect suitor. She had no apparent reason to refuse him and was in no position to accept him. I was not sorry this was so; I could well have understood had she proved unfaithful. Even though he was my rival, I could not help liking and admiring him, and I was almost tempted to tell him what our situation was.

You can imagine our state of anxiety. She was young and we were both inexperienced, and the immediate problems loomed largest in our mind. We thought we had nothing to worry about except the unwelcome attention her pregnancy would attract, and the disapproval of her uncle and other members of the family. This was, indeed, all we had to worry about, but it was nonetheless no small problem. I tried to persuade her to use intermediaries whom he would respect to talk to her uncle, but she did not want to do this. The only thing she could say was that she was dismayed at what had happened, but, since what was done was done and there was no undoing it, our only option was to leave Paris. She maintained it would be easier to make our peace from afar than here at hand, and she added that she trusted I would not abandon her. She claimed we had enough money to leave France, and not return until she was her own mistress. And that this being so, I would have to elope with her, and that she was ready to go anywhere I chose. She concluded by saying that since we were both to blame, it was only fair that we should both share any risks there might be.

I have to admit that this proposal of hers filled me with misgiving. I told her that the most likely result of such a course of action would be to lead me to the gallows: considering her age, which was almost ten years less than mine, and the difference between us in rank and fortune, I should certainly be accused of subornation and rape; and that, if we were arrested, the most lenient penalty we could expect would be for her to be sent to a convent for the rest of her life, and for mine to be cut short at the hands of an executioner. I pointed out that begetting children was not a crime punishable by death, but that rape was, and was moreover one that was never pardoned, particularly when the accused could be presumed – because of the wealth and youth of the girl, if he were of more mature years – to have acted out of self-interest, as would appear to be the case with us. But she would pay me no heed and insisted that we run away together. However much I resisted this course of action, I could not persuade her to change her mind. I opposed it with every argument I could muster, until she accused me of not loving her enough. I am not going to discuss it any further, she said, looking me in the eye – but tomorrow you will see that I have found a way out of our difficulties.

I had no idea what she could mean by this. I was

extremely worried when I left her, and very disturbed by the almost menacing tone she had used when she talked of this new way out of our dilemma. I returned the next day and was fully enlightened as to her meaning. I have been awaiting your arrival for some time, Monsieur, she said, but here you are at last. We are alone, you can speak freely, and tell me, what decision have you come to? Will you abandon me, or will you go with me? I have come, I said, to try once again to make you give up the plan on which you seemed intent yesterday, of leaving France. If we were to do that, I foresee only disaster both for you and for me. My determination, however, is unchanged, she said. But since you are so indifferent to my condition and are ready to abandon me to whatever expedient my despair might suggest, I will relieve you of all your qualms and, at the same, time punish myself for having loved a man who loved me only for his own pleasure, not for myself.

As she said this, she took from a little box a small piece of folded paper which held some yellow powder of a sort I did not recognise. She put three-quarters of this into a silver goblet and mixed it with water. She took the rest of the powder and mixed it with some sweet preserves, and gave this to a little dog she had. The mixture had scarcely entered its body when the animal fell down dead, without a tremor. Looking at this little bitch, I was so stunned by what I had just seen, that I lost all power of movement; but when I saw her pick up the goblet and lift it to her lips, I regained my senses. I threw myself at the goblet, spilling some of the contents on the floor, and throwing the rest out into the courtyard. A large dog, owned by d'Ivonne's coachman, came and licked it up, and died within seconds.

My dear child, I exclaimed, is this the way you have found to escape from our trouble? Yes, Monsieur, this is it, she replied. You have thrown away the poison I would have swallowed and have prevented me from dying before your eyes, but I am glad you have understood the strength of my determination. I still have all the poison I need, and tomorrow you will see me just as my little dog is now. No, I said, taking her in my arms, there is no need for such extremes. I am ready to do whatever you wish. A thousand gaolers devising new tortures would be as nothing to me compared to the horror of seeing you dead. I will take you when and where you please. Your fate and mine are in your hands. All I ask is that you give me all the poison still in your possession. Here it is, she said, handing me another small paper packet, which I threw into the fire without opening. It is no matter, she said, seeing what I had done. I will have no trouble replacing it should you break your word. For yourself, you need have no fear – I will never desert you. And have no concern for your life: I have sworn absolute loyalty to you, and my word will exonerate you. If it is our fate to be arrested on our way, I will proclaim your innocence for all the world to hear. When do you wish us to depart? I said. Tomorrow, she answered, without hesitation. But, I said, we have made no preparations – either for our departure or to make sure we have at least one day's headstart on those who would pursue us! It does not matter, she said. I have money, and we must take the risk. There was nothing I could do to dissuade her. We decided to make for Lyons, and from there proceed to Avignon.

The next day, I found her where we had agreed to meet. The only companion she had with her was her chambermaid, in whom she had confided. Not having made any preparations, we were obliged to take the first coach we found; and we covered seventeen leagues from Paris quite comfortably before we were arrested, on the third day after our departure.

On discovering that Mademoiselle Fenouil was missing, the alarm had been raised; no one knew what had become of her. Her family searched everywhere, and in the end, when it became clear she was not in Paris, without telling you how they knew which route we had taken, it suffices to say they found it out and followed us, and we were taken by surprise while still in bed. I did my best to defend myself, but I was outnumbered and overwhelmed. I was roughly handled, but I was less concerned about my own welfare than about how I saw she was being treated. The man in whose hands we found ourselves had, by right of birth, a certain authority over her, which he asserted to the full. I was in despair, but there was no way I could come to her aid except by attracting their attention towards myself. I begged them to expend their anger on me, and not to mistreat her – but these people were pitiless and were deaf to my pleas. If I felt for her, she was also suffering with me. I was tied and bound, like the vilest criminal. She cried out, saying that I was her husband, and asking to know by what right or authority we were being separated, and why I was being punished, when she was the one who was to blame – all to no purpose.

We were taken back to Paris. I was thrown into a dungeon, and she, who had refused to return to her uncle's house, was placed under the custody of a court officer. My trial followed, and, as I had predicted, I was accused of subornation and rape. I defended myself and tried to the best of my ability to show that I was innocent. I knew Mademoiselle Fenouil would not be offended if I revealed that it was she who had made all the advances in our relationship. I showed all her letters. I told the truth as it was, but things did not look good for me, and probably my adversaries would have won the day, if she had not striven in every way to save me, as she had promised she would do. Neither the threats nor the promises of her family could sway her: she refused absolutely to give me up. We were both brought before my judges; their presence did not prevent her from throwing her arms round my neck, her face bathed in tears. She asked my forgiveness for all I was suffering for her sake. She vowed to them she would never desert me; she said I was well aware she was not afraid of death and whatever my sentence was, she would not outlive me. She went down on her knees in front of the judges and begged them to return her husband to her. She asserted that it was she who was responsible for what had now happened to me; that I had only agreed to leave with her when I had realised she was intent on poisoning herself; and that I had snatched the poison from her hands. She continued to plead my innocence with such anguish and such force that my composure gave way. I had been able to accept my own suffering with reasonable fortitude, but seeing how she fought for me was more than I could bear. My heart seemed to stop, and I fell in a swoon. When I came round, I found myself lying on a bed. I learnt later that the judges had realised that I was not such a villain as they had at first supposed, and, being moved perhaps by the devotion displayed by Mademoiselle Fenouil, and discovering that those who had brought the case against me had done so not without malice, they had used what discretion the law allowed, and interpreted it as generously as possible for us.

Even the public prosecutor said – with an integrity worthy of his high position – that though the seriousness of the charges brought against me would normally force him to call for the full force of the law in all its severity to be applied, the scenes he had just witnessed had made him reconsider his original judgement, which had been too harsh, and persuaded him to impose a more lenient sentence. They knew Mademoiselle Fenouil's age, and among several other rulings handed down, it was decreed that she should be returned to the care of her relatives, or to a convent of their choice, until she came of age, and that I should be banished from France for exactly seven years. The term of my exile would thus fall just a fortnight short of the date on which Mademoiselle Fenouil would reach the age when the law allows a young woman the right to determine her own future. I was ordered to pay all the costs of the trial, to be responsible for the child's board and upbringing, and to pay a large sum in damages to the mother. Against her family's wishes, she had herself declared legally independent and renounced all the claims the Court had awarded her against me. Our promise of marriage to each other was declared null and void. Neither of us appealed these rulings.

Shortly afterwards she gave birth to a boy, who is alive and well, and whom you will shortly see with his mother. I was released from prison. I made arrangements for her to receive my letters and for hers to be forwarded to me. I used a very loyal friend, who has not let us down. I left the same day, without seeing her, and have never seen her since the cruel day when we appeared before the judges. I didn't go far from France. I have spent nearly all the time in Holland, Germany, Spain or Italy, except for the last two years, which I have spent in Portugal with you. Using my own name, I took out a certificate when I left France, and I obtained another on my return, so that my accusers cannot cause me any trouble for not having spent my full seven-year term of banishment outside France, and an additional month or more outside Paris, where I will not return until Mademoiselle Fenouil wishes. She should be here at nine o'clock. There is still some time, it is not yet eight o'clock. Since I have received a large number of letters from her (including a very long one yesterday evening) in which she has told me in detail everything that has happened to her since I left, I can tell you it all just as well as if I had been in Paris myself all the time.

A few days after the birth of her child, when she was just nineteen years old, she went into a convent and stayed there for three years. Then she left and went back to her uncle's, and pretended she had lost all interest in me. My name was never mentioned in her presence, nor did she ever mention it herself, either in front of the family or to friends. She made no sign of trying to find out what had happened to me. She often went secretly to see our child. She withdrew from society completely and appeared to have given herself up to a life of piety. Talk about our affair had exhausted itself, and no one was aware that we were communicating with each other regularly by letter.

Her manner of life made people forget the past. She received several offers from suitors who would have been more than pleased to marry her. There was one in particular, whose family was of equal standing to her own, and who knew all about her adventure with me, and who nonetheless loved her with all his heart. She refused them all; the latter she treated even less civilly than the others. In order to put an end to all these solicitations, she was forced to declare outright that she planned to live alone and would never marry. She made this declaration shortly before news of my death was received, for we had decided that if we let a rumour such as this circulate, she would be left alone and avoid harassment, and her life would be easier. We were able to introduce the rumour in the following way.

I had taken another name and was known as Saint-George, as you are aware – since it was only when we arrived at La Rochelle that you learnt my real name. It so happened that, while I was in Spain, I met a young Frenchman in Madrid, also called de Jussy. He was a Parisian and was neither a merchant nor a member of the Ambassador's retinue, but, like me, just travelling around the country. I asked him about his family and, as far as I could discover, we were not related. I didn't tell him my name, but I felt obliged, because we were of the same nationality, to make a few suggestions concerning his conduct, which was licentious in the extreme – this was the more necessary since we were in a country where jealousy is the rule, and husbands consider they have the right to avenge their honour if they think it is threatened because someone is on too friendly terms either with their wives or with some other female member of the family. He paid no attention to my advice. He maintained a certain style of life by means of the presents he received from some wealthy benefactress – a situation which is not uncommon there. In the end, when I returned from a trip one time, I heard he had been murdered.

Since I was one of his acquaintances, I was told of his death. I persuaded someone at the French Embassy to pen a letter addressed to my relatives, saying I was dead; I asked that it should be stated in the letter that the deceased had requested that, in the case of his death, the family should be notified – which was true. The Embassy even provided a death certificate indicating where the grave was to be found. This all took place in such a way that even now my relatives believe me to be in the next world. It seemed to me that if they themselves believed this was true, they would be more likely to convince others. However, so that Mademoiselle Fenouil should not be deceived by this story, I wrote to her in my own hand telling her the truth. I had the whole packet, which was addressed to my brother, forwarded to her, saying she should do with it as she thought best. I entrusted all this to a French merchant who was passing through Madrid from Cadiz on his way back to Paris. He took the packet to Duval, my intermediary, to whom I had addressed it. (It is he who has been our go-between; you will meet him soon, he is coming with Mademoiselle Fenouil this morning.) He gave it to her, and they consulted with each other as to what would be the best thing to do, and they decided to make use of it.

Duval therefore took the packet addressed to my brother back to the merchant who had brought it and asked him to deliver it, explaining that it was a communication of some importance, but that he and my brother were not on close enough terms for him to deliver it himself. This merchant therefore took it to my brother, who asked him all sorts of questions about me, but all the man was able to tell him was that all those of French nationality in Madrid were saying that someone from Paris by the name of Monsieur de Jussy had died recently. My brother went into mourning and had a Mass said for my soul. Mademoiselle Fenouil sent word to me that he behaved very well, and that he has taken as much interest in my son as if he had been his own child. These are obligations which it will be incumbent on me to repay tomorrow. The news of my death spread around Paris, and my relatives wrote to His Excellency the Ambassador to have it confirmed. They received the same reply as Monsieur d'Ivonne who had also wanted to satisfy himself as to the truth of the story. So the only people in Paris who do not believe I am dead are Mademoiselle Fenouil and Duval. How surprised the others will be to see me alive and well!

The belief that I was dead had the desired effect, and d'Ivonne left his niece in peace. My relatives stopped sending me money, but this was no hardship. On the contrary, I had more than I needed. Mademoiselle Fenouil was now her own mistress and received the income from her property, and didn't spend even a tenth of it – her only servants were a young lackey and the same chamber-maid she had previously had, whom she had taken on again in spite of her uncle – so she sent me more than I wanted. Moreover, since I had nothing to do in Lisbon, I started to take an interest in several shipping ventures. I made a considerable amount of money, which I am bringing back in letters of credit. I have kept Mademoiselle Fenouil informed of what I have been doing, and she supported me wholeheartedly. Seventeen months ago, I asked her not to send any more money, but to save whatever she did not use in order to prepare a place for us to live in when I returned. This she agreed to do, and proceeded as follows.

She pretended to be dissatisfied with her chamber-maid and to dismiss her from her service. This young woman, in conjunction with Duval, then rented a house in a district very distant from that in which Monsieur d'Ivonne lived. Mademoiselle Fenouil gave her all the money needed to decorate and furnish the house completely. Furthermore, she tells me that there are servants waiting there whom she herself has never met, and that I shall find the house well furnished and in good order, with nothing lacking; and that when she comes to meet me, it will be in my own carriage.

It will be soon enough to hear all the details when I see her. And I think I shall not be proved wrong if I tell you that I expect to find she has been absolutely faithful and true to me. Having waited seven years can certainly be considered something exceptional, the more so when one takes into account her uncle's efforts to influence her against me, which should not be overlooked. Of course it is true that, for the sake of her good name and self-esteem, she had to be faithful to the alliance she had formed with me; but, on the other hand, it is also true that it is somewhat unusual for members of the fair sex to be particularly sensitive on this matter of loyalty and reputation, especially if they are besieged by as many potential suitors as she was. After all she and I have suffered, I certainly hope that we will now live happily together for the rest of our days. Her family can no longer interfere: she is her own mistress, having attained the age of twenty-six. I still have the promise of marriage we made, and we both want to renew our marriage vows, and put to rights anything we did formerly which was not strictly in accordance with the law; and, as far as I know, no one is in a position to prevent us from doing so. She and I will now make arrangements for a quiet ceremony. We made ourselves talked about enough before; now it is time to put an end both to our separation and to all the tittle-tattle, and give our child the settled home he should have.

So, continued Jussy, that is the story you have been wanting to hear! And what I would like to do now is to ask you to stay here and wait with me until Mademoiselle Fenouil arrives, and to remain with us until our marriage takes place, if, as you have told me, you have no more pressing business to attend to, and to serve as our witness, and thus see the conclusion of our story. Indeed, I would have been happy enough to take the post-coach from La Rochelle, as you wished. But the measures I was obliged to take in order to have news from Mademoiselle Fenouil every day, and to be able to arrange the proper time and place for our meeting, required me to proceed with more deliberation, as you now understand.

I am too delighted, I replied, at having a part in such an unusual affair as yours not to wish to see it to a conclusion. Not only will I serve as your witness, but I am ready to stand by to give you any other support you may need, though I cannot deny my unhappiness at the way you treated Mademoiselle Grandet, who is someone for whom I have the highest regard. However, I will keep the matter in mind only in order to bring about a reconciliation between you two, if I am able to do so. I swear, said Jussy, I have suffered from the deepest pangs of remorse over that episode ever since it happened. I am ready to beg Mademoiselle Grandet's forgiveness as soon as she is willing to see me. Mademoiselle Fenouil has described her to me as one of the most virtuous and charming women in France, and tells me that she is greatly admired for her exemplary manners and behaviour. I do not say this just on the spur of the moment – here are letters from Mademoiselle Fenouil, which you can read for yourself, and you will see I am saying only what she had written. And I am ready to make whatever amends I can to Mademoiselle Grandet for the way I treated her, and I am sure Mademoiselle Fenouil feels as I do about this.

At this point, Des Frans broke off his narrative and addressed Madame de Contamine. It was this, Madame, that I was discussing with Madame de Mongey some little time ago, when you tried to divine the topic of our conversation. Pray do not let me cause you to interrupt the story, said Madame de Contamine amiably. There will be time later for us to discuss whatever we may wish. At present, continue Monsieur de Jussy's story: we all beg you to proceed. Des Frans therefore resumed the narrative.

Seeing that Jussy was genuinely repentant about the way he had misused Mademoiselle Grandet, I told him that, as far as I was concerned, I forgave Mademoiselle Fenouil for her part in the matter, since she recognised the injustice that had been done, and acknowledged it had been undeserved. We discussed the matter for some time. But to return to my narrative: I am intrigued, I said to Jussy, by the portrait you have painted of your mistress, the example she provides of fortitude and loyalty must be unique in this century! One day I will tell you the experiences which have made me so firmly convinced of the shallowness and inconstancy of the female heart – you will then understand that I have reason to deplore the deceit and treachery of their sex.

You are ungallant, Monsieur! interrupted Madame de Contamine. These words will hardly endear you to your audience! Patience, Madame, replied Des Frans. My comments are not directed at you. A person who is injured is allowed to voice his distress. Tomorrow you will learn what has led me to my conclusions. Today, allow me to repeat to you my conversation with Jussy. The story of how Mademoiselle Fenouil remained true, I said to him, proves to me that there are exceptions, and I am delighted to hear this, since her devotion was to the benefit of a worthy person, whom I regard as my friend.

At that moment, we heard a carriage stop at the door of

the inn. I went to see who it was, and saw a smart, gilded carriage with coachman, three lackeys in livery and four beautiful pied horses. Everything both looked, and was, new. A man, a child and a woman dressed in the height of fashion stepped down from the carriage, followed by a neatly attired lady's maid. I had no doubt but that this was the arrival of Mademoiselle Fenouil, a deduction which was confirmed when I saw Jussy, who had immediately gone to meet them, take the child in his arms. He brought him into the room and handed him to me, and then went to the door, as the child's mother entered. Nothing could be more touching than the reunion which now took place. She tried for a time to restrain the expression of her joy at seeing him again, but, noticing this, he said, Have no fear– this is one of my friends, and very soon he will be one of yours. She then abandoned herself to the pleasure of taking him in her arms. They remained in each other's arms for more than a quarter of an hour, without saying a word; and it was fortunate that she was seated, for when Jussy made to move away, she had fainted. We revived her, and they renewed their embrace – but I feared she might faint a second time and separated them in order to prevent this. They both had tears in their eyes and were so overcome that they could not utter a word. Indeed, it is not difficult to imagine the pleasure they must have felt at being reunited after so much tribulation and such a long absence. Is this not an example of two people triumphing over misfortune, and owing their happiness to their loyalty and devotion to each other?

These first embraces gave place to others. Jussy embraced Duval, who had arrived with Mademoiselle Fenouil, and I greeted her, and found myself admiring one of the most beautiful women you have ever seen. The reunited couple were asking each other a thousand questions. I intervened and, calling both Jussy's valet and my own, had breakfast served. The newly hired lackeys also came in, but we said nothing in front of them which would reveal the true situation. Without giving more precise details, Duval merely told them they were to serve breakfast to their master and mistress, which they did. In the course of the conversation, and in their presence, Mademoiselle Fenouil remarked on how she had left her convent only that morning, to come and meet Jussy, and how Monsieur Duval had been responsible for hiring all the servants. For, she continued to Jussy in such a way that she was overheard, since you were not here in Paris, I had no wish to maintain a household; I preferred to remain in the convent till your return. When the servants had left, we conferred as to what should be done next. Everyone said what they thought would be best, and Duval's opinion won general acceptance. Both Jussy and Mademoiselle Fenouil had their birth certificates, as well as that of their child, and a copy of the court order which had dictated their separation. Therefore, said Duval, the obvious course of action to take is to present a request to the Archbishop of Paris, laying everything before him, and asking him to allow you to marry with the least delay – even today if possible – in order to avoid any further tussles with the law and to put an end to any gossip. What you say is reasonable, I said, and makes good sense. And that is what I had thought of doing, said Jussy. I am glad we are agreed on this, for if we were to make a formal application, who knows how long we might have to wait for permission to marry?

It was decided therefore that we should all proceed to Paris, to Jussy's new home, and that, as soon as we were there, Duval would find someone in authority who could take prompt action. Duval and I mounted our horses, while the others rode in the carriage, and we all took the road to Paris. Jussy's house was pointed out to me as we passed, and then I continued on towards this part of town, where we are at present. That was when I met you, near the Pont Notre-Dame, he said turning to Des Ronais. I accepted your offer

209

of a roof over my head and went with you to your house – but stayed only long enough to refresh myself and put on clean clothes. I didn't tell you where I was going, as you might have wanted to accompany me, and I didn't want you to become involved – I had some fears that things might not resolve themselves as smoothly as in the event they did. Moreover, I had promised Jussy not to reveal the news of his arrival. I returned to his house and remained there until yesterday afternoon.

I had barely returned when Duval came in bringing a notary with him. Laying all the relevant papers out for the man to see, we explained the situation to him. He approved of what we were planning to do, and drew up the request in his own words, which Monsieur de Jussy and Mademoiselle Fenouil then signed. He took it away and within an hour was back, bringing permission for them to marry in whichever church in the diocese they wished, and with instructions to the priest or curate concerned to give the blessing. To facilitate things even further, the notary had brought with him a relation of his, who was curate of a parish just outside Paris, and who was ready to officiate at the marriage ceremony whenever they wished. Since there was no chance of Monsieur d'Ivonne discovering what was happening or where his niece was, and since she wished the marriage ceremony to be properly conducted, they determined to go to this parish that same evening, so that they could be married at midnight in conformity with all the rites of the Church.

The notary and the curate joined us for supper. They were well entertained and, moreover, were handsomely recompensed for all their services. We asked them not to say anything about the events under way in front of the servants, who would be told the facts only when there was no longer any danger of discovery. This they promised. A second coach was hired, and they rode in it with Duval and myself. We also took with us in this carriage all that would be needed for a wedding breakfast, of which we would partake after the Mass. After a good supper, we all set out in the direction of this parish. There, Jussy took all his new servants into the presbytery and told them his name and as much of his story as he considered appropriate, finishing with the information that he and Mademoiselle Fenouil were about to be married, and that when they returned to Paris they were free to speak to anyone they wanted to about the matter. They were better pleased at being taken into his confidence in this way than they would have been if he had distributed all his wealth among them, and they all seemed ready to be dismembered and cut into slivers rather than let anyone say anything against their new master and mistress.

Everyone was in high spirits. While the bride and groom were in the church with the curate, the notary, Duval and myself waited outside – and provided the means for the servants to drink to their master's health. When midnight struck, we went into the church, the marriage ceremony took place, and the child was legitimised. We acted as witnesses, along with four parishioners. A certificate was drawn up which we all signed and then we ate a hearty breakfast. It was about four in the morning when we made our way back to Paris, each one returning to his own home, except for me, who slept at Jussy's house – where we were all still in bed at noon when Duval made an appearance. He and I went together to rouse Jussy and his wife. They rose, and during lunch it was decided that they would make the announcement of their marriage to d'Ivonne and their relatives with a dramatic flourish. This they would do that very evening, Tuesday. They did it in the following way.

When we had finished eating, Madame de Jussy went by carriage to her uncle's home – where she had been living until the day before. He was extremely surprised to see her in such finery, since she had always dressed simply and with an appearance of piety up till then. He asked her where she had been since the previous morning. In reply, she showed him her birth certificate and said that, now she was over twenty-five and able to do as she wished, she had moved into a house of her own and had come to invite him and his wife and children to do her the honour of having supper with her that evening. Nothing could have given him a greater surprise than this response. She promised to send a servant to show them the way, if they were willing to come, and then left them to consider their answer. There was all the more for them to ponder, as her servants had passed the news on to d'Ivonne's household that she had been married the night before. They were at a loss to figure out whom she had married, since their conviction that Jussy was dead misled them completely. There were enigmas they could not unravel: How could Jussy have come to life again? How had the pair remained in communication for so long, while nobody suspected it? How could they have arranged the marriage? And by what magic had Jussy arrived home so precisely as his banishment expired and Mademoiselle Fenouil came of age? They decided, all things considered, to accept the invitation and went for supper with her that evening.

They found a large company there, for Jussy had invited his two brothers as well as two friends, and his wife had also invited a few of her good friends, so the party already numbered fourteen when d'Ivonne and his wife arrived with two of their children, a boy and a girl. Their surprise increased on seeing this large assembly. The room where the guests were gathered was perfectly furnished, with everything as it should be and nothing lacking. Dinner was served, and we were summoned to take our places at table. Jussy was not there; his wife performed the role of hostess. There was a certain air of subdued uncertainty as we took our seats, which I, who was only there to see what

212

happened, could not help but find diverting. I had some trouble restraining my amusement at Monsieur and Madame d'Ivonne's wariness. Meantime, in order to set the stage, Madame de Jussy had put me on her left, and had her son next to her on the right, with an empty place between him and Duval. The silence continued as we seated ourselves; then Madame de Jussy turned to one of the lackeys and said, Go and tell your master that we are waiting for him, and ask him to come and join us. To which the lackey responded: He is just finishing a letter he has been writing. This intensified the astonishment of d'Ivonne and his wife even further, and it reached its height when Jussy walked into the room, preceded by a lackey carrying a torch. He was not wearing a hat and looked like a man who was in his own home and master of the house. But even I was surprised to see him so well-dressed. The fact was, everything had been to hand before he arrived; all that was needed was for the tailor to make a few final adjustments. I beg your pardon for keeping you waiting, he said, as he came into the room. D'Ivonne and his wife recognised him and let out a startled cry. I have been brought back to life, he continued, and have come back to Paris and to my wife, and I ask for your friendship, and assure you that I am ready to reciprocate with my own sincere friendship towards you.

It is impossible to describe the amazement of D'Ivonne and his wife. D'Ivonne stood up and left the table abruptly without giving an answer. He realised that there was nothing to be gained by allowing his feelings to provoke him to violence. On the contrary, if it came to exchanging blows, he stood to lose both the fight and his honour. He walked out of the room, followed by his wife and daughter – in spite of everything we said to try and make them stay; for we did not allow Madame de Jussy to leave the table and go after them. Only the son, who did not share his parents' pique, remained to partake of the meal with us. Jussy and his wife told him the whole of their story, and he expressed his approval of what his cousin had done, and offered his good wishes to her husband and herself, for which they thanked him warmly. They asked him to try and make his father see reason, so that an amicable agreement could be reached to conclude his guardianship of his niece and the oversight of her affairs during her minority; and they asked him also to point out to his father that it had been necessary for her to act as she did, for the sake of her good name and reputation. This young man, who is sensible, agreed with all they said, and promised to do all he could to bring about a reconciliation with his father. We ate a very good supper. The company was in cheerful mood and took to singing. And since there were so many of us, we sent for some fiddlers and started to dance, and had an impromptu ball until three o'clock on Wednesday morning – the day before yesterday. I went to bed more exhausted than if I had travelled fifteen days in a row by post-coach! I left the newly-weds to their slumbers and have not seen them since. But as I owe them a visit, I will call on them tomorrow morning, and you, gentlemen, he said to Des Ronais and Dupuis, may accompany me if you wish. And after that, if Madame de Mongey is prepared to receive a visit from them, I make bold to predict that she will be satisfied with their apologies and accept their expressions of remorse. The two men agreed to the arrangement for the following morning.

I am grateful to Madame de Jussy, said Madame de Contamine, for the example she has set. Because of her loyalty, I can readily forgive her fault. Indeed, she has wiped it out and, at present, is deserving of our esteem, though her example is not one that should be imitated. I hope Madame de Mongey will forgive the lack of consideration with which she was used by Monsieur and Madame de Jussy. I no longer harbour any ill-feeling towards them on that account, replied the charming young widow. It has all

214

MONSIEUR DE JUSSY & MADEMOISELLE FENOUIL

evaporated on hearing what Monsieur Des Frans has told us. If I could be sure of that, said Des Frans, I would bring Monsieur and Madame de Jussy here tomorrow, so that the apology and its acceptance could be made public and everyone be satisfied. Would you doubt the word of the Oracle? said Mademoiselle Dupuis. I know Madame de Mongey. She is sincerity itself and, since she says she forgives them, I am certain it is so. Furthermore, even if you were not willing to bring Monsieur and Madame de Jussy for the sake of Madame de Mongey, I beg you to bring them to please Madame de Contamine and myself. I should be very surprised if Madame de Contamine is not as impatient as I am to meet such an exceptional man as Monsieur de Jussy. And even more, added Madame de Contamine, such an exceptional woman as his wife. I am absolutely determined to see her tomorrow, even if it means posting a lackey outside her door to find out where she goes to Mass.

To be true to each other after a separation of seven years! mused Mademoiselle Dupuis, in a tone of wonder, her eye resting on Des Ronais. And with never the least hint of a misunderstanding between them! Aha! said Des Ronais, I see you are making comparisons, and I am not completely forgiven! It is not Jussy who has my admiration, interrupted Des Frans. After all, there is nothing remarkable about a man who remains true. It is Madame de Jussy whom I admire, for women as a rule are deceitful and incapable of fidelity.

Take care, or you will bring our anger on your head, if you talk to us about women in that way! exclaimed Madame de Contamine. Madame, he replied, I have already told you that I regard all of you who are present as saints and paragons in our time. It gives me the greatest satisfaction that all my friends have fallen into good hands; but for myself, who have not had the same good fortune, do not expect me to refrain from expressing the views I have formed from my own experience. You have less cause for complaint than you think, said Dupuis.

And even if Monsieur himself had good reason for his opinion, said Madame de Contamine, do we have to allow that, because one member of our sex was unfaithful, he should claim the same is true of all of us? We are more temperate in our judgement of your sex, she continued. We are all ready to sing the praises of Monsieur de Jussy; but on the other hand, there is not one among us who does not blame our friend here – indicating Dupuis – for his flirtations and philandering; or who does not condemn Monsieur Des Prez, who abandoned poor Mademoiselle de l'Epine – whom we all knew – in so heartless a fashion. We praise what is praiseworthy, and blame what deserves to be blamed; we do not paint all with the same brush!

Have you finished? enquired Dupuis, his arms folded across his chest. It is disappointing when a woman with as much good sense as you speaks ill of someone, with insufficient evidence for her assumptions. When you know the facts, you will perhaps not be so ready to blame me. And as for Monsieur Des Prez, he is more to be pitied than blamed; and you, Madame, who judge him only by the label on the outside, you yourself would acknowledge this if you knew the whole story, as I do.

Will you not tell it to us, then? suggested Madame de Mongey. Mademoiselle de l'Epine and I were boarders at the same convent, you know, and I must admit that since her death I have taken an aversion to Monsieur Des Prez, and I would like to be able to see him in a different light, since in all other contexts, he seemed to me like a very respectable person. I will be happy to do so, Madame, replied Dupuis, and if the others present would like to hear his story, I will tell it to you. Everyone wanted to hear it, and he was about to begin, when Madame de Londé appeared at the door of the room. He went towards her, and everyone else rose and welcomed her. So, Madame, he said, has a successful conclusion been reached? Yes, she replied happily. The relative you had appointed to speak on your behalf presented the position satisfactorily and has obtained your mother's consent. What good news! And what a pleasure to hear it from your lips! he said. Are we to understand from this, said Madame de Contamine, that both cousins are soon to have their hearts' desire come true? For my part, said Dupuis, my marriage with Madame de Londé can take place as soon as she wishes. And as for me, also, said Des Ronais, my marriage with Mademoiselle Dupuis can take place whenever she likes. That being so, said Des Frans, both marriages must take place on the same day, so that there will be no question of the happiness of the couple who marries first rousing the jealousy of the other pair. We will name a day some other time, said Madame de Londé, but for the present, Madame Dupuis, who cannot leave her bedchamber, has sent me down to ask you all to go upstairs and take supper with her. You see, she is already treating me like a daughter, using me to carry her messages – which I am quite happy to do; or perhaps she had something else to say to the other party involved in our negotiations, which she didn't want me to hear. But by now it will have been said, so let us go up to her!

Everyone left the salon and went upstairs to Madame Dupuis's room. Her son took Madame de Londé's hand, Des Frans escorted both Madame de Contamine and Madame de Mongey, and Des Ronais led his fiancée upstairs. They made a circle round Madame Dupuis's bed, but her niece, Mademoiselle Dupuis, and Madame de Contamine made a sign to Des Frans that they wanted a word with him in private, and he moved with them to a corner of the room, where they conversed in whispers, but with much gesturing and for a considerable length of time. We shall discover elsewhere what they were talking about.

Des Ronais seemed disturbed by their discussion, and Madame de Contamine teased him spiritedly about this when they sat down to eat.

They had an excellent meal at Madame Dupuis's bedside, and she was cheered to see so many young people in such good spirits around her. Des Ronais was tackled and taunted for being worried about the conversation in which his fiancée had taken part and from which he had been excluded. He stood up for himself stoutly and with good humour. They talked of jealousy, and gradually the conversation veered towards the subject of Des Prez. Madame de Londé said she had heard part of the story and would like to know the rest. Her fiancé needed no further encouragement and, everyone having settled down to listen, he began in these terms.

The Story of Monsieur Des Prez and Mademoiselle de l'Epine

It was about two years ago, on my return from a journey I had been making with the King in connection with some matters I was involved in at the Court of Appeals, that I heard that Marie-Madeleine de l'Epine, the oldest of three sisters, had died in pitiful circumstances only about three months earlier. This news distressed me, not because I knew her well, but because she had been one of the most beautiful young women in the neighbourhood. Everyone spoke ill of Monsieur Des Prez; I heard so many reports about the heartless way he had behaved, that, though I didn't recognise the person I had known in these descriptions or in the things he was supposed to have done, I thought he must be guilty. He was not in Paris when I arrived and only returned about three months later.

As we had always been good friends, I went to see him. He was pale and listless, as if he had been ill. When I went into the room, he was sitting with his elbows on a table, his head between his hands. He rose when he heard me enter, and my words seemed to bring him out of a reverie in which he had been lost. There was an open letter in front of him, in what appeared to be a woman's hand. We embraced. I expressed my sympathy for the unhappy state I could see he was in, commiserated with him, and tried to console him. The blow is here, dear friend, he said, pointing with a finger to his heart. I shall never recover. And tears came into his eyes. He picked up a piece of paper which had been lying on his table, kissed it, and put it in a purse which he wore at his waist, like a reliquary. I saw it was a portrait of Mademoiselle de l'Epine. He sighed and spoke to me so incoherently, and with so little sequence in his thoughts, that I was moved by his suffering. I suspected what the cause of his trouble might be, and in order to distract him from his misery, and to see if my guess was correct, I said: You should not have been given the letter you were reading, when you have been ill and are still so weak. You should have been spared from reading it, for, unless I am mistaken, it is this letter which has caused the sadness which overwhelms you at present.

I have not been ill, he answered, and it is not this letter which causes my distress; it merely reaffirms it. I think I know the hand, and recognise Mademoiselle de l'Epine's writing, I said. You are right, he answered. It is indeed from her. But how can you have received a letter from her, I said, since, according to what I have heard, she is dead? She is dead, indeed, he replied. And would to God she were not. I would not be here, but she would not be lost to me for ever.

With these words, his grief broke out anew, even more strongly than before; his tears brimmed, and his constant sighs told me that there was more in this story than those from whom I had heard it had known. But, I therefore asked him, why are you so distraught by this young woman's death, when you abandoned her during her life? Abandoned her! he exclaimed, clasping his hands together and raising his eyes to heaven. My God! Could anything be further from the truth? It is what most people believe, I said. What most people believe is of no concern to me, he said. But you, who know me, could you believe that? And should you not rather have defended my name? Appearances are all against you, I said. Everybody else may believe appearances, he said. I do not care to disabuse them. But rather than have you think so ill of me, I must tell you the truth – though it is hardly worth enlightening you, if you have so little esteem for me. I should be glad to hear the truth, I answered, whenever you are willing to tell me it. I cannot do so here, he said, but let us go out, and while we walk I will tell you the true course of events as they happened. I therefore took advantage of his willingness to tell me his story.

Taking my carriage, we followed the Vincennes road. While we were in the carriage, he scarcely opened his mouth; at least, all I heard were sighs and a few inarticulate murmurs which I could not understand because of the noise the wheels were making on the rough road. As soon as we reached smoother ground, where the carriage made less noise, I asked him to start his story. I couldn't get two consecutive words out of him, but, finally, once we had reached the woods, he had me stop the carriage and got out, without saying a word to me. I followed. He asked me to tell my people to wait for us, and when we had gone some distance, so that we could be sure we would not be either overheard or interrupted, he began to speak.

In order to erase from your mind the false information you have heard, all I need do is tell you exactly what happened between myself and Mademoiselle de l'Epine. Then you will understand that I am innocent, and also learn about the poor young woman's misfortunes and my own – I say 'young woman' – she was in fact my wife. And, most important of all, you will understand why my heart is forever burdened with the knowledge that I was the innocent cause of her death.

You know that it is my misfortune to be the only son of a man who is extremely powerful in the judiciary of our country. I call it my misfortune, for if my father had had less influence and authority, and there had been less cause to fear what he might do, I would not be as I now am, the most miserable of men. Marie-Madeleine de l'Epine, whom you knew, was the eldest child in a family of three girls and a boy, whose father had died, leaving them to their mother's care. He was Italian, of a good family, though not rich. He had come to France with Cardinal Mazarin, in whose employ he had remained till his death. His widow was left to oversee the family's affairs, among which was a wretched lawsuit – the cause of my misfortune. It was a dispute of long standing, which is still not resolved to this day, though it should have been settled long ago. My father was in a position to exert considerable influence as to the outcome.

The family lived not far from our residence, and the mother came frequently, hoping to advance this affair. There were powerful arguments on her side, but had I been the judge, the most powerful would have been the charming young lady who accompanied her. You saw her and can remember her appearance. She was tall and comely, of a very pale complexion, and had the most beautiful fair hair imaginable. Her face was oval, and she had blue eyes, as is most often the case with blondes; but rather than the languid beauty common to blondes, she had a lively, vivacious beauty. Her voice was winsome and appealing, her manner full of charm, seeming both to appeal for tenderness and to offer love. The appearance was not misleading, though the pleasure of the senses was not a dominant part of her nature. Her character was honourable, sincere, open and generous; she was capable of loyalty to the last breath in her body. She deserved to have everything a woman can hope for. She was imaginative, slow to determine on a course of action, but decisive, once the resolve had been taken. She was unselfish, a good friend, a most faithful mistress. She had little interest in wealth or position. I have often heard her say that if the choice were hers, she would prefer poverty and a tranquil life, rather than a life of luxury and high position which could be bought only at the price of one's integrity. With me, she was compliant and ready to please, though by nature her manner could be sharp. I have often known her to do something for me which she knew would please me, but which she would have done for no other reason. She was passionate and unreserved with me, though not immodest, and she often took me in her arms and sought my embrace when I knew she would have been happy if I had been less ardent. In a word, she was the most desirable woman and mistress you can imagine.

I saw her in a room where my father received those with whom he had business; she and her mother were waiting outside his private office. I was dazzled by her beauty, and believing myself to be merely acting out of courtesy, though I was in fact responding to the first stirrings of my heart, I offered to introduce them directly to my father. Taking the mother's hand, I showed them into his office. Allow me to present these ladies to you, Father, I said. They have been waiting some time, and I thought I should bring them to your notice, since their appearance would seem to justify your special attention. I make bold to hope you will render them any service you can.

I left them there and I knew the mother had time to explain her case fully, as they were closeted with my father for more than an hour. I was outside his office, as if by chance, when they left, and asked if their mission had been successful. Yes, Monsieur, replied the mother, and we are greatly indebted to you. I have told your father about all the delays and petty quibbles that beset the case, and I trust he will soon be able to ensure that a just settlement is reached. If it depended upon me, Mademoiselle, I said, the matter would be settled today. She thanked me, and they took their leave. I noticed that the daughter's colour heightened whenever she looked at me, and that, when my glance fell on her, her eyes turned away.

I set a servant to watch and tell me the evenings when they came out to take the air on their doorstep – that is, the young lady and her sisters, not the mother, in whom I had no particular interest. I joined them there frequently. Sometimes we would walk around the fort adjoining the Porte Saint-Antoine, or in the open fields beyond, but I never had any private conversation with the daughter. I was made welcome because of the service I had already rendered, and the ones I might be able to render in the future.

When the weather no longer allowed us to go walking, I joined them to play cards in the evening. We played for very low stakes and only for the sake of companionship. And to provide a pretext for going every evening, I made a suggestion which would ensure that our meetings would continue in the same way for some length of time. I said that our winnings and losses were in themselves insignificant, but we ought to devise some scheme to make them provide us with additional entertainment. I suggested we elect a treasurer: the winners each evening would forego what they had won, and the losers would pay what they owed into the treasury. In this way, when a sufficient sum had been collected, we would organise an outing for which no one need pay and which all would enjoy. The idea was accepted, and the society was formed. We had eight members: the two older sisters, two young ladies from the neighbourhood, and their four admirers – of which I was one. There is no need to tell you their names – they are of no importance to my story. We were all required to be there every evening, though Marie-Madeleine's young brother would stand in for anyone who was unavoidably absent, in which case the absentee would be obliged either to pay any losses he incurred or give him as much as he would have won. These conditions aroused some disagreement, both mother and daughters opposing them, and in the end it was agreed that the young ladies should be exempted and only the men would pay if they failed to appear. The men wanted the fine to be a heavy one, but we were not able to carry this point either. In any case, our funds would not have profited much: everyone had his own reasons for being there, which ensured we were not likely to absent ourselves. The girls' forfeit was to give each of the young men a kiss. And thus we played every evening. Our treasurer was Marie-Madeleine. I sought in vain to speak to her alone and made no progress in my efforts to further our acquaintance. No one could have been more reserved than she was. Things continued in this train for nearly four months. She knew very well that I was not indifferent to her, and that it was more than our card games which brought me to her house, but she was so proficient in eluding me that I was quite unable to engage her in any private conversation.

On St. Martin's Day, we counted the money we had accumulated, and though we had kept our stakes low, there proved to be enough for us to arrange a thoroughly enjoyable outing. Since the company was so congenial, we had one of the pleasantest evenings I have ever experienced. Even so, our coffers were not exhausted, and everyone was so pleased with our society, we decided to prolong its existence so that we could celebrate Midnight Mass and Advent and conclude with a good supper and a dance on the feast days. On the basis of our previous experience, we had no doubt that we would have sufficient resources to have a very special celebration by that time. Our little society reconvened with even more enthusiasm than before, and our funds grew accordingly.

But in spite of all my efforts, I still made no progress with Mademoiselle de l'Epine. She still spent all day with her mother and sisters, and in the evening the fact that there was always a group of people present gave her every opportunity to avoid me, without any appearance of this being intentional. But I was impatient to speak to her and bring matters into the open between us. I was too much in love to remain forever in uncertainty, so being unable to speak, I wrote this note:

I believe you must be aware of what I feel for you. I have spoken till now only with my eyes, but I think they have spoken clearly. The presence of so many people who are continually with you, and your assiduity in denying me any chance to speak privately with you, have forced me to remain silent all this time. If you are not yet aware of my love for you, I must blame my eyes, which are unpractised in this language. But if you have seen and understood their message, I must accuse you of either indifference or hard-heartedness towards me. Release me from my uncertainty. My whole happiness depends on your reply.

As I put this note in her hand, she gave a movement which made me fear that she would refuse it. But she took it, blushing, and without looking at me. I noticed that evening that she did not play with her usual light-heartedness. I returned the next evening and placed myself next to her. She made a pretence of dropping something and, as she bent as if to retrieve it, put a note in the basque of my jerkin. I was too eager to see what it might say to tolerate any delay. I left the company, asking the mother to take my place temporarily, and went into the next room to read what it said. It was brief, consisting only of a suggested rendez-vous for the following day: I was to meet her at the Sainte-Chapelle, while her mother was away overseeing her affairs at the Palais de Justice. I returned to my seat, delighted in the knowledge that at last I was to have a meeting which would enable me to speak with Marie-Madeleine.

I was there at the appointed time, and she arrived a moment later. The Mass, which had provided the excuse for my presence, came to an end. Everyone left, and we two remained alone in the church. Our time was too short to be wasted. I went towards her. So, Mademoiselle, I began, am I to learn today what my fate is to be? I do not know, she answered, what your fate will be, but for myself I fear no good will come of your desire to know me better. If I heeded the presentiment I feel in my heart, I would tell you to stifle any affection you may feel for me. I would even ask you to cease your visits to the house, and I would never see you again. Your presentiments are sombre indeed, I said. Is this all your heart can say? Does nothing counter these forebodings? Indeed, she answered, it must say something even more powerful, since now that I am with you the resolve which I made yesterday, and which brought me here today, fails me. It was not to break off a special relationship with you, since none exists, but it was to beg you not to contemplate forming one, and to say that I feel for you no more than duty and courtesy require; but ... She stopped there, her eyes full of tears. Continue, Mademoiselle, I said. What is this 'but'? What can I say, she answered, with a blush. I find I no longer feel the same as I did when I set out this morning. The holiness of the building in which our meeting was taking place did not prevent me from taking her hand and kissing it, nor from thanking her with a warmth of feeling which I had never experienced before, and which all but overwhelmed me.

We could not pursue our conversation any further in this place; our presence would have shocked anyone who entered the sanctuary. I led Marie-Madeleine to a nearby bookseller's and we entered the store. Her mother would pass this way on her return. The owner of the bookstore was a friend of mine, and we were able to discuss our situation fully and freely here. I thanked Marie-Madeleine for her sincerity. She said that I should not conclude from the openness with which she had spoken that her sense of virtue was any the less strict and that she could hardly account for what had happened to make her express her feeling so boldly. She said she had loved me from the first moment she had seen me, long before she had ever spoken to me, and that it was in the hope of speaking to me, or at least of seeing me, that she had accompanied her mother to my father's chambers. She was telling me this, she said, so that I would not imagine her feelings for me had arisen merely out of gratitude for what I had done, or out of any hope of gain; it was her heart alone which had singled me out.

I said all I could to convince her that what she said filled me with joy. I expressed my love for her in the liveliest terms possible. I believe you are telling me the truth, she said, and I hope so. But nonetheless, you have led me into taking a step which I fear I may repent for only too long. You love me, so you tell me, and I believe you. I love you and am telling you so, but what can come of this? It is clear, we were not born for each other. Though my family is honourable, it is not of the same rank as yours in France, and as for fortune, you are a hundred leagues above me. And I will never do anything which would lead me to forfeit your respect ... These are the reasons which made it seem necessary to refuse to see you again, for I see no possibility of a happy outcome either for you or for me. For you, because, as well as the time you will waste on me, you will antagonise those on whom you depend; and for me, because everyone will see I cannot expect to marry you, and therefore our acquaintance, even if innocent, will be interpreted to my detriment, and I shall pay with my reputation for the pleasure I have in seeing you.

I told her that I had thought of all these things myself, but that my decision was taken. I accepted that there was no hope that we could be openly and happily united in marriage during my father's lifetime; but at least, I said, we were free to love each other, to say so to each other, and to marry without his knowledge, since I was of age. I would have no difficulty finding a priest who would be willing to marry us, I added, if she would consent. After that, we could seek refuge in the provinces, or abroad, for as long as my father's anger persisted.

Her answer to all this was to turn her head away and say it was an impossible dream, and that she could not agree to a marriage which would lay me open to my father's anger and force us to leave the country – supposing we were lucky enough to be able to do so. For, she said, supposing we were able to find a priest foolhardy enough to risk your father's wrath, if the marriage should come to his knowledge, powerful as he is, he would not fail to declare it clandestine and have it annulled. You would be released from your vows, she said, and I would be sent to a nunnery for the rest of my days, to be scorned and vilified – and, moreover, very likely discredited in your eyes, once I had given myself to you. It is this that I fear most, she continued. All else is of no importance to me, but you would cease to love me, and without your affection I would sink into despair. Even if you remained loyal to me, it would be merely an appearance of love and would not prove strong enough to withstand your father's displeasure and the offer of another wife whom he would find for you. I assured her, with all the arguments and professions of devotion that a man so deeply in love as I was could use, that her fears were unfounded. She wavered, but I was unable to win her to my point of view.

After some time, her mother arrived and found us, but without suspecting why we were there together: far from it. I am glad to find you here, Monsieur, she said to me. I need some help. I offered my services. She asked me if I knew a certain person, whom she named. I said he was a good friend of mine, and that I was sure he would help her in any way he could. She said that it was within his power to have some money returned to her which he had ordered to be seized. She said that the order had been rescinded in the case of all the others affected, but not in her case, since it dated only from the previous day and this had prevented its repayment. She said she was not asking him to do anything which would damage his own interests in any way, since the whole thing in fact was nothing but a ploy on the part of her adversary in the lawsuit, who had requested the seizure in order to forestall a demand for payment which had been made against himself. I took her to see my friend, who, at my request, gave her all she asked for. She thanked me, received her money, and I accompanied her to her home.

I went to her house that evening as usual. Marie-Madeleine seemed melancholy and absent-minded. We asked if she was feeling unwell. She said no, but gave as her explanation that, when she and I had been at the book-seller's where her mother found us that morning, we had read a story about two lovers whose love had cost them their lives, and that this tale had disturbed her. I did not like this supposed story, or the way she used it, and wrote to her about it the next day; but she did not answer my letter, and I could not persuade her to agree to another meeting, in spite of many requests. I could not even extract the briefest note from her. I was unhappy, but I was consoled to observe that this behaviour cost her some effort.

We all attended Midnight Mass and had a pleasant evening together. New Year arrived and provided the occasion for exchanging gifts. I presented one to every member of the society, so that I could give one to Marie-Madeleine. A prayer book, a pair of gloves, a walking stick, a tobacco box, sufficed for most, but not for her. As well as a pair of gloves, which I gave her along with my gifts to the others, I presented her with a beautiful watch, which sounded the hours, accompanied by a letter, in which I did not speak of love, knowing that others would see it. Instead, I made it a light-hearted affair, saying that since there was some discussion almost every evening as to when our game should end (which everyone wanted to prolong in order to swell the society's coffers), and since our watches were never in agreement, we could settle the matter by allowing her to decide henceforth: we should all be happy to leave it to her, just as we were all happy to entrust her with the society's funds. This letter was read out aloud, and though she had wanted to return the watch to me, she was persuaded to keep it. This was what I had hoped for. I gave her another letter, in which I explained my other reasons for the gift. These were that I was not unduly concerned whether our games came to an end early or late, but that, since I thought of her throughout the day, I wanted to make sure she thought about me, at least when she wanted to see the time. I asked her to let me know a time when we could meet, and begged for another rendez-vous, but no reply came. Since it was now Twelfth Night, and the end of the Christmas season, we had our three suppers together on consecutive evenings. Carnival time came and went – but, in spite of its relaxed, festive atmosphere, I still made no headway. Nonetheless, I was certain she loved me. The way she sometimes looked at me confirmed what she had said. This was not enough for me, however. But then events took a turn which did more to help my cause than anything I myself could have done.

My father had grown annoyed by my constant attendance at the home of Mademoiselle de l'Epine. He had said nothing to me during the winter, or at Carnival time, but when my visits continued even during Lent, he began to be afraid that the mother – whom he knew to be a fortune-hunter – would lure me into some commitment which would not accord with his plans for me. It was not that he was worried about the outcome, but he preferred to forestall the problem, rather than allow the situation to reach a point where he would have the trouble of intervening and taking action.

He began by joking about it, but seeing this had no effect he eventually forbade me to go to the house. I neither obeyed him nor told either the mother or daughter about the prohibition. He got it into his head that it was the mother who was inciting me to defy him, and this made him angry with her. He could have caused her trouble with her lawsuit. He did not do so, however; he merely made her afraid that he might; for although he was by nature ill-tempered and sharp-tongued, this never affected the integrity of his legal dealings.

Mademoiselle de l'Epine was extremely surprised when the investigating magistrate in her case told her my father was displeased with her. She wanted to know the reason, since, when we have done nothing wrong, it does not occur to us that anyone will find anything to criticise in our actions. She told me that very evening what the magistrate had said. I knew very well what the reason was, but I was careful not to tell her this. The next morning, she came and asked me if I could arrange for her to see my father. She was quite unaware of what the trouble was. Her daughter and I had been so cautious, and had had so little time together in private, that she had no cause to suspect us. However, I didn't want her to know of my father's suspicions, so I told her he was unable to see her, and that he was engaged on a case which would keep him busy for some time. I told her to return home and stay there: I promised I would see what I could do and let her know if an opportunity arose for her to see him during the day. She believed me and prepared to leave, but as I was showing her out we came face to face with my father. He had left his office by way of a hidden doorway which opened on to a private stairway and was crossing the courtyard. The fact that I looked surprised confirmed his suspicions. It was not me you wished to see, then, Mademoiselle? he said. I beg your pardon, Monsieur, she said. I had come to ask you in what way ... And I too, I have been wanting to speak to you for quite some time, he interrupted. Be good enough to step into my office with me, and I will tell you my sentiments. She followed him, and I stood there, more dead than alive.

I remained outside the office door and heard everything. He spoke to her very politely at first, and then in the tone of one who will brook no opposition. I have no doubt, Mademoiselle, he said, that your own and your daughters' behaviour is as much beyond reproach when you are in your own home as it is in public. I don't suppose either you or they merely affect the virtuous appearance that I have always noted in you, nor that you leave it on your doorstep when you return home. I am sure your home life is as well ordered within as it is outside the house. Nevertheless, my son comes to your house every day, in spite of my having forbidden him to do so. I do not wish to believe it is you who encourage him to ignore my orders, but his assiduity is public knowledge, and the subject of gossip, in which you might find yourself included – which might be to your disadvantage. I urge you to ensure this is not the case. Refuse to give my son entry to your house. I do not suppose that you are so unaware of the ways of the world as to imagine that his intentions are honourable; and if any of your daughters were so foolish as to believe this was so, and let herself be deluded by his interest in her, I can promise you it will be the worse for her. I believe, as I have said, that all is innocent, but people will talk, and that reason alone should persuade you to put an end to these gatherings.

Nothing could have taken Mademoiselle de l'Epine more by surprise. If she had followed her first impulse, she would have made an angry retort. But she needed my father's help, and this persuaded her to adopt a milder tone. I cannot say if your son has an attachment to anyone in my house, she said, but I swear I have seen no evidence of one and that, if one exists, those for whom it is a subject of gossip have a clearer insight into what goes on in my house than I do myself. The only reason I have for allowing your son to visit our house is that he is your son, and might in future, as he has in the past, provide the means for me to approach you about my affairs. He has been one of a group of young people who amuse themselves with card games. I know of no other reason for him to come to my house. I am well aware my daughters would not be eligible prospects for him, since in this country questions of wealth and property are all important in marriage. And they are too well brought up to do anything which would in any way bring into question their good name. But tell me, Monsieur, I beg you, which of my daughters is it who is singled out by the gossips? None of them is singled out, he answered. It is my son's regular visits and attendance that are a subject of reproach. Then it is nothing but empty talk, she responded. I promise to put an end to it, and this very day, I will ask your son to refrain from honouring us with his presence. And I will do so in such terms as to convince you that there has never been any question of a motive which could give you offence in the welcome he received in my home. There is no need to make a drama out of it, Mademoiselle, he said, or to chase him away with a big stick. Anything of that sort would be attributed to ruffled pride on your part and would only add further fuel for the gossip-mongers. A quiet dismissal would best serve the purpose. She promised to do as he asked. Then she introduced the vexed subject of her lawsuit. He said he would give her every assistance and did not fail to do so from that day.

The rest of the conversation was of no interest to me, so I walked away, not knowing what to do next. I knew the reception that awaited me if I went to Mademoiselle de l'Epine's house. But not to go was as good as having already been refused admittance. In the end, I therefore went the following day, having by then written a letter which I was able to slip into the hands of Marie-Madeleine. This is what it said:

> *Your predictions are beginning to come true, Mademoiselle. The loyalty I swore to you is going to be called on to prove itself. I know what reception awaits me at your mother's house, and cannot escape it any longer, since I cannot live without seeing you. Not seeing you yesterday was too painful an experience for me to repeat, and I must face whatever sermon your mother has in store for me. The order to absent myself from your house will be a death sentence for me, but at least I shall see you once more. How troubled is my spirit! Why did I not speak to you yesterday? I would have urged you to hide your feelings. I know what they are, but do not let them be apparent to anyone else! Do not let your eyes speak. Put on a show of indifference. But no! I should die of grief, if I did not read love and tenderness for me in your expression. It is vital now that we make arrangements which will enable us to meet. Your reluctance is no longer acceptable. Let me know where we might see each other; it is for you to decide, but as for tomorrow, I shall attend Mass at the Convent des Minimes. I will be there at eight in the morning and remain till after midday.*

I was able to give her this letter without being noticed. I took my usual place at the table next to her. Everyone was there and knew that I was to be expelled from the company. We all remained silent for some time, and then Mademoiselle de l'Epine, the mother, began to speak. You have been deceiving me, she said. You have put me in danger of losing your father's esteem, which you know it is essential for me to retain. I don't know why you have acted in this way, but I know it could have serious consequences for me. Your father is displeased by your constant visits and attendance here. I gather he fears some unfortunate attachment might develop. I think, Monsieur, that you will understand that I

235

must take any action necessary to prevent making an enemy of him. Therefore, although I have been honoured by your visits – indeed, more than your father thinks I deserve – I would ask you to bring them to an end. If I did not have a lawsuit to worry about, she added, with a touch of asperity, or if it were already settled, I would perhaps not be so subservient to his wishes. I tell you this to let you know that it is against my own inclination that I must ask that you do not make any further visits to us here. It is not sufficient that your conduct is in fact innocent – I must also ensure that appearances do not mislead. This, at least, is the gospel that was preached to me, and whose lessons I could take further. It seems that people have been insinuating that there is a reason for your visits which could be damaging to the good name of my daughters. And it is even more important for me to protect that than it is for me to ensure I do not forfeit the good opinion of Monsieur Des Prez – though their whole fortune depends on him. You are too reasonable to be angry with me because of an action I am forced for so many reasons to take.

You are right, Mademoiselle, I replied. My father could indeed cause you problems, as he has said, and I would not want to be the cause of any trouble for your family. What has brought me here all this time has been the fact that it is impossible to find such pleasant, congenial company any-where else. I shall leave, however, without blaming you, since you had no choice but to take this action, and I assure you I will remain the best friend you could have in the world, and promise also that you can count on me if I can ever be of service to you. I also want you to promise not to think badly of me. I do not think I have given you any cause to do so, and it would not be fair to blame me for a mis-guided notion my father has taken into his head. I would even ask you to allow me to come and remind you from time to time of my goodwill towards you – but I will make my visits so infrequent as to cause you no further embarrassment. This request was granted. Thus it was that I was banished from Mademoiselle de l'Epine's home; but if I no longer saw her daughter every day, this did not mean my affairs progressed any the less quickly.

Marie-Madeleine came to the Minimes, where I had told her I would attend Mass the next morning, but she could stay only long enough to arrange a meeting for the following day, at a church in a remote corner of the faubourg. I met her there, and we remained together for more than three hours, parting at length only with the greatest reluctance. I told her I couldn't live without seeing her, and if she didn't take pity on me, I should certainly take refuge in a monastery – if my grief didn't kill me first. She said the same was true for her. So then, I said, all this pain and these regrets do nothing but make us the more unhappy. We must do something. Sooner or later, our meetings are bound to be discovered, unless we can find a safe location for them. This would have to be in a private room somewhere, and you would be in the worst possible situation if you entered such a place, unless you were my wife. Therefore, I continued, consider what I am proposing. I am of age and can give myself to you. I may be dependent on my father for what I inherit from him, and he has the power to prevent me from visiting you at your mother's house, but he is not master of what I will inherit from my mother, nor can he dictate to whom I give my heart and my loyalty. Accept the means I offer for us to belong to each other – which no one has the right to deny us!

What means is it that you offer? she asked. So long as my virtue is secure, and so long as I believe myself to be innocent, I am willing to do as you wish. What I suggest, I said, is that we should marry, unbeknown to anyone but the priest and the witnesses. Then let us do so, she said. I agree to whatever you wish. And if I am to be unhappy, let it be for your sake. I cannot escape my destiny. Whatever your love for me, it does not equal what I feel for you. I say this so that you will understand why I am ready to comply with what you suggest, and that I do so only because my passion for you is too strong to resist. You will have no need to repent of what you are doing, my dearest Madelon, I said, kissing her hand. I promise you, when I have made all the necessary arrangements, you will even be able to tell your mother about our love for each other. You may be sure I shall take care to do no such thing! she exclaimed. It is she more than anyone else of whom we need to beware. She would sacrifice me rather than risk losing her lawsuit, and I would be in a convent in no time at all. Then how can we see each other, if no one will help us? I said. Time and chance will provide opportunities, she said. But what is your plan? What do you intend to do? When everything is ready, I will let you know, I said. Rely on me. My love makes me impatient, and I will waste no time. But how am I going to convey my letters to you and receive your replies?

That is not the most difficult part, she said. I have already thought of a way. Do not use a servant or a go-between. When you have a letter for me, you can deliver it yourself. How can I do that? I said. Do not do it often, she said, to avoid being caught, but make a white mark on the wall opposite my window, when you have a letter for me. I will leave the windows open, and when you pass by in the evening, you can throw it in. I will keep the key to my room with me, so that no one else can go into it, and I shall be the one to find the letter. As for my letters to you, our timing will have to be a little more precise. When I have a letter for you, my flowers will be on the side of the window near the ramparts. If they are on the other side, expect nothing. When there is a letter, you must walk beneath my window at exactly eleven in the evening, whether there is a light in the room or not, and pick up what I drop from the window.

There are not many people about at that time, and I will make sure you are there. In this way, we can exchange news of each other.

After this conversation, I returned home. I saw a malevolent gleam in my father's eye, but acted as if I had not noticed it. I didn't doubt that he would have me followed, so for a whole week, I neither saw my beloved, nor did I even write to her. I also spent less time at home than I had been doing previously.

My precautions were justified. I was indeed being followed, and Mademoiselle de l'Epine was informed of this, to allay her concern. Three or four times I was aware of seeing the same face as I went on my way. I pretended not to have noticed this, but on one occasion, when I was near the Jesuit College, in order to check whether there was indeed someone following me, I sent the lackey who was accompanying me off with the pretext of some errand I wanted him to do. As soon as he had left me, I jumped into a cab, as if I did not want to be seen, and had the cabman take me to the Hôtel des Mousquetaires in the Faubourg Saint-Germain, where I hoped to find a cousin of mine. Not only was my cousin there, but, even better, he had a group of friends who were going to dine at Meudon, and he told me that I would be welcome to join them if I wished. I accepted the offer. A little later, I saw my man at the door of a bar, pointing me out to another man. I gave no indication that I had seen this. We got into our carriage, went to our gathering, and had a rollicking good time. While we were there, I noticed the second man; and shortly after I returned home, the first man, whom I had seen that morning near the Jesuit College, appeared at the house. I was tempted to confront him, but thought better of it and ignored him. I asked my father's servant – whose duty it was to answer the door – who the man was, but he didn't know. All he could tell me was that he had come to the house about ten that morning and had spoken with my father. In the afternoon, my father, not knowing where I was, went to see Mademoiselle de l'Epine. Happily, he found her at home, with her three daughters, who were working together on a piece of tapestry.

This information made me even more circumspect. I wrote to Marie-Madeleine so that she would not be surprised that I had taken so long to do what I had promised. She wrote and told me about the extraordinary visit my father had paid to their home. It seemed he had thought that she and I were together. She warned me to be extremely cautious and not to confide in anyone, to make sure there could be no risk of discovery. Her letter also spoke of her undying love and a thousand other sweet nothings that are of no consequence to an outsider but mean everything to a lover. I took great care therefore all through Lent and the Easter season – that is to say, for nearly two months – with such success that all suspicions were dispelled, and I could be certain I was no longer being followed. I was then able to start preparations to put my plans into action.

Several times I had noticed a man who came to the house to do some copying for my father's secretary, and thought he might be the sort of person who could help us. I liked his face and hoped he could be useful. I told the servants to send him to see me the next time he was at the house. He came and, as a way of leading up to what I had in mind, I asked him to write out for me some love letters of the kind which were currently in vogue, at the same time urging on him the need for secrecy. The next day, I asked a servant to show me where the man lived. He had promised to complete the letters in two days, and I knew the work could not have been done in such a short space of time. But my purpose was not to collect the letters, but to see whether the building where he lived might provide a suitable meeting place for Marie-Madeleine and myself. I found it would serve our purpose well: the rooms were large and clean, and the building was in an out-of-the-way neighbourhood. I even saw a sign advertising rooms for rent, which was exactly what I was looking for. The man was surprised to see me. The shoddiness of his furniture made it clear that his means were limited. I sent out for some food and invited him to partake of it with me, and on the pretext of paying him for the work he had already completed, I gave him a small sum of money, by which I won his gratitude and cooperation – for my friendliness had already given him a favourable impression of me. He had a wife who appeared to me not too strait-laced, and whom I thought might not be unwilling to be involved in a little intrigue. I decided it was to her I should in due course lay open my case. I left, as I had come, without ado, but my generosity had established me in their good opinion, as was apparent on my next visit.

This took place two days later. I had seen the man at my father's house, so knew he was not at home. However, I made it a pretext for my visit that I wanted to see the work he was doing for me. His wife would have gone to fetch him, but I persuaded her my business was not urgent, and there was no need for this: I was happy to wait for his return and would spend the time conversing with her. I sent out for some food, which we ate together, although she showed some reluctance to do so at first. I sent my servant back to tell the man I was waiting for him at his house. If his wife had been young or pretty, I would not have done this, but there was no danger on this score: she was old and ugly enough to preclude any suspicion of impropriety. She was astute, and that was all I required. The first topic of conversation was her own situation. She complained about how hard the times were: her husband earned scarcely anything – it was a struggle to make ends meet. That is to say, I said with a laugh, that if you found a means of earning a few extra pennies without any risk attached, you would not turn it down? Assuredly not, she answered, with feeling. And can you keep a secret when necessary? I asked her. Indeed I can, she answered. I have never been a tongue-wagger. That is a novelty in a woman, I laughed. But if it is true, I continued in a more serious tone, and if you are of a mind to do a good turn for some people who could use your services, listen to what I have to say. There would be fifty gold louis in it for you, once the matter was settled, and after that, twenty louis a month for some considerable length of time. What is more, this is all without risk of running foul either of God's commands or of the law. All that is needed is that you be discreet and keep the matter to yourself.

Her eyes lit up at this prospect, with a joy which seemed sincere. She promised that if all this were true, I could be more explicit. I made her swear that, whether or not she agreed to lend her assistance, she would not reveal what I told her. This she swore, by all the oaths I could require of her, and she has kept her word. My father still has no idea that she and her husband were involved in what followed.

I therefore told her it was I who needed her help; that I was passionately in love with a girl whom my father would never allow me to marry, since, though of good family, she was not rich; that the girl loved me, but would never consent to anything but marriage. I told her also that the girl's mother would not countenance the marriage, for the reasons I have given you, and which I explained to her. So, I continued, we wish to marry without anyone knowing that we have done so. This girl, I said, is not yet of age, but I am. We need a room where we can see each other when we wish, a room which is for our use alone. It will be necessary to ensure absolute secrecy, because my father's anger would strike not only me, but would fall on her, and be disastrous to her mother and all her family. This is the situation. Are you willing to give us your assistance?

Have you, she answered, given due thought to what you

242

are doing? As regards the Church, it seems to me you will encounter no little difficulty in marrying secretly, for what priest is there in Paris who would brave your father's anger and conduct the service? Or if you wish to register your vows in a civil court, the case is even worse – your father would surely hear of it the very day it happened. As far as a room is concerned, there is no problem. It would be up to you to make sure you were not discovered. But how will you blind the mother to her daughter's behaviour? How will your sweetheart be able to come to your rendez-vous without arousing suspicion? And how will she hide the fact if she becomes pregnant? As she certainly will – a woman who is in love does not take a man into her arms for long without the result becoming apparent!

These questions surprise me, I said. We shall be very prudent in how we arrange our meetings. Prudence is a rare commodity when people are in love, she interrupted, looking away. It will not be in short supply in our case, I said. Of that you need have no fear. We have already proved how prudent we can be, since there is not a single person who even suspects our friendship. If she becomes pregnant, I continued, we shall tell her mother, and there will be no problem. She can be confined in the room where we have been meeting – it is easy enough to invent a visit to the country or a stay in a convent. Then, said the man's wife, if you have anticipated and prepared for all these problems, I am ready to help you.

Then the only remaining question, I said, is how to arrange our marriage. Yes, she agreed. And that is the biggest problem of all! As far as the civil authorities are concerned, I said, there is no promise of marriage between us, and no reason why they should be involved. Indeed, a promise of marriage is not what we are interested in, and would not satisfy us. Nor am I looking for a priest in Paris to marry us – my father would not fail to hear of it. What is it

243

that you intend to do, then? the woman asked. What we need, I answered, is a priest who will marry us in secret. We do not even care about a marriage certificate. But, she said, no priest has the authority to marry you in such a way, and the marriage would be defective. What a stickler you are! I exclaimed. It is not necessary for our marriage to be valid in other men's eyes – since we are not even asking to have it certified. The young lady in question requires only that she be at peace with her own conscience, and before God, by virtue of the fact that we have received a priest's blessing on our union. For the rest, she is ready to put her trust in my devotion. In that case, what is all the fuss about? she said. Let her think it is a priest who performs the ceremony. You will have difficulty finding a genuine priest to marry you in secret, but you will find a thousand pseudo-priests who will dress up for the part and appear to do so. What sort of a scoundrel do you take me for! I exclaimed, astounded by her suggestion. I have no intention of committing a sacrilege, and damning myself in God's eyes! Like her, I want to be truly married, both for the sake of my own conscience and peace of mind, and so that I feel myself bound by the sacrament. You do well, she said, to take precautions against yourself. The young lady must be very much in love, to give herself to you on such slender security! And you, will you be true to her? Yes, I answered, there is no doubt of that. Then you are one of a kind! she said, turning her head away. These marriages made for love are short-lived. I give you two months before you tire of her – or God has made you of different stuff from the rest of men.

I trust, I said, you will not make remarks of that sort when you meet my future wife! Nor will you ingratiate yourself to me by such talk! Have no fear, she laughed. If I were ten times as cynical with her as I am with you, it would be only so much wasted breath on my part. Far from changing her mind, I would merely be making an enemy for myself. A young woman in love listens only to her heart, or her lover. It sounds as if you speak from experience? I said. That may be, she laughed. Time was when I had my value. But what do you say, then? I concluded. Are you ready to help us? With all my heart, she answered, though I can see I am letting myself in for trouble!

And for my part, I told her, I promise that I will never reveal that you helped us, and that, whatever happens to my wife and myself, your role will never be known. I trust that will be so, she said. And I believe, she added, I have thought of a priest who might serve your purpose. I will go and see him today, and tomorrow, if you will be good enough to call here, I will tell you if I have been successful, and what we have been able to agree on. I promised to do so. And this, I added, putting ten louis into her hand, is over and above what I mentioned before, and is to pay for the secrecy you have promised. I then left, very pleased to have found a woman apt in the ways of the world, who could be relied on to look after our interests.

I informed Marie-Madeleine of what I had done, and asked her to meet me the next day, so that I could let her know what I would learn from the woman, whom I had arranged to see at nine o'clock. I went to see the good woman the next morning, using the same pretext as before. Her husband, to whom she had conveyed the gist of our conversation, was there. He was reluctant to let his wife do as she had promised, and it was only after considerable persuasion that I was able to obtain his agreement. His wife told me she had seen the priest, as promised, but that he was unwilling to give any undertaking until he had spoken to me. She said she would go and bring him if I wanted. In any case, she said, I could be sure that she had not given anything away: she had spoken to him in confidence during confession and had not mentioned any names; and he did not know me and would not know who I was if he saw me. If he agreed, she said, then the matter was settled; if not, we were no worse off than before. She said he was very poor, the sort of priest that Normandy supplied in plenty to neighbouring provinces, but he was nonetheless a genuine priest and honest. I sent out for victuals, stipulating in particular that there should be good wine, to put our cleric in a good humour. Then I let her go and bring him.

She returned shortly with him. Here is the person I have brought to see you, she said, introducing him. You can take as much time as you wish, and discuss your affairs to your hearts' content. She had the key to an empty room next door. The room was to rent and is the one which my wife and I used subsequently to meet in. I opened the conversation. I believe you already know the subject I wished to see you about? I said. Yes, Monsieur, he said. The matter has been mentioned. But since women are not always particularly clear, perhaps you yourself would explain what it is you want of me. I decided the best explanation might be in terms of money. I summarised our situation briefly, and then, letting him glimpse what I had in my purse, I said, this is the subject: if you want it, it is yours. If you refuse, that is your decision. It is not often one has a chance to come by fifty louis with so little trouble and so little risk. He said that, before getting to that point, it would be as well to clarify certain facts, and launched into a sermon, which was the more unwelcome as he was an indifferent preacher. He expatiated on the duty of children to obey their parents. He discoursed on the misfortunes liable to befall those who neglect this duty. He quoted inappropriate examples from history and the Scriptures of how God's curses fall on sinners, until I became seriously weary – when someone came in to announce that our meal was ready whenever we wished to eat. I seized his hand and led him into the room where the meal was laid out.

He was clearly not used to good food, for he ate heartily

whatever was put before him, though it was not of particularly high quality, and drank only a few mouthfuls of water tinged with wine. I have never seen anyone eat so well and drink so little. However, it was enough to set his thoughts moving in a different direction. The sermon started anew, but its text had changed, and now centred on the devotion that married couples owe each other, and here he spoke more to the point. I responded. St Paul was quoted by both of us. I made it clear that I knew what duties marriage entailed, and that it would not be out of ignorance if I did not fulfil them. I swore undying love and devotion for my wife, and finally overcame his resistance. He said he would not only marry us, but was even ready to give us a marriage certificate, if both she and I accepted the conditions he would lay down to ensure our mutual constancy. These were: that we should each write and sign in our own hand a promise, whose wording he would dictate; that we would at a later date amend by a second ceremony anything deficient in the original, as soon as there was no longer any reason for secrecy; that the reasons for this secrecy should be stated in our promise; that our undertaking should be sealed by a confession of our sins and by a solemn oath that we would recognise and abide by the sacrament he would administer; that these promises would be signed not only by us, but also by him and the witnesses to our marriage, after the benediction and before the consummation. The one I wrote would be given to my wife and remain sealed, and would have a declaration on the envelope, witnessed by a notary, that the contents were the expression of my own free will. Far from resenting his insistence on such precautions, I was grateful to the priest for requiring them. I promised to do all he asked, and undertook that my wife would do the same.

Everything having been settled in this way, we agreed to meet again in the same place at nine o'clock the next day.

247

To prevent any change of heart on his side, I gave the priest some of the money I had in my purse. I gave the rest to our hostess, so that she could buy furniture for the room, and since I did not have enough with me, I took her husband home with me to give him a further sum. I asked her to buy whatever she thought would be most suitable and attractive. I made a note of the tableware we would need, so that nothing would be overlooked. She did what I had asked, and the next day I found the room furnished and in good order.

I didn't know how I was going to let Marie-Madeleine know about what I had done or about the meeting I had arranged for the next day; but she had thought of a way to keep herself informed. For when I went home and was about to enter the house, I saw a poor old woman who showed me a scrap of paper and indicated that I should take it. I did so and gave her a generous reward for having brought it. On it were the words: *Be at the place where we met the last time at three o'clock.* There was no doubt who it was from, and I went to the church that afternoon. I thought I had wasted my time, as it was locked when I got there, but, on turning my head, I saw her, and she made a sign that I should walk ahead. I waited at the corner of a side street, and told her that, if she wanted, I could take her to a place where we could talk at length and in safety. She declined at first, but when I told her where it was, she agreed. We had both discharged the cabs we had used to get to our meeting place, so I sent for another, which took us to our room. We went there, a child gave me the key, and I took in two chairs. It will not be long now, my dear one, I said, before we belong to each other. This is the room where we will be able to express our love freely. It is here, I continued, throwing myself at her feet, that I hope to become the happiest of men, being united with the most adorable person on earth. Do not prostrate yourself, she said, her eyes shining with

248

tears. It is your happiness I want. But I fear that for me this will bring only cruel catastrophe! Alas, she continued, why did fortune put such distance between us, when Heaven made us for each other? I fear that, in trying to bring you happiness, it is the opposite I am doing! I tried to dispel these gloomy thoughts from her mind, and thereafter she refrained from expressing them, but I am sure she was constantly beset by fears of the tragedy which befell her, and the state I should be in for the rest of my life after losing her. Tears filled Des Prez's eyes again at this point in his narrative, but eventually he resumed his story.

I told her what I had done, and said I had given my word on her behalf. I asked her if I had gone further than she wished, and if she was displeased that I had taken matters so far. She answered that what she had said was what she had meant: whatever I wanted, she would do; and that she would not fail to be here in this room again the next morning. She told me that the letter I had thrown in through her window the previous day had made her so impatient that she had wanted to talk to me without delay, and had therefore written the note I had been given, entrusting it to a poor woman with instructions to deliver it into my hands, and promising, over and above what she herself paid her that I too would reward her; she had even promised her a further sum the next day if the letter had been safely received – which a reply would confirm.

I asked her how she was going to be able to arrange to come to our room on future occasions when we wanted to meet. You need not worry about that, she said, there will be no problem. I shall be there whenever you want to see me. Do you think your mother is going to leave you free to do whatever you want? Yes, I think so, she said. And since you ask me how this will be possible, I shall have to tell you. I do not want her to know at present about the plans we are making, but once the marriage is an accomplished fact, I shall tell her. You are of age: she cannot have any objection on that score. She would prevent our marriage beforehand if she could, for fear of crossing your father, whom she fears and dislikes – she still resents how he behaved about your visits, and will never forget it. But if we have taken matters into our own hands, and the matter is settled, it will be in her interest to do everything in her power to keep it secret and prevent your father from finding out about it; for, if he did, she would be afraid he would accuse her of having encouraged our union, in which case he would take his revenge by giving her no further help with her lawsuit.

You are right about that, I said. But will she consider our marriage valid? Will she accept that such a ceremony as we are to have is legal and binding? If our marriage is not valid, I will not consent to it either, she said. Haven't you told me that the priest has demanded all sorts of precautions? Yes, said I. Well then, that is why I am convinced that, since our marriage is to be valid and legitimate, there will be no point in hiding it from her. But did you not promise to give yourself to me, I said, so long as your conscience was satisfied? I still make that promise, she said, but if I am the only one who feels the marriage has been performed in accordance with the law, you need not expect any great haste on my part to keep my promise. On the other hand, if it will satisfy my mother too, my promise is good and I will abide by it. In my estimation, the marriage will be legitimate and indissoluble so long as the man who gives it his blessing is in fact a priest. I require no more than that; but as for my mother, she might need something more. Surely you understand the difference? I give myself to you without reservation. I am content if I am your wife in the eyes of God, but I leave it in your hands to ensure that I have not been deceived and will not be shamed in the sight of men.

No, I said, throwing myself at her feet again, you will not be deceived. I will never abuse your trust in me. You will be my wife in the sight of both God and men. Nothing but death will separate us. I hope it is so, she said. I hold too good an opinion of you to believe that you would ever abandon me. Or if you do, I shall at least have the sad pleasure of knowing that you violate a sacrament and vows that even the most independent minds respect. And at least, if I am at fault in men's eyes, I shall believe in my own innocence before God.

Our hostess, who had been out making purchases on our behalf, returned, followed by several men carrying what she had selected. We behaved as if it were nothing to do with us. When the woman caught sight of Marie-Madeleine, she exclaimed at her beauty and praised her with the enthusiasm of someone who was an authority on the subject. We had a light meal there, and then Marie-Madeleine left, promising to return at nine the next morning. I left soon after, having given instructions for some suitable food to be prepared for us to eat the following day.

Marie-Madeleine and I arrived at almost the same time the next day. She gave her approval for the way the furniture had been arranged, and found it all satisfactory, considering in how short a time it had been done; and indeed, everything had been well chosen. When we had inspected it all, I asked our hostess to go for the priest. While we were waiting, Marie-Madeleine's misgivings returned, as I could tell from the sudden sadness which suffused her face and the tears in her eyes. There is still something which you are unhappy about, dear one? I said. I beg you, be as happy as I am. My joy is not complete unless you feel it equally with me. I feel it as much as I can, she said. But I cannot help looking towards the future, and I acknowledge, it fills me with fear. But do not let this disturb you, she added. It is only for you that I worry. For myself, nothing matters, and provided you are contented, if it is true as you say that your happiness depends on our union, I shall never regret what I am doing.

I shall never be happy unless you too are happy, I said. You may be certain of that. And though all my happiness indeed depends on you and on being united with you, I would willingly give this up, if I thought it could be the cause of the slightest distress to you in the future. I believe, she said, that this is how you truly feel at present. I am even sure, she added, with a certain melancholy, at least I feel I ought to be, that my misfortunes will never come from you, and that it will not be you who contribute to them. But somehow, it is impossible for me to believe that I was born to be happy. Whatever misfortune befalls me, however, I will never accuse you of being the cause. I shall blame the fate which leads me on, and the star under which I was born. She could not express these thoughts without being bathed in tears and, though I did my best to dispel her fears, I could not help but be affected.

The priest arrived. We spent more than an hour alone with him, and, as he found himself in the presence of a young lady who was not only – as I had told him – extremely beautiful, but also – as he had not expected – well dressed and with a bearing which commanded respect, his words were serious and full of good sense. He gave us a little sermon on the engagement we were about to enter into. He pointed out that it was to us the Scriptures spoke when they said a man must renounce all others when he takes a wife, as must a wife when she takes a husband. He said we would have to be even more scrupulous in following this injunction than other married people. Indeed, he said, those who marry at their parents' behest have some cause for complaint if they are not as happy in their union as they had hoped. They can say to their parents: 'You chose my wife, or husband; you are to blame for giving me someone so ill-natured, or whose conduct is so reprehensible. If I had been able to choose for myself, I would have chosen better, and I would be happier; but you wanted me to leave the choice to you, and my willingness to do so has cost me my peace of mind, and perhaps even my eternal salvation, should I fall into sin because of the chains which bind me to this person whom I cannot love and who is so ill-suited to me that our life together with its endless discord is an image of Hell.' You, however, said he, do not have this excuse. You have made your own choice and must resolve never to leave each other.

You, Monsieur, he said to me, are taking this young lady, whose fortune is less than your own. It is this worldly consideration which forces you to secrecy. But God is not concerned with your wealth, and the sacrament of marriage is once and for ever. If you fail her, it is not she whom you will deceive, but yourself. You cannot flout God's law with impunity. Therefore, you must be ready to share equally with her all the risks she faces, and never abandon her, come what may.

You, Mademoiselle, he continued, addressing Marie-Madeleine, you are giving yourself to this gentleman. You know what is required of a virtuous woman, but you will have obligations beyond the loyalty and obedience which are generally required. The love this gentleman has for you has persuaded him to marry you, but you must be aware that this love is as nothing and can vanish, unless it is preserved by your own devoted, submissive and unimpeachable behaviour. You must strive to deserve his love and esteem, since the least mis-step or cause for complaint that you give him may become a serious failing or crime in his eyes, which you cannot erase and he cannot forgive. It may give him cause to lose respect both for yourself and for the sacrament, and should this happen, the law might indeed support him. All the priest said was undeniable.

He readily accepted the invitation to dine with us – since it was too late for lunch. Our hostess, whose husband was away in town, served the meal to us at table, and we ate in a festive spirit. After dinner, the priest made Marie-Madeleine and myself each write out a promise of marriage, or rather, a lengthy statement, in due form, which I believe would be upheld by a court of law. They were alike, only the names and genders were reversed. We swore absolute secrecy to each other. Then I asked him when he would be willing to give his blessing, and he said, not until he had seen us at Mass and heard us at confession. We could not dispute this – it was stated in our marriage promise. We agreed on a time for our confession: myself the next day, and my betrothed, the following Sunday; and then, at six o'clock on the Monday morning, we would be married. He promised he would be in his chapel at these times, and then he left us.

Marie-Madeleine and I remained alone in our room. She said she thought he seemed to be decent and honest, and that she thought her mother would not find fault with what we were doing. Indeed, except that the Royal Edicts regarding the announcement of the banns had not been followed, nor the recording of the marriage in the parish register, everything was in accordance with normal practice and no one could say the marriage was not valid. She seemed satisfied. She examined everything in the room minutely and was pleased with it all. I told her I had pro-mised to give our hostess fifty louis, and I made her take a purse and pay her share from it. She called the woman and told her to take away what we had not eaten of the dinner. I am very pleased with the way you have furnished our room, and am grateful for what you have done, she said. Monsieur Des Prez promised you fifty louis, that is twenty-five from each of us. Here is my part. The woman took the money – after showing a little reluctance. It seems we shall be here on Monday next, Marie-Madeleine continued, and I will be offering the dinner. Here is the money. Take it, and do us proud! It is my wedding, and I want to enjoy it. The woman promised to do as she had been asked, and then left the room.

Being left alone again, I tried in vain to bring forward the conclusion. No, no, said Marie-Madeleine. You will not take advantage of my weakness like that. I saw that I was wasting my time and did not insist. I asked her how she would be able to keep the appointments we had made, particularly on the Monday, since she might be out the whole day. On Sunday, she said, I shall go to church with one of my sisters, and then I shall go and see a lady who is a good friend of both my mother and myself, and I shall ask her to send for me that same evening, with the story that a pleasure party outside Paris is being arranged for the following day. I know she herself would not be interested in such a party, but I shall have a pretext for leaving the house the next day. I shall tell her that I wanted to go to Mont-Valérien, but that I have not been given permission to do so. I am sure she will do this for me. Or at worst, if I disappear for the day, I shall have a scolding from my mother, and I have had plenty of those when nothing serious was involved, and on this occasion I am willing to run the risk and not worry about the consequences. Anyhow, one way or another, I will be there, she said. We embraced, and she left.

I sent for a locksmith and ordered a lock with three keys, so that Marie-Madeleine, the hostess and myself would each have one, and since it was still early, and her husband had returned, I stayed a little longer with them. I promised that either I myself, or friends of mine, would find some regular employment for him. I have done so and, God willing, I shall make myself responsible for his well-being for the rest of my life. His wife was overcome both by her gratitude, and by the beauty of my wife-to-be, and could not sing her praises enough. She formed such a strong affection for her from then on that there was nothing she would not do for her. And this poor woman, at present, is almost my only consolation, since she was so saddened by my wife's cruel death, and I am certain her regret is as sincere as my own.

Tears came to Des Prez's eyes once again at this point in his narrative. As I left this house, he continued, the following Sunday afternoon, I met the priest who was to conduct our marriage ceremony the next day, and joined him in his walk. Without any deliberate direction in view, our steps led us into the Jardin des Capucins, in the rue Saint-Honoré, which is a long way from my father's house. We sat on a bench and a Capuchin monk of the priest's acquaintance joined us, and as I didn't know them well enough to have any subject of conversation other than religion, we got into a deep discussion on that theme. By the most unlikely chance in the world, my father happened to be in this garden at the same time and, seeing me in the company of a priest and a monk, wanted to discover what we were talking about. I could not have chosen a more apt subject: we were deep in discussion about the prodigal son and the question of sincere conversion and a return to God after a season of profligacy and disorder. And to tell the truth, the way these two men were discussing their religion touched my heart. And though I had heard the same things many times, I was so moved that I had tears in my eyes. I turned to wipe them and disguise my emotion, and caught sight of my father half-hidden behind a trellis. You can imagine my astonishment! With difficulty, I tried to suppress my surprise at seeing him there. He noticed this and said, 'There is no great problem. You could do worse than spend your time this way. I did not know you were interested in such matters'. I did not say a word. I made a deep bow to him, and walked away with the priest.

When I got home that evening, however, I heard that he was in a terrible rage against me and that he had asked two or three times if I were not home yet, and had refused to have supper without me. I thought that all was lost, and that he had overheard something about my marriage while I was talking to the priest, though I didn't recollect having mentioned it at that time. I was in despair, but I was wrong: the cause of his anger was quite different. I have never known what he had against the religious orders, particularly the Mendicants, but he hated them like the plague. As soon as I had left the convent gardens, he had asked the gate-keeper if I went there sometimes. The man had said yes, which was true, because Gallouin – who is your friend as well as mine – had entered this order and had lived there for a time, and I had often visited him. This reply, combined with what my father had overheard me saying to the two churchmen – added to the fact that I had dismissed my manservant a week or so earlier without apparent cause, refusing to replace him by any other in my father's pay – all this had convinced him that I wanted to become a monk. He reasoned that I had dispensed with this servant and taken to going everywhere on foot so that my movements could not easily be tracked. He was correct about the facts, though his deduction about the reason for them was mistaken.

He had already given vent to his anger against the monastery; it redoubled when he saw me. On my life, Monsieur, he said, you have found a fine way to show your gratitude! Are you afraid you will go hungry, or not be able to earn your bread, that you have decided to beg for your livelihood? If I believed you had sunk so low, he added, in a towering rage, as to skunk into a monastery, I would wring your neck in two seconds – or lock you up in some hole where you would be at least as well confined. Devil take you! he continued, you miserable scum. You will not throw yourself away so while I am alive, that I promise you!

I was not sorry to discover that this was what he feared. All I needed to do was to promise him that I would not make any commitment of that sort without his consent. He continued his diatribes against those who adopted the religious life – which did not much distress me, since I had no desire

257

to take that course myself. Throughout supper, he spoke of nothing else, tearing their behaviour and reputation apart. I do not know what makes him hate them so, but far from offering them charity, he gives them insults whenever he sees one of their number. He is nonetheless a very generous person, but it is only old people, orphans, or the halt and lame – those who are unable to work – who receive his alms. But this reminds me of an incident I once saw which I must tell you about.

He was in front of the house one day, overseeing the repair of a lead pipe which brought water into the house. While he was watching the plumbers and pavers at work, a sort of hermit came up and asked for alms. In reply, he pointed to the workmen. These men are working, he said. They are earning their living and are not a charge on the public. And if the mindless charity of Christians did not give sustenance to so many useless mouths, we would not have so many tramps and lollabouts in France. Do you understand? The holy man was taken aback and moved away.

To return to my account: he made such scathing comments about 'bowl-rattlers', as he called them, that all the servants thought he knew for a fact that I had made up my mind to join the Capuchin brethren and that it was so that no one should find this out that I had dismissed my serving-man. This is how the rumour which spread throughout the neighbourhood started. He sent for my former servant and, in front of me, ordered him to stick to me like my shadow and to report back to him everything I did. And if he failed to do so, he told him, look at me carefully: you see a man who will have you hanged. Remember what I am promising you. I am a man of my word, and I shall know whether you obey me. That was warning enough to me. It was clear that from the next day, I was going to be saddled with a permanent companion. I forestalled this, leaving by the garden before daylight, and taking so many twists and turns before heading for the church I was going to, that the devil himself would not have been able to follow me.

I arrived exactly on time. Everyone was there waiting for me in a little chapel, whose doors were closed immediately after I entered, and since we were all there and no one not involved was present, Marie-Madeleine and I were promptly married. The doors were then opened, and the priest said Mass in public. My wife left first, and the others followed, while I stayed behind and gave the priest an appropriate recompense for his services. I invited him to join us for the wedding breakfast. He came, and my wife also gave him a generous sum of money. Before our meal, he brought out the promises of marriage which had been in his keeping for five days, and we signed and dated them, and also had four other people who were present certify them; these were: our host, two merchants who lived close by, and an officer, all of whom were friends of our priest whom he trusted. He made us swear in their presence to what he had required of us, and that we would treat our marriage as valid and inviolable. He gave me the promise my wife had written, and then led me into the vestry, where I placed what I had written in an envelope, in the presence of two lawyers, and sealed it with my seal, and on the envelope I stated that I had written and signed what was within with my own hand, and that it contained my free and uncoerced will, in case of death or accident to me, and that I wanted it to remain secret for the reasons given. The lawyers thought it was my will that I was giving to the priest for safekeeping.

We then returned to the house, where he gave the envelope to my wife. Here is all that can humanly be done to secure the inviolability of your marriage, he said. And, before God, let your conscience be clear. Your marriage has been properly sanctified. Keep this envelope and its contents. Do not open it unless it is needed; and when you do open it, make sure you have trustworthy lawyers on hand on whose probity and friendship you can rely, he concluded. After that, he had no more to say, and I believe she was entitled to consider me as her lawful husband, which she did, and gave me reason to take pride in her.

When she arrived, Marie-Madeleine had been wearing a dress and simple jacket, and I was pleased with this lack of show. Although it was more than two weeks after Easter, it was not yet warm enough for light clothing. But while the priest and I had been absent, she had transformed herself, and on our return we found her dressed with the utmost elegance and in a manner calculated to dazzle and please. Her dress had a skirt of blue brocade with silver stripes, and a bodice of the same colour, which, without being overtight, showed off her figure to advantage. Under the dress she wore a petticoat of white satin, edged with lace and a silver fringe. The dress was trimmed with Spanish lace and silver piping. Her shoes were of black Moroccan leather, with silver straps and diamond buckles, and her stockings were of black silk with a silver thread at the back and sides. Her hair was beautifully coiffed, and she had a string of fine pearls at her throat. The whole effect was utterly charming. We and our witnesses ate an excellent dinner, but though it was good in every respect, I found it tedious. Soon the meal was cleared away, the company departed, and at about two o'clock, she and I were left alone.

Here Des Prez was overcome once again by melancholy and gave vent to sighs of the deepest despondency. Those happy moments are over for me, he said. I shall never see her again. She is dead. And a score of similar expressions of grief and despair escaped his lips. At last he resumed in a more tranquil strain: I remained with her till seven in the evening. During the afternoon, we partook of the remnants of our dinner – with even more appetite than we had had at the meal itself. We arranged to meet again in two days' time, since she was unable to return any sooner.

I gave her one of the three keys I had had made and left writing materials on the table, since we had agreed that whenever one of us came, which would be as often as possible, we would suggest a new meeting time if we were alone and could not wait for the other, and that we would also use this means to keep each other informed of our affairs. I paid our hostess what had been agreed, and she promised to take care of our room. I gave her another of the keys, and then I left, convinced that I was the happiest of men.

The only concern which remained was the question of my servant. To overcome this difficulty, I arranged for another room to be rented in a neighbouring house which belonged to the same landlord and, with his permission, I had a communicating doorway cut between the two, so that Marie-Madeleine did not use the same entrance as I did. In this way, my servant, who came to the man's house with me, and always stayed upstairs while I was there, had no chance of ever seeing her come or go. When she was in the room, which I knew because we had arranged a piece of string which she could pull as a signal, I sent my servant out on a series of errands which he would do one after the other. When she was not there, my hostess went to fetch me any messages she had left, and I wrote a reply there and then. In this way, I never went into the room while my lackey was present, and never when my wife was not present; and on the pretext of further writing tasks, I was able to go to the house every day.

I told you my wife was quick-witted and inventive. Let me give you an example. We had spent an afternoon together one day. We were to meet again in three days, since she thought she would not be able to come sooner than that. However, unexpectedly, she was free the next day and wanted to let me know. I was walking on the ramparts with two of my friends, when she saw me from her window, and wrote me a note: *I'm going to our room; meet me there.* She came to where we were, and as we were walking in front of her, she called out to me. I turned round and saw her. Here, Monsieur, she said gaily, here is a note which just fell out of your pocket. I pity your mistress, to have such a careless lover! And she gave me her note as she passed by. My companions knew her quite well, but since I was never seen with her, and no one on earth suspected our relationship, they merely teased me for my carelessness. I read the note and then tore it up with a show of indifference, so that they were convinced it meant little to me. We continued our walk and eventually left each other to go our separate ways – though I was not the first to suggest I had other business. I found her and complimented her on her presence of mind, but warned her to be careful and not take such chances too often.

One day, I saw her at Mass and thought she didn't look well, which worried me. I went to our room the following afternoon, not expecting to find her, but she was there, and asleep. Our hostess, who had heard me come in, made a sign that she wished to speak to me, and indicated I should not make any noise. I had been about to go into our room, for my servant had not followed me. The woman told me my wife had arrived about an hour earlier and told her she had such a bad headache that she had not had a wink of sleep the night before. She told me that Marie-Madeleine had lain down the minute she arrived, not expecting me to come that day, and had fallen asleep. If you take my advice, she said, you will let her sleep for a while. She needs the rest. Go for a walk and then come back. I did so, but when I returned, more than three hours later, she had returned home, though only a few minutes earlier, leaving this note on the table:

I did not realise a husband was required to respect his wife's sleep, particularly in a place where he is well aware it is not the need for rest which has brought her there. I thank you for your discretion. Do not be concerned for my health. I am pleased to tell you I am well, and there is no danger that you will catch any illness from me, as you seem to fear. I have had a wasted journey, which would not have been the case only three months ago. In those days your affection was not so respectful as it has now grown. However, I am loathe to lose what I came for, and I shall return tomorrow, when I hope you will make amends for the disappointment I have had today.

I thought there was wit in this note, and a tender novelty in her complaint that my love had grown lukewarm. I wrote one to her in the same vein, teasing her as she had teased me.

I did not wish to interrupt your sleep as I believed your indisposition was not invented and that you needed it. You may sleep as long as you like today, as I predict I shall be unwell when you read this note. I did not wish to catch whatever was ailing you yesterday, and neither do I wish to let you run the risk of catching my indisposition. You have so often refused, or accepted unwillingly, what I owed you, that I am sure you are not anxious to be paid. I therefore trust you will allow me to defer future payment for three months. In that time my love will regain the vivacity it lost in a similar space of time, and will no longer be so respectful.

I told our hostess about the note and my reply, and gave her instructions as to what she should do. I returned early the next day, before Marie-Madeleine arrived, and hid when I heard her coming. The woman told her I had left in a temper the previous day after writing the note which was on the table. Oh my God! she cried when she read it. Can he have taken such a simple jest amiss and lost his temper in earnest? I saw that she had tears in her eyes, and didn't want to make her suffer any longer. I left my hiding place, embraced her, and our peace was soon made.

I asked her if she would like us to go out for a walk together, and she agreed; and that is the only time we ever walked together out of doors – we were quite certain we would not be seen by anyone in that neighbourhood. We were walking home, when the Devil, who never leaves well alone, provided us with an extraordinary experience.

It was the most beautiful time of year. The fields were full of grain which was ready for harvesting. There had been a gentle rain that morning, which had settled the dust and made the earth firm. The sky was hazy, and there was a little breeze which tempered the heat of the day. I have told you my wife was bold and spirited when she had made up her mind to some action, and the following incident is proof of this. The height of the rye, which was above a man's head, the complete solitude, and my love for Marie-Madeleine prompted the notion in my head of the pleasure it would be to lie with her out here on the grass. I asked her to come with me into the field of rye; at first, she found a thousand reasons to refuse, but I insisted, and eventually she acquiesced. This is not the only occasion which proved to me that she sought only to please me, discounting her own inclinations. Indeed, it almost seemed as if she foresaw what was going to happen to us. We made our way into the field of rye, therefore – never imagining that anyone had seen us.

I proceeded to satisfy my fantasy without delay – when suddenly, I felt a man's arms clasped around me. These arms were long enough to take hold of me, but not to prevent me from breaking loose, although the man had thrown himself bodily on top of me. My wife gave a shrill cry and leapt up from where she had been, as I threw myself to one side. I still had my wits about me and seized hold of the man's two arms. Meeting a degree of resistance he had not expected, he was by now beginning to doubt the success of his unwarranted intrusion. I held him tight. Draw my sword, I said to my wife. Strike him, kill the knave, whoever he is, don't hesitate! She was about to do so without further ado when the man began to beg for pardon and plead for his life. At this, I told my wife to hold the point of the sword to his throat and to pierce him through if he made the slightest attempt to raise himself. She did as I had said; I let go of his arms and stood up, straightening my clothing. I took the sword from my wife's hands and told her to return to our home. And as for you, I told the fellow, whom I now saw was nothing but a country yokel, you are as good as dead.

This ruffian, stunned by this reversal of fortune, did as I told him. He had no choice: I had my sword at his vitals as he lay on the ground, and he dared neither move nor shout; I would certainly have finished him off had he done either. And when, after a good length of time I knew Madame Des Prez would be far enough away for there to be no further fear of insult or discomfiture, I allowed him to get to his feet. Come with me, I said, I will pay you your grain! From what he told me, he assumed it was merely some riff-raff he had come across in the field, but he could now tell from our behaviour that he had been quite wrong. I led him in the opposite direction from that which my wife had taken, until we reached an outlying district, and there, as payment for his insolence, I broke my stick across his back. Two lackeys, to whom I was known, who were waiting for their master who was in a garden nearby, added their weight to the thrashing I gave him, and this, I believe, removed any further desire on his part to make such a mistake again. Some distance away, I had seen a woman dressed in black going in the direction we had come from: I made her my scapegoat. I asked these servants if they had seen a woman in mourning. They said yes, but she had been walking quickly and was already some distance away. They thought, as I intended they should, that she was the person I had been with, and I did not remove this impression. I merely begged them to say nothing about the incident and paid them for their trouble. My father heard of the incident the same evening. He was curious enough to ask the lackeys if they had seen the young woman. They told him she was very pretty, that she had been wearing mourning, and was about twenty-eight years old, but that they did not know her. Thus it was clear that all suspicion had been deflected, and I felt the more relieved as these same lackeys knew Marie-Madeleine as well as they knew me. My father taunted me light-heartedly about the affair that evening at supper, but was far from annoyed and only made a joke of it. I'd rather see you there than in a monastery, he said. Only take care who it is you are dallying with. If the woman you were with today is someone you picked up in the street, you did right to use no more than a stick and give the fellow a hiding, but if she was a married woman, or a widow, or a young girl who has a reputation to think of, you should have left the blackguard on the spot, or her reputation is finished should he ever see her again.

That was all he said. He was right, but I was quite sure the fellow would not recognise her again. Once I had settled accounts with him, I had gone back to see my wife. I was in despair at having so carelessly put her in such a position, and at the fact that anyone but myself should have seen her as she was, particularly a rascal of a peasant of that sort. She was in tears. I consoled her not by commiserating with her, but by treating the matter as a joke. I related how I had made him pay for his curiosity, and we completed what he had interrupted, and parted good friends.

We spent the spring, summer and winter in idyllic happiness. I was the most contented of men. I thought my wife more beautiful and more delightful than ever. No two hearts have ever been more in harmony. When we met in company, we greeted each other civilly but with apparent indifference. Even her mother was deceived and complained that I no longer took any interest in her affairs. She asked one of the young men who still frequented the house to see me and find out if she had offended me in any way. Her concern was not entirely disinterested: she still needed my help as an intermediary with the friend whom I have previously mentioned. My wife informed me of this, and we agreed together that, in reply, I should assure her that I was as devoted to her as ever and would render her any service I could, but the reason I no longer attended her at her house was that my father had absolutely forbidden me to do so: it was more for her sake than for my own, I said, that my visits had ceased; and indeed, were I my own master in the matter, I would be a most assiduous visitor.

We met at the Palais de Justice, therefore, and I accompanied her wherever she had need of me. I lent her money. In her presence, I spoke to her daughter only to ask for news about our little society. I had even taken the precaution of asking my father if he had any objection to my offering my services to our neighbour in this way. He said that, on the contrary, he was delighted for me to do so, and would even encourage me, his only objection to my visits to the house having been the consequences he feared they may have.

It was impossible to credit that two people who behaved towards each other in public as Marie-Madeleine and I did were in fact husband and wife, and it was a strange experience indeed to pass one another – as frequently happened – and greet each other just as one greets any other acquaintance, only a quarter of an hour before or after sharing the tenderest of embraces.

She became pregnant towards the end of September. She told me so, and I was not upset – it was natural enough. There was no difficulty in hiding the fact, and it didn't prevent our meeting each other. But, as there are a thousand misadventures which can happen, however cautious one is, I persuaded her to accept some money which I had often offered her and which she had always refused. So the winter passed, until her condition began to become so apparent that it was no longer possible to conceal it, and it became necessary to consider revealing the situation to her mother. She had thought it would be easy to do this, but when it came to the point, she discovered all sorts of difficulties which she had either not foreseen or had underestimated. She was afraid her mother would not be pleased that she had married without her agreement, and particularly that she had married me, since her mother had reason to fear my father's anger and vengeance. And she was afraid her mother would consider our marriage no more than a liaison. I made light of these fears, and did my best to reassure her. After all, I said, our marriage is something I do not regret. Do you regret it? No, she said, I do not regret it. I would do it again if I had to.

I suggested a way out of the problem – and would to God she had accepted it, for then she would still be here with me: Well, then, I said, do not return to your mother's house. Stay here in our room, and do not leave it. No one will come looking for you here, and you can have the child and no one will know. Write and tell your mother that you are in a convent: whether she believes it to be true or not matters little. Even if she herself does not believe it, it will be in her interest to convince others that it is the truth. Meantime, I will see you every day. And if the time comes when you can safely let her know where you are, then you can do so. But don't go out any more among people who know you, particularly near your home, where your condition will be noticed.

You are right, she said. But I must tell my mother, and I beg you to let me do that. But how will you go about it? I said. That is something I will have to think about, she answered. But before speaking to her, I would like to talk to ... That I absolutely forbid, I said, interrupting her. No one else must know of our relationship. And if I were believed, you would not even tell your mother. Well, then, she said, giving me a kiss, will you do an errand for me? Do you still love me? I love you more than ever, I said, and it is because I love you that I do not want you to put yourself in a position which may cause you distress. As for any errand you may want me to do for you, of course I will undertake it, so long as it involves no risk to you. What is it you wish me to do? I want you to send for my mother to come here whilst you are with me, and for us to be together when I tell her what we have done. We shall have to let her anger run its course, whatever words it may put into her mouth. However extravagant her fury, we must just endure it. When it is exhausted, we shall be able to make her see reason, both by our contrition and by showing her where her own interest lies.

I agree with all my heart, I said. I will be happy to throw myself at her feet if necessary. I will endure anything, so long as she does not lay a hand on you, so long, that is, as her temper confines itself to words. As for that, said Marie-Madeleine, I would gladly accept a few slaps in the face if that would settle the matter! But if you are here, it will be up to you to prevent it coming to that. She will listen to reason, and when she sees that what is done cannot be undone, she will have to resign herself to it, at least to the extent of keeping it secret. But you are quite certain you want to tell your mother? I continued. It is against my better judgement! I fear you may come to regret it; but it is your wish, and that is enough to make it my wish also. But remember, I repeated, it would be better for you to remain here, and neither go home, nor tell her where you are – but just write and say you are in a convent. I fear what the results of this

move might be, and if I, like you, paid heed to my presentiments, I would have you take my advice. Put yourself in
my place, she said. She is my mother, after all, and even if
she were able to convince everyone else I were in a convent,
what doubts would still be tormenting her? What would she
be thinking? In God's name, she said, embracing me, do
this for me!

Very well, I said, with a shrug, I will not stand in your way.
Just decide on a time, and I shall be here without fail. I want
us both to be here, she said, before my mother arrives, since
we will have to send for her. Very well, I said, just tell me
when you want the meeting to be. Tomorrow morning, she
said. My mother has no business to leave the house for and
will be at home. I will send her a note and a carriage, and we
will wait for her here. This is what she wrote:

> *Something which has just happened to me, my dear mother,
> and which requires your presence, leads me to write this note to
> ask you to take the carriage which I am sending and to allow
> yourself to be brought in it to where I am. I can only explain
> the matter by word of mouth and in the presence of those who
> are here with me.*
>
> *Your daughter and humble servant,*
>
> *Marie-Madeleine de l'Epine*

She sent this note with the carriage that had brought her,
having told the coachman to return here if Mademoiselle
de l'Epine came alone, or to go to a certain church if she
brought anyone with her, where I would have gone to escort
her to the room. But she came alone.

While we were waiting for her, we had been considering
how we would conduct the meeting, and had decided that it
should be I who received her and spoke to her first, because
I did not want my wife, in her present condition, to face the
wrath of this woman, who had the reputation of being a

270

veritable she-devil, which in fact she was. I wrote out a copy of my promise of marriage so that I could show it to her without allowing her to have the original. I was able to do this without opening the packet which belonged to my wife, since the only difference between the two, other than the names, was that the genders were reversed, as I have already said. I therefore copied from the one my wife had given me. I had barely finished writing when I heard the carriage stop at the door. Madame Des Prez went into the next room, and I locked the door after her, let down the tapestry which hid it and drew some chairs in front of it. Since it was higher than the floor of the room I was in, it was now completely invisible. I then went down to meet Mademoiselle de l'Epine.

She was quite taken by surprise, not having expected to see me there. Come in, Mademoiselle, I said, giving her my hand. It was I who sent for you. Your daughter merely wrote on my behalf. Where is she, Monsieur? she asked. She is at Mass, I replied, and will be here shortly. She climbed the stairs and came into the room. I went down again, and dismissed the carriage to make sure she could not take it into her head to attempt a sudden departure. I returned, closed and locked the door of the room and removed the key without her noticing that I had done so. She admired the furniture and asked to whom the room belonged. I cut her questions short and invited her to take one of the chairs near the connecting door; thus my wife was able to overhear what was said.

Have you any idea, Mademoiselle, I said, seating myself close to her, why your daughter could have sent for you, and not be here waiting for you? No, Monsieur, she replied. I have no idea. Can you tell me why? Yes, Mademoiselle, I said. I can easily tell you the reason. It is because of something she did without consulting you. And only in this respect – that she did not consult you – did she neglect what

271

would strictly speaking be her duty to you. And she believed your regard for me would be sufficient to persuade you to overlook this neglect, if I made the request. She thought, I continued, it was permissible for her to marry without your consent, since she believed I would be able to obtain your agreement. The deed is done, and no amount of dis- approval on your side can undo it. I must also tell you that she is in her fifth month of pregnancy and has been my wife for more than ten months.

Her interruptions as I spoke were so frequent that I could scarcely finish. What! she exclaimed. The hussy is married! She is pregnant! I will strangle her! Where is she? It is you who seduced her. Wait till I tell your father! He'll have you locked up in Saint-Lazare! I'll never let her out of the house again. Am I not to be pitied, I, who taught her to know right from wrong? I am ruined! My lawsuit is lost! I shall be forced to beg on the streets! Let me get my hands on her! I'll strangle her! The wretch! The strumpet! The jade! And she went on in this fashion for so long that I can no longer remember what she said.

I thought that, if I interrupted her, it would only prolong the outburst: not only would it provide further fuel for her rage, it would also give her time to catch her breath; on the other hand, if I said nothing, she would eventually run out of invective of her own accord. I therefore let her have her say. She was in a furious temper, spitting out fire and venom. She searched above the bed, behind it, under it: everywhere she thought her daughter might be hiding – but she did not suspect there was an adjoining chamber. She demanded again: where was her daughter? So that she could strangle her, as she most certainly intended to do, she said. And indeed, I was heartily glad that I had saved Madame Des Prez from this frenzy. She tried to leave, but since the door was locked, and I had the key, she could not do so. She began her ranting again with renewed ferocity, and I began to think she would leap at me and scratch my eyes out, but she did not do so. Her anger, even though at fever pitch, lasted more than two hours without slacking, and without giving me a chance to open my mouth. When I saw that the outpouring was at last beginning to flag, I decided it was time for me to speak, and since with some people it is better not to humble oneself, as this merely reinforces their grievances, I adopted a tone as high-handed and forceful as her own had been.

I said without mincing words that it was true I had married her daughter without her consent, since I didn't need her approval either then or now, and that I would do the same again if it were still to be done. I said I didn't think I had dishonoured her family by marrying her daughter, nor that her daughter would be blamed for giving me her hand. I said I was of age, as she well knew, and that if she were so shocked and displeased by our marriage she could take whatever steps seemed appropriate to her. She could go as she had threatened and complain to my father, who would take his own revenge on her and her ill-temper, and relieve me of the need to do so. I said the worst that could happen to me would be a short stay in Saint-Lazare, and I pointed out that I could reinstate myself in my father's good graces by abandoning her daughter. I said it would be she herself who would lose any credit she had in the world if, through her action, her daughter were to lose her status as my wife and be seen merely as the plaything of a man to whom she believed herself to have been legally married. I declared that her lawsuit, which was so dear to her, would not be saved by this action; my father, who was a man of honour and probity, far from approving of such heartlessness would consider her a shrew and a termagant for putting a sordid financial interest above her daughter's well-being. I said that everyone would despise her, and she would find herself with as many enemies as there were decent people who heard of such infamous behaviour.

However, if she took the other path, as honour and prudence dictated she should, there would be no such problems. I repeated that her daughter and I had been married for over ten months without anyone – herself included – suspecting it, and that we could continue in the same way. All that she needed to do regarding her daughter's pregnancy was to let it be known that her daughter had asked to spend some time in a convent and make it appear that she was taking her to one. The birth could take place in the room where we were. I would do all in my power to bring her lawsuit to a satisfactory conclusion, the more so, as her interests were now my own; she would not be forced to borrow money to pursue it, as I had resources she could count on; and furthermore I would do everything she could expect of a good son and a good son-in-law. On the other hand, I would move heaven and earth to avenge myself if she took any action detrimental to my wife or myself. I could easily safeguard her daughter from my father's wrath by taking her away from Paris. I admitted it was true I would not be able to refuse the annulment of the marriage, but, I continued, putting on a semblance of anger, neither can anyone prevent me from giving her what she would need to live independently of her mother. You can be sure, I said, that you would never see your daughter again. In less than an hour, she could have left Paris, and I would not leave her until I had established her in a place where her only concern would be that I remain faithful to her, and she need never again fear your unkindness and hard heart, nor my father's anger. Do as you please, I added, opening the door, you may leave when you wish since you refuse to act reasonably. But think before you decide. Take care not to lay in store for yourself remorse that will stay with you the rest of your life.

I had been right to think that a certain forcefulness of manner would serve better than an appearance of humility.

She asked me where her daughter was, but in such a way that I could see her anger was subsiding. Your daughter is not far away, I said, and can hear you. She was wise not to expose herself to your violence. She is free to come into this room when she wishes, but if she came before I called her I would make my displeasure known and you would both see that I am her husband and her master. As I, in my turn, now put on a show of anger her own temper evaporated completely. But, Monsieur, she said, if this came to your father's ears – and I am only worried because of him – what might he not do? When I saw that she was becoming amenable, I pointed out how easy it was to keep the matter secret: having done so for a considerable length of time already, we could continue to do so. She began to agree and asked again to see her daughter. I said there was no hurry and I would allow my wife to come when she herself had quite recovered her composure.

I then assured her that the principal point was that our marriage was fully legal, and that it could not be annulled without my consent, or barring some exceptional occurrence. I described all the measures we had taken, and to convince her I said she could see the priest who had performed the marriage ceremony. She asked me to send for him.

He had not expected such a summons and was somewhat surprised when he arrived, but swiftly recovered his aplomb. Since he himself had devised all the safeguards, his reputation depended on their being effective. He made it clear that every possible precaution had been taken to ensure that the marriage conformed to the requirements, both of the Church and of the law: since it had been sanctified by a priest, and since I was of age and was free to marry. He spoke so convincingly that she had no argument left. She asked again to see her daughter. I thought that there was now nothing to be feared. I moved the chairs, opened the door to the other room and, taking my wife by the hand, led her to her mother, at whose feet she threw herself. Her mother picked her up tearfully, and my wife, also in tears, made her apologies as best she could. I embraced them both, delighted that Mademoiselle de l'Epine had finally come round to accept the fact of our marriage.

In an instant, our peace was made. I invited my mother-in-law and the priest to stay for dinner. There was no longer any need to dissimulate before her, and indeed, had it not been for my carelessness, our relationship would not even yet have come to light. We agreed that Madame Des Prez should return to our room the next day and remain there until the birth of the child. That evening, when she got home, with everybody present, she would ask her mother to let her spend some time in a convent, and the day after that, her mother would make it appear that that was where she was taking her, but would in fact bring her to our hideaway.

Mademoiselle de l'Epine was the first to leave. My wife remained alone with me. She told me she had been surprised by the uncompromising tone I had used in talking to her mother, but realised it had been the right approach, since it had achieved the result we wanted. My answer was to give her a kiss, and as I embraced her, I said, So, at last, dear child, I am allowed to have you to myself, and to spend some nights with you. Her only reply was an embrace and a smile which showed more tenderness than any words could have expressed.

I told her she should buy all she might need that day, so that she would not have to leave the house again. She said she had everything she needed, but that if she later wanted something, our hostess would get it for her, and there would be no need for her to go out. This woman, who was devoted to my wife, offered to take care of her, and as this arrangement perfectly suited my wife, I accepted and told her I would be grateful for her services and would recompense them; moreover, this would mean we would be able to do without some other servant, who might not prove trustworthy. When everything had been settled in this way, I left, having promised to dine there the next day with my wife and her mother.

All that we had resolved was done, and I found them both there the next evening. We all ate together, and I bade my wife to eat well and not to stint on her food. I slept with her for the first time and spent several nights with her during the four months she was there, though I did not do this frequently, for fear of arousing suspicion. We could have continued in this way until after her confinement, had it not been for the disaster which occurred, which was caused by my carelessness, and which cost Marie-Madeleine her life and engulfed me in despair, and which also accounts for the false opinion the world has of me. I must tell you the rest of the story, but allow me to pause a moment; the painful events I must now recount overwhelm my spirit. Indeed, Des Prez was bathed in tears and seemed more dead than alive. It was some time before he could continue. Eventually he proceeded with his story.

I hadn't seen her for two days. The time for the child's birth was approaching, at least it appeared so, and she was extremely uncomfortable. She was feeling more unwell than usual and, not knowing what had prevented me from visiting her, she wrote me a note, using our host to convey it to me. I read it and hastened to go and visit her. As I crossed the courtyard, I met my father, who asked me to accompany him into his office. He spoke about a government position that he was endeavouring to obtain for me, and he also said a few words about a potential alliance he had in mind for me. Although he spoke of it only as a distant prospect, it nonetheless threw me into such turmoil that I did not know how to respond. I took out my handkerchief to hide my disarray, and the letter I had just received from my wife fell out without my noticing it. I left without picking it up. I went out and saw my wife – for the last time in my life. After our initial embrace, she told me that she was unwell and that she was not being properly cared for in the house where she was. She begged me to allow her to accept her mother's offer to have her go home for the baby's birth, which she was sure would be within the next week. She said that her sisters and brother were aware that she was married, though they did not know to whom, and far from blaming her, they were extremely eager to see her, and that the secret would be just as safe there as it was here, since she was using the same midwife as had attended her mother in the past.

Mademoiselle de l'Epine was present and heard what my wife said. She added her support to the request, and I let myself be persuaded. One may have presentiments about the future, but there is no way one can escape one's misfortune. There were a thousand reasons which should have made me refuse to allow such a move, which I pointed out to them, and to these reasons I added my own pleas. I had told them a hundred times that I wanted to be in the room with my wife at the child's birth; that I was dismayed at the suggestion that she move now; and was totally opposed to the idea. But, to our misfortune, she brought to bear all the power she had over me to make me change my mind and give my approval. In her present condition, I did not have the heart to refuse the request which she made with hands joined as in prayer. So, against my better judgement, I consented, and this was the cause of her death.

We arranged for her to be taken to her mother's house at eight o'clock the next morning. In the interval till then, her mother would prepare everything needed to receive her and provide for her comfort. I stayed with her until late that evening and was frequently tempted to withdraw the permission which she had extracted from me. And as I did not expect to see her for a considerable time – not until after the child's birth – we made the fondest and most tender of farewells. Alas! he exclaimed, in a flood of tears. We did not know our farewells were for ever, and that we would never see each other again!

I returned to my father's house, where I did not notice anything amiss, although in fact my position there had totally changed since the moment earlier that day when I had left it. Not being warned – since no one knew of the change – I walked of my own free will straight into the trap and lay myself open to the mortal blow my father was preparing for me. When I had left his office, he too was about to leave, and crossing the room, he walked past the place where I had been standing, and saw a letter on the floor which had not been visible from behind his desk. He picked it up, and assuming it to be one of those he had received that morning, he threw it onto his desk without paying it any attention. But – and notice how Fate conspired against us – the addition of this letter made some others tumble off his desk, and, once again, he picked these up. This second time, the unfortunate letter had fallen open on the floor, and he noticed it was in a woman's hand. Had this not been so, he would have treated it with as much indifference as he had the first time. But seeing a handwriting with which he was not familiar, he opened it and read:

Have you abandoned me, my dear husband? How can it be that, in my present enervated state, as I await the moment when I shall be delivered of the precious burden you gave into my keeping, offspring of your tenderness and our union, two whole days pass without your visiting me? Alas, even at its most robust, my health suffered when I spent a day without you, and now, when I most need your presence and encouragement as my moment of trial approaches, you seem to have forgotten me. In God's name, I beg you, come today, if you wish to save your wife's life.

Marie-Madeleine de l'Epine

You can imagine the anger that the reading of such a letter provoked in my father. Those who have a natural tendency to violence are more to be feared when they act silently than in any visible outburst of emotion. Without saying a word, he determined to separate us for ever, by depriving me of liberty, and by putting every imaginable pressure on the mother and daughter. He went as usual to the Palais de Justice. He gave orders for a sergeant-at-arms and some foot soldiers to arrive at six the next morning at the office of the Flanders Coach Company, which is located at the end of the rue Saint-Martin. He obtained the necessary authorisations and did everything with such secrecy that none of his people heard of it. He dined in town and returned home only in the evening, giving orders that I was to speak to him as soon as I returned home, which was at around eleven. He said nothing to me which gave me the slightest suspicion. He asked me if I would be free the next morning, and said he wanted to take me somewhere that he should have shown me long ago. I thought he meant to take me to see the father of a girl he had spoken to me about. Thinking this to be the case, I said I would go anywhere he wanted with him, and that my only appointment was at the Court of Appeals. Very well! he said. We will go together at six to where I want to take you, where neither you nor I need stay long.

We got into his carriage at exactly six the next morning, on the longest day of the year, June 19th, unhappy day, which I shall remember for the rest of my life! He stopped the carriage at this office of the Flanders Coach Company and took me into an upstairs room. Since the man I thought we were going to meet was from outside Paris, I thought he must have recently arrived in town and be lodging there, and I went upstairs without a qualm. But the instant I entered the room, I was seized by four stout fellows, whose first action was to remove my sword. I was more dead than alive! You will not be here long, my father said. You will soon be taken elsewhere. Here is my evidence, he continued, showing me the fatal letter. Do you recognise it? I wanted to throw myself at his feet, but he turned his back on me, and addressing the sergeant, said: Do not allow him to speak to anyone, and in half an hour take him without causing any sort of disturbance to where I told you.

Then he left and apparently went to Saint-Lazare to give orders for my reception there. The sergeant who had been left in charge asked me to undress and handed me a suit of clothes to put on. These were clothes of my own which were new and of finer quality than the ones I was wearing. I asked him why I was to wear fine clothes to go to prison. These are your father's orders, he said, so that people will think you have gone into the country. I could see that if I did not do as I was asked, these fellows would do it for me, so I took off my coat and donned the new garments. I learnt later that a man who was about the same age and size as myself had been given my clothes to wear, and, with my servant following, using my horses, the two of them had ridden through the streets at a gallop. This good-for-nothing of a lackey of mine had been found drinking in a bar later on, and had told several people that I had left for the country and was not expected to return for some time. This is how the rumour started that I had deserted my poor wife; she, for her part, received much worse treatment and was in much worse case than myself.

I tried to protest at being used in this way, given the fact that I was of age. The sergeant refused to listen. I threw myself at his feet and offered him my purse, containing fifty gold louis, my diamond, my watch and a note for whatever amount he named, if only he would let me write a message to my wife and promise to have it delivered to her. I swore by every oath I could think of to share my whole fortune with him if he would do this for me, and threatened he would feel the full force of my resentment if he refused. He was as impervious to my prayers and offers of riches as he was to my threats, and I was taken off to Saint-Lazare at about eight o'clock – at almost the same moment that my poor wife was breathing her last.

My father returned home when he left Saint-Lazare and went on foot to Mademoiselle de l'Epine's. His arrival took her by surprise, the more so when he made it clear why he had come, in such terms and with such fury as could only be attributed to a complete loss of self-control. He called her the most despicable of creatures. It was in vain that she swore she had had nothing to do with our marriage, and that, if her daughter were there, she would be treated as she deserved. Her protestations were to no effect; he still called her corrupt and contemptible and described my wife as a hoyden and libertine, swearing he would have her locked up. His rage was at its height when Madame Des Prez herself arrived at her mother's door. She had a key, which enabled her to let herself in without knocking, and the length of the passage had prevented her from hearing the goings-on upstairs. She had paid off the men who had brought her, thinking that, having arrived at her mother's house, she had finished with their services; and since the cook, the chamber-maid and the lackey had crept upstairs to hear what was going on, no one warned her of my father's presence.

She therefore went upstairs, unaware of what was taking place. At sight of her, my father's wrath knew no bounds. He used language which she was not used to hearing: she fell fainting on the top step and slipped down more than twenty stairs. Her mother, whose natural tenderness should have been roused by such a sight, treated her – even in that pitiful state – worse than a wild animal would have done: far from offering the help she so sorely needed, she disowned her as a daughter, refusing to have her in the house. See, she said to my father, does it look as if I am the one responsible for their marriage? She sent for another sedan and had the rustics who came with it take my dear wife, half-dead and bleeding as she was, by the arms and feet like a dead animal, put her into the conveyance and carry her off to the Hôtel-Dieu. What unutterable barbarity! Could any viler example be found of putting self-interest above the well-being of one's own flesh and blood!

However violent my father's anger had been, he was dismayed at such a harrowing sight. His heart was softened by the very heartlessness of this unnatural mother, and his shock was such that he could not say a word. He felt pity for a young woman whose beauty he had admired, and whose misfortune he began to regret. He had wanted to put an end to her marriage, but not to cause her death, or that of her unborn child. He was ashamed of the excessive anger which had possessed him, and left the house more disturbed by what he had witnessed than the cruel mother herself had been. He sent word to her to say it was not his wish to prevent her providing whatever attention her daughter needed in her present condition; in fact, he urged her to care for her daughter's well-being and that of the child. Mademoiselle de l'Epine, for her part, from what she has told me, only behaved as she did for effect, and in order not to lose credit in my father's eyes, and was distraught at the desperate turn events had taken. She had only sent her daughter to the Hôtel-Dieu to make a show of indifference, but with the intention of going to fetch her back to the house straight away.

She therefore went off to the Hôtel-Dieu where she found her daughter in the most wretched straits – a young woman, beautiful as an angel, elegantly dressed, whose life was drawing to a close. She wanted to take her home, but my wife was too ill to be moved. All that could be done for her was to put her in a small private room. My poor wife was dying. After her first swoon, she had been brought back to consciousness by the movement of the conveyance in which she was being carried, but had fainted again without having the strength to utter a word. When she regained consciousness a second time, she found herself on a filthy bed in a place I can scarcely bring myself to name, in the company of five thousand beggar-women – the sad flotsam and jetsam of all the disreputable purlieus of Paris.

What despair! With her life ebbing away, she barely opened her eyes. Then she was carried into the room I have spoken of where her mother was. They tried to revive her, but she was already too close to death. For an hour, she gave no sign of life, except for looking around vacantly in all directions. At last, she opened her mouth and asked for me. They told her I was not there. She asked for pen and paper. They tried to dissuade her, since writing would only further drain her strength, but she was so insistent that in the end they complied. She wrote until she was overcome by convulsions, and it is this piece of paper you saw in my hands and, which I wear over my heart. Read it, he said, passing it to me. I took it from his hands and, with great difficulty, read the words:

I am near death. I had not expected so many misfortunes to follow each other so closely. I am not concerned to decide who caused my death as I wish to forgive everyone. Farewell, beloved husband. All that remains of me will be your memories. I feel your child, he is dead. I am dying too. If I could embrace you before ...

This was all I could read, the rest being ill-formed and trailing. He took back the paper from my hand, kissed it,

284

and replaced it over his heart. Then, with great difficulty, being overcome with tears and sobs, continued his sad tale.

She was racked with convulsions, as I said, and could not complete the letter. Consciousness returned a little. She asked for absolution, which was given. She gave birth to a stillborn child and died a quarter of an hour later, in pain and bathed in blood, without a word of condemnation against anyone. There, he said, his tears flowing, there, my darling wife, was the end of our love, and this is the loss which I must live with for ever. At this point, his distress was redoubled, and though God has not given me a heart which is particularly attuned to the suffering of others, I could not refrain from joining my tears with his. I was indeed touched by what he had recounted. And I see that all of you who have been listening feel the same way, said Dupuis, looking around him at those present, all of whom had tears in their eyes. Finish your story, I beg you, said Madame de Contamine. Then we will tell you what we feel about this sad tale. Dupuis obeyed.

As for me, said Des Prez, when he had somewhat regained his composure, while this was happening, I was, as I have said, being held at Saint-Lazare. I was not told of her death, which occurred just as I was arriving at this monastery-prison. I remained there for a whole week in a state of unimaginable torment. One or other of the saintly brethren stayed with me constantly. They tried to offer me consolation and gradually brought me to the understanding that there were worse things for me to endure than my loss of freedom. Eventually, they told me of my wife's death. It was then that I felt the weight of my captivity, since I could neither take revenge nor my own life, as, in my despair, I wished to do. I said and did a thousand senseless things. For three months they tried without success to provide some sort of consolation to my spirit. I am told I was delirious, and my grief had too much real cause to be assuaged.

These pious monks treated my sorrow with respect. They accepted and understood my affliction, with the hope of bringing back my reason; if they didn't fully succeed, at least they calmed the rage which would have made me commit murder. I was not released until they saw that I had recovered enough for there to be no danger of my resorting to violence, but rather than returning to Paris, I went to Normandy and stayed on the property of my brother-in-law, Monsieur de Querville, and came back to Paris only a week ago.

The first thing I did on my return was to go to the Hôtel-Dieu, where I wept for my poor wife. I asked to see where she was buried. She and her child share a grave. I fainted when I was shown the place. I can never return there – it is too painful. I was told that her mother had carried off a note that my wife had written. I went to see her, and she gave me it. It is the one you have just read. I now live only to avenge myself on that harridan. Though she pleads for me to forgive her and does her utmost to convince me she was not to blame, and expresses the deepest sorrow for her daughter's death, I shall do everything in my power to foil the settlement of her lawsuit. I intend also to avenge myself on that scoundrel of an officer who arrested me and cruelly denied even the smallest favour I asked of him – the sad consolation of at least sending a word to my poor wife. As for my treacherous lackey – though he bore the least blame – I have already settled my account with him. And when I have taken care of all of this, I shall see what destiny has in store for the rest of my life. Now that you have heard the whole story, and know what I have suffered and lost, do you not agree that I am less to be blamed than to be pitied? And do you still believe it is true, as they say, that I abandoned my poor Madelon and caused her death? I, who would give my life – nay, a hundred thousand lives – if I could buy hers back?

There, ladies, said Dupuis. That is the story Monsieur Des Prez told me of his life, and if his grief was not sincere, I cannot read the truth in a man's eyes. He had several reasons for not making his marriage known, first among which was that the place where she died does dishonour to his wife's memory. Secondly, though he was not responsible for her death, if he were to clear his name and prove his innocence, he would have to reveal his father's part in her death – through his unbridled temper – which is not known at present, since only the members of Mademoiselle de l'Epine's household were there at the time. Neither would his dead wife benefit from this being known, but only her mother, whom he has sworn to destroy. For my part, I feel the greatest compassion for him. No one could feel a grief more deeply than he feels his. He swore that he would remain faithful to the memory of his wife, and has done so to this day. Whatever lengths his father, while he was still alive, went to, he was never able to persuade him to marry, and now that Des Prez is his own master, and himself holds one of the highest positions in the legal profession, the life he leads proves that he has renounced all interest in the female sex and that his only preoccupation is the vengeance he seeks. The officer who arrested him and took him to Saint-Lazare has felt its effects and has been forced to flee the country. Des Prez looked into his history and found sufficient evidence to have him locked up under the harshest conditions in La Grève. Only by escaping the country did he save his skin, and even now Des Prez still pursues him.

Monsieur Des Prez, the father, took such a dislike to Mademoiselle de l'Epine after the act of heartless cruelty he had witnessed that he could not endure her presence, and, with his son's encouragement, he voluntarily excluded himself from further participation in her legal dispute. It has still not been settled, since all Des Prez's friends either argue against it or contrive to delay a decision. Therefore she is still frustrated and no nearer her goal. Des Prez wants the children, not the mother, to profit from any award. They were heartbroken by their sister's death. It seems unlikely that any conclusion will be reached during Mademoiselle de l'Epine's lifetime. Meanwhile, he found a good living for the priest who had married them, and has arranged permanent employment for the man who gave them his help. He has taken on the wife, who looked after their room, as his housekeeper. In a word, if he showed, and still shows, an implacable enmity towards all those who thwarted or opposed him, he demonstrates equally his gratitude to those who helped him or Marie-Madeleine.

If all this is true, opined Madame de Londé, he certainly is more deserving of sympathy than blame. I pity them both, said Madame de Mongey, they did not deserve such misfortune! I too feel sympathy for them, said Madame de Contamine, but I cannot refrain from noting that nearly all marriages of this sort, concluded without the consent or knowledge of the couple's parents, come to grief. Monsieur Des Prez is a living example, condemned to lasting unhappiness – if what Monsieur Dupuis has told us is true. It is indeed, I can vouch for that, said a voice out of the blue. Everyone looked in the direction it had come from, and saw Monsieur de Contamine, whom his wife ran to welcome. This is a fine way to behave, exclaimed her friend, Manon, to come in like that and startle people out of their wits! It is also a fine way to behave, retorted Monsieur de Contamine, greeting the whole company, to keep married women from morn till night and force their husbands to come looking for them at midnight. To tell the truth, I am beginning to rebel at the way you are leading my wife astray. Hurry up and get yourselves married, he said, and give up this scandalous lifestyle that you indulge in at present! Now, now, said his wife, calm down. You won't have long to wait.

The two parties have reached agreement. Ask Monsieur Des Ronais, whom you see here, his opinion. Well, I never! exclaimed Monsieur de Contamine. Is this really you? I can hardly believe my eyes. So, old friend, have you seen reason at last? What do you have to say for yourself? What I say, answered Des Ronais, is that if it were up to me, we'd consider the ceremony a formality and take it as done. You'll find it done soon enough! said Monsieur de Contamine. Marriage has a strange effect. It changes things out of all recognition, so that they lose three-quarters of their value. Allow me to thank you for this kindly observation, said Manon, making a deep curtsey before Monsieur de Contamine. Indeed, we women are hard done by, said Madame de Mongey. Here is Madame de Contamine, who never tires of telling us that she is the happiest woman in the world, that each day she loves her husband more and more – and see how he pays her back! Well, the fact is, said Madame de Contamine, I pay no attention to what he says. What counts is what he does, and in this respect I am well satisfied. And if you are all scorned by your husbands as I am by mine, I say, get married – you will be none the worse for it!

You see, ladies, continued Contamine, still in a bantering tone, it is not I who put words into my wife's mouth. She is satisfied with what I do, which means, to say the least, I am not useless where women are concerned. Should anyone else among you, on her recommendation, need my services ... Everyone here is suited, interrupted his wife. Each peahen has her peacock, and it is no use your flaunting your feathers. Stick to me, you will not do better. So be it, he said, what one has is better than nothing.

Madame de Londé, Dupuis and everyone present joined in a general conversation, which was short, since the hour was extremely late, and all were standing, preparing to leave. Everyone returned home after having agreed on a time when they would meet for dinner the next day, at the home of Madame de Contamine, who wanted to entertain the company, and where Des Frans promised to bring Monsieur and Madame de Jussy. Monsieur and Madame de Contamine left together, Dupuis escorted Madame de Londé to her home. Madame de Mongey stayed with Manon, and Des Ronais and Des Frans returned together to the former's house.

As soon as Des Ronais was alone with Des Frans, he asked him about the conversation he had been having with Madame de Contamine and Manon before supper. Why, were your ears tingling? said Des Frans, laughing. Not at all, replied Des Ronais, also with a laugh. I was told you were talking not about me but, on the contrary, about you. I can guess what the two ladies were telling you, and they assured me that you would tell me. Yes, said Des Frans. I did agree to tell you, but I don't know if I can do so without sounding conceited and earning your ridicule. I already know the gist without your telling me, said Des Ronais. I can hazard a guess and am sure I am right. You were talking about Madame de Mongey – and Madame de Contamine and Mademoiselle Dupuis were trying to persuade you that you could not do better than seek an alliance with her. You are right, said Des Frans. They gave me the most glowing picture of this lady's merit. And did they also tell you, asked Des Ronais, of her single-minded devotion to you? They did their best to convince me of it, said Des Frans.

Well, I myself can confirm that it is true, said Des Ronais, and if you take the advice of your best friends, you will not lose the chance to make her yours. Madame de Contamine and Mademoiselle Dupuis have only said what I myself was planning to say to you. And it was certainly not at her request that they spoke to you. I know she was extremely reluctant to tell anyone her feelings, and it was only shortly before the death of Monsieur Dupuis that she confided in his daughter. She did so just then because she refused a very advantageous match, which Monsieur Dupuis, who loved her like a daughter, had wanted her to accept. It was only the most recent offer she has refused since being widowed, and it was so advantageous that people interpreted her refusal as implying that she had given up any intention of remarrying. But I can assure you that it is only because of you that she has refused all offers so far – and my information comes from a source that cannot be doubted.

But, said Des Frans, I have never felt for her that ardent devotion which stems from a shared sympathy, which is so essential to a happy union. What are you saying? said Des Ronais. You did not love her? I have always had the highest esteem and admiration for her, answered Des Frans, but it was not love which accounted for my frequent attendance on her. Then why did you tell her it was? asked Des Ronais. She took you at your word and has loved only you since then. It is true I told her I loved her, said Des Frans, with a sigh. But I was only using her to conceal another unhappy passion which I will tell you about tomorrow. This other passion is no longer an issue, said Des Ronais. Since Silvie is dead (for it is she you are speaking of) what matters is that you should acknowledge Madame de Mongey's worth. She is beautiful and has a fine figure; she is virtuous, and of a suitable age – she is no more than twenty-five or twenty-six years old, at most. She is rich – not only as sole heiress to her parents, but also through what came to her from her husband and from bequests from her brothers and an aunt and uncle. Moreover, she loves you. Take it from me, if you do not know this already – it is much better in normal circumstances for a man to marry a woman whom he does not love, but who loves him, than for him to marry one whom he loves, without being loved in return. I am stating this starkly, but it is undeniably true. Think about it, and you will agree. Madame de Mongey is a very personable woman, but even if she were of less attractive appearance, her intelligence, her gentle nature and her virtue, all of which she has amply demonstrated, would justify your affection and would ensure the comfort a man could wish for in his home life. Let us go to bed, said Des Frans. When I have told you my story tomorrow, see whether you still advise me to marry. Let us leave it until then. With these words, they each retired to their room.

They were woken the next day by Dupuis, who scolded them for being still abed at nine o'clock. They took a carriage and went to Jussy's house, only to find he had even then not risen. Des Frans informed him he had come to invite him to take breakfast with two of his friends. Gladly, said Jussy, rising to meet them and leading them into another room, where he left them while he dressed. This did not take long, and after they had exchanged the usual salutation and greetings Des Frans asked for news of his wife. Jussy said she was still asleep – the day had not yet dawned for her. You are already sleeping in separate beds? jested Des Frans, with a laugh. No, no, answered Jussy good-humouredly, we are not yet tired of each other; and if you want to see her, I will show you one of the prettiest sleeping beauties in Paris. He took him by the hand and led him into the room they had first been into, but instead of finding his wife in bed, they found her already at her toilette. I thought you were still asleep, said Jussy. I heard some mention of breakfast, she said, and I wanted to make sure of my share. Very good, he said. Hurry, and we will wait for you. They did not have long to wait.

Des Ronais and Dupuis expressed their admiration when she appeared, and she received their compliments with wit and charm. Des Frans informed them that he had arranged to take them to see Madame de Mongey, who would be at Madame de Contamine's, in order to bring about their reconciliation. We shall be happy to come with you, said Jussy. I used to know Madame de Contamine and even oversaw some business matters for her at one time. No, that is not the Madame de Contamine I am talking of, said Des Frans, it is her daughter-in-law. So, Monsieur de Contamine is married, is he? said Jussy. Yes, and his wife is as illustrious for her adherence to the path of virtue as yours is for her constancy, answered Des Frans.

Madame de Jussy blushed and said she would like to know the story of this Madame de Contamine. Des Ronais recounted it to her and her husband after they had eaten breakfast. I am looking forward to meeting this exceptional woman, said Madame de Jussy when he had finished the recital. If you are looking forward to meeting her, said Dupuis, I can assure you that she is extremely eager to meet you, as are all the others to whom Des Frans told your story, and they will all be there – quite a crowd, in fact – at Monsieur de Contamine's house, where Monsieur Des Frans is to tell us of his adventures. If all these reasons were not enough to persuade me to be there, said Jussy, the fact that Madame de Mongey will be present would in itself be sufficient – the more so since you tell me, said he to Des Frans, that you have a special interest in her? Let us go as soon as you are ready. It is past noon, said Des Frans. They will be expecting us already. Let us be off, then, said Jussy, and so they departed, Des Frans and Jussy in the same carriage. Dupuis went for Madame de Londé, and Des Ronais left a little later with Madame de Jussy, who had wished to make some slight adjustments to her dress to make sure she could hold her own in the illustrious company she was joining.

All the ladies arrived at about the same time. Madame de Contamine received them in her role as hostess. She and Madame de Jussy exchanged the politest of greetings and, from that moment, formed a friendship which to all appearances will last a lifetime. Jussy and his wife expressed their profound apology to Madame de Mongey, who accepted it graciously. Madame de Londé arrived with her husband-to-be and charmed all those assembled. It was indeed an exceptional group that was gathered here. One could not have found in all of France five more beautiful women. They noted and admired each other's dress and appearance, and exchanged compliments with wit and grace, and in due course this formality gave way to a more relaxed conversation. Des Frans spoke alone with Madame de Mongey for some time. No one knew what was said, but it was noticed that the attractive widow had blushed.

The company sat down to eat. Madame de Contamine placed Des Frans between herself and Madame de Mongey; the others were seated as their hearts chose. The forthcoming marriages – of Des Ronais and Manon, and of the latter's cousin, Dupuis, and Madame de Londé – provided the subject of conversation during the meal. It has to be said, Jussy maintained, as the conversation progressed, that if a wife is an encumbrance, it is a necessary encumbrance. That is so, agreed Contamine. They are a necessary evil, and if one can do without them altogether, one is fortunate. How these creatures malign us! said Madame de Jussy with a shrug and a laugh. Surely, only those who are unhappily married can share such an opinion! said Des Ronais to Contamine. And as far as we can see, you have no cause to complain of your choice. I do not complain about my wife, answered Contamine. There are some women, even a large number, who are far less reasonable than she is. But however happy one's marriage, there are many moments when a man regrets the loss of his freedom. I am not talking, as you see, about those with unhappy marriages. I am talking even of people with the most loving of marriages, like myself.

What is this I hear! his wife interrupted in great surprise, with tears almost springing to her eyes. Have I done something to displease you? No, not yet, he said, but the very question might come near to displeasing me. Let me continue what I was saying. I do not think there is a better marriage than mine anywhere in the world. I love my wife more today than I did when I married her. I am sure – or think I can be – that she also still cares for me. Now be quiet and let me finish, he said to her, seeing she was about to interrupt once more. But nonetheless, he said to the company in general, I am sometimes tired of the constraint it imposes. So you would have people live in disorder, consorting with each other as they pleased? said Madame de Londé. Here is another one, exclaimed Contamine, looking at her. What a miracle it would be to find a woman who would hear you out to the end of a sentence! No, Madame, I am not the least in favour of anarchy. What I am saying is that a wife's solicitude can be a burden to her husband. Let me give you an example. I often return home with my head still full of business concerns. I am preoccupied. My wife thinks I am in a bad temper and her untimely efforts to humour and console me make me lose the thread of my ideas – which I can never again recapture. The same thing happens when I am working in my study. I do not dare to tell her to leave me alone, for fear of upsetting her, so that, out of consideration for her, and because of her concern for me, there are often occasions when I wish, if not that I were not married, at least that I were not so beset by my wife. Thus there are disadvantages in marriage which a husband discovers only by experience, and since I have found them to exist, I am sure others find them too.

Well, said Des Ronais, continuing the conversation, I only hope my betrothed will make my life miserable in the same way when we are married. What! So that I shall be able to hear you, too, tell all and sundry, as Monsieur de Contamine has just been doing, that your wife dotes on you too much! Manon chimed in.

You see, said Madame de Contamine with amusement, what terrible hardships he has had to suffer? Now that I understand, she turned to him, I will make sure you have no further cause for complaint. In future, I promise, I will always wait for you to come looking for me. So you will go to the other extreme! he said, laughing in his turn. Too far in either direction is too far, as you would be the first to let me know if I were at fault.

One thing is certain, Des Frans began, whether a woman loves her husband, or does not love him, she ... Enough! said Madame de Contamine, putting her hand in front of his mouth to stop him. Here we have some sort of amphibious creature, she said, indicating him, whose nature I cannot quite fathom. But whether he is a fully fledged man, or merely a fledgling, he takes it on himself to criticise our sex, and tears our reputation to pieces, more than if we were actually guilty of doing him any harm!

From what I understand, dear ladies, said Dupuis, coming to the defence of his friend, his entanglements with the fair sex have not brought him great joy. I do not know the whole story, though I can guess at much of it. I only know (as I mentioned to him in Des Ronais's presence) that it has something to do with a necklace, which it is said he stole. Whoever it was who told you that, Des Frans interrupted in considerable surprise, must have supernatural insight! It was indeed I who took the necklace, but whatever can have led you to suspect that this was so?

So, said Madame de Contamine, speaking to Des Frans, how long do we have to wait before you tell us your story? I am quite ready to tell it, he answered. There is no longer any reason for me to hide what happened. I am the only one who will suffer from having the memory of my disgrace reawakened. All of you here are masterpieces created by Heaven and Nature – the latter formed you with beauty and grace, and the former endowed you with all the virtues that are admirable in a woman – so you will not be shocked by what I have to tell you. I am only anxious to show you that my own experience gives me the right to vent my spleen against womankind and would lead me to believe that they are all deceitful. Or, if that is too sweeping, I at least have been too ill-used by them to be able to say anything good about them if I am being honest.

I have only ever loved one and she betrayed me; and I would have nothing more to do with women for the rest of my life if I did not know that there are women in the world whose virtue has been tried and proved. If a woman is genuinely good and virtuous, she has my admiration. But there are so few of whom this can be said that you must not be surprised if I base my opinion on what is true of the majority, and consider the rest as miracles that Nature produces only rarely.

Stop your diatribe there, Monsieur Des Frans, Dupuis interrupted. As you see, I know a lot about your adventures, although you have never spoken to me about them. Gallouin, who played a considerable part in them, was, as you know, a close friend of mine. He died a penitent, in the odour of sanctity; let us not disturb his memory. However, in spite of my respect for Madame de Londé – his sister, who is here with us now – and for his memory, it is incumbent on me, in order to exonerate Silvie, to say that there are parts of your story about which you yourself do not have the full facts. I have told you that Gallouin did not know that Silvie was your wife, and therefore had no idea that he was doing you an injury. And that Silvie was perhaps under the influence of a force which human nature itself could not withstand, and which no woman's virtue could have resisted: to put it bluntly, Gallouin was master of some terrible, and even dangerous, secrets. I will explain more fully perhaps some other time. Silvie, though guilty to all appearances, might have been innocent at heart. That is all I have to say; you can tell us your story when you will. Madame de Londé knows what I have told her about you.

And I think everyone here is impatient to hear you. For my part, I will tell you how I know what I know when I tell my own story, as Madame de Contamine has asked me to do.

Everyone was indeed impatient to hear a story which, from what little they had heard, seemed so surprising. The table was cleared, the servants were sent away, and Des Frans was asked to begin. He said, turning his head aside, that by agreeing to tell his story, he was going to cover himself in shame and embarrassment. He remained for a few moments silent and lost in thought. Then he began, in the following words.

The Story of Monsieur Des Frans and Silvie

I am the oldest son of one of the best families in the region I come from, but less wealthy than any of my relatives, since my father followed a military career, which is not the best way to make a fortune, unlike his two younger brothers, who went into the field of finance and tax collecting, which offers more fruitful opportunities for amassing wealth. This wealth, it is said, is not always obtained by the most honourable means, but it provides power and standing enough in the world for people to disregard the method by which it was acquired. It is for this reason that I have less credit in society than my uncles and cousins.

My father was killed at the siege of Valenciennes, serving with the armies of Monsieur de Turenne and Monsieur de la Ferté; and an older son that he had had by a previous wife was killed a short time later, fighting under the command of Monsieur de Grammont, leaving me as his only heir, under the guardianship of my mother, a woman who, though of high birth, had brought little in the way of property to my father on her marriage. All of this, in addition to the debts left by my father which had to be paid off, reduced my mother and myself to a very lowly state, compared to the prominent position enjoyed by my father's younger brothers, and put us, in a sense, under their protection.

I was still a schoolboy when my father died, and I felt his

loss keenly. I felt it even more strongly when I saw how my uncles now assumed a superiority with respect to my mother and myself, which I had not been accustomed to – my father having always instilled in me a sense of the position to which my birth entitled me, one which now exceeded that allowed by my fortune. He had always spoken of his brothers with scorn, because of their employment, calling them Jews and thieves who soaked the public. This had taught me, young as I was, to feel an aversion for them, and I have always found it difficult to tolerate their demands of me, and have never felt the respect and obedience for them appropriate in a young man towards those to whom he is accountable – those who have a right to judge his behaviour and to discipline him when he is at fault.

When my schooling was completed, my uncles obtained a junior post in a government office for me. I started in this employment, but being of an independent nature, I did not take readily either to the strict hours during which I was required to be present in the office, or to being at the beck and call of my superiors. The Director complained to my uncles. I heard about his complaint, and angry words were exchanged between us. I returned to Paris without permission, leaving the office and its stacks of forms and papers to anyone who wanted them. My family was very surprised to see me back in Paris and asked for an explanation of why I had returned. I told my uncles I found working with their Director intolerable, and that our personalities were incompatible. But I told my mother what I really felt: that even if I were the most impoverished and least fortunate gentleman in France, I would not stoop to become one of those who persecute the peasants and the ordinary people; that I had a sense of honour and was not heartless enough to be party to the cruelties inflicted on the poorer orders on the pretext of raising taxes for His Majesty; that I was too humane to stand by and watch the hardships which they suffered. I told her that, far from persecuting them and ruining their livelihood, as my work had required me to do, I would prefer to give all I had to relieve and reduce their suffering. I said my father had been right to look on my uncles as Jews and usurers, and that the flunkeys they employed were like bloodhounds, who merely did their master's bidding. In a word, I concluded, it was clear I was my father's son, and, like him, I did not intend to become either a taxman or a debt collector: such occupations accorded neither with my conscience nor my honour.

My mother, who had a longer acquaintance than I with the ways of the world, did not wholly concur with my point of view. While she had tolerated my father's principles in his lifetime, they were not her own. She believed nothing was of greater importance than being rich, and since she was unable to stifle this conviction, she resented the superior airs and extravagant finery of her sisters-in-law – who were nothing but the daughters of merchants and tradespeople, but who dressed with a great deal more show than she was able to afford – she, who in my father's time had looked down her nose at them. She therefore made a number of apt and reasonable observations in response to what I had said. I should have profited from them, and there have been times since then when I have had reason to regret not doing so. But I was destined to court misfortune and, instead of listening to her good sense, I reproached her for wanting me to follow a way of life which, I told her, would cost me my immortal soul. I said my father had inspired me with a nobler sentiment, by which I intended to live, whatever others might say; and that if she had loved my father during his lifetime, she would prove it by her respect for his memory, and not violate it and her own birth by encouraging me to adopt a calling he would have deplored. I expressed my feelings on the matter so strongly that my words fell short of the respect I owed her, and I walked out, leaving her with a sense of bitter doom in her heart. She fell ill as a result, but told no one what had caused her distress. She spoke of it only to me, and this she did with a tenderness and affection that aroused such contrition in me that I promised to do whatever she wanted. Her health improved; she worked to mend relations between my uncles and myself, and the outcome was that they found another place for me, more acceptable than the previous one, about eighty leagues from Paris. Must I tell you how I behaved, and how it ended? Indeed, I cannot escape, since I am making this confession to you ...

This post was in the Ministry of Customs and Excise and was concerned with collecting the tax on alcohol. I had no great knowledge of the subject, but I had an assistant who took care of everything. All I needed to do was add my signature to the documents he prepared. It didn't take me long to become as expert as he was, however, and I soon discovered the little dishonesties he practised.

I was required to be permanently in my office from eight in the morning till midday, as well as from two till six in the afternoon. This was no great hardship in the winter, or even for the first part of the spring, but when the weather became good enough to tempt me out of doors and into the fields for some fresh air, and when I saw other young people of my age out walking and amusing themselves, the office to which I was confined became like a jailhouse for me, and I made up my mind not to be imprisoned in it.

Since I was anxious this time to remain on good terms with my mother, and not to upset Messieurs Des Frans my uncles, I told them all sorts of untruths, which I can no longer remember, though one was that I had fallen sick. They soon found that this was not the case, and plenty of good ink was expended in reproving me, and though their reprimands were justified, this did not prevent me from reacting angrily. One noontime, I received three bulky letters by the same delivery. I read them, ate my lunch, and then reread them, casting about in my mind for some new excuse, since the previous ones had not been sufficiently convincing. This preoccupied me for some time. I had forgotten that I needed to be back in my office, and it was nearly three o'clock when someone came to tell me that a large number of people were waiting to see me. I returned to my desk and found there, among the others, an official in the municipal government, a tax farmer, or 'Elu', who had come to obtain authorisations on some tax exemptions to which he had a right.

Since he considered himself a personnage of some importance, indispensable to the country's welfare and not to be trifled with, he began by taking me to task, addressing me as if I were some lowly office boy or factotum. At another time, I would have answered him roundly, and defended myself – or I might have paid him back for humiliating me, as I did some time later – but at that instant I remembered that my accounts were not in order – even my register was not up to date – and that if I did not placate him it could get me into trouble with the regional Superintendent, who unfortunately happened to be in town just then. This Superintendent was a man of upright and honest character, who consequently had limited patience for government clerks who were not conscientious in their duties. Not only would I be blamed for my absence, but he might well take it into his head to look more closely at my records, and the result might be very disadvantageous for me.

These thoughts passed through my mind in an instant, and I let the Elu say all he wished. I even attended to him first, hoping by this means to satisfy him and send him on his way. But he was not so easily mollified. On the contrary, his sermonising continued: that this was not what the King expected of those who served him; that precise hours of duty were prescribed, during which it was incumbent on me to be present in my office, so that an official (I am not sure he did not add 'of his importance') would neither be kept waiting, nor have to send for me. He said he would be making a complaint to the Superintendent (whom he referred to moreover none too respectfully, barely giving him his official title), who would be more than ready to teach me my duty, since I did not as yet seem to be fully aware of it. This was what I most feared. I therefore heard him out, with such self-control and patience that even I myself was surprised. I overwhelmed him with civility. I owned that I had been in the wrong. I showed him the letters I had received, in an effort to offer an excuse for myself, but he was unmoved and told me that I could just as well have read them, not in my private quarters, but in my office – after having dealt with his business. I contained myself until I had seen him off the premises and into the street, but I was seething inwardly, and promised to even the score and make him regret the way he had treated me.

I began that evening to make a serious effort to bring my accounts up to date. It was not long before I had done so. Everything was in order within four days and I no longer feared a visit from the Superintendent – the only way the Elu could have caused trouble for me. News of the harangue he had subjected me to soon spread around the town. He boasted of having put me in my place so effectively that I had not dared say a word to defend myself. People found this surprising, as I did not have a reputation for forbearance. When anyone mentioned the matter to me, I admitted it was true and said, since I was in the wrong, there would have been no point and no honour in trying to defend a bad cause. I began to acquire a name as a man of moderation who would not be drawn into a dispute. Efforts were made to reconcile the two of us, and the Elu made some sort of apology for having lost his temper. I avoided all further discussion of the matter, merely repeating that I had been in the wrong and biding my time – while still resolved to have my revenge. I had nothing to fear: my affairs were in order, and I was ready to account for them; moreover, I was not unduly anxious to remain in this employment.

He returned about two weeks later with a fairly large packet of papers which he needed to dispatch without delay. Messengers, whose time was being charged to his account, were ready and waiting to leave and carry them to their various destinations as soon as they were signed. He was doing some business, buying and selling wine and using fictitious names, and needed to have these papers approved. It was only ten in the morning, and everything could have been completed in a quarter of an hour, but I suddenly thought of a way to repay him for the insulting treatment he had meted out to me. I received him with the utmost affability. I turned over his papers one by one, chattering the while on a variety of matters. We discussed the goings-on in the town, the news of the Court, and of the war. I employed every commonplace one can imagine to prolong the conversation, allowing time to slip by. He was a man of strong opinions, and prided himself on his knowledge of politics and local events – as if he were the editor of some local news-sheet. I expressed some disagreements, in order to make him develop his argument. He began to flounder, and I made my point. It struck twelve just as I reached the last of his documents: all that was needed was a signature, which could have been given in a moment. He thought this was what would happen and that his business would thus be completed. I had been chatting to him with such familiarity that he took me for a simpleton. He was wrong. I rose and announced coldly that he would have to return at two o'clock. His face fell. He begged me just to add the final signature. I refused. I have not forgotten the lesson you gave me, I said with some dignity. The King requires me to be in my office at two o'clock. But equally, I have not forgotten that I am to close my office at twelve noon. His protestations were in vain; he had no alternative but to accept my decision. He was furious, and even more so when I gave my servant instructions, in front of him, to go and invite two men whom I knew were his mortal enemies to have lunch with me. He left, and by way of farewell I said cheerily, 'Till two o'clock, then, Monsieur.'

The two men came, and I told them how I had treated the Elu. They were heartily amused and thoroughly approved of what I had done. We ate our lunch, and I went back to my office at precisely two o'clock. The Elu was too angry to come back himself; he sent a servant to collect his papers. It was not one of his own servants that he sent, but even if it had been I would have done the same thing to annoy him. I refused to hand the papers over except to the person who had originally brought them. The servant came back bringing a note. I gave it back to him, saying he must tell his master that I did not wish to keep papers in my possession other than those for which I was directly responsible, but that I could only return his into his own hands. He was miserly, and his envoys and couriers were being paid for their time, as I have said, and eventually he had no alternative but to come himself; but he was so gruff and ill at ease that I could not refrain from laughing. This made him even more angry, and he would have started another argument with me, but I no longer feared the Superintendent and was so much master of the situation that he realised his only escape was through the door. The two men with whom I had lunched enraged him further by their laughter and by imitating his manner to each other – without saying a word. They spread the story round, and, as it was only a small town, everyone had heard it before the day was out, and the Elu had been given a nickname he has never shaken off, for since that day he has been known not by his own name, but as 'Monsieur l'Elu at two o'clock'. The story even reached the ears of the Superintendent, who merely laughed at it. And indeed, an official of the Elu's rank was not a sufficiently elevated personnage in my estimation to have the right to order me about and tell me what I should or should not do.

I had had my revenge, but I was still a mere clerk in an office. It shamed me – the son of a valiant soldier who had died serving his King – to be spending my life in a remote province, in a dusty office, while other young men, whose equal I was in birth, were either in the Musketeers or serving in other posts which enabled them to win honour by their military exploits, and doing what I would have wished to be doing. My mind and spirit were so overwhelmed with this thought that I actually became ill. The Superintendent found a temporary replacement for me until I recovered my health. This substitute was a young man from Paris, of the same age as myself, with plenty of common sense. He was in fact your brother, Madame, Des Frans continued, turning to Madame de Mongey. When I regained my health, I had no wish to reclaim my post. I wrote to those responsible, recommending that my replacement be retained, and made the same representations to the Superintendent, to whom I explained my own reservations about my work. And my uncles, who were satisfied with his work, and had other plans for me, allowed him to have my place. His official nomination to the position was sent to me, and I handed it to him myself. He was extremely grateful – more grateful than he need have been, for I was indebted to him, since it was through him that I first met you. I am genuinely saddened by his death, which I heard of from Monsieur Des Ronais.

No longer having any employment in the provinces and nothing to do there, I returned to Paris and remained here longer than I expected, awaiting instructions from my uncles, who had at present found no position of the sort they wanted for me, for they wanted to choose what I was to do. And since the season for military campaigns was over, I was forced, as ill luck would have it, to spend the autumn and winter in Paris. I say 'ill luck', for had I been anywhere else, I would not have gone astray as I did – through no other fault than my own, though it seemed as if I was under some force which I did not understand, and which has led me to believe that, even if our actions appear entirely voluntary, we can nonetheless say that our life is not always governed by our free will; but that it is the stars that rule the major events and their outcome. Indeed, all my reason could do was to show me the disaster that lay ahead, and my own weakness, but it did not give me the strength to save myself.

I went to Mass at Notre-Dame on Nativity Day, the 8th of September. I had placed myself near one of the pillars. A grey-robed Sister of the Order of St Vincent de Paul – those who care for foundlings – came up to me and asked if I would serve as godfather to an infant who was about to be baptised, who had been found abandoned only the previous night. It is the practice to choose someone who appears to have a certain standing in society and make this request of them, in the hope of receiving a gift towards their charitable work. I did not refuse the request. The Sister asked me whom I would like to invite to be godmother to share the duties with me, and I pointed out a nicely dressed young woman, in half-mourning, who was accompanied by a girl whom I took to be her servant. The Sister went to speak to the young woman, and I thought it seemed she did not immediately acquiesce. I went and presented myself; she responded politely, in a manner that persuaded me she was no ordinary person, and she agreed to serve with me as a godparent to the child. I sent a lackey who was with me to find a carriage, telling him to meet me at the Foundlings Hospital. I gave the young lady my hand. She had a servant-boy with her as well as her lady's maid, which added to the favourable impression I was already forming. We stood godfather and godmother for the child, in the usual way, disputing between us as to who should choose a name, and in the end, since the infant was a girl, it was she who made the choice. The orphans of the institution came and asked for alms, and as these poor children do indeed deserve our compassion, and since I was beginning to have the wish to make my companion think well of me, I gave a sum which was, if not in keeping with my means, at least in keeping with this wish; and she for her part gave what was a handsome amount for a woman.

Since my gift had been sufficient to buy me some favour, I asked the Sister if it would be possible to arrange for us to lunch at the Hospital. I told her that, since I had not yet eaten, the odours which abounded – even though this was a children's home, not a hospital – were making me feel slightly queasy. In fact, I have always suffered in this way if I am deprived of a meal. I am not sure if the Sister accepted my word for it, or whether I was indeed, as she said, beginning to look faint. She took me into a small refectory, and my companion followed. We were given some pieces of beef straight from the pot, and some grilled lamb cutlets. I told my companion I would rather have given her other food than this, but that I had not dared ask her to accompany me further afield. I said I had not wished to see her depart without at least wishing her good health, and had seized on the first idea that came into my head. She accepted this explanation, though claiming that if she had thought I was asking for refreshment only because of her, she would have refused. She had been convinced I really did need sustenance, since I had suddenly turned pale, and for that reason she had agreed to accompany me here, rather than cause any delay, she said.

My servant had brought a carriage, and I handed her into

it, and her servant-girl, who had been with us all the time, climbed in after her. My companion dispensed with all those excessive niceties which a certain segment of society indulge in – tediously exaggerating and reiterating expressions of gratitude or delight. From her behaviour, I judged she not only knew the proprieties, but also knew how to combine a decorous modesty with an honest and open manner – something one learns only in the company of people of quality. My good opinion of her thus increased the more. The ease and naturalness of her conversation, and the versatility of her expression, reinforced this opinion, and I came to the conclusion that one could not find a more beautiful or accomplished person.

Since it is she who was the cause of all my wayward behaviour and of all my misfortunes – which resulted from the love for her which filled my heart; and since it was her beauty and her admirable qualities alone which can excuse the violence of my passion and the ardour of my pursuit, I owe it to you to draw her portrait, so that you can understand that the excesses I fell into stemmed from the fact that she was the most beautiful and fascinating person one can imagine.

I realise, dear ladies, Des Frans added, interrupting his narrative, that what I have just said is somewhat ungalant, but I beg that you forgive my incivility and attribute it to my need to paint her as more attractive than perhaps she was. She was no more than nineteen years old, a little above average height, and a delight to behold – so slender that I could clasp her waist – even fully dressed – within my two hands. She had wavy hair, which was a foot longer than her own height, and of the most beautiful chestnut colour you can imagine. To have it combed, she stood on a table and her maid and her aunt (whom I will soon be telling you more about) occupied themselves with the task. Her forehead was smooth and white; her large wide-set black eyes had a languid look. Sometimes, though, her gaze could be so piercing that one could not meet it without turning away. Her eyebrows were of the same colour as her hair; her nose was well formed, narrow and slightly aquiline. Her snow-white complexion and naturally rosy cheeks produced a delightful effect. She had a small mouth, given to laughter, and full red lips. She had an oval face; her teeth were white and even; her chin rounded, with a little dimple. Her neck was of a dazzling white; her skin was soft and delicate. Her breast rose and fell with perfect regularity as she breathed, testament to her perfect good health. Her bust was small and firm, and she sometimes said to me in jest that a woman's breast was large enough if it was sufficient for an honest man to cup in his hand. Her arms and hands were plump. She walked like a princess. She could dance to perfection and sang equally well, and played both the piano and the guitar with competence. She was neither thin nor buxom, but perfectly proportioned, somewhere between the two.

That is the very portrait of Silvie, said Des Ronais. It is she whose picture I was painting, said Des Frans. You have given us the portrait of a woman of perfect beauty, said Madame de Contamine. As far as appearance goes, said Des Frans, no one could be more beautiful. Her intellectual qualities appeared to be of equal merit – she had more wit than all other deceiving women combined. She could dissimulate; she could change her voice and expression as promptly and effortlessly as the best actress might after spending hours carefully studying a role. She appeared totally sincere, but she was fickle, duplicitous and bent on pleasure, especially sensual pleasure, in pursuit of which she would sacrifice everything: honour, duty, money and virtue. She was bold to the point of effrontery. In a word, she incorporated every beauty in her person, and every vice in her character, though she knew so well how to disguise the vices that her appearance gave a completely false picture; and I myself, after having known her extremely well for two years, would have sworn she was honest, faithful and selfless – that is to say, I would have sworn she was as full of good qualities as she appeared to be. I only found the contrary to be true after marrying her.

You were married? said Madame de Mongey. Yes, Madame, answered Des Frans, I was. I am not surprised that this astonishes you. For my part, said Dupuis, I thought as much. For better or worse, continued Des Frans, it was so. And this is the secret I am grateful to my family for having preserved, and I beg you all to reveal it to no one. I still have reasons for keeping the fact hidden. But let me continue: I have even more surprising things to tell you.

When we left the Foundlings Hospital, I accompanied her to her home. She lived some distance away, but not far from the neighbourhood where I myself lived. She lived with a woman who was thought to be her aunt, but who was in fact no such thing. Silvie invited me into the house; I accepted. It was an attractive building, and her rooms were magnificently furnished. Her aunt was not present, and I was alone with Silvie, on whom I can have made no very favourable impression – I was too disturbed to be able to conduct a reasonable conversation. I merely asked for permission to call on her again – permission which was granted politely enough. It was all I could hope for.

I was a changed man when I left her, and so lost in thought I hardly knew myself. My love for her never increased – from that moment I loved her with my whole heart. The rules of etiquette required that I should let some time elapse before paying my next visit. I wished to conform to these rules, but was unable to do so. That very evening, I returned to walk past her house. She was sitting outside the door with some other young ladies who were her neighbours, but there was no man with them. I walked back and forth until eleven o'clock, when they went indoors. I returned the next day and saw her set out with several young ladies for a walk outside the ramparts. They sat on the grass and began to sing. Silvie sang the following lines from Arethusa's part in Lully's opera *Proserpine*:

I fear I shall give way
His persistence knows no bounds
And if he were to stay
I know my heart's response.

Her voice was divine, and I could not resist the temptation: I walked towards her and she recognised me, greeting me politely. These girls were daughters of the bourgeoisie, and since my dress indicated a somewhat nobler rank, they received me well. I took Silvie's hand: those who were watching were somewhat surprised by the freedom of this gesture, but we were not unduly concerned about this. You have a lover whose pursuit you may not be able to resist, my dear friend? I said, helping her to rise. How happy he must be to inspire such an emotion in a person like you. Oh no, Monsieur, she answered, laughing. The sentiments expressed in my song are not my own! The melody is new and pretty, and I have been told I perform it reaonably well – that is my only reason for singing it. It has no special meaning for me, she said. But I will not repeat the rest of our conversation. It was too long for me to remember it all. But everything she said delighted me. I admired the aptness of her ideas and the way she expressed herself. I was thoroughly charmed.

I accompanied her home. On the way, I invited her and her friends into a lemonade shop, but she refused. You have not been fasting today, she said, smiling, and we are not at a Foundlings Home now! I do not believe that you are feeling faint. I do not feel as strong as I might, I said. Your presence

causes a weakness in my heart, and I therefore need sustenance to help me regain my strength. You seem to be
subject to these attacks of weakness, she said, but it is fortunate that they occur only where there is an eating place,
or other remedy near at hand. However, this evening, you
must forego the restorative: your health will not be endan-
gered even if you suffer a little discomfort! But you do not
know, I continued in the same bantering tone, if I have
some new heartache, that no simple nourishment will cure.
I am certain that your good health will ensure your recovery, she answered. At least, your indisposition cannot be
grave, since it does not prevent you from laughing. You are
hard-hearted, I answered. And you are hard to believe when
you plead you are unwell, she replied.

We reached her front door, where we found her aunt, to
whom I introduced myself. Silvie informed her that it was I
who had served with her as a godparent two days before,
and we exchanged formal greetings. I then went on my way,
my mind occupied with delightful thoughts. The beauty of
Silvie's voice when she sang had done nothing to diminish
her charm for me, since I have loved music all my life. The
next day, I paid a visit in due form, during the day. I found
her more appealing than ever; she performed on several
instruments, which she played delightfully. We spoke of this
and that, and though I stayed for three hours, it seemed like
only a moment. I returned later in the day after supper and
said that, since I was a neighbour, I had come to pass the
evening with her and her companions. The weather was not
good enough for us to go out walking, and we spent the
time dancing to the accompaniment of songs. I was completely overcome and had no further resistance to offer. I
have never seen anyone dance so captivatingly. When I left,
I was walking on air. I could not explain what had happened
to me, except to say that I had never encountered anyone so
charming or so accomplished.

A few days later, I arranged for us all to make an excursion outside Paris, that is, Silvie, her aunt and the three neighbours who were her usual companions. Inevitably, a meal featured in our entertainment, and I made the best arrangements I could. My companions seemed pleased with the outing, but I was not, since I had not had enough time to organise the event as I would have wished.

Coming down the steps outside the inn, Silvie tripped. My immediate and anxious concern revealed the interest I took in her. I sent a man with all speed to fetch a carriage from Paris, for, being on foot, we had come only a quarter of a league. She was grateful for this attention. Her foot swelled, and she was obliged to stay in her bed, to which I had carried her, for two weeks. I remained with her constantly, leaving only at mealtimes – and if she had wished, I would not have left even then. Her aunt was remarkably tolerant. Aunts are not usually so amenable. No hindrance or limits were placed on my visits; my presence was accepted without question. Though both women knew what brought me there, nothing was said. Only my eyes and my actions made it clear. I was certain these were understood, and though Silvie remained very reserved with me, I felt sure I could read her secret feelings in her eyes.

Eventually I spoke. I said I loved her more than anyone had ever loved before, and asked her to whom I should speak to ask for her hand. She dispensed with the display of affected modesty that young ladies usually employ in such circumstances. Instead, she said she was flattered by the sentiments I had expressed and grateful for the honour I did her. But she begged me, for my own good, not to give way to a temporary emotion which I might one day have reason to regret. I swore my eternal devotion. I told her my love was for all time and proof against any eventuality, and that, loving her as I did, I could never repent of any commitment I made to her. I said she was the first person I had ever loved, and that she would certainly also be the last. I do not flatter myself, she said, with the belief that I am either beautiful or deserving enough to inspire such a strong emotion. Listen to what I have to say, she continued. Choose a more deserving object for your affection. You think you love me: you are mistaken, and I too would be making a mistake if I were to believe you at your word. You know neither who I am nor what I might be. Perhaps I am so much above you in station that I should be misleading you if I allowed you to continue your attentions to me. Or perhaps I am so much beneath you that you would come to feel shame over any attachment you showed for me. Therefore, both for your sake and mine, separate yourself from me while you can still do so with honour.

No, Mademoiselle, I said. It is no longer within my power to free myself. Your advice comes too late. In all that you have said, the only thing that gives me cause for fear is an inequality in birth. I do not wish for a difference in your favour – it would be to my disadvantage and despair. If your birth is so far above mine that I cannot hope to aspire to your hand, my distress will prove to you the sincerity of my devotion and respect – which no distinction of birth could increase. But if your birth should prove inferior to mine, my love will overcome all obstacles. Take care in what you say, she repeated. Make no protestations you may come to regret. Let me remind you once again, you do not know me, or who I am. I know you, I answered, as I shall always know you, as the most beautiful and accomplished person in the world. Nothing else is of any importance. It is you yourself who delight me, and you alone . . . It is your own wishful eyes which imbue me with all these qualities, she interrupted. If they were unblinkered, my attractions would be less potent. Believe me, do not persist in this blind devotion. I am not worthy of such sentiments. Recover your former self and proceed with more caution. And to ensure that you will not

316

one day come to hate me more than you now love me, do not depend so much on an attachment which could bring you shame.

I made every effort for a long time to persuade her to tell me more about herself, and to find out what her feelings for me were, but I could discover nothing. I could see by her behaviour that I did not displease her, but I wanted her to declare that it was so, and this she refused to do. It was not that I had any jealousy. I had never seen a man either in the house or in her company. I was the only one who called on her. I made enquiries of her neighbours and was told that the house was a veritable convent – that no man was ever seen there. Moreover, she herself rarely went out, and when she did, it would only be to visit friends in the neighbourhood to do some needlework. She never went anywhere beyond the immediate vicinity. More often, the young ladies who lived nearby would come to her house with their sewing and handwork. These were her only visitors. Nothing was known about her family: I was told only that she and her aunt had been living in this house about eighteen months, and that they had been wearing deep mourning when they first took up residence. They lived very quietly and I was the only man who ever visited. This information threw me into paroxysms of anxiety. I longed to discover who she was – but the time for this had not yet arrived.

At this point, my uncles found another position for me, but since it was outside Paris I was unwilling to accept it, and told my mother that though I realised how indebted I was to her and my uncles, and though I had resolved to do exactly as they wished, I begged her not to insist that I accept the type of position they were offering. I said that, because of my distaste for such duties, I would be doomed to make enemies for myself, and my good name would be destroyed without benefiting my fortune. I told her my conscience would never be at peace in such an occupation. I admitted it was necessary for me to establish myself in some profession, but I begged her to leave the choice to me. I intimated that the law would be more acceptable to me, and that I believed I would be reasonably happy in some judicial function. I pointed out that my father's legacy was not completely exhausted, and that, as a result of her good management, it would be possible to purchase an office of some sort for me and thereby not put the family to shame. She accepted all of this, or at least appeared to. She conferred with my uncles, who agreed to let me do as I wished. I therefore resumed my legal studies. What a transformation! I, who had formerly had such a deep-seated hatred for the law, or anything to do with pen and parchment – who had hankered after and breathed only the sword and the battlefield! – I was returning to my studies and was on my way to spending my days haunting the corridors of the Palais de Justice in a drab and dusty robe! I was not pleased with myself, or with the direction in which my infatuation was leading me. But it was not the only unfortunate step that love has led me to take. My passion dominated everything. It was stronger than I was. I sacrificed all to it: my honour, my integrity, my family, my fortune – and my choice of profession. I saw nothing except through the prism of my love.

Since my visits to Silvie were too frequent and too pro-longed to be kept secret, word of them reached my mother's ears. She knew that I was madly in love and it was obvious that this was why I had refused my uncles' offer, but she was good enough to refrain from revealing this fact to them. She knew that I would not yield to pressure, so she tried to influence me through kindness and understanding, but this proved no more successful. Silvie seemed ever more beautiful. Every means possible to remove me from Paris was tried. Appeals were made to my honour, or I was tempted with ways in which to improve my fortune, but I rejected everything. Silvie inevitably knew of the opportunities I was giving up for her sake, and knew that the decisions I made were the result of my love for her and her hold over me. She pretended to make efforts to bring me back to my senses, which it was clear I had lost. But her efforts only had the opposite effect.

Meantime, I was still endeavouring to uncover the mystery of her birth and often tried to persuade her to enlighten me, but she would tell me nothing, and I would have remained in ignorance if some information had not fallen into my hands in a surprising fashion.

I was leaving her house one evening in January. It was nearly midnight. The night was extremely dark. Earth and sky were all completely black. My way had been lit by a lackey carrying a flaming torch, but this was blown out by the wind; no lantern remained lit, and I was groping my way along. I heard someone nearby and asked who was there. A man's voice asked if I was not Monsieur Des Frans. Yes, it is I, I answered. What do you want? Here, he said, my orders are to deliver this packet into your own hands. Do not try to find who sent it, but look into the truth of what it contains. It is in your interest to do so. He handed me a sealed package and walked away. I cannot say I lost sight of him, as I had never been able to see him. I called, but he did not answer. I walked on, in considerable unease as to what anyone was communicating to me in this extraordinary fashion. I tore open the envelope, there and then, as if it were possible to read it – when I could not even see what street I was in! I realised the futility of what I was doing and, thrusting the whole thing into my pocket, continued on my way to my mother's house. As soon as I reached my room, I opened the packet and, by the light of a candle, saw the first words:

Notice to Monsieur Des Frans concerning his love for Silvie

319

There were three sheets of paper covered with very small writing in a man's hand. It was clear they would take some time to read, so I took them to my bed with me. I will not repeat the contents in full – I cannot remember the exact wording. However, the gist was: that I thought this girl whom I loved was a vestal virgin and came of good family; that the engagement into which I was rushing headlong horrified those who had my interests at heart, and my friendship with her was shameful in every respect; it was pitiful to see me so deceived by a girl who had so little merit. I was told she had never known her father or mother, and that she had been brought up in the institution where she and I had served together as godmother and godfather. She had been abandoned at birth by her parents, and taken to this Foundlings Hospital, where she had remained till she was eight years old. My correspondent admitted that she was beautiful, and said it was because of her beauty that Madame la Duchesse de Cranves – who had no children of her own – had taken her into her home. Silvie had lived there till the age of eighteen, and it was there that she had learnt the social graces and been educated in all that a girl should know. Though she had been surrounded by nothing but examples of virtue, her own conduct had come under suspicion, though the writer could not categorically assert that it had been criminal. Yet it appeared Madame de Cranves had not been entirely content, since in her will, she had not bequeathed to Silvie all she had promised: only a small sum of money, some furniture and an annuity. There had been a rumour that Silvie had been in league with one of Madame de Cranves's ladies-in-waiting – the one most trusted by her mistress, by the name of la Morin, with whom Silvie was now living and who passed for her aunt; and that some jewellery had been taken, along with a considerable sum of money that the Duchess had held in cash just prior to her death, and which had not been found thereafter. The story was that this theft had been instigated by a young man named Garreau, the Duchess's secretary and overseer, who had told the two women where the money was kept. It was further said that this young man had pledged to marry Silvie; indeed, it was he who was rumoured to be her lover. This was what people thought, but nothing had been proved, because the man had been arrested on suspicion of theft by the Duchess's heirs and had died in prison.

The writer of these pages urged me to reflect on all these matters concerning Silvie: her birth, her actions, the suspicions of theft and licentiousness. Finally, the writer said he refrained from giving me any advice: he believed I was too sensible and well born to do anything unworthy of a man of honour, and scion of a distinguished family, and he regretted that I had been so blinded by my attraction to this girl. A copy of this letter, it was stated, had been sent to my mother. The letter had not been delivered to me at my home, as that would have made it appear that it came from my uncles, and this was not the case. It had not been given to me in daylight, for fear I should see the messenger, who was also the writer, and who had not wanted to confide the task to anyone but himself. I could put the information contained to Silvie in person, without showing her the letter, and she would not be able to deny that it was true. In any case, certain people who were named, and whose address was given, could tell me all I wanted to know about Silvie, since they had known her over a long period of time in Madame de Cranves's household, where they had been servants from the time when Silvie first arrived until the time of the Duchess's death.

You can imagine how I felt as I read this. At one moment I was inclined to dismiss it all as invention, and at the next I thought it may be true. I could fix on neither one opinion nor the other. I remembered that Silvie had always refused to give me any indication of what her birth or family might be. This lent credence to the view that what was written was true. There were innumerable ways I could respond to these revelations, but I could settle on none of them. I spent the whole night considering what action I should take. I read and reread the letter. I cursed its author for having enlightened me. A moment later when my reason reasserted itself, I recognised that I was greatly indebted to him for having rescued me at the brink of a shameful abyss. In a word, a struggle was being played out within me between my love and my honour. At nine the next morning, I had still resolved nothing, when my mother came to my room, holding some papers in her hand. I know what you have come to tell me, Mother, I said. The letter you have in your hand is mentioned here. This is a fine revelation! she said. So, you know now the truth about the young woman, but you have not seen the warnings I have been given. Here they are, she said. Read this paper, then bring it back to me in my room as soon as you have finished. She threw onto my bed a piece of paper similar to the ones I was already holding in my hand. It was headed:

To Madame Des Frans on the matter of her son's behaviour

It told her that I had been given enough information to unseal my eyes about Silvie, but that no course of action had been proposed, because it was better for me to take my own decision about how to act, rather than be provided with advice. It was presumed that I was honourable and responsible enough to make a proper choice, whereas I would resent being told what to do: a good outcome was more likely to ensue if I acted of my own free will, but it was for her to determine how to convince me of the shocking and disgraceful nature of my attachment. The writer suggested that I would benefit from a period of time abroad, and that the diversion of travel, or of some employment in the provinces, would allow time for my unfortunate passion to subside. According to him, Silvie and la Morin were extremely dangerous. He claimed that as soon as I started visiting them, they had resolved to ensnare me. Silvie was to give the impression of being more virtuous than was perhaps the case, and la Morin would play the role of her aunt, allowing me complete freedom to visit her supposed niece, while the latter would allow me no privileges. They had made enquiries about my family to determine whether I would fulfil their requirements, and were satisfied on this score, having learnt that I was an only son and my own master, without legal guardians, and that I was sufficiently wealthy to provide them with the comfortable style of life they sought. They were convinced that, when I was deeply enough ensnared, and as inextricably in love as possible, they would be able to persuade me to ignore or dispense with any parental or family consent to an alliance. The only stumbling-block was the question of Silvie's birth. They had tried, with the bribe of a hundred gold louis, to tempt a penniless gentleman to vouch for Silvie as his daughter; he could do this with apparent validity, as his own daughter, who was about the same age as Silvie, had recently died while travelling to Paris from her home in the country. The letter to my mother contained the name and address of this gentleman. It also hinted that Silvie had perhaps offered him something else – a fact which it might be possible to elicit from him, as he was wont to imbibe his wine freely, and his tongue was liable to run loose when he was in his cups. The writer of the letter stated that the two women were so certain that their plot was going to succeed that la Morin had allowed herself to tell a former member of Madame de Cranves's staff, whom she thought she could trust, that Silvie's beauty was making her fortune and that she was about to wed a rich young man of good family.

This missive concluded by advising my mother that, if I

remained obstinate and persisted in my intention of marrying Silvie, against all the dictates of honour and virtue, she should resort to whatever means she could find to prevent the marriage, even if this meant serving an injunction on Silvie and la Morin for attempted subornation, and even if it meant having me locked up, under the jurisdiction of my family, and deprived of my freedom of movement temporarily. There was no time to be lost, she was told; she should act promptly, for once a religious ceremony between Silvie and me had taken place, it would at best cost a great deal of money to undo the affair, supposing this were even possible – not to mention the shame which would torment me and cause me eternal regret, as soon as my passion – or the charm I was under – subsided, as it inevitably would, once we were married. The writer of the letter insisted that he was not motivated by any ill-will towards Silvie, but only by the concern he felt for a well-respected family, and by his sympathy for a young man who was blinded by a shameful and unworthy infatuation, and was about to bring about his own downfall, unless prevented from doing so.

This gave me further food for reflexion, as you will readily understand. My mind was made up. The picture I had been given of Silvie was sufficient to make her repugnant to me. I rose from where I was sitting and went to my mother's room. So, my son, she said, what is your decision? Can there be any doubt? I answered, with a disdainful laugh. I should think myself unworthy to be your son if I did not realise I had been wasting my time over this woman. I thank the author of these pages, and consider him – without knowing who he is – as the best friend I have, someone who has saved me from disaster. There is no need to employ the desperate measures he mentions. I loved Silvie: I would be lying if I denied it. But I did not know her, and what I have learnt can only make me despise her. I beg you not to return to the subject. I am mortified by it, and shall remember her only as a subject of merriment and scorn. The whole world would be entitled to treat me as a laughing-stock if I took the matter seriously. Find some pretext for me to leave Paris forthwith – some errand for me to undertake, an ambassadorial expedition for me to accompany, a military campaign for me to join – some expedient such as you suggested previously. I am ready to leave. My change of heart is genuine – that you may count on.

What a relief it is, she said, to see you recovered from your foolishness! I believe you are being honest with me. I will never refer to the matter again. There is no need to dwell on past mistakes. There is no more to be said on the subject. I even think this experience may make you more prudent in future. Was Silvie always prudent in her conduct with you? she continued. Yes, I answered, she was. Her virtue and modesty – which I believed to be genuine – were not the least part of her attraction for me. Certainly, if she had betrayed the least hint of indiscretion, I would have been less devoted to her. You were not so badly matched, after all! laughed my mother. One deceiver deserves another! But she was smarter than you, and she fooled you. Here, she said, take these papers. I have no more need of them. I will see your uncles at dinner. I am beginning to weary of all these efforts to protect you and keep you out of mischief! And I begin to fear their patience will be exhausted, like mine. Every day one is back at the starting point with you! For Heaven's sake, this time at least, for once in your life, try to buckle down to an honest train of life! Give people a chance to say something good about you! If this experience hasn't taught you a lesson, nothing ever will! Promises are all very well, she said, but I won't be happy until you are safely out of Paris. Be off with you, and buy two horses, one for you and one for your servant.

I swore to her that my heart and my mouth spoke as one and that I was ready to mount a horse and ride off that minute, and that I would never again look at or give a thought to such a despicable creature as the one with whom I had but recently been entranced. In a word, I said exactly what someone truly repenting of his follies would say, and I would have sworn that I meant it. But I did not yet know the extent of my own weakness. Or rather, perhaps what I did not know was that my destruction was written in the stars, and that I was destined to succumb to the peril which threatened, and did not have the strength to escape it.

Scarcely had I left my mother's room than I became prey to a thousand uncertainties. I had no wish to see Silvie: I considered her unworthy even of my disdain. My indignation and scorn could not have been greater, yet my anger made me think it would be a pleasure to find out more about the deception that was being hatched against me, and that it might be gratifying to cross-examine this gentleman, my would-be father-in-law. I knew his name – Rouvière – and had his address. I made my way to the inn where he had his lodging, found him and approached him, on the pretext of seeing two horses, which I claimed to have been told he had for sale. As chance would have it, there were indeed two horses for sale at this inn, but belonging to some other gentleman. I saw them, and since the man to whom they belonged was elsewhere, I had to await his return. Everything conspired to forward my design. I asked Rouvière if he would join me for lunch while we waited. He was more than willing, and we went to a nearby eating house.

I plied him with drink, while excusing myself from indulging, saying I was recovering from some illness. This was readily believable, as I was out of sorts. Just then, the Marquis de Querville, the owner of the horses, and brother-in-law of Monsieur Des Prez, whose story you have heard, arrived. As he was eager to sell his horses and I was eager to buy them, we soon came to an agreement, and I had the animals sent to my home. I invited Monsieur de Querville to stay and eat with us to seal the bargain, and he was ready to do so; but midday struck and he was obliged to leave us, telling us he had some business of the greatest importance to which he must attend, but if I could wait half an hour, he would be back. It suited me perfectly to be left alone with my man for this time. I promised Querville that we would be there when he returned.

The two of us were now alone, and I questioned this man, Rouvière, about his family, what part of France he came from, his property, his fortune, how he occupied himself, and why he was here in Paris. I accompanied each question with a large glass of wine. He answered me as if he were kneeling before his confessor. He was, it appeared, a gentleman from Le Mans. He was extremely poor, since he had attached himself and his fortune to a prince who had exhausted both his own wealth and that of many another who had supported his cause during the troubles. Rouvière seemed well informed about these matters; indeed, he spoke as if he had been a participant in them. He deplored his misfortune. He told me he had had a daughter whom he had hoped to place with some noblewoman, and that he had been bringing her to Paris, but that on the journey she had died, at Illiers, after only two days of illness. He had continued on to Paris, in order to approach the son of this prince whom he had followed, to make a claim for a pension, which would enable him to eke out a living in his declining days, or perhaps to seek some employment with the army whereby he would at least earn his food. This all accorded with the information in my mother's letter, and I was about to ask him if he did not know Silvie and her aunt, when he brought the subject up himself.

He told me he had counted Madame la Duchesse de Cranves among his acquaintance, and that she had died about two years previously, a source of regret to him, because she would have given him assistance; at the very least she would have taken his daughter into her household. His daughter was at least as worthy of help as another young woman whom Madame de Cranves had rescued from an orphans' home, he declared. Without betraying any particular interest, I asked him what he meant by this, and he told me the story of Silvie as it had been written to me, word for word. He had nothing good to say about her, or about the young man who had died in prison. He concluded by saying that yet, when all was said and done, there were those who were lucky and those who were unlucky in this world. For in spite of all her misdoings, she had nonetheless found herself a good match, a young man who was enormously rich, with no dependants, only a mother, a devout woman interested only in her religion. This young man asked for nothing better than to marry Silvie. It was true, he added, that the suitor did not know the story of her birth or of her unsavoury escapades. But, he went on, with a laugh, beauty is apparently all that counts. La Morin, he continued, who poses as her aunt and who was an accomplice in the theft I mentioned, wants me to give a little help in promoting this marriage and has promised me a sizable inducement – a hundred gold louis! And how could you be of help? I said. She wants me to assume the guise of Silvie's father, he answered, and sign the contract of marriage – passing her off as my daughter. If I added a little nobility to her escutcheon, this would not diminish her appeal in her lover's eyes, it seems! But, I continued, a deception of that sort, were it ever to come to light, could have serious consequences and get you into trouble with the law. Yes, indeed, he said, but where is the law going to find me? I have neither hearth nor home. And besides, who is going to look any further and cause trouble? Not Silvie or la Morin, and the husband will believe whatever he is told and look no further. And if he did look further, he would find I had a daughter of the age of Silvie, who had lived quietly in the provinces, in a convent with my sister. No one in those parts knows of my daughter's death. And Silvie has been living a very retired sort of existence, keeping herself to herself, unknown and in an out-of-the-way neighbourhood. And after her marriage, she expects to live in Poitou, where it is said her husband-to-be has property.

But in one way or another, I said, such facts often come to the surface. That is not what worries me or makes me hesitate, he said. Once I have the money, I shall not stay in these parts long enough to be in any danger. What is it that makes you hesitate then, I asked. I have some misgivings, he answered, about deceiving a young man of good family who is honourable and upright. But I will overcome those scruples if Silvie gives me what I want. What more can you ask then, I said with a laugh. Isn't a hundred louis enough for you? Yes, he said, as far as the money goes, I am quite satisfied, but I wouldn't mind stealing a march on my supposed son-in-law. In a word, I would not be unhappy if there were some truth in it when I said Silvie belonged to me – and this is what I want before I agree to sign anything. You understand what I am saying? This is a scurrilous condition you are imposing for your assistance! I said with a laugh. Isn't it enough to deceive the young man so callously, without robbing him further? Maybe, he said, shrugging his shoulders. But you are being overscrupulous. Am I not as good as a general factotum or manager in Madame de Cranves's service, with whom Silvie was involved, so the duchess's butler tells me? And if the husband is to be a cuckold, does it make so much difference whether there have been one or more incumbents before he takes over the lease? And ... But, I interrupted, the husband will discover that he is not the first owner of his property. He would need to be more perspicacious than the Devil himself! Rouvière answered. Even doctors and midwives know little enough. I wrote to Silvie, he continued, and she refuses point blank:

she pretends to be all sweetness and innocence. But if she won't agree, I won't help her. She is young, comely and beautiful. I have committed a thousand sins of the flesh in my time, with far less pleasant companions – one more will not make my conscience that much heavier!

All this was said in such a straightforward, uncomplicated way that I could not help but laugh, in spite of the indignation I felt towards someone so dishonest and dangerous; and in spite of the confirmation it gave me of the dastardly trickery they were planning. He gave further proof of it all when he continued: And it will soon be settled, for they are urging me to give my word, and then they will reveal Silvie's supposed birth and background to the young man. I had another note from la Morin yesterday evening. Here it is, he said, handing me a piece of paper. See whether I am lying or telling the truth! I knew la Morin's handwriting as well as I knew my own, and recognised what I saw to be hers. I read the note. This is what it said:

You are taking your time, dear Monsieur, and causing unnecessary delay. Our compact should have been settled two weeks ago. Silvie and I are tired of waiting, and she is ready to break off discussion with you. There is no question of her complying with your request. She will never agree, even if this is to be the end of our negotiations. She would rather consider increasing our offer to you. Your suggestion is shocking in a man of your age, and she is justly horrified. Be at our usual meeting place at noon tomorrow, and we will see if agreement can be reached on a new offer. If not, we shall approach someone who, if not less mercenary, is at least more honourable than yourself.

On reading this note, I suddenly felt a desire to have it myself. I took a slip of paper from my pocket and, since my companion was too drunk to notice the difference, put it in place of the note he had handed me. I then said to him: The subject is indeed crystal clear, and if I were in your place, I would not keep such notes about my person – it could only too easily give substance to suspicion. Here is what I would do with it, I continued, and tearing my own slip of paper to pieces, I threw them into the fire. This did not provoke any reaction in him other than laughter. That is what I would have done myself, he said, and is what I did with its predecessors. But, I said, I have made you miss your appointment! I've missed plenty of others! he rejoined. It is as well with these women not to appear too anxious to play their game. But why do you need a meeting place? I asked. Would it not be easier to meet at Silvie's house? You could speak more freely there, and without fear of interruption? Not on your life! he said. That would ruin everything. It is imperative that I should not be seen with her – and her intended is at the house every minute of the day. If he were to see me before our agreement is made, it would be goodbye to the whole arrangement. Both he and the neighbours would recognise me if I had been seen visiting her. So we meet at the other end of Paris from where she lives – in the Tuileries, near the big pond – and choose a time when there is scarcely anyone around, particularly now when the weather does not tempt people to be out walking. Our arrangements are in place. As soon as we have reached agreement, and Silvie has performed her little dance, I shall return to the country. She and la Morin will inform the young man that I am her father, and tell him to write to me – and to post the letters himself, so that he feels confident that there is no finagling. I shall receive the letters, show them around a little, reply to them, and then return to Paris. Silvie and her betrothed will come to meet me in their carriage. I shall greet them as my soon-to-be son-in-law and daughter. I shall stay with her, and only then will I be seen, with la Morin taking her place as if she were my sister. This is how we intend to proceed. What do you think of the plan? he asked. Is it not well conceived and unlikely to fail? It is excellently planned, I said. The pigeon will undoubtedly be snared. Indeed, the scheme is admirable, but I would be a little afraid in your situation that it may turn into one of those tragedies where the first act takes place at the Châtelet and the last before the Hôtel de Ville. I don't think there is any fear of my turning into a hero of that sort, he answered. As soon as I have seen those two married, and seen what sort of a birdbrain the young fellow is – and perhaps having extracted another contribution from him – I shall disappear into the furthest reaches of the country.

He continued talking in this vein a little while longer, which gave time for Querville to return. I paid our bill and did not regret the time spent: what I had learnt was worth the price. Querville and I went to a more reputable establishment to eat. Rouvière was still with us. While we were having dessert, two gentlemen of Querville's acquaintance appeared and a conversation was struck up, during which Querville asked the new arrivals if they wanted to give him a chance to get his revenge. They agreed, and some cards were brought. They asked if I would like to make up their number, as fourth member of the party. I am no card player and, moreover, I thought it likely these were some of those card sharps that abound in Paris, but since I only had a little money with me and was willing to lose it, I agreed. My suspicions proved groundless. Querville and I played against these two and won so handsomely that we had to pay for what they had ordered. In fact, I won three times the value of the horses as well as my expenses.

When they had left, Querville told me he was very glad to have recovered his money, and that these two, who had cleaned him out only two days earlier, were the sons of bankers. It was because they had left him penniless that he had been forced to sell his horses, and, he said, if I wanted to sell them back to him, he would take them and give me an extra ten louis into the bargain. I said I couldn't do this because I had already sent the horses to my mother's, and he accepted this excuse. We went on to the opera and then had supper together, Rouvière having left us and found somewhere to sleep off his wine.

It was very late by the time we separated. There was a hard frost; the night was calm and beautiful. A servant from the tavern where we had been eating came to light my way home with a torch – for my valet had not returned since taking the horses home for me. I was slightly tipsy, and it occurred to me it would be amusing to pay a visit to my former sweetheart and watch her disarray and embarrassment when I confronted her. I cared so little for her now that I thought I could take my revenge and would enjoy laughing at her expense. I little knew my own weakness. I went right across to the other side of Paris – from the Palais-Royal to near the Bastille – and I was so taken by the thought of how I would enjoy my little comedy that I didn't think to tell the man who was carrying the torch to wait for me, and he went back to the inn, assuming I had reached home when I went into the house of my deceitful mistress. It was by now so late that the two women were preparing to go to bed.

What is it that brings you here at this hour of the night? said my erstwhile beloved as soon as she saw me. Does one come calling at nearly midnight? What have you been doing, that we have not seen you all day? I have been concerned for you!

Why, I heard a scrap of news, I answered jocularly. A mere nothing – but which could be enough to lead your venerable supposed aunt, Madame Morin, also Monsieur de Rouvière, gentleman of Le Mans, and you yourself, my dear child, to the gallows. On hearing the name of Rouvière and on perceiving my outrageous manner, so different from my usual behaviour, the two women's faces fell. I laughed out loud at their surprise. On my life, I went on, addressing Silvie, if you want to have a little romp with a man, I would have thought myself as good a candidate as some old codger! And instead of asking a hundred louis for the privilege, I would have paid you good money myself! And what of all the time I have spent courting you – that ought to count for something too! Of course, I would not be able to say you were my daughter. And by the way, dear Madame, I said to la Morin, your charming brother failed to meet you at the Tuileries today. Here is the message you sent him – you had better write another immediately, to prevent further delay. There is no time to lose. If Rouvière insists on his request to know his daughter more intimately you will have to look for another would-be father – someone less lustful, though it may mean paying more for his cooperation. And those who brought you up and nurtured you, I said turning to Silvie, how dear they were to you! How sad that Garreau died in prison! I hear you were so much in love with each other you would have been happy to be united together in death before the Hôtel de Ville! But what is postponed is not gone for ever! There will be another chance for you and your worthy aunt!

They were both in a state which it is easier for you to imagine than for me to describe. I was enjoying the opportunity to give full rein to my wish for vengeance. The two women remained completely silent: their disarray was beyond description. I found the scene – though silent – highly entertaining. Farewell, my fine friends, I said. May God take you back into his fold, lest Beelzebub – with whom you have been consorting – carry you off for good!

I intended to leave after this flourish without awaiting a reply, but I was prevented from doing so. Silvie rushed to the door, which she closed. I tried, somewhat roughly, to push her aside, but she would not desist. Instead, she threw herself at my feet, her eyes streaming with tears. What are you doing, faithless one? I said. Allow me to leave. Be grateful that I refrain from taking a vengeance which would be within my rights. No, Monsieur, she said, clinging to my leg with all her strength, and preventing my departure. You will not leave until you have heard me. I demand this, in the name of all you hold most dear. And what can you say to me? I asked. Do you expect me still to believe your impostures? No, she answered. I will not try to justify myself. I have done wrong. But at least if you allow me to explain the reasons for my misdeeds, I shall appear less culpable. I do not deny that I have done wrong, but there was more misfortune in my crime than intention to wrong you. Indeed, I embarked on the path of deceit only because I was afraid of losing you, and if I had loved you less, I would have done nothing for which you could reproach me!

At that moment, I turned my eyes towards her and was lost. She was still at my feet, and cruelty itself would have relented at the sight. She was weeping; her breast, revealed through the half-open folds of her simple bedgown, her hair which was loosened ready for the night and which fell about her body, her beauty which was all the more ravishing in her humiliation, and, last of all, the baleful influence of my Star which led me on – all these combined to make me see in her only the one I loved, the idol of my heart. If I may say it without impiety, I saw in her a second Madeleine. My anger melted; I raised her from the ground; I let her say all she wanted. I paid no attention to what she was saying. I no longer belonged to myself. A thousand thoughts beset me, each one outweighing the one which had preceded it. Or rather, though alive and breathing, I was insensible to all around me: I was no more aware of my surroundings than if I had been dead. I remained for some time in this state. Eventually I regained my senses, but I was unable to rally my powers of judgement. I told her only that I would return the next day, when I had regained some composure; and that she should look at the papers I would leave with her and see what explanation she could give, since she could not deny the facts they contained. I made her promise that she would return them to me, and for surety I had no disquiet about taking a ring of great value which she was wearing on her finger. As I left, I threw a glance at la Morin, which rekindled all my ire, and set her trembling from head to foot. My hand went to my sword, and I might have done her injury, but fortunately the guard became entangled in the knot of ribbons which was attached. The short time it took to release it allowed me pause to reflect on what I was about to do. It was unworthy in me to kill this woman. Instead, I left her to her fate and contented myself with the thought that sooner or later the public executioner would call her to account for all her perfidies.

All this violent agitation had taken its toll on my physical well-being. The effects of the wine I had drunk had disappeared, but I was in a pitiful state and so enfeebled that my only recourse was to knock at a house two doors away where I saw a light, and from where I sent for a sedan to carry me home.

The following night was no more tranquil than the preceding one had been. Quite the contrary. The weakness I had discovered in myself in the presence of this woman, the return of my earlier feelings for her – which had occurred against all expectations – the collapse of all my resolution, and my shame at such weakness in myself: all these things, following hard upon my previous turmoil, threw me into such a state of irresolution and apathy that I felt both disgust and pity for myself. Weak in both body and mind, I fell sick of a fever. I had no desire to live and had so little strength it seemed unlikely I should long continue to do so. I hoped death would deliver me from the misfortune which had always accompanied me, and from that which I believed the future would bring. I was at the lowest ebb. The conflict raging within me robbed my life of all hope and meaning. In the state I was in, I would certainly have welcomed, or at least been indifferent to, a sentence of death. But I did not die; my destiny was not yet fulfilled. I had not yet reached the depth of shame which awaited me. I was saved by the very indifference I felt towards preserving my life: for a week, I refused all food, and at the end of that time, my fever left me.

During my illness, a messenger had been sent frequently on behalf of someone unknown, to enquire after my health. I was certain this unknown person was Silvie. I was grateful for this concern on her part. I wanted to find her innocent and, in spite of the proof I had been given of her treachery, I hoped that, when I heard her explanations, she would appear less guilty. With this hope, the first visit I made on my recovery was to see her. But before telling you what happened there, I must explain that my mother – who did not know, or even have the slightest suspicion, that I had been weak enough to go and see Silvie – had paid little attention to the fact that some unknown person was taking an interest in my health. She had assumed that my illness was caused by the inner struggle involved in my efforts to follow the dictates of honour and stifle the yearnings of my heart. The fact that I had obtained the horses and sent them home that same day had convinced her that I was determined to part for ever from a woman who had so deceived me and renounce all contact with her. My illness, in my mother's eyes, revealed the strength of my feelings and the effort it cost me to repress them. My plight aroused her sympathy. She didn't mention Silvie to me, but was as considerate towards me as if she had been my best friend. The role she played – so much more unselfish than should be expected of a mother – her concern in trying to understand my feelings, her tenderness in caring for me: all

337

of this, added to the respect I had always had for her, made me feel I would be unworthy to live if I repaid such a good mother by slipping back into a situation which I felt to be as dangerous as she did – and whose anguish would inevitably shorten her days. I therefore made my decision: I believed I had persuaded myself that I would abandon Silvie, and it was in this belief that I paid my visit to her.

My short illness had changed my appearance considerably. My spirits were sunk even lower than my physical condition. I had intended to return the diamond I had taken from her and reclaim the papers I had left with her, while bidding her a final farewell. I hoped to have the strength of character to do as I had resolved, but it was not long before I realised my mistake. She was extremely pale, and her changed appearance took me by surprise; she was in a state of weakness and dejection equal to my own. Her pallor and dull eyes revealed a sweetness in her beauty which I had not seen there before. It was my misfortune to discover new charms in her every day. I was saddened to see her thus. The sympathy I felt reawakened all my love. My resolve was forgotten and, far from the severity with which I had intended to treat her, my only concern was to console her. What shameful weakness I displayed! I wiped away the tears I had caused. I begged her not to weep, to attribute my harsh words to the first rush of anger which had flooded over me, for which I had been sufficiently punished by my own regrets and the state to which they had reduced me. I begged her not to increase them by her reproaches. In a word, I did everything I could to reassure her and to prove that her hold over me was in no way diminished.

This gentle and humble manner – so different from what she had expected – revived her spirits a little. Her sighs and tender looks pierced my heart. She saw how my determination faltered and seized on the moment, so auspicious for her – not, she said, to justify what she had done, but to let

338

me understand the reasons for it, and to prove that she did not deserve the insults and abuse I had treated her with.

Here are your papers, Monsieur, she said. Take them back. I know both the handwriting and the author. Scoundrel that he is, he is nonetheless right to say he does not act out of hatred for me. Indeed, he acts, on the contrary, out of unrequited love. But, Monsieur, she continued, taking my hand, are you willing to listen to what I have to say? Yes, Mademoiselle, I replied, I will listen. Not in order to change my mind – my heart already believes you – but so that you are satisfied.

Very well, then, Monsieur, she continued. I do not dispute the facts. What you have been told is true in every circumstance as given to you, but it is false because the motives behind it were not known to your correspondent, and are known only to Monsieur le Commandeur de Villeblain, to Madame Morin and to myself. And these are what I will reveal to you.

I was delighted to hear her provide a witness such as le Commandeur de Villeblain, since he was a close relative of my mother, an absolutely reliable man, someone incapable of involvement in any deception. Through him, therefore, I would be able to separate truth from falsehood. I made no sign of what I was thinking to Silvie, but gave my fullest attention to everything she said. She continued as follows.

It is true that I never knew either my father or my mother, but I know who they were. It is true that I was not born of a legitimate marriage, but am I responsible if their union was not preceded by a wedding ceremony? It is true that I was abandoned, and that I was taken from the orphanage at eight years of age, but it is also true that Madame de Cranves, who took me into her home, knew my parentage long before she saw me. But, Monsieur, I must tell you how this came to be.

Madame la Duchesse was the sister of Monsieur le

Marquis de Buringe, who was my father. He died in Candia, serving with Monsieur de Beaufort. He was wounded and, before he died, had time to make a will in his own hand; or rather, he wrote to Madame de Cranves, his sister, saying that, since he was preparing to meet his Creator, he wanted to cleanse his conscience. He told her about an affair he had had with one of his mother's ladies-in-waiting, which had resulted in the birth of a girl; and that, not being in a position to care for the child (being the youngest of three brothers and very young at the time, and destined, more-over, for the Order of Malta), he had been obliged to leave the child in the care of an orphanage, having no one he could ask for help, the infant's mother having died in childbirth. He told Madame de Cranves the day of my birth, the time, the place, everything by which I could be identi-fied, and expressed his regret that he had not recognised and cared for me himself on becoming the head of his line after the deaths of his two brothers. He admitted the shame he felt at having left his child in an orphanage for so long. He asked her, as his sister and sole heiress, to care for me, and to treat me with generosity. He made no other bequests, but left all he owned in her keeping, to be passed on to me, his daughter. This letter was delivered unsealed to Madame de Cranves by Monsieur le Commandeur de Vil-leblain, in whom my father had confided on his deathbed, and who was named in the letter, asking him to ensure that his dying wish was carried out.

Madame de Cranves, when she took me from the orphanage had her reasons for not making her brother's will public. She showed the letter only to the directors of the orphanage. Madame Morin, in whom Madame de Cranves had absolute confidence, was sent to identify me from among the other girls of my age. I was shown to Madame Morin. Madame de Cranves came to visit the girls when we had just reached the age at which our instruction was beginning. Monsieur de Villeblain accompanied her. Madame Morin was to kiss me. This was the sign they had chosen. She did so, and Madame de Cranves, when she saw me, declared that all this precaution was not necessary: she would have been able to pick me out from a hundred thousand others because I was the living image of her poor brother, the Marquis de Buringe. She asked the directors to allow her to withdraw me from the orphanage, gave a very large donation, and took me home with her.

That, Monsieur, is how I came to live with Madame de Cranves. It was not, as you see, by chance, since I was in fact her niece. You were right to say I must regret Garreau's death. It was he who had this letter in his keeping, since Madame de Cranves had given it to him, as you will learn. But if you will do me the kindness to confirm what I have told you, the directors of the orphanage are not all dead: they can confirm the truth of what I have said, and are too honourable not to do this for me. Also Monsieur le Commandeur de Villeblain – whom I shall call as my witness in a matter of even greater importance – is still, thank God, in perfect health. It is more than eighteen months since I have seen him, but Madame Morin saw him at the Hospice in the rue Saint-Antoine not long ago. He will tell you the truth of the matter and let you know if I have lied in the least syllable. This then is what I had to tell you regarding my birth.

As soon as I went to live with Madame de Cranves, she took every possible care with my education, which would seem proof enough that she took more interest in my welfare than would be the case if it were purely a question of charity towards someone of no special significance to her. One would not have a mere orphan taught Italian, or how to sing and dance, and play musical instruments, or all that goes to the training of a girl of some birth. She went to a great deal of expense on my behalf. And finally, for someone who was no more than a simple member of the household, as your informant claims I was, one does not provide a lady companion, such as Madame Morin, as well as a personal chamber-maid and a servant-boy. I still have the same three attending and serving me as when I lived with Madame de Cranves. Your correspondent cannot prove that this is not so, and therefore refrains from mentioning it. But now I must broach the major accusation – the question of how I have conducted myself.

The good-for-nothing accuses me of having an illicit affair with Garreau. He even claims that Madame de Cranves was displeased with me and that this was made plain in her will. Here is the real explanation.

The Duchess wished to provide for my future by arranging a marriage for me. She considered Garreau as a potential match. He was an intelligent young man, of pleasing appearance, who came of a distinguished family of lawyers. If I say too much in his praise, you will start to be suspicious, so I will say no more. Madame de Cranves knew that I did not displease him, and spoke to him on the subject. He admitted that he loved me, and she therefore thought the match would not be inappropriate, and gave him permission to discover what my feelings were. Garreau was very assiduous in his attentions to me, and we resided in the same house, and it is this that gave rise to the rumours which were bandied about. I could not refuse to accept his attentions, when Madame de Cranves had intimated that she had selected him as a husband for me, though no one except Madame Morin knew this, and we had been told not to make the matter public. I was already the envy of all the other servants, as a result of the unusual way I had entered the household, and because I was treated as a daughter might have been, although there was apparently nothing to warrant this special treatment. The chief fabricator of these rumours, and manipulator of this resentment, was Madame de Cranves's butler, one Valeran, about whom I had already had to complain to Madame de Cranves for his disrespectful manner towards me, for which he had received a severe reprimand and had once been temporarily dismissed.

Before finishing what I have to tell you about myself, Monsieur, she continued, I might add that this man, while serving in her house, had married one of Madame de Cranves's chamber-maids and was quite ready to undermine the good reputation of her household. He had said openly to me that Madame de Cranves – who was ailing – would not last much longer, and I would therefore do well to find friends for myself who could make sure I would continue in a style of life similar to what she had provided for me. He continued further that it was no use deceiving myself: whatever she left me in her will, he said, her heirs would see to it that the testament was overturned, at least insofar as my inheritance was concerned. I would therefore be wise to prepare some protection for myself, and he could provide that protection. I received this suggestion with the contempt it deserved – accompanied by a slap on the face. I threatened to report what he had said. I was unable to do so that day. Valeran's wife was with Madame de Cranves the whole day, and I did not wish to bring the matter up in her presence. This proved to be a mistake on my part.

His wife told him that I had not mentioned the matter to Madame de Cranves, and this emboldened him to come to my bedchamber that night. I don't know how he was able to get into my room without either the girl who slept by the door or myself hearing him. All I know is that I woke with a start when I felt his cold hand on my stomach. I screamed for help. He seized hold of me in an attempt to silence me – leaving bruises that were visible for a considerable time. The people who came to my aid freed me from his grasp. I went straight to Madame de Cranves – just as I was, wearing nothing but my nightgown – to lay the case before her and demand justice, though her rooms were far removed from my own. Valeran's wife did all she could to stop me, even throwing herself at my feet several times, but I was not to be deterred. I made my complaint and obtained satisfaction. Madame de Cranves allowed me to remain in her room and sleep there, and the next day Valeran was dismissed and left the house to the accompaniment of a beating from her footmen, which I witnessed. She forbade the Swiss guard who kept the gate ever to let Valeran into the house again, on pain of losing his own employment.

Thus Valeran was turned out, but after two months he was allowed to return, because Madame de Cranves, who was good-hearted, listened to his wife, of whom she was fond, and who interceded for him; also because he had been a family servant who had been with her, and her father before her, for a long time. He promised he would mend his ways. I added my own voice to the pleadings of his wife; otherwise Madame de Cranves would not have relented, as she herself acknowledged when she addressed the assembled household. So Valeran recovered his position and asked my forgiveness, kneeling there with everyone present, while I sat at table with Madame de Cranves. He was only allowed to rise when I gave permission, since Madame de Cranves wished to teach him a lesson. Instead of humiliating him further, after that I did all I could for him. I overlooked how he had assaulted me, though I still took care to avoid any sort of conversation alone with him. But since I had driven him to despair, and his love for me had converted itself into rage and anger, it was he who instigated the gossip among the servants about my conduct in connection with Garreau, since none of them knew any reason why Garreau should be visiting me. I learnt that Valeran was the source of the gossip from one of the footmen to whom he had been talking. In the end, I could no longer refrain from making a complaint about this.

Monsieur le Commandeur de Villeblain was visiting the house at the time, and I had no reason to hide my grievance from him, the more so since he had always appeared interested in my welfare, and since Madame de Cranves (for the reasons I have explained to you, but which I was not then aware of) generally told him all that happened to me and everything that I did. No other member of the household but myself – be they lady-in-waiting, squire or secretary – was ever invited to sit at Madame de Cranves's table. Monsieur de Villeblain had stayed for dinner, and there were just the three of us at the table.

Valeran came to clear the plates, as was his custom. Be good enough, Madame, I said to the Duchess, either to give Valeran (I did not prefix his name with 'Monsieur') your instructions or allow him to explain himself to you. It is not right that he should make the allegations that he does about me. Whether they are true or false, it is not proper that you alone should not hear them. I then turned to Valeran and addressed him coldly. Valeran, I said, would you be good enough to tell me why you take it on yourself to criticise my behaviour? And to make me the subject of your impertinent conversations with others of your kind, such as footmen, for instance? If you know of anything reprehensible in my conduct, why do you not tell Madame de Cranves, rather than prattle about it with people like yourself who can do nothing to correct it? I hoped my leniency in the past might have made you more sensible, but you continue to spread untruths about me. Tell us now, here in front of Madame de Cranves and Monsieur de Villeblain: either admit you are a cheat and a liar, or tell them how you come to know of the misconduct you accuse me of. Is this something new? said Madame de Cranves. Yes, I said, indicating Valeran with my hand. This worthy person is bringing discredit on your house. If he is to be believed, you are honouring a girl of questionable virtue when you receive me at your table and allow me to sleep in your bed. And I ask you to intervene and judge between us in this matter.

Valeran was more dead than alive as I said this, but he was in an even worse state when Madame de Cranves addressed him angrily: Leave my house, Valeran, she said, and never return unless you resolve never to speak of Silvie except with the same respect as is due to me myself from a wretch like you. You ill repay the generosity shown towards you when she persuaded me to take you back. Mademoiselle, she said turning to me, do what you will with him: it was because of your intercession that I allowed him to return. I leave his fate in your hands. Mete justice to him as you think fit. Let him be beaten, or let him stay. I will not intervene. But if any more of this nonsense comes to my ears, I shall hold you accountable – and myself too. I absolutely forbid you to tolerate any disrespect from anyone in this house. I give you the same authority over my staff as I myself have. Do what you wish with this good-for-nothing. You have my approval for whatever you decide.

Monsieur de Villeblain then addressed me: Mademoiselle, he said, I beg you to pardon him. Turning to him, he said: Monsieur Valeran, you are lucky that Mademoiselle has made her complaint only to Madame, and not to anyone else, for had it been otherwise, even respect for her might not have prevented someone exacting punishment on her behalf. You do not know who she is, but believe me, you will do well to treat her with respect. Monsieur, I interrupted, that is all I ask. Tell him, said Madame de Cranves, what you wish to become of him. Your decision will be our command. I beg you, Madame ... I began. Address your words to him, she said. Well then, Valeran, I said, let it be understood: this is your second offence. I am prepared to forget it. But be sure, this is your last chance. If there is one more repetition, you will pay in full for all your previous misbehaviour. Leave us; see to your duties. But remember, from now on, my tolerance is exhausted.

It seems to me, Silvie said to me, that my position could

not have been made clearer than that. At the time, I still did not know that I had the honour of being Madame de Cranves's niece. I had acted as I did simply because she had always told me to consider myself on a different footing from the other members of her household and not to tolerate any discourtesy. Valeran was thoroughly mortified by what had taken place. However it is he, Monsieur, who has taken it into his head to communicate with you and your mother by means of these letters. I know his handwriting well, which moreover he has not even taken the trouble to disguise – merely telling you not to show the letter to me. The loss of face he brought on himself at my hands was the result of his trying to interfere in something which did not suit him. After that, he became more prudent. He did not dare to say anything more about Garreau and myself. Garreau, however, was not satisfied with words and gave Valeran a beating, right there in the house, thus making himself Valeran's sworn enemy.

Valeran did not dare cause any more trouble during Madame de Cranves's lifetime, but after her death he found a means of avenging himself, for it was through his doing that Garreau was put in prison, where he died, with a cloud of suspicion still surrounding him after his demise. It is now time for me to tell you about this and prove my innocence to you. In doing so, I shall also be proving Garreau's innocence, for indeed, we acted in concert, his cause and mine being one and the same in the 'theft' that Valeran claims we carried out in league with Madame Morin.

I have told you that Madame de Cranves had selected Garreau to be my husband, but she fell ill just as we were to be married. Just before her death, she had received a large sum of money – the last payment on the sale of some land which had belonged to the late Monsieur le Marquis de Buringe, my father. I can therefore say that this money belonged to me, and still belongs to me, since she who by law was his only heir, had intended the money to be mine. Her plan had been to recognise me as her niece on my marriage, and to settle the money on me in the marriage contract and in her will; but having the money already to hand, she changed her mind and decided to give it to me during her lifetime. She was concerned for me, and didn't want me to have to go to court after her death to defend my inheritance against other potential claimants who might be extremely powerful and could have disputed the articles of her will. Such people, because of their standing, might have been able to have her will declared invalid, leaving me, who would lack protection, penniless and without resource. It is true that there was the letter from my father, whose authenticity she trusted, which could prove my birth, but others might have cast doubt on its validity and argued that my claim to be her niece was unproven. Then challenges and investigations would have ensued, with their expenses, and the outcome might not have gone in favour of a girl who had no ally. To forestall such eventualities, she consulted Monsieur de Villeblain, who spent a long time discussing the matter with her, and who was still with her when Garreau and I were sent for, along with Madame Morin (the only one of we three who knew the truth about my birth), and went to her room.

It was then that I learned who I was, and you can imagine the joy I felt. She entrusted the letter I have told you about to Garreau's keeping, after certifying its authenticity with her own signature, and asking Monsieur de Villeblain to do the same. Garreau received it with the greatest happiness, as proof that I came of a noble family, and was not of unknown parentage, as he had up till then believed – as I myself had done and all the others in the household. Though, as for myself, the distinction with which Madame de Cranves had always treated me, and occasional words that she had let fall in unguarded moments when her heart was overflowing, had given me some suspicions of the truth – suspicions now happily corroborated.

She told Garreau she had changed her mind as to how we would be married, giving the reasons I have just explained to you, and in order, she said, to safeguard you both from any sort of disagreement with my other heirs, I am giving you the money I received from Monsieur d'Anet immediately. Take it, and keep it safe, but I want it to be in Silvie's possession until you are married, and thereafter it will belong to the survivor. I shall prevent any possible dispute by declaring that I have already disposed of the money, without saying what I have done with it. I will also put into Silvie's hands some small pieces of jewellery, in the presence of those who will have some claim on my inheritance after my death, and then what I bequeath to her by my testament will be such a small amount that my niece and nephew will have no quarrel with it.

This was the reason, Monsieur, Silvie continued, why Madame de Cranves left me in her will only ten thousand francs, some pieces of furniture and a lifetime pension of twelve hundred livres. It was not, as Valeran claims, because she was displeased with Garreau and myself. We did as she wished. I took the money and put it in a safe place which I have at my disposal, and I still have the whole amount. I gave Garreau a promise of marriage which I signed, and he did the same for me, and as the money was in my possession, my promise also contained an article declaring his right to one-third of it. These two documents were approved and countersigned by both Madame de Cranves and Monsieur de Villeblain, whose instructions we were following; and Garreau and I made a promise to them that we would marry at the earliest possible time. Here, Monsieur, is the promise I received from Garreau which I still have. The paper she handed me was indeed what she claimed it to be.

349

The very next day after this meeting, Monsieur le Marquis d'Anemace and Mademoiselle de Tonnai, nephew and niece of Madame de Cranves – she on Monsieur de Cranves's side and he on hers – the sole heirs of the Houses of Cranves and Buringe, of which the Duchess was the dowager and beneficial owner, came to see her. She sent for Monsieur de Villeblain, and as soon as he arrived I was called to her room. When everyone else had left the room, she spoke to her niece and nephew as follows: My death will soon make you the masters of all I possess on this earth. I have made a will which will not offend you. The strongest article concerns Silvie, whom you see here. I leave to her my small pieces of jewellery. I am glad to have this chance to tell you this; and so that you will not ask her for them, and to make sure there is no question about their ownership, I will hand them over to her now, in your presence. And indeed, she had them brought. Here you are, my dear Silvie, she said, handing them to me. Keep some, in memory of me, and sell the rest, if you wish, to pay for whatever you may need, and for your marriage. Here, I give them to you. They are yours. I took them from her, with tears in my eyes.

Then, turning to her niece, she said: The small items of jewellery are too insignificant to be of interest to you. Here are my more valuable pieces, which I give to you. You are not in need. Keep them, in memory of me. Monsieur, she said, turning to Monsieur le Marquis d'Anemace, you would have cause to complain if I left you out when I am disposing of all I own! I am leaving my house and its furniture to you, with my silver, my horses and everything that is here. It is up to you to take the requisite action to ensure that nothing is removed unlawfully. I make an exception of my clothes, my hairpieces and that furniture which Silvie has had the use of, and which I leave to her, and regarding which I would ask that you rather be generous towards her than quibble with her. These are the instructions you will find in my will, and I am pleased to be able to tell you in advance what they are. I am also leaving her some money and a small lifetime income. Don't contest any of this, I beg you both. She deserves your consideration. I commend her to you. Promise me to do whatever you can for her. I do not tell you my reasons for asking this. They gave her their promise and have kept their word, honoring her memory. I have nothing but praise for the way they have behaved.

She then told them they would find little or no money in cash after her death, since she had disposed of it according to the dictates of her conscience. But also, she said, they would find she had left not a penny of debt, since after becoming a widow, and following the deaths of her two brothers, she had paid off all the debts owed by the Houses of Cranves and Buringe. She commended Garreau to them, as a young man who was both faithful and devoted, and who, by his good stewardship and hard work, had played a large part in enabling her to pay all her creditors. Then she signalled to me that I should leave, and she remained alone with them and Monsieur de Villeblain for a very long time. I am certain they spoke of me, for when they came out of her room they both embraced me tenderly and promised me their friendship in such a way that I felt sure they had been told of my birth.

They were married to each other about a year ago, and people of their rank are so well known in society that I am certain you must know who they are. You may consult them as further witnessess who can verify the truth of what I have told you. They are both in good health, and their word can be trusted.

As Monsieur d'Anemace was young and had no people dedicated to his service among Madame de Cranves's servants who would look after his interests should she die; and as she might have taken it amiss if he had put aside or removed her furniture or silver during her lifetime, he

charged Valeran with responsibility in this matter and promised to retain him in his service in the future. This he did,
after Madame de Cranves's death – though Valeran did not
remain with him long, as his rough, insolent manners led to
his dismissal. Monsieur d'Anemace had also promised him
a reward. He had asked me also to keep an eye on his
inheritance, but I was not in a position to do so. When
Madame de Cranves died four days later, I was too overcome by grief to think of anything but the loss of someone
who had been such a kind and generous protectress. All I
could do was retire to my own room with Madame Morin –
to whose care Madame de Cranves had entrusted me, telling
her not to leave me until my marriage had taken place.

It was because of Valeran that I first discovered how my
position had changed. The Duchess's eyes were barely
closed in death when he came uncouthly into my room, to
which I had withdrawn, and, on the pretext of obeying
orders from his new master, he began, without the least
consideration, to remove the gold and silver trimmed covers
from my bed and my chairs. Madame Morin drew my
attention to what he was doing. His insolence, combined
with the sorrow with which I was afflicted, made me act with
extreme vigour. I called some servants, and when I had
enough to protect me from his violence I went up to him
and slapped him with all my force. I then went to find
Monsieur d'Anemace and asked if he had given Valeran
orders to dismantle my room. He apologised profusely for
the man's effrontery and made him return to me all that
had been removed and, at the same time, made him bring
me some torches, a pair of candle-snuffers in a holder, a
ewer, a covered bowl, a goblet and some other items of
silver. I still have all these pieces, and the furniture which I
have at present is that which I used in Madame de Cranves's
house.

This was not all. Valeran knew that Madame de Cranves

had received a large sum of money about ten days before her death. He told this to a lawyer in whose hands Monsieur d'Anemace had placed his affairs, and this man believed what Valeran told him. An inventory was made, and this sum, which is what I had and still have, was not found. They asked Garreau what had become of it: he said Madame de Cranves had disposed of it without telling him what she had done with it. Valeran claimed Garreau had stolen it, and on his accusation Garreau was arrested and imprisoned. Monsieur d'Anemace was not in Paris. Nonetheless I found him and pointed out the injustice done to a man whom Madame de Cranves had recommended so highly to his care. I reminded him that she herself had told him that she had disposed of any cash she had had on hand, and I explained to him what it was that motivated Valeran's actions. Monsieur d'Anemace was astonished at what had happened to Garreau, which was in direct conflict with the orders he had given on his departure. He wrote expressing his disapproval of all that had happened, and saying that he himself would apologise to Garreau as soon as he returned to Paris. He came two days later, but Garreau had refused to leave prison until his accuser withdrew the charge against him and cleared his name. There was not enough time for this. Garreau had been so roughly manhandled by the men who arrested him, led on by Valeran, that he had suffered some internal injury, from which he died on the fifth day of his imprisonment. And I have so far been unable to retrieve either the Marquis de Buringe's letter, or the promise of marriage which I had given to Garreau.

These are the facts about the theft that Valeran accuses us of – Garreau, Madame Morin and myself. I leave you now to decide for yourself the truth of the matter. As for the jewellery, Monsieur d'Anemace himself has not asked for it, for he knew very well what his aunt had done with it. But since no one among Madame de Cranves's household staff knew what had happened to it, while everyone knew she had a large quantity of very beautiful pieces and was surprised that none were found among her possessions after her death, it suited Valeran to paint me as guilty of theft.

That, Monsieur, is all I have to say in justification of my conduct, and I believe it shows my innocence quite clearly. You can investigate the truth of what I have said – I have offered you credible witnesses whom you may consult. The only remaining point concerns Rouvière, and on this score I make no effort to claim innocence. It must be held against me. It was a fraud which I was willing to countenance – but if this deception makes me a criminal, are you the one who should condemn me? No, you do not condemn me, she continued, with a tender glance. You are too well aware that it was with the aim of making myself appear worthy of you that I agreed to this deception. I preferred that you should think me the daughter of a lowly, penniless gantleman, rather than claim to be of a more illustrious lineage which I could not prove without causing a stir and setting tongues wagging in a way which would offend you.

I will not try to exonerate myself by blaming others. You remember how reluctant I was to answer you when you wanted to know about my family? My birth – which I would be proud of in other circumstances – would, I thought, seem hateful and shameful in your eyes, and I did not dare reveal the truth. I tried to blind you; but Rouvière must have told you how much I was to pay him and the conditions I imposed on him for the privilege of passing as his daughter? He was to remove himself permanently from Paris and, for this, he received additional payment. You have met the man – while I scarcely remember having seen him when our negotiations first started. And consider whether our attempt to deceive you would really have succeeded: how could I reconcile what I owned with the pretence of being his daughter? And could you not have checked my name on the register which you and I signed as godparents, just five months ago? Does this not prove that it was only the question of my illegitimate birth which was the stumbling-block and which I was trying to hide? Does this look like a work of treachery undertaken by people accustomed to live by cheating? In no way could it be so construed! The haphazard way in which it was cobbled together must prove it was not the work of practised fraudsters! My attempt to deceive you was revealed to you by a rascal, and I am in despair – not because the deception was discovered, but because I was dishonest with you. You know now what my birth was, and where I come from. Although the fault of my birth is not mine, it makes me unworthy of you. I can no longer hope to win your heart, which I have forfeited through my dishonesty, but at least if you distinguish the flaw of my birth from the transgression I actually committed, you will no longer despise me, and that is all I ask. You must admit that there is more misfortune than misconduct in what I have done.

I will leave you now, Monsieur, she said, happy that I have had the opportunity to disabuse you of the false accusations levied against me by a worthless wretch. For it is true, Monsieur, that although my birth was not sanctioned by marriage, and is improper according to our laws, yet I have inherited the strict sense of honour and probity of my forebears. My virtue is untarnished, and I can promise that it will remain so, since I did not weaken even for you. I allowed myself the flattering hope of a life with you, she continued, with tears in her eyes. That hope has vanished, but the place in my heart which I gave to you, no other will occupy. My days hereafter will be spent in a convent, withdrawn from the world, where my innocence and piety will prove to you that, without the crime visited on me by Fate – the involuntary misfortune of my birth – I was worthy to belong to you.

There are only two things I would ask of you. You thought my ring beautiful. I beg you to keep it; it will cause you to think of me sometimes and to accept that it was my misfortunes, not my faults, which separated us. And secondly, I would ask you not to think ill of Madame Morin. All she did was on my behalf. She thought she was acting for the best; what she did was done only to make me appear more worthy of you, by trying to hide from you what I would so dearly love to be able to hide from myself. She never suggested that I act in a dishonourable fashion. It was Rouvière who wrote making an improper suggestion. I tore up his letter in anger; luckily, I have found the pieces. Here they are, she said, handing me some torn scraps of paper. You can piece them together. Madame Morin answered for me, according to my instructions. You are mistaken if you question her devotion to virtue. She has lived for many years in Madame de Cranves's house, which has always been a veritable temple of propriety. If she were not truly honourable, she could not have remained there so long, nor would Madame de Cranves have given her a position of confidence. It was Madame de Cranves's decision that she should be my companion and guide, and Madame Morin sees in me a member of the family to which she is devoted.

This is all I ask of you. Grant me these two requests, and I shall be content to leave the world behind. But above all, do not seek to see me. All commerce between us must end. Seeing you would cause me the greatest distress. Nor do I want to be the cause of any complaint your honoured mother may have against you. Leave me, Monsieur. Break the chains which can only cause you shame. Return to your former self, and let me go to my convent, with the sad consolation that it was at my behest you left me, not because you deserted me. I will keep you no longer. I bid you a last farewell.

She rose from where she had been sitting, close to me,

after having talked at this great length, and without a single word of interruption from me. I looked at her and saw her eyes full of tears which she was struggling to hold back, but which were brimming there in spite of her efforts. She was about to leave in order to hide her emotion from me, but I drew her back and made her return to where she had been seated. I threw myself at her knees and took and kissed her hands. I wept as she did, and found no word to say. I had been pierced through the heart by her farewell. I remained for a long time in that position. Our hearts were both riven with pain, and we remained motionless save for our eyes. What is it? she said at last. Why do you keep me here? Why do you not leave? Ah! How could I? I answered. That was all I was able to say. After that, I was not even able to open my mouth. She raised me up, and I took a seat, where I remained for more than an hour, insensible, as if in a daze. All I remember is that she was no less distraught than I was.

At last, I roused myself and, without saying anything, I offered her the ring which I had taken from my finger, but she refused to take it. I said farewell, but my eyes belied my words. How beautiful she was at that moment! Indeed, no one in my place would have been able to resist her charm. How fraught with expression, and how inconclusive, was the adieu spoken by our eyes! I told her I would bring her diamond back some other time, and that I did not consider our farewells complete. She replied only with her eyes.

I returned to my mother's house more pensive than I had been when I left. I was at odds with everything. I was at odds with myself. I now saw this same Silvie whom I had so despised no longer as a cheat and dissembler, but as someone adorable – unfortunate in her birth, and innocent in her conduct. If she had practised any deception on me, she had been acting only out of love and devotion. I interpreted the dishonest stratagem she had thought to play on me only as revealing her ardent love for me, employed only out of fear of losing me. I saw only her dazzling beauty, which had always enthralled me. I no longer remembered the resolutions I had made to leave her, nor the scorn which I had so arrogantly heaped on her – except to crave her pardon for it. My gibe – that she would pay for her crimes at the hands of an executioner – now seemed an outrageous slur, which I could not expiate even with the last breath in my body. How could I escape the Star which ruled my fate? I was wholly at its mercy.

I abandoned myself to my destiny, though not without remorse. How would I hide from my mother this change of heart, so contrary to the resolution I had expressd to her? By what means could I justify the fact that I was still in Paris, and that I had returned to Silvie? Would she accept the explanations Silvie had given, as I had done? How could I remain in good standing with my uncles, after so many twists and turns? Did I not appear fickle and irresolute – or worse, weak and lacking in character? Though these reflexions shamed me, they failed to change my mind. I went back to see Silvie the next day, no longer arrogant and contemptuous, as on my recent visits, but contrite and submissive. How indeed could I be otherwise, when I thought of my own weakness? I dressed with all the elegance and splendour I could muster – a fact she noticed and appeared grateful for. I found her plunged in sadness. Her room was half-dismantled, and part of her furniture already packed and ready to be removed. She asked me why I had come. I answered that I was returning her conquest to her: that I had been born only for her, and that I could not bear to have caused her such heartache.

She made no great show – as I had expected she might – of her generosity in accepting my apologies. She promised to forget everything. But, she continued, do not attribute our reconciliation to my good nature. I am moved by a stronger force – the irresistible inclination I have for you.

You will have to face your mother's anger, your uncles' indignation, and whatever might result from their resentment. I foresee, from Valeran's warnings to them, what may happen. You will have to endure whatever difficulties this may cause. And I foresee the troubles I in turn shall have to face. I must renounce my decision to save myself by entering a convent. I am willing to forget your harsh words to me, since you are prepared to overlook their cause. We continued the conversation, saying everything possible to each other to persuade ourselves that we were born for each other. I told the servants to put the furniture back in place, and dined with her, while we continued our protestations of devotion the while.

But after all, I said, are we always to be at the mercy of this Valeran? I know him, she answered, he has begun and he will continue. He is a villain who will not stop delivering his unseasonable commentaries. The fury which possesses him will not die down; on the contrary, it will redouble if he discovers that you are still seeing me. But, I asked, is there no way of silencing him? I know of none, she said. I went hoping to see Monsieur le Commandeur de Villeblain this morning, to tell him in general what has been happening and to ask him to give the knave a warning. His kindness to me in the past and the authority he retains over Valeran would ensure that the latter would think twice before trying to do me further injury if the Commandeur were here. But he left Paris only a week ago to take the waters at Barbotans in the Pyrenees, and he is not expected to return till the end of summer. I thought of approaching Monsieur and Madame d'Anemace, but decided not to do so because, apart from the fact that Valeran was dismissed from their service in disgrace, I might have been led into a discussion of matters which Madame de Cranves forbade me to reveal. If he was honest and intelligent, I would ask you to see him, and you might persuade him to desist. Meantime, if you are prepared to do what I ask, I know I could remove any lingering suspicions you may have about the allegations he made against me. I have none, I answered. Nonetheless, she said, I need to talk to him, and you could hear what he has to say for himself if you wish. How do you propose to do this? I asked. All I have to do is to send for him, and you yourself can hear how he defends himself. After the harm he did you, I said, he won't come. I would agree with you, she said, if I did not know him. But since I know what a ruffian and knave he is, without wit or judgement, with no shred of decency in his soul, and without shame, I am sure he will come – he may even think that I shall be grateful to him. I agreed to do as she wanted, and she wrote this note:

I wish to speak to you, Monsieur. Come to my house at once. I am alone and am waiting for you. Follow my messenger.

She sent her lackey with this note and told him to tell the recipient she was alone. What are you going to do when he comes? I asked. I want him to tell me why he acted as he did: why he sent such messages to Madame Des Frans and to you; why he sought to ruin my reputation in that way; and how he discovered the things he told you. I wish to know, in a word, what his motives are and what he was hoping to gain. I want to hear how he explains himself.

We continued to talk thus while awaiting Valeran's arrival. But, Monsieur and Madame, said Des Frans, breaking into his narrative and addressing the master and mistress of the house: I don't know if listening to me has given you a thirst, but all this talking is certainly making my throat dry! One needs to be a more experienced hero of a novel than I am to tell such a long tale without interruption! Let us have an interlude! Everyone was in agreement. They all sat down to a luncheon, during which they discussed what they had just been hearing, and everyone agreed with Madame de

Mongey, that if what Silvie had said to justify herself was true, she was quite innocent, and was guilty of neither malice nor misbehaviour. It was in fact all true, said Des Frans. About two months after marrying her, I was able to obtain the promise of marriage which she had given to Garreau, and the letter her father, Monsieur le Marquis de Buringe, had written to Madame de Cranves. It was through Monsieur le Commandeur de Villeblain that I had them. Moreover, without being requested to do so, and not knowing that I had any interest in the matter, he recounted to my mother – while I was present – all of Silvie's story, exactly as I have told it to you. If that is so, interrupted Dupuis, Silvie has always been the victim of her lovers – who have themselves proved unfortunate; while honest and virtuous in fact, she has always been wrongly suspected, and in the end, though seeming guilty when she died, she was in fact entirely innocent. Poor Madame Morin – an honest and virtuous woman if ever there was one – paid with her life for her devotion to Silvie and her affection for her. Let us make our observations later when there is more time, Madame de Londé interrupted. At present, if Monsieur Des Frans is able, let him finish his story. I believe everybody is anxious to hear the rest.

I hid myself, Des Frans continued, as soon as I heard Valeran coming up the stairs. What can I do for you, Mademoiselle? he asked as he came into the room. I have just received a note from you. Am I in the happy position of being able to be of service to you? I would do any possible service for you, at the cost of my life or of all that is most precious to me. Be seated, said Silvie, and I will tell you what I want of you. He did not comply immediately, but in the end he was persuaded to take a seat, and she sent her lackey out of the room.

I am extremely pleased to see you, she said to him. You must be aware that it is a matter of some importance which obliges me to send for you. I am aware of that, Mademoiselle, he answered, and that my presence is only agreeable to you to the extent to which I can be of help to you. We are alone, she broke in, although I fully realise that I am running a risk in allowing this to be so. But I am confident you will show no lack of respect for me here. Certainly, Mademoiselle, he said, you have nothing to fear. I am too ashamed of my first offence to repeat the mistake.

If shame for a wrong you had done prevented you from repeating it, I would have no complaint to make against you now. But so be it, what is past is past, and I am prepared to forget what is over and done with. I am even prepared to speak in your favour to Monsieur and Madame d'Anemace, from whose service you were dismissed; and I can promise, any effort on my part to help you regain your position would not be in vain. In return, I ask only one thing: will you do it? Yes, Mademoiselle, he said, if what you ask is within my power, rest assured I will do it. It will cost you nothing, she answered, but it must be agreed. He promised, swearing the strongest oaths. I accept your word, then, she said. What I ask of you is that you answer my questions truthfully. Can you guess what these questions are? He seemed to squirm a little and to hesitate. Where is the honesty you swore to me? she asked. I can guess, Mademoiselle, what they are, he said. You wish to ask about Madame Des Frans and her son. You are right, she said. Tell me why, in your letters to them, you accused me of theft and of being Garreau's mistress. I can forgive what you said about my birth, since you do not know the truth – though I can assert that the most distinguished man in your family would consider it an honour to be a servant to the lowest in mine. Answer me precisely and honestly, for your whole future depends on your doing so. Tell me the truth now, and don't force me to call on others to discover it for me. You can be certain that a man of your position in life could not triumph against me. It were better for you to earn your pardon through your honesty.

His self-assurance was undermined by her imperious tone. He tried, however, to twist his answer and began a lengthy explanation. These are not the facts I wish to know, she said. Tell me precisely: What proof have you of my relations with Garreau, or of the theft you spoke of? I spoke of it, he said, only as a suspicion, and as knowing of it only by hearsay. You yourself were the source of the rumours, she said. Why did you revive them, after the attention the matter brought you from Madame de Cranves and myself, while Monsieur de Villeblain was with us? Why did you continue to spread it around? Ah, Mademoiselle, he said, What does jealousy not force us to do? You know my feelings for you only too well, and I was in despair on seeing that Garreau was preferred to me. He deserves to be called Monsieur Garreau by a man such as you, she said. But what did you hope to gain? He was a bachelor, while you were married. He had a right to aspire to my hand, without offending me, whereas you did not. That is true, Mademoiselle, he said. But taking your position as it appeared to be, I did not consider I insulted you by admiring you. Very good! she said. That is to say, your motives were hardly honourable. But why did you take it into your head to repeat the same stories and untruths to a man who seeks my acquaintance and friendship, and who was unaware of them? Was that to please me? What did you hope to achieve?

Ah, Mademoiselle! he answered, throwing himself at her feet. You do not know yourself if you believe that a love you have once ignited in a man's heart can ever be extinguished. My feelings for you have not diminished – though my respect has increased. I wrote to Monsieur Des Frans to turn his heart against you, and to his mother to ensure she would not allow him to enter into an alliance with you, and that she would force him to give you up, if he would not do so voluntarily. My passion for you is stronger than my reason. I realise that the distinction between his station and mine is immense, but hoped that, if he abandoned you, you might eventually be persuaded not to refuse to take the place left by my wife's death.

So your reason was the hope that despair might lead me into your arms? And that, though scorned by another, I would still please you. These are sentiments we might expect of such a man as you! But no – leave your illusions behind, once and for all. I put aside the question of the sudden death of your wife – who was in good health only a month ago. But if it was your doing, as seems possible, the crime was wasted. The distance between us is too great to be bridged. But at last, I have learned your reason for writing those letters, and I am glad to know it. But tell me, how did you know that Madame Morin and I had made enquiries about Monsieur Des Frans and his family, and how did you know all the rest of what you wrote? I wrote it because I guessed it was what happened, he said. I see, she said. That is typical of your nature: you concoct a pattern of conjectures, pass them off to others as facts, and then come to believe them yourself!

And as for Rouvière, she continued, how did you make his acquaintance? Ah, Mademoiselle, he pleaded, allow me to refrain from answering that question. No, she answered. This is something I need to know. Very well, Mademoiselle, he continued. I will tell you. But it will make you dislike me even more! On the contrary, she said, the more honest you are, the more kindly disposed I will be towards you. Give me the answer! What can I say? he said. My wife's death had made it possible for me to think of aspiring to your hand. I set out to find you and discovered where you lived, and in a bar not far from where we are now I heard that a young man of quality was apparently courting you. I followed him one evening and learnt with dismay that he was Monsieur Des

Frans. I looked for a way to cause a rupture between you, so that I might win you – by whatever means. I was pondering how this might be done when I ran into Rouvière on the Pont-Rouge. He was on his way to the Tuileries. It did not take long for us to renew our acquaintance. I knew him as a man capable of anything, ready to undertake any dubious scheme, and who, once embarked, would stop at nothing. I decided to confide in him and persuade him to help me, whether by wile or violence, in my design, but just as we reached the Tuileries he told me he did not have time to hear me out, as he had a meeting with someone who knew me and it would not be wise for me to be seen. I left him, the person arrived, and I recognised Madame Morin. I hid so that she would not see me, and waited until their conversation – which lasted a considerable time – was over, before catching up with him to ask what they had been discussing at such an unusual hour.

I know the man's weaknesses. I took him out to dine and discovered the intrigue he was involved in. Thus I was in a position to do what I wanted, that is, to delay the conclusion of your arrangements with him. I persuaded him to add a supplementary demand and talked to him about you and Monsieur Garreau and Madame Morin, using whatever calumny came into my head. I knew there was no question of your agreeing to any arrangement which would be to the detriment of your good name and reputation, and was certain his indecent proposal would be rejected: all I wanted was to delay any agreement being reached, so that I could have more time to write my letters and advance my own plans. So I made him write to you there and then from the place where I had taken him. I had the letter delivered to you and made him swear to stick to his demand.

I then wrote to Madame Des Frans and to her son. I was convinced he would never visit you again, and that my letters would never come to your eyes. I felt sure that his anger would be directed only at Madame Morin and Rouvière, both of whom I was ready to sacrifice in the hope of advancing my own plans. This is the truth, Mademoiselle. These are all the misdeeds that my love of you has led me to commit. I do not dare to tell you my love will never die, for I see the anger in your eyes. But I would ask you, if I dared, why you – who claim to be of such high birth – would be willing to pass for the daughter of Rouvière. It is true, he is a gentleman by birth, but he has forfeited that distinction by his conduct.

I made no agreement to answer your questions, she said. That is something which must remain a mystery to you. But, in admitting that you wished to destroy my reputation, and were willing to sacrifice Madame Morin and Rouvière, are you not afraid that I might persuade him to take his revenge on you, and avenge me for your disrespect and the harm you have done? I doubt you would reap much honour if he were to confront you. I assume you have not grown more valiant than you used to be, while he is considerably more accomplished than Garreau was – whom you never dared meet in honourable combat.

But have no fear: I promised to forgive your misdeeds, and even to do you a service, and will keep my word. But take care to mend your ways, and to speak of me only with the respect you owe to those who are your masters. Remember what Madame de Cranves and Monsieur le Commandeur de Villeblain have said on the subject. Had the latter been in Paris, I would have made you pay dearly for your interference. Listen to me and make no further attempt to meddle in my affairs, or in those of Monsieur Des Frans. What business has a good-for-nothing like you to stir up trouble among the members of a distinguished family? And by what authority does such a one as you advise that a charge of unlawful congress be brought against me, or that a man who never did you any harm, whom you do not know, and whom it is indeed in your interest not to know, should be confined in a secure place? If I had revealed your identity and told him it was you who had written those letters, you might well be lying dead by now. All I need do is let him know this, and were he to give free rein to his anger, you would receive a thrashing you would not survive. Take care, I repeat, or your foolishness will bring dire misfortune on your head. You have my pardon, as I promised, but remember you are the only enemy I have in the world and I shall hold you responsible should anything untoward happen to Monsieur Des Frans or to myself. Enough, she said, rising. Remember what I have said, but forget me, if possible, for my peace of mind and for your own. Never come here again. My rooms are besmirched by the presence of a knave such as you. I shall be dining with Monsieur and Madame d'Anemace and will let you know of their response. With that, she dismissed him.

I came out from where I had been hiding. So, she said, what do you say? My opinion, I said, is that he is a consummate scoundrel and a man to be feared. I might not have restrained myself from making him pay for his misdeeds there and then, even though you were present, had I not thought of another way of avenging you – through another miscreant who is no better then he – Rouvière. I must devise a means to draw them into a fight with each other. It should not be difficult to do so. By tomorrow at the latest, I am sure it will be done.

I see now why you remained so patient while listening to our exchange, said Silvie. You have my approval to do what you suggest, and, as you heard, I made a similar threat to him myself. There is no doubt but that one of them will wreak our vengeance for us and dispatch the other; but I don't see how it can be done without our names coming to light. Someone will seek to separate them, and they will reveal the subject of their quarrel; we shall be implicated, and my reputation will suffer. The story will do the rounds of Paris and come to the ears of Madame Des Frans. People will embellish what they hear; even if nothing is added, appearances are already bad enough to damage both our reputations. It would be better, she said, to leave those two malefactors to their own devices. Fate will take care of them for us. What you say is true, I said. But I will take care that your name is not mentioned.

I then told her everything I had said against her to my mother, and how troubled I was by the promise I had made that I would leave Paris, and by the problem of how I could now gainsay it and remain here without my mother guessing why I was doing so. For what reason can I now give her, I said, after the adamant declaration I made? If we were to have rendez-vous and meet privately, she is not a fool, and would soon have someone follow me and find out everything I do. If she sees that I have been deceiving her, I am afraid she will adopt the harshest measures against me. And what I fear even more is that you might be the one to suffer, for I do not think it safe to count on the kindness she has always shown me in the past. For it is often the case that people who are generally mild-tempered know no bounds once their patience is finally exhausted. My mother is one of these people. My violent and exaggerated outburst against you, I continued, convinced her that I had given you up completely. What will she say if she finds out that I have changed my mind, have continued to see you, and have been deceiving her? These are the problems we owe to Valeran's interference! Silvie cried, bursting into tears. There is no way to escape them! It is better for us to separate! I foresee nothing but difficulties which will overwhelm us if we refuse to give each other up.

These lamentations and counsels of despair are not what I hope to hear from you, I said. My heart will not permit me to think of leaving you. I only told you what I had said to my mother so that we could try to think of a way to remain true to each other, yet protect ourselves from the unfortunate consequences that seem to threaten us. And which are in fact inevitable, she added, interrupting me. But, she said, tell me, do you have the fortitude to endure an absence? For Heaven's sake! I cried. What are you going to suggest? I see no other alternative, she said. It would be for you to decide how short or how long to make it. But that is the only solution. You are telling me to leave you? I asked. Yes, I am telling you to leave me, she said. See how much I love you, she continued, since the fear of losing you forces me to such desperate measures. You cannot ignore the promise you gave your mother; your apparent readiness to go and your seeming indifference to me will remove any suspicion she might have. You will not be followed, no one will ask how you spend your time, and you will be able to find some excuse for hastening your return. All the storms which threaten to engulf us will dissipate while you are away. We will be able to correspond with each other. I do not anticipate that either you nor I need fear any of the dangers an absence can entail. Your return will be the proof of your love. I cannot believe that after what has passed you are ever going to leave me for another; and for myself, I think that the deceit I contemplated – which now fills me with shame – should prove to you that I shall be true to you. In other words, I believe that we are each confident of the other's heart; at least, I do not foresee any infidelity on your part or on mine. Agree then, my dear love, she said, taking my hand in hers, let us triumph over ourselves first. It is the key to triumphing over others.

We reached no conclusion that day. This course of action seemed too desperate for me to agree to immediately. We arranged to meet the following day, when we would come to a decision. I returned to my mother's house, apparently calm, but in reality in cruel distress.

On my way home, I thought about what Silvie had proposed, and realised she was right and the plan she suggested was necessary. I ate supper with my mother. Well, Mother, I asked, have you been able to see my uncles? Shall I be leaving soon to undertake some service for them, or shall I be going away merely to please myself? I have had a great deal of trouble convincing them, she answered. So many changes of heart, one after the other, on your part, have made it difficult for them to credit that you have really sown your wild oats and that this time you are to be trusted. But finally I pledged myself as your guarantor. You are to leave in four days, with Monsieur le Cardinal de Retz, who is returning to Rome. You must be properly – even impressively – equipped and provisioned, since your position will require that you spend freely and make appearances in public. Your uncles and I will provide the means for this initially. It will be good for you to travel and see other parts; and Italy has much of interest to offer. In a year or two, when you are a little older and have proved yourself, we will find a permanent position for you; but at present your uncles are not prepared to give you any serious responsibility. They are afraid you are still too rash and unpredictable. So you will be spending from your own inheritance. This will make you more careful, but they will put you in a position where you will be able to more than recoup your outlay in due course.

This was what she told me, and it did not surprise me. And your Silvie? said my mother. You haven't said a word about her. How are things between you? I leave that to your imagination, I answered. I have not even seen her since reading that letter and the warning you received. And if she were the only person in Paris, I would not care if the whole place fell down! Very good, she said. That is the right way to think about it. Keep those sentiments in mind, and you will find peace, honour and good fortune!

In spite of what I said, I had in fact made up my mind to

see Silvie the next day and to send for Rouvière. In the event, I did neither. I had barely woken when Querville, the man who had sold me his horses, came into my room and asked for a word in private. I sent my servant out and asked Querville what he wanted of me. I will come straight to the point, he said. My acquaintance with you is of recent date, but I know no one else in Paris. I have therefore come to you and am taking you into my confidence, and asking for your help. After that, he explained the problem he had, and I could think of no one but Rouvière who could help him in the circumstance. He had got himself embroiled in some youthful escapade which necessitated a two-week delay in his marriage, which was due to take place in two days' time. I went back with him to the inn where he was lodging, where I met his father, who was one of the leading members of the Parliament of Rouen.

I then went to look for Rouvière. Though he was still lodging at the same inn, he did not take his meals there, not being able to afford to do so. As soon as he saw me, he launched into a tirade of reproaches, and if I had been disposed to take offence, we would have discovered which one of us could outmatch the other. I let him have his say and vent his spleen, and then I told him I was the Monsieur Des Frans concerned in his negotiations with Silvie. I told him about the information my mother and I had been given by Valeran, and what Valeran had said about him in the letters – which I embellished in the retelling. And to prove that what I said was true, I showed him the passages where he was mentioned in the letter Valeran had addressed to my mother, which I had brought with me for the purpose. Fortunately, Rouvière recognised that it was indeed Valeran's handwriting, and changed his tune on seeing it. He began to make excuses for his part in the projected deception, saying that, not knowing me, he had been ready enough to help Silvie out, the more so in view of his parlous financial state, which had made the prospect of earning a hundred louis irresistible to him. His long-winded excuse provided some further vindication of Silvie and Madame Morin and gave me added evidence of Valeran's malice, for he had tried to persuade Rouvière to kill me, saying I was the cause of all his difficulties. Rouvière fulminated against Valeran with the greatest ferocity and told me terrible things about him. I stoked his anger, while making it appear that I was damping it down. When I had produced the reaction I wanted, and he had the bit between his teeth, he was ready to stride off, sword in hand and demand satisfaction of Valeran. I accompanied him back to the inn and persuaded him to let the matter rest for the time being. He said no more about Valeran, but he avoided the subject in such a way as to convince me that he had made up his mind to settle scores and rid the world of his presence.

When he had calmed down sufficiently, I told him that if he was willing to do something for a friend of mine, I was sure this friend would reward him in such a way as to compensate in some measure for what he had lost because of Valeran. He promptly asked what service the friend needed. I told him about Querville's problem, using an assumed name. He thought about it for a while, then said with decision: It's as good as done. You can tell your friend that I will take care of his problem before noon tomorrow. He can count on me. Let him appear to want the marriage to go ahead, but I promise he will not have to proceed until it suits him. Since this man of Le Mans was a man of action, I had no doubt he would be as good as his word, and I told him thereupon that it was Querville who needed his help. He was delighted to hear this, for, as he said, he is a good sort of fellow – down to earth, with a deep pocket, and he knows how to drink with a will! I was impressed at this summary of the qualities needed to be counted among this man's friends, but I made no comment.

As Querville had left with his father to go and see his fiancée, we had to await his return. I was not worried about going to see Silvie since my meeting with Rouvière had turned out so well, and I had not needed to mention her. He had not even asked if I had made it up with her, so discreet was he where she was concerned.

At last Querville arrived. He and Rouvière spoke and agreed on what had to be done, which was performed the next day. But since this has nothing to do with my own story, I will save it for some other occasion, when I will tell you Querville's adventures, as he related them to me in Rome – since he was forced to leave France after his marriage to escape the aftermath of a duel at which he had been present.

I went the next day to see Silvie and told her what I had said to Rouvière about Valeran. Valeran had seen Rouvière the previous day and had told him he had confided in someone who turned out to be a traitor and had told Silvie everything. Silvie, he said, had then sent for him, Valeran, and asked him to get rid of the traitor – who was me. I also told her that Rouvière was determined to avenge us all. She was worried by this, for fear of her name being involved, but this did not happen. In fact, on the same day on which Rouvière had settled Querville's affair for him, at the very time when I was talking to Silvie about him, he killed his enemy with a single sword stroke through the heart – at which Valeran fell to the ground without a word. As for Rouvière, he took himself off – I don't know where he went. I have never heard of him since.

That was how Valeran perished – the result of his interference in other people's affairs. Rouvière did him a kindness, however, preventing him from ending on the scaffold. In fact, four or five months later, I discovered Silvie had been right, and that he had poisoned his wife. In spite of that, we felt some regret, she and I, for having been in part responsible for the death of a man – even though he deserved it. We never spoke of him again after his death, any more than if he had never existed. No one could ever find the name of the person who killed him – Rouvière had covered his tracks so well. I only recognised him from the description I was given. In fact, you are mistaken about that, Des Ronais interrupted. I know Rouvière's life almost by heart. He died in prison not long ago. He had had eight interrogations, the records of which I have read. The fact of his death, and the intervention of honest and prominent people for whom he worked prevented any trial from taking place. Apart from that, we know everything there is to be known. His life was a succession of setbacks and wrongdoing, all of which turned out badly for him, but all were a source of amusement for those who, like the average law-abiding person, know little about the life and escapades of a scoundrel. We can laugh at his misdeeds and mishaps some other time. But for the present, let us hear the rest of your story.

For myself, Des Frans continued, as Silvie and I had concluded it was necessary for me to leave, I made up my mind to our separation. During the next two weeks while I was still in Paris, I didn't visit her any more in her home. But we met elsewhere every day. I bade her goodbye at a place four leagues outside Paris. We made arrangements to exchange letters safely. She asked me if I would let her keep Madame Morin to live with her and serve her. She reminded me how Madame Morin (who didn't dare show herself and always disappeared when she saw me) had always been with her, but said that if I had any objection she would not keep her any longer. She added, however, that Madame Morin was the only person she felt able to confide in, since she was the only person who knew her; and that she would miss her sorely, having been used to her companionship since she was a child; but that all these considerations counted as nothing if I had the least reservation.

I was grateful to Silvie for making this request so honestly. I told her that it was true, I had some misgivings about Madame Morin; I could not help remembering the letter she had written to Rouvière. When she informed him, I went on, that you would not dream of considering the demand he had had the effrontery to make, it was clear that she had spoken with you about it and perhaps entertained the possibility that you might agree to it. You are wrong, Silvie retorted. It was Rouvière who put the proposition to me in a letter, and Madame Morin, to whom I showed this letter (the one which I had torn up and gave you in pieces), was thoroughly disgusted by the suggestion. In any case, I said, I trust you so absolutely that I would not wish to deprive you of a companion who means so much to you. All I can do is urge you not to be influenced by any questionable advice from her. You are still mistaken! she said. She is on your side, and your interests are her interests. It was only because I was so afraid that the story of my birth would repel you, and because I begged her to, that she agreed to make contact with Rouvière. And I swear to you that no one is more delighted than she that I have chosen you. And no one could be more ardent than she in your praise. I wish with all my heart that you would make enquiries among people who have known her for many years, for they would tell you that her reputation is known to be impeccable. In that case, I answered, keep her. I give my consent with all my heart.

This exchange between Silvie and myself had been taking place in a hostelry where our meeting was taking place, and at the conclusion Madame Morin appeared from behind a bed where she had been hiding and assured me of her undying loyalty. She tried to persuade me that she had said nothing to Silvie which could be construed as indelicate. I broke in on this speech and asked her to arrange for dinner to be brought to us. She went and left Silvie and me alone.

Silvie was right, Dupuis commented, to tell you that Madame Morin was known as a perfectly respectable person, as I have already said. I accept that that is so, answered Des Frans. Monsieur le Commandeur de Villeblain spoke to me about her in the same vein after my marriage, but her moral principles were not perhaps invariably inviolable. Her principles never faltered right up to her death, said Dupuis. Listen to what I have to tell you! said Des Frans.

I was left alone with Silvie, as I said, he continued. I tried to wrest some favour from her which would ensure she remained true to me – and was obliged to be satisfied with verbal assurances that her loyalty would withstand every test. She forced me to take one of her diamonds, incomparably superior to the one I already had, and to keep it as a memento of her love; and she promised to keep on her finger the one which I returned to her. She wanted to give me a purse filled with gold coins, which I refused, for indeed I did not need it. We exchanged portraits and separated.

I was away for only five months, including both journeys and the time spent in Rome. I accompanied Monsieur de Créqui, ambassador to Rome, on his return to Paris, making use of this as my excuse. My heart had already been calling me home for some time. I had heard from Silvie several times and had written to her very frequently, but since our letters consisted only of expressions of our mutual and undying love for each other, you will excuse me from quoting from them. I informed her of the day when I should return, and she came to meet me – at a distance of eight leagues outside Paris. Nothing could have been more tender and affectionate than our reunion. I was madly in love with her and thought she returned the feeling in equal measure. I told her I had resolved to marry her, if she would consent, without consulting my family. I explained my reasons to her, which were that my mother would never give her consent, not only because of what Valeran had said about her, which my mother still believed, but also because she would not allow me to marry yet, saying I was too young. I made it clear that, if I spoke to my mother, and she refused her consent, as appeared only too likely, her opposition would be so insuperable that we would never be able to marry during her lifetime.

Silvie understood my reasons. Not, she said, that there is any danger your mother might find me unable to compete in terms of wealth with anyone else whose hand she might seek for you. I have as much as you could hope to receive, whoever you married, and more than you would look for. But because she will think that I came into possession of this wealth by dishonest means, as Valeran told her, and because she is not aware of my extraction and the circumstances of my birth, she would not wish you to marry someone of whom it was known only that she had been disowned and abandoned at birth. I did not wish to speak so bluntly, I said. But you are right: these are the reasons which would make her withhold her consent. The fact is, said Silvie, of all the members of your family, you are the only one I wish to marry. I myself need no one's consent, and you are legally of age. Therefore, I will marry you as soon as you wish. I accepted the money she had brought with her, so that I might appear to have husbanded my resources carefully when I showed it to my mother. Our decision was reached. We proceeded together towards Paris, separating only when we were at a distance of one league.

I can only repeat – that it is destiny that determines whom we marry. I was greatly in love with her, but in spite of this I frequently wished I could delay the marriage. I felt a terrible reluctance within myself. But I did not let this show. On the contrary, from the moment we reached the decision I have just told you about, I did my utmost to hasten the conclusion. And at that time, since there were fewer restrictions on how marriages should be conducted than there are at present, I was able to make all the necessary arrangements within three days.

We drew up a marriage contract in which she called herself Silvie de Buringe, natural daughter of the late Marquis de Buringe and of Lady Marie Henriette de —. It contained no acknowledgement that I had received anything from her. I undertook to provide her with a lifetime pension, and she gave me six times as much money as was required to establish this annual income at the rate current at the time. It was she who insisted absolutely on this arrangement. I have no relatives, she said, and at present I have no heirs to consider, and if, as time passes, I have any, they will be children and you will be their father, and there is no better place to put what belongs to them than in your hands. If I die before you, she continued, and leave no children, I would not wish to leave you in need in any respect, or in danger of falling into debt. All I have is mine alone, and I leave it all to you. If you die first, whether you leave me with children or not, there will be nothing when you are gone to keep me in the world. I have no interest in who inherits from you, since I shall certainly withdraw into a convent for the rest of my days, where the pension which Madame de Cranves settled on me and that which you have given me will be more than sufficient to cover my needs.

Tell me honestly, said Des Frans, interrupting his narrative, have you ever heard of anyone acting in a way that was more disinterested and selfless, more straightforward and more generous? As well as all her money, she also forced me to take her jewellery, which was worth almost as much as the money. If I were to die and leave her young and widowed, she would have been in a position to make a brilliant marriage with someone in a very different station from myself. Her marriage with me would have removed the barrier of her birth; and her wealth, in money alone, was far

beyond anything I could have expected – without mentioning her jewels and her furniture, all of which were
extremely beautiful and valuable. But no, to prove that she
loved me alone and had no other consideration in mind,
and that without me the world meant nothing to her, she
disposed of everything in my favour and, overcoming my
objections, forced me to accept it all. By parting with all
rights to her property on her marriage, she made it certain
she would have no alternative on my death but to spend the
rest of her life in a convent.

No, the more I think about this, and the more I
remember what she did, the more I have to say to myself
that women are incomprehensible! After a gesture of such
generosity, how could I hesitate? The arrangements were
made and we were to be married in two days' time, when, on
the day after the contract had been drawn up, I received a
letter from Monsieur le Comte de Lancy urgently begging
me to return to Rome with all speed, saying he awaited me
impatiently. It was he whose influence had enabled me to
return from Rome, and I had sworn to be back there when
he needed me: without this pledge he would not have given
me the support which allowed me to come back to France.
It was now necessary for me to leave Paris within four days to
allow time for a journey of three hundred leagues.

To tear myself away from Silvie at that point without
marrying her was more than I could immediately bring
myself to do. I told her of the dilemma I was in, and she
tried to persuade me to stay in Paris another two days at
least. I explained that it was a matter of honour, and that
the Bishop of —, who had transmitted the letter from his
brother, the Comte de Lancy, would notify the latter of any
delay or dilatoriness on my part; besides which, my word
had been given and my honour was at stake. She wept: I
would have weakened, but since it was an affair of honour
which could not be resolved without my presence, I

remained firm. I did not have the strength, however, to deny her request while I was with her. But I returned the keys of her coffers to her, which she had forced me to take, left her, and went to the Bishop and asked him to notify his brother that I would set off post-haste. Since the former had been enjoined to urge my immediate return, he was delighted to do as I asked. He questioned me about the nature of the affair, but I did not think it right to enlighten him, any more than I had explained it in detail to Silvie. He wrote his letter and as he did so, I took my pen and some paper, and while he was writing to Rome, I wrote to Silvie:

If I were less moved by your tears, I would have said my goodbye in person, but seeing them I feared my resolution would fail me. It is a matter of honour which requires my departure, dear Silvie, and I would consider myself unworthy of you if I did not submit to its command. Leaving you, my heart is more deeply stirred by your affection than I can tell you. Forgive my absence. I dare to believe that you share the pain it gives me, but, dearest Silvie, it will not be for long. The distress I feel on leaving you should prove to you that I put my word and my honour above all else: it is on my word and my honour that I promise to return to your side a month from today. Take good care of yourself on my behalf: I shall not be well satisfied if your distress allows you to neglect your beauty during this time. I hold you responsible for your well-being, and should it have suffered when I return, I shall believe that you take no pains to please me.

I also wrote to my mother, telling her of my departure. I gave both these letters to the chaplain with instructions not to deliver them until I had left Paris. I then mounted my horse and rode off. I reached Rome four days earlier than expected, which gave me time to rest until the day which had been chosen to bring the affair to a conclusion. It concerned the Comte de Lancy, and my part was that of a friend only. You can guess what sort of thing it was. He had indulged in some dalliance which had come close to being his ruin, and had two rivals who hated him with a vengeance. The matter was concluded to our satisfaction.

That evening, I received a letter from Madame Morin telling me that Silvie had fainted on reading my letter, thinking I had abandoned her; that she had fallen into a fever, with pain on one side of her body; and that she had been bled twice on the day I left, the same day on which the letter had been written. I immediately requested leave to return to Paris, which I received only with difficulty, through the good offices of Monsieur le Cardinal de Maldachini, since our ambassador needed the support of all the Frenchmen he could muster, particularly those who could cut some sort of figure. I caught the post-coach and was the only passenger. I did not reach Paris as speedily as I had hoped. Crossing the Alps, we were attacked and I was wounded by the bandits who make a living there and in the mountains of Savoy. Everything I had was stolen, leaving me with only the shirt on my back – excepting only the ring which Silvie had given me, which by great good fortune was left. I don't know how this happened, except that it must have escaped the thieves' notice in the dark. My postillion's concern for me was so rudimentary that he abandoned me to the robbers' mercy; or it may have been than he was in connivance with them, for he certainly took me by a route I had not used previously, telling me it was shorter. And in fact I don't doubt that he delivered me up, since I have heard that others have suffered the same experience. As they say – if it were not for the people of the Dauphiné, one could say that the Normans were the most rascally people on earth. Excuse the digression! I lost enough to make it a painful memory for me. They took, among other things, my portrait of Silvie, which I regretted the most bitterly, though not the longest, for I still had the original to whom I would return; it was the absolute lack of money which caused me the most suffering.

I reached Grenoble only with the greatest difficulty and in such a state – I must have been unrecognisable. I went to one of the meanest hostelries in town, since I was in no shape – on the strength of the torn shirt which covered my body – to present myself at a more prestigious establishment. By good fortune, a Carmelite monk happened to be passing: I called him and told him the plight I was in. He believed me and took pity on me. I gave him the diamond and asked him to pawn it and bring enough money for me to live on till I could receive word from Paris. He went and brought a jeweller back with him, who took my diamond and gave me, so he said, all the money he had. I was thus able to move to the inn where I had previously lodged, the best in Grenoble. I had new clothes made, but could not proceed on my journey immediately, as I was not well enough to travel. I wrote that day to my mother, telling her what had happened to me, but as I doubted she would have enough money in the house to send me what I needed, I also wrote to Silvie and asked her to send me some. It was as well I did. I don't know why my mother has never liked to keep money in the house. I believe it is because she is afraid someone will cut her throat and steal it. Her habit was to put everything in the hands of her brothers-in-law and obtain from them as much as she needed to live on for two weeks at a time at most. The first news I received from Paris did not come from her. My uncles, Messieurs Des Frans were away from home, and my mother had to borrow some money. Silvie, who had ready cash available, had lost no time. As soon as my letter arrived, she sent me far more than I needed. This is the letter I received from her by return of post:

Your misfortune is the reward for the hard-hearted way you treated me. Far from condemning the bandits who robbed you,

I would have thanked them if they had treated you on your outward journey as they did on your return. I am, however, happy that your diamond escaped their hands, for without it your very life would indeed have been in danger; you would have been in truth the Knight of the Sad Face; but I do not regret the other things they stole from you, except inasmuch as their loss delayed your return to me. I am sending sufficient funds to enable you to replace what was stolen. The postmaster will give you this sum. Return home as soon as possible; however, give mind to your health. If you want me to meet you when you return – as I expect – let me know the day, the time and the place. Farewell, dear love. I feel as if I am delaying the postman, that he is waiting for me to finish my letter so that he can speed on his way. And that he will not be in Grenoble as soon as he should be. And that I am stealing time from myself, since you will not be able to set out until he arrives.

I received this letter and the money and went straight away to retrieve my diamond. I thanked the Carmelite monk, whom I took with me to the postal agency, explaining that I would receive a letter and some more money from my mother, and asking him to return these – when they arrived – to Silvie's address, which I gave him. I hired some horses to take me as far as Lyons. In Lyons I caught the stagecoach, and Silvie met me eight leagues outside Paris. We planned how we would proceed from there, but waited till about eight in the evening to return to Paris; that is, since it was October, until after dark, so that I should not be seen.

Silvie embraced me on our reunion with more ardour and eagerness than ever before. The fear of losing me had made me even dearer to her, from what she said. We had agreed that I should not let my presence in Paris be known, and that I should not show myself there until we were married. We now had an opportunity which would enable us to marry and keep the fact a secret. My mother, in particular, would be far from suspecting I was getting married in Paris when she believed I was far away in Grenoble. Moreover, I would not be sorry to have a few days which I could devote to the pleasures of being newly married. I would therefore not make my return known until I had heard from my Carmelite monk, who was to forward the letter and the money from my mother. She would then have no reason to think I had not been in Grenoble when they arrived.

These were the plans I had been making on my return journey. When I told them to Silvie, she said I was the master, and my wish was her wish. I did not write until the next day to the people who were arranging the marriage licence and the formalities for our wedding. The licence had already been obtained, but since the wedding had been postponed I did not know whether it was still valid, and I thought the next day would be soon enough to find out. Madame Morin joined us for supper, and we ate with relish, since our minds were at ease. After the meal, it was a question of where I should sleep. Silvie wanted me to have her bed, and I said that would suit me perfectly, so long as she did not desert it herself. We were in the highest of spirits, both she and I. Since we were on the point of being married, I could take liberties which at another time would have been improper, but which were now permissible, so we discussed the matter at some length and with some amusement without tiring of it, and could not have laughed more. In the end, she slept in her bed and I slept in Madame Morin's.

As it had been a very long time since I had had a peaceful night in a good bed, I slept until late the next morning. When I awoke, I found that everything I needed to enable me to cut a respectable figure had been prepared and bought for me – there was even cloth to make a fashionable outfit and a tailor to measure me for it. I thanked Silvie for her forethought, for I was indeed in need of replacements for all I had lost. By evening, I was sufficiently well turned-out to be fit to appear at a wedding. During the day I had written to the people who were ensuring the wedding arrangements were in order; in spite of their zeal and efforts, we had to wait till the next day for the authorisation to be delivered. So I spent a second night like the previous one, but I did not sleep so well and rose earlier. I went in my dressing gown into Silvie's room. She was asleep, but Madame Morin, who was there, told me she had slept little that night. They had been chatting together all night long, and Madame Morin asked me not to disturb her mistress, since she had only just gone to sleep, saying there would not be another chance for her to rest for some time, nor for me, either. So I slid into the bed beside Silvie, without waking her, and since I hadn't slept well I also fell asleep. When I awoke, Silvie was no longer there. She was up and had dressed in the room next door, where I had spent the night. This provided the subject for much more jovial comment on her part, and she teased me with all the sparkle and wit you can imagine. Since it was late by this time, we ate lunch.

At about six in the evening, the people who were to act as our witnesses arrived, among them, the principal occupant of the house where Silvie was living and two of Madame Morin's relatives. We had an excellent supper, which had been prepared without fanfare, for fear anyone in the neighbourhood might notice if there were any unusual activity. At midnight, we went to St. Paul's Church, which was only a few steps away and where the marriage ceremony took place. It was about two o'clock when we returned to the house. We had another good repast, then everyone took their leave and Silvie and I went to bed; in love as we were, I can leave you to imagine the rest.

I remained at her house for a week, going out only to

Mass, and that so early in the morning that I went back to bed when I returned. What a life! A man would indeed be happy if such an existence could continue indefinitely! Though she pleased me infinitely, I had eventually to desert her. I received news from my good Carmelite in Grenoble, who had faithfully done all he had promised, and I sent him some books in appreciation of what he had done for me. And then I had to think of separating from my wife. The next day, we arranged an outing some six leagues outside Paris with a few people who knew our secret, using this as a pretext to cover my return to Paris. We left at six in the morning in a hired coach. I wore the clothes that had been made for me in Grenoble. We went to the Plessis, on the Fontainebleau road, so that it would appear as if I came from that direction. We separated about three o'clock. Silvie and her group returned to Paris, and I went on to Fontainebleau where the Court was in residence, and where I hoped to find friends who would not fail to report that they had seen me. And in fact I found several there who had heard of my misadventure on the road near Grenoble. To console me, they took me to supper and to the theatre, and gave me the opportunity to win two hundred louis from them.

I returned to Paris the next day, taking the water-ferry from Valvin so that I would not tire myself unduly, and went to my mother's, arriving two or three days earlier than she expected. She thought I would be arriving on the carriage from Moulins, where she had asked me to check on some minor business we had there. Once again, I had to have new clothes made, and, of course, I went out that evening – you can guess where I went!

It was about six weeks after my return to Paris and after my marriage that Monsieur le Commandeur de Villeblain – who, as I told you, was a close relative of my mother – came to dine with us at the house. I received him with my most civil and courteous manner, and resolved to find out, with my mother present, whether what Silvie had told me was true, since she had cited him as her most reliable witness. With this in mind, I brought up the subject of his absence and found out that he had returned only the previous day. I had been with Silvie all that day – I had even slept with her – though my mother thought I had been to Versailles, which is where I had claimed to be going the previous day in connection with an appointment I was interested in. I knew for sure therefore that Silvie had not spoken with him. This was in addition to the certainty that he was not the sort of man who would ever lie, whatever the situation. We moved on from a discussion of his travels to the subject of the war, and then to that of the war in Candia in particular. He had taken part in the fighting, and among those of note who had died he spoke with regret of Monsieur le Marquis de Buringe, who, he said, had been an outstanding officer and a close friend of his, a brave and honourable man. He spoke of the Marquis's family, mentioning Madame la Duchesse de Cranves. This was what I had been waiting for. Do you remember seeing in the Duchess's house, I asked, a young girl by the name of Silvie, whom the Duchess had taken into her home in an unusual act of charity? Yes, indeed, he said, and I have some acquaintance with her, and would be happy to be of service to her if I could. I have a high regard for her. If I knew where she was living at present, I would pay her a visit

You are very generous towards her, I said. It is unusual for a man such as you to have any concern for a girl in her position. She is worthy of my concern, he said, from several points of view of which you are unaware. Moreover, when I left Paris, she was becoming known as one of the most beautiful and accomplished of women. You are right, Monsieur, I responded, to say that no young lady could be more accomplished than Silvie, who benefited from

Madame de Cranves's desire to give her every opportunity to cultivate her abilities. If Madame de Cranves, he said, was so attentive in providing for this girl's education, it was not purely out of charity. There were other powerful reasons, and I have heard the Duchess say that Silvie was so pleasant and likeable that she pursued through inclination a course of action she had initially undertaken out of duty. Why, Monsieur! I exclaimed. You are surely not suggesting that we question the good name and respectability of the Duchess! You would certainly be totally misguided if you were to harbour such suspicions, he laughed. Madame de Cranves was the very epitome of honourable and upright behaviour. And if Silvie had a special place in her household, it was as a result of some other circumstance which in no way reflected on the Duchess personally. But, he continued, apparently you are acquainted with Silvie?

Indeed, he knows her, as I can tell you, interposed my mother. He knows her so well that had he not been apprised of her dubious character, I don't know what might have happened! You surprise me, Madame, said the Commandeur, when you describe Silvie as someone of dubious character! I have never heard any suggestion from Madame de Cranves – who knew her at close quarters – that anyone had accused her of any conduct which fell short of a rigorous standard of virtue. Then she must have changed a lot since then, said my mother. If one attacks the reputation of a girl like Silvie, the Commandeur continued unruffled, one must have some very convincing evidence. Mere hearsay would not suffice. I admit, he said, I take an interest in anything concerning her; I would not believe without proof that she had brought discredit on her birth and upbringing.

What is that birth, then, Monsieur? I asked. One does not commonly find persons of illustrious birth in the place where she spent her childhood. If you hadn't broken with her, he said, in a gentle voice, as I see you have, and if you still counted yourself among her friends, I would tell you who she is – even though, by so doing, I might not please certain people of high rank, who wish to appear not to know her, though in fact they know very well who she is, since they were told and her claims were proved to them in my presence – though Silvie herself does not know that this is so. And if I told you, you would agree that, as far as the family to which she belongs is concerned, you could find those whose lineage is inferior with whom an alliance would nevertheless do you honour. And as for wealth, it goes without saying, you would never find anything to equal hers. This much I am quite sure of. But I do not believe a word of what is said about any reprehensible behaviour on her part.

I must give you the facts, Monsieur, I said, and prove that I broke with her only as a result of irrefutable evidence; and I rose to go and fetch from my desk the warning letter which Valeran had written to my mother, which I had kept for the sole purpose of showing it to him, to see whether what he would tell me accorded with what Silvie had said. He took it and read it from beginning to end. When he had finished, he returned it to me, and spoke again. I am astonished, he said, at what I have just read; but if the person from whom this letter comes is no better informed about Rouvière than about the rest of what he says, I can assure you that he is either mistaken – if he honestly believes what he has written – or is an out-and-out rogue, if he has made these accusations in order to injure the young lady in question. If you know who he is, this report-monger, he continued, I could provide him with more accurate information, if he deserves to be so treated; if not, I would take other measures to deal with him. No, Monsieur, I said. I do not know who he is, and I merely keep this letter as a means of preserving me from temptation.

Well then, he continued, I think I will have to tell you what I do know for certain. Preserving the reputation of a person such as Silvie is a good enough reason for me to reveal a secret which was confided in me by someone who is now dead, and at the risk of alienating some who are still alive – who, however, would forgive me for the sake of defending the reputation of a young woman who is a blood relative. Are you willing to hear what I have to tell you? My mother urged him to proceed, even before I did.

He related the circumstances of Silvie's birth; her upbringing at the Orphanage; her removal to live under Madame de Cranves's roof; her intended marriage to Garreau; the gifts of money and jewellery she received from Madame de Cranves; Valeran's disrespectful behaviour and gossip-mongering; the education she had received while with the Duchess of Cranves; and finally, he recounted to my mother all that Silvie had told me privately, the facts being the same in every detail. He added only one thing, that Silvie had never been told, and still did not know, who her true mother was. Silvie believed it was someone by the name of Monglas, a lady-in-waiting to Madame de Buringe, but this was not so. This person, who had indeed been secretly married, died in childbirth, whereas Silvie's mother – a woman of very high birth – died much later. She had had a liaison with the Chevalier de Buringe – later the Marquis de Buringe – on the strength of a promise of marriage which he had given her. They loved each other sincerely (the Commandeur added) and had pledged to marry, but since neither was in a position to do so at the time, they had not dared to let their relationship be known and had been forced to relinquish Silvie to the orphanage – while providing signs by which she could be recognised. When his older brothers died, Monsieur de Buringe – not having as yet made his vows – returned to France intending to marry his mistress and reclaim their child, but discovered that she had been forced to marry M——, in spite of every attempt on her part to resist the marriage. It was in order to save this person's reputation that he had told his sister that Silvie's mother was a lady-in-waiting who had died in childbirth. His mistress's desertion had turned him against all other women and he refused to marry, and had been killed in Candia; he had not been long outlived by Silvie's mother.

But what I don't understand, the Commandeur continued, is the deceit which Silvie plotted with Rouvière. I know the man, he added, and though he was born a gentleman, if justice were done, he would have been dispatched by the hangman more than thirty years ago. It makes me suspect something, and if you don't mind lending me that letter, I will look into the matter; and, if only to satisfy myself, I will ask Silvie about it tomorrow. I would go today if I knew where she was. Do what you like with it, I said, handing him the letter. It is of no consequence to me; and I assure you, whether she is innocent, misjudged, or guilty, I would never again consider marrying her.

You must be terribly ill-disposed towards her, said he, to speak so vehemently. I take no offence, however, in spite of the warm interest I have in her; but I assure you, she has changed greatly if you are right about her. I can even assure you that she is not the sort of young person who would throw herself at a man or take the lead in establishing a romance, nor would she readily lay herself open to rebuff. I was delighted to hear him give such warm praise to someone for whom I cared so deeply. My mother, who saw Monsieur de Villeblain almost ready to break into a reproach at what I had said, was herself startled by the bitter tone of my words, and by the derogatory way I spoke of Silvie to a man whom she respected greatly and who had a personal knowledge of the young woman in question. She apologised for me and signalled to me to leave them.

I did so, after reiterating my profuse expressions of respect to the Commandeur. His servant told me where he

was staying, which fortunately was not far from Silvie's
house, to which I immediately made my way; and without
saying a word, I made her sit down, and lay pen, ink and
paper on a table before her. I was laughing and put the pen
in her hand, and hardly giving her time to ask what I was
doing, I directed her to write according to my dictation. She
wanted to know what this was all about, but I merely dictated the following note:

> *My spies are everywhere, dear Monsieur. I am grateful to you
> for having so generously defended me just now at the house of
> Madame Des Frans, against the accusations of her son – who
> is a complete dunderhead. I shall be pleased to tell you what-
> ever you wish to know about my behaviour. I have not done
> anything which would make me unworthy of your good opin-
> ion. The kindness you have always shown towards me requires
> that I give you an account of what I have done. I await your
> visit, if you will be good enough to come to my house.*
>
> *I am, Monsieur, your very humble and obedient servant,*
>
> *Silvie de Buringe*

I took the letter and sealed it, and then put it in front of
her. Write the address, I said. To whom? she asked. To
Monsieur ... Monsieur ... I repeated 'Monsieur' five or six
times. For pity's sake! she exclaimed, seeing my laughter,
Who is it? The Commandeur de Villeblain, I said. At this,
she let out a cry of delight, leaping up to hug me. Is he in
Paris? she asked. You have seen him? Yes, I answered. Do as
I say. She wrote the address and sent her footman to deliver
the letter, telling him to wait for the Commandeur's return
if he were not yet home. He did not delay. I barely had time
to give Silvie a summary of the conversation which had
taken place at my mother's house when the footman
returned to tell us the Commandeur was on his way. She
went to greet him, and I disappeared for a few moments.

There is no need for me to tell you how delighted they were to see each other. He asked her how she could possibly have come to know so quickly about a conversation which had only just taken place. I have a familiar spirit, she answered, who tells me everything that is said or done at Madame Des Frans's house. He wastes no time, he said laughing. No, but seriously, how did you know? I am not deceiving you, she answered, also laughing. It is my familiar who reported to me. You will see him; and if you will do us the honour of dining with us, it will give us great pleasure. Here, she continued, calling me, Come and join us. This is my friendly spirit, she said as I came into the room. Could I have any better informant? Indeed! You are right, Madame! answered the Commandeur, and I have been in error, addressing you as Mademoiselle! I understand perfectly now why you spoke as you did, he said to me, with an embrace. What I said about Silvie must have delighted you! I played the role of simpleton – and you were speaking the truth when you said you would never again consider marrying her, for, as far as I can see, the deed is already done – without your mother's knowledge?

You are right, I answered. And neither my mother nor any other member of my family is aware of it. You saw the reasons I had for acting in secret when you read the letter a good-for-nothing knave wrote to my mother. I said when my mother was present that I didn't know who had written it, but my wife told me it was the same person, Valeran, whom you spoke of, and indeed, it was he. My mother believes what the letter says is as true as Holy Writ, and I didn't think I could persuade her otherwise, having nothing would prove its falsity. So I thought it better to proceed without informing her, rather than risk losing Silvie by asking for my mother's consent, which I know she would have refused. So my intention is to appear wholly indifferent to Silvie, in order to deflect suspicion.

Before I married her, I talked to Silvie about the letters my mother and I had received, and heard her explanation. I am glad I believed what she told me. During the conversation at my mother's house today, I tried to direct the subject towards Silvie, not to discover if what she had told me was true – I never seriously doubted it – but so that you yourself could provide my mother with the information simply and directly, not knowing of our marriage. It gave me the greatest pleasure to hear what you said. I was delighted to hear you speak so warmly of Silvie, and I was exultant when you became heated in her defence, and I would have led you on even further, to give my mother even stronger proof – except that I was reluctant to deceive you further.

I would not have relinquished my defence of the daughter of a man who was dear to me during his lifetime; to whom I am indebted in many ways; whose memory I will always cherish; and who, beyond all this, left his secret in my keeping and asked me, when he died, to be as a father to his daughter. It was for these reasons that Madame de Cranves always discussed with me everything that concerned Silvie. I was well aware, I answered, how good you have been to her. She can tell you how I dictated the note she wrote asking you to come here. I thought it better not to surprise you as you left my mother's house, by telling you then that Silvie was my wife. You were not pleased by what I had said, and you would not quietly have listened further to me. Moreover, such an unexpected piece of news would have given you a surprise which might well have been noticed, and have made it necessary for me either to reveal what I had been taking great care to conceal or to add further to the deception, which I preferred not to do. So, instead, I had my wife invite you to come here, and was the more willing to do this since you had indicated you would be glad to see her and speak to her. You acted wisely, Monsieur, he said. But what I wish to discover now is how your wife explains the episode concerning Rouvière, for, to tell the truth, I am troubled by it. And then, I should like to know what happened to her after the death of Madame de Cranves and, finally, how your marriage was arranged. I can well understand your interest in all these matters, I said, and we will be only too happy to tell you the whole story, both to satisfy your own curiosity, and also in the hope that you might pass on to others whatever you learn. It is more likely to be accepted and believed from your mouth than it might be if it came from anyone else.

I am happy to be your intermediary, he answered. You can count on me to do anything I can for you. I am delighted to see you two young people united, for the two of you are like son and daughter to me: you, Monsieur, he said, speaking to me, are the son of the best friend I ever had, of whom I may say I arranged his marriage with a cousin of mine; and you, Madame ... he would have continued, turning to Silvie, but she interrupted him to exclaim: You are related to each other? Yes, Madame, answered the Commandeur. Madame Des Frans and I are the children of two brothers. Ah, you rascal! she said to me, giving me a tap on the cheek. You never told me! You thought I was only telling you fibs! And you, Monsieur, she said, addressing the Commandeur and embracing him, you have been a good parent and a true father to me. He responded warmly to her enthusiasm and told me she was the daughter of a man to whom he was extremely indebted. Therefore, he said, both for your own sakes, and in memory of your fathers, I will do all I can for you and render you any service in my power.

We thanked him for his kindness and goodwill, and then Silvie told him all that had happened to her since Madame de Cranves's death: how we had met, how our marriage had been arranged. It was only when it came to Rouvière that she was embarrassed, and it was I who told him this part of the story, but I did not reveal that it was I who had set him up for the fight with Valeran. The Commandeur told us he was pleased to be informed about these events. He praised both Silvie and me where our conduct deserved praise, but he did not exonerate her for the deceit she had been prepared to practise on me. He insisted that honesty is invariably preferable to any alternative. She did not try to defend a bad cause, saying only that she would not have acted as she had done if she had been able to say that she was the daughter of Monsieur le Marquis de Buringe, but that since she had nothing with which she could prove this, she had thought she might employ this artifice to provide herself with parents; she truly regretted the intended duplicity and had shed many tears over it. He told her that – rather than benefit her – this deception might well have rebounded to her detriment; that untruth has only a short lifespan, whereas truth lives for ever. If Rouvière's death was in keeping with the sort of life he had lived, he said, she would have been more shamed by the supposed relationship than by being born the lowliest of commoners, since, in whatever station it pleases God to place us, we are responsible not for our birth, but only for our actions. She acknowledged the wisdom of this, as you will understand.

Monsieur de Villeblain ate supper with us, and he and I decided what measures we could take to reclaim the letter the Marquis de Buringe had written to Madame de Cranves, and the promise of marriage that Silvie had given to Garreau, from the courts of law or from Garreau's heirs. This we did the following day, and I still have both in my possession.

Silvie went out of the room for a moment to order the supper. She sent someone to call me out so that she could have a word with me, and asked if she had my approval to invite Monsieur de Villeblain to take his meals at her house in future. I said I already had it in mind to do so, and we then returned separately to the room. We sat down at table, and Madame Morin took her usual place. Monsieur de Villeblain spoke of her in terms which put an end to my suspicions. I wish to God there had never been cause for me to renew them! During the meal, Silvie said to Monsieur de Villeblain that, as he had no home of his own in Paris, and was therefore obliged to take his meals at a common table with other lodgers in the establishment where he resided, and accommodate himself to other people's whims and habits, something which was not always pleasant for a man of his age, and an arrangement which did not always provide all the comforts and convenience one could wish for – because of all this, and since he was living only two or three doors away from her house, she begged him to retain only his living quarters there and to take his meals with her. She said she would not order a more elaborate table for him, but that she had some excellent wines – such as he would not find at his lodgings! She said she would be delighted and honoured if he would accept her offer. I added my entreaties to those of my wife and, after some resistance, he accepted, on condition that his servants would not eat here and would only come to the house when called.

Meantime, as my wife had put a very considerable sum of money into my hands (and wished moreover to sell some of her precious jewels), she wanted me to buy a government appointment for myself, which I agreed to do. I initiated negotiations for an extremely attractive position and offered to pay for it in cash. This came to my mother's ears, and she asked me how I came to have such a large sum of money at my disposal. I told her some friends were lending me it, but I could see she was not entirely convinced and would inevitably begin to have suspicions. I preferred that she should know the truth, rather than leave her to be troubled by doubts, and I asked Monsieur de Villeblain to see her and tell her everything.

He went immediately, taking with him Monsieur de Buringe's letter, which we had recovered a short time before (we had torn up the promise of marriage from Silvie to Garreau). He arrived at the house as if there were no particular reason for his visit. He knew I was not there, since we had dined together at Silvie's. But nonetheless he asked for me. My mother told him I was not at home, and asked him what it was he wanted to see me about. I came, he said, with apparent nonchalance, and pulling some papers from his pocket, to finally remove from his mind any doubts he may still harbour about Silvie, and to restore the esteem he originally had for her and erase the distorted picture painted in these papers. I have discovered the whole truth, not only from her, but from others who can be trusted. I know all there is to know, and she is innocent on all counts. I was not wrong when I was unwilling to believe that she would stoop to any unworthy action. On the contrary, it is your letter-writer who deserves to be sent to the gallows. My mother, being curious, like all women ... Continue your story, Monsieur, Madame de Contamine broke in. We can do without your comments on the nature of women! I crave your pardon, said Des Frans. I was carried away by what I was talking about, and inadvertently slipped into a generalisation, forgetting that it might not meet with the approval of some of my audience. So, my mother told him she would be extremely happy to know the whole story. This is what he had anticipated. He pleaded Silvie's cause before her as if it were his own daughter he was defending, and staked his own honour on the truth of what he said. He showed my mother the reasons for all that Silvie had done, condemning only the incident concerning Rouvière, which he had not wished to omit, and in recounting which, because of his great love for Silvie, he sought to minimise her guilt.

When he had convinced my mother about Silvie's innocence, he began to speak to her about me. He showed her the advantages Silvie was able to give me and had already given me. He tried to make her understand that I would immediately acquire some standing, without owing my fortune to anyone else. He told her he was convinced I could never find a better match, and that he himself was willing to speak to me and try to repair my relations with Silvie, for he was sure I still loved her. And as for Silvie, he continued, she still loves him. So, Madame, if you will give your consent, I am certain our efforts would not be in vain. What do you say?

I think like you, Monsieur, answered my mother, that our efforts would not be in vain. Let me be even more sincere with you than you have been with me. It is quite clear what the situation is: my consent is not needed. The appointment my son is buying has removed the scales from my eyes: this is where the money comes from. They are married already, is that not the case, Monsieur? she said. He, who was the very acme of honesty, admitted that this was so and did all he could to win her approval for what was already done. And, he told her, we would be the happiest and most contented of couples if she could bring herself to pardon us for having acted without her consent.

He went on to say that he was absolutely convinced that Silvie's virtue was untarnished, and that my mother would find herself fully rewarded if she brought Silvie into her home, and would never regret it if she accepted her as a daughter-in-law. He said, if she wished, he would arrange for Silvie to speak to Monsieur and Madame d'Anemace, and was certain that they would be willing to acknowledge her relationship to them, for the sake of the family she now belonged to, and would indeed confirm all that he had just told her. And furthermore, he said, the accurate account Silvie had given me of her past ought to count in her favour. Far from criticising what I had done in marrying Silvie, continued Monsieur de Villeblain, he admired me for it and would have done the same himself had he been in my place. She should not be surprised that I had said nothing to her: I had feared, with good reason, that she would refuse her consent, and that she would vigorously oppose my wish and intention, if she had had the least inkling that I planned to make Silvie my wife when she had set her mind against it; that I realised the nonsense and falsities that a scoundrel had conveyed to her had etched themselves so deeply on her mind that there was nothing I could say which would erase them. For all these reasons I had been right to say nothing to her. He read her Monsieur de Buringe's letter, which gave undeniable proof that Silvie was his daughter, and as for everything else she claimed, he assured her that he himself had seen it with his own eyes.

Having said all he could concerning the practical issues involved, he turned to address religious and emotional considerations. He said that Silvie and I were certainly made for each other. He recounted the extraordinary way in which we had met. He pointed out how the hand of Destiny was visible here: the instant inclination we had felt for each other from the very first moment; the futile attempt which had been made to separate us; the change of heart I had undergone, which made it impossible for me to leave her. All this, he said, was evidence of the most steadfast love that two people could have for each other. A further proof of Silvie's devotion to me was her generosity in bequeathing and sacrificing all she owned to me. All of this taken together, he said in conclusion, has the appearance of a marriage made in Heaven and smiled on by Destiny. God had certainly made us for each other and our marriage had satisfied His will, and should be respected.

My mother listened to all he had to say without interrupting him. For some time she remained uncertain what decision she should make. She considered the matter long and hard before coming to a resolution. At last, she answered Monsieur de Villeblain as follows: If I did not trust you absolutely, Monsieur, I admit I would not believe a word of all you have said. But since I know you are the most honest and most honourable man in the world, and am certain that no lie could pass your lips, I cannot doubt that what you have told me is the pure truth. I believe it solely because it comes from you. If it had come from my son, I admit, I would have called him a liar. But from your mouth, I am convinced it is nothing but the truth.

But, Monsieur, put yourself in my place, and tell me what you would do. I have an only son who marries without my knowledge: this is already a serious blow for a mother. Added to that, he marries a girl whom he knows I believe to be a thief and a cheat, without family and without morals – for, after all, I have only come to believe this is not the case as a result of what you have just told me. To what shame was he exposing me? To what difficulties was he exposing himself? If I had learnt of this marriage from anyone other than you, I would have died of heartbreak, and I would have bequeathed to him nothing but curses, and the scandal this would have caused would have deprived him and his wife of any respect and consideration in society. Without taking any of this into account, he marries his sweetheart.

I myself may no longer believe all I had heard about her, but will I be able to convince my brothers-in-law that all I had told them was false? They know it was because we had been warned about her disreputable character that I dispatched my son to Italy at such short notice. And will they be able to convince all those to whom they have spoken that they had been misinformed? Imagine for a moment that they believe what I will now tell them – which I think unlikely, for, if the truth be told, they are well aware what he is capable of, and what I am capable of doing to shield and protect him – if I now tell them he has married this girl, far from believing me that she is not the worthless deceiver we had thought, they will think I am blinded by my partiality, that I have let myself be misled once again and am trying to mislead them in my turn. He will be completely undone in their eyes and will have no credibility left. They will still think of Silvie as a foundling, think her wealth was stolen, and believe that everything I originally told them, and that accords with appearances, is true.

You may tell me that my son no longer needs them, and that he has no need to worry about what they think. That may be true as far as he is concerned, but what about me, who have no other child – if I take his wife into my home and treat her as my daughter-in-law, and see her misused by everyone else in the family as a nobody? And besides, Monsieur, she continued, how do you explain away the deception she was prepared to practise on him? She couldn't prove she was the daughter of Monsieur de Buringe? A fine excuse! You were able to get possession of the letter – why could she not have done so? Only young fools and visionaries would accept the excuse that it was because she loved my son so much and was afraid of losing him. The deception was too cleverly conceived and arranged to be taken merely as the result of youthful desperation. In my opinion, anyone who could design a strategem of that sort is dangerous and makes me wary. It seems to me a little too knowing and artful a scheme for a girl who is not yet twenty years old. I cannot pardon that and, were it for that reason alone, I will never accept her into my household.

She loves my son, and I am grateful to her for that. She loves him, he is her husband, and so in this she does no more at present than her duty. I accept it is true that if she had not loved him, she would never have given him such a large sum of money. I agree with you, she has paid a good price for him! I like her generosity. I like her character and her strength of mind, in giving up everything for him. I hope to God she will never repent of what she has done, and that her love for him remains true. But I cannot forgive the rest.

So, Monsieur, let me tell you frankly what I have decided. I will never receive her to live in my house. I could never feel comfortable with such an artful, scheming person. As for the marriage, I did not approve of it, nor do I disapprove of it. He can live with her as he likes, and I will not oppose or hinder him. Indeed, I will treat her as a daughter-in-law in private, but not in society, for the reason I have given you, which is the low esteem in which she would be held. I will let her visit me here, and I will visit her, but I insist absolutely that the marriage be kept secret during my lifetime, so that I will never have to suffer the chagrin of seeing a daughter-in-law whom I have acknowledged scorned by the rest of the family. It is in my son's interest therefore to accept this condition to avoid a breach within the family, and to protect his wife's reputation, or rather, in order that she should not lose it completely.

Let her live in her own house, and he may continue to live in mine, to prevent unwelcome chatter. He should let her move to a house where she is the sole tenant, so that people do not become aware of their relationship. He should pay only the rarest of visits to her during the day. Provided they keep the matter secret I will not interfere, since their marriage is already solemnised, and she does no wrong in receiving him. But I do not want anyone to think of her as my daughter-in-law, for she is no credit to me. This then, Monsieur, is what I have resolved, and nothing will make me change this decision. If my son will keep his marriage secret, we can remain good friends, and I will forgive his lack of consideration for me; but if he wants to proclaim it openly, I do not wish to see him ever again – even less his wife.

This was all the Commandeur de Villeblain could obtain from her, and he had to acknowledge the good sense of her decision and admit the validity of her reasons for taking it. He was good enough to come to Silvie's where I was waiting for him. We did not have to ask him to tell us what had been said. Without prompting, he reported the conversation word for word. I had hardly expected my mother to accept the situation so calmly, and I recognised that she did so because of the complete confidence she had in Monsieur de Villeblain and because of the care he had taken in putting our case before her. I thanked him for what he had done, but I was afraid Silvie would not be happy with the outcome, which I felt was particularly hard on her. I was pleasantly surprised by her reply when I expressed this fear.

You do not know me very well, she said, embracing me. It was you I wished to marry of all your family; therefore it is of no consequence to me whether your uncles know that I am your wife or not. They have not met me, and I have no desire either to know them or to be known by them. With regard to your mother, I am very satisfied with the way she is prepared to accept me. She knows that I belong to you by a marriage sanctified by the Church, and she is ready to accept our union. She does not wish our marriage to be known, and I understand her reasons for that. She herself believes in my innocence, and that is sufficient for me. I wished to see my reputation cleared in her eyes, for your sake. She knows the truth, that is all I care about. What others think of me is of no importance. By keeping our secret, we not only can enjoy the pleasures of marriage, but will find them augmented by a spice of mystery. I have more than one reason for being pleased with the arrangement she has decreed – the principal one being my fear that you may cease to love me, which would inevitably happen if I were the butt of scorn on the part of your family. I should see your love evaporate, for one does not continue to admire what is rejected by others. I accept the conditions

404

Madame Des Frans offers us, and I beg you to accept them too.

I was delighted by this unselfish response, and Monsieur de Villeblain was pleased by it also. We sat down for our meal and agreed that I should immediately buy a government charge and look for a house where Silvie could live, nearer to my mother's, and more comfortable than the one she was in at present.

It did not take me long to find such a house. There were plenty available in the neighbourhood, which was formerly the most popular in Paris, and is now the most deserted, since the area was cleared and replaced by the new construction in the Butte Saint-Roch. The house had a garden with a hidden gate which gave on to a narrow alleyway, on the other side of which was my mother's garden, so that from one gate I crossed straight to the other, and could come and go at any hour of the night without disturbing anyone. All I had to do was to procure a key, which I did. Silvie came to lodge there, and soon afterwards I bought the house. It is this house which I am planning to move into now, since I intend to sell or rent the other one, which is neither so pleasant nor so comfortable, being of a much older style.

The beauty of the new arrival caused something of a stir in the neighbourhood. You were the first person, said Des Frans to Dupuis, to mention her to me. I pretended not to know her. I had determined to hide from everyone the fact that she was my wife, for the reasons I've explained. I saw her only rarely in public and I made it appear that my affections were engaged elsewhere. Keep to your story, said Des Ronais, in an attempt to save Madame de Mongey, who was blushing slightly, from embarrassment. We all know about this. There is no need to bring the matter up again.

You are right, admitted Des Frans. And it is not the only fault I have been guilty of in my life. There were certain times when I visited Silvie, and as I was often with all of you and Gallouin, she asked me to tell her who you all were. I sang your praises to her – as might be expected, since you were my friends and decent, honest people! I told her too much about Gallouin, though, and it was he, in the end, who injured me where I was most vulnerable. She liked you all and spoke well of you all, but since she had not yet learned to dissemble, she spoke most highly of him. At the time, I didn't give this a second thought. But, whether through jealousy, or hindsight, or hatred for him, it now comes back to me – and I think it really was so.

She had been living quietly, with very few visitors, but nonetheless appeared to be a person of some distinction; and though her household was modest, it was adequate for her position and gave a favourable impression; and finally, she was always impeccably dressed, with pristine linen, fine embroidery and beautiful jewellery – which she loved and of which she owned a considerable quantity. In a word, she gave the appearance of being a young woman of very good family and extremely wealthy, so in due course all the young, unattached dandies began to think she merited their attention. She did not like having a large company in attendance and restricted her salon to a small but select group, which gathered nearly every day, either at your house (said Des Frans to Madame de Londé) or at her own house, where Madame Gallouin, your mother, allowed you and your sisters to appear regularly. Gallouin was one of the number too, as was also Monsieur Dupuis. It gave me pleasure to see how everyone was attracted to Silvie. I noticed – but without qualms – that Gallouin was particularly attentive and began to be accepted as her most assiduous admirer. But since – thank God – I am a good Parisian and incapable of jealousy, I was unconcerned. On the contrary, I was delighted to see her so happy, and – far from opposing this more sociable lifestyle – I encouraged her to

spend more time in company. When she and I were together, she joked with me about the offers and overtures she
received. She would have liked to lead a quieter life, such as
she had had in the rue Saint-Antoine – with the company of
girls and women only, and without men – but I was opposed
to this. How could I have foreseen that someone who had
done so much for me, and whose affection seemed to grow
every day, would prove unfaithful? Only a prophet could
have foretold this.

She had already been living close to my family home for
three months without having seen my mother, except in
passing. They were both eager to meet and have some
conversation together, but what pretext were we to use to
introduce her into the house, without revealing the real
reason? I could have brought her in the back way through
the garden, but my mother would not allow this. She
thought Silvie attractive from what she had seen of her. Her
beauty and her manner were pleasing and what she heard
about her from other people increased her curiosity. She
wanted to find out if her mental abilities matched her
beauty; she believed this was so, but wanted to prove it for
herself. Monsieur le Commandeur de Villeblain, who had
been away from Paris and who had now returned, settled
the matter. He took Silvie to my mother's house and
introduced her as a relative of his (which she was in a way,
since he was my uncle). And then my mother repaid the
visit. I was delighted to hear that both were well satisfied
after these meetings. The Commandeur left shortly thereafter to return to Malta, where he died about three years
ago. He had been sadly moved at the news of Silvie's death,
which I had given him, without daring to supply any details.
While he had been in Paris, he had done all he could to
smoothe relations for us with my mother and my uncles,
acting like a real father. My mother and Silvie visited each
other frequently, as if out of politeness, but in reality out of

a combination of duty and inclination, for my mother certainly developed a genuine affection for Silvie, which led her, in conjunction with Monsieur de Villeblain, to tell my uncles about our marriage. It had even been agreed that the marriage should be made public, and this would have been done had I not had to leave suddenly just as the announcement was about to be made.

The purchase of the appointment I had been interested in had never been completed. We had not been able to agree on the price, and furthermore Silvie and I had begun to feel less sure about it, because it entailed responsibility for tax money – which in the end belonged to the King; and if there were any irregularities or ends left untied in accounting for it, this might lead to investigations which could ruin a man, unless he were someone of a much more careful and more mercenary disposition than I was. I therefore broke off the deal, preferring to aim for an appointment at Court, like the one I have been in discussion about for the last two days. I was on the point of concluding my purchase of a position of this sort when I received news that there had been a fire in the manor house of a fine estate which I own in Poitou – almost the only property of my father's remaining in my possession.

This made it necessary for me to mount my horse and depart immediately. I found the disaster was even worse than I had been led to expect. My tenant farmer had been arrested – accused of deliberately setting fire to the house, to hide his theft of a quantity of furniture and silver which was being stored there on behalf of a gentleman of the neighbourhood who was in financial difficulties. My own finances were seriously jeopardised by all this: not only did my tenant owe me a great deal of money, but also it had cost my father more than fifty thousand francs to build the house that had burnt down. I was therefore obliged to institute legal proceedings against both my tenant farmer and against this gentleman whose fault it was, according to his own written deposition, that the fire had been started. This was what I was advised to do by business friends and by my lawyer.

Because of this, I was away from Paris for more than four months. I finally grew impatient and decided not to wait for the verdict to be reached in the local court, and, feeling certain it would go on appeal to the High Court in Paris, I left the matter in the hands of my lawyers and returned home. Wanting to have the pleasure of surprising Silvie, I gave her no warning of my return. I am now reaching the tragic part of my story. You are about to hear of my utter humiliation, my violent rage and my shameful weakness.

I had, as I've told you, a key to the gate of Silvie's garden and house. I had told no one of my return. No one expected me. I wanted to arrive when everyone would be asleep, and indeed I reached her gate at two hours after midnight. I found it closed only on the latch, so that no key was needed to open it. I blamed this on the negligence of the household servants, not suspecting the true cause. I went up to Silvie's room as quietly as I could, to surprise her in her sleep. But it was I who was surprised when, by the light of a candle which had not been extinguished, I saw a man's clothes lying on an armchair beside the bed, and two people sleeping in it together – namely Gallouin and, in his arms, my perfidious Silvie.

What a sight! What fury and despair seized me! Imagine how I felt! I had my sword in my hand ready to thrust them through one after the other – but she made a slight movement and my hand was stayed. My eye fell on her breast, which I worshipped. My fury left me and dissolved into anguish and despair. Is such weakness possible? I was afraid of the disgrace she would suffer if I gave way to my anger – I was fearful for her honour at the very moment when she was cruelly besmirching my own! I could not bring myself to wreak my revenge with an act of cruelty which – though justifiable in the heat of the moment – belied both my tender feelings for her and my innate humanity. What honour is there, I thought, in stabbing a woman to death? What honour in attacking an enemy in his sleep? I believed these thoughts sprang from my sense of chivalry and decency, though in reality they were merely the offspring of weakness. My faithless love was wearing a necklace whose clasp was unfastened. I contented myself with taking this necklace as evidence which would convince her I had caught her in the act, committing the greatest crime possible for a woman. Then I left.

I agree with what Monsieur Des Ronais has said: one does not die of grief. Hardly had I left the house when I began to repent of not having exacted my revenge for such a monstrous injury. The next moment, I was grateful that I had resisted such a temptation and had spared my own reputation, saving myself from becoming the laughing-stock of all our acquaintances. I was in no state to be able to think of taking any rest. I turned on my heel and rode straight back to my estate in the country. There I made the arrangements that would enable me to take my revenge and thereby appease my anger and my shame. I could not forgive her: the injury was too great. But having spared her life in that moment of weakness, I resolved to make her spend what remained of it confined within four narrow walls, on a diet of bread and water, making her punishment fit her crime – if not by its immediacy, at least by its duration. I felt a sort of pleasure in depriving myself of her company, since she had made herself unworthy of my love, and in the thought that I would take her from her lover without his knowing what had become of her. I therefore wrote a letter to her, saying I would soon be in Paris. In reply, I received a letter which still makes me tremble whenever I think of it, and which redoubled my anger and scorn for her. It was filled with reassurances of her eternal love, sorrowful complaints about my absence, and anxious longings for my speedy return.

Yes, faithless one! I said to myself. Your wish will be fulfilled. I am returning to Paris. But I am returning to make sure that, by your suffering, you wash away both my shame and your crime. I arrived in Paris at last, so exhausted and so unlike my former self that I was hardly recognisable. I stayed at my mother's house and didn't go to visit Silvie, as she had naturally expected I would. On the first morning after my return, I received a message from her complaining about this indifference. I did not reply. She became impatient and came in person up to my room.

I received her icily. She tried to overcome my unnatural reserve. I did not wish to reveal my feelings and my plan of revenge so soon, and I wanted also to have my revenge on her lover before I took it on her. I did not respond to her endearments, excusing myself by blaming the fatigue of the journey. She was even brazen enough to say it was not any sensual pleasure she cared about, but only that she wished to have the joy of hearing the reassurances of my love. What a state I was in! I was on the point of losing my self-control and giving free rein to my bitterness and anger. Every loving gesture and remark she made was a mortal blow to me. Her love had never appeared stronger or more devoted, but the more ardent it seemed, the more impervious I was to it. But I would certainly have given way either to my anger or to my weakness for her if my mother had not come into my room just then, and her presence saved me from the intolerable conflict of emotions warring within me.

I went out that same day and, after searching high and low for Gallouin, eventually found him. He was extremely polite to me. This was not what I wanted from him. I picked a quarrel and made him draw his sword. I wounded him and, having him on the ground, would have completed my vengeance had others not intervened and dragged him from me. Since it was I who had started the quarrel, everyone was against me. I returned to my mother's: I had taken some of the money Silvie gave me there, and I now collected what I would need for a long journey, leaving the rest in a safe place. I told my mother I was leaving to escape the hand of the law. She knew that I had started the quarrel, and guessed there was more to my action than she was aware of, especially since I was not known to be of a quarrelsome disposition, particularly where my friends were concerned – with whom I was usually easy-going and tolerant. She asked me what the quarrel had been about and asked with such insistence that, after giving her many supposed reasons which she was too astute to accept, in the end I told her the real one.

She was no longer surprised at how changed I had been on my return. She was more surprised that I had been able to master my anger and resist the impulse to kill them both on the spot. She asked me what I intended to do. I made up some story, which she accepted. She was heartily grateful that no one yet knew of my disastrous marriage. I told her I would stay in the country only long enough to assuage the bitterest of my anguish, and that I would return to Paris in a few days to have my marriage annulled and free myself from this ignominious bond. I decided to send a letter to Silvie asking her to come in about a week's time to a place which I indicated. I asked my mother to deliver this letter to Silvie. My mother refused; she would never lend her hand to anything dubious or deceitful, and in order to avoid having to visit Silvie or receive her visits in future, she left Paris that same day and went to stay twenty leagues away, with her brother, Monsieur le Comte de Villeblain. It was fortunate that Madame Morin was no longer alive. She had expired shortly after my discovery of my wife's perfidy – in which it seems she must have been implicated, since she used normally to sleep in Silvie's room. There were rumours that her death, which had been sudden, had not been entirely natural. I made no effort to investigate whether these rumours were accurate. Whatever the truth, I was not unhappy to hear of her death, as it relieved me of the need to decide what to do with her. I had planned to have her accompany Silvie, but I had also thought this would alleviate the hardship of Silvie's punishment too much.

I left Paris without seeing Silvie, but to allay any suspicion she may have entertained about my intentions, I wrote her the most loving letter I have ever written in my life – the more tender in appearance because the less so in fact, a thing of artful contrivance, not of genuine feeling. I received her reply a week later at the address I had given her. I had said, among other things in my letter, that my greatest sorrow on leaving Paris was to be separated from her, and she said in her reply that she was ready to follow me to the ends of the earth.

This was what I had hoped she would say. I wrote again immediately and told her I did not intend to return to Paris. I said I was tired of having to take so many precautions when I visited her, and that I wanted our marriage to be made public. I told her I had made all the necessary arrangements in the country house so that she could come and live there, since I intended now to establish myself outside Paris; and that if she loved me as much as she had always claimed, she could prove it by joining me there. I added that the sooner she came, the more sure I would feel of her affection. I also said that, if she came, as was my expectation, she could sell her furniture and her china, since it could be replaced at a better price outside Paris. I asked her to let me know what carriage she would take and on what day she would be arriving at a town I indicated, which was barely a league distant from my property. I asked her to be careful not to talk about me, nor say she was my

413

wife, for fear the people I was hiding from should hear of it and have her followed in order to find out where I was.

She did exactly as I had asked; but if I had been surprised to find her in her own home in the arms of another man, she was just as surprised in her turn at the way I received her. I had hired a man – a reliable fellow from Poitiers. I told him I had been having an affair with a beautiful Parisian girl whom I had seduced, who was coming to be with me, unbeknown to her parents, and that I could not go to meet her since it was possible she was being followed, in which case I would be recognised. I told him what he was to do, and he followed my instructions to the letter.

My property, as I've told you, is about a league from a town in Poitou where the Paris–Bordeaux coach stops overnight. He went there in the evening and asked for a person named Madame de Buringe. She answered. He gave her a note which I had written in which I told her I had had a fall, which prevented me from coming to meet her myself. I mentioned also the possibility that she might have been followed. I asked her to leave her lackey and maidservant at the inn for that night, saying I would send for them the next day. She herself was to ride the horse I had sent and accompany the bearer of the message, who would bring her to my house. All this was done.

My man brought her to where I was waiting in a part of my house which had escaped the fire, and which had been repaired to serve my purpose. She saw no one but myself. I took her up to a room where the only furniture was a rough camp-bed with a straw mattress, without sheets or blanket, and a three-legged wooden stool, such as one sees in the country. There were no wall-hangings, no fireplace or chimney, and no window, except for a small round skylight, covered with an iron grating. Although the sun had already set, there was enough light left for her to discern these objects.

414

What is this place, Monsieur? she said. This is nothing but a prison cell! This is where you will be living, Madame, I answered. This is the place which has been reserved for you. Here you may bewail your crime and my shame until the day you die. No sentence of death pronounced on a criminal can ever have had more effect on him than these terrible words had on Silvie. She was unable to produce a word in reply. She fell at my feet without voice or movement, but as I had prepared myself over a long period of time, my heart was hardened and I was unmoved. I tasted the first moment of pleasure from my vengeance. After the misery I had been through because of her, I had reached a state of insensitivity and looked on her with the utmost scorn. My disdain for her merely increased. I felt no pity. I searched through everything she had brought with her and removed anything she could have used to take her own life. My aim was to treat her like a condemned criminal, whose life has been preserved for the sole purpose of serving as a warning to the public.

I shook her violently, but she showed no sign of reviving consciousness. I took a cruel delight in feasting my eyes on her – a sight both hideous and touching. How my heart had changed towards her! I have asked myself over and over how I could have summoned so much cruelty towards a woman whom I had previously idolised – whom I still idolised! I left her. And for fear I might fall prey to some vestige of remorse, I was unwilling to stay in my home. I went instead to have supper and sleep with an acquaintance who lived three leagues distant. I didn't return until fairly late the next day. I sent the same man who had met Silvie off the coach to bring her two servants to the house. I kept them with me. It had been I who hired them for Silvie in the first place, and I was certain they had played no part in her fall from virtue. I told them they would see her soon, that she had gone to stay with a female relative. I planned to send them both back to Paris at the first opportunity. But as I did not want anyone else to know where she was, I did not retain the services of the man who had accompanied her to my house the first night. I gave him a sum of money sufficient to enable him to leave the province, and even the kingdom – which he had every reason to be willing to do. My only intention at that time was to keep Silvie confined within that cell, her whereabouts unknown to any other soul, until the day she died.

I went to see her and found her still stretched out full length on the floor. She had recovered from her faint, but not from the shock, and she had not moved in more than sixteen hours. There is no way I can describe the state she was in: it was unimaginable. She looked at me, but instead of a doting lover or compassionate husband, she found an inexorable judge and master. See here, wanton jade! I said, dangling her necklace in my hand. Is this not proof? Your lover was saved from my vengeance, but you will not escape: you will pay in full what is owed to my vengeance. In reply, she threw herself at my feet, the tears flooding from her eyes. I was unmoved and gave her nothing but a disdainful smile. I threw her a parcel of rags, which might have served the lowliest of peasants. I made her take off her own clothes; I forced her to cut off her own hair – the longest, most abundant, most beautiful I have ever seen – which I burnt there and then with the aid of a candle – a sacrilege I still mourn. I gathered up the clothes she had been wearing and made her put on the tattered shreds I had brought. I allowed her neither socks nor shoes. These, then, were the physical conditions I forced her to live in; as for food, I took her black bread and water every three days.

Meanwhile, the brouhaha over my fight with Gallouin had been smoothed over – and this had been done more promptly than I had expected. I had intended to return to Paris in due course, but I no longer had any desire to do so.

I wrote to my mother and told her how I was treating Silvie. She took pity on her and begged me to pardon her. She was horrified by the harshness of the punishment I had chosen. She wrote to me, saying it was too inhuman, and she would never have let her leave Paris and come to me if she had known what I intended to do. Rather than be Silvie's judge and tormentor, she said, I should make her agree to the annulment of our marriage and, after that, have nothing more to do with her, or else make sure she went to live out her days in a convent. In a word, she said my vengeance was barbaric, and not in keeping with the honour of a reasonable man. Her advice was good, but I was not yet ready to heed it. In fact, I kept Silvie on this regimen of bread and water for three months, during which time I set about having the house rebuilt, making it larger and more beautiful than it had been before, as I now expected to spend the rest of my life there, and my interest in its rebuilding was the only pleasure I had. I amused myself sometimes by visiting Silvie, to taunt and deride her. Many times she threw herself at my feet, not asking for pardon – she confessed she was not worthy of it – but begging me to let her die quickly and free her from an existence worse than death. I would leave her without deigning to answer.

In the end, time allowed my fury to abate. I realised that her misery did not increase my happiness. I was torn by a thousand competing emotions. My remorse for the way I was treating her began to torment me – a remorse which avenged her for her suffering. Horror at what I was doing assailed me, and I began to understand the agony I was inflicting on her, and to feel pity for her. This pity rekindled in my heart the love I had had for her, and I was ready to forgive her, to ask her forgiveness for the way I had treated her, and to take her in my arms again – on condition only that she mend her behaviour.

I sent her servant-girl and the lackey on separate errands

some distance away. I went to visit her and took her diamonds back to her, her clothes, linen and lace, and all the finery I knew she loved. I told her to dress as she used to do, and led her to some rooms in the house which had been redecorated and properly furnished. I forbade her to tell anyone how I had treated her and told her to explain to anyone who asked that she had been away and had just returned. I gave her back her two servants when they returned from the errands I had sent them on, telling them their mistress was now home again. I no longer fed her on bread and water, but on the best delicacies that the local farmers and huntsmen could provide. I refrained for a long time from visiting her. I myself did not understand what it was that held me back. I let her know she was free to go out walking or to Mass if she wished, and she used this permission, without abusing it. I was happy when I was told that day by day she was regaining her health and figure.

It was more than a month after she had left her prison before I saw her. I sent one day to ask if she would like me to join her for dinner. She replied, saying I was the master and could do as I wished. I went. Her languour, the weakness from which she was not yet fully recovered, her timidity in my presence, the downcast eyes, which she did not dare raise to meet my own – and, even more than all of this, my inclination and the fatal attraction she held for me – made her seem more appealing than ever before. I cannot describe how disturbed and confused I was when I left her. I realised the danger I was in, and in my disarray as to what course of action I should take, I walked into a wood which was on my property. There I soberly examined my feelings for her. I realised that if I allowed her to remain with me, I should inevitably fall back into my previous dependence on her. I knew my love for her had not diminished; that, rather, it had grown more violent. It had been as strong as ever even while assuming the mask of revenge. I knew I was at the mercy of my passion for her, which was stronger than my will-power. I was in danger, in a word, of demeaning myself and covering myself with shame in one way if not another; and even worse, I was in danger, I felt, of giving way to a violent impulse which could reassert itself once again, as had happened in the past. I knew that it would take only one moment of rage to destroy a life which I had up till now preserved. I recognised I had done well not to discharge her maid and manservant, because they knew her and their presence had at times enabled me to master the urgings of my despair – or rather, of my disappointed love – which might otherwise have led me to end her life.

I understood therefore that our separation, and her removal to a convent, were absolutely necessary to prevent me from either descending into an abyss of shame and ignominy, or from taking her life. Having reached this conclusion, I went back to her room with my mother's letter in my hand. She threw herself at my feet, in tears. She was wearing a white satin house robe which I had often told her I found more appealing than any other attire she had. Though the dress was informal, she had taken every care with her appearance. It was clear her aim was to win back my affection. My first response was to feel gratitude for this but, a moment after, I saw it as a new attempt to ensnare me.

There is no need to abase yourself in this way, Madame, I said, raising her from the ground. I no longer have any intention of persecuting you. Read this, I continued, handing her the letter. You will see the advice I have been given, and which I shall follow if I have your agreement. If not, you are free. You can go and live wherever you please. The decision is in your hands. I am ready to return whatever I have received from you. But give up all hope of any further communication with me. You have made me too unhappy, and I have treated you too badly for a true reconciliation between us ever to be possible.

I gave her time to read the letter. Her eyes were so full of tears, she had trouble reading it to the end. She immediately made her choice: to retire into a convent. I was delighted at this decision, and I set out to select a suitable one. It was not long before this was done, but it was necessary to deliberate for some time with the nuns on the conditions of her residence in their institution. I said she was married and wished to be able to leave and return whenever she liked. The nuns were afraid that so much freedom of movement would violate the general rule of seclusion adhered to by their order, but in the end the generous sum of money which I was ready to confer on them in return for providing a secure lodging for Silvie and her maid was sufficient to obtain their agreement. She did not abuse this right to come and go as she pleased; in fact she never once left the convent after she first entered it. I informed her when the arrangements were completed, so that she could put her affairs in order and be ready to accompany me to her future home, since I was to take her there. She sent a message inviting me to dine with her. I did not trust myself and refused her even this consolation.

Early the next morning, I went to her room, having been informed that she had risen. I did not wish to see her before she was fully dressed. Any disarray in her toilette could have made me falter in my determination. How beautiful she was! How her beauty moved me! Tears came to my eyes; she knew me too well not to be aware of how disturbed I was by her presence. She tried to increase the disorder I felt, perhaps hoping to weaken my resolution. She told her maid to leave the room, as she wished to speak to me in private, and the girl went out for a moment. I suddenly saw the consequences such a tête-à-tête might lead to, and dared not risk them. I called the girl back and left the room myself. Silvie followed me, with tears in her eyes.

I had given her an authority to take whatever money she

wanted from a new farm manager I had, promising in writing anything she asked up to the limits of my revenues from the estate. I also gave her letters of credit for large sums of money by means of which she could obtain funds either in the provinces or in Paris from people to whom I had entrusted almost all she had given me. I gave her some cash and a note detailing what I had done with the rest of her wealth. She was reluctant to accept any of these, but I insisted that she do so. Then I conducted her into a small carriage; her maid, who was unwilling to be separated from her, followed her into the carriage, and I mounted a horse, as did her lackey – he is still in my service, the man who regularly accompanies me – and we proceeded to the convent which was to be her home thereafter.

She entered the building without a word, but she was in tears and her step was unsteady. She asked to have a moment's conversation with me before I left. As there was a grille between us, I did not refuse. She was so enfeebled she could barely stand upright, and sat when I said I would not listen to her otherwise.

Then it is for ever, Monsieur, she said, in tears. It is without hope of return that I am separated from you? It was your doing, Madame, I said. Our destiny was in your hands. Through your actions, we have both been made miserable, me far more than you. You are not a prisoner here. You may leave should you wish. Provided we are apart, it is of no concern to me where you may be. It was within your power to have made our union one which would be envied, but your infidelity has made it otherwise.

Ah, Monsieur, she said, weeping. I cannot undo the past. I accept the justice of what your anger drove you to do. I will not attempt to justify my conduct. It was, to all appearances, wholly criminal. I feel as though the torpor that overcame me was a dream. The more I think about it, and the more also I think about the feelings I have always had for you, the less I understand how my infidelity came about. I do not blame Fate; I do not blame the temptation of my senses: I was forced into what I did by some supernatural power. I accepted without complaint the punishment you imposed on me; I was ready to accept a future within the walls of a convent: but I had not foreseen the anguish there is for me in being separated for ever from you. No, though in body and spirit I shall be more tranquil here than in the first room where you kept me – whatever ill-treatment I had to suffer there – I cannot agree to remain here, because you will be too far away. Mistreat me, imprison me, but do not remove yourself from me! Put me in a dungeon, feed me on bread and water, treat me with the worst cruelty your injured love can devise – if I know you are nearby, my suffering will not plunge me into the despair I should suffer if you are far away. It will be less fearful a punishment for me. Do you not have bolts and chains, barred windows and locked doors in your house where you can confine me more surely than if I am here? I will remain there for the rest of my life! That is what you promised! Punish me. But do not deny me your presence. I beg you, allow me to see you – even though you come only to punish me!

It is no longer possible, Madame, I said. If I were guided by the love I used to have, and perhaps still have for you, I would yield to your arguments. But I must listen to what my honour dictates. How could you be faithful to me? How could you love me – your persecutor, when you betrayed me – your ardent and passionate lover? You are free, either here or wherever you wish, to lead a tranquil life. But I can hope for no repose, other than death, which I will seek and which I may find sooner than we think. My life can only be one filled with confusion, shame and despair! Farewell, Madame, may you . . .

Enough, Monsieur! she interrupted. Let us then dispense with polite banalities. I will talk no more of matters which give you pain. Take my jewels. I left them under the mattress on which I slept last night. They are the only possessions I have left in this world. Here are the papers and the money you gave me. I do not need them. I gave you all I had. I give it to you again, with the certainty I shall not regret doing so. I lived only for you, and, losing you, I have nothing left to live for. I have no desire for the things of this world. My life will soon be over, but what little time I have left will be spent in such a way as to prove to you that I have truly repented of a crime which was involuntary. Do not attempt to see me, I beg you. Help me to forget you. Do not enquire after me. I will persuade myself that you are dead. That will be enough to shorten the burden of my life. I will try to stifle the thoughts I shall have, not of the world, which I leave without regret, but of you. I shall die before long, a victim at one and the same time of our legitimate love, and of what was in verity a crime – yet sure of my own innocence. My virtue never left me. My God! she continued, in a torrent of tears, through what charm is it possible that these contradictory truths abide in me? Alas, it is in truth often the children who pay for the crimes of the parents! It is I who have borne the punishment for my parents' illicit love. Forgive me, Monsieur, she added, looking at me, when I am dead, for all the distress my life has caused you. Do not still hate me. I deserved your love and earned your hatred; but my misfortunes, in the end, deserve your compassion. Farewell, Monsieur. Think of me no more, and you will live more contented. I pray God may favour you with his grace and take me for victim. With this wish, I take my final farewell from you.

With these words she withdrew, bathed in tears. The sight brought tears to my own eyes, as the memory of it still does. Ah God above! I cried, as she left, is it possible that a love so tender and so passionate can be so ill-fated! I was almost ready to call her back, and remained there motionless in the convent parlour for a very long time. And then I returned to my home, where I stayed a certain while, a prey to remorse and the anguish of my lost love. The papers and money which I had given her, and which I had refused to take back from her, were brought to the house at a time when I was not there, and handed to my farm steward in a sealed box. There was no letter. I found her jewels where she had told me they were hidden. I was moved, but not influenced, by these gestures.

I decided to leave France, as a means of escaping the constant turmoil in my mind. I wrote to my mother and told her of this decision, which received her approval. I asked her to take charge of my affairs. I gave my steward instructions to go from time to time to Silvie's convent and enquire if she needed anything; and to make it worth his while to treat this duty seriously, I promised in writing to give him double any amount she took from him. This incentive was fruitless – she never asked for a penny; nor would she ever see or speak to him, or to any other visitor, having absolutely renounced the world from the time when she was no longer able to see me.

As for me, I left about a month later, without ever going to her convent, although my thoughts turned constantly in that direction and would have led me there. As I had no particular inclination to take any other road, I set out towards Paris, intending to bid my mother farewell, and to hide from every other acquaintance. I reached the place where Monsieur de Jussy recounted his adventures to me on his return from exile – and then went no further. I could foresee all the reproaches my mother would make to me, and could not muster the equanimity to face them. Indeed, how could I have borne to hear all she would say? Rather than proceed, therefore, I wrote to her and told her, among other things, that Silvie refused absolutely to agree to the termination of our marriage – which was true; and that even if she had agreed, I myself would have been unable to do so. I told her I was paralysed by a misery which never left me, and wished only to end it by seeking death.

I set out for Italy without awaiting her reply. Nothing held any interest for me. I wished only to die. So much pain was unendurable. I fell ill, but since I had no reason to preserve my life, I ignored the bouts of fever and it was not until I reached Lyons that my strength failed me. Making no effort to save myself, I attempted to continue my journey, but collapsed and had to be carried to Grenoble. My fever grew worse, and I could go no further. Since I was known at the inn where I was staying, every possible care and attention was given to me. I grew delirious. In a lucid interval I sent for the Carmelite father – the one I have spoken of before. He came, and during one of the rare moments when my delirium left me I was told that there seemed no hope of recovery for me and I should prepare myself for death. It was the Carmelite father who conveyed this to me. I knew as soon as he opened his mouth what he had to tell me, so was prepared for what I heard, and when he told me the doctors had resigned all hope, I embraced him and said I had never received better news. I spared him the need to prepare me for death, but I asked him to prepare me to meet it as a true Christian, and asked him to stay with me to the end.

While I had been in the grip of this fever, there had constantly been on my lips the names of Silvie and Gallouin, and after hearing my confession the Carmelite father was fully aware of the state of my mind and heart. The recital of these facts brought on a recurrence of the fever, and I imagined I was once again holding Silvie in my arms, in peace and perfect harmony. It seemed that Gallouin had come to tear her from me and, being unable to do so, was stabbing her while I held her. My delirium increased and, in the end, they were forced to tie me down. Afterwards, the Carmelite – who had been present all the time – described the wild contortions that had seized me and the extravagant things I had said, covering me in confusion. I completed my confession and asked for absolution. His response, and the instruction I received from him, touched me more than anything I have ever heard. He refused to give me absolution unless I promised to forgive both Gallouin and my wife. He told me I had failed in my responsibility – which was to ensure she should not be exposed to temptation. He said her fall from virtue therefore was in no small degree my own fault, not only because I had been absent for four months, but also because I had insisted on her entertaining a wide circle of acquaintance and engaging in society, when she would have preferred to live more quietly. He reminded me that we must forgive our enemies. He made it clear to me that conjugal chastity is required equally of both partners in a marriage, and that it is only because a man is stronger and has less fear of public obloquy that he does not feel constrained to conform to the same standards of virtue as a woman. In the end, he presented me with so many arguments that I could not refuse the obligations he placed on me, and I gave a sincere undertaking to fulfil them. I asked him to write to Silvie saying that I was ready to forgive her and forget everything; he did so, and I signed the letter, but since it was not my handwriting on the envelope, she never took it nor opened it – having vowed to cut herself off absolutely from the outside world.

I received the last sacrament. Everyone believed I was on the point of death, but the crisis passed and hope was revived. The Carmelite father, who never left me, was careful to uphold me in the resolve to be reunited with my wife; and having made this resolve, I was more at peace and my health improved daily. I remained in Grenoble only because I was still weak from the number of times I had been bled. The first time I went out was to the cathedral, which is dedicated to Our Lady. On the way there, I happened to glance into a small store which we were passing, and saw the portrait of Silvie – the one the bandits had stolen from me when I was crossing the Alps. The sight of it reawakened the whole force of my love for her, and I fell in a faint. The Carmelite father thought this was a lingering effect of my illness. But my servant, acting on the spur of the moment, seized hold of the picture, and cried: 'Here is the portrait of Madame!' The father then understood the situation and spoke to the shopowner, who told him the picture had come into his hands by chance, and that he had received it from someone he did not know. I took it from my servant and kissed it with tears in my eyes. The shopkeeper, when he knew it had been stolen from me, let me have it for whatever price I was willing to offer him. I carried it off and have kept it ever since.

Having retrieved her portrait, my determination to return to Silvie was strengthened even more, and I grew impatient to get back on to my horse and start the homeward journey. It was just over two months since my arrival in Grenoble, and nearly four since Silvie had moved into the convent. I requested the Carmelite father to come with me to Paris, and he agreed to do so. We covered as many miles each day as my enfeebled state permitted. Finally we reached my property, where the first news I received from my farm steward was that Silvie had died only two days before.

This intelligence, for which I was so unprepared, threw me into a quagmire of despair. I forgot her infidelity and remembered only how much we had loved each other. It was now that my devoted Carmelite companion employed every effort in endeavouring to console me. I need hardly tell you of the profound remorse I now felt: I blamed myself for her death and wanted to punish myself for it. My sword was taken from me, or I would have used it to kill myself. For more than six months I was closely watched, as if I were a madman, until eventually – though not giving up my wish to die – I gave up the idea of killing myself. It was due entirely to the good offices of the Carmelite father that I overcame my utter despair – this I must acknowledge.

He went with me to the convent where Silvie had died. My anguish returned in full force. I had a tombstone and memorial erected at her grave, embellished with every ornament and tribute my devotion could suggest. Her maid was still at the convent, still in mourning for her mistress. She knew the whole story of what had happened, Silvie having told her a part, and the Carmelite the rest. She treated me like a barbarian and a monster – with justification. The Carmelite calmed her. I wished to provide her with an income so that she could live comfortably in the world, but she preferred to remain in the convent, where she could remember and mourn her mistress. I settled a sufficient sum of money on her to give her an honourable station in the convent, and have secured a grave there for myself, when God pleases to call me, next to that of my beloved Silvie. And to ensure my wish is carried out, wherever I have travelled since then, I always carry a copy of my will with me and sufficient funds for its provisions to be carried out.

Eventually we left this melancholy place, to which I determined never to return in my lifetime. I accompanied my good Carmelite monk back to Grenoble and showed my gratitude for all his kindness to me with a gift which he said was excessive. At his insistence, I stayed for some time in his monastery, until he was satisfied he had restored me to a stable frame of mind ... If I had ever had the slightest urge to take up the religious life, I would have remained there for the rest of my days, but I have no taste for the monotony of such an existence. I left and continued on to Rome, where I found Monsieur de Querville, who had preceded me and taken refuge there some time earlier.

Monsieur de Lancy, Querville and I went to Hungary. The

fact that I had no desire to preserve my life made me a fearless fighter. People attributed actions, which were in fact the fruit of my despair, to exceptional valour on my part. We were present at the battle of the St Gotthard Pass, where the Turks were defeated. I acquired a considerable reputation, but it meant nothing to me, and since my aim was to find death, and since peace was now established between the Emperor Leopold and the Turks, I made my way to Portugal, where war against Spain had flared up. A peace treaty was signed soon after, but unwilling to return to France with Monsieur de Schonberg, I remained in Portugal where I made the acquaintance of Monsieur de Jussy – here present. He knows the sad life I led there.

I was still in Portugal two years ago when I received the news of my mother's death, which grieved me in no small degree. But I had renounced all ties with my homeland. I had no intention of returning and, had it not been for Monsieur de Jussy, I would still be living there, far removed from a place which brings many cruel memories to my mind. It is true, nonetheless, that it has given me some pleasure to see my native land again. One never loses the love of one's homeland, and the comfort I have found here has made me decide to make my stay permanent, even though I am still burdened with a deep sorrow over Silvie's death. She died like a saint and remembered me with her last breath. I fear I shall, for the rest of my life, despite her betrayal, remember her with too much tenderness.

There was not a single person among those who had heard Des Frans tell his story whose eyes were not bathed in tears. He himself was overcome with weakness, overwhelmed by the memory of so much sadness. He soon collected himself, however, accepting the consolation offered by those around him. I admire your moderation and self-control, said Monsieur de Contamine, once Des Frans had recovered from the turmoil of his emotion, but I cannot applaud it. I would have acted differently. Although, thank God, I am not violent by nature, I would certainly have killed both lover and mistress on the spot. You were justified and would have had nothing to fear. And, if I could have kept it secret, I would have included Madame Morin also in the retribution. These three murders would have been legitimate.

You are right, replied Des Frans. I should not have stifled my first impulse, but should have killed them. However, I do not regret having acted in a gentler, more humane way. If they had died as they were, in a state of mortal sin, I should forever have suffered pangs of guilt. As it is, I am guiltless in the death of Madame Morin, and both Silvie and Gallouin lived to make a sincere repentance for their crime.

Your comment befits a truly Christian and honourable man, said Des Ronais. But I must say, I cannot understand how you had the strength of mind not to take Silvie back, when the pain of separating yourself from her cost you so much heartache – particularly since you had resisted the urge to exact immediate retribution when you discovered them. I must admit, I was so touched and moved by your account of her farewell, that I would readily have forgiven her and taken her home with me, had I been in your place!

I too would have done so, interrupted Contamine. And so long as I was sure my dishonour was not known to anyone, I would have hoped not to repent of doing so; after all, being a woman, she would have been dependent on me – a servant, to do my bidding. Not to mention the fact that – let us face the truth – she had already paid for her crime with a harsh punishment!

It would not have been for those reasons, said Jussy, speaking for the first time, that I would have taken her back. It would have been for my own sake. Here is my wife, he went on. I have no fear that she will ever be unfaithful to me – and I would not be grateful to anyone who told me she had been. I love her at least as much as you loved Silvie, but if I caught her in the act, and did not avenge myself there and then, I would not punish her further, except by despising her if her guilt were secret, or by separating from her if it became known. But I would not put myself through so much misery to pay for the crime of another – not to mention the chatter and gossip I would wish to avoid. Nor would I act as her jailer and tormentor – while still idolising her in my heart! And, frankly, your punishment exceeded that which the crime deserved. I do not understand how one could be so hard-hearted!

In addition, said Dupuis, it was not her own weakness which led her to err. She felt this to be so, and I know it was so. Here, he continued, is the letter she wrote to Gallouin about six months after she left Paris. Shall I read it to you? Everyone wanted to hear it. It was written in the following terms:

If I did not feel sure that you love me as much as it is possible to love, I would not relieve you, as I now do, of the anxiety you must be feeling about what has become of me. Our relationship was too criminal to continue. It was more heinous in God's eyes than you knew because I hid from you the vows I had made and the commitment I had entered into before meeting you, and which I violated when I knew you. I have already been punished for this as much as it is possible to be punished in this world, both in mind and body. I have suffered all one can suffer without dying. I have sincerely repented, and still repent, for having given a sort of consent to what passed between us. It was, however, a consent in which my heart had no part. It has caused me a pain and confusion which will endure as long as I live – a space of time which will be longer than I would wish, yet too short to expiate my fault. I write to say farewell to you for ever. Think of me no more. I have no wish to think of you, and will not do so. If I must think of you

431

as I write this letter, it is less for your sake than for my own. Remember your promise to keep secret what happened between us; never violate it – or rather, forget everything, even my name. This is the first letter you have received from me, and it will be the last; think of me no more; you will never hear of me again. Alas, my life had been innocent; it had run in quiet paths, which had lulled me till I was insensible to danger. I believed my devotion to prudence and virtue would protect me for ever. How mistaken I was! It is an error I will not repeat; I know my weakness too well and am humbled by it. The walls and grilles of a convent will protect me henceforth from occasions such as led to my undoing. Dear God! Is my virtue then dependent on locks and bars? Take no pride in having triumphed over my weakness! God ordained my downfall, in order to teach me humility. He used you only to punish me. Take care lest, having served His purpose thus, He may have no further use for you. Do not attribute my surrender to your own merit or powers of persuasion: you would be mistaken to do so; it was the result of the blindness into which God led me. His succour and support had deserted me, and I would have strayed from the path of virtue as easily with another as with you. This is certain. And it is certain also that in my heart I was indifferent to you. Thank God, my lapse from virtue lasted only one day; but to redeem myself in His eyes I must pay for it for the rest of my life. I shall never leave the convent. There is nothing in the world to hold me; my retreat is final. I have lost the only thing which could keep me in the world. I think of you with regret and shame. I will not say which convent I am in, for I never wish to hear your name, nor that you should hear mine. Though I could blame you for all my misfortune, and for having disturbed the even and untroubled course of my life, which without you was happy and peaceful, I do not wish you ill. God, who knows my innermost heart, knows that I ask for you only favours and blessings. Alas, I am not worthy to have my prayers answered. I hope you are spared a punishment such as mine. Live in peace and happiness in the world if you are able to do so. But be aware that you have aroused God's anger, since it was you He chose to be the means by which my inno-cence was destroyed. For this, I would wish you to feel remorse, which will bring you back to God and to His service. Have you not already concluded that a victory so easily won was obtained only because a force stronger than yourself was fighting with you? A man of much greater merit than yourself, whom I loved with all my heart, made far greater efforts than you to overcome my virtue. My resistance faltered, but though my heart was on his side, I did not succumb. This victory led me to believe my virtue was invincible. What confidence I had! How misplaced was such confidence! I believed I would always remain mistress of myself, and easily rebuff any assault on my virtue, having repulsed so many. I had no qualms about my power, since it had never failed me. And what was my shame and despair after my ignoble defeat! I can only repeat: some other power, added to your own, was responsible for your victory. Be assured that you were nothing but the instrument, in God's hands, for my humiliation. I fear the consequences for you of this. I am concerned for your salvation, for which I pray. Farewell. Through you I fell into an abyss of ignominy and remorse, for which I am doing penance: it is in the interest of your eternal salvation that you should think to do the same.

That is Silvie's style, said Des Frans. She writes as one who truly repents of what she did. She does not say she was married – or rather, her reference to her marriage is so imprecise that it gives only a suspicion of it. She has an admirable facility of expression, said Des Ronais. She has the universal instinct of a woman, said Contamine. I don't know if I should say what I think in front of Monsieur Des Frans? Yes, said the latter. Speak your mind, without con-straint. My impression, Contamine therefore continued, is that Silvie's farewell to Gallouin had less to do with repentance and a veritable return to God than with frustration at having left her lover in the world, where he might readily find some other to console him. Frankly, her repentance, in my opinion, was not very sincere. At least, it seems to me, that she has this in common with the damned – she would like to see everyone else in the same position. This is why, since she herself was confined in a convent, she wants him to share the same fate! Her wish was granted: he did enter a monastery – and it was because of her that he did so.

I cannot allow Monsieur de Contamine so to tarnish the shining example of virtue provided by Silvie, merely on the strength of such an unfounded suspicion, interposed Madame de Jussy angrily. I cherish her memory. I look at her life with admiration: her suffering and the hardships she endured make Monsieur Des Frans a monster in my eyes! I would go even further. I beg pardon for my outspokenness, but it is not in my character to dissimulate. His wife's renunciation of the world and her death have won my respect and esteem. If Silvie was reluctant to lose Gallouin, she continued, addressing Monsieur de Contamine, why did she give all she owned to the man who had persecuted her? Why leave herself destitute for his sake? Why bury herself alive in a convent, when its doors were open for her to leave whenever she wished? And if her repentance were not sincere, why persevere in it till her death? Yes, it is beyond doubt, she said, that Silvie was innocent; and however involuntary her penitence may have been in the beginning, it was sincere in the end. Having heard what she said in her farewell to her husband and in her letter to Gallouin, I cannot doubt this. There is a touching and persuasive fervour in the way she expresses herself which cannot be feigned. There is more in this story than one sees at first sight!

My cousin does not tell us what he thinks, said Manon. I

would prefer it, dear cousin, if you did not try to make me take part in the discussion, he replied. Forgive me, Monsieur, Madame de Londé said to him. Mademoiselle Dupuis is right. It seemed you wished to make us believe that my brother had used some sorcery, some artifice or magic – if I may use the term – to overcome Silvie's resistance? Both Silvie and Gallouin are now dead, Madame, he said. And both died in a state which should make us respect their memory. Let us forget what they did during their lifetime.

Monsieur Dupuis is right, said Madame de Contamine in order to change the course of a conversation which was becoming fraught. We cannot do better than leave their memory in peace. Let us forget the sad thoughts left by Monsieur Des Frans's story. It is time to think of supper. Meantime, let us have some amusement! Come, ladies, said Contamine, rising from his seat. I have always been told that a woman's first idea is her best one. Let us do as my wife suggests! Everyone rose and went into the garden to enjoy the fresh air and to give the servants time to prepare the table. In order to provide some entertainment and cheer everyone's spirits, Madame de Contamine performed a song, and several other members of the company followed her example. However, the concert was of short duration, since the meal was soon ready to be served.

During the meal, the subjects of conversation were light, and everyone did their best to divert Des Frans's spirits, since, in spite of his efforts, a deep veil of sadness had descended on him. No one mentioned Silvie, not only out of concern for Des Frans, but also for the sake of Madame de Londé, in front of whom no one wanted to raise the question of her brother's role in Silvie's story. It was very late in the evening by the time the friends dispersed and went their separate ways. They promised to reassemble the next day at Des Ronais's house, where they were all invited for the midday meal. Madame de Londé – who was shortly to marry Dupuis, and who knew that he was going to tell the story of his own life the next day – was reluctant to be of the party and tried to excuse herself. Her feelings were understood and respected, and Manon, who knew that Des Ronais would subsequently tell her all she had missed, promised to leave with her as soon as Dupuis began his tale. On this condition, she agreed to join the group for the meal the next day. Madame de Mongey was not entirely happy either, as she was uncomfortable about going into a house in which Des Frans was living. But Manon, who realised what she was thinking, but did not consider it a sufficient reason to allow her to absent herself, promised to accompany her to Des Ronais's house (where Des Frans was staying). When all these questions were settled, everyone left, each returning to his own home. Jussy and his wife left together; Dupuis accompanied Madame de Londé to her home; Des Frans and Des Ronais accompanied Madame de Mongey and Manon to the latter's house, and then went back together to Des Ronais's house.

So, there you are, said Des Frans to his friend, as soon as they were alone. Now that you know the whole of my story, do you still advise me to remarry? Yes, more than ever, answered Des Ronais. You should do so to provide solace and comfort for your future. You will find peace and tranquillity in Madame de Mongey's arms; you will forget the distressing memories of your ill-fated connection with Silvie. We will talk about it again another time! At present, I must make preparations and give orders for the reception of the fine company we are to entertain tomorrow. You will readily understand, he continued, that I want everything to run smoothly, since, as well as Contamine, Jussy and their wives, Madame de Londé and our friend Dupuis are coming. Not to mention, added Des Frans with a smile, your own charming sweetheart! And yours too, said Des Ronais, also smiling. You will learn from Dupuis some of the reasons which should influence you to consider marrying Madame de Mongey. He will not have to gloss over anything he might wish to say, since Madame de Londé is not going to be present: and perhaps he will prove to you that Silvie's infidelity – which is your reason for not wishing to remarry – was not of her own free will. In any case, even if it had been, it should not deter you from thinking of a second marriage, especially when the person concerned is a woman of impeccable virtue. But, for the present, I wish you good night. And at that, he left Des Frans, and went to his own room, where he sent for his servants and gave them orders for what was to be done the following day.

Very early the next morning, Dupuis came to the house, and while Des Ronais was occupied elsewhere – having been obliged to go out on an extremely urgent matter – Dupuis had a very long conversation alone with Des Frans, in the course of which the latter was moved repeatedly to lift his eyes heavenwards, to utter loud exclamations and frequent sighs, the session ultimately concluding in a deluge of tears. When their guests arrived, Des Frans was forced to pull himself out of his reverie and occupy himself with the duty of welcoming the visitors, for Des Ronais, in his own absence, had asked Des Frans to do the honours of the house. The latter therefore made great efforts to hide the sadness which his conversation with Dupuis had engendered – and succeeded in doing so. Dupuis went to fetch Madame de Londé, returning with her a short time later, while Des Frans remained at the house to entertain Monsieur and Madame de Jussy, Madame de Mongey and Manon.

Des Ronais arrived back eventually and offered his excuses to his guests for not having been at home himself to receive them. His apologies were accepted – and in fact, there had been good cause for his absence. Only Madame de Contamine, to provide a touch of light relief for the company, pretended not to be satisfied with his reasons and chaffed him for having entrusted someone else with the duty of receiving his fiancée. He defended himself in equally light-hearted vein, but she pushed her point, until he begged Contamine and Madame de Mongey to come to his rescue and put an end to her false accusations. Far from doing so, however, they allied themselves with her. So did everyone else present, so that the poor Des Ronais – attacked on all sides – went down on his knees, joined his hands, and begged them all for mercy, and in particular asked pardon of Manon. It was granted, and this episode, which was accompanied by much mirth, provided that spirit of joviality and good companionship which completes the pleasure of a dinner party.

A splendid meal had been provided. Just as they sat down at table, Monsieur and Madame de Terny had arrived at the house. This couple had been to call on Manon, and hearing that she was having dinner at Des Ronais's, they had thought to follow her. They were warmly welcomed. The company was now complete, and a very agreeable meal ensued, with de Terny's good-natured humour contributing not a little to the general enjoyment. Des Ronais had overlooked nothing in his desire to ensure the best possible cheer for his guests and had ordered such a profusion of good dishes that the ladies professed themselves shocked, saying they had believed themselves to be his friends, who could come to his house for a simple repast without fuss and fanfare, but they realised they were mistaken, since he treated them with so much magnificence and ceremony. In fact, the dinner was superb. Des Ronais said, with a laugh, that it was all Des Frans's doing. Des Frans assured them he had had no part in the arrangements. There was much laughter and good humour. The ladies sang some drinking songs and praised each other's performances. Nothing needed for a perfectly pleasant and joyful occasion was lacking.

After the meal, Madame de Londé and Manon took leave of the company on the pretext of a visit and promised to return for supper. When they had left, Dupuis was called on to keep his promise and recount the story of his life. He was prepared for this, and was ready to proceed. He sent for a bottle of wine and a glass to be placed beside him, so that – as he said – he would not have to wait until he was thirsty to drink. He sent the servants out of the room and told his audience to stop him as soon as they grew bored; after which he began his story.

The Story of Monsieur Dupuis and Madame de Londé

Since it is only right that, having heard all of your stories, I should also tell my own, I will now do so, even at the risk of laying myself open to your disapproval. My behaviour has not been altogether blameless – I acknowledge that. I know that I have acted like a knave and a rascal at times. But, to balance the record, there have also been some comical moments. All of you, he said, addressing his friends, have shown yourselves to be veritable heroes of loyalty and devotion to the one you loved – whereas I ... I have been the very epitome of fickleness and inconstancy. There is no one but Madame de Londé who, after having first driven me to despair, has in the end been able to win my devotion. Before her, it was quite otherwise. I always did exactly as I wanted. I cared only for pleasure and amusement, and if I did not like what I found, whether because it did not come up to expectations, or merely because I lost interest, I had no scruple about discarding it. If Madame de Londé were present, I would not speak as frankly as I am doing, but since she has absented herself from our company, and since I trust you all not to reveal anything I say which might offend her within the next week – at the end of which she and I are to be married – I will recount things exactly as I see them. When she and I are married, I shall be the first to make her laugh at my adventures, and show her what a miracle she has achieved in reforming me. Until then it is better that she should not know about them. I am also not unhappy that my cousin Manon isn't here, not only because, like all young women, she has a tendency to chatter, but also because there will be things in my narrative which it would not be suitable for an unmarried woman to hear. All that being said, and having requested your discretion, let me proffer a word of wisdom, which is the following: there is nothing so dangerous as to leave an eighteen-year-old youth who has plenty of money at his disposal to his own devices and accountable to no one for his behaviour. This is the situation I was in when my father died.

You are well aware, he said, turning to Des Frans and Des Ronais, how I spent my college days, and what my tutors thought of me. I was, to put it bluntly, one of the most incorrigible rapscallions in the college. My escapades were like something out of a picaresque novel, and if I wanted to take up your time with the pranks of a juvenile, I could relate these exploits, but at present I am telling you about adventures which, if not more serious, at least had more influence on the course of my life.

You know my family background: I have only one brother, with whom I was never on very good terms – a situation which is not unusual. He was ten years older than me and for that reason thought he had the right to criticise me and assume some authority over me – an authority which I rejected so energetically that he stopped even speaking to me. It was not that he was afraid of me – he was more malicious than I was. But having made up his mind I was not worth troubling with and would never amount to anything, he preferred to let me do as I pleased, rather than lay himself open to my violent temper. And since he moved to the provinces some years ago and rarely visits Paris, we live without contact and almost unaware of each other's exis-tence. It is true, moreover, that while my father was alive, the lack of brotherly affection between us was exacerbated by my mother's preference for him. He was the spoilt child – for she was easily taken in by appearances. From his outward behaviour, one would have taken him to be quiet and respectable. In fact he was no more so than I was, and my easy-going, open character was more to my father's liking. So I was my father's favourite, he was my mother's.

My father's preference for me, however, gave me no particular advantage. I was too young when he died to have benefited in any way except for a few presents he gave me as a child, but these did not do much towards establishing my fortune, because my brother – whose inheritance had been settled on him while my father was alive – had taken for himself the best and most valuable of the household effects; and after my father's death, my mother had no inclination to do anything for me. I got what was due to me from my father's side, and nothing more, but this being the case, I had no obligation to anyone and had the satisfaction of being completely independent. I did not exhaust my inheritance, however, since I had access only to the income, which I spent as I felt inclined. But since all I needed was my food and drink, it is not surprising that I spent my time in idleness and dissipation. I am now a completely reformed character, and this has been true for some length of time. My conversion began through the good offices of a certain widow and was completed by Madame de Londé, who succeeded in making an honourable man of me. That is enough of an introduction. I will now get to the substance.

And to start with, I have to say that the proverb according to which a young man's first sexual encounter is always with either an old or an ugly woman was not true in my case. The first person I fell in love with was beautiful, had a fine figure, and was no more than nineteen or twenty years old. This is how it came about. When I first went to school, I was a boarder, but when I was a little older, I boarded only during the winter, and in summer ate lunch with my tutor, and in the evening returned to my father's house. I was not yet thirteen years old, and in the second form, at the time I am talking of. (It was more than three years later that I passed my oral examinations in the Physical Sciences, and that was a week before my sixteenth birthday.)

One evening, I was returning home. It was extremely hot. Right in the middle of the road, just at my feet, I found a fan. I picked it up and raised my eyes to see where it had come from. I saw a young woman at a first floor window, who called out: Don't worry, leave it, dear child. My servant will fetch it for me. Allow me to bring it for you, Madame, I answered, and went straight into the house. The young servant was just inside, on the bottom stair, and tried to take the fan from me, but I refused to give it to him, and, being roughly the same age as he was, I resisted his efforts to take it with a threat and carried the fan up myself. Here is your fan, Madame, I said, handing it to her.

I thank you, young sir, she said. There was no need for you to give yourself the trouble to bring it to me. My servant was coming to fetch it. Yes, Madame, I answered, but then I would not have had the pleasure of coming in to your house and being close enough to see you properly. This answer made her laugh. She asked me about my schoolwork, and I answered, if not with much wit, at least without reticence – indeed, with a boldness bordering on cheekiness. That is another of my good qualities which I forgot to mention to you. People have always said that they never saw a youngster who was bolder or more sure of himself for his age than I was. (You must decide for yourselves if I have changed since then!) Our conversation concluded with an invitation from her for me to come and share some little pastries with her the following day. I clearly remember telling her she did not know what might come of a promise to take breakfast with a schoolboy who was always up betimes in the morning. Come at any time you like, she said. I will be ready for you.

I promised to come, and did as I promised. I should tell you that she had several times remarked that I was a handsome young fellow, and I had as often told her that she was a beautiful lady. Though she spoke French perfectly, she had a slight foreign accent, which I found very attractive, as indeed it was – I was not alone in finding it so. She was something between a girl and a woman, or both at the same time. She was from Malta, and while not married to him, she had left the island to be with a man of quality who brought her to Paris and quietly provided her with all she needed in order to live a comfortable life. In other words, she was the mistress of a Commander of the Order of Malta. She was a plump, cheerful young woman, with large black eyes, dark hair and an ample white bosom – a warm, good-natured person. It was she who was responsible for my initiation.

I went at six the next morning. A fine time to visit a woman! I banged on her door, just as I would have banged on my classroom door, or at the entrance to my school building. It was her young servant who opened it. He was none too pleased at having his sleep interrupted and would have closed the door in my face, but I was too quick for him. I pushed him aside and woke my sleeping beauty, who wanted to know who it was. It is me, Madame, I said. I have come for the cookies you promised me. Ah, yes, she said. Come in, my child. She told the young servant to open the windows, and sent him off to the pastry shop. We were left alone. I sat in a chair close beside her, and she questioned me as she had done the day before, in a way that was suited to someone of my age, but since I was precocious, my little attentions soon caused her to change her manner. Because of the heat, she needed to loosen her clothing, revealing among other things a pair of breasts as delightful as any I have ever seen. I had sometimes made free with the servant-girls at my father's house, to their annoyance. I employed the same procedure now. I used both my hands and my mouth, and told her I wished I could suckle at her breast. In a word, imagine how a shameless youth might behave when no restraint is imposed. My childish ardour amused her. I became emboldened. Nature is the best teacher, and I let myself be guided by her and met no discouragement. The sparrow found its nest and must have given satisfaction, since I was given permission to return. Her pleasure can have been only moderate, for I was not mature enough to set her passions alight. That then was my first experience, which was followed by a great many more – the Devil alone knows how many. She urged discretion, and I was careful to comply. Our commerce lasted more than two years. There is no need to tell you what became of her, but during this time I was constantly with her, because I found such pleasure in her company, and she found ways of doing many kindnesses for me.

She and the Commander never went on any excursion into the country without taking me. He had no idea that she had any attachment to me other than the pleasure of my childish prattle and was only too willing to include me in their outings. My pockets were always full, and I earned considerable prestige among my schoolmates because of the plentiful supply of sweets I always had at my disposal.

Because of this liaison, I no longer wanted to board at school, even in the winter. It was also because of my Maltese mistress that I took my schoolwork more seriously. She made me feel it was a point of honour for someone as grown-up as myself not to be in trouble with his tutors because of a lack of application to his studies. She also said that if my progress at school were not satisfactory, they would think it was because I spent too much time going back and forth, and would make me a boarder again, which would prevent me from seeing her.

It was this argument which carried the most weight with me. I therefore studied to such good effect that my tutors were satisfied and my father was more pleased than ever with me. He knew that I was constantly at this woman's house, but why should he be any more suspicious than the Commander – particularly since he knew only what she herself wanted to be known, namely, that she was a foreigner married to a Frenchman who had brought her to Paris? This is how the Commander let himself be known, and he took great care to hide the cross of his Order, especially when he came to see her. Eventually, our friendship came to an end because she moved away.

It was only a short time later that I left school. My father had always intended me for the army, and my military training began. The equerry of the Duc de Ledune was a close friend of both my father and my uncle, and they asked him to take charge of my instruction in horsemanship. I therefore attended his riding school – but not for long. Among my fellow students there was a young man from the Dauphiné whose appearance was very misleading: he looked like a little saint, but was in fact as mean as the Devil. Our master was angry with him one day and gave him a cut with his whip while he was on horseback, which made him sit up with such a start that I couldn't help laughing. 'Sit up straight,' the master instructed him harshly. The young fellow didn't say a word, but made a face at which I laughed out loud. I was a mischief-maker just as he was. As soon as he had dismounted, he started a quarrel with me. Our master pretended not to hear, but made up his mind that he would give me a dose of the same medicine. It was my turn to show my paces, and I mounted my horse. I had not noticed, but the curb-chain of my horse's harness had come undone. I had scarcely completed my first circle when I felt the whip strike me across the back, just as it had with my predecessor, who, the tables turned, now let out his own peal of laughter.

I glowered at him and pulled my horse's head round to rush at him, but our riding master caught hold of the reins. 'A good horseman,' he said, in a glacial tone, 'should never mount his horse without casting his eye over the harness. Your curb-chain is not fastened.' That was enough for me. I finished the exercise for that morning with my mind made up that it would be the last I ever spent under such a rigid master. I said nothing that day, but I never returned, and I went elsewhere to learn the skills of horsemanship.

I did my military training under a master and in company with a number of tough Parisian youths, with whom I became acquainted. They assumed at first that I was some inexperienced innocent. I realised that if I was to be accepted as an equal, I would have to pick a fight with one of them and beat him. This I did and, thereafter, we were all on the best of terms.

My father arranged for me to take lodgings with an engineer who taught me all about fortifications. I had left home because of a little dispute with my mother over a pretty chamber-maid of hers, whom she had dismissed, she said, because of me, since the girl was also serving me in my bedchamber. My mother may have been right – though she had no proof. But she looked at me so sourly that I begged my father to let me leave home. I had another reason for wishing to do so, which was that my brother had arrived back in Paris. My mother welcomed him like a spoilt child. I compared her affection for him with her indifference to me, and this made me hate living at home. I repeated my requests for permission to move out of the house. There were occasions when my father took my part, and this sometimes caused a certain chilliness between him and my mother. In the end, I pleaded with him to allow me, like Jacob, to give place to my older brother, pointing out that all the disputes that arose because of me were unpleasant and did me no good. He naturally wanted to be master in his own home and was distressed by the lack of harmony in the family, so he allowed me to take up lodgings, as I have said.

I remained in these lodgings all winter, after which, since I was now of an age to handle a musket, my father had me enrolled in a company under the command of one of his friends. Before I left to join my company, my father wanted me to pay my respects to Monsieur d'Alamogne, whom he knew well, and in whose regiment I would be serving. He gave me a letter to take to him. Monsieur d'Alamogne was not in Paris, and I decided to go to Versailles in order to deliver the letter to him there. Before leaving, I called on my father to tell him what I was planning, and to ask if there were any other errand I could do for him. Just as I turned the corner of the street, I happened to see my brother going into a house which I knew to be occupied solely by a number of young women of easy virtue. I thought at first I must be mistaken and, to make sure, I left my horse at a tavern where I was well known, and went into the establishment just mentioned. I had barely crossed the threshold when I heard my brother's voice and was able to recognise him through a keyhole.

I have already said that his prudish manner made my mother think he was a latter-day Cato. He had recently married a beautiful young girl in the provinces, who was wealthy and of good family, and though the duty of conjugal fidelity dates from the creation of the world, when God made a single Eve for Adam, my brother did not see the need to subject himself to this rule. Since his marriage and return to Paris, his way of life had appeared even more sober than before. He was his mother's second voice and, like her, never missed an opportunity to preach morality. Indeed, if his doting mother were to be believed, it was almost time to start a movement towards his canonisation. I myself was kept informed of all he did in Paris by one of my father's servants who liked him no better than I did, because of his pious airs, which infuriated all the household. Since his return to Paris about six months earlier than this, I had never spoken to my mother without her launching into a panegyric about her exemplary son, who, she suggested, should serve as the model for my own behaviour. She knew that I sometimes went to Madame Martine's establishment – the house of dubious repute which my brother had entered. She had done her best to catch me there and had promised to put me to shame, should she find me; indeed, she would have made no secret of it, but I was too clever for her, and her efforts had always been wasted. Neither had she been able to have the establishment closed, as it was quiet and discreetly run.

I determined to open her eyes once and for all with respect to my brother, whatever might come of it. I told a servant to call a cobbler who had a shack at the corner of the street, and I took him to the tavern where I had left my horse, so that I would not be seen talking to him. I have to go to Versailles immediately, I told him, and I haven't a sou. I have just asked my mother to lend me some money, but she refused. I told her I would go and steal it from Madame Martine's, and that is what I am going to do. Go and tell her you've seen me going there. She will come and look for me, for fear I do something foolish. Do this for me, and I will make it worth your while. He showed some reluctance to do my bidding, but I knew he was one of my mother's spies, and I threatened to give him a good hiding if he didn't look sharp and do as I asked. So he went, and I, for my part, made as if I was going into Madame Martine's. But I took off as soon as I saw him go into our house and went to await the outcome at the tavern.

I had not been there long before I saw my dear mother appear. The heightened colour of her face bode no good. She had come on foot, followed by her coachman and two footmen, and as soon as she had disappeared into la Martine's, I leapt on to my horse and returned to my father's house by a roundabout way. I said nothing to him about the affair, in case my ploy misfired. I soon saw it had not. A moment or two later my mother returned all flustered, with my brother following in such confusion it was clear my plan had succeeded. Indeed, she had found him sitting on the knee of a young temptress, holding her breast in one hand and a glass in the other. Both mother and son had been caught out.

I had not seen the comedy itself, but I was present at its sequel. I had spoken to my father and he had given me some money and invited me to stay for dinner at the house, asking in fact for it to be served earlier than usual. The four of us sat down at table. No one said a word. My mother was in such a state that she hardly dared open her mouth, either to eat or to speak. My brother likewise was struck dumb. But as for me, I could not refrain from laughing: without doubt, both the actors and the occasion warranted it. My father was at a loss. Is it because your younger brother is having dinner with us that you are so out of sorts? he asked. Is he not one of the family as much as you are? Why the devil do you look so disgruntled? And as for you, what are you laughing like that for? It's not difficult to understand, I said, with a titter. My mother went thinking to find me at Madame Martine's honourable establishment and, instead of me, it turned out that the cobbler, her spy, had made a mistake – it was my brother who was there!

There was no way he could deny it. The lackeys who had gone with my mother were the ones who were serving us at table, and they too could not refrain from laughing. I thought my father would be angry, but he wasn't. On the contrary, he too began to laugh. I don't know what he might have said to my brother later in private, but for the moment he simply said it was disgraceful in a married man;

and at least, if he was not restrained by the fear of God, he should fear to lose the respect of his fellow men and, above all, fear the surgeon.

That was good enough for me. I completed my errand to Versailles and, very soon after, set out for Flanders, with the expectation of participating in my first campaign, but this was not to be. Our battalion remained in garrison at Amiens, where all we did was drill and exercise. I grew bored and was about to ask leave either to return home or to join that part of the army which was under the command of Monsieur de Turenne, when I received letters from Paris informing me that my father was at death's door and was asking for me with great urgency.

I was readily granted leave, and I returned home with the utmost speed, arriving barely in time to see my father before he died. There is no point in recounting his last words. I did not fully profit from the advice he gave me, and others did not fully abide by the instructions which he left for them to carry out. He died too soon for me, since I had just reached an age where I could begin to achieve something, but, through lack of guidance, I achieved nothing. And this was the more so, since peace was made, leaving me to pass my youth without occupation.

My father died towards the end of July, and I was left to my own devices and spent the winter in Paris, in the company of vagabonds and wastrels, who, like me, were not worth much. We caroused furiously, particularly at Carnival time. But before I go any further, I must tell you about as madcap an incident as any you can imagine. There were eight of us in the group – one of whom was Gallouin. He and I were the only ones who had servants, but we dismissed them whenever we wanted to go incognito. On the Thursday before Shrove Tuesday, there was a big ball in the Faubourg Saint-Germain. We decided to go in fancy dress. We went to an old-clothes dealer and picked out the most grotesque outfits we could find. We drew lots, and it fell to me to have a devil's costume, complete with tail and claws. We went off to have supper – that is to say, as we usually did, to drink like fish – after which we went to the ball, in two carriages, whose coachmen not only made us pay more than the coaches themselves were worth, but also in advance, which was our mistake – since as soon as we went into the ballroom, the scoundrels took off, and we never saw them again.

When we left the ball, we called for them, but they had disappeared. We were a long way from home. What were we to do? We saw a light still on in a tavern and went in. They gave us something to drink, but could not put us up for the night. There was nothing for it but to start out for home on foot. The night was pitch dark and, having drunk so much, we found the path too narrow and became separated as we straggled along, each one making his way as best he could. I had no idea where I was and nearly broke my neck when I bumped into a cobbler's hut. Having realised what it was, I decided to wait there till morning. I bundled myself up inside it and went to sleep on the wooden plank that served as the counter. Since I had drunk so much wine, I slept as soundly there as I would have done in a good bed, and gave no further thought to my companions than if they had never existed. I intended to stay there only until daybreak, when the water-sellers would be about, but once asleep I was incapable of rousing myself again. And apparently, the cobbler whose hut it was had also been out revelling the previous night, and it was nine o' clock before he appeared.

I had woken up in broad daylight, chilled to the marrow, with no idea where I was; but after struggling to collect my thoughts, I remembered what had happened. But I couldn't bring myself to go out in daylight dressed in my devil's costume, and, in spite of the cold, I would have stayed where I was till nightfall, if the cobbler had not come to wheel his shack to some other place. He thought the Devil himself had taken possession of it and let out a terrified shriek, which made everyone in the busy street turn and gawp. Seeing that I was discovered, I decided to escape from my hiding place and take to my legs. I jumped to the floor, pulled the mask over my face, showed my claws, and since everyone believed I was indeed a real live devil, they promptly made way for me. As soon as I got outside, I ran off as fast as my legs would carry me, not knowing where I was going, and, at a turning in the street, found myself in the middle of a funeral procession. The priests took to their heels, and as I got on a level with the corpse, those who had been carrying the coffin dumped their burden, and turned tail. I was amused at their panic, but didn't stop running until I reached a tavern and flung myself headlong inside. Fortunately, it was the very one where we had been drinking the night before, and some of the locals recognised me, and everyone's terror subsided.

I thought that would be the end of the matter, and that all I need do would be to send for my servant to bring me some clothes, and find a coach to take me home. But I was wrong. The alarm I had caused in the funeral procession, the fallen corpse and broken bier – all this convinced the relatives and the worthy assembly that it had been an ambush. They surrounded the tavern, and threatened to kill me, so to escape from the hands of this riff-raff, I was forced to send for a sergeant-at-arms. He did not know me, but he knew my name. In order to find out if I was telling the truth, he went to my mother and told her my story, at which she laughed heartily and sent her carriage with my servant, as well as the two who were in her service. I changed into my own clothes and was thus able to command sufficient respect from those gathered there to be able to make an honourable exit.

This escapade however was not enough to persuade me to

dissociate myself from these companions. The following Sunday, which was the last in Carnival, we were in a house which belonged to one of our number, but which was uninhabited as builders were at work there. We used to meet here, where we had freedom to do as we pleased. The only furniture was a few planks, which we used for chairs and a table. We had a dozen earthenware plates to eat from, some pots without handles which we drank from, and three old wooden candlesticks. The only things that were always clean and fresh were the bottles, as they were constantly being replaced. We built a fire between two paving stones. A bed consisted of two or three bundles of straw covered with an old piece of linen, and served both for ourselves and for the worthy young ladies who were included in our society. In a word, it was a veritable flophouse, and we enjoyed ourselves there in our own way better than we would have done in the most magnificent palace in the world. We had good cheer and a warm fire; we drank excellent wine and ate succulent morsels – often with our fingers and always without tablecloths and napkins. One of our diversions was to invite three or four ladies of the street to join us, ply them with wine, then entice them into an argument with each other, until they fell to exchanging punches. It was highly entertaining, and still would not offend me – nothing is more ludicrous!

That Sunday, then, we decided to stop at nothing. We heard a pastry-seller outside selling cakes and called to him. He came in and was surprised to find us in such a squalid place. We gave him something to drink, to give him heart, and then, as we had planned, we forced him to gamble with us, making him stake up to four times the value of his wares. When he lost, he wanted to go and fetch the money to pay his debts, but we refused to let him leave. We would try him, we said, according to the laws of the land. We tied him up like a criminal, and four young ladies played the roles of

454

Judge, Registrar, Clerk of the Court, and Public Prosecutor. We cross-examined him, demanding to know why he had been gambling when he did not have the cash to pay his debts. The poor fellow hardly knew what was going on. We men were the litigants and the plaintiffs, and the young ladies were his judges. Opinions were heard, and in accordance with the conclusions of the slattern playing the part of the Prosecutor, the one acting as Judge pronounced sentence that he be condemned to be hanged. It was only because we were so inebriated that we could have allowed the charade to reach such a point, for the poor man was half dead with fright. As if to carry out the sentence, we made him climb up on a crane, which the builders had left in the courtyard, a rope was fastened round his neck (which we cut without his knowing that we had done so), and then we threw him from a height of one foot on to a heap of plaster and manure. His hands were tied, so he could not raise himself. Our intention had been only to give him a fright, and in this we could not have succeeded more completely, for indeed he had a terrible one.

Our first reaction was to laugh at the success of our prank, but we didn't laugh for long. The poor fellow lay on the dungheap unconscious and without movement. Our high spirits soon changed to misgiving, and we began to repent of our folly. We used all the means we could think of to revive our poor victim. Eventually he regained consciousness, but was weak and feverish. We carried him in front of a warm fire and plied him liberally with wine. We then sent for a surgeon, to whom we admitted exactly what we had done. He bled him and reprimanded us with all the severity we deserved. He insisted that we provide everything needed to cure his fever, as well as whatever would make it worth his while not to spread the story round. This we did, and I thank God, he recovered in a reasonably short time. It was a week before he was able to return to his master, who, by this time, since it was Lent, had no more need of him. We looked for work for him and found him a place as a cook in the household of a man of good standing, and subsequently, when it was all over, he was the first to laugh at the fright he had had. Gallouin and I resolved never to take part again in a prank so dangerous as this, which had come near to costing a man his life.

It was in this way that I spent the first year after my father's death. These two samples will suffice to paint the picture. Gallouin, as I said, was one of our group, even one of its leading lights, and it was at this time that he became acquainted with mysterious secrets which pass our normal understanding. For myself, I assure you, I had no desire to dabble in these matters, having no stomach for such things. Be that as it may, the life I led at that time was one of pure self-indulgence, and the only thing that could save me from the pernicious influence of these companions was for our association to come to an end. And with the beginning of Lent, followed by Easter, and another religious festival which occurred at about the same time, our meetings did indeed cease. If this had not been the case, and if I had not changed my way of life, it was clear, even to myself, that I was heading for disaster. So I mended my ways, but not to such an extent that I renounced all pleasure and amusement. I merely discarded what had been excessive and scandalous.

I therefore began to cultivate a more respectable style of acquaintanceships, and to take an interest in my neighbours. The first of those to whom I addressed my attentions was Sophie, who subsequently married d'Espinai. I was unaware that she had an established admirer. If I had thought she already had one, I would not have wasted my time pursuing her. But this young lady took such pains to keep the truth hidden that I believed her to be free and unattached, and in this belief I began to pay her court.

Though she is not a beauty, she is pleasing enough in her person and, all in all, not unattractive, at least as far as I was concerned, as I was not looking for anyone of great distinction.

She received my attentions quite well initially, and I thought my suit was progressing. But it was not so, and I began to perceive that her warm response was intended primarily to awaken jealousy in another. At some other moment, I might have dismissed a piece of deception of this sort with a laugh, but I resented the fact that I had been made a dupe. And indeed, she had allowed me certain liberties which, while innocent in themselves, had led me to anticipate more. I did not think d'Espinai intended marriage, and therefore I did not think I would be doing him any great injury if I taught her a lesson. I thought their relationship was illicit. It was not so, but I allowed myself to believe it was.

I found out one day that he was at her house. She had never explained to me the reason for his frequent visits. She had been hiding the truth from me, and I intended to repay her for this deception. Knowing that he was there, I also went and walked straight into her room without knocking. I found them in a situation which perfectly suited my purpose. They were beside the fire, he in an armchair, and she on a stool between his legs, her elbows on his knees, her head on his stomach, and he had his two hands round her breasts, one on each side, like two pistols on either side of a saddle.

Hearing me enter, she turned her head and leapt up in anger at having been discovered in such a compromising situation. Indeed, she exclaimed with a heavy scowl, this is a fine way of making a call on one's friends! Indeed, said I, imitating her manner, in your position I would have made sure my door was firmly closed to prevent such calls! Allow me to enquire, she said, why you are here? I am looking for a pair of contented lovers, I said. I have found them and will now leave. And I walked out. D'Espinai ran after me in great haste. I thought he was going to make trouble, but on the contrary he implored me not to tell anyone what I had just seen. He said he intended to marry Sophie, and since they were on this footing, she accorded him certain favours which would be considered improper in other circumstances, but which were legitimate in these. He said he would be greatly in my debt if I promised not to mention what I had seen. My reply was that he must take me for a fool, and that I would rather be hanged than keep silent, that Mademoiselle Sophie had been deceiving me, and that, though I had been her lover first, she had never allowed me such liberties. (I did not wish to admit that he had been well received by her before I had started to visit her; I wanted to make out that their relationship dated only from the time when they had made up after their quarrel.) As for your intending to marry her, I added, that is an unlikely tale! I will believe it when I see it, not before! But one thing you may be certain of – I will not be used as a foil to disguise your liaison with her! This did not put an end to his pleas, but they made no impression on me and I left without giving the promise he wanted. He would have struck me had he dared, but he feared I was stronger than he.

That very evening I went to see Sophie and brazenly offered her a very dishonourable condition on which I would remain silent about what I had seen – namely that she do the same for me as I had witnessed between her and d'Espinai. In reply she would have scratched my eyes out had she been able to do so. I defended myself against her physical attack, but did not silence her verbal assault, since all my life I have enjoyed hearing women rant and curse, so long as their violence is restricted to speech. But since she was no fishwife, my enjoyment was only moderate: after her first outburst, she returned to her pleadings, and I to my offer.

My dear young lady, I said, do you think you can use me

as a cover, to divert attention from your real liaison? You told me I did not displease you; you allowed me to take certain small liberties, which, if they became known, would sully your reputation; it would seem not to be in your interest to offend me, and yet, suddenly, I find I am rejected in favour of another! And on top of this, you then beg me to remain silent about your fickleness. You clearly take me either for a saint or a cretin. One can address requests of this sort only to someone like a monk, who might fear having his own indiscretions revealed. But, in this day and age, for a man like me, who has no such fears, it is asking too much! I should soon be the dupe of every worthless minx in town if I let you get away with the way you have treated me! And all considered, it seems to me you have got the worst of the deal, for I believe I am worth at least as much as d'Espinai. You are worth ten times as much, she said, but you are not offering to marry me, and he is. If your intentions were serious, I would have preferred you, and I would still prefer you! I am most grateful, I said, mockingly, and I began to hum the tune: 'I do not want the milk if another has the cream'. At this she broke down. She wept, she protested, and I left her.

Since neither she nor her suitor were of any interest to me, I bandied the story around, spicing it with details of my own invention, and it was received with general amusement. The result was that I speeded up their marriage, since they brought the date forward in order to put an end to the gossip. When I saw that they really did intend to marry, I thought I was within my rights to hinder them and make a sham of their union.

I had heard my dissolute companions talk of a substance which deprived a man of his natural abilities for a con-siderable length of time and made him useless to a woman. I asked Gallouin to obtain some for me, which he did. It looked like pure spring water, it was so clear and sweet. I put some in a small phial and resolved to devise some stratagem to administer it to d'Espinai. It was a dastardly thing to do, but I didn't give it much thought. And I did something even worse. I went to Sophie and hypocritically told her I had come to apologise and do whatever she asked to make amends for having told the unkind stories about her lover and herself. I said I was full of contrition and ready to do whatever she asked to prove that I was truly repentant. To do her justice, I must say she is not one to harbour resentment. She forgave me wholeheartedly, even inviting me to her wedding. I took my perfidy even further and said she should be satisfied with her victory, that it should be enough for her to have humiliated me, without adding the cruelty of asking me to be present at a ceremony which would break my heart. I have come to see you, I continued, only because of my sincere regret at having wronged you. My feelings have not changed. Though I still love you, I will not trouble you again. I cannot bear to see you in another's arms. I will leave Paris and take my despair elsewhere. I wish only to beg forgiveness from you and your betrothed for my foolishness and my slanders.

It is strange how ready people can be to overestimate their own worth. Sophie was prepared to believe she had really aroused in me this tender yet violent passion. She swallowed the bait and told me it would cause her great distress if I left Paris. We were reconciled; she even wished to make peace between myself and her fiancé. At that moment, he arrived. I offered him the most fulsome compliments. He was overjoyed at his triumph in winning Sophie's hand and was highly pleased with himself. To seal our reconciliation, Sophie sent out for lunch to be brought in, and I was able to slip the liquid unseen into a glass of wine which d'Espinai drank. When I left them after the meal, we were to all appearances the best of friends. This took place early in January.

I went to spend Carnival and Lent in Brittany on Monsieur de Rohan's estate, with one of his officers who was a friend of mine. It was after Easter before we returned. I made enquiries as to how Sophie was and learnt that since her marriage she had appeared as sour as a quince, and her husband no better; in a word, they were not a happy couple. I took this to be the result of my potion and went to see Sophie. She was pleased to see me, but I found her much changed. I asked if she had been ill, and plied her with so many questions, and swore so convincingly that I would not betray her, that in the end she said: The stories you told about Monsieur d'Espinai and myself before we were married were a pack of lies: the poor thing is quite without manhood, and I am still as much a maid as I was before our marriage. What are you saying! I exclaimed, feigning surprise. Are you telling me you are lodged at the Inn of Wasted Time? Alas! that is so, she answered, in such a plaintive tone that I was tempted to laugh. I told her how dismayed I was to hear this, and began to reawaken her frustrated passion. I maintained that she should not waste her youth with a man who could not make her happy, but should remarry. Indeed, I promised to wed her as soon as she was free. She compared my ardour with her husband's impotence and wept with despair. I thought to take advantage of her disarray and came near to doing so, but was prevented by the arrival of her husband, who appeared at that moment.

She took to heart what I had said: she was made of flesh and blood, and not immune to desires which d'Espinai could not satisfy. He tried to dissuade her, but she determined to follow my counsel and recounted to me every last word that she and her husband exchanged. The poor man believed he had been bewitched – and the best part was that neither of them had any suspicion of the part that I had played in the comedy.

461

Eventually it became common knowledge that Sophie was seeking a separation from her husband. But since the promises I had made were too binding to be broken without causing me serious trouble if she ever became free, I thought it expedient to undo the charm before any adjudication was made on the request. I arranged for a letter to be sent to Sophie's mother, in an unknown hand, stating that d'Espinai's frailty came as the result of a potion he had drunk, whose effect would disappear four months to the day after his marriage. The letter begged her to persuade her daughter to delay the separation from her husband until the end of that time, when she would no longer have reason to be dissatisfied with him. Her mother conveyed the contents of this letter to Sophie, who passed them on to me. I said it was an imposture, bewailed my misfortune, and appeared to be in despair, an emotion which elicited Sophie's gratitude; and I persuaded her to proceed with her demand for a separation and an end to her marriage. But the truth was, I was satisfied with what I had done, and was content to take my revenge no further. I explained the whole story to Gallouin, who promptly came to the rescue. He knew the antidote, and, without my even being present, he took d'Espinai out for dinner and ordered veal stew for him, to which he added the drug which would return his manhood to him. Gallouin did not refer directly to his symptoms. He merely encouraged him to overcome his reluctance to approach his wife, making him drink more than was his wont, in order, he told him, to dispel the black humours that had been curbing his virility. And then he left him, confident and in good heart, after reminding him of Montaigne's dictum that Bacchus and Venus make good partners.

Sure enough, d'Espinai's manhood returned and he announced the fact to his mother-in-law, who left him alone with his wife. The latter, anticipating a repetition of earlier disappointments, was at first unwilling to allow him to approach her, but her resistance provided the final stimulus he needed, and with the determination instilled by the wine he had drunk, he overcame her reluctance, and the deed was done.

After this, his manner changed completely. He was no longer apologetic and deferential towards his wife, and he was no longer willing to tolerate the frequent visits I paid her. Whereas previously he had not dared to make any objection to them, he now confronted her on the subject and absolutely forbade her to see me. She reported this to me, telling me how distressed it made her. But since the prohibition suited my purposes and was in her best interest too, I told her that since it had been she who had sought the annulment of her marriage, she must now, for her own peace of mind, endeavour to regain her husband's trust and submit to his authority, even at the price of sacrificing me. I said that, for myself, however painful it might be, I would forego my pleasure in her company rather than be her undoing. She was none too pleased at this lukewarm retreat, as she made clear to me. But I didn't care. I haven't spoken to her since. I think, at the bottom of her heart, she had no really strong feelings for me, although we had been good friends. So that was how the first entanglement after my reform came to an end. You see how complete my conversion had been! I had played the part of a scoundrel in this affair, but this was nothing in comparison with what followed, which I will now recount to you.

The heroine of this next adventure was Célénie, whom you all know. She was young, unmarried, attractive and of a pleasing figure. Her complexion was dark, and her bright black eyes were the sort which speak of love. Her birthday was in May, and all, or nearly all, those born in this month tend to be of an amorous nature. I felt sure I should not be wasting my time if I paid her court. And indeed, in her case,

I loved her enough to want to marry her, but only until she had yielded to me; after that, I no longer thought of making our union permanent.

We were neighbours and I had known her for a long time. I had first spoken to her at a wedding, which she had attended dressed as a peasant. She was carrying a little basket with two eggs and a cheese in it, like a country girl, and she looked charmingly pretty and appealing. It was so warm that she had removed the velvet mask which had covered the top half of her face. What a pleasure it would be to break those eggs of yours! I said to her. It is Sunday today, she replied. We do not make omelettes on Sunday. It is not in order to make an omelette that I wish to break your eggs, I said, but so that you would bring me some milk. I have a cow which gives me more than I need, she said. Do you know how to make curd? I said. Of course, she said. And I also know how to make butter and cheese. Don't you give any to your cat? I said. We don't have a cat, she answered. But you are a mouse who would be well worth catching, I said, and I wish I were a rat and could be your country cousin. I am looking for a town rat, she said. I think they are more handsome and refined. Have you found one today? I asked. No, I have found no one who will buy my wares, and I am going to take them back home, she said. Will you sell them to me? I asked. Gladly, she said. You may even have them at a bargain price, for I am weary of waiting and eager to return home.

At this point someone came and asked her to dance, and our conversation was interrupted. She then danced with me, and then, after dancing with someone else, when I tried to find her again she had disappeared. I went to see her the next day, and told her I had come to conclude our deal. She laughed and said it was not market day. This led to a lengthy conversation, which I will not repeat, and to many others which I had with her over a certain length of time.

In the end, I proposed marriage, and this led to the

subject of her older sister, who was about to be married. As you all know, there were three sisters who married at long intervals one after the other – and all of them more than six years after they would have wished. We talked about her sister's marriage, and it was clear to me that she too wanted to be married. I told her I would ask for her hand, and that I didn't think the offer would be refused. You are right, she said, your offer will not be refused, but neither will it be accepted, because it has been agreed that my oldest sister's dowry will be paid in cash, which my mother has been making every effort to raise, and all that is left now is in the form of goods and property and will not be easy to transform promptly into money. And furthermore, my mother will not allow me to marry until Toinon too is married. She is older than I am, and it is right that she should take her place as a married woman before I do; moreover, I am not sure you love me sincerely. And what reason do you have, I asked, to doubt that I love you, and do so with all the devotion possible? I am afraid, she answered, that your attachment to me is nothing more than a diversion to help you forget the beautiful Sophie, who is now married to Monsieur d'Espinai. You cannot deny that you were in love with her – and that you still love her.

I acknowledge, I answered, that I loved her with all possible tenderness. I acknowledge that I am truly sorry for having spoken scurrilously of her. And I acknowledge that my hopes were rekindled when I heard of her intended divorce. But you must agree that the way I withdrew and relinquished my claim, rather than cause any difficulty between her and her husband, was the act of an honourable man. And of someone who truly loved her, she interrupted. Yes, that is so, I said. That is my character, I went on. I shall always put the happiness and tranquillity of a girl or woman I love before my own. I shall treat you with the same consideration as I had for her. My character will not change.

I admit, she said, that your behaviour was that of an honest man, and if I were sure you loved me as much as you did her, it is true I would be willing to love you too. I assured her she need have no qualms as to my sincerity, and told her that the best means to convince her of it would be for me to ask her mother for her hand, and I begged her to let me do so. She agreed, but added that she was afraid my suit would not be successful.

As I really did love her, the next day I sent my proxy to make the proposal, which her mother received, with Célénie present. The gentleman who spoke for me was articulate and competent, and performed his duties perfectly. Both the younger daughters were present in fact. He said he had come to make an offer of marriage for Célénie which she would not be able to refuse. The older sister, Toinon, flushed with dismay when it thus became apparent that the person concerned was Célénie, not herself. Her mother noticed this, as did both Célénie and my intermediary. The mother said, in her reply, that my offer was an honour both to her and her daughter, but that she could make no commitment for Célénie until Toinon's future was settled, for since Toinon was older it was only right that she should be married first. But what she could offer would be to arrange for both marriages to take place at the same time; and she begged me to remain patient until such a time, which might come sooner than even she thought. She was obliged to proceed in this way, she said, because it might be considered strange, and might damage the prospects of her older daughter, if the younger one were to marry first. This was the answer my spokesman brought back to me.

Célénie reported the dialogue that had taken place to me word for word, as well as describing her sister's chagrin. So that means, dear Célénie, I said, taking her in my arms, that we must wait for your sister's future to be settled before we ourselves can be happy. This is the answer I expected my mother to give, she said. There is no alternative but to accept it. No alternative? I said. And what if your sister doesn't find a husband for another four years – do we sit here patiently and wait to grow older? And it will be four years, you may be sure, or even longer, for who the devil will take her? She hasn't a single feature that could attract an honest fellow. I knew I could say this, since there was little affection lost between the sisters, and it was true, her sister was neither pleasant nor good-looking. But what is there we can do about it? said Célénie, with a smile.

There is a way, I said. If you will do as I say, we can be married before her and in spite of her. It depends on you, and whether your strength of will is as strong as your affection for me. If it is a question of will-power, she said, I have plenty of that. Tell me what you would suggest. We must become man and wife, I answered, in fact, without benefit of a ceremony. That is a risky way of proceeding, she said. It is the only one available, I answered. Your mother has no objection to my proposal; it is only because your older sister is unmarried that she refuses to allow us to be happy, but if we make a stronger case for our marriage, she will have to make the best of it. I give you my word, I said, embracing her, I will make you happy. You know that I am to be trusted, and there is no reason for you to fear that I would desert you, just as I am certain that you will not desert me. Think about it, and you will agree that what I am suggesting is both reasonable and possible. You are not being serious, she said. It may be possible, but it does not follow that it is reasonable. I did not say any more about it that day, hoping that time and opportunity would eventually bring her round to my way of thinking – and relying on the aphorism which says that a girl who listens is half-convinced; and I was proved right. I left her and went my way. Her mother, who had welcomed me warmly when I arrived, was equally civil when I left, which cannot be said of her sister, who looked sourly at me.

I returned two days later and found that the household was in some disarray: Toinon, who could not tolerate the idea that her younger sister was preferred to her, was not hiding her displeasure, and Célénie was maintaining that she could not help it if I found her more attractive than her sister. Toinon claimed that it was Célénie who had been making the advances, something the latter roundly denied. Their mother had intervened, but had made no impression on Toinon, who was as ill-spirited as she was ill-favoured. Célénie, however, remained silent, and their mother, seeing that the quarrel had abated, had gone out. There was still tension between the two girls when I arrived, and Toinon, when she saw me, said with an unpleasant sneer to Célénie: Here comes your intended! Soon he will make you happy!

I am delighted, I said, if my presence, rather than displeasing your sister, gives her pleasure. I am in your debt for telling me this. She herself has never let me know as much, and I did not know I was so fortunate. It is possible my sister is mistaken, Monsieur, Célénie said. You should not believe everything she says on the matter. What! my dear Célénie, I replied, Would you deprive me of the pleasure of knowing the kind things your sister tells me? I would not wish to deprive you of them, she answered, if she did not imply she knew what my thoughts were; and I should be delighted if the kind things she said were meant good-naturedly and came from a generous heart. Whatever the motive for Mademoiselle's words, I said, I shall always be grateful for anything she does to promote my happiness. You are welcome, Monsieur, said Toinon. I will leave you and my sister to discuss your own affairs. I can see my presence is not needed and I do not wish to be in the way.

Célénie tried to call her back. What is it, I said, that causes this bitterness between you and your sister? She can't accept the fact that it is me you love, Célénie answered. She thinks that she should have your heart, and that I have stolen it from her. If you were to seek her hand, she would become soft and gentle, and she and I would be good friends again. I thought this may be the case, I said; not because she imagined she loved me – but because she was furious that I had asked for you before anyone asked for her. This is the problem we have already talked about. It is for you to decide whether you are going to let yourself be a hostage to time and spend the best part of your youth waiting for someone to take pity on her! You are very hard on her, laughed Célénie. She is not so ugly as to need pity, and there are those who will look more favourably on her than you do. It is true, my lovely Célénie, I said, looking at her, my eyes are charmed by you and find nothing else pleasing. I wish your sister were as beautiful as you, so that her good fortune could hasten our own. But that is a futile wish. You could make me perfectly happy, and – if I may say so – you would find happiness yourself at the same time. Let me ask again what I asked before. I am sure your heart is in agreement with mine, if you have given thought to what I said.

Yes, she said, I have given it some thought. It is true that what you suggested would afford the quickest way to hasten my mother's approval for our marriage. But you must admit that it is fraught with hazards. I see none, I replied. What hazards are there? You might change your mind, she answered. I would lose your esteem if I gave myself to you on the strength of your word alone. The gossip my behaviour would cause were it to become known, and the shame I myself would feel if I were so to forget myself and my upbringing. These reasons are only valid for the outside world, I said. Why would you feel shame with me? Does a woman feel shame with her husband? Would not any rumours about our engagement to each other be justified? It is ridiculous to think I would esteem you less. On the contrary, I would know that you love me and have absolute confidence in me, and I should love you more for that reason, since it would be of your own free will that I received your favours. My love would be compounded with gratitude, as well as desire. Your fears of finding me untrue are not justified. Have you forgotten that you said you trusted me? The fear you express does me an injustice! But if neither my word nor my oath satisfy you, I will put in writing whatever you wish to dictate, and that you may put your trust in. It would be unreasonable to imagine that I could deny both what I had put in writing and the request for your hand I have already made to your mother. So make your decision, my dear Célénie, I continued, throwing myself at her feet and kissing her hands. Do not refuse to ensure our happiness, since it is within your power to do so. And I argued so forcefully that in the end she yielded. However, we resisted the temptation to act precipitately, for we were afraid someone might come into the room, but we agreed to meet the next day, when both her mother and Toinon would be paying a visit to her oldest sister, who was married and unwell.

On this occasion we were not so circumspect. She had sent the servants off on errands and we had arranged a signal, so no one saw me enter. Her bedroom windows were almost closed, and I could barely see well enough to write what she dictated to me. She thought she had taken every precaution – but the piece of paper was in fact worthless. I wrote whatever she wanted, and when she was satisfied I also had what I wanted.

Whether it was because I did not find all I had hoped for, or because I was fickle, as soon as she had given herself to me, I no longer had any wish to marry her. Far from revealing this to her, however, I wiped away her few tears and renewed my caresses. Thereafter, we met in various remote locations and borrowed houses. At the same time, I continued to visit her in her home as usual. We conducted our lives in this way for a good while, and then, after about four months, she told me she was pregnant. This did not please me, but I did not let her know this. On the contrary, in order to extricate myself from this affair, I made myself appear more in love with her than ever.

It was at around this time that my Pont-Neuf adventure took place – at which you were present, said Dupuis, interrupting his narrative and addressing Des Frans, who laughed at the memory of this incident. What adventure is this? enquired Madame de Contamine. Another of your dubious pranks? Not exactly, Madame, answered Des Frans. There was nothing deceitful or underhand about this incident. It was all out in the open, for everyone to see! Monsieur Dupuis can characterise it however he likes. I will make no attempt to do so. It was, said Dupuis, an act of madness, stupidity and brutality. Do you think those are the right words to describe it? he asked, laughing. I want to hear what happened, said Madame de Contamine. Certainly, Madame, said Dupuis. I have no intention of hiding anything from you.

As I have said, Célénie and I met in furnished rooms, which we borrowed, and of which there is a large number in Paris, for the benefit of fortunate lovers. We had one of these. It was during the heat of summer, and very often we took delight in being completely naked. This is doubtless not very respectable, but we were both too young and indifferent to propriety to worry about this. One day, I decided I wanted to go swimming. There were six of us, one of whom was Monsieur Des Frans. We went under the Pont-Neuf. The others stayed near the boat, but Gallouin and I, who enjoyed swimming and diving, clambered up onto the bridge, made our way to the second-storey windows of a house built on the bridge, and jumped from there into the water. There was a crowd of people watching us as we fell.

Among them was a good-for-nothing soldier on the parapet of the bridge – where the scum of the populace come to defecate and dump their refuse – and with his foot, he directed some filth towards us. I looked up to tell him to stop – and some of it landed full in my face.

You can laugh! Who wouldn't? All those who were watching laughed too. I didn't laugh! I plunged my head into the water to wash the filth off, and making my way between the boats, I reached the steps. I climbed up them naked and within reach of all the cart drivers' whips, and they didn't spare me! I climbed up on to the Pont-Neuf and caught up with my knave of a soldier, who had thought he was safe. I laid hold of him by the hair and punched him on the nose three or four times, and then threw him into the river, jumping in after him myself. His fall from the bridge, combined with my attack, had stunned him. The weight of his clothes was pulling him under the water, and he would have been a drowned soldier, if he had not been rescued. I prevented our boat from going to his aid, and the boatman did not dare to argue with someone as incensed as I was. My friends caught up with me. I was in a flaming temper, and all bloody from the whiplashes. Nobody laughed – I would not have tolerated it if they had. We put our clothes on again, and I had the boatman take me to the Quai de Conti where the wretch had been taken. Our arrival was enough to silence the mob: the presence of our lackeys made it clear we were not to be trifled with.

I found the soldier lying on the ground, with more than a thousand people milling round, among whom were more than forty soldiers, like himself. Though he was dying, they could not restrain me from breaking my cane across his body. And his comrades did well to keep out of my way. We went back across the bridge, where we found some people still laughing at what had happened to me, whom I dealt with in such a way as to remove anyone else's inclination to laugh at me. I came back to the Quai de l'Ecole, where not a single cart driver remained. I had our lackeys slash all their paraphernalia to pieces and do as much damage as they could. Then my friends took me to my carriage, and I got into it with them, still in a towering rage, both because of the damage to my person and because of the mockery I might incur for the way it had been received. I had been thinking of Célénie, to whom I dare not show myself. For a whole week, my shirts stuck to my skin, and it was more than six weeks before my scars were healed. But in the end, I recovered and thought no more of it.

Célénie had told me she was pregnant, and I no longer had any wish to marry her. I had become aware that it was my family, my property and the position I could give her in the world – in a word, her ambition – that had played a bigger part in obtaining her favours than her love for me. She was grasping; true generosity, and the consideration for others that one would hope for in a wife, were virtues she did not possess, or did not wish to employ. I had noticed at times an excess of emotion which was pleasing in a mistress, but which I thought would cause alarm in a wife. All of these observations had made me resolve that I would never marry her. Speaking of her pregnancy, she had indicated that she would have to inform her mother of it. This put me in a quandary, and I had asked her to wait a little time, with the excuse that we needed to be careful how we broached the matter, though really it was to give me time to contrive some expedient which would extricate me from my predicament.

At about this time, her sister became engaged. It was a very advantageous match, and I was delighted, not for her sake, as I cared little for her, but because it removed one difficulty – and by means of this marriage, I planned to obtain my liberty. I redoubled my attentions and gifts to Célénie, in order to strengthen her attachment to me, so that she would do whatever I asked, and I was successful in persuading her that I loved her too much ever to leave her. A girl who has a high opinion of herself, and is convinced of her own beauty, can always be manipulated if one plays on her conceit and her susceptibility to flattery.

I hadn't ever spoken to my mother about Célénie. I hadn't told her I wanted to marry her or that I had asked for her hand. I was not of age to marry without my mother's consent, but I had assumed she would give it, or had thought I could do without it. You see how much I cared for my filial duty! It is true that her attitude towards me and her lack of interest in what I did might appear to release me to some extent from a strict observance of this duty. In any case, I certainly knew I was doing wrong, and it is certainly true also that I made no effort to improve my behaviour.

She found out that I had made the request for Célénie's hand, discovering this, in fact, while my brother was in Paris. Both he and I were living at home, but were careful to keep out of each other's way. We avoided any need to speak to each other and had not even seen each other since his return. All our relatives were dismayed at this state of affairs between us, and an effort was made to remedy it by speaking to us individually. My uncle took it on himself to talk to me. He sent for me and said everything a good man and worried relative could say to a young man who is in danger of ruining his life. He wanted me, since I was the younger one, to make the first steps towards a reconciliation with my brother. He said our feud was like a dagger in my mother's heart, and that it jeopardised the whole family.

I answered that my mother had only herself to blame, and that she knew that the only thing I owed her for was the fact that she had brought me into the world; and that this debt was so common and general that in itself it counted for nothing, and had to be accompanied by other actions, which would have shown I was her son not only by blood, but also by affection – something she had never done. I said it was because I knew very well she had no affection for me, and had never had any, that I had thought she would be glad if I did not eat at home, and this was the reason I did not do so. I added that if she would prefer that I did not live under the same roof as her and my brother, she could tell me so: I should not be surprised by a further sign of rejection, such as this, and I would go and live elsewhere, even though the house was mine, and neither of them had a shred of right to it, since in the division of property it had fallen to me. I said that I had never dared to show the affection I actually felt for her; on the contrary, never having seen myself treated by her as a son, I had gradually become accustomed to not treating her as a mother. I said that, as far as my brother was concerned, far from wishing him ill, I would be happy to be of service to him, at whatever cost it might be; but I admitted that the difference between my mother's treatment of him and myself stung me. It was because I had been so cruelly rejected and sacrificed – even though I was as legitimate as he – that I found it hard to meet and talk to him.

My uncle found this explanation plausible, and my other relatives, including my mother, found it not unreasonable. It was four months since I had seen her, much less talked to her. A meeting, to which I agreed, was arranged. But it passed in complaints and recriminations on all sides. It did not improve my fortune, and left my brother and myself still at daggers drawn.

Our relatives were invited for dinner at the house. I joined them, though with some misgivings. I still felt bitter, because my mother – though she had claimed a few days earlier to feel some affection for me – had not in any way changed her treatment of me, and seeing my brother's position so far above my own in every respect made me feel humiliated. During the meal, there was talk of Célénie and of my offer of marriage to her. I was careful not to reveal either what my actual feelings were or what the present situation was. On the contrary, I claimed it was a matter of honour that I fulfil the undertaking I had made. We had all drunk a considerable amount, and I was being teased and ridiculed. I did my best to defend myself, but since everyone was against me, my arguments were torn to pieces. I had tolerated all their taunts with the air of someone who could take a few jibes, but eventually my brother went too far. Since he was judging Célénie from his own well-established position, and since, to tell the truth, she was not a very good match for me, he talked of her with contempt. He called her a real hussy, with no qualities to recommend her. I responded in a way that should have warned him to go no further, had he had even the slightest respect for my feelings, but he continued to pour scorn on both Célénie and myself, concluding his remarks in a mocking, countrified accent, saying, 'Pon me wurd! If her's like to be wun on't famly, us'll need to mack 'er welcome!' My only reply was a slight inclination of the head, which went unnoticed. But I resolved to pay him back for this insult he had made in my presence to a girl he believed I cared for.

I determined to fight it out with him, but could not challenge him there and then because of the presence of our guests. In due course, they left, and my mother, after saying her farewells and wishing them Godspeed, withdrew to her room. My brother had thrown himself down on a daybed, and I had taken a book in my hand. As soon as I was sure my mother was out of earshot, I ran to the door and bolted it, and went towards my brother. Now, Monsieur, I said, unsheathing my sword, let us see whether your sword is as ready as your tongue! The time has come for you to answer both for my mother's preference, and for your disparagement of Célénie. Don't be such a simpleton! he said. I was only making conversation. I wasn't intending to insult you! I am not asking for excuses, I said. I am telling you to

476

defend yourself. And hurry – the time is too short to be wasted on words. When he saw that I was in earnest, he took his sword in his hand.

I have already said he could be more spiteful than I was, and now he proved it. He stayed on the defensive for some time. Zounds! I said. You are sparing me. Let's see how long that will last! And I pressed him more closely than I had till then, and wounded him. When he felt his blood flow, it roused his anger to the same pitch as my own. We no longer spared each other. We both saw blood and were ready to fight to the death. One or the other of us would certainly have remained there, if my mother and the servants – who had run back to the room on hearing the rumpus – had not knocked down the door. They arrived in time to save my life: the tip of my sword was entangled in the tassel of ribbons which hung from his sword handle and he was pressing me hard. I had no alternative but to throw myself bodily at him, so that we were wrestling each other, and, as I was much punier than he, I would have been the one to succumb. We were both wounded in three places, on the arms and the body. Our blood and our anger combined to make us lose all reason, and we were not in control either of our words or our actions. The servants were transfixed, and my mother was weeping and crying out, as a woman would. I would not wait to hear what she said. This, Madame, I said as I went out, is what your unequal affection has led to. Au revoir, Monsieur, I continued, addressing my brother. We will conclude this anon, and I will have my revenge on you, or you will have yours. Just so, he said. We will soon find each other, since we will each be looking for the other.

I went up to my room, where I intended to remain only long enough to have my wounds dressed. I meant to go to the room where Célénie and I met, but I was not able to do so. No sooner had my wounds been attended to than my uncle came into the room, and I was overcome by weakness and taken to my bed by my servant, who was helped by the surgeon and his assistant. I was in worse case than my brother: his wounds were more damagingly placed, but they were more superficial than mine. Two thrusts had pierced my upper arm only half an inch apart, and the third was in my armpit. Soon after I had recovered from the spasm of weakness, my mother came into the room. My anger was spent, and Monsieur Dupuis spoke up to defend me. I pretended not to have noticed the fact that my mother had stayed with my brother until it was clear he was out of danger, without giving a thought to me. Instead, I quietly asked how he was. She said he was in great pain. I am sorry, I said. But it would not have happened if he had been content to mind his own business and leave me alone. This made my mother angry and she showered me with reproaches, so that in the end I asked her to leave me, so that I could rest. I wanted to leave the house immediately. My mother would not allow it, and my uncle, to whom I appealed, also forbade it. He said I should not be so headstrong and ready to act always on my first impulse.

To bring my account of this unfortunate episode to a conclusion: it was hushed up by the family; the servants were ordered not to speak of it. I let Célénie know about it, and she came to see me. I made arrangements to marry her from my bed, if my life were in danger. She thanked me and wept copiously. My brother was in bed only two weeks and saw her one day as she was leaving. He treated her with great civility and told her the same story as we had ordered the servants to tell: that we had been attacked by thieves.

As soon as he was able to leave his room, he came to see me. I was surprised by his visit, which I had not expected. We embraced. He said he was dismayed by what had happened, and that, since I took his teasing so to heart, he promised not only never to repeat it, but also to persuade my mother to consent to my marriage with Célénie. I said in

478

answer, that he ought to be satisfied with the advantage he had over me in age and in fortune, without adding further injury to my self-respect by treating me as something worthless. I also said I intended to forget the past, and thanked him for his offer, but said that I did not need my mother's consent and would rather never marry than ask her for it.

My answer was not very conciliatory as you see, but such as it was, he did not take it amiss. I went to visit him, in my turn, and he received me cordially. My mother was greatly pleased by our reconciliation, which proved to be genuine, for since then, we have lived together on good terms, without ever interfering in each others' affairs, unless we were asked to. He has offered several times to return the part of my inheritance of which he has the benefit; but realising it was in good hands, and since it would not enable me to obtain a position as attractive as the one he has, and not wishing to establish myself in one that was inferior to his, I have told him to keep it. I have let him know that I am going to marry Madame de Londé, and since this is such an honourable match, and one which is distinctly advantageous to me, he has made generous offers to me which I had not expected from him, and which prove to me that, in the long run, blood runs thicker than water and that a brother is always a brother.

As for Célénie, who, as I told you, came to see me, and who thanked me for having defended her so staunchly: she listened to my reasons for not wishing her to reveal her pregnancy. I pointed out that since her sister was about to be married, it would be better for us to defer our own wedding, so that people would not say we were marrying because we had to. I said it was in our interest to hide the truth, because, if her mother found what the situation was, and so knew it was impossible for me to withdraw from my commitment, she would give Célénie a less advantageous settlement than she would if I had less incentive to proceed with the marriage. Moreover, I said, the dispute between my brother and myself would not lead to any benefit for me if I did not try to improve my mother's opinion of me. I said she was beginning to regret her previous harshness, but that she would doubtless feel it had been justified if the present circumstances came to her ears. It was important, I said, for me to encourage the seeds of her more favourable attitude towards me – which did not necessarily come from a real change of heart. It would not be advisable to give her any new cause to criticise me, for she would not fail to use it as a pretext to renege on all she had promised to do for me.

This reasoning, although not particularly convincing, was sufficient to influence Célénie. It is true that it was accompanied by marks of tenderness which would have persuaded the least trusting girl in the world. So she promised to hide her pregnancy. She is tall and well built, so this was easier for her than for a woman who is small or of average size. She attended her sister's wedding in her sixth month of pregnancy without anyone noticing her condition. When it was no longer possible to hide it, she took to wearing a loose, flowing garment and complained of being unwell, so that she could remain in bed, or wear a house-robe, and, in the event, she was successful in hiding the truth.

If I had not been an actor in this comedy myself, I would doubt that it was true, but her success proved it was possible. I saw her every day, but no one gave any thought to these visits: her sisters had moved out and only her mother remained at home, and she had always thought of me as a son-in-law, and having given her the same reasons with respect to my mother's hoped-for generosity as I had given Célénie for deferring our marriage, I was given all the freedom I wanted to visit and talk with her daughter. I expressed concern to her about this illness and even used it as one of the reasons for postponing the wedding.

The good woman was not sorry for our marriage to be somewhat delayed: paying for two celebrations one after the other would have strained her resources. Thus, since we all had our reasons for preferring a later date, none of us urged the other to bring the marriage forward, although every one of us pretended to wish for it as soon as possible. Célénie left her bed every evening, and we often went out for a walk together, and when she was in her ninth month I took her to see a very competent midwife, who could tell us when she could expect to be delivered of her burden. This woman was called la Cadret and lived in the rue Saint-Antoine, at the corner of a little street in front of the rue Geofroi l'Anier. She told us Célénie had two more weeks to wait and, until then, all she need do was to eat well and amuse herself. I gave the woman the money to buy clothing for the child and to hire a wet nurse; and two weeks later I brought Célénie back to her.

As I said, I would not believe what I am about to tell you had I not seen it with my own eyes. You know where Célénie lived, and I have told you where la Cadret lived, so you know the two places are far apart; however, Célénie made both journeys there and back on foot, and refused to make use of the sedan chair which I had ordered ready for her use. This convinced me that, however delicate a girl may be, she can do whatever may be necessary to hide a mistake of this sort and avoid falling into the abyss which her lack of virtue has opened before her.

I went to see Célénie that evening, as usual, and found her in a loose house-robe. It was November, and we walked to la Cadret's at around seven in the evening; though it was late in the season, the weather was mild and quite pleasant for walking. Our timing was impeccable: Célénie had barely entered la Cadret's house when her pains began; and this same Célénie – who had groaned pitifully on the first occasion she allowed herself to run the risk of becoming pregnant – gave birth to a little girl, with no other sound than a deep sigh – notwithstanding the difference there is between the pleasure of the one and the pain of the other. It was nine o' clock when we left – and, however much I tried, I was unable to persuade Célénie to use any conveyance on her return home.

The child was put out to nurse, and I had her cared for until she was six years old, when she died of smallpox or some other illness which her nurse gave as the reason for her death; this was about two years ago. But that evening I took Célénie home. She kept her bed for four days – no more! If she had been married, she would have taken six weeks to get over the birth.

I had the infant baptised under my name and hers, but not as legitimate; and since I no longer had any wish to marry Célénie, I exerted every effort to finding some acceptable way of extricating myself. I thought that an absence might provide the solution, and looked around for a suitable opportunity, and even contacted my former friends. There is one more ludicrous adventure I had in their company I must tell you about, which took place at the house of this same midwife, who had attended Célénie.

Four of us were coming home from having supper in the rue de la Mortellerie one night at about one in the morning. We were on foot, and it suddenly started to rain so heavily it might have been the second Flood. We didn't know where to go for shelter at that time of night; moreover, it was so dark we scarcely knew what street we were in. I saw a light, and it was at la Cadret's house, where Célénie had given birth only two weeks earlier. In fact, the child was still there. La Cadret put us in the same room that Célénie had been in, and we lit a fire to dry ourselves by, and to keep us warm for the night and while we waited out the bad weather.

This room was separated only by a partition from another

room where la Cadret was busy attending a young girl who was bringing forth in pain the fruit of what she had received in pleasure nine months earlier. There is nothing unusual about this in a midwife's house, and we found some amusement in the circumstance. The girl was very young and was not facing her pain with much fortitude, but crying out at the top of her voice; and among her barely coherent screams I distinguished three or four times the word: Butter! Butter! We had spent the evening drinking and needed something to help us overcome the excess of alcohol we had imbibed. When I heard the word 'Butter' repeated so often, I ran to the door of the room where the girl was, and half-opened it. Save some of the butter, I said to la Cadret, to make us some onion soup. This interruption, which I had made on the spur of the moment, worked in an unexpected way. First, it made la Cadret burst into a great gale of laughter. I followed suit, partly because I saw her laughing, and partly because, at the same time, I saw the poor young creature lying grotesquely on her back in front of the fire, her knees up and spread apart. This young demoness began to join in the laughter, and with such gusto that it propelled the child into the world. They gave us some butter for our onion soup, and since I had helped in the delivery more than anyone else, I was nominated to be the child's god-father. It was not a magnificent ceremony, but it was Bacchic: we didn't leave the house and the dinner table till evening.

To return to Célénie: I persuaded her that, in order to allow for her thorough recovery after giving birth, it would be prudent for us to cease our private meetings and live chastely for a time; and that this would not be possible if we continued to be neighbours, as we would never have sufficient will-power to resist our impulses when temptation arose; and therefore it would be better for there to be a greater distance between us. She was not easily persuaded but, by dint of repetition, she eventually agreed to let me go to the country until Carnival-time, when, I promised, I would return to Paris and we would thereafter remain together for ever.

She was in bed with a slight fever the day I took leave of her; and as I was leaving, I noticed that her dressing room was open. I laid my hand on a purse which I saw there, and in which I knew she put documents and papers of importance to her. I took it and inside found the promise of marriage I had given her. No harm will be done if I take this! I thought. If I am going to marry her, this promise is unnecessary; and if I do not want to marry her, there is no point leaving something in her possession with which she can create trouble for me. So I tore the paper up, without compunction, and even with a certain light-heartedness, and left for Brittany with no further thought of Célénie than if I had never seen her.

I didn't return to Paris throughout the winter, nor even for a good part of the spring – not until twelve days after Easter, in fact. The first piece of news I received was that Célénie was going to marry Alaix, whom you know. I didn't believe it at first, but since the banns had been published, there was no room left for doubt. I went to see her in the afternoon. She was surprised, but not disconcerted, to see me. Her future husband was also present. Here is Monsieur Dupuis, she said, introducing me, of whom I have spoken several times. So it is you, Monsieur, I said who are going to marry Mademoiselle? That is so, he replied, since Mademoiselle has been good enough to consent to be my wife. You could not find a young woman possessed of more admirable qualities of every kind, I said. One has only to see and know her to be of this opinion. I perfectly agree, Monsieur, he answered. I found this conversation too stifling to continue, so I left them and went to find her mother.

So, Madame, I said to her, I find that, in spite of your

promise to me, it is true that you are giving Célénie to another? Have you forgotten that she was promised to me? That was so long ago, Monsieur, she answered, and you seemed to have so completely forgotten the agreement yourself that, when she told me of her inclination for Monsieur Alaix, I did not believe I need consider myself bound by it any longer. So you are telling me, I said, that she loves him and is unfaithful to me? I do not wish to stand in the way of her happiness, I continued, but at least I hope you will allow me a moment of conversation alone with her? Not that I would try to make her change her mind. One would have little hope of reversing a girl's change of heart, but there is something which is important to me which I would like to clarify by having a few words with her. I won't prevent you from settling any questions there may be between you, her mother said. You may talk to her whenever you please; but I don't think you will get very far, nor that she will break off her engagement to Alaix. That is why I wish to speak to her, I said, and I beg you to arrange for me to see her in private tomorrow morning. Then I left, consumed with anger at Célénie.

In one sense, I did not care that Célénie was getting married, since I did not wish to marry her, but I didn't want her to have the privilege of discarding me. I wanted our separation to come as the result of my rejection of her, not as a result of her change of heart. It was a question of my self-respect. I didn't want to marry her, but I didn't want her to marry Alaix in preference to me. Before deciding what course of action I should take, I wanted to talk to her. This I did the next morning, without further delay. I went into her room. She was up, but not yet dressed, and I found her negligée more appealing than all the finery women adorn themselves with, thinking to heighten their beauty.

Is it true, then, my dear Célénie, I said, that you are untrue? I had refused to believe all that people had written to me about your engagement. I thought I could be sure of your constancy, after all that has passed between us; but since this is now apparently forgotten by you, I returned post-haste to remind you of it. Tell me truthfully, does your choice of Alaix come from your heart, or from your mother? Is it submission to your family, or your own unsteady affection, which has torn you from me? Do you hope to drive me to despair? she said, in a tone full of disdain. Is it not enough for you that you cruelly took advantage of my weakness for you, and my trust in you? Is this the time to tell me you still love me, now that I am on the point of belonging to another? Are you not the most despicable of men – not only betraying me, but also removing the means to prove your treachery? Did you not heartlessly steal back the promise of marriage you had given me? Did you not leave with barely a word of goodbye? Did you send me news? Did you even let me know where you were? How could I then write to you to let you know what was happening to me? Go, and leave me in peace! Let it be sufficient for you to know that I will forget what I did, and that I will not exact the vengeance that a despicable scoundrel such as you deserves.

Very good! I said. Your reprimand is to the point; but now, I have returned, repentant, wholly yours, ready to marry you. What do you say? It is not too late to save you from the terrible mistake you are about to make. Marry you! she exclaimed in fury. I would rather be tied to the gallows than to a man as deceitful as you. It appears you no longer love me, then, I said. I do not love you, she said. I hate you with all my soul. I would prefer the company of the vilest of demons to yours! You do not mince your words! I said. They are still not strong enough to express all the repugnance I feel for you, she replied.

I must admit that I was dismayed by her display of pride and scorn, which I had not expected. I liked her all the

486

better for it, and at that moment I renewed my sincere determination to marry her and take her from Alaix. With this thought in mind, I continued: What, dear Célénie, have you forgotten that you are bound to me in such a way that for your honour's sake you must make it permanent and innocent? Have you forgotten that a child is waiting to receive from you the recognition that God and Nature, and your own conscience, forbid you to refuse? I have forgotten all, she said disdainfully. But I have not forgotten, I said proudly. It is clear that an appeal to your honour merely hardens your heart. I must use other means to bring you to reason. I have ways of making you keep your word – or of ensuring that your infamous behaviour becomes common knowledge. You have the choice. Make your decision. I do not intend to waste time in further argument.

Ah, traitor! she exclaimed, the tears springing to her eyes. You are determined to bring about my downfall. Here, she said, laying bare her breast. Pierce me through the heart if you are not satisfied. At least, when I am dead, I shall be free of all your persecutions. This is not the time, I said, to play the dramatic heroine. The question is: Will you marry me or not? I will never marry you, she answered, not if my life depended on it! In that case, I said, we shall have to see whether your betrothed is still willing to have you after I have spoken to him. Are you so despicable as to do that? she said. What is our marriage to you? You do not love me. All of this is pure comedy to you, for in truth, you would not know what to do if I took you at your word. You are wrong, I answered, I am utterly serious. You say I took the promise of marriage I had given you. Give me a pen and paper. I do not need ink – I will give you another, written in my blood, in which I acknowledge your child, and that it is only in order to marry me that you are breaking your engagement with Alaix. Send for a notary. I will sign a contract. What more do you want? Are not such guarantees worth as much as the

one I took from you? And is it, I added, I who should be
urging you to accept this offer, which your virtue requires
that you accept, and should it not rather be you who are
urging me to make it?

You are a knave and a cheat! she said, sinking into a seat
and weeping. I threw myself at her feet and renewed my
protestations, and in order to make our peace I tried to
reclaim my former privileges. I lifted her from her chair and
carried her to the bed. She did not cry out, but defended
herself with a ferocity which surprised me and which convinced me that it is not possible for a man to have his way
with a woman who is unwilling. I was exhausted before she
was. The struggle left us in the greatest disarray. She
escaped from my arms and threw herself on my sword,
which I snatched from her hand. She leapt at my eyes and
scratched at my face: in an instant it was covered with blood.
At this, my anger flared uncontrollably and I dealt her a
heavy blow – a deed more worthy of a street tramp than of a
man of my rank. I was overcome by shame at having committed such an action and was unable to utter a syllable.

All this had taken place without a word being exchanged
between us. She went back to where she had been sitting,
weeping still. With the aid of a mirror, I wiped the blood off
my face as best I could, and in this sorry state I walked out.
To conceal both my disfigurement and the self-reproach I
felt for having laid my hand on Célénie other than to caress
her, I kept my face hidden behind my kerchief, and
returned to my room, full of rage at what I had done and at
the condition I was in. It looked as if all the cats in Paris had
been sharpening their claws on my visage. It was nearly a
month before I was able to go out again.

As soon as I reached home, I wrote Célénie a promise, in
my own blood, as comprehensive and binding as I could
make it – since I had no intention of going back on it. With
it, I enclosed a letter, expressing my affection as tenderly as

I knew how, asking her forgiveness for everything in my conduct which had displeased her. I reminded her that a woman's virtue lay in complete devotion to the person of her husband, whom she should be ready to accept in her arms at all times, and that she should have considered me as her husband from the moment she first gave herself to me; I said further that her honour, her virtue, her child, her salvation, indeed every consideration in this world and the next, required that she remain true to me. I begged her to take account of all this and not to throw me into despair by marrying Alaix. And I promised to be the same sort of person for her as she should be willing to be for me. I concluded by threatening to destroy her reputation if she refused to listen to reason, and promising to ignore her errant behaviour if she broke immediately with Alaix. There was nothing more I could do. I kept a copy of the letter and of the promise – or rather, I did not destroy the rough drafts I had made, not feeling calm enough to spend time recopying them. If I had looked carefully into my heart, I would certainly have seen that it was not love which dictated my actions, but an arrogance which would not allow me to accept Alaix as a rival and which made me feel it would be shameful to allow him to replace me in Célénie's affections.

I sent the letter and the promise sealed together, telling my servant to give them to no one but Célénie. She knew him, as he had been in my service for more than four years. On his return he recounted how he had asked for her, how she had been sent for, but that when she recognised him, she almost refused to take the package, but when he told her it was of the greatest importance, she had finally done so. She had then shut herself in her room, and while he awaited a reply, he had made enquiries about her marriage. He had been told that Célénie herself, at dinner, had persuaded all concerned that the ceremony should take place that very night, with no further delay, and that she had in fact been closeted with Alaix when he had asked for her. He told me that when she had read what I had sent, she had come to look for him, had told him that her reply was what he was about to see, at which point she tore the papers he had brought to pieces, and burnt them in the kitchen fire.

This narration plunged me into a rage. I sent for one of those scribes who congregate under the vaults at the Church of Les Saints Innocents. I sent my servant back to Célénie's home and told him to keep note of all that happened. I had the scribe make a fair copy of the letter I had sent to the faithless Célénie, as well as of the promise, for I was fully determined to send them both to Alaix if the marriage took place. I also had the scribe write out the details of my liaison with her: the name of the midwife and where she lived; the child's name; the parish where she was baptised and the date of the baptism; where the child was being cared for and the nurse's name. I included everything and concocted a highly unflattering portrait of his intended wife for Alaix.

My servant returned around three o'clock in the morning. He told me there had been a great supper at Célénie's home, at which she had appeared quiet and reticent; and that after the supper they had all been to the church, where the marriage had taken place. They had then gone to Alaix's house, where they were to sleep, and where the guests had been served a wedding breakfast. My man had been able to hide himself in a narrow space behind the nuptial bed, which was curtained off by a tapestry, and where there was a window which gave on to an alley below. He installed himself on the window sill. He is a reliable and enterprising fellow! It was as much out of his own curiosity, he told me, as out of the need to report to me, that he had put himself in danger of breaking his neck when he jumped from the window on to the paving below.

He had had to wait a quarter of an hour before he heard

Célénie come into the room with her mother, her sisters and some other women who attended her, and who had exchanged a fair number of crude remarks as they undressed her, remarks which she had received with tears and sighs, like a novice. I don't know how I stifled my laughter, my servant said, when I heard so much nonsense spoken in such serious tones! Finally, he said, the noise ceased, and I concluded the beauty was in bed awaiting her husband, who arrived soon after. He kissed her, and said that now she belonged to him and could not refuse him. For some time, said my man, the only noise was that of doors closing, but after that there was no lack of entertainment. It started with shrieks and groans from Célénie, and loud calls for her mother, interspersed with so many absurdities that, for fear of giving myself away by laughing out loud (he said), I leapt out of the window. I landed on the pavement below, doing no damage to myself other than getting my hands and coat covered in mud from that filthy alleyway. Then I came straight here to tell you what I had seen and heard. I am only sorry you were not there yourself to enjoy the comedy!

On hearing this recital, I shed any concern I might have had about protecting this shameless woman's reputation. I told my servant all about our affair, and I read him the letter and all the other things the scribe had written out for me. I added a note to my letter to Alaix, telling him that I had been informed of the funeral dirge that had accompanied the loss of his wife's pseudo-virginity, and that I was shocked at her pretence of innocence. I said it was for him to decide what measures to take, and how much esteem he could still feel for his wife. I did everything I could to destroy Célénie's reputation and undo her in Alaix's eyes; to tell the truth, I was grateful she had given me the means to do so. I put all the documents together, one inside the other, in a packet, which I gave to my servant, trusting to his devices to ensure

491

it reached Alaix that very morning, before the newly-weds arose. Since he understood my desire for revenge, he made sure my wishes were carried out to the letter. He gave the packet to a man he knew and asked him to deliver it promptly, saying he should have taken it the night before, but had been out drinking and had failed to do so, and now his master needed him for other matters; he therefore begged this acquaintance to be responsible for it, and instructed him to tell Monsieur Alaix, if asked, that he would discover who the sender was when he read the contents. And he made it clear that the packet was to be handed to Alaix the minute he awoke, as the matter was of extreme importance.

This was done, as I subsequently learnt. Barely had Alaix opened his eyes than a lackey, thinking his diligence would be rewarded, gave him the packet. Alaix had a fire lit, put on his dressing gown, and read the whole thing from start to finish. Imagine what his feelings must have been! Devil take these damned scribblings! he said on concluding his reading. And whoever went to the trouble of sending them! His lackey was ordered out of the room, but, not having expected this reaction from his master, and piqued by curiosity, he remained to listen at the keyhole. Well, Madame! said Alaix to Célénie. Here is a paean of praise to your virtue which I have just received! Célénie trembled at this, and even more when she saw what he held in his hand. The copies of my letter to her, of my promise of marriage, together with my letter to Alaix, left her in no doubt that he was thoroughly informed of her past: I wonder how she felt at that moment! She could no longer pretend innocence. It was impossible to deny the truth, and highly unpleasant to admit it. She made up her mind, however, to the latter course, and this was the most admirable thing she ever did. She was also, no doubt, aware of her husband's nature and reckoned that he was not one to be unduly concerned about who had lived in his apartment before he took over the lease. She rose at once and threw herself, weeping, at his feet, offering more promises that she would henceforth live an honest woman than perhaps he felt any need for. Above all, she promised never to see me again in her life.

Alaix must have accepted this pledge and forgiven her, for they are now living happily together. Her adventure didn't cause any gossip because of Alaix's good sense, and because they both had good reason to keep quiet about it. For my part, I had exhausted my malice and had no further wish to pursue her, believing that, by making her forfeit her husband's esteem, I had done enough. I don't know how he feels, but whenever I meet her she refuses to look at me, or if she does, her eyes are filled with fury – which doesn't worry me, as neither of them is of any further interest to me. This, then, was my second adventure, one which, I am sure, has convinced you that I am an utter scoundrel. And I admit that – though my actions made it appear that my desire to marry her was sincere, and made it look as if my behaviour stemmed from despair over her desertion, and that she was more to blame than I – yet the truth is, I would have been in an embarrassing position if she had left Alaix and returned to me. There would have been no way to avoid marrying her; and there is no question but that she did the right thing. She is assuredly happier with him than she would have been with me. As you see, I am unburdening my sins on you. You will give me absolution when I have told all.

Though I told Alaix that his wife had deceived him, the next part of my story will show you that, on the other hand, I have too much of a sense of honour to deceive my friends, or to allow them to be deceived.

One of these friends, by the name of Grandpré – a companion of my days of youthful debauch – was of a good bourgeois family and was hoping to marry a girl from a family of roughly equal rank to his own. He described her to me. The pair had known each other for a considerable time, and he frequently sang the praises of her beauty, her figure, her voice, her wit, her manner – so much so that I wished to meet her myself. One day he introduced me to her, and so we became acquainted. I discovered that Mademoiselle Récard was of a lively, free-thinking turn of mind, which was in harmony with my own, and attracted me to her. I made a great deal of progress in a short space of time – but would have got no further in a hundred years had I not used a degree of subtlety in my approach. She had found a way, as will become apparent later, to satisfy her needs without the help of those she met in society. Her manner, to all appearances, was free and easy, though the fact is she was a deceitful jade. She was of medium height, with a somewhat coarse, sallow complexion. Her mouth was rather large, but one forgave this defect since she had beautiful teeth which fully compensated for it. Her eyes were brown and sparkling. She was rather thin, and her downy skin was always pale: these are all traits which indicate a weakness for the pleasures of the flesh. This was the opinion I reached the first time I saw her.

Grandpré was, and still is, a perfect gentleman and, as I have said, a close friend. I told him my opinion, and his answer was that I was a very poor judge of physiognomy, and that Mademoiselle Récard was the most modest and reserved young woman to be found in Paris. Attempting to change a lover's opinion about his beloved – especially if one has only conjecture to go on – is about as useful as trying to change the colour of a negro's skin by washing him with soap and water. I said no more, but instead decided to keep a close watch on his intended bride and to take advantage, if I could, of any frailty I might find. Although the portrait I have drawn of her is not very flattering, it is nonetheless true that she was a very amiable person and

494

worthy of an honest man's devotion, if she herself proved to be honest and virtuous.

In my dealings with her, I discarded the respectful manner which I usually employed with women, adopting instead a manner more suited both to her character and my own: that is, I used a bantering tone, which proved so effective that in less than a month I had gained the right to touch and kiss her breast. In company, I behaved with the greatest reserve and would have scrupled even to touch the tip of her finger; I was never free in my speech, nor ever ventured a double meaning in what I said. But when we were alone, I behaved with the utmost freedom, and though we never reached the final chord, I was at liberty to enjoy all the melody which precedes it. I was not happy to be delayed so near the conclusion and would certainly have overcome the last barrier had she herself not realised that her guard was tumbling. I must tell you what it was that obliged her to take more rigorous precautions against herself.

Her little bitch was in heat, and in order to prevent the animal from going off and finding a mate for itself, she was careful not to let it out of her room. I pitied the creature's distress and hoped I might use it to provide an illustration for its mistress. You will see if I was mistaken! I looked for and found a handsome dog, exactly what was required. I carried it to Mademoiselle Récard's and set it down on the floor. Soon, it had made acquaintance with Orange, the little bitch. I pointed out how well the two understood each other, and said we could take lessons from the animals on how to behave. I made as much of this example as I could. At last, Orange allowed herself to succumb to the dog's advances. I pointed this out to Orange's mistress, saying she should show herself as amenable. But where the ultimate favour with a woman is concerned, one cannot proceed as with any other request one might make. It can only be obtained when, like a needle with its thread, as the proverb says, one thing leads imperceptibly and inescapably to the next. Mademoiselle Récard, moved by the example before her eyes, and by the ardour of my caresses, which were becoming more than playful, was on the verge of surrender. I saw in her eyes, which shone with excitement, that she was ready to yield. The blush which suffused her cheeks revealed her waning resistance, and a spot of saliva at the corner of her mouth betrayed the turmoil within. I had already lifted her from her chair – the weakness of her refusal implied consent. I was turning in search of a more comfortable resting place, when a servant-girl came into the room, whom at the time I inwardly cursed, but who in fact had done me a good turn.

We were both in a state of obvious agitation, whose cause the maidservant easily guessed. While she turned red, I grew pale with anger and annoyance, but the moment had passed, and the young lady from that time on took such great pains that, for a whole month, during which my assiduities continued undiminished, she never allowed herself to be alone with me again. We talked together in situations where we were not overheard, but we were never alone in places where we could not be observed.

It was during one of these conversations that she was generous enough to tell me that she loved me with sincerity and tenderness, and that she would consider herself fortunate if she were able to spend her whole life with me; and that she believed I loved her too, and that if I therefore wanted to approach her mother to ask for her hand, she on her side would give her agreement so readily that she was certain the marriage could take place. I trembled at this proposition: I had even less intention of marrying her than Célénie, and, indeed, she was Célénie's inferior in every respect and, though I liked her well enough, I did not esteem her sufficiently to consider making her my wife. I thought of her unfaithfulness to Grandpré, and of the way she had all but yielded to temptation with me, and realised my honour would be far from safe in her keeping.

With these thoughts in mind, but assuming an appearance of sincerity, I told her that I was in despair at being unable to accept her offer, and that, had I been my own master, I would have accepted it without a moment's hesitation; but, I told her, I was wholly dependent on my mother and my family and would be in danger of being disinherited, my mother having all but concluded an alliance for me. I lied and said I was not of age to dispose of myself against my mother's wishes, but that, if she would trust my oath and a promise signed in my own blood, I would be true to her all my life and would find a means of breaking off the engagement my mother was in the process of arranging. A promise of marriage to a girl such as Mademoiselle Récard held no terror for me. I would as happily have made fifty such. She could see that I was not being honest and was merely toying with her, and decided to relinquish her hopes of marriage to me and return to Grandpré, who, it is true, had been harbouring a certain amount of jealousy over my close friendship with her.

He discussed the matter with me and asked me if I really intended to marry her. I told him I did not, adding that he was well aware I was not in a position to marry. If that is the case, he said, let me implore you to stop visiting her. If you intended to marry her, I would withdraw, since I am sure I could not compete with you for the heart of a girl you wished to please. But since you do not intend, as I do, to make her your wife, I beg you not to spend so much time with her. I promised with no regret to do as he asked, and kept my word. I even tried to enlighten him about the dubious virtue of his intended wife. I told him, after securing his promise of secrecy, about the incident with her pet dog and what had almost taken place between her and me. He wouldn't believe me, or didn't want to believe me, and it seemed certain that she would have become his wife had chance not intervened and proved that she was unworthy to be so.

During that period of debauchery and indulgence in my early youth, I used to know all the women in Paris who presided over what were known as 'the nunneries of Venus', and although it was more than three years since I had had anything to do with any of them, I still knew where most of these establishments were. One of these 'abbesses', known as la Delorme, had premises behind the Hôpital des Quinze-Vingts, in the rue Saint-Nicaize. I knew that the whole house – which was not very big – belonged to her. I happened to be alone and passing nearby one day when I saw our virtuous Récard leaving the building. I thought I must be mistaken, but having reached the rue Saint-Honoré, and approaching more closely, without being seen by her, there could be no doubt but that it was she.

I went back to la Delorme's house. She remembered me and welcomed me warmly. I asked her how business was. It goes from bad to worse, she said. She fulminated against the police lieutenant, the city commissioner and the 'good order' they were intent on establishing in Paris. I interrupted her to ask if she had not recently taken on some pretty new young girl? You would have found exactly what you are looking for, she said, had you been here just a few minutes ago. A young girl such as you are describing has only just left. This one is not in it for the money, she continued, for she will take none. But she is particular about her clients, and I introduce her only to those whom I know and can trust absolutely. I recognised our charming Récard in this description. I found her behaviour infamous and had no qualms about taking this opportunity to unseal my friend's eyes. If I were an out-and-out rogue, I would have used my discovery for my own amusement. But Grandpré was too good a friend and la Récard too contemptible for me to use the information for my own advantage.

There is something to be said for this young woman's behaviour! I said to la Delorme. I like her independence. Does she come here often? Yes, she answered. She will be here at eleven o'clock tomorrow morning. She was here today for more than an hour, waiting for a gentleman who did not come, as it had been arranged he should. She does not accept just anyone, as I told you, being concerned about the consequences. But can you not send for her? I enquired. I don't even know who she is, my brothel-keeper replied, let alone where she lives. She only comes here because one of my girls is away. All I know is that she comes of a good family and does not wish to be recognised, and takes all sorts of care to keep her identity secret. Are you sure she will be here tomorrow? I asked. Definitely, the woman answered. She was quite certain about it and would not let me down. She even gave me the money to pay for some lunch to be prepared. As I said, she is not interested in the money. On my word, I said, I will be here at that time too! I would like to meet her. Do you want to check on my good health? No, she said. I know you are careful. I just wish you had come earlier and had met her today!

Here, I said, handing her money. Have some food ready for us, and if the young lady is all you have told me, you will have earned my gratitude. You know me. I can be counted on. By the way, I added, I won't hide anything from you. I am engaged to a girl whose home is not far from here, and am soon to be married, so I need this to be absolutely secret. That is, I do not want anyone to see me. Make sure no one else is here when I come. And, above all, do not play any tricks on me. If this girl has any infection, you will be the first to pay for it. She does not want her name to be known. She is right. Nor do I wish mine to be known. Tell her merely that I am a friend of yours. Have no fear, she said. Just come. I assure you, you will be well satisfied. I therefore confirmed the rendez-vous for eleven , the next morning, but to be certain, I resolved to be there by ten.

That evening, I looked for Grandpré, and found him with his sweetheart – he, who had been living all this time on thin gruel, while she feasted to her heart's content! I told him I needed to speak to him and would wait at home for him. He promised to come, and did so.

How can I be of service to you? he asked as he came in. It is not so that you should be of service to me that I asked you to come, I answered, but so that I could be of service to you. Among my friends, you are the one I esteem the most, and with whom I would always try to share any piece of good fortune. You know how to appreciate a beautiful woman: as good friends we need feel no shame in acknowledging this. Tomorrow I have a rendez-vous with a young woman of great beauty and charm, and would like to introduce you to her too. I am obliged to you, he said, but I dare not take any risks. You will not take it ill if I refuse, since I am to marry Mademoiselle Récard in a week's time. I must be prudent. I want to make her happy, at least on our first night together! After that, I can see your young lady. If you saw her, you would not refuse, I said. Never mind. You wish to be careful, and I esteem you for that. But come with me, nonetheless, and then do as you wish. I would like you to see her. Allow me to refuse, he said. I know my weakness, and if the young lady is as delightful as you imply, I might lose my resolve. So let me imagine her, without seeing her. For God's sake! I exclaimed in frustration. The fact is, you are being terribly deceived! Just trust me and say nothing to anyone, and I will enlighten you about something that is of the utmost consequence to you! In that case, he said, I will do as you wish. Well then, I continued, do what you will in the event: the person I am talking about is none other than your virtuous fiancée, Mademoiselle Récard herself! Ah, Monsieur Dupuis, he said, one does not make such assertions unless one is in a position to prove their truth! Accusations far less serious than this have led friends – brothers even – to cut each other's throats! I am not about to cut anyone's throat, I said, least of all yours; and there is no better way of proving what I say than by letting you yourself come face to face with this paragon of yours, in the temple of Venus! If you do not wish to accompany me, provided you have not breathed a word, I promise you that, before noon tomorrow, I shall have breached the last hurdle with her! Do you understand me now? Can I speak more plainly than that? Ah! Can what you are telling me be possible? he said, in great distress. I don't know if it is possible, I said, but I know it is a fact! At that, he railed against her, against the mother who had borne her, the nurse who had raised her, and these lamentations continued for upwards of two hours. Since this made things neither better nor worse, I let him say what he would until his despair was exhausted.

But, said he eventually, how can I verify what you have told me? She will surely take every care to ensure she is not discovered. There is no problem there, I said. So long as you do exactly as I say, and do not appear until you are convinced that what I have been telling you is true, I can arrange everything. Grandpré agreed to this. I made him eat supper and stay with me overnight, so that he could not do anything which would make the plan go awry. I gave instructions to my servant, whom I knew I could trust – this was not the first time he had served me and proved reliable in a delicate situation.

We rose just before ten and went to la Delorme's. I posted my man in a bar opposite. When the young lady in question approached, he was to signal to us, by blowing one of those whistles such as charcoal vendors use to announce their presence in a neighbourhood. I warned him to keep out of sight, since she knew and would recognise him. Grandpré and I went in, and I introduced him to la Delorme as the

501

brother of my betrothed, whose discretion could therefore be relied on, and asked her to send for another girl whom she trusted, as we both wished to be entertained.

It turned out to be a day for adventures with women who had secret lives: the person whom la Delorme brought for my companion was a married woman whom I met frequently in society and knew, as the saying goes, as well as the back of my hand. That story has nothing to do with the one I am telling you at present, however. All I need say, is that she was extremely surprised to see me. I promised I would not reveal her and have kept that promise, as she deserved, since she reformed her ways and has subsequently led a more honest existence.

Grandpré was in a state of acute anxiety. I was not in the least worried, until I heard it strike eleven, and then I began to fear some contretemps – but not for long. I heard my valet's whistle, the sign that our nymph was on her way. I hurriedly made Grandpré and the other woman hide behind the bed, and sat down myself in an armchair between the table and the fire – it was becoming cold enough for one to be needed. My back was towards the door, and I had a book in my hand. The windows were closed, and there was little light in the room; moreover, I had on a new coat which I had never worn before. La Delorme thought the two others were already out of the way and happily occupied. She was thus all the more frank in her speech, which suited my purpose.

Ah! she said, so your friend found the young lady I brought to his liking? And for you, here is the young lady I promised. You can enjoy yourselves and not have any fear of catching anything! These words left no room for doubt, as you see. Mademoiselle Récard, who had just come into this very ill-lit room from being outside in full daylight, did not recognise me. I took her from la Delorme without a word. I kissed her, and to initiate the acquaintance I placed one

502

hand on her breast and the other under her skirt. She did not demur, and responded warmly to my kiss. It looks to me, said la Delorme, as if you two intend to make love merely by feel, without a word spoken to each other! See, she said, if the young lady is not beautiful! And she drew open the curtains. I was not surprised to see Mademoiselle Récard – it was what I had expected. But the same was not true for her – and her surprise was enough for the two of us. She let out a loud cry – Oh, my God! Oh, my God indeed, I repeated, running to bolt the door, and returning towards her. She was more dead than alive and wept like a sinner caught in the act. I did not expect the pleasure of meeting you in such a place as this, Mademoiselle, I said. But we neither of us came here with the intention of weeping. It was more a desire for pleasure which brought us, and I hope I shall not be disappointed. Let us not deny it – we both came to the ball, we had better make up our minds to dance together. What a disaster! she said, weeping. Not necessarily, I said. Am I not an honourable man, and one of your friends? How about it, I went on, addressing la Delorme, there is no reason for Mademoiselle to have wasted her money. Let us have some food. And to Mademoiselle Récard, I said, Come, sit down. We will discuss the rest later, and I took off her hat, gloves and scarf.

La Delorme went out to see to the food that had been ordered for us. The beautiful Récard also attempted to leave, but I was too quick for her. Easy, my little lady, I said. There is someone else for you to see. This time, I locked the door and pocketed the key, and taking her by the hand I led her to the table. We are ready for you now, Monsieur de Grandpré, I said loudly enough for him to hear. Here is your virtuous bride, gentle as a lamb, and ready to satisfy you without benefit of lawyer or curate.

At this, Grandpré left his hiding place, sword in hand, ready to pierce her through – and her cries rose to a higher pitch. I threw myself at him. What's this nonsense? I exclaimed, laughing. Sheathe your sword! Contain yourself! Don't let your anger bring you to grief! Ah, bitch! he said – and nothing more, for he fell to the ground in a swoon. I rushed towards him and, with the help of the woman who had been with him, I laid him on the bed, while we left la Récard to take care of herself, since there was no way she could escape. As soon as she had seen Grandpré coming towards her, sword in hand, she had let out a scream and rushed for the door, where she now stood, weeping. La Delorme was on the other side, also crying to high heaven, demanding to be let in. I asked the other woman to take care of Grandpré; I urged our weeping beauty back towards the fire and went to the door and opened it a slit, like the peephole in the door of a prison cell, letting la Delorme in – all amazement at the goings-on in her establishment. As I was not in the least perturbed by any of this, I quietly reclosed the door, returned to the table, and drank a large glass of wine. Grandpré regained consciousness; I hid both his sword and my own, and explained to la Delorme what all the trouble had been about.

This gave rise to a new pleasure: the unprecedented experience of hearing this woman – who derived her income from the vice of the populace – castigating the beautiful Mademoiselle Récard for her immoral behaviour, urging her to reform, and generally laying down the laws of propriety better than any ordained preacher could have done. This all took up some time; it was beginning to get late for dinner, so I gave orders for the food to be served and obliged everyone to sit at the table. The disgraced Mademoiselle Récard threw herself at Grandpré's feet, begging his forgiveness, a request he answered with a kick. I didn't altogether disapprove of this treatment, and consoled her somewhat heartlessly with the observation that girls who took up this profession needed to be tough and had to expect a little mistreatment of that sort on occasion. I made her sit at the table, which she did unwillingly, and what is more, I made her eat and drink – though she had no heart for either. Grandpré came through the experience better than I had expected, and ate and drank with some appetite; but the truth is, I was the only one there who really enjoyed the repast.

After we had eaten, I asked Grandpré if he were going to let la belle Récard leave just as she had come – pointing out it would be only fair for him to have his revenge for all the times when she had refused him, now that she had put herself in his power. He led her by the hand – she was as quiet as a lamb, there is nothing more docile than a girl caught in such a place. She lay on the bed, and when he saw that all her resistance was gone – he struck her across the face with his gloves. Enough, strumpet! he said. You are beneath an honest man's contempt! – and left her there. Her tears now flowed even more freely than before. Then it was my turn. I will not be hard on you, my dear young lady, I said. I do not have the same grievance as Monsieur de Grandpré. I came here hoping only to meet a pretty girl and am delighted it was you. But at that moment, I decided to make her pay for what she had done to Grandpré – at least until his anger was exhausted, and until he himself begged me to have pity on her. I made her take off every scrap of clothing and examined every part of her body, and while still naked I made her drink to my health and that of her lover – in a word, I did everything that an unmitigated ruffian might do to a guardroom harlot – except take the final step. I mortified her and humiliated her as much as I could, until in the end Grandpré begged me to give her quarter and let her be.

I was ready enough to do so, as my only aim had been to assuage his sense of betrayal. Moreover, I made him pro-mise to keep the matter secret – to which he agreed the more readily as his own reputation was involved. I promised that I likewise would not speak of the matter if she gave up this shameful behaviour; and I have never previously mentioned this affair – and wouldn't have spoken of it to you if she had earned my consideration, but she has become a veritable Messalina. Shortly after the events I have recounted, she found a respectable man whom she married, and during his lifetime she even lived very properly with him, but this has not been so since she was widowed. As for the other woman whom la Delorme had brought, as I was the only one who knew her, I promised not to reveal what I had discovered about her, and she has earned my discretion, since I am certain that her behaviour has been entirely honest since then. As for Grandpré and myself, we left the place without any other achievement than having taught Mademoiselle Récard a lesson and relieved Grandpré of any wish to marry such a depraved creature.

I would tell you what I know of Gallouin at this point, since it was at about this time that he became a monk; but I think it is better to wait until I tell you how I came to know his sister, Madame de Londé, as those two parts of my story are connected.

Before that, I have to tell you the story of my acquaintance with a widow, whose name you will allow me to conceal. The amicable way in which our relationship ended, the love and trust we felt for each other, and the friendship which still exists between us require that my lips remain sealed as to her identity. This affair is exceptional. It starts with the sort of actions one would expect of a cheat and scoundrel, but concludes with a man of wholly reformed character; and I can testify that it was she who succeeded in extricating me from the bad company which had previously influenced me, who set me on the right path, and who completed my transformation into a man of honour.

My brother had sent me a bank draft, which required that

I go to a well-known banker to receive payment. This man was busy with courtiers and men of affairs who were sending money abroad, and I had to wait for him to attend to me. While I was waiting, I leant against a window which looked onto a small garden. It was a very low window, on the first floor. Below, there was a thick arbour of vines, which prevented those within its shelter from either seeing or being seen; but it did not prevent me from hearing the two women who were conversing there – or, indeed, from hearing them so clearly that I caught every word of the exchange, although their voices were not raised. The conversation concerned their husbands – one alive, the other deceased. One of these women was shedding hot tears. She was the wife of the banker whom I had come to see; and the other, consoling her, was her sister, who had been a widow for about six months. This latter was trying to persuade her companion that she herself had been even more unhappy during her husband's lifetime than the distressed one was at present. I knew that they were sisters, and that the cause of the younger one's tears was the philandering and infidelity of her husband.

Is there a woman in the world more miserable than I, dear sister? said the unhappy one. Before our marriage, my husband wooed me with all the assiduity and tenderness imaginable. You yourself saw all that he would do for me. Did I not have reason to be sure of his devotion? Yet we have been married less than a year, and the wretch looks for solace elsewhere! It would not be so bad if the mistresses he chose were worthy of him, but he runs after any little vixen he meets – that is what I cannot forgive! Two worthless chamber-maids I had for only a short time have been through his hands – even my cook was not too paltry for his attentions and has had to be dismissed. Am I mistaken, sister, she continued, or am I not still as beautiful as I was before I married? And am I not a thousand times more

507

beautiful and pleasing than my slut of a cook? I am younger, in any case, and incomparably more desirable. And now that I have only monsters working in the house – since I am careful now to engage nothing but ugly old women – he takes it into his head to run after street women! In all honesty, sister, is such treatment tolerable?

No, it does not seem so, her sister consoled her. Your husband is at fault and is indeed to be blamed. But I do not think you should let yourself feel hurt by it. Do you not have frequent opportunities you could use to avenge yourself for his inconstancy? Ah, sister! the first one exclaimed. What are you saying? I have never loved anyone but my husband, and I still love him; nor do I find myself particularly tempted by any other man's embraces.

Then why are you so dismayed by your husband's inconstancy? asked the confidante. Why not let him have his little escapades? In order to make you feel better, all I need do is tell you what happened to me. I have been a widow for six months. I spent three years with my husband, which is very little considering how much in love he was when we married. The whole family thought I was the luckiest woman in the world, and he the most faithful husband in Paris; and indeed, neither you nor anyone else ever heard me complain that his love for me had cooled, nor that he consorted with women of the streets. Yet in reality I had far more reason than you to complain! What would you do if your husband, having caught an infection from the loose women he frequented, then passed it on to you, forcing you to seek a surgeon's help – you, who weep so many tears merely because your husband is less ardent than he was? But that is what happened to me, though it was something I never spoke of. I always concealed the sort of life he led, though he was far more promiscuous than your husband. And why did I do this? It was because, having thought about it, I came to the conclusion that we all seek our own pleasure in this world, and that, if I had allowed myself to do exactly as I pleased, I would possibly have done worse than he.

Ah, sister! exclaimed the unhappy one. Is it possible for an honest woman to talk as you are doing? And to think of being unfaithful to her husband, and of imitating his reprehensible behaviour? Heaven forbid, replied the widow, that I should seek to instill such sentiments! No, sister, one must preserve one's honesty, come what may. One does not follow a bad example, and I wish only to make a comparison with men. You are talking like a young bride, and when you grow tired of your husband, as he is beginning to be of you, you will understand better what I am saying. Be honest, she continued. It is impossible that since your marriage, you have not experienced the pleasure of love? Were it otherwise, you would not feel any jealousy. I admit, agreed her sister, that I have enjoyed the legitimate pleasure one can experience in marriage, and that I am in despair because my husband now seeks his pleasure elsewhere, bestowing his embraces on others.

Why then, said the widow, do you say that you are indifferent to the pleasure of a man's embrace? Why, said her sister, because one can enjoy this pleasure when it is legitimate, as it is with a man to whom one is married. Nonsense! replied the widow. It is not legitimacy that determines the degree of pleasure we experience; rapture is not dependent on a contract or on the blessing of a priest! Looked at rationally, marriage is nothing but a publicly acknowledged agreement between a man and a woman that they will live together; and this agreement is sanctioned by the law to avoid the disorder that would arise if we did not each have our own husband or wife; and in particular, the disorder that would ensue if a woman could give herself at any time to the first person who caught her fancy. What a man does with a woman who is not his wife is no different

from what he does with his wife. His enjoyment of a particular woman, however, diminishes gradually, and he seeks a
new pleasure through diversity – though the experience is
essentially the same. Something which is less readily available appears more exciting and provides more occupation
for his imagination. A woman would behave in the same way
if she dared. It is only the fear of what people will say, and of
the possible consequences, which restrains her; and a
woman's resentment of her husband's roving eye usually
has less to do with her love for him than with her reluctance
to be deprived of his caresses, and with the injury suffered
by her pride – since she remains convinced she is no less
attractive and no less able to satisfy her husband than anyone else. Look into your heart, she continued. Have there
not been one or two men you have seen since your marriage
who could have tempted you? Even if you will not admit it, I
am sure it is so. And had you been able, or had you dared to
approach them without danger or scandal, you would not
have stifled the impulse.

These are questions, sister, which I cannot answer, the
neglected wife replied. What would become of the world, if
people could do whatever they wished with impunity? Yet
there are countries, the widow insisted, where women are
free to live as they please; there are even countries where it
is considered their duty to search out men, in order to save
them from worse sin! Now if you asked these women if they
would like to exchange their state for ours, do you think
they would agree to do so? And they would be right to
refuse, because their only law is that of Nature. Nature's law
is in conflict with the harsh laws which a sense of honour,
unknown to them, imposes on us and enshrines as our
preeminent duty

Indeed, the widow continued, what other pleasure is
there for a woman in this world which can compare with
that of love? Is it not so that we may enjoy this pleasure

tranquilly and in security that we are prepared, when we take a husband, to call him our master, to make his will our own, and tolerate his wayward humours? I talk of course in terms of what is true according to Nature, and with respect only to our life on earth – and I ask you again, without the physical pleasure which binds us to the opposite sex, what woman would be willing to marry? Which of us would be willing to give herself to a single man, and put up with the heartache and despair this entails, if she were free to enjoy this pleasure with whomever she chose without risk or shame? There would be no such thing as marriage in the world if, while remaining single and independent, we could take any man we wished into our arms without criticism or untoward consequences; and our lives would certainly be happier if love and desire were our only guides. We should then be in the position of those women I mentioned earlier, who would refuse to change their way of life for ours. It is for this pleasure alone that we who live here forego our precious liberty. We sacrifice everything for this pleasure!

It is true, the young wife said, that what you are saying describes our natural inclinations. But, dear sister, were we to follow these inclinations, we should be no better than wild animals! You are right, answered the widow, we should then be no better than the animals. Yet I have to say, it seems to me that Molière spoke wisely when, in Amphitryon, he put these words in Mercury's mouth: 'Where love-making is concerned, the foolish animals are not so foolish as we like to think.' Indeed, I think this is true, and in my opinion, they are extremely lucky not to be subject to this cult of honour, which men, rather than Nature, have imposed on our sex. Since, then, we are agreed that this is how a woman feels, should we be surprised that this is how men also feel? It would on the contrary be a great deal more surprising if they did not have the same disturbing emotions, and if they did not give way to them, since in this respect the law weighs heavily on us, and not on them; and since custom, which is unforgiving to us, seems to authorise, or at least to tolerate, a different standard of behaviour for them, though indeed they are more at fault than we are, because they claim to have greater intellectual powers and moral strength than we have, which should enable them to resist the prompting and temptations of Nature. Though, she added, we should not be too hard on them for their infidelity, since we would do the same if we dared: we would try to seduce them, as they seduce us, if it were not that such conduct brings greater disgrace on us than it does on them.

I lived honourably with my husband, the widow continued, as a woman should. I followed the customs of the country in which, by God's will, I was born; if I had been able to disregard them without incurring harm or provoking gossip, I would have done so. But I hold that it is in subduing the whims and longings of her heart that a woman's virtue lies. I am a widow. I have been virtuous and hope to remain so, but this would not be so were I to allow my senses to rule my conduct. And I believe there are very few women who are not like me in this respect, that is, who are not restrained purely by the fears of pregnancy, of catching some disease or, at the very least, of becoming the butt of scandal. There are very few women who are virtuous for the love of virtue itself, or from the fear of God. Yet these are the only guiding lights we should follow. But if we examine our hearts, we shall see that it is concern for appearances which dictates our behaviour, and that we are motivated by worldly considerations rather than by the desire to save our souls.

You are opening my eyes to much that is very true, said the young wife, ideas to which I had never given thought before. There are very few women, remarked the widow, who would admit to the truth of what I have been saying, except among themselves; but nearly all would admit to its truth if they examined themselves honestly. And I have only said all this to you, dear sister, she continued, to help you understand your husband's peccadilloes. He will come back to you in the end, and be the more considerate to you. A loyal wife always wins her husband back in the end. There is some justice on your side if you blame his behaviour at present, but do so silently. Do not show any jealousy, as this will only add to his aggravation; be ready always to let him return to you and, while blaming him, take great care neither to hate him nor to imitate him. For on this point, we are all – men and women alike – more in need of compassion than of reprimand. Above all, refrain from reproaches, and avoid both bitterness and scorn, as these would only increase his discomfiture and provide justification for his negligence.

One could not have been more surprised than I was to hear a woman talk such good sense about sexual morality, and speak so openly on a subject about which women are usually extremely reticent – for I swear, I have not invented a single word of what I have just related: on the contrary, I have omitted a considerable amount, which I have forgotten. Of course, she was talking to another woman, who was her sister, and did not know she was being overheard. Nevertheless, I thanked her in my heart for having spoken so honestly, and thanked her with a gratitude as sincere as if she had actually been speaking to me.

I was eager to know who she was and, if possible, to speak to her in person. I made my way down into the garden and found the two women there. I knew immediately which was the widow by her garb of deep mourning. She was very beautiful. Her hair – as one could tell from the little that was visible – was as black as her dress. She had a pale, smooth complexion, and the reddest and most beautiful mouth I have ever seen; her eyes were bright and lively, with a level, self-confident gaze; her neck and hands were of an exquisite delicacy, and I found her whole appearance infinitely pleasing. I had already had an introduction to her thinking, and the sight of her completed her conquest. Her manner was not in the least downcast; on the contrary, I seemed to detect in her an air of good spirits rather than of self-pity. Her sister was also a very attractive person, and if I had not already been favourably predisposed to the charms of the widow, I would not have been unwilling to offer consolation to her sister for the cooling of her husband's ardour. She was, at nineteen or twenty years old, three years younger than the widow. She was dressed in high style, in half-mourning, but her air of sadness did not appeal to me. It was the widow who had stolen my heart, while her sister won my sympathy.

I made a turn of the garden, which, since the garden was small, did not take much time, and then retraced my steps, with the intention of speaking to them, but they rose before I reached them, and went into a room which led directly from the garden, and whose door closed behind them. They both had admirable figures, as I was able to see as they walked away, but the widow was somewhat taller than her sister, and her gait was more relaxed, so that her bearing revealed a confidence which her sister did not share. I left the garden utterly charmed by her. I asked a manservant who these two ladies were, and he told me, mentioning the widow's name. I asked him where she lived, as if out of idle curiosity, and he also provided that information. I went back to the spot where I had originally been waiting, saw the banker, who gave me my money, and then left the building, my heart filled with this new passion.

That evening I went to the street where the widow lived. I had supper with one of my friends in an eating place not far from her house. I went there on three or four successive days, trying all the time to devise some stratagem which would give me an entry to her house – and could think of none. Even the fertile brain of my manservant, Poitiers – whom you already know by hearsay, and in whom I had confided – could produce no acceptable stratagem. Neither he nor I had any acquaintance in the neighbourhood.

He had suggested that I could deliberately provoke a quarrel with one of the widow's servants, and then – 'your attempt to rectify matters,' he said, 'will give you a pretext for talking to the man's mistress.' I was almost disposed to follow this suggestion and would have done something of this sort, when my incomparable servant came and said he had found a perfectly honourable means by which I could become acquainted with her. What is it? I asked. I have just seen a woman water-carrier leaving the widow's house, he said, a woman who is so far advanced in pregnancy that she will be giving birth at any moment. And how does this affect me? I said. It affects you, he replied, because you and the widow are going to be the child's godparents. Leave it all to me!

Four days later, the woman's husband (whose occupation was that of general porter) came and asked me to be godparent for his child. I had never met him before, but it was my enterprising manservant who brought him to the house and presented the request, as if it had been the man's own idea, when in fact he had instigated the whole thing himself. I don't know how he had planted the notion in the man's head. I agreed to do what he asked and, while talking to him, asked who the baby's godmother was to be, and in reply he named my charming widow. I asked if she had already agreed, and he said, no, but that he would see her and had no doubt she would readily do so. I instructed Poitiers to accompany him, and they left together.

The widow, in her turn, when asked to serve as godmother for the child, asked who the godfather was to be. It was Poitiers who answered that it was to be his master, who was a man of quality. And, he added, I was sent to determine whether the godmother was someone whom it was worth his while to see, and if not, he would not come. Ah, indeed! she laughed, he is ready to rely on your judgement then? Yes, ma'am, my irrepressible servant retorted. He trusts my eyesight. Well then, will he come if I accept? Yes, Madame, answered Poitiers, he will come, and bring his carriage for you himself. I shall be most grateful, she said. But tell me, you who have such good eyesight, will it be worth my while to come and see him? If my master were not the most handsome, most gallant, most honourable gentleman in France, I would not remain in his service a quarter of an hour, he answered. Yes, Madame, it will be worth your while, and you may even be sorry that you had not met him sooner. If the master, she answered, showing her amusement, is worth the valet, he must be quite exceptional. I am eager to meet him. Let him come to see me whenever he likes. I shall be glad to receive him. It is for you to name the time for him to call on you, Madame, said Poitiers. My master will defer to your pleasure, and your convenience will determine when he comes. Did he instruct you in all these niceties? she asked. He did, Madame, he replied. He told me what I should say, providing the godmother was attractive, and it was on that condition that he told me to make the necessary arrangements. So you think I am attractive enough? she said, laughing. As an angel, answered Poitiers, and I am certain my master will find you even more beautiful than I do, because his insight will show a thousand amiable traits which are beyond my ability to see. But, Madame, to enable me to complete my mission, be good enough to name a time when he should come. Tell your master, she said, that I am happy for him to choose his own time. No, Madame, I have been given orders to discover your preference, and I shall be in disgrace if I neglect them. Very well, she said. Let us say this afternoon at three o'clock. I shall be ready, if he will be good enough to come for me.

Poitiers returned and reported this conversation and its outcome. It amused but did not surprise me. I knew that Poitiers was impudent, and capable of initiating and conducting all manner of intrigues. It was for this reason that I liked him. I left him in charge of all the arrangements for the baptism and for the meal which followed. He acquitted himself well – even better than I had expected.

He told me that he had found my beautiful widow in indoor attire, but that he was certain she would change and appear in all her finery. I also put on my most fashionable clothes. I asked my mother to lend me her carriage, or at least to allow me to use her servants' livery. She lent me both her carriage and her servants. I therefore arrived at the house of my companion godparent in an impressive carriage, attended by three stout footmen, seated behind, creating as much of a show as I could. Poitiers was there to introduce me to her.

To my shame, I admit I was so overcome by her beauty when I saw my widow at close quarters that I could barely utter the necessary courtesies as required by good manners. She interpreted my incoherence incorrectly. Your servant misled you, she said. He gave you a portrait of me which persuaded you to come, and you now find the original was not worth the trouble. No, Madame, I said. He did not mislead me. It would be impossible for him to overstate your beauty. But though your beauty outshines any other that I have seen, I admit I wish I had not come, for I shall not be able to escape from here without surrendering my liberty, and that is something I may come to regret. Your fear is flattering, she said, laughing, but with me you have no cause for concern. It is not my way to take another person's possession and keep it without their consent. But if my liberty was left in your hands, would you not feel free to do with it as you wished? I asked. If it were left willingly in my keeping, she said, what danger would there be? So, what reason is there to be sorry that you came here? It is not that I shall regret surrendering my liberty into your beautiful hands, I said. It is only if you are careless with it that I may come to regret it.

So! You are laying down conditions already? she laughed. You are too cautious on a first meeting! Do not take the matter so seriously! This will lead you only to trouble and anxiety. Live one day at a time. It is of little moment to you, I replied, because you are used to receiving such offerings – you are not surprised that I am compelled to relinquish my liberty into your keeping. I will not attempt to decide whether it is because I am used to such declarations, or because I do not take them very seriously, that I am not unduly concerned, she said, still showing amusement. Such protestations may trip too readily off the tongue to be sincere.

I do not know whether you are justified in scorning them merely because they are impulsive, I said. But I can testify from my own present experience that the very first sight of beauty such as yours prompts both love and admiration, and you should not accuse my love of being insincere, but merely its expression, for tumbling out too hastily. It is not one or the other separately which I may suspect, she said, but the concurrence of the two: I would find your declaration altogether more credible if we had been acquainted for a little time, because I would then be able to believe you had perhaps discovered some merit in me to justify it. If that is what you want, I said, all is well! Every day of my life I will tell you I love you, for every day I shall discover some new charm in you, and you will have to admit that my protestations are based on what I see, and what is.

In that case, she said, all you would be doing would be praising me very prettily each day for something newly observed, proving that for the rest you are relying on imagination, and that my merit lies in your head rather than in my person. Would that be merely a supposition, I said, if I said that you are the most beautiful person I have ever seen? And would it be a supposition if I said also that you alone have more wit than all the other women I have ever known put together? As far as my beauty is concerned, she said, laughing, I know what to believe: my mirror tells me the truth. As for my intelligence, if what you say is true, I can only feel sorry that you have in the past met only women who were simpletons! And yet you seem to me to have too much good sense to have spent your time only with women of that sort. It is true, I answered, that I have known women in my life who were considered witty and intelligent, but I have known none who could equal you, and it is no mere supposition when I tell you this.

It would be embarking on too long a discussion, she said, were we to try and prove or disprove your contention. Let it suffice, therefore, for me to assure you that I am not unhappy that you have this good opinion of me. But this discussion is not what you came for! It was for you and me to attend a child's baptism and become its godparents. I think, if you are ready, it is time for us to proceed.

And so we went. I offered my hand to lead her to her carriage, into which I climbed after her, and my carriage followed behind. The ceremony followed the usual pattern, and Poitiers had arranged everything so well that we had a very proper repast in a suitable and well-chosen location. In fact, the whole event went better than I would have anticipated. The widow was pleasantly surprised. It was clear to her – as I was pleased to note – that the preparations had been made in advance; and in all honesty, if my man had had two days to put the arrangements in place, I doubt they could have been improved upon.

I accompanied my companion godparent to her house and stayed for some time. Before leaving, I asked if I might call on her again. She agreed to this, and I subsequently visited her every day.

Since she was a widow, who preferred to be independent and lead her own life, and since, in fact, she was accountable to no one but herself, we soon became very friendly. It was clear I did not displease her, as I noted with pleasure – since I liked her better every time I saw her, and, indeed, I did discover each day some new charm in her. She received many visitors, among them, some who became too deeply involved for their own peace of mind, but since I had no reason to quarrel with any of them, and since, if I went into detail it might provide an indication of a name I do not wish to reveal, you will allow me to say no more on that point, except to note that, if anyone's presence became troublesome, they were no longer made welcome.

I adopted with her the same approach as I had used with Mademoiselle Récard, except that I was less brazen and more discreet. I was a model of civility and good manners in public, while when I was talking to her privately I tried to be light-hearted and tease her good-humouredly.

I was by then old enough to be thinking of marriage, and she would have suited me perfectly; but before talking to my mother, or to anyone in my family, I wanted to have her consent. She was young, extremely beautiful, with a fine figure, very intelligent, and very wealthy. She had had one child by her late husband, a daughter who was one and a half years old. She was of good family and the widow of a financier, also of good family; both he and his father had probably sold their souls in order to acquire the wealth she now enjoyed. They had both improved their position in society by means of government appointments which they had held. In a word, she was exactly right for me. However, although she loved me as much as a woman can love a man, she had resolved never to remarry because she wanted to remain her own mistress. You will see in what follows her strength of character.

She had been a widow for about ten months, and I had

known her for three or four, when one day while I was at her house, we were talking about a widow who had not remarried, but who had become pregnant. There were a number of people present, and everyone expressed an opinion. It was said that her lover had promised to marry the woman, but in the event he was the first to make light of her predicament and to gossip about it in society. This gave me my opportunity: I merely made a passing comment about the woman, expressing sympathy for her, but I railed against the man, whose behaviour I qualified as befitting the most treacherous and blackguardly of scoundrels. Yes, I continued, I am not a woman, so it is not self-interest which makes me speak; but if I were – and if I had been weak enough to give myself to a man – as would undoubtedly have been the case – and if he had betrayed me and talked of it and belittled me – not even as in the present case, which is an example of the last word in perfidy – but if he had given even the merest hint to anyone of any intimacy between us, not all the torturers in the world, concocting new horrors, would prevent me from killing him – either with my own hands or with the help of intermediaries. My God! I added, does an honest man brag about his conquests! It is despicable, unworthy of a gentleman! But such behaviour is only too common among Frenchmen; and though I am French myself, I consider it so indefensible that I would be ready to avenge a woman so treated, even if I did not know her or have any connection with her.

Just as I uttered these last words, the man in question came into the room. He was the brother-in-law of the widow and lived in the provinces: it was there that he had ensnared the woman we were talking of, and it was in Paris he was making her the butt of his amusement. She had recently followed him here. I myself had never met him before. He was well dressed, good-looking, and appeared to be of robust physique, but I felt sure I was tough and ruthless enough to match him in a fight, and since I had my own reasons for what I was doing, I had no qualms about crossing swords with him. My charming widow, whispering in my ear, told me who he was, intending to warn me and ensure my good manners. You underestimate me, I responded to her. I am a forthright person and will speak my mind when it comes to voicing an opinion about cheats and miscreants. I will not provoke an open quarrel here in your presence, but I cannot disguise what I think. What was the subject of your conversation, dear ladies? the man asked as he seated himself. We were discussing, said the widow's sister, the importance for a respectable woman of not seeing her reputation besmirched, considering all one hears of the snares and pitfalls which some among us have not escaped. There is much to be said on that subject, said the man. There are at the present time so many women who disregard the rules of good conduct, their number is quite beyond calculation!

I share your opinion, I said, that there are many women whose conduct is not above reproach (I do not refer to women of loose behaviour – who do not deserve our attention – but to women who may take a lover, such as the person we were talking of, and whose conduct can therefore be considered reprehensible – though the term is perhaps too strong and does an injustice to a faithful mistress): I will allow that there may be a large number of such women, but there would be far less bother and scandal in society if there were not so many knaves around, in whom these women have placed their trust, and who do not have the decency to maintain a discreet silence about their liaisons.

Indeed, I continued, still without indicating that I knew who he was, we have all now heard about this young lady from the provinces, Mademoiselle de Gironne, who allowed herself to be seduced. No one knew this two days ago, and no one would ever have known, had her lover been a man of honour; but he found it acceptable to tell about the mistress he had deserted, revealing himself at the same time as a scoundrel – since it is known, I hurried on without allowing time for anyone to interrupt, that he had promised to marry her, and since it is known also that he had bound himself to secrecy. And now he thinks it is enough to say she was a widow, and should have known from experience what is likely to be the result when a woman keeps company with a man. Is that a good enough reason to betray one's mistress? Even if it is true that he could renege on his promise to marry her – since the law does not require him to keep it – yet, is it not the action of a churl to deceive a woman with the word 'sacrament', when he has no intention of proceeding to a marriage ceremony? Could he not have told her in private that he no longer wished to marry her, and that she had no power to make him do so? She could have bewailed her error and the perfidy of her lover, but would have been forced to accept the reality of the situation and need not have become the plaything of our scandal-mongers and the laughing-stock of the town. But no – not satisfied with having taken advantage of a woman, and breaking his promise to marry her, he must cap it all by throwing her reputation to the dogs. My God! I concluded hypocritically, joining my hands together, and raising my eyes to heaven, Where is sincerity? What has become of good faith? What has happened to that charity which teaches us to turn a blind eye to the faults of others? And since when has it been acceptable to admit – much less to proclaim – one's own knavery and bad faith? Is it not true, Monsieur, I went on, addressing myself directly to him, that such a person has lost the right to be respected and deserves to be shunned by society?

Everyone was looking at me, and the ladies in particular were grateful in their hearts for what I had said. The widow, who had told me who he was, did not know what would happen next and was extremely surprised at what followed. The man was in a state of acute embarrassment and was quite at a loss as to what answer he could make, since all I had said was undeniable. He had brought no complaint against his mistress: she had not been unfaithful, and she had no failing for which he criticised her. There was nothing but his own infidelity which had led him to discard her, and the only shred of justification he offered for doing so was that she was a widow.

You do not answer, Monsieur, I said, still addressing him. Is it that you disagree with what I have said? It is clear, he answered me, that you have interests of your own here which you are hoping to promote by expressing these opinions. I have no such private interests, Monsieur, I said, with a certain self-righteousness. The only widow present who is free to marry is Madame here, and while she does me the honour of allowing me to attend her salon, I do not aspire to claim with her the same liberty as that accorded by Mademoiselle de Gironne to her lover, and the insinuation that you make – and in her presence – that I may one day be granted this liberty is a slur on her character, while your claim to discern some ulterior motive for the opinions I have expressed is without foundation! I did not express an opinion in order to win the approval of Madame. It is the injustice of the situation itself which makes me speak as I do. It appears, however, that you have some reason for disagreeing with what I have been saying?

There are circumstances in the incident you were discussing which could change the interpretation of it, he said. If that is so, I said, I accept that the matter could be seen in a different light. But I find it difficult to believe that there are such considerations: the man would hardly have refrained from divulging them – we would have heard of them as well as all the rest. He would use them to exonerate himself and would not limit himself to the fact that his mistress was a widow to make light of his inconstancy. He might thereby be able to avoid the charge of perjury and do less injury to his own reputation.

You are not aware, one of the ladies intervened, addressing me, that it is Monsieur de Beauval himself to whom you are speaking. I do not know, Madame, I answered calmly, whether this gentleman is Monsieur de Beauval, the same who was Mademoiselle de Gironne's lover. I do not have the honour of his acquaintance. But I can only say that it is difficult to believe that the affair we are discussing can be connected with this gentleman, who has every appearance of being a man of honour. Are you of the opinion then, Monsieur, said the man, addressing me, that a man's good name depends on his not taking whatever pleasure offers itself, and in avoiding any attachment unless he is ready to be bound by it for the rest of his life?

I believe, I answered, that a man's honour depends not only on refusing to deceive a woman such as the young lady in question, but also in refusing to deceive even his worst enemy. A man's good name depends on his sincerity and probity, on his compassion for those who are less fortunate, on returning the affection of those who love him, on showing gratitude for any kindness he receives, and on the absolute confidence others can place in his word. I see none of these in the abandonment of Mademoiselle de Gironne. It is not in my nature to mince my words. I expect no gratitude from Mademoiselle de Gironne, whom I do not even know. Nor do I fear your resentment enough to disguise my sentiments. I feel both sympathy for the young lady, and indignation and disgust at the way you behaved, and I cannot refrain from expressing these.

You have made your position quite clear, he said. I would not like to have you as my judge! I shall never be that, I answered. I do not sit in any court of law and, if I did, I would be under an obligation to base my judgements on the laws of the land. Which you consider defective, he said. No, Monsieur, I replied, they are just. I would not wish to change them, but they are the laws of men and cannot be perfect; and if you will deign to hear what else I have to say, you will realise that I am not motivated by the desire to make a favourable impression on Madame, as you implied earlier.

Let us consider the law as it relates to the present case. It was designed with great wisdom, and with the intention of regulating the behaviour of widows, who, by their status in society, are mistress of their own actions and may choose to marry whom they please – or indeed to remain unmarried, if they please. This absolute freedom could give rise to scandal and disorder in society if the law did not exert some restraining influence. The law, therefore, gives no protection to a widow who becomes pregnant and does not oblige the man responsible to marry her – even if a promise of marriage were made. The law is indifferent to matters of family, age and wealth. The result is that a man can entice a widow into a liaison with legal impunity. However, should a man deliberately so deceive a widow, he is no less guilty before God (or indeed before men) than if he had seduced an unmarried girl. And it is not the action of an honest man, in my opinion, to rely on laws which were enacted merely for the promotion of good order in society to relieve him of a moral responsibility. Look into your own heart, Monsieur, I said. I am sure you will find your conscience is not wholly tranquil; or at least, I am sure, even if you consider yourself innocent in the eyes of your fellow men, you do not feel confident that God will treat you as his child, to let you enter into His inheritance, you – who deny this recognition to your own child, condemning him to illegitimacy!

Since all those present agreed with me, and as the man's discomfiture was increasing every minute, far from condemning my outspokenness, the company applauded the position I had taken, and together we made him so ashamed of his behaviour that he promised to return to his mistress and she was sent for right away. A marriage contract was drawn up without delay, and four days later they were married. I don't need to tell you how she thanked everyone, and myself particularly – her lover having explained that it was I who had convinced and converted him. Since they were both from the provinces and returned there the following week, this incident did not become well enough known to have reached your ears, and the names of the parties involved will not reveal that of my widow. The fact that I had come so strongly to the defence of the woman did me no harm in the eyes of the widow. She believed me to be someone who would be incapable of revealing a secret affair, and I realised that the only thing which now held her back was the danger of pregnancy. I overcame this fear with a wholly dishonest ruse, as I will now tell you. The day after the conversation I have recounted, I returned to her house, and she told me that she had been extremely pleased with my intervention and thanked me for it, and said that she was delighted that the pair had been reconciled. I spoke as I did, I told her, out of conviction, and because that is what I believe. But I admit I was shocked by the man's indiscretion. At the very least, he owed it to his mistress to keep the affair quiet; and if I deserve any credit for speaking out as I did, I should want it to be for having emphasised this point. As for the rest, I said nothing a child could not have explained as well as I did. But it must be said, I added with a laugh, the woman was exceptionally naive, and the man a complete innocent! Is it really possible that neither of them knew the secret of making love without untoward consequences? (This, said Dupuis in an aside, is where I used a totally reprehensible falsehood to trick her.) If it were me, I can do whatever I want with a woman without her running any danger of pregnancy. Nothing could be simpler!

You know such a secret? said the widow eagerly. Yes, I do, I answered. Are you in need of it? No, indeed not, she answered laughing. But would you be scoundrel enough to use it? Yes, without a second thought, I answered, so long as it was to extricate a woman from a situation I was responsible for, and if I loved her, and she loved me and deserved not to lose her reputation. I noticed that the widow was paying close attention to my every word and drinking in my poisonous boast with fascination. We discussed the subject at some length, and then the conversation turned to other topics. But I was convinced that she believed I could save her from a difficult situation if by misfortune she should find herself in one; and I was proved right in thinking it was solely the fear of unwelcome consequences which had prevented her from yielding to me, and in believing that, when this obstacle was removed, I would find no other. This became clear two days later when I arrived, as was my habit, between three and four in the afternoon. I saw her through the window. She had a book in her hand, but I was so far away, I assumed she had not seen me, and did not wave. When she did see me, she moved quickly away from the window. This surprised me, and I went in, intending to ask her why she had done so. Anyone less practised than I would have been surprised at what he found. Let me paint the picture for you, dear ladies.

She was no longer reading a book. She was stretched out on a daybed, lying on her back, her head flung back and to the left towards her shoulder, her left arm resting alongside her body on the bed, her right arm reaching out from the bed on to a seat, where she had laid the book; her left leg and thigh were on the bed, her right leg outside the covers, somewhat crosswise. Her skirts and petticoat, displaced and above the knee, revealed the most perfectly formed calf and plumply curved thigh one can imagine, their delicate whiteness enhanced by a black silk stocking, secured by a scarlet garter with a diamond buckle. She was wearing a simple house-robe over a black skirt of gauzy silk crêpe de Chine and the black underwear of a widow. Her neck and throat were uncovered, but a kerchief covered the lower part of her face. In this delightful posture she pretended to be sleeping. In fact, she was not.

I understood why she had disappeared from the window. It was clear that she had been preparing the moment for a long time. I acted as if I believed she was asleep. I gently closed the door of her chamber and went quietly towards her. I left the handkerchief as she had placed it, but I did not leave her skirts as they were. She maintained the pretence of sleep until reaching the height of pleasure, when she made as if suddenly awakening, and her feeble efforts to escape from my arms only heightened the ecstasy.

I must admit that I have never had so much pleasure with a woman as I had with her, nor have I ever known one who was more beautiful or whom I loved as much. The anger she feigned after the above incident seemed neither too exaggerated nor too mild to me. I pretended to believe it was justified, but the truth is, I had been delighted by what she had done. I threw myself at her feet and begged her forgiveness as if I alone had been responsible. She forgave me, the pardon was sealed; I was perfectly happy with her, as she appeared to be with me. I left, promising nothing but secrecy, and I have kept to this commitment, and will do so for the rest of my life. The honourable way in which she brought our relationship to an end ensures that I shall admire and love her for ever, and nothing will induce me to reveal her name. Her sincerity with me demands that I show every consideration for her, and that I take care never to damage her reputation or interests in any way; and what remains for me to say about this adventure will demonstrate this.

For the next two years we saw each other nearly every day,

without the least problem or discord arising between us, because of our understanding and respect for each other. To all appearances, I was a good friend, a man of no particular importance to her. She was not troubled by suitors, since she had frequently stated that she had no desire to remarry, and since she had refused proposals which any other woman would have considered extremely advantageous. I knew she loved me with affection and loved only me, not only because she accepted me as her lover, but through a thousand little acts in which she showed this every day – little surprises she prepared when I least expected them, or the way she deferred completely to whatever she knew would please me. Whenever the occasion offered, she was more than ready to do me a service; she frequently tried to persuade me to take money to buy a government appointment for myself, but I always refused – unless she would agree to marry me, which she would never do. We had no secrets from each other. She told me everything she did. She followed my advice in everything, and in all ways. She wanted to do whatever pleased me at all times, and I had no wish other than to please her. She turned me into a thoroughly honest man, and I am totally indebted to her for delivering me from the bad company I had formerly kept. She combined the ardour and intensity of a mistress with the tenderness, concern and faithfulness of a wife.

Thus, since I no longer consorted with anyone but her and had no expenses (since the only present she would accept from me was my portrait), I was able to afford a carriage and the better lifestyle which I enjoy at present. And though this entails considerable expense for someone with my income, I have been able to maintain it and yet to have more money at my disposal than had previously been the case. It is true that I have not wasted a halfpenny on gambling or any other unnecessary expenditure.

Neither intimacy nor constant companionship has dimmed our ardour or our respect for each other. I admitted that I had overheard her conversation with her sister and told her of the efforts I had made to become acquainted with her. She admitted that she remembered having seen me in the garden at her brother-in-law's house, and that she had been attracted to me when I first arrived at her house, and had guessed that I had planned our meeting as godparents to the water-carrier's child. She told me that as a result of my outspoken comments to Beauval, she had decided to give herself to me, since what I had said had convinced her that she could trust me. She admitted that it was true she had been afraid of the possible consequences of a liaison, and her decision had been sealed by the secret I claimed to have. She admitted that she had set the scene for our first embrace, and that she had pretended to be asleep solely to save her from the embarrassment of a first encounter of this sort face to face in broad daylight. She had been waiting for me at the window for some time before she made her quick retreat, and had deliberately provided the opportunity I had taken. Indeed, she said, had I let it escape, a second one would have been extremely unlikely, as she would have been mortally offended. And finally, she told me that, as I had doubtless noticed, she loved me more than any woman had ever loved a man.

At these words, I took her in my arms. My dearest love, I said, we were made for each other. I know that I shall love you for ever; I am sure you will love me for ever. Let us be united for ever. Let everyone know of our union. Give me your hand in marriage. Your heart is in my keeping, and mine in yours. Let us save ourselves from the need to keep our love hidden. No, she said, with a kiss. I know you. You know me. We are not tormented by guilt, so let us remain good friends and lovers, as at present. We shall love each other better and longer this way. I shall always be your mistress, loyal and faithful to you; and I count on your feelings remaining the same always for me. I could never extract any other answer, however much I pleaded; even during her pregnancies, I was unable to persuade her to marry me.

After we had known each other for two years, she told me she was in her fifth month of pregnancy. I didn't want to tell you before now, she said, for fear of distressing you. Tell me honestly, do you know of a remedy? No, my dearest love, I said, throwing myself at her feet. It was only because I knew your feelings that I lied and said I knew how to avoid this eventuality. I do not love you the less for having done so, she said, embracing me, I esteem you the more. You are too honourable to desert me or allow my situation to be known. I beg you to be discreet, and to help me in every way you can to hide the situation I am in. What has happened does not upset me in the least, dear love, I said. Marry me. I ask for nothing better. You cannot now refuse what I am so eager to offer!

I would accept if I loved you less, she said. Your desire to marry me proves the sincerity of your affection – I need nothing else. But as for marrying – let us not think of it, I beg you. If God preserves my life, our child will be well cared for, I will see to that. If I die, I will give you all that is needed to provide the child with a place in the world. It is my child, she said, a love child, for whom I do not have to relinquish my independence. He will not suffer because I refuse to make him legitimate; he will be the dearer to me since he is the child of my heart. He will be well provided for, I promise you, and if he reaches manhood, he will not regret his birth. But do not talk of marriage between us. Where my fortune is concerned, whatever you want is yours. (This was something I did not doubt, after what she had offered to do for me, which I had always absolutely refused.) And as for my position in society, she added, I shall never remarry; I shall always be yours, as your loyal mistress, but not as your wife. I love you too much to allow you ever to become indifferent to me, or to weary of me and scorn me. Eventually I should grow to fear your disdain and cease to love you.

Therefore, let us not think of marriage, dear friend, she continued, embracing me again. What do you want with a wife and the encumbrance of a household, since you have the chance to be free and to enjoy all the pleasures of marriage without its troughs and pitfalls? I know more than a hundred couples in Paris, she said, who would be happy if they lived as you and I do. But as they cannot escape from each other, they cannot stand each other. If they were not bound to each other any more than you and I are, they could separate, and they would feel as you and I do towards each other and live in perfect harmony. I have told you what my life was like with my husband, and I protest that I will never take another! On that I am resolved! I shall never change. Let it be so, then, I said. I will never speak of it again unless you bring the matter up yourself. After that, we renewed the caresses which were never stale between us.

The child was delivered in the widow's own home, in complete secrecy, since together we had been able to arrange everything with the utmost care. The midwife remained incommunicado for a week in quarters arranged for her in the house, without even windows. She did not know where she was, or who she was attending: I had brought her in my carriage, and I returned her to her home, blindfolded. The widow's chamber-maid (as well as two who subsequently replaced the first one) knew nothing about the birth. Our first child was a boy. He is a lovely child, and she adores him and devotes so much attention to him, I am certain she will always love his father. She had twin girls about a year later, and another daughter about fifteen months after that. These last three children died in infancy, and secrecy was so well preserved that there is not a soul who has even the slightest suspicion of any of this.

In the end, after five years without ever growing jealous or wearying of each other, and still as much in love as we had ever been, we broke off our intimacy by mutual consent, but not without the shedding of sincere tears on both sides. But there were very strong reasons which persuaded us to bring the liaison to an end – reasons which you will allow me to refrain from revealing to you. The widow and I write to each other frequently; she is certainly the only woman in the world whom I believe to be completely frank and truthful. I hold her in the greatest esteem; you will allow me to say no more about her and her present life.

All that I have told you so far will certainly have convinced you that I am an utter scoundrel, and that my widow was of a highly sensual nature. But, gentlemen, put your hand on your heart – is there one of you who, in my place, would not have done as I did? And ladies, if you were as honest as the widow, you would admit, as her sister did, that what she said was true; and as for what she did, though your prejudice may make you condemn it, I am sure, in your hearts, you understand it and agree that she was justified. And you will concur that there are few or none of you (I mean, not only here among my present listeners, however unconvinced you try to appear, but among women in general) who would not behave as she did, if they hoped for a similar outcome. But trust and discretion are rare in the century in which we live because there are very few honourable men – and even fewer faithful mistresses!

At this point in Dupuis's narrative, his cousin, Manon Dupuis, returned alone. Dupuis asked where she had left Madame de Londé. I left her at my aunt's, with her brother, Monsieur Gallouin, and they request that you be so good as to send for them when you are ready to eat dinner this evening. Willingly, said Dupuis, and as soon as my story is finished. However, interrupted Des Ronais, before you take it up again, this would be a good moment for us to break off and have some refreshment. How lucky we are that Mademoiselle Dupuis arrived just now and made the thought of food occur to you! Madame de Contamine teased him. Otherwise you might never have thought of it. Des Ronais was the butt of further jibes during the collation, and Dupuis's narrative was discussed, everyone expressing an opinion about what he had related. You, dear reader, will easily imagine the sort of conversation that took place.

There have been some indelicate episodes in the adventures I have recounted so far, said Dupuis after they had finished eating, but the ladies did not interrupt me, and I deduce from their silence that they were not offended. There were only married women and a widow present, said Monsieur de Terny. What offence would they find? And besides, they all share the widow's sentiments. There is no reason why they should have appeared shocked. So, go ahead, and finish your story. Embellish it all you wish!

There is nothing licentious in what remains to be told, said Dupuis. But I will tell it with complete honesty, which would not be the case were Madame de Londé present, or if I did not trust you not to pass it on to her – though there is nothing which is not to her advantage. Whereas there is little that is to mine, for, to tell the truth, I used to think my attachment to her would take the same course as the others I have had and end the same way. Instead, it almost ended in tragedy – a tragedy of which I would have been the hero – while it looks now as if it will end in a marriage, more like the ending of a comedy – a marriage which cannot take place too soon for me.

I will have to take you back to the days of my youthful depravity, before my reform. Gallouin, as I have told you, was one of the wildest of our band and learnt occult secrets which I did not wish to know. If he had imparted them to me, I would certainly have tried their influence on his sister. He took me to his home one day to dine with his mother and all the family – that is to say, his mother, his two sisters and a young brother who was destined for the Church, and who was only twelve or thirteen years old at the time – but who is now head of the family, the same who will be coming here for supper this evening with Madame de Londé. There was also an ecclesiastic at the table, whom I took for the boy's tutor, but who was in fact the spiritual guide of the mother, Madame Gallouin, and one of those men who drive the children, the friends and the domestics in a household to distraction, once they have wormed their way into the confidence of the master and the mistress.

Gallouin and I planned to spend the afternoon in our usual dissolute fashion. To prepare ourselves for this, we turned the conversation during the meal to topics such as eternal life, the four ends of man, the little value to be attributed to earthly concerns, and other sober reflections of the sort. Before proceeding any further, I must make it clear that, dissolute as our pastimes were, we kept them secret, and that when we were in what is called honest company we dissembled so well that we too were accepted as upright members of society. That being said, let me return to the cleric who was sharing our meal that day – and who soon began to irritate me. It seemed to me that what he was saying was premeditated and aimed specifically at Gallouin, to whom, with the use of borrowed names and the pretence of a general discourse, a severe upbraiding was being addressed. This deduction was the more inescapable since the cleric was delivering a hail of invective against the vices of youth – which was not relevant to the mother or the daughters, nor to the young boy. Later that evening, Gallouin told me I had not been mistaken, and that it was in order either for me to receive my share of the lecture, or with the hope that my presence would silence the man, that he had taken me home with him that day; and that he had been anticipating this sermon for more than a week because of some petty misdemeanour he had committed, which he told me about. He listened to the man's harangue with phlegmatic composure, either because he was indifferent to what was said, or in order to make it look as if he did not realise it was directed at him. Since I was not constrained by the same considerations, I could not remain silent and challenged the ecclesiastic's assertions.

Really, Monsieur, I said, you would do better to enjoy your meal, rather than doing so much damage to your lungs and getting into a pother over the vices you describe. I do not think there is anyone here who is in need of your instruction, for I see no one here who is given to the ill-behaviour you so deplore. If your remarks are intended for Monsieur Gallouin (and they do not seem applicable to anyone else here), I must tell you, you are wasting your time. He and I are good friends – I know the sort of person he is, and I can assure you your apprehensions are misplaced.

My remarks are not addressed to anyone in particular, Monsieur, he said. I make them merely by way of general conversation. In that case, I countered, you are giving yourself unnecessary anxiety, creating monsters and chimera merely for the pleasure of doing battle with them. Gracious me! the mother interjected, Monsieur is by no means attacking creatures of his own imagination! What he is describing are vices to which all young people are prone, and I don't imagine my son is any less likely to fall prey to them than anyone else. Is it for my benefit, then, Madame, said Gallouin to his mother, that the good cleric here is deploying his rhetoric and laying these commonplace observations before us? All your worries about my conduct are merely the product of your own curiosity: you know what I am referring to. But for heaven's sake, let go your fears and trust me. You think I am dissolute, and as far as I can see, Monsieur has taken your word for it and believes so too, and is as deceived as you are. If you knew how I spent my time, you would discover there was nothing in my behaviour which conflicts with your sense of propriety. You may be more ready to believe my friend here, who perhaps has a higher standing and authority than myself, if you wish to enquire of him. Oh, indeed, his mother retorted, you would have me believe on nothing more than your word that you spend all your spare time in church!

You would not be so far wrong as you think, Madame, I said, in a sober tone of voice. Your son lives an exemplary life. There is an uncloistered monk who could enlighten you about this. He is your son's spiritual director. And if you wish to confirm what I am saying, I continued hypocritically, this saintly man is a relative of mine, a cousin of my mother, whom you know. And since the topic has arisen, I believe I ought to tell you that your son, even though he is the oldest in the family, himself had the wish – and perhaps still has it – to adopt the monastic life. He was only dissuaded from doing so by the forceful arguments put to him by my kinsman, who emphasised the need for complete detachment from the world, an unassailable sense of vocation, and the need to be proof against the appeal of secular distractions – an appeal which tends to reassert itself in those who make too early an undertaking to follow the religious life.

Indeed, his mother replied, you would be giving me plenty of matter for thought if I were of a humour to believe you. There is not a syllable which is not true, Madame, I said, and you will agree that, by enquiring of holy and enlightened churchmen such as the one whom I have mentioned, you will be able to confirm for yourself the truth of my words. And what I have told you about your son is true: he wanted to enter a monastery and will probably do so one day, if you are not careful. Would to God that he should do so; I would consider him fortunate, she answered, weeping. I am not yet ready to take this step, said Gallouin. I have been made aware of the seriousness of such a decision. I cannot forsee the future, but for the present, however anxious I may be to put your mind at rest, my friend's relative presented such strong arguments against my intention that I have postponed any immediate action.

After this, since no one can speak more convincingly about religion than those who themselves have none, or very little, such as hypocrites and the pseudo-pious, Gallouin and I threw ourselves into further discussion of the matter, overwhelming the poor cleric and reducing him to silence. It is true that he was not one of the most erudite of churchmen. The mother, reassured by hearing her son talk like an anchorite, had tears of joy in her eyes; and I was transformed in her opinion into the most mild-mannered and God-fearing young man in Paris. We were so carried away by our performance that we found we had committed ourselves to paying a visit to my ecclesiastical kinsman. This promised to be an unappealing adventure, but we managed to come through it with honour. Those who are sincere in their beliefs can always be duped by a Tartuffe. The man of God whom we were visiting – who would have been one of the most pious priests in Paris, had he not had such a delicate palate, nor been so nice about his dress, nor so particular about his living quarters, nor so fond of money (all of which are vices typical of his calling) – would have sworn, after we had called on him a few times, that the two of us were models of high-minded and upright behaviour. As a result, Madame Gallouin's maternal tenderness towards her son was rekindled, and she developed the highest respect for me – all of which provided a source of great mirth for Gallouin and myself.

I soon began to grow weary of playing such an unnatural role, however. The effort of presenting a polished exterior was out of character for me, but I had to persevere or forego the opportunity of seeing my friend's delightful sister, the present Madame de Londé. You are all acquainted with her, so I will restrict myself to telling you things you do not know about her. Since she is a great beauty and has a superb figure, one is at first sight dazzled, but there appears to be little below the surface until you have known her for a very long time; for, though she is as intelligent as a woman can be, and is in fact very well read, this does not become apparent until one has spent a lot of time in her company. Her personality is gentle, but strong and assured. She speaks little, and what she says is always serious, until, as I have said, a long acquaintanceship has allowed her to relax. Her virtue is unimpeachable, at least as far as I have been able to discover; that is to say, she has driven me mad and forced me to love and dote on her, against my intention, by dint of refusing and denying me. If I were to believe what her late husband told me, she is a woman in appearance only, with none of a woman's weaknesses within. But if I believe what I myself have seen, she is a woman through and through, with a heart as tender as can be, but with more self-control and strength of character than anyone should be allowed to have. What I shall tell you about her will show you – better than all the outward descriptions I could give – what sort of person she is.

She was only seventeen years old when I first noticed her – for, until then, I had only seen her in passing. I found her charming, and my masquerading as a youth of pious bent was not unconnected with my desire to know her better, since it ensured I would be well received by her mother, who had a high regard for me – which was not entirely deserved. I often talked to her daughter in her presence, and though the latter spoke little, what she said was always sensible and to the point, and I could not help but fall in love with her. Gallouin had maliciously told her that I planned to enter the Capuchin order as a monk. She believed him, and we had talked about this possibility while her mother was present. I had neither denied nor confirmed it, nor indeed said anything which could be considered definite about my future intentions.

About a month after our conversation, I found her alone for the first time, for her mother had a rule never to let her daughters out of her sight. On this occasion, however, the younger daughter who was ill had called her, and she had gone, leaving the older one alone, at her tapestry, and it was at that moment that I arrived. She asked me if her brother were still thinking of entering a monastery. I told her I did not know – he had not confided in me for some time, and all I could say was that he still visited my relative frequently, but I did not know what they talked about, since they limited themselves to matters of no importance when I was present. And as for you, Monsieur, she continued, do you also intend to hide yourself away in a monastery? I had at one time thought of doing so, Mademoiselle, I answered, with a heavy sigh, but I find my thinking has undergone a change. God has made it clear to me that I am not called to a life of contemplation. I believe I shall achieve a more dependable happiness in the world, and I find I am too interested in society and contemporary events to disengage myself wholly from them and renounce them. I am pleased for your sake, she said, that you have come to this decision. In my opinion, a man who is capable of serving his king and country, the public and his friends, should not bury himself away for life from his contemporaries, failing to use the talents God gave him, and depriving the world of valuable skills. I am grateful to your relative for having deflected you from your earlier inclination.

My change of heart cannot be attributed to the influence of my uncle, I replied. It has come about from my having seen someone who has a more powerful effect on me than he has ever had. The sight of this person has made me realise in a flash the truth of what the good cleric had been saying to your brother and myself. He warned us that, after taking vows of poverty and chastity too hurriedly, it sometimes happens that the sight of a beautiful young woman, to whose hand one might have aspired, overwhelms the feelings of a man committed to the cloistered life, causing him all the more suffering since they cannot be acknowledged. It is then, he said, that one might regret the liberty which would have enabled one to express these feelings. Furthermore, he said, this worldly love, if denied and repressed, can lead one to neglect and hate the vows one had too hastily pronounced. Thereafter, he said, despair can follow, until in the end the cloister becomes a prison, or rather a hell, from which there is no escape. I now see the wisdom of his words only too clearly, I said. I would die of rage and despair, if I were at present forced to repress the feelings which fill my heart. Such turmoil would certainly be my death, seeing that, even free as I am at present, I do not dare reveal my feelings to the one who enchants me, nor tell her how my heart is filled with the most tender and passionate love for her.

Yes, dear lady, I continued, throwing myself at her feet, it is because of you that I have abandoned – not my piety and religion, which are not in conflict with the ardent love I have for you – but the intention I had formed of retreating to a monastery. It is because of you alone that I do not turn my back on the world. You will no doubt be surprised by my declaration, but I can no longer bury the flame which you have lit in my heart. I have never experienced love before, and I would never have done so if your beauty had not presented itself to my eyes and convinced me that you alone are worthy to enslave me. I shall love you for ever. You alone are the mistress of my destiny. It is for you to decree what is to become of me, but you should be aware that I cannot live without loving you, and without telling you of my love.

She was so taken aback by this declaration that she did not know how to reply. I was happy to note the trouble which revealed itself in her eyes and her gestures, and which I took to augur well for my suit. She was about to speak when we heard her mother returning. I was still on my knees. Go, she said. I am too overwhelmed to give you a reply at present. I left her, happy at least that I had made my feelings known, and hoping soon to receive a favourable response, but in this I was disappointed: I was unable to discover whether I had made an impression on her heart or not.

It was when I had reached this point in my relations with Mademoiselle Gallouin that her brother confided to me the story of his love for Silvie, enjoining me to secrecy. You were not in Paris, Dupuis continued, turning to address Des Frans. You returned shortly thereafter; you picked a quarrel out of thin air with him, on some trumped-up pretext – in the German fashion – and a fight ensued in which you inflicted a dangerous wound on him. I admit I was glad I was not called on to be present, as I would have had to take sides, and would not have known which to choose. I have to say, however, in all honesty, that appearances were so much against you, I was so much in love with Gallouin's sister, he was so badly wounded, and in such grievous condition as a result, that I would probably have taken his part and felt compelled to try and avenge him. Knowing what I now know, I can only crave your forgiveness, but I was ignorant of the cause of your quarrel at the time and trust you will not hold this admission against me.

No, of course not, answered Des Frans. Knowing what I now know, on the contrary I would have blamed you if you had not been ready to defend your sweetheart's brother – love must always take precedence over friendship. But continue your story, I beg you. I am anxious to hear what happened next. Certainly, said Dupuis. I am about to tell you the part that concerns you – a part which will fully rehabilitate Silvie in the opinion of everyone who hears it. I am betraying a promise of secrecy, but since the two people involved are now both dead, there is no longer reason to abide by it; and moreover, it behoves me to explain the actions of a woman whose heart was always chaste, and whose purity would never have been sullied had not un-natural secrets and the power of evil been used to overcome her virtue.

I went to visit Gallouin on his sickbed, and he, having made me swear not to reveal what he was about to tell me, recounted everything that had happened between himself and Silvie. He told me that he fell madly in love with her at first sight and did everything possible to gain an introduc-tion to her circle, and had succeeded; that you yourself had taken him with you to see her several times; that it had been very clear there was some familiarity between you and her, so that he had not dared reveal his own feelings to her while you were in Paris, for fear of being rejected if her heart were already engaged. All he had been able to do was to establish a little group of friends, which included Silvie and his sis-ters, so that he could have the pleasure of seeing her as often as possible. He said that when you left to visit your estate, after the manor house burnt down, he had taken the opportunity to make his feelings known to her, and had used every means – tears, declarations of love, promises and constant attendance – to win her heart. But she had always refused to accept any gift. He had several times proposed marriage and had met with nothing but resistance: she had always resolutely rejected any proposal, whatever form he presented it in. In his absolute desperation, he said he was even tempted to hold a dagger to her throat and threaten to kill her and then himself, if she would not submit to his embrace – which, knowing her resolute character, he expected would be the case. Whatever the result of such a tactic might be, he had made up his mind to employ it, he said, unless the use of one of the secret charms he had learned about during his dissolute youth should prove effective in overcoming her resistance.

To ensure the success of this charm, he needed some of Silvie's own blood, as well as something she wore next to her skin. So, to obtain some of her blood, he chose a moment when she was working on some embroidery, in the company of his mother and his sisters, and making an awkward turn, he knocked her on her right arm, so that she pricked herself with the needle. As if the movement had been accidental, he begged her pardon and knelt before her to offer his help, pulling from his pocket a white handkerchief which he had put there in readiness, and used it to wipe the blood from her left hand, and was then able to keep the bloodstained handkerchief. As for something which touched her skin, he thought of the necklace which she wore constantly, and while seeming to tease her, he tore the ribbon, and so was able to take the necklace home with him to repair. He replaced not only the ribbon, but also a silken thread which held the pearls, after dipping them in the mixture he had prepared, which contained some of his own blood as well as Silvie's. The next afternoon, he took this necklace back to her.

You would not believe (I use Gallouin's words, said Dupuis) the result this produced. Though the incantation which I pronounced, and the mixture – containing blood from both of us – in which I soaked the ribbon and the thread, had both been powerful, I was startled at their prodigious effect. Silvie had scarcely replaced this fateful string of pearls round her neck, when her eyes began to sparkle. She gazed at me with love and tenderness, and I had no further resistance to overcome. She forgot everything for me, and this same Silvie, who had never shown the slightest wish to please me, hastened to receive my caresses, with an eagerness – or rather, an insistence – bordering on indelicacy. It was she who urged me to spend the night with her. She gave me the key to her garden and promised to dismiss her servants early, so that no one should see me. The only person she was in the least worried about was Madame Morin, and I promised to ensure she would not trouble us. It was only by giving my word to return for supper with her in no more than an hour that Silvie would let me out of her sight, and as I left she threw her arms round my neck and there were tears in her eyes.

Indeed, I was somewhat astonished myself at this display of excessive emotion, but though an artificial triumph such as that has little charm for an honest man, my passion was so overpowering that I felt no remorse about pursuing my criminal path. The only reason I left Silvie at that moment was to go and prepare a sleeping draught of simple herbs for Madame Morin – the only person about whom Silvie appeared concerned – for this woman normally slept in her room, next to her bed. That afternoon, Madame Morin had been with my mother and had been teaching a new tapestry stitch – which was much in vogue and which she had mastered – to my sisters. She would be returning for supper with Silvie, for she was her almost constant companion. Madame Morin was highly esteemed and respectable, and someone for whom Silvie had a great regard, having, she told me, been raised by her. Madame Morin would certainly not have sanctioned our conduct. But Silvie at that point counted only on me and insisted that we avoid at all costs being discovered by her. Alas! (said Gallouin as he continued his story and with tears in his eyes) I sacrificed this honest woman in pursuit of my crime!

I made a concoction, he continued, of this and that – the sort of drugs one can find at any apothecary's, which I do not need to name, returned to Silvie's and added the mixture to a chicken stew which I knew this woman was specially fond of, and of which she ate a large portion – while I playfully dissuaded Silvie from eating any. What was left was eaten by the servants. Madame Morin had scarcely finished her supper when all she wanted was her bed, where she fell into such a deep sleep that no amount of noise could rouse her. I left the house, as was my wont, by the front entrance and returned by way of the garden, to which Silvie had given me the key. No one observed me; all the servants had fallen into the soundest sleep. Only Silvie was there to receive me, which she did with the utmost impatience. She used every means to try to awaken Madame Morin and, finding it impossible, she was satisfied, and wasted no time in urging me to join her in her bed. She preceded me, and I was not far behind – and our subsequent exhaustion plunged us into the deepest sleep.

I awoke first, ready to recommence our embraces, but the reckless, passionate Silvie of the previous night was no longer there. She remembered all that had happened the previous day and into the night, but hated what she had done. I now found only a fury: she tore herself from my arms, calling for help and summoning her servants at the top of her voice. She was so distraught that I was obliged to grab my sword from her hands to prevent her from killing either herself or me. Her servants, who had partaken of the drugged stew, must have been suffering from its effects, for none of them made an appearance even though she cried out for them to come for more than an hour. As for Madame Morin, she could no longer hear anything. I saw that she was dead.

This discovery, and Silvie's distress, made me view my actions of the previous night with horror. I didn't tell Silvie what means I had used to cheat her virtue, nor did I tell her that Madame Morin was dead. I begged her forgiveness. I also pointed out that were any of this to become known, it would be disastrous for her reputation. Once again I asked her to marry me. She spurned the proposal, saying she considered me a monster. The only thing she asked was that I should never reveal these events to anyone. I swore to respect this request. If I divulged the least hint of what had taken place, she said, it would cost not only my life, but hers as well.

I noticed that she was no longer wearing the necklace. I said nothing, but understood that the charm had ceased to work. I then left the house, truly repenting my crime, which had gained me nothing and had cost the life of a woman who did not deserve such an end. None of Silvie's servants awoke till after midday and were still dazed even then. But poor Madame Morin, who was too far advanced in age, and whose constitution was too weak to withstand the strength and quantity of the drug I had given her, was found dead in her bed.

Silvie did not accuse me of this death, for fear its cause would be investigated. She sent to ask for the return of her necklace, and I went to see her to enquire if she had made a thorough search for it in her bed and in the room, but she refused to receive me. I thought the necklace must have come undone in the tumult of our love-making, but I now doubt this, since it has never come to light. And in order to allay her fear that someone may have entered the room that night and taken it from her neck, I was obliged to send word to her that I had taken it, and that I would keep it all my life as a keepsake of my love for her. I sent twenty times its value to her, but she has always refused to receive anything from me. If I sent her a letter, she burnt it in front of my messenger – except for the first one, which she read. And even worse than this, since that disastrous day, she refuses to leave her house, for fear, it seems, of meeting or seeing me.

I have to admit (Gallouin continued as he recounted his tale to me) that I am still disturbed by the disappearance of the necklace, but, after all, it cannot have been Monsieur Des Frans who took it from her neck, for he was a hundred leagues away, in Poitou. Nor can it have been any of Silvie's servants: not one of them would be bold enough to steal it from her person, at the risk of waking her and being caught in the act. I cannot fathom what can have happened; and if I were credulous enough to believe the Devil could carry something off, I would believe it was he who had taken it. Whatever the truth of the matter, I am convinced it is because of Silvie that Monsieur Des Frans wanted to kill me. But after all, does he think that she belongs to him, and has no right to speak for herself? I am madly in love with her – this you cannot deny after what I have told you I did to make her mine. And I will marry her, in spite of him, if only she will agree. As soon as I am recovered, I shall use every effort to persuade her to marry me.

This, said Dupuis (resuming the narrative himself, and no longer quoting Gallouin), was how Gallouin spoke to me in the days immediately following his injury. But a few days later, we were startled to hear that Silvie had suddenly disappeared. She had sold all her possessions, dismissed her servants and moved from her house, without saying where she was going, and accompanied only by a maid and a servant-boy. For more than a week we had no further news. Had he been able to, Gallouin would have been out searching for her, but for more than two months he was confined to bed and could not leave his bedchamber. I did my utmost to discover what had become of Silvie, but had no success. In fact, I was wasting my time, as she had used a false name when hiring a carriage. This made us think again, and Gallouin now had no doubt but that she was with you, said Dupuis, addressing Des Frans, and he felt certain he would obtain some information from you if you came back to Paris. He was eager therefore to promote the reconciliation that your mother – who returned at about this time – was anxious to effect with his mother, with the aim of reestablishing good relations between you two. It was with this in mind that he agreed to, and signed, everything Madame Des Frans asked for.

But four months after he had recovered, he was still at a loss as to what to think, until he received the letter Silvie wrote to him from her convent. It enabled us to deduce the truth, and we no longer had any doubts. The use of words like 'promise' and 'commitment' persuaded Gallouin that she was married and, because of the way you had picked a quarrel with him, that you were her husband. He now felt certain that you must have found her with him that night, and that it was you who had removed the necklace. And he concluded it was you also who had sent her to the convent. The only thing he did not understand was how – hot-headed as you are – you had resisted the impulse to kill both Silvie and himself on the spot. He was amazed at your restraint, and earnestly hoped that he would be the only victim of your vengeance and that you would spare Silvie, who was innocent.

Gallouin told me that he had reached these conclusions, and I agreed that they were probably correct. You saw that I was not surprised when you told us what had passed between you and Silvie, nor on hearing that you were married to her. Gallouin bewailed the fact that a woman who deserved so much better had suffered such misfortune in her life and bitterly bewailed the part he had played in her downfall. So many distressing events ...

At this point, Dupuis was interrupted by sobs from Des Frans and expressions of commiseration from the entire company. Everyone mourned the death of someone so beautiful, so admirable and so virtuous. Everyone shed tears for her; the discovery of her innocence reawakened Des Frans's dearest memories, and his grief over her demise was as touching as if her death had but newly occurred. He was near to dying of grief. Madame de Contamine expressed the sentiment that there was no punishment sufficient to expiate Gallouin's crime. In spite of the fact that he had repented, she reviled his memory and would have cursed him beyond the grave, had her husband not imposed silence by asking Dupuis to proceed with his story, so that both Des Frans and the rest of the company might be distracted from these distressing memories. Dupuis complied.

So many unhappy events following one after the other had a profound effect on Gallouin. He made confession to a priest, during his illness, of all the misdeeds of his youth and came to feel a sincere repentance for them. He contemplated all the wrong he had done in his life. He was afraid the existence he had led up to the present, and which would continue unchanged in the future if he remained in the world, would be like a downhill slope and lead inexorably to the baleful end which had been predicted for him in his horoscope, and he came to the decision to adopt the monastic life. And this he did.

My mind is made up, he said to me one day. I see the disorders of my previous life; I see what little satisfaction the pleasures of the world can give. I recognise the failings of my nature, which I must conquer. This is what my reason tells me, and fear forces me to take the action my reason prescribes. What is it you fear? I asked him. I will tell you the source of my fear, he said. Keep it to yourself, if you think it best. Listen. This is what haunts me.

You and I did our studies together. and you know my tutors were well pleased with my work. But I noticed even when I was very young that, whatever praise I received, my mother always looked at me with tears in her eyes. I was aware of this for more than twelve years, but was never able to understand the reason for it. In the end, when my studies were completed, and after my father died, I begged her with such insistence to explain what troubled her that she could no longer refuse and told me something which has frequently given me anxious thoughts.

There used to be a man in Paris, who was very well versed in astrology, and who drew up horoscopes for a large number of important people, and his predictions as to how they would die came true in very many cases. My mother, giving way to a weakness which can be pardoned in a woman, was curious to have him draw up my horoscope. He predicted I would die by hanging and strangulation. Good God! I burst out, interrupting Gallouin's words. I was not overdisturbed by this, he responded calmly. I don't believe in such predictions. I know there is nothing in them and, besides, such beliefs are contrary to my religion. Also, my rank protects me from death by hanging. If I were to die by an executioner's hand, it would be the axe and the block I would have to fear. This is what I said to my mother with a laugh when she told me the reason for her tears.

However, he continued, I am ashamed to say, this prediction keeps returning to my mind. And tell me, even you, who are my friend, if I were arrested for what I did to Silvie, and for the death of Madame Morin, and you were my judge, could you save me from an ignominious end? Does not such a dastardly crime make me unworthy of the rights attached to my birth, and deprive me of the sad distinction afforded by my rank? Without a doubt, the prediction of my horoscope would be fulfilled. I admit the thought fills me with horror, and Silvie's letter, which reinforces these fears and seems to foretell some greater disaster, has made my decision final. My mind is made up. I will withdraw from the world and enter a monastery, both to do penance for my crime and my sins and to forestall their consequences. Nothing I said could influence him, and it was with great sadness on my part and great joy on the part of Madame Gallouin that he became a member of the Capuchin order.

He showed Silvie's letter to his confessor, who instructed

him to make every effort to rectify the erroneous judgement you may have made about her (Dupuis continued, turning to Des Frans), even if this meant revealing the truth about his crime; to ask your forgiveness; and not to defend himself against your anger with anything other than tears. He submitted to these conditions with true Christian humility, and before being accepted into his order he went to your estate on foot without informing anyone. He made every possible enquiry but could neither find you nor discover your whereabouts. In despair at his failure, he returned to Paris. He made no enquiry about Silvie, having been expressly forbidden to do so. On his return, he took his vows. Only after this did he tell me what I have just told you about his visit to your estate. He lived like a saint for the rest of his life, which ended as had been predicted, though it is not yet time for me to speak of this. I cannot refrain from a reflection on his conversion and adoption of the religious life, which is this: if it were only those who truly repent and truly believe who entered our monasteries, there would be fewer monks but their lives would be more edifying.

To return to Gallouin's sister, Madame de Londé, whom I loved sincerely: I attended her brother constantly during his illness, and this provided frequent opportunities for me to see her, but she took great care not to speak with me alone, so that I never again had an opportunity to speak to her privately. I wrote to her twenty times, but she refused to receive my letters. However hard I tried, I found it impossible to discover her feelings. I had not yet come to any understanding with her, though I believed I noticed she was not indifferent to me. When her brother went into the monastery, he took with him all my pretexts for visiting the house, and, losing my opportunities for seeing her, I also lost the habit of being in love with her. In order to console myself for this loss, and for the pain of seeing my friends disappear into a monastery, or into the provinces, or into the serious professions they now embarked upon, I became attached – as I have told you – to my delightful widow, who occupied my attention so fully that I was prevented from looking elsewhere. My relationship with her lasted five years and more, and during this time I heard, with considerable indifference, that Mademoiselle Gallouin had married Monsieur de Londé.

If I thought you were capable of saying anything to her, Dupuis continued, interrupting the train of his story, I would not be speaking as frankly as this – but you are all trustworthy people and I depend on your discretion, both with respect to what I just said and to what remains for you to hear. So, he continued, resuming his narrative, I forgot all about her. Yet it was written that she would be my real passion, and that I should love her more than I had ever loved anyone else – not even excepting the widow, and more even than I had thought myself capable of loving.

She had been married for more than three years then, and it was more than five years since I had seen her, except in passing, and then only rarely, and without speaking to her at all, when she came to my notice at a time when I least expected it. The way it happened was quite unusual. I was walking alone with a book in my hand, thinking of the adventures of my past life, and particularly of the true pleasure one enjoys in the arms of a faithful, loving mistress, such as my widow, with whom I had broken off my association less than a week before, and who still filled my thoughts. These meanderings had led me insensibly to a house which belonged to the secretary of Monsieur, the King's brother, on the outskirts of Paris. I went and sat down on a bench at the entrance to a long avenue, which led in one direction towards Paris, while in the other the countryside stretched as far as the eye could see. I had only just sat down, when I saw a tall and very fashionably dressed lady coming towards me. It was a warm day, but she wore a half-mask of velvet, which prevented me from recognising her immediately. She was alone and was walking very slowly. She looked behind her from time to time. Here is someone come for a romantic tryst, I said to myself. A moment later, a woman in more menial garb came up and spoke to her. I couldn't hear what she said; I only saw that the lady gave an impatient gesture and sent the woman away. As far as I could see, we were the only people in the park. The lady continued to walk towards me. I noticed that she was of a very pale complexion and that her blue eyes were not unknown to me. I was charmed by a beautiful hand which was visible. I tried in vain to rally my ideas: I was far from having any thought of Madame de Londé.

I noticed that the lady looked long and hard at me, and turned several times to look back when she had passed. This indicated to me that she knew who I was, while I did not recognise her. She turned and retraced her steps coming back towards me, her eyes still fixed on me. I am not by nature reticent, but I imagined the situation to be something quite different from what in fact it was. I thought she was here for a rendez-vous with her galant. It was quite the contrary: she was here to disrupt a rendez-vous.

As I did not expect any particularly favourable development from this encounter, and as she continued to look at me, I went towards her. You have the advantage of knowing who I am, dear lady, I said, and you are hiding your face from me to ensure that no one but your lover may see you in this solitary spot where you await him. I do not know who he is, nor who you are, but if I may judge from what I see, either he is extremely captivating, or you are very much in love, since you allow him to keep you waiting so long, when it should be he who arrives first. But allow me, on the strength of what I can see – your hand, your arm, your eyes, your figure and your bearing – to offer myself in his place, and I am sure you will not regret the exchange. At least, you will not find in me the indolence and half-heartedness which I find inexcusable in him.

Since you do not recognise me, she answered, I will pardon your temerity in presuming to judge my reasons for being here alone. It is true that it is an errand of love which brings me here, as I assume it is with you also? No, I answered, you are mistaken. I am unfortunate in love. My mistress has cruelly left me. I am here without reason. I wandered here without design, and it was chance which kept me here to occupy the place left vacant by your indifferent lover. You would not think me worthy of your attention if I did not offer to console you in the absence of this other – who, it may prove, is not my equal.

As I said this, I raised my hand to the half-mask she wore, to see her face. You are too bold, she said, staying my hand. If I wished to be seen, I myself would remove the mask. Since I have not done so, it is clear I wish to remain unseen, and you are indiscreet to attempt to see me against my will. It is only fair that we should be on an equal footing, I said. I am sure you know me. Why do you not wish me to know who you are? It is true, she replied, that I know you. You are Monsieur Dupuis, and it is also true that I do not wish you to see me because you would recognise me. Who can you be? I asked. I respect your wishes and will not touch your mask, but I shall remain here until your lover appears, to reproach him for his tardiness. And if it is my husband I am waiting for? said the lady. If it is your husband, I shall find I have been much mistaken in my surmise. But I shall nonetheless make you pay for your refusal to be seen. And how will you do that? said she. If it is your husband, I said, the appointment was certainly not for you to meet him at this time of day, and I shall make him suspect that you came here to meet me. When I see him, I shall know who you are, and the whiff of jealousy he will inhale will be your penalty and will make you regret your refusal to show your face. Your threat is ingenious, she said, but its malice is not in keeping with the air of piety and devotion you wore formerly, which made you appear, five years ago, halfway to being a saint or, at least, like someone ready to adopt a monk's garb.

As I had never adopted a sanctimonious pose except at Madame Gallouin's, I understood immediately whom I was talking to, and determined to keep up my play-acting, and pursue this adventure as far as it would take me. It is true, I said, I did formerly intend to withdraw from the world, as some of my friends have done. But the religion I had and still have in no way contravenes my wish to know who you are, as I have no unworthy designs. Moreover, it is true, I would have entered a monastery long ago, if a sentiment which has always occupied my heart were not in conflict with the complete disengagement from the world which is required by the religious life. I was prevented by my love for a person of exquisite beauty – someone of a similar build to yourself, though not so tall nor so rounded in figure. But I was nothing to her, since she married another. I cannot say she was unfaithful, since she had never given any pledge to me, though she knew I cared for her. But, I continued, with a great sigh, I have remained constant, unmoved by all others, and will remain true to her and never embark on any other sentimental attachment. (I could make this assertion, being quite certain my intrigue with the widow was unknown to anyone but ourselves.)

Such a long-standing and unrequited devotion may be difficult to credit, said Madame de Londé. There is nothing which could give anyone cause to doubt it, I said. You, who know who I am – name one woman or girl who has received my attentions or whose name has been linked with mine in any way during the last five and a half years since I declared my feelings to the one I speak of. It is certain I have had no connection with either woman or girl, nor have I sought any. The aloofness of the person I have mentioned and her indifference towards me over a long period of time when I was able to visit her home daily persuaded me that my company displeased her; and having no reason to go to her house when her brother left it, I felt I would be doing her a service by no longer forcing my presence on her. I have always loved her without hope. Her marriage nonetheless led me to despair, and I formulated a plan to go and stab myself to death before her eyes, but a remnant of the religious teaching I had received reminded me that by taking my own life on earth I put my eternal salvation at risk. Since then, I have led a pitiful existence. I have sought solitude; books and sorrow have been my companions; my friends – whom I no longer see – think of me as some sort of wild creature. I have avoided all opportunities not only of speaking to her, but even of seeing her, in order not to cause the least breath of scandal, and not to give her the slightest displeasure. Whenever, by chance, I saw her in the distance, I fled, since, if by misfortune I encountered her, it only reopened an unhealed wound. I never enquired after her and have no idea what has become of her, except for the most general sort of reports which have reached my ears, to the effect that her scorn for me has been repaid by her husband's infidelities. It even gives me some solace to know that she is not entirely happy. Good God! I added, looking to the heavens, how could anyone married to such an incomparable person not find his whole happiness in her? How can he deride the caresses for which I would forfeit the last drop of my blood? I bewail her misfortune, I said, wiping away a tear which I had conjured up, and will always do so. And it was with my thoughts dwelling on her that my reverie led my footsteps to this place – which I had never entered before. But how is it, I said, looking up at her in surprise, and by what secret charm, that someone unknown to me has drawn from my mouth something which I have always hidden with so much care, and of which even my best friend – her brother – is no more aware than anyone else in the world?

Is what you have just told me really true? she asked. Would it were not so, I said, with tears in my eyes, for then I would not be leading this sad life. Yes, it is true, true as I have told you, and true that I have told you without knowing who you are. This lady, she said, would be grateful to know of your constancy. Why do you not speak to her?

The language of love is so unfamiliar to me, I said, that if I were in front of her, it would perhaps be impossible for me to express my feelings to her. Tell me her name, she said. Perhaps she is among my friends and I can be your spokeswoman. I would willingly tell you her name, I answered, but I must know into whose keeping I am confiding the secret in which the whole happiness of my life resides. Take off your mask, and I will see if I can make you my confidante. If that is the price you require for revealing your secret, we may each carry our own away with us unshared, she answered. Mine is not heavy, I said. I have been carrying it too long to find it a burden. You are losing more than you realise, she said, in not revealing it to me. You gain nothing by not knowing it, I said. At least I lose nothing, she replied. That is true, I said, but I do not see that I lose more than you. You count it as nothing, then, she said, that you forfeit the pleasure of seeing a beautiful woman like myself? There is no place empty in my heart to receive such pleasure, I said, and since receiving the impression which is engraved there already, I obtain no greater pleasure from seeing the most beautiful women in the world than I have from seeing a beautiful painting.

I own, she continued, I would be very happy to learn the name of this woman who reduces all others to insignificance in your esteem, and who inspired you with such a lively and enduring passion. I am almost inclined to reveal my face to you. No, I replied, do not do so. I would not tell you my secret after all. I have cherished it for so long that I am not ready to part with it out of simple curiosity and a wish to see your face. The terms of our bargain have changed, then? she said. Yes, they have changed. I withdraw my offer. And in my heart I am ready to beg my mistress for forgiveness for having felt a moment's curiosity about another. Whether you are beautiful or ugly is of no consequence to me.

You are uncivil, she said. This paragon of yours must have a perverse effect on you to make you so harsh on our sex. On the contrary, I said. If she had taught me to be less honest I would wish to see you, to take pleasure if you are beautiful and to scorn you if you are ugly. I cannot say, she replied, if you would take pleasure in seeing me or wish to reject me, but I cannot bear the idea that you may think that I am ugly, and before I leave I will show you the truth. However, I should tell you, she went on, that once you called me beautiful. And I do not believe I have changed so much since then.

I may have said so, I answered. But it may have been out of civility rather than honesty. It may be that you are indeed beautiful: your manner and everything I see about you attract me because they remind me of her. But whoever you are, your beauty could not equal hers. Before I leave, she said, you may decide if my beauty is inferior. And whatever the decision, I declare you are the only man in the world uncourteous enough to have made such remarks to me, and I intend to force you to ask pardon for them. You may be certain I shall not do so, I said. And ...

I was on the point of continuing, but this same woman who had already spoken to her came and spoke again to my masked companion. It doesn't appear that anyone has come, Madame, she said. The birds have flown elsewhere, and the hunt has yielded no game. Then my steps have been wasted from that point of view, said Madame de Londé. Farewell, Monsieur, she said, turning to me. Keep your secret safe. There is merit in your discretion. You are forgetting, Madame, I said, retaining her, that you do not wish me to believe you are ill-favoured. I am glad you have reminded me, she said, disappearing into a small stone shelter beside the path along which we were walking. See, then, Monsieur, said she, removing the mask, were you mistaken previously when you said I was beautiful? Or was I mistaken when I believed you?

I knew very well, as I have said, that it was Madame de Londé, but I pretended to be amazed to the point of ecstasy. I took two steps back, supporting myself on the door of this building, as if to prevent myself from falling. I uttered a single exclamation – Ah, my God! and allowed my hat, my gloves, my book, my walking stick to fall to the ground, as if I had lost the strength to hold them. And then I threw myself at her feet. Ah, Madame! I said. By what unexpected chance have you appeared before my eyes? Was I not unhappy enough without discovering anew what I have lost? I am undone. Madame, you know my secret. I can no longer keep it hidden. It is for you to decide how I am to conduct myself towards you in future. I have always loved you, but the fear that you might discover this is no longer there to rule my behaviour. In the past, I have hidden from you, but I will no longer have the strength to do so. Do not tell me I must. I would not be able to obey. From now on, I shall seek all possible opportunities to see you, with as much determination as I avoided such occasions in the past, to prove to you that I have lived and will always live only for you.

I was wrong to make myself known, she said. I have been led into a strange adventure. I forbid you, however, ever to think of seeing me. Such a prohibition is pointless, Madame, I interrupted. I should be deceiving both you and myself if I promised to respect it. No, I continued, encircling her knees with my arms, I cannot help but love you. I shall die unhappy, but I shall at least die with the solace of having told you that I die for love of you.

I have the gift of being able to summon tears to my eyes at will in the presence of a woman. At this point, I allowed my tears to flow with abandon. My performance was taken as a sincere expression of feeling, and tears came to her eyes, too. In short, she was deeply touched. She raised me from the ground, an action for which I was grateful, as the gravel was biting painfully into my knees. She sat down on a bench in the shelter, and allowing me to sit next to her, wiped away her tears and talked to me charmingly, giving a general confession of the events of her life during the past five years.

She said she had loved me since she first saw me when I used to visit her mother's house. She had refused to make any response to my declaration since she was of an age where she was too timid to enter into any sort of understanding, and she was all the more unsure of herself as a result of her mother's constant warnings. She would rather have married me than anyone else, if she had dared to make her feelings known, and if my assiduities had given her encouragement. However, she had heard that I had a secret involvement with some other woman, and she had therefore consented readily enough to a match which her mother had arranged for her with Monsieur de Londé. She said she had lived and still lived quite happily with him, because his roving eye relieved her of attentions he would otherwise have addressed to her. She left him free to follow his fancy not only because her feelings for him were not of a nature to arouse her jealousy, but also because her temperament did not incline her towards many of the duties which marriage imposes on a woman. Her husband's flirtations did not upset her, but caused her amusement, and she had come to this parkland just to catch him out in a tryst which she thought he had arranged with some pretty young woman of no consequence. My outing has not succeeded in its purpose, she continued. Instead of him, I found you, and seeing you has renewed in my heart the inclination I used to have for you. I thought I had forgotten you, but I was mistaken, and I couldn't resist the sudden wish to talk to you. I did so without considering what might be the result. Your declaration, which I did not expect, both surprised and delighted me. I revealed my face because I wanted to, feeling sure I was the person you were speaking of. I thought it was nothing but a simple jest – but I realise I was wrong. You assure me that you have always loved me, and I never forgot you. And I admit I still love you. But if you persist in wishing to see me, I foresee only difficulties which will cause me much distress, and which will not make your life any happier. That cannot deter me, I said. At least I shall have the pleasure of seeing you.

It will not be in my house, she said. It will be wherever possible, I said. I shall even seek out occasions on which to see you. It will be against my wishes if you do so, she said. I am no longer able to control my need to see you, I replied, throwing myself at her feet again and making use of my facile gift of tears. My passion overwhelms me and I am no longer master of my conduct. I have to see you, whatever may come of it. If you take pity on me for what I have suffered during the last six years, and if you make it easy for me to see you, we may avoid awkward meetings which I could not forestall on my own. Otherwise, if you leave me to my despair – which is no longer necessary now you know the truth – I may give way to the excess of my emotion. My passion, which I cannot subdue, and which overpowers my reason, may make me disregard propriety, so that you become a target for gossip; and you will regret, too late, that you were not more tolerant in helping me to conserve the little good sense remaining to me.

You are trying to impose conditions on me with a knife to my throat, she said, beginning to cry again. What would become of me, she went on, if I allowed you to see me in private? What would become of my reputation? Your virtue is in safe keeping in my hands, I said. The recital of my unhappiness, my suffering and despair will not cause any-one with a temperament as calm and equable as yours to take pity on me and forget herself. Nonetheless, I do not wish to run any such risk, she answered. What is to become of me, then? I said. We must come to some agreement before we part, and it is for you to decide what it shall be. Either allow your compassion to comfort and control me, or use your cruelty, and by dooming me you will also bring injury to yourself.

The woman who had accompanied Madame de Londé had remained silent all this time, but she now intervened in our conversation. Your feelings will not always be at such a pitch, Monsieur, she said. My mistress's good nature and generosity will temper their violence. And you, Madame, she said, when you have thought it over, you will see that it is in your interest to respond prudently to a passion which has suddenly been reignited by this unexpected meeting, after being suppressed for six years. Yes, Monsieur, she con-tinued, you can rely on me to see what arrangements can be made. You will be able to see Madame. I am in her service, and I will make it possible for you to visit her. But I will have to rely on you to do exactly and punctually as I tell you. You have saved my life, I exclaimed, rising from the ground and embracing her; and you have saved something even more precious to me – you have saved Madame de Londé's reputation. Talk to her. Make her agree. I will agree to anything you suggest, answered Madame de Londé, so long as I never find myself alone with you.

It was therefore agreed that I should go and visit this waiting-woman, assuming the name and guise of some relative of hers, and that we should then make arrange-ments for Madame de Londé and myself to meet, as often as we could without exposing her reputation to any risk. This being decided, I took my leave. I did not accompany her to her carriage, since I might later have been recognised by some footman on visiting her house. I went home very satisfied with my encounter.

I have to complete my self-portrait for you, even though you will see me as I merit. I had been putting on a performance, as you have seen. I was still preoccupied with the affair I had been having with my widow, which had ended only recently. I now began to form the hope of replacing it by a similar liaison with Madame de Londé. In my mind, she was already my mistress. I assumed she would be an easy conquest. She was no longer, I told myself, the timid and reserved Mademoiselle Gallouin. She was now a married woman with a grievance against a husband she had never really loved. She would be a faithful and tender mistress. She was a sensuous woman, like the widow, who would not be unhappy to repay her husband for his infidelities, and who rebuffed his caresses only because she loved me and wanted no one else. In a word, I took the conclusion for granted and considered her already in my arms – thinking the journey over before I had hired the coach.

The next day, I went to see this woman, whose name was la Mousson, and who is still in Madame de Londé's service. I came purporting to be her brother, as we had arranged. She told me she had two reasons for having offered to help us: the first was that she had been moved by our plight; and the second, that she wanted to see her mistress with some amusement to lift her mind out of the dark mood which often descended on her. She did not know whether these low spirits could be attributed to the fact that she had always been in love with me – which, however, was something she had never mentioned – or to her husband's neglect. According to la Mousson, he was a strange character, though Madame de Londé had never seemed disturbed by this, either when talking to her or to anyone else. It is no use her saying that her husband's flirtations don't worry her, said la Mousson. She is a woman and, in my opinion, that is enough to make one doubt her supposed indifference. Tell me, she said, where would you find a beautiful young woman such as she is who is content with a husband who never shares her bed and who never speaks to her in private, day or night? Did she get married so that she could live like a nun? Upon my life! she continued with some spirit, one gets married to share one's life with another and to work at making a third! Try and raise her spirits, Monsieur, she said. I will do all I can to help, I promise. I thanked her for her concern, and a present which I forced her to accept confirmed her loyalty to my cause. She went to tell her mistress that I was there, and came back to report that it was only with the greatest difficulty that she had persuaded her to see me, but in the end she had agreed. Here is your chance! said la Mousson.

Madame de Londé did indeed appear, and Mousson prepared to leave us but she was called back. You seem very afraid, Madame, I said, of having a moment's private conversation with me. You may talk as much as you wish, she answered, and say whatever you like, but I absolutely refuse to find myself alone with you: you will remember that it was only on that condition that I agreed to receive you. There is no one but Mousson to hear what we say, and I trust her. Considering what she already knows, nothing will surprise her, provided you confine yourself to speech – a stipulation I am determined to enforce, and to which you agreed. Should you attempt anything other than conversation with me, you may be sure that at whatever cost, I shall refuse ever to see you again in my life.

This is what she said, and what she observed to the letter, so that after six months I was no further advanced than on the first day. I received as many protestations of love as I could wish for from her mouth – which I was not even allowed the pleasure of kissing! Frankly, I was not content to be making love like the angels – this method did not suit me, as I told Mousson, who said she did not understand it either. She said that since I had been seeing her mistress, she was no longer so unhappy, she was looking more beautiful than ever and her complexion was more dazzling than it had been. She said perhaps it was my own fault if I was not making more progress. I answered that she herself knew only too well that I was doing all I could, but that her mistress was proof against all methods of attack, and that it was her own presence (since she never left us) that was hindering my advance, and that I would be infinitely pleased if she could find some pretext for leaving Madame de Londé and myself alone for a time. She said it was not within her power to do so, since her mistress had expressly forbidden her to let us out of her sight for any reason whatsoever, on pain of being dismissed. Nevertheless, Mousson did take pity on me, exposing herself to having this threat carried out, which indeed happened – and it was only through my use of prompt and forceful measures that she was able to regain her position. Here is what happened.

Mousson told me one evening that Londé was away from home, at a place which was two leagues outside Paris, and that his habit was, on these occasions, not to return home to sleep. If I wanted to come early the next morning, she said, she would show me to the room where her mistress slept. I flung my arms round her and hugged her when she made this offer, and immediately accepted, as you can imagine. And she did indeed take me to her mistress's bedroom and leave me there. I allowed myself certain liberties which I had not been granted previously, at which the sleeper promptly awoke and was extremely surprised to find herself in my arms. If she had merely tried to defend herself, I would have proved the truth of the proverb 'Surprise is half the battle', but she began to yell for help with all her lungs, and I had no alternative but to beat a hasty retreat. As I escaped, her servants came into the room from the side which joined her husband's quarters on the main staircase, and Mousson, who arrived at the same moment, heard the answer she gave when they asked her why she had called them: she had woken with a start, she said, and had felt as if she were being held in a dragon's claws. An admirable story! I thanked her inwardly for the compliment! Then, as soon as she was dressed, she dismissed Mousson from her service on some trumped-up pretext, part of which was that she had forbidden her ever to leave her bedroom until she was awake and dressed.

Mousson, who is really devoted to her mistress, came in great distress to see me at my home, to which I had hastily returned. I realised there was no time to be lost. I told her what she must do, and she followed my instructions. I myself went immediately to the monastery in the rue Saint-Honoré where Gallouin now resided. He and I were still good friends, but I had never told him of my feelings for his sister, nor did I mention them now. While we were talking about indifferent matters, someone came to tell him he was wanted at the door, and we went to see the caller together.

It was Mousson. I have come, Reverend Father, she said, to beg you to make my peace with your sister, who, in a fit of temper, has just dismissed me. I was at fault, I admit, but I begged her forgiveness. I beg you to see if you can mend matters for me. I will see what I can do, he said. There is no time to lose, Father, she said. If Madame engages someone else to replace me, there is nothing we will be able to do! Who is this woman, Father? I asked Gallouin. She seems devoted to her mistress. She is my sister's waiting-woman, he answered. You must do as she asks, I said, and make peace between them. Will you not go round to your sister's straight away? This woman looks trustworthy. I add my appeal to hers: I too will feel obliged if you bring about this reconciliation. And if you wish to go immediately, I will accompany you. I have not had the pleasure of seeing Madame de Londé since her marriage, and I should be happy to offer my greetings to her. Very well, he answered, we will go and have lunch with her: it is Friday – they will not need to make special provision for us. I will give you a note to take to your mistress, he said to Mousson. I dare not return without you, Reverend Father, she said. She will not receive me back unless you are there. My sister must be really angry! he said, laughing. Go then, and wait for us at her door. We will be there as soon as you are.

We set out without delay and found husband and wife about to sit down at table. Londé had only just arrived back. At any other time, I would have been annoyed that he was present, but as it was, I was very happy to see him there because this made it certain his wife would not be able to ask for an explanation which might have embarrassed me, and would not have led to the outcome I wanted.

Londé did not know me, never having seen me, since, whenever I had visited his wife, I had chosen a time when he would not be present; and the household servants were far from recognising me, dressed as I now was, since I had always presented myself as someone of no standing when I had visited the house. I therefore behaved as if it was the first time I had seen Madame de Londé since her marriage. I could not miss the opportunity of accompanying your brother, I said on entering, which gives me the chance to offer my heartfelt greetings, and to assure you that I am delighted to present my respects on your marriage. After which I doffed my hat to her with a flourish. She received this compliment coldly, replying curtly but with civility. I then greeted Londé, Gallouin having told him who I was. He responded effusively, with the warmest of expressions, to which I gave the best response of which I was capable at that point.

We all four sat down at table together, and it was then that Gallouin, the Capuchin monk, pleaded Mousson's case before his sister. At this point, Madame de Londé lost some of her composure and was so adamant in her refusal to take her back that everyone was surprised. Her brother and her husband both asked what great crime the woman had committed that could have so angered her. She concocted the best reasons she could – which all seemed trifling, since she did not give the real one. I looked at her with a smile, and this threw her into complete disarray. She reddened and, pointing to me, said: There is the gentleman who knows my reasons better than anyone, and I am certain he understands them well enough, if he deigns to tell us what he thinks.

It is true, Madame, I said, that I can guess your reasons. This woman cannot be both innocent and at the same time displease you. But, Madame, for all sin, there is forgiveness. I can assure you, after what I have heard her say to the Reverend Father, that this person cares greatly for you, that she will give you no further reason to complain of her, and that she will serve you better in future. I am so certain of this, on the strength of her words and her honest appearance, that I am ready to add my own prayers, if they have any weight, to those of your husband and the Reverend Father your brother – though indeed these ought to suffice by themselves in a matter of this nature.

This is a fine sort of introduction for Monsieur – parading our domestic spats before him the first time he does us the honour of a visit! said Londé. Let the woman remain in your service, he continued, and let's have no more nonsense! Bring Mousson here, he said to a footman. And as soon as she appeared, he said: Here you are, back in your mistress's good graces again. Confound it! Let's have less of this – one moment best of friends, next moment ruffled feathers between you! As for the rest of us, he said, Let's talk of other things. Which we did.

We spent part of the afternoon together and then separated, without my being able to exchange a word with Madame de Londé. I dropped a little snuffbox as I left, to give me a pretext for a subsequent visit, even if Londé were present, because I was afraid that, without Mousson as an intermediary, it might be a long time before I had a chance of talking to Madame de Londé; and I wrote this letter to her that very evening:

Your anger serves no purpose, nor would my repentance for having caused it, since I see no prospect that I shall learn to conform to the rules you lay down. You yourself are to blame for the violence of my feelings and your cruelty is responsible for my lack of respect. I am driven to despair not because I saw you as you were, nor for having embraced you and stolen your favours (I would do the same again though I earned your hatred for it), but because your severity robbed a fortuitous occasion of its conclusion. I hardly know how to describe my feelings for you at present. Give me a means of explaining them to you. I love you madly and I hate you with all my soul for your cruel resistance. I hate you for causing my despair, and the disastrous consequence I foresee – while at the same time I am filled with admiration for the very virtue which causes my distress. How is it that you can arouse such conflicting feelings in me? Cruel and inflexible as you are, I adore you; what would I feel if you took pity on me? You should not punish your waiting-woman for my intrusion and the surprise I caused you: she had no part in it. I had tricked her the first of all and had spent the night in your apartment without her knowledge – and if your door had not been locked from within, I would have done at midnight what I did by daylight. Take thought on the state you have reduced me to, both for your own sake and mine; I implore you, decide what is to become of me. I will bring my life and my sword to lay before you. Be ready either to see my end, or to treat me less harshly. My resolution is taken. Either, with my own hand and in your sight, I will become the victim of your cruelty, or you must make my life less desolate and more bearable.

I returned to her house the next day, no longer in my disguise. Dupuis had replaced the brother of Mousson. I spoke to the latter and she told me that her mistress was still at such a pitch of anger against both her and myself that she had not yet dared to have any conversation with her. She had said only that she did not know I was in her rooms (which we had agreed to say), but her mistress had not appeared to believe her. I wanted to give my letter to Mousson so that she could deliver it, but she begged me to understand that she could not be seen to be involved in any such communication. So I asked her at least to be near her mistress when I gave her the letter, to which she agreed, and we went into Madame de Londé's room together.

I had come with the excuse of asking for my snuffbox, and had entered without Madame de Londé's knowing of my arrival. I have come to ask you, Madame, I said, to be good enough to enquire among your servants if any of them has found a small snuffbox, which I believe I must have dropped here yesterday? It was given to me by someone particularly dear to me. She sent a maid to make enquiries. Leave this place, you insolent ruffian, she said, with a mixture of hauteur and scorn in her voice to which I was not accustomed and to which I would have retorted with indignation had I not heard steps in the anteroom. I tried to hand her my letter, but she refused to take it, and I threw it unsealed into the space between her bed and the wall. She saw this and tried to make me take it back, but was thwarted in this by the return of the girl with my snuffbox, which I took and promptly departed.

She must have read my letter, for I found it impossible for more than two months to exchange a single word with her except in her husband's presence. I have to admit that this behaviour, which would formerly have been enough to stifle my interest, only strengthened my admiration, and from being one of the most dissolute of libertines, I was reformed and became what I now am – the most sincerely devoted and faithful of men, believing my whole happiness to consist in loving a woman as beautiful, amiable and virtuous as Madame de Londé. So what followed, which you are now about to hear, came to pass with a genuine acceptance on my part, and without any deception or charade; although until then, almost all I did had been prompted by guile and self-interest, not by genuine feeling.

Her refusal to address a single word to me forced me, in order to have access to her, to become a member of Londé's set. I took part in all his activities and gradually became his confidant. He was not in the least reticent about his amorous distractions – on the contrary, he was the first to discuss them with his wife and to display them as trophies.

But, I said to him one day when we were alone at his country house, are you not afraid of your wife's resentment? Young, beautiful and attractive as she is, what excuse do you have for giving yourself to other women, who do not compare with her? You do not know her, he said. There can be no other woman in the world as cold as she is. She would have made an excellent nun: the vow of chastity would have been no hardship for her. When I want to use a husband's privilege and make love to her, she is reluctant and constrained – I would need swords and knives – and I have no desire to take her by force all the time, as I would have to. But, I said, is there no love between you? Did you marry without affection for each other? As for her, he said, I cannot say if she has ever been in love; but, for my part, I was madly in love with her, and I still love her tenderly. I was the most devoted and faithful husband in France for more than eighteen months and would be still, if I had not become aware, once my first passionate ardours had been assuaged, that she accepted me in her arms only as a conjugal duty because I was armed with a marriage certificate, not because of any attachment to my person. We discussed the matter, and she did not disguise the fact. On the contrary, she freely admitted that her lack of ardour was part of her nature, and that in fact she was not particularly drawn to the pleasures of the senses. Since then, I have recognised that she preferred to be left alone to lead her life in her own way.

I thought perhaps, he continued, that if she were made to feel a little jealousy, and if I were to show a little indifference and infidelity, this would awaken a reaction, but I was wrong. She is amused by my little affairs. And – far from being distressed by them, I'll be damned if, for the last eight months, when I have left her quite alone, she hasn't been looking more radiant and seemed happier. That certainly is surprising, I said, since a woman is usually more beautiful when she is enjoying the company of a man. Yet it is true, he continued, that celibacy has made her more beautiful, and I have acquired the habit of not thinking of her as my wife, but only as a good friend. But are you not afraid, I asked, that she will grow weary of her solitude in the end and wish to find her husband again? I would be only too happy if that were to happen, he answered. I would become as faithful again as I once was, and it would save me plenty of trouble and heartache – not to mention expense. Why do you not have her brothers or her confessor speak to her? I asked. There is no need for an intermediary between us, he said. Madame de Londé knows her duty, and I could enforce it if I wished. But I want her affection and her embrace only if they spring from her heart, not because she is instructed by anyone else. And I fear this will not happen, unless she is to change completely.

Only a few days ago, I went to see her in her bed, intending to spend a few moments with her, he went on. She responded as an honest woman can and should to her husband. I lay down beside her, but when I wanted to go further she said she knew it was my right, and that her body belonged to me, and that she would not therefore refuse me if I insisted, but if I wished to please her, I would not demand that she submit to my embrace, which she would do reluctantly and out of a sense of duty and to the mortification of her soul. What would you expect me to do? I left her, as I think any other man in my place would have done, unless he were a heartless brute or a sadist.

What you tell me is beyond my understanding, I said. How does she spend her time, then? I have watched her quite closely, he answered, without her knowing that I was doing so. I thought at first that she had some clandestine affair and that it was because of some secret lover that she was so cold towards me. I found I was completely mistaken. She sees no one but her servants, and occasionally some relatives – and even that, so infrequently that I am almost ashamed myself. Sometimes three months will pass without her leaving the house except to go to Mass or to hear a sermon; and so she spends her time annoying her waiting-woman and sending her into a pother; and the latter knows how to turn the tables and do the same with her, as you saw yourself a short time ago. There was nothing unusual about it, for they can be the best of friends at midday and locked in a quarrel before nightfall.

She also spends time with some young women she has who work for her from morn till night. She was responsible for all the furnishings and decoration in her part of the house – the chair covers and armchair covers and bedcover – all the sewing and embroidery, with fringes and tassels, some done in gold thread. I imagined it would take a hundred years for it all to be done, but she finished it in less than two. Let me point out that she had twelve girls there working for her, at such a pace and with so little time off that they started to call the place the 'penitent's nunnery'; and two or three of the girls, when they had finished the time they had agreed on, refused to return for three or four months, in spite of the fact that she paid and fed them well. What is also extraordinary is that during all the time she was working on this scheme and had people working there, no man except her brothers or myself and a few of my friends whom I invited ever came into the room. I am quite sure of this.

She has no entertainment that I know of except that sometimes she invites the servants up to a large room she has, or into her antechamber, and has them all dance and sing in front of her, and she herself sometimes joins in; or else they tell amusing stories. I have often found her occupied like this, and it is because she gets to know all her people so well that they are so fond of her, though they often give her considerable annoyance and manage to rile her too. But then all they need to do is ask for pardon – and it all starts over again two days later!

Only two weeks ago I had been knocking on the door for an hour, and when I went up to her rooms I heard the devil of a racket going on. I found her sitting at a little table by herself, and all the servants were up there with her celebrating Twelfth Night. Her coachman was King, and she had made him drink until he couldn't take another mouthful, and he was telling stories which made her laugh till she cried. There was nothing for it but to sit beside her at the table, where we had to serve ourselves because she made my coachman and footmen join the others who were there. We remained there and this wild party continued until two in the morning, with the servants having the time of their lives. I found it all as entertaining as she did, not least because she had had the wicked idea of making a palfreyman, who comes from Poitiers and speaks only his own patois, sit next to a scullery maid, who knows only her own incomprehensible Norman dialect, and said she wanted to have them marry each other. These two told each other stories which would have tried the gravity of a Cato, and I have to say, I wasn't bored while I was there.

What an extraordinary woman she is! I said. It is not that she is a fool, he explained. She likes a good laugh when the mood seizes her, as you see. She can even be somewhat cunning, and to prove that her frigidity is just part of her nature, and not a whim, let me tell you about an incident that took place about three months ago, in the house we are in at present. I was having some work done here, particularly in the gardens, and a little peasant girl, a local beauty, caught my eye – just a young thing and as pretty as an angel. Townspeople and outsiders are often less well received by young women of this sort than yokels from their own area. I have noticed this to be true in several situations of this sort. On this occasion, however, my little peasant girl was willing enough, and we had little difficulty coming to a verbal understanding with each other – it only remained for us to find a suitable place to meet. She was in either her father's or mother's sight all day long, often enough in the sight of both, since she worked along with them in the gardens. In fact, our agreement was made in their presence – on her side with the hope of a present, and perhaps a little prestige. The parents could hear nothing of what we said, but they would have seen anything we did. It was while I was walking around and watching her at work on the vegetable beds that I spoke and that she gave her replies. We soon found ourselves in agreement and arranged a meeting. It proved so much to her liking that she said we should try and find a way of seeing each other with more leisure and less constraint.

It occurred to us that her father and mother went to Paris taking vegetables to market at Les Halles every Wednesday and Saturday morning. To do this, they left the village at one or two in the morning at the latest, and often they even left the evening before, on Tuesday or Friday. We agreed that I should sleep in the country on Tuesdays and Fridays, and that she would come and join me as soon as her father and mother had left and the rest of the household – which included two other children – had gone to sleep. I took one of my lackeys into my confidence to enable her to get into the house and to my room. There is always one of these good-for-nothings around, but the one I chose was a witless fool.

Having made our plans, I took care to keep our rendez-vous. I liked the little peasant girl. This went on for about four months without Madame de Londé noticing, but eventually she realised that I regularly spent the night away from home twice a week, and always the same two nights, and so she suspected some intrigue and mentioned it to me with a laugh. I replied, in the same light-hearted tone, that I only went to keep an eye on what the carpenters and pain-ters and other workpeople were doing. She merely laughed at this, saying she didn't think I was being entirely honest.

Women are always curious, and she took it into her head to find out the truth. She questioned my rascal of a lackey to such effect that the imbecile told her everything. She instructed him not to report their conversation to me. Having found out at what times the girl came and left, she laid her plans. She arrived an hour before the girl would be leaving my room. She stopped her carriage some way from the house so that we should not hear it, and came into the antechamber outside my room, and prevented my lackey from making any noise. She waited quietly for the girl to come out, and caught her at my door. Imagine the latter's surprise at being discovered by my wife, whom she knew quite well. Stop a moment, my child, said Madame de Londé. Don't be afraid! I'm not going to hurt you! Looking at her closely, she recognised her and forced her to take some money, then let her go without a further word. She came into my room and found me in bed. The last thing I was expecting was to see her there. I knew very well I could catch you in the act, she said, kissing me. But I forgive you. She is young and pretty. Then she turned and left without waiting for an answer.

I was very surprised by all of this, Londé continued. I returned home to Paris for dinner and could not escape her teasing, which was quite amusing and didn't disturb me in the least. For, such as you see her, looking as serious as can be, let me tell you, there is no woman who can be more witty and droll than she is, nor who can make you laugh more when she is in the right frame of mind. I wanted to prove to her that I had not completely exhausted myself with my little peasant girl. No, no, she demurred. You cannot be expected to work night and day. And fended me off with a laugh. Such is the character of my wife!

I have to agree, I remarked, that it is quite unusual, and that I would never have thought a woman could be so indifferent to the pleasures of the senses. However, there is no doubt that this is the case, he said. And that is not the only incident which has convinced me of it. I have no rival to contend with, I am very certain of that. She gives me my freedom, and I demand nothing of her. I live with her and do as I wish. I could make her behave as my wife if I wished, but I have no inclination to assert my marital rights, and no suspicion that she is in love with another. So, without being any the worse off for it, we are both free and live together as good friends – or rather, like brother and sister – since we take our meals together; and that is all we do, although we are a man and a woman, and do not dislike each other; for in truth it is because I love her a great deal that I do not force myself on her.

If anyone but her husband was telling me such a story I

would certainly not believe it, I said. Yet it is true, and if all married people had as much consideration for each other as Madame de Londé has for me and I for her, he answered, we would not see so many unhappy households. Though if everyone were similarly to follow a pattern of life which suited him, it would be very necessary, both for the peace and salvation of the individual and to maintain order in society, for the rules of honour and courtesy to be carefully observed, as they are between her and me. You are asking for the impossible, I said. I know that, he answered. Not only because women like Madame de Londé are very uncommon – Nature does not produce many like her who are immune to both sensual pleasure and to jealousy – but also because it would be very difficult to find another husband like me, who loves his wife as much as I love mine, and who nevertheless prefers to forego the pleasure of sharing her bed and of having legitimate offspring, rather then cause her the least distress or displeasure.

All that Londé told me about his wife made me believe that it was because she loved me that she neither sought nor accepted his attentions – for he was, to do him justice, one of the most handsome and attractive men in France and a person of real merit. I therefore blamed her resistance to him on her attraction to me. Perhaps this was so, but it did not help me to make any progress. As for her alleged frigidity, I always believed it to be a mere supposition and an illusion. In my company, Madame de Londé was invariably so reserved that I was never able to have a private word with her; nor, since the time I had made my way into her bedroom, now more than six months previously, even with Mousson present. And so, whether it was my admiration for her devotion to virtue, or the very strength of my love in itself – such as I had never experienced before – or because of the two combined, I came to love her so much that I could no longer endure life without her.

I began to hate her husband and would have liked to see him dead. Knowing it was impossible to have his wife while he was alive, I was frequently tempted to cut my throat and his, or to do to her what Tarquin did to Lucretia. Such thoughts didn't stay with me long – the thought of committing a crime has always horrified me. I regretted not having learnt the secrets her brother had wanted to show me.

However, as you know, my dear cousin, he said (addressing Mademoiselle Dupuis), during this last summer I fell ill. A high fever and the heat of summer made me delirious. You told me that I talked incessantly of Madame de Londé and that in my ramblings I revealed all that was on my mind, even the thoughts I had had of stabbing the husband or violating the wife. You told me of your dismay at these revelations, and how you spoke to Madame de Londé; how she had found it difficult to decide what she ought to do, but had eventually determined to visit me. This she did, and though I showed her every respect, my ravings were nonetheless wild and extravagant.You told me how sorry she had been to see me in such state, but that she had said nothing more than that, except that she begged you not to allow anyone but the most discreet of friends to see me, because of the way her name was constantly on my lips, either praising or blaming her.

You told me that she had said her husband was planning to visit me, but that she had asked you not to allow him to do so. And in fact he did come twice, and you told him I was not well enough to receive visitors. In the end, my youth and strength saved me, as you know; but with my renewed health came a redoubled passion for this woman, which propelled me into a final act of desperation. Because of what I had said during my fever, of which you had informed her, she was more than ever on her guard, and it was always with a certain amount of disquiet that she saw me. She took care not to be alone with me, and avoided speaking to me with such assiduity that all my efforts were vain. I tried to speak to her even in Mousson's presence. Even in this I failed. My life seemed like torture to me, and I settled on the plan either to terminate it in her presence or to force her to give herself to me to prevent me from doing so. There was madness in this plan, it is true – perhaps my fevered brain had not recovered completely; there was certainly a turmoil of rage within me. But that was what I nonetheless determined to do, and one thing I cannot fathom is that it never entered my head to turn the point of my sword against her, not even in order to frighten her.

I waited more than six weeks for an opportunity, and then one evening I slid into the small antechamber which led into her bedroom. I hid behind a folding screen which, not being in use at this season, was stored there, and waited motionless until I saw that she was alone. She had eaten her supper in her room, since Londé was not at home. The servants were all so far away, eating supper in their turn, that they didn't hear the first cry which escaped her when she became aware of my presence. She was kneeling in front of a small altarpiece when I went into the room. She tried to move away. It is too late, Madame, I said, preventing her from leaving. My life has nothing further to offer me, and I have nothing to lose. I have come to die in your presence, since I have no hope of softening your heart towards me. I read my death sentence in your eyes: witnessing it being carried out will be a spectacle worthy of your cruelty, I added, closing the door which opened onto the great staircase. As I returned I drew my sword from its scabbard: she was more dead than alive and so penetrated with fear that she did not utter a word. I was undoubtedly at such a pitch of emotion that I would have pierced myself through the heart if she had not saved my life. I steadied the handle of my sword against the wall, with its point against my ribs, and threw myself on it with all my force – as one sees in the paintings depicting Ajax.

This desperate action was enough to bring Madame de Londé back to life. She was no longer afraid that I was about to rape or kill her. She hurled herself towards me as my sword passed through my body between the ribs. She seized hold of it and drew it out. The blood flowed as if from two fountains. Oh, my God! she cried. What have you done? This is nothing, Madame, but the beginning! Give me my sword and let me finish, I gasped, trying to take the sword from her hand. Your cruelty will not relent until my last breath is drawn, and I have come to expire in your sight. But, carrying my sword with her, she ran to call for help. The kitchen where the servants were at supper was so far away that she would not have been heard and I should probably have died without help except that, as chance would have it, Mousson had left her napkin in her room and had come for it. She heard her mistress's voice and came into the room. You will imagine her shock on seeing her mistress, ready to swoon, the bloody sword in her hand and myself with blood pouring from my wounds.

It was at this point that Madame de Londé embraced me. For God's sake, she said, take thought for your life. I swear I will be in your debt for doing so. But take thought also for my reputation, I beg and enjoin you! It is your wish, Madame, I said, and it shall be so. Mousson led me into her room and went to search for a surgeon, who came and dressed the wound – in Madame de Londé's presence – opining that it was extremely serious and could put my life in danger.

I remained sequestered in Mousson's room for six weeks, until I was recovered sufficiently to be moved. I had remained there in absolute secrecy: not a soul knew of my presence except Madame de Londé, Mousson and the surgeon who dressed the wounds. I then returned to my home, or rather was transported there, in such weak condition and so different a person that I was hardly recognisable. I was not yet restored to health and the surgeon visited me daily. I believed my mother, not fully persuaded of my reformation, was not alone in the suspicion that I had been obliged to take refuge all that time at the surgeon's, to be cured of the ravages resulting from my dissolute way of life. This was an error of judgement that I could, however, have forgiven easily enough, though Madame de Londé, since becoming a widow, has told me that my mother in fact knew where I was all that time.

To return to Madame de Londé: my wounds were dressed in her presence, and she herself helped the surgeon. I saw her every day, for she spent as much time at my bedside as she could. My action had in the end convinced her of the depth and strength of my love, and she looked after me with such tenderness and became so gentle and loving that I thought the fulfilment of my happiness was assured once my health was restored. Perhaps these apparent promises were intended only to speed my recovery so that she could send me home the more quickly. Or perhaps she was not deliberately deceiving me, and it was my conceit and inflated opinion of my own worth which misled me. Whichever it was, it was with this hope in mind that I left her house; but since then, much has changed.

I was not yet well enough to go out of doors when I received the news that Londé had died of pleurisy at his country house just outside Paris, after an illness of only two days. This did not sadden me to any great degree, but it grieved his widow. Indeed, he was mourned by all who had known him, as he deserved to be. Because of his death, when I next saw his widow, two months after I first went out of the house, I did not pursue the promise she had seemed to make. I allowed her first tears to flow freely and went to wipe away those which followed. On my second visit, I found her alone except for Mousson – as I had asked the latter to arrange. I threw myself at her feet; she raised me and embraced me. We looked at each other with tears in our eyes. I could not speak to her of Londé. I spoke to her only of myself. I expressed my love with the same ardour as ever, but added that I had now banished its violence and excesses. You are now your own mistress, I said. You are now in a position to decide for yourself whether you will satisfy my dreams. You are free to yield without guilt to the love you told me you had always felt for me. She embraced me again and promised to give herself to me as soon as propriety allowed. I begged her to bring the date forward as much as possible, and she agreed to do so. She asked me however to allow it to appear that the pressure for her to remarry came from her family, and that she was cutting short her mourning only in deference to their wishes and urging, not because of her love for me.

I had recourse to her brother, the Capuchin monk, to whom I told all. He spoke to the family, and Madame de Londé agreed to shorten the period of her mourning by six months, allowing it to appear she was yielding to their request. I saw her every day and was pleased to notice that the waiting time was as tedious for her as it was for me. I saw nothing in her behaviour which did not disprove the coldness of which Londé had accused her. On the contrary, I saw her filled with love for me, and there were only twelve days left before our marriage was to take place, when once again we saw it delayed by the death of her poor brother, which I will now tell you about, and in which he met the unfortunate fate predicted for him.

He was known as an effective preacher, and since entering the monastery he had dedicated his life to serving others. He had been chosen to take part in a mission during Lent, on Low Sunday. He asked us not to celebrate our marriage during his absence, and this we readily agreed to, since the day we had appointed for our wedding was shortly after his expected return. The mission was at a location only two days' journey from Paris, and we were to be married on the second Thursday after Easter, which would in fact be two days after his return.

On Easter Saturday he had been performing the duties of his mission in a locality to which his zeal and charity had led him. He was returning with a brother monk, who was his companion on this mission, to the monastery two leagues distant where they were staying, when the most appalling misfortune occurred. They were travelling on a little-used path through a forest. There were in the forest at the time robbers who had been causing mayhem and committing terrible crimes. They were being pursued by agents of the law and were trying to make good their escape when they saw, by the light of the moon, these two hapless Capuchin monks. The scoundrels pounced on them and stole their monastic garb, hoping to escape in disguise. To prevent the two monks from alerting the police, they killed them, and in order to hide the traces of their crime, they hung them in the trees. All this was in vain, however, as they were caught three leagues further on, and admitted on the wheel their iniquitous deed. But this did not save the life of Gallouin or his companion, whose clothes they had discarded in a ditch.

The loss of such a good friend and holy man caused me much pain, and still does. And however serious the injury he did you, continued Dupuis, addressing Des Frans – not knowing he was doing it, since he was unaware of your marriage – I am sure you are too discerning and honourable not to have some compassion for him, considering his sincere repentance and his sad death. You know what I think, answered Des Frans. I have forgotten that he ever did me any offence. I weep for him as much as you do. And I am sure that anyone who hears of his death, so long as they have the least shred of humanity, will shed tears for him. We will talk about it again later, but for the present continue with your story.

It is finished, said Dupuis. For I do not think I need tell you what sorrow this misfortune has caused his family, and particularly his sister and myself, a sorrow which is still unhealed. This unhappy event is still so recent, and his loss will leave an emptiness in our hearts for so long, that it is not surprising that we have not yet celebrated our marriage. But, at last, all the obstacles are now cleared away; we are all agreed; our marriage contract is ready to be signed. All that she and I wish for is to belong to each other. And I hope we shall be married at the same time as my cousin, Manon, and Monsieur Des Ronais.

There were one or two more delays before these two marriages took place, and the marriage of Madame de Mongey and Des Frans occurred shortly thereafter.

END